THE
PERCY WESTERMAN
OMNIBUS

Three Famous Books

THE PIRATE SUBMARINE
CAPTAIN CAIN
THE FLYING SUBMARINE

LONDON: NISBET & CO. LTD.

PRINTED IN GREAT BRITAIN BY
MORRISON AND GIBB LTD., LONDON AND EDINBURGH

PUBLISHERS' PREFACE

O N the ground that one cannot have too much of a good thing, the Publishers are issuing in this one volume three complete books by the world-famous writer for Boys, Percy F. Westerman. In this volume will be found 874 pages of magnificent, adventurous reading.

By the common consent of Boy Readers this author is second to none as *the* yarn spinner. He may always be relied upon to rouse the utmost interest and to keep it at an intense point from cover to cover.

Known to his friends as " The Skipper," Percy F. Westerman is a great believer in life in the open air; towns and cities are an abomination to him. Actually he lives afloat on a tidal river in the south. A first-class craftsman and a practical handyman, he has himself built a fascinating home on the roomy hulk of an ex-Thames barge; here he can pace his own quarter-deck and keep a look out on the world. On board he may be found surrounded by mementoes of various adventures and wanderings. A great dog lover, his favourite is perhaps a tremendously shaggy, bobtailed sheep dog with an intense faithfulness and keen intelligence.

On the barge Percy Westerman writes his books, mostly at night, for by day there are many other interests to follow—sailing, motoring ashore and afloat, travelling and a hundred and one things in which his alert, energetic personality delights. In the summer months especially he will cruise far afield, but never without two or three dog friends. This love of the open and an unconventional life is reflected in all his books.

The Publishers feel that they are rendering a real service in giving this most popular author in Omnibus form.

CONTENTS

THE PIRATE SUBMARINE

CONTENTS

CONTENTS

THE PIRATE SUBMARINE

CHAPTER I

A PAIR OF ROGUES

"THAT'S done it! Scrap brass has fallen another thirty shillings a ton, Pengelly. The slump has knocked the bottom out of the market. We're in the soup."

Thus spoke Tom Trevorrick, senior partner of the firm of Trevorrick, Pengelly & Co., ship-breakers, of Polkyll, near Falmouth. He was a tall, powerfully-built man, standing six feet two and a half inches in his socks, red-haired, florid featured, with a high though receding forehead and a heavy protruding jaw. His rich deep voice had a plausible ring about it—a compelling, masterful yet persuasive tone, that had largely influenced the shareholders of Trevorrick, Pengelly & Co. to part with their money with the absolute certainty of a pre-war ten per cent. return.

Paul Pengelly, aged thirty-three, or three years older than the senior partner, was of different build and temperament. Trevorrick represented the Celtic strain of Cornishmen; Pengelly had dark curly hair and sallow features—legacies of

I

an Iberian ancestor, one of a handful of survivors
from a vessel of the Spanish Armada that had
been cast ashore on the rock-bound Lizard.
History does not relate why the Cornish wreckers
spared the lives of the olive-featured mariners,
but it does record that the shipwrecked Spaniards
took wives of the Cornish maids, and lived and
died in the country of their adoption.

Pengelly was slow of speech, stolid in action
save when roused to anger. Of an argumentative
nature, he acted as a foil to his partner's exuberance. If Trevorrick suggested a certain course,
Pengelly almost invariably went dead against it,
not that he disapproved of the scheme, but simply
as a matter of habit. He was secretive and
cautious ; but he never hesitated to do an under-
hand action if he felt reasonably secure from
detection.

He was a man of many parts—a jack-of-all-trades
and master of a few. Given to building castles in
the air, he would soar to dizzy heights in planning
fantastic schemes. Some of them might take
definite shape ; then, almost without warning, he
would " chuck his hand in " and cast about for
something else.

Eighteen months previously, Trevorrick and
Pengelly had met for the first time. Trevorrick
had just left the Royal Navy. He had been a
lieutenant-commander attached to the Portsmouth submarine flotilla. He had not resigned
under the favourable terms offered by My Lords
to redundant officers ; he had not been " axed "
under the Geddes Scheme. He had been court-

martialled and dismissed from the Service under circumstances that could not be termed extenuating.

Trevorrick was at a loose end when he encountered Pengelly. He had a limited amount of capital. So had Pengelly. The latter's latest scheme appealed to the ex-lieutenant-commander. Just then, hundreds of ships of all sizes were being sold out of the Service for breaking-up purposes. There was money to be made out of the business, with very little capital required for plant, while surplus destroyers and submarines could be bought at a flat rate of one pound per ton, subject to the condition that they had to be broken up.

Of the hundreds, nay, thousands of people who patronise the little steamers plying between Falmouth and Truro—or Malpas, according to the state of the tide—few are likely to notice a small creek on the starboard hand of the picturesque river Fal. Fewer still know it by name.

Its entrance is narrow, between steeply rising, heavily wooded ground. Although barely twenty-five yards in width across its mouth, it carries nearly thirty feet of water at Springs. Two hundred yards up, the creek widens out. One bank retains its precipitous, tree-clad nature. The other dips, forming a wide bay, with a flat belt of ground between the shore and the high ground beyond.

On this site, hidden from the Fal by a bend in the channel, stood a derelict shipyard. A century ago, when Falmouth was at the height of its prosperity as a packet-station, the shipyard teemed with activity. It enjoyed a brief and illusory spell of life during the Great War, when it again sank into obscurity and neglect. The two slipways were left to rot, two tidal docks were allowed to silt up. The buildings were ruinous and leaky. The whole concern was in the hands of the Official Receiver.

To the delectable spot came Trevorrick and Pengelly. They looked at it. Trevorrick lost no time in declaring that it was " the " place ; Pengelly asserted that it was not. The big man had his way, and thus the Polkyll Creek Shipbreaking Company came into being.

They started modestly upon their enterprise. The heaviest item for plant was the purchase of an oxygen-acetylene apparatus. At first, ten hands were engaged. Pengelly wanted to obtain them locally. Trevorrick, as usual, overruled him, and as a result inserted in a Plymouth paper an advertisement for ex-Naval and Mercantile Marine men. They received shoals of replies and could pick and choose, without having to pay Trade Union rates.

" We'll have unmarried men," declared the senior partner. " They won't be wanting to run away home every five minutes."

" Married men are more likely to stick to their jobs," objected Pengelly.

" No one but a born fool would chuck up a job nowadays," retorted Trevorrick. " They are none too plentiful."

In due course, the shipbreaking yard began to function. A destroyer and a submarine were purchased at Devonport and towed round to

Falmouth and up the Fal to Polkyll. The scrap metal was sent up to Truro in barges and thence transferred to goods train for the Welsh smelting works. So profitable was the venture that three more vessels were bought for demolition, twenty additional hands taken on, and the firm of Trevorrick and Pengelly became a limited liability company.

So far, things were going smoothly. The two principals got on amicably, which was rather to be wondered at, since Trevorrick was apt to boast that he had had heaps of friends and had never been able to keep one of them. No doubt, the totally dissimilar physical and mental characteristics of each kept them in a state of mutual docility; but already Pengelly was tiring of the monotonous work, and Trevorrick was scheming to get away to a livelier spot than the dead-and-alive Polkyll Creek.

Then, slowly but surely, came the slump. The shareholders had their first dividends—ten per cent.—paid out of the capital. Another dividend was shortly due and there was no possible chance of it being forthcoming, unless Trevorrick and Pengelly drew upon their capital—a step that each was firmly determined not to take.

" Are we in the soup ? " asked Pengelly, in reply to his partner's pessimistic declaration. " What do you suggest ? "

" Pack up and clear off," replied the senior partner. " Lay hands on all the ready money we can possibly get hold of, and make ourselves scarce."

" How about the shareholders ? " asked Pengelly.
Trevorrick shrugged his shoulders.

" Shareholders have lost money before to-day,"
he remarked. " That's their affair."

" That's all right as far as we are concerned, if
they take it lying down," objected the other.
" S'posing they don't ? What then ? We
wouldn't be safe for twenty-four hours in this
country. We might try our luck abroad."

It was Trevorrick's turn to offer objections.

" Don't fancy the idea, especially with a warrant
hanging over my head. Fellows who issue
fraudulent balance sheets (Pengelly winced) get
it in the neck pretty badly when they're caught.
I've no fancy for seven years behind prison bars.
And there's another thing. How long could
either of us hang out abroad with what money
we can lay our hands on ? Six months. After
that—*phut* ! "

" Then what do you suggest ? "

" Depends," replied Trevorrick. " Fifty thousand apiece and a snug hiding-place in one of
the South American republics."

" Takes some doing."

" It can be done."

" How ? "

The two men looked at each other, trying to
fathom the depths to which either would be prepared to go.

" How ? " asked Pengelly again. " Holding up
a bank, for example."

" Try again."

" Highway robbery, perhaps."

" Sort of," admitted Trevorrick. " For ' high-way ' substitute ' high seas,' and you've got it."

" Piracy, by Jove ! " ejaculated Pengelly, with a gleam in his eyes. It was a case of blood will tell, and Pengellys had in bygone days sailed under the Jolly Roger ; more than one had made a public spectacle at Execution Dock. " That's funny, deuced funny," he added, after a pause. " I've been thinking of that myself."

" It'll require a jolly sight more than thinking," remarked Trevorrick grimly.

" It's risky."

" Course it is. So's everything, if you go the wrong way about it. Take shipbreaking : you might get cut in two by a chunk of steel plate, or you might try the business end of an oxygen-acetylene flame. That's happened before to-day."

" You—I mean, we—would probably be caught inside of a week," said Pengelly, resuming his habit of raising objections. " Aircraft and wire-less don't give a fellow much of a chance."

" Not if we played our cards properly."

" Don't see how," rejoined the little man petu-lantly. "And when we're collared——"

He completed the sentence by a double gesture —a circular motion of his right hand in a horizontal plane followed by a rapid vertical movement.

" Better that than seven years," said Trevorrick coolly. " But you're showing the white feather already."

" Surely you're joking about it ? "

" Never more serious in all my life," the senior partner hastened to assure him. " The audacity

of the thing is in our favour. Ask any naval
expert. He'll tell you that piracy, except in the
Red Sea and the China Station, is as dead as Queen
Anne. I'm going to show the blamed experts
that they're talking through their hats."

" But——"

" Don't start butting in with your confounded
' buts,' " exclaimed Trevorrick, with a tinge of
asperity. " You say you've been considering the
matter. How far have you gone into the practical
side of it ? I can make a pretty shrewd guess.
You haven't even scratched the epidermis of the
problem. I have. Cast your eyes over this."

From his pocket-box, Trevorrick produced a
leaf of a notebook. On it was written in small,
carefully-formed letters, the following :

1. The vessel.
2. Crew.
3. Maintenance.
4. Cruising limits.
5. Communication with shore.

" Now," continued Trevorrick briskly, " I've
gone deeply into the question. We'll run over
the various items. Then we can discuss details ;
but remember, I want constructive, not destructive
criticism. Here I am trying to put you on to a
get-rich-quick scheme. That's the main idea.
It's for your benefit—and mine. First, the ship.
I propose adopting R 81."

R 81 was the Polkyll Creek Shipbreaking Yard's
latest acquisition. She had been towed round
from Devonport only a couple of days previously
and had been placed in the mud-dock alongside

the rapidly-disintegrating hull of her former sister-submarine R 67.

" Bless my soul, man ! " interrupted Pengelly, heedless of the senior partner's caution. " You'd never get her outside Falmouth Harbour."

" You're bearing in mind the Admiralty inspector," declared Trevorrick, purposely refraining from showing displeasure at the interruption. " He'll be here to-morrow or Friday. After that, it will be three months before he shows up again. Then I can manage him all right. No, I don't intend to offer him half a crown to look the other way. But there's not the slightest reason why we shouldn't hoodwink him. The moment he goes after his next visit, we'll start operations. R 81 goes under the covered shed ; R 67 will be moved into R 81's berth. It's not altogether a stroke of luck that we haven't started cutting into R 67's hull below the waterline. When the inspector comes again he won't see R 67. She'll be broken up entirely as far as he's concerned. R 67 will assume R 81's number. We'll leave enough of the hull for that. The pirate submarine, ex-R 81, will already be nearing completion well out of the sight of the official eye."

" Trevorrick, I always thought I had the bump of imagination," declared Pengelly. " I give you best."

" Imagination isn't of much use, unless you put it to a practical purpose," rejoined the other. " What I'm proposing can be done ; more, it's going to be done."

" But——"

" There you go again," interrupted Trevorrick tolerantly. " Carry on, then. Trot out your objections. We'll argue all along the line as we go. What were you about to remark ? "

" We'll assume that you've bamboozled the Admiralty Nosey Parker, whose business it is to bind us to our contract," said Pengelly. " You've got the submarine fit, more or less, for sea. You'd have to take her down the Fal on the surface. There's not enough water to submerge. Day or night, you'd be spotted ; and there'd be questions asked."

" Pengelly, your Christian name ought to be Thomas, not Paul," remarked Trevorrick, in a bantering tone. He could afford to try to be facetious. He knew enough of his partner by this time to realise that the greater the objections the latter raised, the more chance he, Trevorrick, had of gaining his case—as he almost invariably did. " I'm going to take her out of Falmouth as a surface ship. I'd defy any one to think her to be otherwise than an old tramp without they actually came on board, which I don't intend that they should. We've got the materials. In a couple of months we'll build up a superstructure, rig dummy masts and funnels, and there you are. What have you to say against that ? "

" Top-hamper," declared Pengelly bluntly. " What do you propose doing when she dives ? Ditch the lot ? If you don't, she'll roll over when she's submerged. And what speed do you expect you'll get when running beneath the surface, assuming she doesn't turn turtle ? "

" Top-hamper judiciously constructed will make
no difference to her stability when submerged,"
replied the other. " All that requires to be done
is to see that the superstructure, taken as a whole,
weighs the same as the quantity of water it dis-
places—fairly simple matter if we make use of
air-tight tanks and compartments packed with
cork. Speed under the surface doesn't count for
much in our case. Storage batteries are a nuisance at the best of times. No, I mean to submerge
and rest on the bottom in the event of an attack.
She's built to withstand, with an ample margin
of safety, a depth of twenty-five fathoms."

" Armament—guns and torpedoes—then," resumed Pengelly. " That's going to knock you.
Torpedoes don't grow on blackberry bushes, and
you can't go trotting about with a six-inch quick-
firer under your arm. Supposing Elswicks or
Vickers did accept your order for a quick-firer,
you'd have the police knocking you up to know
what your little game is."

" Torpedoes are out of the question, I'm afraid,"
admitted Trevorrick. His fellow-partner grinned
with satisfaction. It was one of those rare
occasions when he scored a point with his objections.
" It's a pity ; they might have come in handy,
especially as they've left the tubes in the ship.
Nothing like a ' tinfish ' to settle an argument.
Guns—no difficulty there. I can buy a 15·2
centimetre quick-firer of the latest pattern—that's
practically six-inch—at Liége and get it delivered
afloat outside Dutch or Belgian territorial waters
for a mere song, with as much ammunition as

we're likely to want. You see, I've made inquiries all along the line already. Next item : Crew I'll skip that for the present ; but, let me tell you, there was method in my madness when I was so mighty particular in the choice of the hands here. Maintenance—that's easily disposed of. We'll help ourselves, supplementing our store with purchases from the shore. Now, Cruising Limits. No need to go very far from home. West Coast of Europe between Finisterre and Bergen offers enough scope for our little stunt ; but it's in the Channel that I hope to play Cain. No, don't get alarmed, Pengelly. I'm not out for British shipping unless I'm forced. Hoist German colours and capture a French vessel ; collar a German and tell him we're a Frenchman. Spin a yarn to a Dutchman while you're going through his pockets. Bless my soul, man, we'll have our fifty thousand apiece in no time. That brings me to the last item : Communication with the shore. We'll have to lay by for a rainy day, Pengelly—show a clean pair of heels before it's too late. We'll have to travel light. Can't carry a pantechnicon of booty with us. We must arrange to have it sent ashore and transferred to a trustworthy agent in South America. I know of at least half a dozen."

" How about the crew ? " asked Pengelly. " We can't show up at some port with thirty fellows tacked on to us."

" No need," replied Trevorrick with a grin. "We're not sentimentalists, nor philanthropists."

CHAPTER II

THE PIRATE CREW SIGN ON

ON the following day, Mr. Chamfer, the Admiralty inspector, arrived.

He was a short, slim-built man with a totally disproportionate sense of his own importance. Thirty years of Civil Service life had got him into a rut. It mattered little how he performed his duties as long as he did them somehow : a monthly visit to the cashier's office at Devonport Dockyard to draw his salary was an assured thing. At the end of every year his salary was subject to a fixed increase. Whether he earned it or not, whether he possessed higher or lower qualifications than his confrères mattered not at all—the annual " rise " came with unfailing certainty. Mr. Chamfer was a firm believer in the principle of following the line of least resistance, namely, to get through his perfunctory duties with the minimum of trouble. Provided he was treated with due deference to his position by the principals of the various shipbreaking firms with whom he had to deal, the former had no cause to complain of irritating demands on the part of the Admiralty inspector.

" Ah, good morning, Mr. Trevorrick ! " he exclaimed. " Fine morning. Business going strong,

I hope ? Let me see : R 81 arrived here this week. Started on her yet ? "

" No, sir," replied Trevorrick, with his tongue in his cheek. " We're engaging ten additional hands for that job. Next time you pay us a visit you'll find that there's not very much left of her."

" And R 67 ? " inquired Mr. Chamfer, consulting an official form.

" She's practically demolished," was the reply. " Do you wish to make an inspection ? "

The inspector gave a quick glance out of the office window. Eighty yards away lay the object under discussion, the gaunt skeleton of a mammoth, the steel ribs of which were being attacked by a swarm of workmen, who gave the onlooker the impression that they were Lilliputians clambering over Gulliver's recumbent form.

" No, thanks ; I won't trouble you," he hastened to reply, as he scribbled, " R 81—work in hand ; R 67 practically demolished," in column six of the official document. " Well, since you suggest it, I will—just a nip. And soda, please. Well, Mr. Trevorrick, your good health and success to your work."

Two minutes later, Mr. Chamfer's car was tearing along the Tregony Road on its way back to Devonport. It would be three months at least before the official repeated the visit, and much was to happen at Polkyll Creek before those three months were up.

" Fancy, that little worm draws as much pay as a full-blown captain ! " remarked Trevorrick to his partner. " You and I have to keep blighters of that sort. Well thank goodness that's over. We'll have the men up now."

The yard-bell uttered its warning notes. Although it wanted half an hour to " knock-off time," the thirty employees of the firm of Trevorrick, Pengelly & Co., promptly left their work and trooped up to the office, wondering whether the bell had been rung in mistake or whether something of an unusual nature was on the boards. There had been rumours, originating goodness only knows where, that the works might have to close down, and that prospect, with winter only a few weeks off, was a dismal one.

They trooped into the large office and found Mr. Trevorrick looking cheerful and self-possessed, with Mr. Pengelly, with a frown on his face, toying nervously with a paper-knife.

Trevorrick wasted no time in preliminaries.

" Men ! " he began. " Present-day conditions of the metal market have forced us to make preparations for the closing-down of the works. If there were any indications of a recovery during the next three or four months we would hold on. Unfortunately, there are none."

He paused, rapidly scanning the features of the dejected men. There was no doubt about their being downcast. He realised that figuratively he held them in the hollow of his hand.

" However," he continued, " there is no reason why the amicable relations between us as employers and employees should not be maintained ; but, let me hasten to remind you that amicable relations won't fill empty stomachs. Mr. Pengelly and myself are anxious to put our sincerity to a practical test. It rests with you whether you decide to take advantage of our offer.

" Before going deeper into the matter, I can assure you of a constant job, paid for at the same rates that you are receiving at present with the addition of a bonus, which might be anything up to a couple of hundred pounds, at the termination of the first year's work. It may entail discomfort, it is of a hazardous nature, although with due precautions there is no danger that cannot be avoided. There is one stipulation I must make—each and every man must be under the strictest pledge of secrecy."

He paused again. The men shuffled uneasily. Several at the back of the room whispered hoarsely to each other.

" Is the job straight and above-board, sir ? " inquired an anxious voice.

Trevorrick looked straight at the speaker.

" Naturally," he replied.

His tone carried conviction. Had he said more in reply, the men might have " smelt a rat."

" Very good, sir ; I'm in it," announced the cautious one. Others joined in accepting the decidedly indefinite offer.

" Any one not wishing to sign on can go," exclaimed Trevorrick. " I won't blame him for refusing a job about which he knows nothing, but there are other people's interests to be safeguarded. What ! All agreed ? Excellent ! Now, Mr. Pengelly, will you please read out the declaration and obtain every man's signature, please ? "

The document binding each employee to secrecy was cleverly worded, concluding with the affirmative that each man admitted his liability to be summarily dismissed for insufficiency of work, bad workmanship, insubordination, turbulence, inebriety or other offence or misconduct contrary to the rules and regulations of the Posidon Salvage Company.

" There you are, men," exclaimed Trevorrick, after the last signature had been obtained. " You now know what is the nature of the work—salvage. I will briefly relate the history of the *Posidon*. Ten or twelve years ago—in 1916, to be exact—the *Posidon*, bound from Quebec for the United Kingdom with a cargo consisting mainly of copper and silver ingots, was torpedoed by a Hun submarine when about six miles S.S.W. of the Lizard.

" An attempt was made to beach her on Looe Bar, but she turned turtle and sank in fifteen fathoms. After the Armistice attempts were made to salve the cargo. Divers went down, found the wreck lying over on her beam ends. There were a few bars of copper found, but of silver not a solitary ingot. The explosion of the torpedo had blown away one side of the strong-room. That discovery brought the salvage work to an abrupt termination.

" Now then. This is where we come in. From a most trustworthy source, I found out what actually did happen to the ingots. The *Posidon* turned turtle and sank, but between the two operations there was an interval. She drifted bottom-upwards for perhaps half an hour. In

2

that position the weight of the copper burst open the hatches and nearly the whole lot was strewn on the bed of the sea. The silver, too, fell through the blown-in face of the strong-room. Consequently, when the ship did make her final plunge, she was two hundred yards away from the spot where she had dumped her precious cargo. Is that clear ? "

A murmur of assent came from the interested listeners. Tales of sunken treasure waiting to be picked up from a veritable Tom Tiddler's ground appeal to most people ; and Trevorrick's breezy, convincing manner did not fail to impress the simple-minded audience.

" You know it's there, sir ? " inquired one of the employees, an ex-seaman diver.

" Certainly, Hunt," replied Trevorrick. " I've seen it. I cannot produce better proof than that ? "

" Any difficulties, sir, in the way of other people being on the same lay ? " asked another.

" The Admiralty, by whom the vessel was chartered, have abandoned her ; the underwriters have settled up and written her off as a bad debt, although it may be possible that they might want to chip in. That's why we must conduct our operations in secret. It's all above-board, you'll understand. I wouldn't defraud any one. I have taken counsel's opinion and have been informed that we have a moral, legal and every other jolly old right to stick to what we can find. But we must guard ourselves against others who may try to jump our claim.

" How ? I will tell you. As you know, the

Admiralty inspector has just been here. I took the opportunity to sound him, and he assured me that there would be no objection on his part against our employing R 81 as a salvage craft. Being fitted with air-locks, enabling a diver to leave and enter at will, she is an ideal proposition for the job. The only difficulty is getting her in and out of Falmouth Harbour. Officious busy-bodies might write to the Admiralty asking why she was being employed instead of being broken up. I mentioned this to Mr. Chamfer. He was most sympathetic and hinted—hinted, mind you —that if R 81 could be sufficiently disguised, there ought to be no further difficulty. That, with your co-operation, I propose to do."

The men's enthusiasm was rapidly rising. Pengelly gave a glance of admiration at his partner. There was no doubt about it : Trevorrick held them in the palm of his hand.

" There's no time to be lost," continued the promoter. " We'll start this afternoon. . . . Carry on, men. Barnard and Marchant, will you remain, please ? "

The workmen hurried gleefully out of the office, leaving the two foremen with whom the principals conferred over certain details in connection with the fitting out of the submarine.

At length Barnard and Marchant were dismissed, and Trevorrick and Pengelly found themselves alone.

" Well ? " queried the former abruptly. " What do you think of the yarn I've just been pitching ? That got 'em, didn't it ? "

Pengelly nodded.

" So far, I admit," he replied. " But——"

" Go on, man ; get it off your chest," prompted the senior partner, now in high good humour.

" S'posing we get R 81 under way. How do you propose to switch over from salvaging to piracy ? That'll take some doing."

" Possibly," admitted Trevorrick. " But I'll do it. You wait and see. By the bye," he continued, abruptly changing the subject. " What was that yarn you were telling me about Chamfer ? —Something about him coming into a pot of money."

" Yes, lucky bounder," replied Pengelly enviously. " Some misguided relative of his shuffled off this mortal coil about two years ago and left him thirty thousand pounds."

" Hanged if I'd stop in the Admiralty service with that little lot," remarked Trevorrick. " Even though he's got a soft billet. I'd blow the lot in a couple of years. ' Easy come, easy go ' is my motto."

" He's evidently of a different nature," said Pengelly. " But why do you ask ? "

" Nothing much," was the response. " Look here, Pengelly, we'll have to throw dust in the eyes of the shareholders. Can we run to another five per cent. ? "

" It will cut into our capital."

" It'll have to," decided Trevorrick. " We'll declare a half-yearly dividend. On the strength of that we might apply for extra capital. And another thing : you'd better run across to Penzance

intention of driving R 81 under the water. In the event of danger he could submerge and " lie doggo " until he deemed it prudent to break surface. Thus, he cut out an important item in the running costs.

Meanwhile, the roar of the oxygen-acetylene plant had given place to the rattle of riveting-hammers and drilling-machines. All hands worked with a zest, prompted by the hope that they were participators in a profit-sharing scheme. To guard against intruders, watchmen were posted by night, while a boom of timber was stretched across the mouth of Polkyll Creek, to which a notice-board was affixed with the intimation that " This Creek is temporarily closed to Navigation. Dangerous. By Order."

By whose order it was not stated. Few craft other than pleasure skiffs ever penetrated the secluded backwater, and the season was too late for picnic parties. Some of the local fishermen were " up against " the infringement of their rights, but a judicious expenditure on beer quickly removed their opposition to the temporary closing of the creek.

Quickly the task of disguising the submarine as a tramp steamer progressed. Vertical girders bolted to her bulging sides formed the framework for the side-plating. She was given a raised fo'c'sle and poop; while amidships, by an ingenious arrangement, was a raised structure that could with little trouble be moved fore and aft. On the structure was the dummy charthouse with a funnel in its wake. Thus, by altering the position of the midship structure, the submarine would present the appearance of a " three island vessel " or one of the coasting type with the funnel well aft. In addition, she was given a pair of stumpy masts with derricks, so arranged to be lowered should occasion arise. Ventilating cowls were fixed to various positions on deck, each with a duplicate base, in order to alter the general appearance. Two boats were carried in davits, each constructed of sheet metal and fitted with valves that enabled them to be easily filled and emptied when the submarine dived or came to the surface as the case might be.

In two months from the time the work was first put in hand, R 81, rechristened *Alerte* of London, was floated out and moored in the centre of Polkyll Creek. If necessary, her presence could be explained by saying that she was about to take a cargo of scrap metal round to Cardiff.

Even at close distance it would be almost impossible for the most practised eye to discover the fake, unless the observer actually went on board. With her black sides streaked with iron rust, her stumpy masts and buff funnel with a black top, she was like many a hundred tramps that nosed their way coastwise from Thurso to Penzance and from Wick to Falmouth.

To complete the deception, Pengelly, who was a skilful penman, made a fictitious " Certificate of Registry " and other necessary ship's papers. Nor was he content with one of each. Six different sets, each in a different name, were prepared and placed on board.

At an early stage in the proceedings, Pengelly
had gone over to Penzance in order to interview
and enlist the services of that tough old salt Silas
Porthoustoc. At the merest hint that he proposed
to run a cargo, the skipper of the lugger's eyes
gleamed.

" What be't, maaster ? " he inquired.   " Spirits,
lace, or what not ? "

" Neither at present," was the reply.   " But
something highly contraband."

" So much the better, say I," grunted Silas.
" Where be tu ? "

" What's the size of your hold ? " asked Pengelly,
without answering Porthoustoc's question.

" Say twelve feet by six an' you'll not be far
adrift."

" That's the hatch ? "

" Ay, of course," replied Silas.   " Reckon as 'ow
I could stow a twenty-five feet spar if I wur put to
it."

" Good enough," agreed Pengelly.   " Here are
your orders : Three miles S.S.E. of the North
Hinder Light, between midnight and dawn on the
17th."

" Good," chuckled the old man.   " Then ut be
Schnapps after all ? "

" Sort of," admitted Pengelly.   " You'll find a
motor cargo-boat waiting for you. She'll show
three long and three short flashes every half-hour,
till you answer her by the prearranged signal. It's
all set down on this paper. Our rendezvous——"

" What'll that be, maaster ? " interrupted Silas.

" Meeting-place," explained the other.   " Will

be ten miles sou' by west of St. Alban's Head. Recognition signals the same. Payment fifty pounds down and five per cent. on all subsequent consignments—and we'll keep you pretty busy. Not much risk, either, if you know your job."

" Guess I knows my job, all right," chuckled Porthoustoc.

" Good ! " ejaculated Pengelly. " If there's much of a lop on outside you'd best run up the West Scheldt. You'll find your cargo waiting for you off Neuzen. Know it ? "

" Find my way in blindfold," declared Silas. " I'd like to have a quid for every lil' keg I've brought out o' they parts. The *Fairy* 'll be on the spot to time, blow high, blow low, maaster."

Having secured an ally, although Silas Porthoustoc was in ignorance of the real project of his employer, Pengelly returned to Polkyll Creek and reported progress.

" We'll slip our moorings on Saturday," declared Trevorrick. " She's practically ready. We took in the last few tons of oil this morning. Men are full of beans and slogging in like buck niggers. Pengelly, old son, it's going to be simply IT and no mistake."

In this optimistic state of mind, Trevorrick perched himself on the edge of a desk and lit a cigarette. From where he sat he could command two views : one over the creek on which the *Alerte* rode sedately at her moorings ; the other along the narrow drive leading to the one and only entrance to the works from the landward side. Half-way down the drive lay a lorry laden with

broken metal. It had been there for the last
month—by design—to prevent would-be dealers
and other callers from driving straight up to the
office.

Suddenly Trevorrick rapped out an oath.

Pengelly started to his feet ; not because his
partner was not addicted to strong language, but
because the vehemence of the other's spontaneous
delivery, following a phrase of self-satisfaction,
warned him that something unusual had occurred.

" That fool ! " hissed Trevorrick.

Pengelly hurried to the window. A car had
stopped by the obstructing lorry, and from it
walked a man whom Pengelly instantly recognised
as Chamfer.

The Admiralty inspector had arrived three weeks
before he was due.

" Confound the fellow ! " ejaculated Pengelly.
" What's to be done now ? "

The spasm of rage evident in Trevorrick's face
had passed. He was smiling grimly.

" Make yourself scarce," he ordered. " I'll deal
with him."

Pengelly knew that tone. He went.

" Stand by when I call you," called out his
partner.

Left alone, Trevorrick preened himself and stood
up to wait the uninvited visitor.

Briskly the little man came into the office. The
two shook hands—Trevorrick cool and collected,
towering a good seven inches over the self-
important little Chamfer. A hawk confronting a
cock-sparrow would have been an apt simile.

" This is an unexpected visit, Mr. Trevorrick,"
began the inspector.   " We officials like to have our
little jokes, eh, what ?   Take you on the hop, eh ?
Ha, ha, ha !   Not my fault, though.   Another
Admiralty minute—confound 'em.   I've got to
send in a report upon the condition of R 81's
Diesel engines.   If disposed of, I must have the
name and address of the purchaser."

Trevorrick realised that he was in a fix.   He
could neither produce the machinery (unless he
gave the show away by taking Chamfer on board
the *Alerte*) nor could he offer his sales book for
inspection, since there was no record of the engines
being sold.

" Rather unusual, isn't it ? " he remarked, playing for time.   Already a scheme was hatching in
his ready brain.   " We've bought R 81, lock, stock
and barrel."

" But you must bear in mind that the Admiralty
has an undisputed right to supervise the breaking
up of these craft until the clearing certificate has
been granted."

" The engines have been removed," announced
Trevorrick.   " One minute : I'll turn up the name
of the purchaser."

He went to a safe behind his desk.   Mr. Chamfer
went to the window overlooking the creek.

" You haven't wasted much time over her," he
remarked, noting as he thought the meagre remains
of R 81.

After that, things were decidedly hazy as far as
the Admiralty inspector was concerned.   He was
conscious of a powerful hand thrust over his face

and a sickly, smelly object pressed tightly over his nose and mouth ; a desperate attempt to breathe, a sort of wild resentment at being thrown off his balance. Then, oblivion.

" Pengelly ! " shouted his partner.

" Good heavens, man ! " exclaimed Pengelly, when he entered the room and stood aghast at Trevorrick's temerity; " what have you done now ! You've spoilt everything."

" Spoilt nothing, except the train of this fellow's thoughts," retorted Trevorrick coolly. " He's our first haul. Thirty thousand you said—or was it fifty ? We'll get a tidy slice of that, Pengelly. We'll take him on board. It will interfere with previous arrangements, I fear."

" How about the chauffeur ? He'll be suspicious."

" Leave him to me," replied Trevorrick, picking up his hat. " Stand by in case Chamfer wants to sit up and take nourishment. If he does, give him some more of this."

He pointed to a bottle containing chloroform and ether.

Pengelly nodded. He was on the point of inquiring how his partner could explain Chamfer's presence to the crew, but thought better of it.

Presently, Trevorrick returned humming one of the latest music-hall ditties.

" That's that," he remarked. " The fellow went off like a lamb. Pitched him a yarn that his master was going down to Falmouth with us in the launch, and that he was to pick him up by telephonic orders to-morrow or possibly the day after at

Penzance. Now, Pengelly, sit down and write. Make out a medical certificate to the effect that ' Mr. Jasper Chamfer is at present under my care, suffering from '—what shall we say ?—' from influenza.' Put any old signature, with M.R.C.P. after it. We'll post it on to Devonport Dockyard. They won't worry to look up the doctor's name in the Medical Directory."

" How do we explain this to the men ? " asked Pengelly, pointing to the motionless figure on the coco-matting.

" Send up Barnard," was Trevorrick's only rejoinder.

Presently the bo'sun—formerly foreman—came hurrying up. His eyes bulged as he caught sight of the unconscious representative of My Lords Commissioners of the Admiralty.

" Do you know this man, Barnard ? " demanded Trevorrick.

" Ay, ay, sir ; 'tis th' inspector. Chamfer's his name."

" Then forget it," returned Trevorrick. " In future and for as long as I think necessary his name's Jones. Got that ? "

The bo'sun nodded.

" The skunk has let us down," continued the senior partner in unruffled tones. " You'll remember he agreed to let us recondition R 81 as a salvage craft. After all our trouble, he went back on his word because we would not comply with his demand for a quarter share. He threatened to report the matter. The fool didn't realise what he was up against. The question is, what's to be done with him ? Any suggestion, Barnard ? "

" Take him with us, sir."

" Smart idea that, Barnard ; very smart. Don't you think so, Pengelly ? We'll act on it. Cut off and tell the hands of what has occurred. Warn them that we must at all costs weigh and proceed at tide-time."

" Ay, ay, sir ; we'll have to fill the fresh-water tank and ship the rest of the dry provisions. I'll tell off a party to swing back the boom."

" And a couple of hands to carry this fellow aboard," added Trevorrick.

" Now pack," he continued, addressing his partner. " We've none too much time. In a way it's as well. It will afford a good excuse to go up Channel instead of proceeding to the mythical wreck of the phantom ship *Posidon*. We needn't worry ourselves about the newly-christened Jones. The crew will deal with him."

" What are you going to do with him when we get him on board ? " asked Pengelly. " Ditch him ? "

" Against my principles," laughed the other. " 'Sides, there's money to be made out of him. You wait."

Throughout the rest of the day the work of preparation proceeded. Amongst other things the wireless aerial was sent aloft. The installation was the original set belonging to R 81, but for good reasons Trevorrick cut out the transmission gear. Communication by wireless was apt to be a two-edged sword. By its use the position of the pirate ship *Alerte* might be located to within a mile. Receiving was a different matter. It would enable the *Alerte* to gain valuable information regarding the presence of shipping in her vicinity.

Jasper Chamfer was soon carried off to the ship. Trevorrick's invention of his cupidity and treachery was only too successful. At the thought that the enterprise which was to make them rich was in jeopardy through the action of the double-dealing Admiralty official, the crew were ready to go to any length to muzzle him most effectually.

At eight o'clock on a rising tide, and with the seven-day-old moon well down in the west, the *Alerte* slipped her moorings

CHAPTER IV

THE FIRST HAUL

IN spite of her premature departure, the *Alerte* was well found for her work. Everything that Trevorrick and Pengelly could provide had been placed on board, or had been arranged for at the earliest possible opportunity. Yet Trevorrick smiled grimly when he reflected that here was a modern pirate vessel proceeding to sea absolutely unarmed with the exception of a service revolver and fifty rounds of ammunition.

Pengelly, whose acquaintance with Falmouth Harbour and the river Fal was extensive, conned the ship from the bows, transmitting his orders to the quartermaster at the above-water steering apparatus. Trevorrick, in peaked cap, bridge coat and rubber boots, tramped up and down the temporary structure amidships. He was feeling rather anxious, not on account of his recently adopted profession, but as to whether the *Alerte* would clear St. Anthony Point without either grounding or being challenged by the Falmouth Customs officials. He was one of those devil-may-care fellows who never hesitate to take risks and face the consequences provided they have had a run for their money. Ignominious capture

3

at this early stage of the proceedings would be the limit of bitter disappointment.

Slowly the *Alerte* smelt her way down the intricate channel of Polkyll Creek. Once her rounded bilge scraped the mud, but without losing way she dragged over the slippery obstruction. Ahead lay the dark, tree-clad hills of the right bank of the Fal.

" Hard-a-starboard ! " shouted Pengelly, supplementing these instructions by ordering the port engine to " go astern."

Even then, under the opposing action of the twin propellers the *Alerte* described a fairly wide turning circle. It was only by a hand's-breadth that she avoided running her nose against the opposite bank.

" Easy ahead both ! " bawled the navigating officer.

The dense wooded ground echoed and re-echoed to the explosions of the supposedly muffled exhausts. If this noise continued, Trevorrick realised that all attempt to disguise the means of propulsion of the *Alerte* was at an end. As far as he could judge, the distinctive sounds would be audible from Green Bank to St. Mawes.

Gradually the river opened out. Mylor Creek bore broad on the starboard beam. Now unchecked by the lofty and narrow banks the noise of the exhausts sensibly diminished, while the rising breeze, hitherto masked by the trees, served still further to stifle the oral evidence of the presence of the mysterious craft.

Then, like a galaxy of stars, the lights of the

shipping and the town of Falmouth opened out. For the next three miles would be the critical part of the run. At any moment the tricoloured lamp of one of the Customs' launches might be seen bearing down upon the outgoing " tramp."

" Lugo Buoy on the port bow, sir ! "

Now the gauntlet was all but run. Ahead loomed the rugged outlines of St. Anthony and Pendennis, with the narrow channel between them, still further contracted by the dangerous Black Rock.

" Ahoy ! What ship is that ? " hailed a voice out of the darkness. Unseen and unheard, a motor launch had swept alongside the pirate vessel's port quarter.

" *Alerte* of London ! " shouted Trevorrick.

" Cargo ? "

" Light."

" Where are you bound ? "

" Truro for Plymouth."

" All right. Heave us a line. I'll see your papers."

" Ay, ay," replied Trevorrick.

His ready brain was working. If things came to the worst, the Customs' launch could be stove in by the simple expedient of dropping a pig of iron into her. He might even take the crew prisoners ; but, he reflected, there was no likelihood of obtaining a ransom for *them*. They would merely be useless mouths to feed.

" Ease down ! " bawled the imperious voice.

" Ay, ay," responded Trevorrick, but made no move towards putting the order into execution.

" Stand-by ! " he bawled, brandishing a coil of rope.

The bowman of the launch caught the flake of the coil and took a turn. Directly the rope tautened, Trevorrick cut it. The launch dropped astern, until under extra throttle she again ran alongside.

It was a gain of a couple of minutes. By this time the *Alerte* was lifting to the fairly heavy rollers coming in from the English Channel. With her additional top-hamper she was rolling pretty heavily.

But by this time the Customs' boatmen had thought better of it. Boarding an outward-bound vessel was not such an imperative duty as examining one " come foreign." It wasn't worth the risk of having their boat stove-in and finding themselves in the ditch on a cold November night. A breaking sea sweeping clean over the canopy decided the question.

Without a word, the motor-launch's helm was put hard over. Listing dangerously, she flung about and disappeared into the darkness.

Thoughtfully, Trevorrick put a stopper round a piece of pig-iron lying in the scuppers.

St. Anthony Light blinked knowingly away on the *Alerte's* port quarter.

" Well ? " inquired Pengelly, stamping aft. He had put Marchant on duty in the eyes of the ship, since there was now plenty of sea-room.

" We'll submerge off Helford," decided Trevorrick. " Wind's off the land. It'll give the crew a chance to exercise. Get the hands to stand by with the mast-lowering tackles."

Twenty minutes later the *Alerte*, with masts and funnel lowered, slowed down a couple of miles due east of Mawnan Chair. A cast of the lead gave sufficient depth.

" Hands to diving stations ! " roared Trevorrick, his words recalling incidents of long-past days when under better auspices he had held command of a submarine flying the white ensign.

Quickly the crew disappeared below. Giving a final glance round, Trevorrick followed Pengelly through the hatchway, which closed after them with a metallic clang.

The throb of the Diesel engines ceased. The silence was profound, broken only by the top of the wavelets against the outer plating of the hull.

The electric lights gleamed upon the grave faces of the crew. With two exceptions they were new to submarine work. They had excuse to feel jumpy, but the sight of their cool and composed skipper gave them a certain amount of confidence.

A gurgling noise announced that the buoyancy tanks were being flooded. Slowly the disc of the depth indicator began to move. Once it started it never faltered until it stopped at eleven fathoms.

The *Alerte* was resting on the bed of Falmouth Bay.

" All shipshape and Bristol fashion, my lads ! " exclaimed Trevorrick, turning away from the control station and drawing off his leather gauntlets. " No anchor watch to keep. We're as snug as fleas in a rug."

The men trooped for'ard for supper. Trevorrick and Pengelly retired to the diminutive wardroom amidships, where a repast was already spread upon the teak swing-table.

" To-morrow," remarked Trevorrick, in the course of the meal, " To-morrow, Tom Trevorrick ceases to exist as such. Henceforward I am Captain Cain—' every man's hand against mine,' you know."

" Then you're letting the hands know early ? "

Trevorrick nodded.

" And what am I, then ? " continued Pengelly. " Captain what ? "

Trevorrick laid down his knife and fork and looked fixedly at his companion.

" Captain Nothing," he replied. " There won't be two captains aboard this hooker. You can put that in your pipe and smoke it."

" But we're on equal terms ? "

" From a financial point of view, yes," agreed Trevorrick. " But mark you, I'm in sole command. There's no getting away from that : not an earthly. You, Pengelly, are second in command ; to be consulted as and when I think fit. You are to carry out my orders unquestioningly. Have you got that ? Good : then don't forget it."

Then, having delivered his ultimatum, Trevorrick's mood changed. He went on with his interrupted repast, chatting on topics that had no bearing upon the subject of the great enterprise.

Presently he inquired casually :

" Has Chamfer recovered his senses yet ? "

Pengelly shook his head.

" I haven't given him a thought," he replied.

The captain stretched out his hand and pressed a push. For'ard a bell tinkled shrilly. One of the crew, tapping upon the door, entered.

" See if Jones is stirring," ordered Trevorrick, glancing at the clock on the bulkhead, which showed that it was twenty minutes past one in the morning. " If he is, bring him along."

In less than a couple of minutes the man returned, followed by the luckless Jasper Chamfer. The Admiralty inspector looked and probably felt an utter wreck. The after-effects of the anæsthetic, coupled with the confined atmosphere of his cell, would have capsized many a man of tougher fibre.

" Stand there," ordered Trevorrick curtly, at the same time motioning to the seaman to make himself scarce. " Unaccustomed surroundings, eh ? "

" Where am I ? " inquired Chamfer tremulously.

" As near as I can say, you're between ten and eleven fathoms beneath the surface of Falmouth Bay," announced his captor grimly. " But I haven't brought you here to ask me questions. I want information from you and—I'm—going—to —get—it."

He paused to let his words sink in.

" You poked your nose into our affairs. I'm going to probe into yours," continued Trevorrick.

" It was my duty."

" That's your affair. Now, tell me. I understand you're worth about thirty thousand pounds. Is that so ? Well, I won't inquire, I'll assume. They say ' silence means consent.' That thirty thousand is an encumbrance. Already you're self-supporting, drawing a fat salary and doing precious little to earn it—doing it mightily badly, I might add. You'll have to disgorge : some of it, at least. How is that sum invested ? "

Chamfer shook his head.

" I won't tell you," he replied, with a faint show of spirit, which his quivering form belied.

" Disobliging blighter," commented the captain. " Very well, then. There's nothing more to be said at present. You'll go back to your cell. To-morrow you will look upon the sun for the last time."

Without giving the Admiralty official another look, Trevorrick touched the bell.

" Remove Jones," he ordered.

" By Jove, man ! " ejaculated Pengelly, after Chamfer had been taken away ; " he would have told. I could see it on his face."

" I didn't look," was the unconcerned response. " To-morrow he'll be as docile as a dove. And while I'm about it," he added, " in future you will drop that tone of familiarity you've been in the habit of using. Remember, as your captain I am entitled to the word ' sir.' . . . You'd better turn in now, Pengelly."

Pengelly got up and went out without a word.

The door had hardly closed when the captain recalled him.

" Good-night, Pengelly."

" Good-night, sir ! "

" Nothing like putting it across the prevaricating blighter," soliloquised Trevorrick. " Without proper respect all discipline goes by the board."

Pengelly, in his cabin, was indulging in different views.

"If the swine thinks he's going to ride the high horse with me, he's mistaken," he muttered. "I'll do him properly when I get the chance."

The night passed uneventfully. At four bells the hands were roused and breakfast served out, every one being given a liberal tot of rum. The meal over and the "traps" cleared away and the mess-deck being cleaned up (Trevorrick was "dead nuts" on routine), the men were mustered in the fore-compartment that previously served as the bow torpedo-room and air-flask chamber.

To them came Trevorrick, rigged out in pea-jacket, gold braided cap, muffler, flannel trousers, and sea-boots. At his right hip was a holster, the flap of which was unfastened to display the butt of a revolver.

"Men!" he began. "Circumstances are against us: luck isn't! That swine of an Admiralty inspector has to be held responsible. He has 'blown the gaff.' Taking advantage of the confidence I placed in him, he has betrayed the secret of the *Posidon's* cargo to the Admiralty. I understand a dockyard lighter with a diving party is already over the position of the ingots. That being so, our original plans are a wash-out. But little difficulties of that description, annoying though they be, don't daunt me. Since Jones has caused the trouble, Jones must pay.

"I'm going to take strong measures. I haven't the faintest doubt that they will attain the desired end. To be brief, I intend to squeeze him to the extent of £20,000. Of that sum, Mr. Pengelly and myself each take £5,000. The remainder— £10,000—will be divided between the hands in proportion to the wages you were receiving while in the employ of Trevorrick, Pengelly, and Co. I have not yet worked out each man's share, but on a rough calculation it varies between £300 and £400 a-piece, which is considerably in excess of the sum originally offered in connection with the proposed, but now abandoned, salvage operations. Later on, I have other attractive propositions to bring forward, but for the present I'll say no more."

It might be owing to the strong spirit, it might be the vision of sudden and easily gotten wealth. Be that as it may, the captain's speech roused the men to boisterous enthusiasm.

Trevorrick left them to discuss matters.

" I said they'd eat out of my hand, Pengelly," he remarked. " One word from me and they'd cut the throats of the first crew of foreigners we came across. Not that that is my intention," he added.

As dawn was breaking, the *Alerte* was brought to the surface. Masts and funnel were set up, the motors started ahead at a modest five knots, a course was shaped to the S.S.E. which would take her well clear of the Cornish coast.

When twenty miles out in the Channel, Trevorrick swept the horizon with his binoculars. Save for a large oil tanker well away beyond the Lizard, there was nothing in sight—which was precisely what Trevorrick had wanted.

" Clear lower deck ! " was the order.

Up tumbled the hands. Under the captain's directions a plank was brought out and placed with his heel resting on the deck amidships, and its outer end projecting five feet beyond the low bulwarks.

" Fall in on your respective sides—port and starboard watch," shouted Trevorrick. " When Jones comes on deck howl at him. Put the wind up him for all you're worth. I'm not going to carry my threat into execution. It won't be necessary, and he's not worth it. . . . Bring up the prisoner."

A combined yell like the howling of a pack of wolves greeted the trembling Jasper Chamfer. With quivering steps he was led to the foot of the slightly inclined plank. Here his eyes were bandaged and his arms lashed behind his back.

Trevorrick held up his hand for silence.

The uproar ceased immediately.

" Now," began the captain in clear, measured tones, addressing the captive. " I will state our terms whereby you may gain your life and, under certain restrictions, your liberty. If within thirty seconds from the termination of my proposal you still refuse a perfectly reasonable demand— there's the plank. You will sign an order on your bankers, authorising them to pay the person named in your letter of advice the sum of £20,000. Having done that, you will be placed on board a vessel bound foreign, you giving the undertaking that you will not reveal your identity nor attempt to cancel your bond within the period of four months. Remember that, if you do, your life will not be worth a red cent. We belong to a powerful and widely scattered society, having agents in the principal ports all over the world. Conform to the conditions and you will be free to return at the expiration of the time limit mentioned. Refuse and your fate rests with you."

In dead silence, Trevorrick pulled out his watch. The blindfolded man could hear the deliberate ticking of the timepiece.

" Ten seconds," announced Trevorrick. . . . " Twenty seconds, ten more to go. Stand by, you men. . . ."

" I agree ! " almost shrieked the tortured man, and with a groan he pitched forward. Trevorrick caught him as he fell.

" The twenty thousand's ours, lads ! " he announced. " Pipe down. Take him below."

The assembled crew broke ranks and were about to disperse, when Trevorrick swung round on his heel.

" Stand fast ! " he ordered.

Months, nay years, cannot destroy the deeply-rooted sense of discipline of the ex-naval man. Smartly the ununiformed crew pulled themselves together and waited immovable, while two of their number " struck " the unconscious Chamfer down below, lowering him through what was originally the fore torpedo hatch.

" Men ! " exclaimed Trevorrick. " We may just as well understand each other. Already you have seen how I deal with those who thwart my

purpose, especially when that purpose is to the
advantage of those in my employ and under my
command. You all know, only too well, what it is
to be up against Fate. So do I. Since the chance
of earning an honest living is denied us—honest
according to the ideas of a certain class of society
that has never to study the question of existence
from our standpoint—there remains another alternative. You know the saying : ' Heaven helps
those who help themselves.' I mean to act upon
that, on the firm belief that Providence will see
us through. We've made an excellent start.
You will naturally feel inclined to ask : How shall
we help ourselves on future occasions ? Already
we have broken the law and incurred severe
penalties by kidnapping a citizen of the realm
and a government official to boot. All of us,
remember."

He paused in order to let his words sink in.

" May as well be 'ung for a sheep as a lamb, sir,"
exclaimed one of the men.

Several of his companions uttered expressions of
assent.

" That's the spirit," said Trevorrick. " Exactly what I expected. Well, my lads, it's my
intention to arm this old hooker. Already
arrangements have been completed to that end.
Then we'll stop the first likely Dago or Hun ship
we fall in with and see what we can do to ease
their pockets. Mind you, I'm not going to run
needless risks. I have your interests as well as
my own at stake. It's going to be a short cruise
but a busy one. When we pay off there will be

no doubt that each of you will have sufficient money to buy a comfortable pub and live the rest of your lives in simple luxury and ease. Think what you can do with, say, three thousand of the best to play with—probably more. Now then; any questions ? "

Questions came; slowly at first, then rapidly. Trevorrick dealt with each at length, replying so suavely and convincingly, that his listeners were metaphorically lifted off their feet. They were not inquiries respecting the proposed methods by which they were to acquire wealth, nor did the questioners seem to trouble themselves over the possible consequences of their lawlessness. The subject that weighed most heavily on their minds was: how were they to obtain guarantees that their shares would actually reach them ?

" Exactly the sort of question I should expect from an intelligent body of men," replied Trevorrick. " Naturally you look ahead. Your horizon isn't six inches from your eyes. But you can see perfectly well that it would be impracticable to run ashore a cargo of booty valued, say, at fifteen thousand and divide it up like a sirloin of beef. We have to employ an agent—a middleman. One is already engaged—a thoroughly trustworthy Penzance man—and you know the word of a Penzance man is his bond. He will take off our loot and dispose of it. The profits of each transaction will be immediately apportioned. Each of you can either have his share posted to any address he cares to give, or it can remain with the agent

till called for in person. In the case of cash and
jewellery, we will, if thought necessary, make the
division on board."

" S'posin' some of us loses the number of our
mess, sir ? " asked a burly ex-stoker, " wot
'appens ? "

" You lose it, I suppose," replied Trevorrick.
" We will all do sooner or later. It will be all the
same a hundred years hence."

Several of the hands laughed at their skipper's
feeble joke.

" But I know what you mean," he continued.
" In bygone days, pirates used to regard the death
of one of their number as a sort of windfall. It
enhanced the value of the survivors' shares. I
have no intention of following that precedent.
Every member of the crew can nominate a next-
of-kin in the event of his losing his life—which I
am anxious to avoid."

" You mentioned pirates, sir," remarked the
bo'sun. " I take it we're to sail under the skull
and cross-bones ? "

There was an ominous silence. The sinister
significance of the term had struck home.

" Now you come to mention it, Mr. Barnard, I
really think we are," replied Trevorrick lightly.
" But there's still time if there's any white-livered
blighter who wants to back out. Now, my lads ! "
he continued in ringing tones, " all those who do
not wish to carry on on my terms—two paces step
forward—March ! "

Not a man moved as directed. Two or three
shuffled and lowered their eyes under the stern gaze

of the self-declared pirate captain. Possibly they
would have taken advantage of the offer had it not
been that the fear of ridicule was stronger than their
inclination to keep within the law.

Trevorrick's smile had given place to a look of
grim determination. His shaggy eyebrows met in a
continuous straight line ; his aggressive jaw shot
forward.

" That's settled, my lads ! " he exclaimed.
" Now, there's something more to remember.   I am
the captain of this craft.   My orders you'll carry
out smartly, at the double, and unquestioningly.
If they're not, there'll be trouble—but there won't.
In the future, you—and others—will know me as
Captain Cain.   Mr. Pengelly here is second in
command ; Mr. Barnard is bos'un, and Mr. Marchant, gunner.   These, under me, are your officers
and must be treated with respect due to their rank.
I insist upon perfect discipline, which alone will
enable us to win through.   If any man has a
grievance against another, there must be no
quarrelling.   He must report the circumstances
to me and abide by my decision. . . . Mr. Marchant, before the men are piped down, serve out a
tot of rum apiece and drink success to the *Alerte*
and all who sail in her."

For the last hour the motors had been stopped.
There was no immediate hurry to reach the rendezvous, and Captain Cain was too prudent a man to
use up oil in aimlessly cruising up-Channel.   Unless
another craft came within sight the *Alerte* could
drift ; but the pirate skipper realised the risk of
his vessel wallowing in the long swell without

carrying way. That would be in itself sufficient to excite the curiosity of any passing shipping.

Presently, after a prolonged examination of the horizon, Captain Cain went below to his cabin, leaving Pengelly in charge of the deck. For certain reasons, the skipper did not desire the presence of his lieutenant.

He touched the bell and, on a man entering to inquire his pleasure, ordered Jones to be brought to him.

The wretched Jasper Chamfer, looking ill and horribly scared, was brusquely shown into Captain Cain's cabin.

" Good-morning," was the captain's greeting, as genial as if he were dealing with Chamfer in his capacity of Admiralty inspector.

" Good-morning," replied Chamfer, almost automatically. He was too bewildered to grasp the significance of his captor's irony.

" Sorry to trouble you," continued Captain Cain, " but there are a few formalities to be observed in the carrying out of our agreement. That twenty thousand ; is it in shares ? "

" Government Four per Cents., redeemable in 1931," replied Chamfer. " Also Six per Cents. Royal Mail."

" Deposited with whom ? "

" My bankers, Trevannion Brothers, Plymouth."

" Manager a friend of yours ? "

" I know him fairly well."

" Good," commented Captain Cain. " Here are paper, pen and ink. First write out an order transferring twenty thousand pounds to my account

4

—Thomas Trevorrick—payable to my bankers, Messrs. Grabaul, Yewgett and Co., Truro."

For some minutes there was silence in the cabin. Somewhere for'ard a gramophone was blaring out that popular ditty ; " Then he knew he'd parted."

Without a word, Chamfer handed over the order. The captain read it carefully.

" Ever heard that story about the Harley Street specialist, Mr. Chamfer ? " he inquired. " Two of the brigands met in Oxford Street. Said one, ' How much did you charge So-and-so for that operation ? ' ' Seventy-eight pounds fifteen and sixpence,' was the reply. ' Extraordinary amount,' commented the other. ' Whatever made you fix that sum ? ' The specialist laughed. ' I made him show me his pass-book,' he replied. Well, I'm not asking to see yours, Mr. Chamfer, nor am I lifting all your little pile. At the same time, I want to make sure of what I have got, so just write a friendly little covering letter to the manager of your bank."

" What shall I say ? " asked the victim wearily.

" Gracious, man ! Haven't you any imagination ? Perhaps that qualification isn't required of Admiralty Civil Servants. Tell him you've been unexpectedly ordered a sea voyage by your medical adviser, and that before you go you must make certain adjustments in your finances. . . . That's right. I presume you won't require a receipt ? "

" What are you going to do with me now ? " asked Jasper Chamfer, tremulously.

" What I told you before," replied the pirate, with

a grin. " A voyage to Jamaica or Pernambuco will do you a world of good. Broaden your outlook on life, Chamfer ; enlarge your mental horizon. But, remember, for the next four months your name's Jones. One hint to the contrary and, by Jove ! your number's up. 'Nough said ! "

Placing both documents in his pocket-book, Captain Cain turned to go on deck.

" You can amuse yourself as you like," he remarked. " You've got the run of the ship. There's nothing to be afraid of provided you hold your tongue."

It was blowing freshly from the west'ard when Captain Cain rejoined his lieutenant. The *Alerte*, with a trysail bent to keep her steady, was steering S.E. by S. making about one knot. Well away to the east'ard a beaten-down trail of smoke betokened the presence of some sort of steam vessel. To the south'ard half a dozen tanned sails indicated the position of one of the Cornish fishing fleets making for home.

" Got it, sir ? " inquired Pengelly. By this time the " sir " came with no noticeable hesitation, though the utterance caused the man to curse inwardly every time he had occasion to address his self-constituted superior officer.

" Yes," replied Captain Cain. " He parted like a lamb. I've an order for the twenty thousand. I'll have that transferred to Saldanha at Bahia. Useful man, Saldanha."

Late that afternoon, and after the sun had set beneath the misty waters of the English Channel, the *Alerte*, with smoke pouring from her funnel, rolled and lurched past Rame Head, rounded Penlee Point and brought up in the sheltered waters of Cawsand Bay. There was no attempt made to conceal her presence. An anchor-lamp shone brightly from the forestay. To all appearances she was just an ordinary tramp that had brought up outside Plymouth Breakwater while awaiting orders, and thus saving harbour dues which she would have incurred had she entered the Catwater.

"I'm going on the beach, Mr. Pengelly," announced the skipper, loud enough for the watch on deck to hear. "Send a boat for me at ten-thirty."

"Ay, ay, sir," replied the second in command, following up by ordering one of the boats to be lowered.

Ten minutes later Captain Cain, in shore-going rig, landed on the sandy beach at Cawsand. A few fishermen were lolling about in the narrow streets of the village. A member of the Coast Preventive Force was talking to the village policeman. Both glanced at the stranger, merely by force of habit. It was not unusual for people to come ashore at Cawsand.

"Can you tell me the nearest way to Plymouth?" asked Captain Cain of the modern substitute of the old coastguardman, not because he did not know, but to give the man an opportunity of questioning him.

Captain Cain was a good walker. In quick time he covered the distance between Cawsand and Cremyll, crossed by means of the ferry to

Devonport, and hastened along Union Street. Here he posted two missives : one in Chamfer's handwriting, addressed to the local bank (that would bear the Plymouth postmark, which was no small advantage); the other to his own bankers, instructing them that on the receipt of securities to the extent of twenty thousand pounds they were to sell out and transfer the proceeds to the firm of Señor Paquita, Calle Rancagua, Copuapó, Chile.

"Guess that fool Pengelly would look a bit sick if he knew," soliloquised Captain Cain, as he turned to retrace his steps. "It's all in the game. If I don't look after Number One, who else will ? "

CHAPTER V

THE RENDEZVOUS

" SAIL on the starboard bow, sir ! "

Captain Cain, binoculars slung round his neck, clambered up the almost vertical teak ladder to the temporary bridge.

It was in the forenoon watch—seven bells, to be exact—of the day following the pirate captain's visit to Devonport. The *Alerte*, ploughing along at an easy five knots, was abeam and nearly five miles to the south'ard of Bolt Tail. All that iron-bound coast betwixt Bolt Head and Bolt Tail stood out clearly in the sunlight. To the west'ard the lower lying ground bordering Bigbury Bay was invisible, while to the east'ard the Start was fading into the grey mists that sweep down when the cold Dartmoor air mingles with the warm atmosphere of the English Channel.

The mist was certainly spreading. Unless Captain Cain were very much mistaken, soon the granite cliffs of Devon would be blotted out by the watery vapour.

" I'll risk it," he decided.

At an aggregate speed of eleven knots, the *Alerte* and the strange vessel rapidly closed. Soon it was apparent that the latter was a collier ; more, she was well down to Plimsoll mark. From the data Captain Cain drew the following conclusions:

She was bound foreign. Evidently she hailed from the Tyne, and since the Welsh coalfields supply the iron furnaces around Swansea with as much coal as they want, it was as futile for a Tyneside collier to carry coals to the Bristol Channel ports as it would be for her to carry that commodity to Newcastle. She was standing too far out to be shaping a course for Plymouth, while her size and draught indicated that she was not an ordinary coasting collier.

"Make our number, Mr. Barnard!" sung out the skipper.

The "number," consisting of four flags of the International Code, was already toggled ready for instant use. The first letter was H, but the combination did not appear in the pages of the list of shipping. Captain Cain had seen to that.

The four-flag hoist had hardly reached the halyard block when the stranger replied with her number.

"KJVT, sir," sung out Mr. Barnard.

Reference to the list revealed the stranger to be the s.s. *Pickfast* of Newcastle, a subsequent signal, AXSR, indicating that she was bound for Kingston, Jamaica.

The *Alerte's* next move was to hoist her Code flag over the letter "H," signifying "Bring-to, I have something important to communicate." To which the collier replied by the single flag "C," indicating "Yes," and at the same time altering helm and stopping her engines

"Lower away a boat, Mr. Pengelly," ordered Captain Cain. "A couple of hands below there and bring Jones on deck."

In two minutes the boat, steered by Pengelly and with Jasper Chamfer in the stern-sheets, was bounding towards the collier *Pickfast*.

Without a word, the grim Northumbrian mate of the *Pickfast* caught the heaved bowline and took a turn. As the *Alerte's* boat swung alongside, a rope ladder was lowered to the accompaniment of an invitation to come aboard.

The *Pickfast's* Old Man had descended from the bridge and was awaiting his visitors. He was a short, thick-set Tynesider, with huge shoulders and bowed legs, a shrewd face and a taciturn manner.

"Eh, lad!" he exclaimed, addressing Pengelly. "What dost want?"

"A passage to Jamaica for this man," replied Pengelly, feeling that it would be a waste of time to beat about the bush. "We'll pay you fifty pounds in cash."

The Old Man threw a quick comprehensive glance over the little Admiralty inspector. He noted also that the would-be passenger was without luggage.

"I'll ha' nowt to do wi' him," he declared bluntly. "I've no call for passengers myseen. Police after him?"

"No, no," Pengelly hastened to reassure him. "All above-board, Captain. He came aboard us in a hurry, I'll admit. We were bound for New Orleans, but had our orders countermanded at

Falmouth. Jones is his name; ordered a long sea voyage for the benefit of his health. Come on, Captain. Fifty pounds easily earned."

"Coals an' bananas: them's my freight," remarked the skipper of the *Pickfast*. "Passengers aren't in my line. Still, it's easy money if he'll take things as he finds 'em. All right, Mr. Jones, I'll take you."

And with the air of a man who has conferred a great personal favour, the captain pocketed the notes and waddled in the direction of the bridge. With equal alacrity Mr. Pengelly clambered over the side and dropped into the waiting boat. The painter was cast off and the collier's propeller began to churn the water.

Mr. Jasper Chamfer had started on his involuntary voyage to Jamaica.

Eight hours later the *Alerte* dropped anchor in Studland Bay. Here she was not likely to be disturbed, nor would her presence excite much attention. Since she flew no signal for a pilot, the pilots for Poole Harbour let her severely alone. A vessel might lie there for a week without attracting official notice, since that anchorage is frequently made use of by craft bound down Channel. Provided the wind kept between sou'-sou'-west and north it was a secure berth, but should the wind fly round to any other point a heavy swell soon rolls into the bay, making it a matter of urgency for the vessels lying there to up-anchor and proceed.

The anchorage suited Captain Cain admirably. He was within a couple of hours' run of his rendez-

vous with the *Fairy*, and by this time Captain
Silas Porthoustoc ought to be on his way down-
Channel with his cargo of arms and ammunition.
Until the *Alerte* received the *Fairy's* Belgian cargo
little could be done to augment the pirates'
treasury.

At length the evening fixed for the meeting of
the pirate ship and her tender arrived. Seven in
the evening, with neither moon nor stars to miti-
gate the darkness of a November night, the
Alerte weighed, gave Old Harry Rocks a wide
berth and shaped a course to carry her well clear
of St. Alban's Head.

At ten o'clock she was at the rendezvous. The
prearranged signals were made, but no reassuring
reply blinked through the darkness.

Midnight came and went. At 4 a.m. the Middle
watch was relieved, but still no sign of the motor-
lugger *Fairy*.

"Old Porthoustoc's let us down, Pengelly,"
declared Captain Cain petulantly. "He's made
a lash-up of things. Shouldn't be surprised to
hear that he's under arrest either at Dover or
Dunkirk."

"Not he, sir," replied Pengelly confidently.

Both men had remained on deck all night, in
their eagerness to welcome the *Fairy* alongside.
Every quarter of an hour the flashing signals from
the *Alerte* stabbed the darkness, but not the
suspicion of an answer was received.

There was practically no wind. It was a belated St. Martin's summer. The air was warm
and moist, with patches of haze sufficient to

obscure the rays of Anvil Point light a bare twelve miles off.

"Flashing light on our starboard quarter, sir!" shouted one of the hands.

"That's her, then," declared Pengelly.

"What's the silly fool doing so far to the west'ard?" demanded Captain Cain, whose temper had not been improved by his long vigil. "Port twelve, Quartermaster. Watch for the next flash and keep her on that."

A quarter of an hour later the two vessels met, the *Fairy* with her canvas stowed and her motor coughing noisily.

"Sorry we'm late," said Silas apologetically, as the *Fairy* was made fast alongside her big consort. "Wind fell light up-along. Motor jibbed sudden-like. Never knowed 'un to play the fule afore. Tide carried us well to loo'ard afore us could get un gwine agen."

"All right, I hope?" asked Captain Cain.

"Ay, an' why not?" rejoined Silas Porthoustoc, as if the question were unnecessary, and that running a cargo of munitions was a mere bagatelle. "I'll come aboard. She'll lie nicely there," he added, jerking his thumb in the direction of the *Fairy*, which was grinding softly against the fender-protected side of the *Alerte*.

Silas, who like many another of his fellow-fisher-folk would have related anecdotes of his wife's sister's husband's cousin or other remote connection, kept up a running fire of family history. Without the slightest provocation, he would launch out details of relatives whom one never knew, never wanted to know and in all probability never did know. But when it came to what he had done he was almost as mute as an oyster. There was precious little *Ego* in Silas Porthoustoc's *Cosmos*.

" What's the matter with your hand, Silas ? " asked Pengelly, noticing in the lamplight that the old man's left hand was encased in bloodstained bandages.

" 'Urt 'un," was the reply, surly and almost resentful, as if the skipper of the *Fairy* had been called upon to make a confession of professional incompetence.

He did not think it necessary to add that the injury had been sustained thirty-six hours previously, when, in a nasty lop off the Nord Hinder, the precious cargo consigned to Captain Cain was in danger of making a swift passage to the bed of the North Sea. Only Silas Porthoustoc's prompt action in jamming the slipping sling had prevented the disaster ; but it was at the expense of a crushed hand and a badly lacerated finger.

As soon as the *Fairy* was secured alongside the *Alerte*, the latter's foremast derricks were swung outboard with the necessary tackle rove. There were cases of automatic pistols, each weapon concealed in an air-tight tin and packed in tallow. The tins bore the name of a well-known firm of tinned beef exporters and the cases were entered in the manifest as containing pressed beef. Three thousand rounds of small-arms ammunition followed, similarly disguised. Then came a crate with a card nailed to it, describing its contents as a sewing-machine. It was: " It sowed death broadcast "; for on the case being broken open there was revealed a machine-gun, firing the same calibre ammunition as that of the pistols, automatic in action and air-cooled. This had been ordered as an afterthought. As that class of article went it was cheap.

The mate and the boy of the lugger next set to work to shovel aside a thick layer of coal in the *Fairy's* hold. This done, they laid bare what appeared to be the lugger's kelson, a long, rough-hewn piece of timber. Under this was passed wire slings. The eyes of the slings were engaged in the hook of the lower block of the *Alerte's* derrick-purchase.

"Handsomely now, my lads!" cautioned Captain Cain, to the man manning the running part of the tackle. "Walk back with her—here she comes."

Torn from its bed of coal the huge bunch of timber rose slowly. By means of grips one end was dipped sufficiently to allow the twenty-five feet of woodwork to clear the hatchway coamings. Higher and higher it rose, the *Fairy* listing acutely during the operation, while even the *Alerte* heeled under the strain on her masthead.

"At that!" shouted Captain Cain. "Swing her gently, lads!"

Inboard swung the derrick, its load swaying eight feet above the deck in spite of the efforts of the hands at the grips.

"Ease away handsomely!" exclaimed the pirate captain. "Stand from under!"

With a dull thud the baulk of timber was

deposited upon the steel deck of the *Alerte*. The slings were cast off, and while some of the hands lowered and secured the derrick, others set to work seemingly to dismember the twenty-four feet of rough pine.

It was an easy task. Snugly hidden between the slabs was the much-wanted six-inch quick-firer. Its mounting followed, and was immediately bolted down to the deck just abaft the rise of the fo'c'sle.

"Carry on, Cap'n Porthoustoc," exclaimed Cain, after the necessary exchange of banknotes had been effected. "Look out for us on the 1st, and we'll have a rare cargo for you. Chenal du Four at sunset. It'll be slack water at nine."

"Very good, Cap'n," replied Silas, touching his grizzled forelock. "Us'll be there."

The warps were cast off, the *Fairy's* motor began to cough and splutter, and ten minutes later the lugger was lost to sight in the darkness.

But the night's work was far from being accomplished as far as the *Alerte's* crew were concerned. The six-inch quick-firer was mounted : it had to be concealed from outside observation. To attempt to screen the weapon from any one on deck would have been a senseless task. The construction of the submarine prevented that. Even her conning-tower stood out gaunt and unashamed when viewed from the deck ; but from another vessel that armoured structure seemed to be merged into the 'midship superstructure and bridge.

A cutter, hitherto carried abaft the 'midship deckhouse, was man-handled for'ard. Unlike the other boats, it was clench-built of elm ; but in order not to impede the *Alerte's* diving capabilities, the garboard strakes had been cut away. It was a simple though lengthy task to saw through the timbers next the keel and cut through breast-hook and transome, with the result that the cutter was longitudinally divided into two parts. Quick-release clips of gun-metal were then fitted to keep the two portions into some resemblance of a boat. The reunited parts were then placed keel uppermost over the quick-firer, a tarpaulin being stretched over all to hide the missing garboards.

Throughout the long night the hands toiled, Captain Cain giving practical assistance besides directing operations. He worked his men hard —he believed in it—but he never spared himself.

It wanted an hour to dawn when the task of making all snug was completed. Dawn ought to reveal the *Alerte* as a harmless tramp, her powerful ordnance stowed away under the boat. But Captain Cain was not satisfied.

" We'll submerge before we stand easy, lads," he shouted. " Eighteen fathoms 'll find bottom. Diving stations, all hands ! "

Down sank the *Alerte*, the tell-tale débris of splinters, shavings, and sawdust floating away as she submerged. She rested on the bottom in a very faint tideway, certainly not more than one knot. The crew piped to breakfast, completed the meal and expected a " stand easy."

They were disappointed. The *Alerte* was to break surface before dawn, lest the operation be seen by a passing vessel. Then and only then, as she cruised towards the French coast, were the hard-worked men allowed a brief spell of leisure.

" Anything in sight, Mr. Pengelly ? " sang out the captain, as he slithered over the weed-encumbered deck to the bridge-ladder.

The second in command was sweeping the horizon with his night-glasses. It was pitch dark —the period of intense darkness between the false and the true dawn.

" Nothing in sight, sir ! " reported Pengelly.

The words were hardly out of his mouth—in fact, Captain Cain had not time to telegraph " Easy ahead," when a loud voice, coming from close alongside, hailed :

" Ship ahoy ! Throw us a line ! "

CHAPTER VI

THE LAST OF THE *IBEX*

" I MUST hand her over to her new owner before the end of the present month, Gerald," declared Rollo Vyse, owner of the thirty-five-feet motor-yacht *Ibex*, to his chum Gerald Broadmayne. " If the worst comes to the worst, I must get professional assistance. You know what that means. Never could stick a paid hand. Be a sport and bear a hand."

" When do you expect to be back ? " inquired Broadmayne.

His chum felt this was a decidedly encouraging question, notwithstanding the fact that the other had used the second person plural instead of the first.

" Saturday evening, for an absolute cert," replied Vyse. " Glass is steady, sea calm. We'd make Southampton hands down by Friday morning, hand over the yacht and check the inventory, and catch the first train home on the following day."

Gerald Broadmayne was a strapping fellow of six feet two inches. In point of age he was " rising twenty-one." By profession, he was a sub-lieutenant R.N., and having just completed

5

a two years' commission on the East Indian Station, was already beginning to be "bored stiff" with his "little drop o' leaf," to quote the lower deck vernacular for the sailor's equivalent for furlough.

Existence in Fowey, even with its mild climate, was apt to be a bit tedious in November, after a prolonged spell under the tropical sun. Yachting was his hobby, although circumstances prevented him from having a small craft of his own. Almost without exception his pals in Fowey had laid their yachts up, and there was not much fun knocking about in the harbour or spending comfortless hours in the Channel in an open or half-decked boat.

The exception was Rollo Vyse, a lad two years his junior, two inches shorter than the Sub, but with a decided excess of girth. His arms and legs were massive and muscular. In spite of his ponderous frame he carried not an ounce of superfluous flesh. His big frame, hardened by almost unlimited physical exercise, was destitute of fat. He would sprint well and run a mile without undue physical distress ; swim like a South Sea Islander and dive like a duck. At school he was a terror with the gloves on. Twice in succession he was the champion athlete of the year of his school. Yet with all these accomplishments, he was far from being brilliant in educational subjects.

Fortunately, or unfortunately (that depended upon the future), Rollo had little to worry about. It was not necessary for him to earn his own living.

He had an ample allowance, provided he kept within the bounds of prudence—which he generally did. In due course, Rollo Vyse would become head of a huge coal combine, when his sole responsibility consisted in affixing his signature to the Annual Report.

Nineteen fellows out of twenty so situated would have gone to the dogs. Not so Rollo Vyse. A thorough sportsman, he had no use for companions whose chief aim was to " sow their wild oats." He meant to enjoy himself—to make the very best out of his youth—and he did.

His favourite pastime was yachting. He did not take it up as a sport. Yacht racing did not appeal to him. It was the lure of the sea that held him. The greatest of the few outstanding disappointments of his early youth was his father's refusal to let him go to sea, either in the Royal Navy through Dartmouth College, or in the Mercantile Marine through that strictly-disciplined yet withal happily-run training-ship, the *Conway*.

Vyse was a yachtsman of the modern school. He knew little about cutters, yawls, and ketches. Seamanship in such he was ignorant of. He never had to handle a craft under sail alone. He had never experienced the thrills of a short thresh to wind'ard with a weather-going tide.

His first craft was the *Ibex*, an out-and-out power boat. Thirty-five feet over all, with a beam of six feet and a maximum draught of three-feet-eight, the *Ibex* was propelled with a pair of petrol motors giving her a speed of about eleven knots.

Her accommodation consisted of a spacious fo'c'sle with two " pipe-rail " cots ; a saloon with settees on either side and a swinging table on the centre line ; abaft a small galley, separated from the engine-room by a steel bulkhead with a sliding door that was supposed to be water-tight. The engine-room was large in proportion to the size of the boat, being nearly nine feet in length, with a narrow, railed-off gangway between the twin motors. Abaft the motor-room was a " sunk " deckhouse, containing the wheel and the engine-room controls. Right aft a large open cockpit with a short deck and coamings.

For nearly a twelvemonth the *Ibex* was Rollo Vyse's pride and delight. She was a good sea-boat, her engines had never once let her owner down. "Vyse's luck" was almost proverbial in Fowey. If he said he would return to harbour on a certain day, he always did so, although on some occasions the Polruan fishermen shook their heads as they climbed the hill and gazed towards the surf-swept Gribben. "That there moty-boat'll drown 'un sure as sure," they would declare ; but the sight of the *Ibex* pounding the heavy seas as she passed the rocky ledges around Punch's Cross, and entered the land-locked harbour, compelled them to admit that for the present their cheerful prognostications were some-what adrift.

But into Rollo Vyse's Eden had arrived the serpent under the name of one Jim Vardo—a good fellow and all that sort of thing, according to Rollo's admission. Vardo without the *Spitfire* was quite all right. It was Vardo *with* the *Spitfire* that upset Rollo.

Why ? Simply because the *Spitfire* did twelve and a half knots to the *Ibex's* eleven.

Vyse was not a racing man as far as marine motoring went, but when the *Spitfire* seemed to make a point of going almost everywhere the *Ibex* went, and overhauled her every time, there was a supercilious, self-satisfied look upon Vardo's face that made even easy-going Rollo Vyse squirm.

" Wait till I get him out in a stiff sou'wester," muttered Rollo. " I'll knock spots off his old orange-box."

But that opportunity never came, for the simple reason that Vardo hadn't the real love of the sea. He himself admitted that he was cautious ; Rollo with characteristic bluntness declared that Vardo was " white-livered." At any rate, the *Spitfire* never showed her nose beyond the mouth of Ready Money Cove when there were white horses in the Channel.

The fact that in smooth water the *Spitfire* could show her heels to the *Ibex* decided the latter's fate. Vyse decided to sell her and purchase another motor-cruiser, larger, more powerfully-engined and capable of developing fifteen and a half knots. Then Jim Vardo's loose-lipped, mealy-mouthed features wouldn't wear that fatuous grin.

Accordingly, the *Ibex* was sold to a South-ampton yachtsman, subject to delivery at that port ; and now arose the problem how Vyse was to get her round.

It was late in the year. His chums rather

jibbed at the suggestion that they should fôrm a
crew. Had it been Cowes week they would have
clamoured for the vacant berth; for although the
Ibex was arranged as a single-hander, and Rollo
often had taken her out alone, the passage between
Fowey and the Wight was rather too long for a
one-man show.

Rollo was getting jumpy. November was well
advanced. No amateur help was forthcoming.
He was about to take the unwelcome step of
engaging a professional hand when a *deus ex
machina* in the person of Sub-Lieutenant Gerald
Broadmayne appeared upon the scene.

It did not take Broadmayne long to make up his
mind. The ability to make a quick decision on
points that require unerring judgment is a characteristic of the naval man who hopes to make
a name for himself in his profession.

"Right-o; I'll come," he replied. "When
do you get under way?"

"In an hour's time," said Vyse promptly, lest
too prolonged an interval might afford his new
shipmate an opportunity to change his mind.
"Provisions and petrol are on board. I'll have
to lay in some fresh tack, though. Heaps of
bedding, too. All you'll want is your kit."

"I'll be at Whitehouse Steps in half an hour,"
declared the Sub. "Must slip off on my motor-
bike and tell my people that Little Gerry is off
on the high seas and pack up a few things."

"And I'll do the same," added Rollo; "although my governor's been expecting to hear
that I've actually cleared every day for the last

fortnight. You're a real pal, old man. Thanks awfully."

Prompt to time, the chums met at the pre-arranged spot. The Sub was rigged out in white sweater, grey flannel " bags " and rubber shoes. Across his shoulder was thrown a black pegamoid oilskin. A suit-case containing clothes of sufficient respectability to enable him to return by train lay at his feet.

Vyse appeared in a thick blue sweater, pilot coat and trousers, the bottoms of the latter garment being rolled over a pair of india-rubber sea-boots.

" Rest of my gear's already on board," he remarked as they descended the steps to the dinghy. " We're going to have a topping run if this weather holds. How about making an all-night run ? We'd be inside the Wight before morning."

" I'm game," replied Broadmayne, dumping his suit-case in the stern sheets of the dinghy.

It was a short distance to row out to the moorings on which the *Ibex* lay. The motor yacht, riding to the first of the young flood, looked smart and seamanlike in the afternoon sunlight. From the short, slender mast fluttered the club burgee, hoisted for the last time on that particular craft. A loose-footed lugsail and small foresail formed the sum-total of the yacht's canvas. Vyse rarely made use of the sails, since the motors never gave trouble. In the event of a mechanical breakdown, the *Ibex* might do four miles an hour with the wind abaft the beam ; but with her light draught she would sag to lee'ard like a barrel.

Rollo disappeared into the motor-room, leaving his chum to stow his gear and make the dinghy fast alongside. Bitter experience in the shape of a painter getting hopelessly foul of one of the propellers had prompted this course. Not until the yacht was forging ahead would the dinghy be allowed to tow astern.

First one, then both of the motors began to purr rhythmically. Vyse appeared on deck, gave a perfunctory glance over the side to see that the circulating pumps were working, and nodded to his companion.

" Let go ! " he exclaimed.

With a splash and a rattle of chain, the mooring buoy was dropped. Slowly the *Ibex* drifted upstream until Vyse from his post in the wheelhouse could see the buoy bobbing twenty feet from the bows.

Putting the helm over, Rollo pulled both levers into the ahead position. Instantly the little craft shot forward, cleared her buoy and headed for the open sea.

" Dinghy on deck ? " queried the Sub coming aft.

" No, she'll tow astern," was the reply. " There's no sea to speak of outside. Give her plenty of painter."

Broadmayne did so. This done, he lighted a cigarette and took up a position slightly in the wake of the helmsman.

Neither spoke much. Both enjoyed the lift of

the following waves as the keen bows of the *Ibex* cleft the dancing waters. They were afloat with a definite object in view. For the present, nothing else mattered.

Rollo Vyse was too good an engineer to attempt to run the motors all out. For one thing, it was bad for the bearings if the engines were run " all out " for any length of time, and he wasn't anxious to deliver the *Ibex* to her new owner with her anatomy resembling a box of chattering scrap iron. For another, he did not wish to cover the one hundred and thirty miles between Fowey and the Wight at such a speed that the *Ibex* would be in the narrow waters of the Solent before sunrise. What he aimed for, was to reach Southampton before noon, thus giving ample time to perform the necessary formalities connected with the handing over of the yacht.

The Start was abeam just as the sun was setting. The *Ibex* gave that dangerous headland with its treacherous overfalls a wide berth, and shaped a course to pass seven miles to the south'ard of that nightmare to cautious mariners—Portland Bill.

It was a warm, almost balmy night. The thick clouds, acting as a blanket, totally obscured the stars, but kept the temperature remarkably high for the time of year. All the same, after having shared a meal on deck, the two chums were glad to don oilskins and mufflers before undertaking their long vigil.

" Aren't you funky of going into the motor-room with that ? " inquired Broadmayne, as Rollo appeared from an examination of the oil gauges of the automatic lubricators, his features glowing in the glare of a lighted cigarette.

" Goodness—no," replied the other, with a laugh. " Haven't you ever seen a fellow shove a lighted cigarette into a full tin of petrol ? "

" Haven't and don't want to," replied the cautious Sub.

" Well, it's not the petrol ; it's the petrol fumes that are the danger," continued Vyse. " There's far more danger from the fumes in an empty petrol can than there is in a full one. The motor-room is well ventilated and there are trays to catch any drops from the carburettors, so you see I am careful. . . . Aren't the engines going beautifully ? Eight hundred revs., and hardly any vibration."

For the next two hours the two sat perched on the low bulkhead on the after side of the wheelhouse, Vyse occasionally touching the wheel to correct the vessel's slight tendency to fall off to starboard.

" We ought to spot Portland Light very soon," he remarked. " That is, unless there's local fog about."

" I'll look," said Broadmayne, unstrapping his binoculars.

Steadying himself with legs set widely apart, the Sub stood erect upon the roof of the wheelhouse.

" Nothing in sight yet," he announced.

The next instant the *Ibex* trembled under a violent shock. For the moment she seemed to lose way. Broadmayne, thrown off his balance,

pitched forward, falling at full length upon the
coach-roof over the motor-room. There he lay,
grabbing at the low brass railing, until, feeling a
bit dazed and shaken, he made his way aft.

" What's up ? " he inquired breathlessly.

" Hit a bit of wreckage, I think," replied Rollo.
" Gave her a bit of a biff. You're not hurt ?
Good, I thought you'd stove-in your deadlights,
old man, by the way you fell."

His anxiety relieved concerning his chum, Rollo
Vyse's next thoughts were for the yacht. As far
as he knew, the *Ibex* had not fouled either of her
propellers. Evidently her forefoot had thrust
down the submerged object sufficiently to enable
the cut-away stern to clear.

" Hang on to the wheel a jiffy while I go below
and have a look round," he said ; and, picking up
an electric torch from a rack in the wheelhouse,
he dived below.

He was gone some time—nearly a quarter of an
hour. When he reappeared, he reported that the
boat was not making any water beyond a slight
trickle through the stern gland of the starboard
propeller.

" I think she must have given her prop. a bash,"
he added. " There's an unusual noise as if the
shaft isn't running true. You can't hear it from
here."

" There's Portland Light ! " exclaimed Broadmayne, as four pin-pricks of white appeared on
the port bow. " Rather close in, aren't
we ? "

" Indraught, perhaps," replied his chum.

" We'll stand out a bit. South eighty east will do."

The Sub made the necessary alteration in helm. Midnight passed. Portland Light was drawing abeam. According to Vyse's calculations, it ought to have been passed a couple of hours earlier.

" Guess there's a hot tide against us," he remarked. " Or, perhaps we aren't doing nine knots. It's all right so far ; we've an ample margin."

The sea had now grown distinctly agitated, although there was little or no wind. Rollo put it down to the backwash from Portland Race, the roar of which was distinctly audible—a disconcerting noise on a dark night. " Now we're closing the Shambles Lightship. We ought soon to pick up Anvil Point. I'll have another look round below and then I'll bring up some hot drinks."

Instead of going down the engine-room hatchway, as before, Vyse made his way for'ard, gaining the saloon direct by means of another hatch. Above the gentle purr of the motors the loud buzzing of a Primus stove was borne to the Sub's ears, a grateful and comforting sound that gave promise of something piping hot within the next ten minutes.

Glancing at his watch, Broadmayne was rather surprised to find that it was nearly two o'clock. By means of rough compass bearings he calculated that the *Ibex* was about eight miles S.W. by W. of St. Albans. A few minutes later the two powerful lights ashore were blotted out.

About that time a vessel showing white and green navigation lamps passed at not less than a mile away. It was too dark to see what she was like, but the muffled pulsations of an internal combustion engine were distinctly audible.

A dazzling light from the *Ibex's* motor-room suddenly attracted the Sub's attention. Peering down the half-open hatchway he expected to see Vyse doing inspection work with his electric torch.

To his surprise, he saw that the light came from under the port engine—a steady flare of yellow light that was already licking the sides of the cylinders.

Before Broadmayne could utter a warning shout the steady flame developed into a sheet of fire. A blast of hot air tinged with tongues of ruddy flame shot up through the open hatchway. Yet Vyse gave no indication that he was aware of the peril.

Quitting the wheel, the Sub dashed for'ard. He could see his chum, sublimely unconscious of the inferno raging the other side of the steel bulkhead, crouching over the sizzling frying-pan on the Primus stove.

" Fire in the motor-room ! " shouted Broadmayne. " Where are the Pyrenes ? "

Even then Rollo showed no great haste until looking up he caught a glimpse of the Sub's startled face.

" All right ! " he bawled—shouting was the only means of making himself heard with the roar of the atmospheric gas stove. " All right. They're in there. I'll get them."

With that he shot back the sliding door in the metal bulkhead. A blast of hot air and flames sent him backwards, half-dazed. Involuntarily he raised one hand to protect his eyes ; then backing through the compartment next the seat of the fire, he gained the saloon.

He had left the bulkhead door open. A tongue of fire licked the panelled ceiling of the saloon. Madly he turned, swarmed up the ladder and gained the open air.

Seeing his chum safe, the Sub did the best possible thing. Descending into the saloon, he fought his way to the bulkhead and closed the door. Then emerging by the same way he had entered, he ran aft over the already excessively hot cabin top and closed the engine-room hatchway. There was a chance—a hundred to one chance—that the flames might die out through lack of oxygen.

" Come aft ! " shouted Broadmayne.

Vyse, now gaining more control over himself, obeyed. By now the motors had ceased to function. The flames, igniting the petrol in the carburettors, had melted the unions of the petrol-pipes. Instead of the inflammable spirit mixing with air and exploding within the cylinders—as it ought to do, two steady streams were pouring direct from the tanks, to add fresh fuel to the flames.

" Thirty gallons in the tanks ! " shouted Rollo in reply to his companion's unspoken question. " I'll go for'ard and turn off the taps. We'll be blown sky-high if we don't."

He placed one foot on the coaming before hoisting himself over the roof of the wheel-house. As he did so, the motor-room skylight blew out with a loud report, sending a pillar of flame-tinged smoke a full thirty feet into the air, and throwing every part of the deck into bold relief by reason of the dazzling light.

" That's done it ! " shouted Rollo.   " We can't save her now. The dinghy, old man ! "

At first the Sub could see no sign of the tender. He fully expected to see her trailing astern, but as the burning *Ibex* had lost all way the dinghy had ranged up alongside the starboard side.

There was no time to save anything. Casting off the painter, Broadmayne shouted to his companion to look alive. Vyse leapt into the dinghy, the Sub followed, giving a vigorous push as he sat down and sending the little cockleshell clear of the floating inferno.

" Where's the other scull ? " demanded Broadmayne anxiously.

There was only one in the dinghy. By some means one had been lost overboard. How or when, they knew not ; nor could they waste time in forming conjectures ; and since there was no sculling-notch in the transom, the only way to propel the little craft was by paddling with alternate strokes on either side.

It was slow work ; but not before the dinghy was fifty yards away from the burning *Ibex* did the Sub boat his oar.

" Now what's to be done ? " he inquired.

" Wait and see the last of her," replied Vyse. " Luckily, she's fully insured."

" You'll be lucky if you are alive to draw the money," thought Broadmayne, for it was a most unenviable position to be in. Ten miles from land,

and almost every foot of that land a frowning, surf-swept cliff, Portland Race to the west'ard and St. Albans Race waiting for them if they attempted to close the land. Although the wind was light, almost a flat calm, there was a steady swell, indicating a strong breeze, perhaps a gale, before very long. Overhead, save for the ruddy glare from the fiercely burning yacht, it was as black as pitch. Not a star was visible. It was only by remembering that the faint breeze came from the west'ard (and it might back or veer at any time) could any sense of direction be maintained.

In silence the two chums watched the passing of the *Ibex*. Amidships, flames were pouring fifty feet into the air. The coach-roof and part of the top strakes had gone to feed the flames, the cracking of woodwork adding to the roar of the burning petrol. Sizzling embers were falling like sparks from a dying squib, hissing as they dropped into the water. It was a question as to what would happen first : whether the hull, burned to the water's edge, would founder before the fire reached the fuel tanks.

Suddenly there was a terrific flash that, compared with the raging flames, was like an arc-lamp and a candle. Almost immediately after came a stupendous roar, like the discharge of a warship's broadside. In the midst of the up-flung volcano of flame appeared the whole of the forepart of the cabin top. With apparent slowness it turned over and over until it fell with a loud splash within twenty yards of the dinghy. Then, with a hiss

like the last defiant note of a dying viper, the last
of the burning wreckage disappeared from view,
leaving the dinghy tossing aimlessly on the heavy
waters, surrounded by a pall of darkness that was
rendered all the more opaque by the sudden transition from the blazing light.

" What's the time ? " inquired Vyse, breaking
the silence.

The Sub consulted the face of his luminous
watch.

" Half-past two."

" And daylight's not till about seven—four and
a half hours. Well, what's the programme ?
What's the coast like hereabouts ? "

" Precious few landing-places," replied the Sub.
" Lulworth Cove, Chapman Pool and perhaps
Warborough Bay. Might make one of 'em ; but
the chances are we'd fetch up on Kimmeridge
Ledges. The closer inshore we get, the more
likely we are to encounter short steep seas. Best
keep well out till dawn."

" Perishing cold job," grumbled Rollo, who,
before going below for the last time had discarded
his oilskin coat. Fortunately for him, the Sub
still wore his pegamoid. " And it's not much use
talking about getting ashore. We can't row ten
miles with one scull."

" That's so," agreed Broadmayne soberly. " I
vote we paddle. Take quarter of an hour spells.
That'll keep us warm. The fellow who isn't paddling can wear my oilskin coat. Wish we'd had our
grub before we started on this little cruise in a
tub."

6

" Luckily we have plenty to smoke," remarked Vyse. " Have a cigarette ? "

The word cigarette brought the Sub's thoughts back to the disaster.

" Wonder how the fire started ? " he asked. " You weren't in the motor-room at all, were you ? "

" No," replied Rollo. " Not the last time. I meant to go directly we'd had something to eat. It's just possible that when we bumped against that lump of wreckage the jar might have started one of the petrol pipes. And then it might be anything : short circuit of one of the high tension wires, for example."

Slowly—painfully slowly—the hours sped. In spite of frequent spells at the scull Vyse felt the cold acutely ; more so than did his companion, for he had been rather badly scorched about the face, and the night air irritated rather than soothed the sting.

Once, when a gentle breeze sprang up, they thrust a stretcher through the arms of the pegamoid coat and lashed it to the oar, stepping the latter as a mast. For about twenty minutes the dinghy maintained a steady rate of progress. Broadmayne entertained hopes of making either Swanage Bay or the sandy shore of Bournemouth Bay. Then the wind died utterly away.

" What's the time ? " inquired Vyse, for the thirtieth time at least.

" Quarter-past six," replied the Sub, without making the least effort to stifle a prodigious yawn.

" Another three-quarters of an hour before dawn, muttered Rollo. " There's a light astern."

Broadmayne looked.

" Shambles Lightship," he declared. " It's clearing a bit. We haven't made much progress. The tide must be setting to the west'ard. Hello, what's that ? "

" What's what ? " asked Vyse, following the direction of his companion's outstretched arm. " Can't see anything."

" There, about a hundred yards off. By Jove, it's a ship."

" It is, by smoke ! " admitted Rollo.

" No lights. She's not making way," continued the Sub, speaking more to himself than to his chum. " Strange—decidedly so. Abandoned, perhaps."

" Listen ! " exclaimed Vyse. " Voices."

Without replying, Broadmayne seized the paddle and commenced to propel the dinghy in the direction of the mysterious vessel. For mysterious she undoubtedly was. No ordinary craft would be lying without way and showing no riding-light. Smugglers, perhaps, but to Gerald Broadmayne it meant shelter—any port in a storm.

It was slow work. Ten minutes' frantic work with the scull brought the dinghy close under the strange vessel's starboard quarter.

" Nothing in sight, sir ! " exclaimed a deep voice.

" By Jove ! she'll be forging ahead in half a shake," thought the Sub, and, throwing down his oar, he hailed the unknown craft : " Ship ahoy ! Throw us a line ! "

CHAPTER VII

THE CAPTURE OF THE *CAP HOORN*

" SHEER off ! " shouted Captain Cain, leaning over the bridge-rails and directing the full blast of his powerful voice upon the still unknown craft alongside. " Stand clear ; we're going full ahead in half a shake."

" Hang on a minute, Cap'n ! " replied Broadmayne. " There are only two of us—survivors of the yacht *Ibex*, burnt late last night. If you won't take us on board you might give us some grub and water. We're famished and horribly cold, you know."

Captain Cain made a brief mental review of the situation, as far as he knew of the facts. He was not a soft-hearted man—far from it. There would be very little risk to the occupants of the boat if they remained adrift for a few hours longer. They were bound to be picked up by some of the up- and down-Channel traffic. He could provide them with a few provisions and then go ahead.

On the other hand, he was quite in the dark as to what the two men in the boat had seen or heard. It was much too early for the *Alerte* to reveal her true character, that of a submarine pirate craft. And it was very disconcerting when he, the captain, was congratulating himself that the *Alerte* had been armed and had gone through additional diving tests under cover of darkness, to find a boat lying alongside with two persons in her who might be remarkably cute in spotting anything out of the ordinary at sea.

The simplest solution was to drop a pig of ballast through the bottom of the boat and leave the two men to their fate. They couldn't keep afloat very long in the open Channel in November. On their own admission, they were cold and famished. They'd sink within five minutes.

But the suggestion was dismissed as quickly as it had been formed. Captain Cain was strongly opposed to taking life wantonly, whether it be man or beast. If occasion arose with sufficient justification for his point of view, the pirate captain would shoot down any one in cold blood or otherwise. Again, he had pledged himself to his crew, and for the present it was policy to abide by his plighted word, that he was against performing any violent act against the crews of British ships, and were not these two men British survivors of a disaster ?

And, judging by the tone of the man who had spoken, one of the survivors was some one of good, possibly high birth. In any case, the pair might prove useful additional hands to the *Alerte's* complement. If they wouldn't, well he'd make them. There was also the chance that the distressed mariners might be people of social standing and wealth. Then there would be a good opportunity to demand ransom. Coming on top of

the Chamfer incident, Captain Cain decided such
a possibility seemed no probability. He would
be lucky, indeed, if he could repeat his previous
success in that direction.

All this flashed through the ready brain of the
pirate captain in a very few seconds. Quickly
he made up his mind.

" Come aboard ! " he said briefly.

One of the hands caught the dinghy's painter.
A rope ladder was lowered down the perpendicular
side of the *Alerte*, and with a final effort to control
their cramped limbs, Vyse and Broadmayne contrived to reach the deck of the pirate submarine.

" Take them below ! " ordered Captain Cain
from the height of the bridge. " Tell Davis to
serve them with a good hot meal. They can
berth for'ard."

With his head swimming and his knees giving
way under him, Rollo Vyse was glad to have the
assistance of a couple of the crew to take him
below. Broadmayne, although feeling decidedly
groggy, still retained sufficient alertness of mind
to take stock of his immediate surroundings as
far as the first streaks of red dawn permitted.

The steel deck littered with kelp and seaweed
was in itself suspicious, unless the vessel were a
trawler and had just emptied her nets on deck.
But there was not the peculiar smell that steam
trawlers cannot get away from.

Directly the Sub found himself below, he knew.

" By Jove ! " he soliloquised. " She's a sub
marine."

In spite of his hunger and fatigue, Broadmayne

puzzled his brains over the strange situation. What was a submarine, disguised as a surface ship, doing in the Channel ? Her officers and crew were not in naval uniform, although several of them had unmistakable indications of having served under the white ensign. The owner, especially, had the cut of a *pukka* naval man.

" Perhaps she's a new type of Q-ship," he thought. " If the manœuvres were on, I could understand it. Won't it be a joke if she is a mystery ship ; and won't the owner feel a bit sick when he finds he's harbouring an inquisitive Sub on board his hooker ? Like his confounded cheek, though, making us mess and berth for'ard."

Soon the two chums were sitting down to a hot, substantial meal. They were not alone. The crew's quarters in which they were sheltering was occupied by the best part of the watch below, about a dozen rather smart and alert men, older than the usual run of naval ratings. The Sub noticed that, without exception, they looked a bit tired and fatigued, consequently he was not surprised to find that his attempts to broach a conversation were resolutely, yet politely, rebuffed.

Foiled in that direction, Broadmayne tried to pick up the threads of the scanty scraps of conversation. Again he was foiled. Every sentence he overheard had no bearing upon life on board. " Shop " in the crew's quarter seemed to be taboo.

He glanced at Vyse. Rollo, having made a good meal, was leaning back on the settee with his eyes closed. The problem offered no difficulties

to the owner of the burnt-out *Ibex*, for the simple
reason that he was comfortably dozing.

The Sub looked at the clock in the bulkhead.
It was a quarter-past eight. Although it was
day, no natural light penetrated the interior of
the hull. The submarine was running on the
surface. The pulsation of the internal combustion engines proved that.

A man clad in blue cloth trousers, sweater and
sea-boots entered the compartment and began
to remove the empty plates.

" Had a good tuck in, chum ? " he inquired.
" All right—best turn in for a spell. There's
your bunks, blankets and all. Captain won't
want to see you afore three bells in the second
dog."

" Thank you," replied Broadmayne. He, too,
was feeling drowsy. Perhaps it was the heat of
the confined space. He touched Vyse on the
shoulder.

" Turn in, old man ! " he exclaimed.

" What for ? " demanded his chum rebelliously ;
then his desire to sleep dominated all other inclina-
tions. Merely kicking off his rubber-boots, Vyse
turned in all standing. The Sub followed his
example, and a couple of minutes later both men
were lost in heavy, dreamless slumber.

Meanwhile Captain Cain, whose almost unbounded energy could keep him going at high
pressure for thirty-six hours without any desire for
sleep, was standing on the bridge of the *Alerte* as
she stood southward at eight knots.

He was at the wheel. With the exception of

one mechanic standing by the Diesel motors, all hands were enjoying a few hours' well-earned rest. Shortly after the crew of the *Ibex* had been taken on board, a wireless message had been picked up that gave Captain Cain an inspiration upon which he determined to act.

The wireless message was from the Norddeutscher-Lloyd intermediate boat *Cap Hoorn*, to the Ushant signalling-station, reporting that she was ninety miles W. by S. of Ushant, homeward bound from Bremen.

Already the pirate captain had " looked her up " in the shipping register. He found that the *Cap Hoorn* was a vessel of 8500 tons, with a speed of fifteen knots. Coming from Buenos Ayres and Rio, she would be certain to have a valuable cargo. It was a risky business to hold her up, but Captain Cain, having weighed the pros and cons, decided to intercept her.

At noon the *Alerte's* crew were roused. Preparations were immediately started to disguise the ship. The funnel was given a different coloured coat of paint ; the masts, previously light brown with black above the hounds, were painted a uniform shade of dark grey. The bridge and funnel were bodily shifted twenty feet aft, and the position of the ventilating cowls altered. Finally, on both bows and astern the name *Alerte* was covered by strips of painted cloth bearing the name *Cimeterre*, and the French tricolour hoisted aft.

" I'm going to put the breeze up a Hun, my lads," he announced. " She's now on her way up-Channel.

She's a lump of a boat, but we'll get her. Remember that for this occasion you're Frenchmen. When we board her, keep your mouths shut and let Mr. Pengelly grease his jaw-tackle. He can speak French like a native and German quite enough to make himself understood. I'm not going to hurt Fritz more than I can help. It depends upon himself. If she heaves to, as I expect she'll do, Mr. Pengelly will take half a dozen hands, all armed, and see what's of use to us——"

"Sail on the starboard beam, sir ! " shouted the look-out man. "Black hull, white top-hamper, two funnels all yellow."

"That's our pigeon," declared Pengelly ; then noticing his partner glare, he hastened to add the previously omitted " sir."

"Very good, Mr. Pengelly," sang out the captain. "Tell off your boat's crew in readiness. Fall in, Q. F. numbers ; signalman, stand by and hoist the I. D."

The *Alerte* and the *Cap Hoorn* were approaching almost at right angles to each other's course. As the positions of the ships went, the *Alerte* would bring the German's port side on her starboard bow, in which case, under the " Rules and Regulations for Preventing Collisions at Sea," the former had to give way.

Nearer and nearer came the huge Norddeutscher-Lloyd vessel, showing the " bone in her jaw " as she flung out a tremendous bow-wave. Unswervingly, both vessels held on. The *Cap Hoorn* blew a warning blast on her syren.

"Hard-a-starboard ! " ordered Captain Cain, at

the same time motioning the alert signalman. Round swept the *Alerte*, until she was on a parallel course to that of her victim. The screens concealing the quick-firer were lowered and the muzzle of the weapon swung round. Simultaneously the signal I. D. (Heave-to, or I will fire into you) was hoisted; followed, without waiting for the *Cap Hoorn's* reply, by LDA—ZMX (Disconnect your wireless apparatus).

The two vessels were now roughly four hundred yards apart. Through his binoculars, Captain Cain observed with considerable satisfaction that the German officers and men were in a state of panic, while the passengers, guessing that something was amiss but ignorant of the true state of affairs, crowded to the side.

The pirate captain rang for full speed ahead. Almost immediately, the pulsations of the motors increased, and the *Alerte* quickly attained her maximum speed, equal to that of the *Cap Hoorn.*

Still the latter showed no sign of stopping her engines. From her bridge a three flag hoist went up.

" WCX, sir ! " reported the *Alerte's* signalman, as he rapidly turned over the pages of the Code Book, adding as he discovered the message, " Signals not understood, though flags are distinguished."

" More bluff ! " ejaculated Captain Cain. " I'll send 'em a message that won't bear misunderstanding. Captain of the gun ! " he continued, raising his voice. " Give her one above the waterline. Knock her rudder-head to smithereens."

The quick-firer spat viciously. Considering the gun-layer had had no previous experience with that particular type of weapon, the result was highly creditable to his professional skill.

The projectile struck the *Cap Hoorn* about ten feet for'ard of the rudder and about four feet above the waterline. It made a clean hole where it entered, but of the devastating effect of the explosive shell there was little doubt. Splinters and slivers of metal flew high in the air. Flames and smoke poured from a jagged hole in the poop. The red, white and black ensign, its staff shattered by the explosion, was whisked fifty yards astern.

Twenty seconds later the *Cap Hoorn's* propellers were going astern; but owing to the rudder-head being pulverised, the massive rudder swung hard over to starboard. Slowly her head began to pay off towards her antagonist. Men armed with fire extinguishers and hoses were seen running aft. With indecorous haste another German mercantile ensign was hoisted and as promptly lowered in token of surrender.

" Look alive, Mr. Pengelly ! " exclaimed the pirate captain. " You know your orders ? "

" Ay, ay, sir," was the reply.

A boat was lowered. Into it went Pengelly and half a dozen men, all armed with automatic pistols. By this time Captain Cain had got way off his ship, the two vessels being now about a cable's length apart.

The boat's crew gave way with a will, their comrades, with the exception of the men at the quick-firer, crowding to the side to watch their progress.

" Mr. Barnard ! " shouted Captain Cain.

The bo's'un doubled aft and saluted.

" What's that man doing on deck ? " inquired the skipper angrily, pointing to Gerald Broadmayne, who, unobserved by the hands on deck, had come up from below and was watching the unusual sight.

" Dunno, sir," replied Mr. Barnard helplessly. " Both of 'em were sound asleep when last I looked in."

As a matter of fact, the bo'sun, in the excitement of the one-sided enjoyment, had completely forgotten about the presence of the two strangers on board. He had omitted to lock the door between the men's quarters and the vestibule immediately underneath the base of the conning-tower.

" All right, let him alone," decided Captain Cain, as he reflected grimly that now the cat was out of the bag, his involuntary guests would have to remain on board at all costs, until the termination of the cruise, wherever and whenever it might be.

" So that's the game, is it ? " thought the Sub. His searching eyes quickly took in the evidence of the incriminating surroundings—the quick-firer trained abeam, with a still smoking shell-case lying close to the mounting; the French ensign floating over a vessel whose crew were British and, for the most part, West-country folk; the men all armed with automatic pistols; least and not last a boarding party on their way to the disabled German liner. " Piracy—out and out piracy."

Like those of the *Alerte's* crew who remained on board, Broadmayne found his interest centre on the boat containing Pengelly and his armed companions.

Before the boat had ranged up alongside the *Cap Hoorn*, the German crew had lowered the accommodation-ladder.

Headed by Pengelly, the boarders ran up the ladder. At the gangway they were met by the captain and several of the officers of the captured vessel ; while gathered at a respectful distance were about thirty of the crew and those of the passengers whose curiosity had overcome their timidity.

There was no sign of resistance. Pengelly, escorted by the German captain, disappeared from view, three of his men following him. The others, with the exception of the boat-keeper, drove the passengers and crew for'ard like a flock of sheep.

" No guts ! " soliloquised Broadmayne scornfully. " Can you imagine a British ship with that sized crew chucking up the sponge ? They'd rush the blighters even if they only had broomsticks."

Presently one of the *Alerte's* boarders at the head of the accommodation-ladder held up a small white flag. It was a pre-arranged signal. As long as it remained held aloft, it indicated that the looters were having things all their own way. Should the Germans turn upon their captors, the white flag would be dropped. Then, and only then, would the *Alerte's* quick-firer pump shell after shell into the huge target presented by the motionless *Cap Hoorn*.

Twice there came the dull report of an explosion. The crew of the quick-firer tautened, the captain of the gun looking inquiringly at the imperturbable figure on the *Alerte's* bridge. But Captain Cain gave no sign. The white hand-flag was still conspicuously displayed at the gangway of the prize. Occasionally he swept the horizon with his binoculars, ready at the first sign of an approaching craft to recall his merry men and seek safety in flight.

An hour and ten minutes after the boat had pushed off from the *Alerte*, Pengelly descended the *Cap Hoorn's* accommodation-ladder. The boat, heavily laden, headed back to her degenerate parent and was hoisted up in davits.

" Well ? " inquired Captain Cain laconically.

" Skinned 'em, sir," replied Pengelly, with a broad grin.

CHAPTER VIII

A PROPOSAL SCORNED

AGAIN the *Alerte* hoisted a signal. It was to give the *Cap Hoorn* permission to proceed.

Steering like a dray, since the destruction of the rudder-head had left her with only her twin screws to manœuvre with, the German liner forged ahead, turned eight degrees to starboard and shaped a course for the invisible French coast.

The *Alerte*, without waiting for her prey to disappear from sight, worked up to a speed of eight knots, steering in a northerly direction, or towards the shores of England.

" What happened ? " asked Captain Cain.

" Went through the ship's papers," replied the lieutenant. " Found that she's eighteen million marks of specie in her strong-room. Blighters swore they hadn't a key—trust Fritz for bluffing or attempting to bluff. So we had to blow off the lock. Then we had a round-up of the first-class passengers. By smoke ! They shelled out like lambs. The proceeds are in that sack "— pointing to a well-filled canvas bag lying against the base of the conning-tower. " It was poor sport relieving a white-livered crowd like that.

And the joke of the whole business is that the
German skipper thought we were Frenchmen. I
told him that war had been declared between
France and Germany, and that he was to proceed
straight for Cherbourg. Warned him that if he
attempted to run for it, or to use his wireless,
there'd be considerable trouble. I'd like to see
what happens when the *Cap Hoorn* gives herself
up to the naval authorities at Cherbourg."

" Unfortunately—or, perhaps, fortunately—we
cannot be present," rejoined Captain Cain ; then
addressing the quartermaster, he ordered the ship
to turn fifteen points to port, or nearly in a reverse
direction to the course she had been following.

" Why ? " inquired Pengelly.   " There'll be half
a dozen French torpedo craft on our track.
Wouldn't it be wiser to make ourselves scarce ? "

" I am keeping the rendezvous in the Chenal
du Four," replied the captain. Being in a high
good humour, he could afford to be affable to his
querulous subordinate. "The news will be wirelessed everywhere within the next few hours
that the *Cap Hoorn* was stopped and plundered
by an unknown vessel masquerading as a French
government auxiliary craft, which, when last
sighted, was steering to the nor'ard. Consequently, every one responsible for hunting us will
reason much as you did—that we're off either to
the English or Irish coasts. They won't dream of
looking for us in the neighbourhood of Ushant.
L'audace, Pengelly, *toujours l'audace* : that's the
winning card. All right ; carry on. Set the
hands to work to remove our disguise. For the

7

next day or so, the *Alerte* will be the *Alerte*. I'll
interview those fellows we picked up this morning.
Tell Marchant to bring one of them to my cabin.
I won't see them together."

Captain Cain was on the point of descending
the bridge-ladder, when he stopped and exclaimed
in a voice loud enough for the watch on deck to
hear :

" We'll make a partial division of the coin at
one-bell, Mr. Pengelly. Pass the word to the
hands."

Going below to his cabin, the skipper began to
make preparations to receive his involuntary
guests. They had come aboard of their own free
will, it was true, but already they had discovered
that getting away from the *Alerte* was quite a
different matter.

Presently the gunner knocked at the door.

" Mr. Broadmayne, sir," he reported.

" Take that chair, Mr. Broadmayne," said
Captain Cain.

The Sub did so. Although giving away the
slight advantage he possessed in height, he
realised that it was decidedly uncomfortable
having to be interviewed with his shoulders bent
to prevent his head touching the sweating steel
roof of the little cabin.

" I suppose," resumed the pirate, with a slight
tone of irony, " that you are already acquainted
with the nature of the craft that has given you
shelter ? "

" I'd be remarkably dense if I weren't," replied
Broadmayne.

" And what, might I ask, is the result of
your investigations ? " inquired Captain Cain
suavely.

" To put it bluntly," rejoined the Sub, " you're
a filibuster—a pirate."

" That's putting the case rather strong," protested Captain Cain.   " The vessel we intercepted
was a Hun.   I was fighting Germans in the high
seas when you were a child in arms, I imagine.
I saw enough to make me vow I'd go bald-headed
for one whenever I had a chance.   That chance
I took to-day."

" I won't question your motives," remarked
Broadmayne imperturbably.   " But I take it you
have no Admiralty warrant to act as a privateer
in peace-time ?   Then, as I said before, you must
be a pirate.   Rather interesting, what ?   I was
under the impression that gentlemen of that type
were as extinct as the dodo."

" Who and what are you, Mr. Broadmayne ? "
demanded Captain Cain.

" Sub-lieutenant, Royal Navy."

" You are—or were ? "

" Am," declared Broadmayne, with a tone that
indicated he was proud of his profession.

A look of disappointment flitted across the face
of the pirate captain.

" Then what were you doing on a private
yacht ? "

The Sub told him.

" Vyse, did you say ? " interrupted Captain
Cain.   " Vyse ?   Any relation to the north-
country magnate of that name ? "

" Son," replied Broadmayne.

The next instant he felt angry with himself for having divulged that part.

" Really ! " exclaimed the other. " That's most interesting. Well, Mr. Broadmayne, I'm afraid I must ask you and your friend to remain on board for the remainder of the cruise. It won't be a protracted one, I assure you. You can have the run of the ship, except at such times when it will be necessary to order you below. Of course, considering we have saved your lives—your dinghy would have been swamped when the sea rose an hour after you were rescued—and that we have to feed you, a monetary payment is expected. But there is one alternative. I don't suppose you'll accept it first going off. That is, if you both care to join us in our enterprise—remember, we are not molesting a single British subject—then you will be entitled to a fair share of the proceeds, which I can assure you are far from being inconsiderable."

Broadmayne made no reply. He was puzzling his brains, but not on account of the pirate's seductive proposition. He had seen the man somewhere, but where ? Suddenly he remembered.

" I am more than surprised to find a former naval officer engaged on a stunt of this description," he remarked bluntly.

Captain Cain's features went a dusky red under his tan. The pulses of his temples were throbbing like steam-pistons.

" How do you know what I've been ? " he inquired harshly. There was a dominant note in his voice Most men would have quailed before it. The Sub showed no sign of trepidation. On the contrary, he felt considerably elated at having found a weak spot in his antagonist's armour.

"Some years ago," resumed Broadmayne, "I was one of a party of cadets who were taken round to Devonport from Dartmouth in a destroyer— the *Calder*, Lieutenant-Commander Sefton. It was one of the usual day instructional cruises, you know. On that occasion the cadets were shown over some of the submarines lying in the Hamoaze. There was a two-and-a-half striper who did the showing round. Some time later, he had to sever his connection with the Service—kicked out, in fact. No need to mention names."

Captain Cain controlled his rage with an effort.

"Quite correct," he rejoined. "However, Mr. Broadmayne, you will please remember that while you are on this craft you will keep that knowledge to yourself."

"I am not in the habit of trading on any one's past," replied the Sub. "But I have a strong objection to attempted intimidation. If circumstances warrant my making use of the information bearing on your former career, I'll do so. And, let me add, I consider your offer that we should throw in our lot with your piratical crowd an insult. My answer, if an answer be required, is NO !"

Without another word, Captain Cain touched the bell-push.

"I'll make this young puppy feel sorry for himself before I've done with him," he said to himself.

The gunner answered the summons.

" Take Mr. Broadmayne on deck," ordered the pirate captain, " and bring Mr. Vyse to me."

Presently Rollo Vyse appeared. He was sorry he had missed an opportunity of speaking to his chum, as he was entirely in the dark as to what had occurred.

To him Captain Cain made a similar proposition, which he " turned down " even more forcibly than the Sub had done.

" So that's your attitude, is it ? " exclaimed the pirate, losing control of his temper. " Very well. Here are pens, ink and paper. You will write a letter to your wealthy parent, informing him that you are detained on board a certain ship and that you will be deprived of your liberty until the sum of one thousand pounds is paid to the person named therein. You will add that it is useless to set the police upon my agent. He knows nothing and is acting in all good faith. Now then, one thousand pounds in Bank of England notes, none of which is to exceed ten pounds."

Lighting a cigarette and picking up a book, Captain Cain feigned to have lost interest in his victim.

For some moments Rollo sat quietly thinking.

" S'pose I'll have to humour the silly ass," he decided, and took up a pen.

For nearly twenty minutes Vyse was engaged upon the demand for ransom. He was not writing all the time. There were intervals when the rapid movement of the scratchy pen ceased, causing the pirate captain to glance inquiringly over his book.

" How will that do ? " asked Rollo at last.

Captain Cain took the proffered paper and read:

" DEAR FATHER,—This is a request to *pay* up.
Broadmayne and I were rescued from the *Ibex*,
which was burnt at sea. There's *no* need to worry.
We're given every *attention* and are comfortable.
But the captain of the ship we're on is going *to*
detain us till our expenses are paid. *This,* he
states, is One thousand pounds. Sounds a *pre-
posterous* sum, doesn't it ? However, that is the
extent of his *demand,* so I hope you'll settle and
let us have our freedom. We're in for a rough
time otherwise. The money is to be in five and
ten pound notes, payable to the person named
below.—Your affectionate Son,

" ROLLO VYSE."

" Is that your usual signature ? " asked Captain
Cain.

" Certainly."

" Very good," continued the pirate, folding the
sheet, putting it in an envelope and placing it
carefully between the leaves of a blotter. " I'll
see that it's forwarded to its proper destination.
You may go."

Vyse went. In the alleyway he gave a grim
chuckle. His letter had been carefully composed.
Several of the words were underlined. To a
casual observer the lines would appear to be the
lavish crossing of the letter " t " in the line below.
Captain Cain had not spotted it. The underlined
words read: " Pay no attention to this pre-
posterous demand." Rollo had no doubt that
when his father received the letter, his shrewdness
would quickly enable him to read the camouflaged
message.

He found Broadmayne pacing the poop. For the present, none of the crew were aft. The *Alerte* had resumed the features she possessed when she left Falmouth. No outside observer would have recognised her as the vessel that had stopped the *Cap Hoorn* earlier in the day.

" Gerald, old thing ! " exclaimed Rollo, after a brief exchange of their experiences, " we've got to get clear of this craft. If we don't, before very long we stand a hundred to one chance of being sent to Davy Jones's locker. The skipper gave me the impression that he's a hard case. I believe he'd sink her with all hands rather than surrender."

" From what I know of him, he is a hard case," agreed the Sub. " But the question is, how can we part company with this vessel ? I'd attempt it like a shot if there were a ghost of a chance. The hands seem to be up to their job. They'll keep a keen eye on us, I fancy. Our only hope, I think, is to enlist the sympathies of some of the men. We'll have to sound them carefully. No doubt we'll find that one or two are fed-up already, and would do almost anything to save their precious necks."

" You mean to say we might be able to bribe them ? "

" Hardly," replied Broadmayne. " They seem to be coining money on this game. I believe there's a share-out coming off very soon. No, it won't be the lure of financial reward. We'll have to play on their feelings a bit."

The thrilling notes of the bo'sun's pipe brought

all hands to the waist. A partial division of the spoil was about to take place.

The crew fell in according to their respective watches. The gunner and the bo'sun were standing on either side of a small sack of gold coins placed upon an upturned cask. A short distance away stood Captain Cain, with Pengelly at his elbow with a book in his hand.

"My lads!" began the pirate captain, "we have now made a rough calculation of the value of the loot from the German hooker. Of course, when the stuff is disposed of ashore, it may be of considerable more value than we have estimated. On the other hand, it may be less. Roughly, the share for each man before the mast is one hundred and ten pounds for this day's work."

He paused. A rousing cheer greeted the announcement. Hitherto the crew had to be content with promises. Now the sight of the bulging sack indicated that they believed in the old adage, "A bird in the hand is worth two in the bush."

Captain Cain held up his hand. Instantly the boisterous cheering ceased.

"As your captain," he continued, "I naturally have your welfare at heart. Here is the money. I would point out the disadvantages of keeping such an amount on board. Some of you might be tempted to risk the loss of their shares at cards. What you do in the fo'c'sle during your watch below is no affair of mine, but I should be sorry to learn that any man has had the ill-luck to lose his wealth—hard-earned or otherwise.

Therefore, I would suggest that, should any one wish to place his share in a place of absolute safety, I will be responsible for its keeping. In other words, I am sending the booty back to England in the *Fairy*. All money entrusted to me will be judiciously invested, and a receipt given for the same. On the other hand, any one who wishes to hold his share can do so. . . . Mr. Barnard, call the roll ! "

The bo's'un began his task. As each man's name was called, he stepped forward to a chalk-line drawn on the deck. Here he stated what he wanted—either the actual coin or a receipt for the same. In the former case, Marchant, the gunner, counted out the coins and handed them to the man. In the latter, Pengelly wrote out a receipt.

About a dozen men took the cash. Of the remainder, a few allotted their share, receiving Pengelly's form of acknowledgment ; the others compromised by drawing a few pounds on account and leaving the balance with the captain.

All this was done in full view of Broadmayne and Vyse. The captain knew they were looking on. Perhaps he hoped that the sight of so much money might make the two men under detention alter their minds about signing-on.

The muster was about to be dismissed, when one of the men stepped forward.

" Well ? " inquired Captain Cain laconically.

" Us of the fo'c'sle wants to know what's to be our attitude to'ards those blokes we picked up, sir," said the man. " Seein' as 'ow they messes

an' berths for'ard, 'ow are we to treat 'em ? Are
they with us as part of the crew, sir ? "

" What are you driving at, Matthews ? " asked
the captain.

The man hesitated.

" 'Tes like this, sir," he continued, after a pause.
" If they ain't hands, then why are they berthed
along o' we ? If they are, it ain't fair on the rest
of us that they don't take part in the routine of
the ship—slackin' about while we are a-workin'
'ard."

It was then that Captain Cain made a serious
mistake. Instead of " ticking the man off " for
attempting to interfere with the captain's plans—
a grave breach of discipline—he temporised with
the delegate.

" The matter will receive my attention,
Matthews," he replied.

" Very good, sir," rejoined the man.

He saluted, turned and went back to the others.
His comrades saw what the pirate captain could
not—a self-satisfied look upon the man's face at
the thought that he had scored off the owner.

" Pipe down ! " ordered Captain Cain.

A minute or so later, he beckoned to his captives.
The Sub and his companion descended the poop
ladder and approached the pirate skipper.

" I can't have idlers on board this craft," said
Captain Cain abruptly. " From now you will
form part of the starboard watch, and stand your
tricks like the rest of the hands. Understand
that ? "

" Very good," replied the Sub coldly. " In the

circumstances, we have no option. We are willing, under compulsion, to do our part towards working the ship, but in no case will we bear a hand at any work of piracy."

" We'll see about that," retorted Captain Cain, with a sneering laugh. " Now, go and report to Mr. Barnard, the bo'sun. Tell him you're placed in the starboard watch."

Without replying, the two chums turned and went to carry out the captain's orders. Purposely they omitted the salute. They expected to be recalled and made to give it ; but Captain Cain feigned to take no notice of the omission.

" I'll break their spirits yet ! " he mused.

But Broadmayne and Vyse thought otherwise.

CHAPTER IX

A DASH FOR LIBERTY

JUST before sunset the *Alerte* entered the Chenal de Four, a dangerous and intricate passage between Ushant and the Brittany coast. Not only does the water on either side of the deep channel teem with jagged rocks—many of them submerged at various states of the tide—but both flood and ebb set at from six to seven knots, sometimes obliquely across the narrow passage. To complicate matters further, the rise and fall of the tide is twenty-four feet at springs and eighteen feet at neaps.

By taking advantage of certain states of the tides, a vessel bound for Brest and the Biscayan ports from the English Channel could save a long detour outside of Ushant by making use of the Four Passage, but, in any case, the utmost caution is necessary. Strangers are, in fact, warned that to attempt this channel without a pilot is entailing great risk.

To Captain Cain this hazardous locality presented no terrors. Many a time during his naval career he had taken submarines between Brest and Portsmouth, and had lurked in the Chenal de Four waiting to turn the tables on the U-boats that preyed on the shipping converging upon Ushant. Now he was going to put the knowledge that he had gained legitimately to a perfectly illegal use.

" Any sign of the *Fairy*, Mr. Pengelly ? " he inquired.

" No sir."

" All right. I'll carry on. Quartermaster, keep those two towers in line—S. 5 E. is the course. Mr. Pengelly, see that the anchor is clear and fifty fathoms cable ranged on deck ready to let go."

The sun set in a vivid red sky. The lights of Kermorvan and St. Matthieu towers sent out their guiding beams. In a couple of hours the moon would rise.

Still the *Alerte* held on. Presently the lookout reported a sail on the starboard bow. Against the still strong afterglow in the western sky the intervening stretch of water appeared to be studded with rocky pinnacles.

" That's the *Fairy*," declared Captain Cain to Pengelly, who had rejoined him on the bridge. " She's brought up in four fathoms off Beniguet Island. No, we won't send out recognition signals. . . . Hard-a-port, Quartermaster. . . . Meet her ! . . . At that ! "

The *Alerte*, her speed reduced to five knots, appeared to be heading straight for a saw-like reef. Another alteration of helm and she slipped past within half a cable's length of this ridge of rocks, eeled her way between two half-tide rocks and settled down on a course S.S.W.

" Stand by ! " shouted Captain Cain, ringing for the propellers to be declutched.

Gradually the *Alerte* lost way. A hoarse order from the bridge was answered by the rattle of cable heaving through the hawsepipe. Snubbing gently at the tautened cable, the pirate submarine swung round head to tide within two hundred yards of the Falmouth lugger owned by the redoubtable Cap'n Silas Porthoustoc.

The *Fairy* had a riding-light on her forestay, but no hail came from her deck. The *Alerte*, having extinguished her navigation lamps, hoisted her anchor-light. To any observant Breton fisherman there was nothing to excite suspicion. Small craft bringing up to avoid a foul tide were fairly common objects in the vicinity of the Chenal du Four.

Since Broadmayne's and Vyse's " promotion " to the starboard watch, the chums had spent much of their time on deck. Their new messmates, now that they recognised them as such, were apt to be either patronising or rudely inquisitive. They looked upon the two chums' predicament—being forced to work without payment—as a huge joke, especially as Rollo and the Sub were obviously men of a different social standing. Hence it was not surprising that the late crew of the *Ibex* kept to themselves as much as possible.

The Sub knew roughly the position of the *Alerte*. Although he had never before been through the Four Passage, he realised from his previous knowledge of Ushant Light that the anchorage was between some of the islands off the westernmost part of the Brittany coast.

" Wonder what that vessel is ? " he remarked, pointing to the *Fairy's* riding-light. " If she's a Breton fishing craft, we might swim off to her."

" Not in this tideway," objected Vyse, for the water was hissing and seething past the side of the *Alerte*. " We might when the tide eases off. It's bound to just before high water. 'Sides, the moon will be up soon."

They waited and watched, conversing in low tones. The *Alerte's* deck was practically deserted. There was a look-out man on the fo'c'sle. Occasionally some of the hands would emerge from the close atmosphere of the crew's quarters for a breath of fresh air. But no one seemed to take the slightest notice of the two chums.

Presently the moon rose behind the gaunt Brittany hills—a huge red disc, that soon appeared to diminish in size and assume a vivid yellowish hue. It was now one bell and the first watch.

" That's not a Frenchman," declared the Sub, as the slanting moonbeams fell athwart the bluff outlines of the Penzance boat. " She's a West-country lugger, I'll swear. Wonder what she's doing here ? "

" Perhaps her skipper's a pal of the pirate captain," suggested Vyse.

" Not likely," objected Broadmayne. " They didn't communicate with each other when we came in. I was looking out for that. 'Sides, it's hardly feasible that a sailing lugger, if she were acting as tender, would show up within a few miles of the great French naval port of Brest. It would be far safer to get in touch fifty miles from land."

" That's so," agreed Vyse. " And that brings us back to our original proposition. How's this for a scheme. The lugger's now almost dead astern of us. The tide's easing a bit. The *Alerte's* look-out is for'ard, consequently he can't see what's goin on aft. We can lower ourselves over the stern, swim off to the lugger and get aboard by her cable, if there's nothing better. We'll warn her master of the undesirable nature of the *Alerte* and offer him a hundred quid if he'll weigh at once and give us a passage to England."

" Then the sooner the better," said the Sub briskly. " It will be another hour and a half before the look-out is relieved. If he misses us, he'll probably think we've gone below. His relief will know we're not."

Their preparations were quickly and silently made. They sacrificed their footgear. Broadmayne took off his black oilskin, rolled it neatly and stowed it away under the platform of the sounding machine aft.

The next step was to drop the after-fall of one of the quarter-boats overboard. Had the *Alerte* been a genuine tramp steamer the fugitives would have to run the risk of being seen through the cabin scuttles, but her cabins being within the hull of the submarine, were artificially lighted.

Broadmayne gave a swift, comprehensive look for'ard. The look-out man was still in the fo'c'sle. He was resting one leg on the low bulwark, and was gazing stolidly in the direction of St. Matthieu lighthouse. Evidently he considered his job a merely formal one, and was making the best of his

8

trick by indulging in fanciful speculations of what he would do with his rapidly increasing wealth.

Giving his companion a reassuring nod, the Sub cautiously slid over the rail, gripped the rope and lowered himself slowly.

" Ugh ! " he mused.   " Feet first ; rotten way to take the water.   I'll bet it's beastly cold."

But to his surprise the sea was fairly warm.   It made him shiver when the water rose above his ankles and knees, but directly he was immersed to his neck he felt no further discomfort.

It was true that the hot tide had slackened. It had decreased from six to about three knots, or a rate equal to that of a brisk walk.   Still hanging on to the rope, he felt himself being swept aft until his feet were almost showing above the surface.

He dare not let go until Vyse was almost at the water's edge, otherwise he would be swept far to lee'ard before his chum was ready to cast himself off.   Keeping together for mutual encouragement was part of the prearranged plan.

Down came Vyse, hand over hand.   The two chums were now up to their necks and still hanging on to the rope.   Both realised that if they were swept past the lugger by some not unusual freak of the tidal current, they were as good as lost.

" Ready ? " whispered Broadmayne.   " Breast stroke : don't speak."

They released their hold and struck out.   The towering hull of the *Alerte* seemed to be moving with great rapidity.   Almost before they realised it, they were clear of the shadow of the poop and were swimming strongly in the moonlit sea.

Now they could clearly discern the lugger as she strained and tugged at her tautened cable. The water was frothing against her stem-band. But for the cable, it looked as if she were forging ahead under power. Every now and again she would sheer madly, so that at one time the swimmers were heading straight for her; at another—it looked as if they would be swept half a dozen yards away from her.

By good luck, Broadmayne grasped the cable. With a jerk that well-nigh wrenched him away, his body swung round in the fierce current. The next instant, Vyse secured a hold.

Then the lugger commenced to sheer again. The cable dipped, dragging both men below the surface. Not daring to let go, they hung on, holding their breath until the iron chain tautened again, lifting them both waist high out of the water.

" You go first," gurgled the Sub.

It was a hazardous business, clambering up on the underside of a vibrating chain at an angle of about forty-five degrees. Although it was not far to go, the difficulty increased as Vyse approached the vessel's bows. There was a danger of being nipped between the cable and the small, iron-shod hawsepipe, with the additional possibility of his arm being jammed between the chain and the lugger's stem-head.

Keeping clear of these dangers, Vyse hung on, looking for a means of getting in over the bows. Suddenly he caught sight of a stout piece of line by which the chain bobstay had been triced up to prevent it being chafed by the cable. It might hold—it might not. At any rate, he decided, if it did carry away, he could make a grab at the bobstay.

Desperately, Rollo made the attempt. The rope gave slightly as he transferred his weight to it. The next instant he had thrown one leg over the massive bowsprit. It was then a fairly simple matter to haul himself up and across the heavy spar.

By this time, Broadmayne was attempting the ascent ; water poured from his saturated clothing as he drew himself clear. He was breathing heavily, but the grinding of the cable and the rush of the tide completely drowned his laboured gasps. With less caution than his chum had shown, he allowed the knuckles of his right hand to be barked by the surge of the chain. Had it not been for Vyse's prompt assistance, the Sub must have relinquished his hold.

For quite five minutes the two men crouched on the lugger's fore-deck, too exhausted to move. There was no one of the crew on deck. A faint gleam was thrown obliquely from the half-closed fore-peak hatchway. Aft, the fluted glass skylight over the skipper's cabin was illuminated from within.

" Come aft," whispered Broadmayne.

In stockinged feet, they crept cautiously past the huge old-fashioned windlass, made their way along the narrow space between the tarpaulined hatch covers, over the hold, and gained the small aperture leading to the cabin.

The Sub knocked softly upon the door.

" That be you, Garge ? " demanded a deep, rolling voice. " Come in."

Accepting the invitation given to the absent

" Garge," whoever he might be, Broadmayne opened the door. Had it not been for the voice, the Sub would have formed a first impression that the cabin was untenanted.

Under the skylight hung a swinging lamp, with a polished brass deflector. Immediately under the lamp was a table that at one time had been polished mahogany. Now it was scratched, tarnished and blackened, the captain evidently being in the habit of knocking out the glowing embers of his pipe upon the table.

At the after end of the cabin was a long book-case above a settee. On either side were seats with lockers under, while above the seats were cavernous recesses with large sliding doors.

One of the latter was partly open, revealing a hairy-faced man lying fully dressed on a bunk, with a heap of blankets covering him from his feet to the point of his chin. Apparently he was still wanting additional warmth, for a coal fire blazed in a brass-lined fireplace—the skylight was shut, and, until Broadmayne opened it, also the door.

Cap'n Silas Porthoustoc's astonishment at the sight of two saturated strangers was quite equal to that of the Sub and his companion, when they caught a partial view of the old man " stewing " in the hot and unpleasantly close air.

" Who are ye, an' what you'm wantin' ? " inquired Cap'n Silas, embellishing his inquiry with half a dozen totally different adjectives.

" It's all right, Captain," replied Broadmayne soothingly, " we've just swum off from the vessel brought up ahead of you."

" Desarters, eh ? "

" Sort of," admitted the Sub.

" An' you'm thinkin' the *Fairy* is a nursery for cut-an'-run sailormen ? " rejoined Captain Port-houstoc. " You'm come tu wrong ship, you'm have. Best swim back along 'fore there's trouble."

" Look here, Captain," began Broadmayne firmly.

Before he could say more, the skipper of the *Fairy* thrust back the sliding-door of his bunk and rolled out, bringing with him an avalanche of blankets, a heavy pilot coat, and an oilskin.

" Wot's this ? " he demanded. " Threatenin' me in my own cabin, aboard my very own ship ? "

" Not at all, Captain," said the Sub hurriedly. " We want your assistance. We'll pay you well."

" Pay me well ! " echoed Captain Silas scornfully. " Can show the colour of your money, belike ? "

" We'll give you a hundred pounds if you'll put us ashore anywhere in England," said Broadmayne. " Possibly the Admiralty will pay you considerably more. The vessel we were on is a pirate."

" 'Slong's she don't do aught to we, I'm content," replied Captain Silas. " Howsomever, a hundred pun' is worth a-pickin' up. But if she be a pirate, as you say, what happens if so be she sends aboard us to look for ye ? "

" If you up-anchor and get under way at once she'll be none the wiser," suggested the Sub. " If you think she'll chase you across the Channel, there's no reason why you shouldn't run for Brest. You'll get your money just the same."

" Can't start afore the tide sets tu south'ard," objected Captain Silas.   " But I'll tell you what : I'll stow you away.   You can lay your life on it, you'll not be found.   A hundred, you said ? "

The Sub reiterated his promise.

Without another word the skipper of the *Fairy* kicked aside a narrow strip of coco-matting, fumbled at a small circular hole in one of the floor-boards, and at length raised a double-width plank about eighteen inches square.

The light of the cabin lamp revealed a cavernous space, with sloping sides and massive oaken timbers.   Floor there was none, the narrow space above the kelson being packed with rusty iron bars.   A cold and evil-smelling draught ascended, while with every roll of the lugger the bilge water sluiced and gurgled over the iron ballast.

" Our clothes are wringing wet," observed Vyse, stating what was an obvious fact, for they were standing in puddles, while the heat of the closed-down cabin caused the wet material to emit a regular haze of vapour.

" Off wi' 'em, then," said Cap'n Silas shortly. " I'll hide 'em.   Blanket a-piece will serve till they'm dry."

The two chums were in the final stages of dis-robing when one of the hands tapped on the sky-light.

" She be hailin' us ta come alongside, Cap'n," he announced.

" Pretty kettle o' fish you've made," he ex-claimed.   " Pirate, you say she be.   Well, 'tain't no use us kickin'.   We'll drop alongside of 'er, an' they

can search till them's tired.   They'll never find you.
Down you go.   Keep clear of yon propeller shaft."

Gingerly the chums gathered the loaned
blankets about them, toga-wise, and dropped down
upon the ballast.   The trap-door was replaced
and the coco-matting relaid.   In utter darkness
the fugitives crouched, listening to captain stamping about before going on deck.

Soon the *Fairy's* motor started, but the shaft
gave no sounds to indicate that it was revolving.
Then came the clank of the pawls of the windlass,
as the cable came home, link by link.   The gentle
purr of the engines increased to a loud, pulsating
roar.   The clutch was engaged, the propeller shaft
began to revolve—perilously close to Vyse's feet it
sounded—and the lugger began to forge ahead.

She had not been under way for more than three
minutes when the motor stopped and her stout
hull quivered as she bumped alongside the *Alerte*.

" Now what's going to happen ? " thought Broadmayne.   " The blighters are coming on board."

There was a terrific din on deck.   Men were
stamping and running about, heavy weights were
dumped down, the hatch-covers over the hold
were thrown back.

The Sub could hear men's voices as they shouted
to each other, but the motor roar intervening
between them and the fugitives prevented the
Sub hearing what they were saying.

" They're making a pretty strict search,"
whispered Vyse.

" 'Ssh ! " cautioned his companion.   " There's
some one in the cabin.   It's Pengelly, by Jove ! "

" All in small packages . . . easily got ashore . . . he told you to do that ? Look here, Silas, you'd better not . . . the cave behind your kitchen . . . we'll arrange all that later . . . part brass rags within a fortnight . . . it'll pay you far better . . . then that's a deal ? "

The Sub broke out in a gentle perspiration. From the scraps of conversation he had overheard, there could be but one explanation forthcoming. Pengelly and the master of the lugger were plotting —against whom ? Captain Cain, without a doubt. That was interesting. But the disconcerting part was : what was the skipper of the *Fairy's* attitude towards the two men hiding in the bilge ? Would it pay him better to give them up, or to keep faith with them and so gain the promised hundred pounds ?

" Mr. Pengelly ! " shouted a voice, which Broadmayne recognised as that of Captain Cain.

" Ay, ay, sir ! " replied the second in command.

The fugitives heard the sound of Pengelly's boots upon the ladder leading on deck. The *Fairy's* skipper followed.

" The old sinner," whispered Vyse. " I thought he was going to betray us."

" I don't think so," replied the Sub. " The promise of a hundred pounds is our sheet-anchor. By Jove ! I can see some interesting developments before very long."

" What developments ? " inquired the other in a low tone.

Before Broadmayne could reply—it was quite safe to maintain a cautious conversation, since the

uproar on deck would deaden every sound below—
a minute shaft of yellow light played upon the
Sub's hand. He knew what that meant. The
coco-matting had been removed, thus allowing the
lamplight to enter the thumbhole in the covering
to their place of concealment.

The next instant the trap hatch was thrown
wide open. Standing close to the opening was
Captain Cain, a revolver in his hand and a sardonic
grin on his face. Behind him were four of the
Alerte's crew. Silas Porthoustoc, chuckling audibly,
was stationed in the narrow doorway, while over
his shoulders appeared the grinning faces of Pengelly and Barnard the boatswain.

" Out of the frying-pan, eh ? " exclaimed Captain Cain mockingly.   " You two have vastly
underestimated the intelligence of the *Alerte's*
ship's company. I'll deal faithfully with you for
deserting, my lads. Now, out you come."

Dejected and humiliated, Broadmayne and his
companion emerged from the loathsome place of
concealment. Their clothes had vanished. Clad
in nothing but Cap'n Silas's blankets, they beat
an ignominious retreat, running the gauntlet of a
fire of rude chaff from the *Alerte's* crew as they
hurriedly went below to their berths. In the eyes
of the rest of the ship's company they were nothing
more or less than skulkers, who took every opportunity of dodging their share of work. And as
such they had no sympathy from the piratical
crew of the *Alerte*.

CHAPTER X

BRUTE STRENGTH

BROADMAYNE and Vyse had not been more than five minutes in their bunks in the otherwise deserted crew's quarters, when the bo'sun entered, storming and raging.

"Skulking again!" he shouted. "Here, you son of a horse-marine, show a leg! And you, you limb of Satan, it's the like o' you as gets the likes o' me into trouble. On deck with you, an' if you don't work like blue blazes, there'll be trouble."

It was useless to refuse. Mildly, Vyse protested that their clothes had been taken away and that having to hold a blanket round one is apt to hamper a person's activities.

"Quite so," agreed Mr. Barnard, with a coarse laugh. "'Bout time you did go into proper uniform."

He went to the doorway.

"Matthews!" he shouted. "Get the key of the slop-chest and rig these skulking hounds out. . . . Give you five minutes to fall in in the rig of the day," he added, "or, by smoke! you won't get even bread and water for the next twenty-four hours."

Well within the stipulated time the two chums

went on deck, each dressed in rubber-boots, blue jersey and canvas jumper and trousers.

" Look lively there ! " shouted the bo'sun. " Nip down the hold and bear a hand."

The hold was almost empty. In one corner was a pile of iron-bound boxes and a number of small sacks, the mouths of which were secured with wire and sealed with discs of sealing-wax.

For some reason the derricks had not been brought into use. Each packet was handled separately, passed from one man to another, until by stages it reached the deck. Here a careful tally was made before the booty was transhipped to the lugger *Fairy*.

" That's the lot, Cap'n Silas," shouted Captain Cain. " You know your orders. Right-o ; carry on and good luck ! "

Quickly the dark brown canvas of the *Fairy* was set. She was riding head to wind alongside the *Alerte*, held only by a bow-and-stern warp.

" All ready ! " shouted Porthoustoc. " Let go, for'ard."

A slight touch of the lugger's tiller gave her sufficient sheer to allow the head sails to draw.

" Let go aft ! " bawled Silas.

" All gone ! " shouted one of the *Alerte's* crew.

Then like a wraith the lugger drew ahead. There was no doubt about her speed and handiness. Without having recourse to her motor, she glided between the rocky pinnacles and was soon lost to sight in the gathering mist.

" Eighteen hours stand easy, men ! " announced Captain Cain. " Clear away and hands to diving

stations.   We'll lie here as comfortably as any one
could wish till to-morrow evening.   If all goes
well, my lads, we'll rake in another twenty thousand
or so before this week's out."

Within twelve hours from the time when she
cast off from alongside the *Alerte*, the *Fairy* was
creeping past the Cornish coast, with the little
fishing port of Mousehole bearing one point on
her port bow, distant about one mile.

The *Fairy* had made a quick and uneventful
passage, averaging seven and a half knots.   Captain
Silas Porthoustoc was almost shaking hands with
himself.

"Lawks!" he muttered.   "'Yes a fair ole
game.   'Ere's that there Cap'n Cain, as he calls
hisself, a-tellin' me to put the stuff in such an'
such a place until such times as they Lunnon
men—fair sharks they be, drat 'em—come down
wi' a moty car an' take it away.   Then there's
that Pengelly—I don't like him much, but 'e's a
sight better'n t'other un—says 'e, 'Don't 'ee du
it, Silas.   Hide the stuff in cave behind your
kitchen, an' we'll share the profits.'   Well, I
dunno.   There's one thing, they girt swells from
Lunnon won't handle the stuff, or my name's not
Silas Porthoustoc ; nor will that Cap'n Cain.
An' tes more'n likely as 'ow Cap'n Cain an' Mr.
Pengelly 'll row an' finish by blowin' holes in one
another's skulls.   That bein' so, I collar the lot."

He interrupted his dreams of avarice by glancing
skyward.   The wind, hitherto strong, had died
away, which was just what he wanted.

" Garge ! " he shouted to his mate. " 'And that there topsail. We'm not puttin' into Newlyn —tide don't serve. We'll bring up inside Clement's Island. She'll be quite all right. If you an' young Bill want a spell ashore, you can, 'slongs you'm board come eight t'morrow morn."

Garge jumped at the suggestion. His home was at Newlyn. It was an easy walk from Mousehole. Young Bill, Garge's nephew, could go with him.

Accordingly the anchor was let go and the sails loosely stowed. The *Fairy*, being one of a type common to Mounts Bay, would excite no curiosity. She was registered as a fishing craft and, in fact, was one except when Captain Silas had undertakings of a more hazardous and withal more profitable nature in hand.

The mate hailed a passing boat, and uncle and nephew were readily given a passage ashore.

Left to himself, Cap'n Silas paced the deck till nightfall, relieving the monotony by exchanging bantering speech with the crews of the outward-bound Mousehole fishing fleet, most of whom he knew.

After sunset he hoisted the riding-light, went below, and prepared and ate supper.

Shortly after midnight Silas went on deck. Everything was quiet. Softly he brought the dinghy alongside, muffled the rowlocks with cotton waste and then proceeded to load up with the precious cargo received from the *Alerte*.

Deeply laden, the dinghy was rowed shorewards, right into a small cave about a mile to the southward of Mousehole village. Here the cargo was unloaded and buried in the firm white sand forming the floor of the cave, at fifty yards from its mouth.

Silas, when he worked, *did* work. Normally easy-going and of a lazy disposition, he had the gift of toiling with almost superhuman energy when circumstances required. And this was one of them.

Ten times during the long December night did the dinghy, well down in the water, make the double passage between the *Fairy* and the cave.

At a quarter to eight, Silas, looking fresh as paint, rowed ashore, this time to Mousehole to pick up his crew. Two hours later the *Fairy* entered Newlyn harbour, where her captain received the condolences of the fisher-folk on the news that his trip had proved to be singularly unfortunate. The *Fairy* had not brought back so much as a solitary fish.

Captain Silas Porthoustoc, with his tongue in his cheek, went home.

His cottage was situated on the hillside beyond Mousehole. When ashore, he spent much of his time gardening, and so poor is the Cornish soil that to grow anything worth having the ground has to be plentifully manured. Hence, it occasioned no comment when Captain Silas toiled up the hill with a wheelbarrow full of seaweed, since seaweed is an excellent fertiliser. Had any one, sufficiently curious and daring to risk incurring the old skipper's anger, investigated what was under the seaweed the result would have surprised them.

In three days, Silas made forty-eight trips with

his wheelbarrow. At the end of that time his garden still required more manure; but every ounce of the booty from the *Alerte* was snugly stowed away in the cave behind the kitchen of Silas Porthoustoc's cottage.

Darkness had fallen when the *Alerte* rose to the surface, after her eighteen hours' repose. Before the moon rose the crew had set up the funnel, masts and rigging, and by nine in the evening she was shaping a course slightly to the west'ard of the Casquets—that dangerous and frequently fog-bound ledge of rocks six miles west of Alderney.

Up to the present, Captain Cain had not put into execution his threat of punishing Broadmayne and his chum for their "desertion." For one thing, he meant to make an example of them before the crew, and consequently waited until the men had had their greatly-wanted rest; for another, he believed in "prolonging the agony," or delaying the actual punishment in order that the thought of it would prey upon the minds of the culprits.

From information obtained through the medium of Captain Silas Porthoustoc, the pirate skipper of the *Alerte* knew that a small French steamer, the *Surcouf*, was leaving St. Malo for the French islands of St. Pierre and Miquelon, lying off Newfoundland. Amongst other items, she carried the sum of five hundred thousand francs for the treasury of these Gallic dependencies and a quantity of valuable silver plate, the private property of one of the chief officials of St. Pierre.

An hour before sunrise the *Alerte* stopped her engines. She was then nine miles W.N.W. of the Casquets. By means of her wireless she learnt that the *Surcouf* would not clear St. Malo earlier than ten o'clock, or two hours before high water.

That interval gave Captain Cain his opportunity to carry out his threat to the Sub and Vyse.

All hands were mustered on deck. Seized by a couple of the crew, Rollo Vyse was hauled to the up-turned boat that formed the screen for the quick-firer. Although boiling with rage, Vyse kept his feelings under control. Resistance was useless. He might easily fell his two captors, but he could not hope to defy the whole crew success-fully. At one moment he harboured a scheme to break loose and hurl himself upon the pirate captain ; but to do so, he would have to run the gauntlet of a dozen active and strongly-built men. So, in the circumstances, he made up his mind to take his gruelling with as much fortitude as possible.

Stripped to the waist, Vyse was secured to the boat, his arms over the keel and his ankles lashed to one of the gunwales.

" All ready, sir," reported the bo'sun, who held a formidable-looking whip of plaited sennet, terminating in a triple leather thong.

" Give him a dozen to start with, Mr. Barnard," ordered Captain Cain. " We'll see how he likes that."

The bo'sun drew his fingers caressingly through the thongs, spat upon his palm after the manner of

9

horny-handed sailor-men, and prepared to enjoy himself.

"Belay there!" exclaimed the captain. "Where's the other skulker? Bring him on deck."

"I am here!" announced Broadmayne, stepping forward from the wake of the conning-tower. "I don't suppose it's any use protesting——"

"It isn't," interrupted Captain Cain grimly.

The crew roared with merriment.

"Then I won't," continued the Sub. "But I will point out that you're exacting the penalty before trial. We haven't had a chance to defend ourselves. Now, Captain Cain, I'll make a sporting offer. I don't suppose you have boxing-gloves on board, so I'll challenge any man in the ship, yourself included, to a five-round contest with bare fists. If I win, then my friend goes unpunished. I don't ask for any favour on my own behalf. In any case, the hands will see a sight worth seeing."

"Good lad!" shouted one of the crew, and about half a dozen others applauded. The proposition appealed to their love of sport. They were ready to witness the comparatively tame spectacle of a man being flogged; but they vastly preferred to enjoy a fight with the gloves off.

"Silence!" roared the Captain.

"Garn! Be a sport!" retorted another of the crew brazenly.

Captain Cain strode towards the delinquent. Three steps did he take, then he stopped abruptly. Perhaps for the first time he realised that main-

taining discipline over a crowd of rogues—rogues
of his own making—was a different matter to that
of the old days, when his authority was backed
by the King's Commission. The early successes
of the cruise had turned the men's heads. Between
themselves, they held the creed that " Jack's as
good as his master," but as yet they dare not
profess it openly. Nevertheless, Captain Cain felt
that he was playing with a volcano.

" Good idea, my lads ! " he exclaimed, without
betraying his suspicions. " Who'll uphold the
reputation of the ship to the extent of five
rounds ? '

There was a long pause. Several of the men,
great, deep-chested fellows who were good at a
rough and tumble, were thinking about accepting
the challenge, but the sight of the tall, well-built
Broadmayne, who in addition had youth on his
side, made them think twice—or more.

" Blime ! " ejaculated a bull-necked, bullet-
headed fellow, " wot are we all a-hangin' on to the
slack for ? 'Ere goes, ole sport. I'll take you on."

The speaker looked, and undoubtedly was, a
tough proposition. An ex-first-class stoker, he
had been employed as a coal-heaver at Millbay
Docks until, after a term of unemployment, he had
been engaged at the Polkyll Creek Shipbreaking
Works as a hammerman. In spite of being
nearly forty years of age, he was in the pink of
condition and as hard as nails. Three inches
shorter than Broadmayne, he was certainly heavier
and possessed the doubtful advantage of three
inches in girth. The muscles of his arms stood

up like egg-shaped stones under his firm flesh.
The sinews of his chest were like whipcord. But
there was one defect that the Sub was quick to
notice. Like many a man of his build, the ex-
stoker was disproportionately weak in the lower
limbs.

All the same, Broadmayne realised that he had a
heavy task in front of him. If he were to more
than hold his own, he must avoid a direct blow of
the other's shoulder-of-mutton fist, and trust to
science and agility to counteract the fellow's superabundant reserve of brute force.

" My chum's my second," declared Broadmayne.
" Cast him loose."

Somewhat to his surprise the men did so, Captain
Cain raising no objection.

" Whatever happens," whispered the Sub,
" you're free for the time. That's something."

" Be careful," cautioned Vyse. " Try tiring him
out."

" I mean to," rejoined Broadmayne.

Already the rough preparations for the contest
were complete. The slightly curving steel deck
made a sorry ring, destitute of matting. Two
ropes had been stretched from rail to rail, two others
crossing them at right angles.

Pengelly was appointed referee. Barnard, the
bo'sun, acted as timekeeper, conspicuously displaying a handsome gold watch, lately the property
of the captain of the *Cap Hoorn*. Captain Cain,
perched upon the upturned keel of the quick-firer's
screen, watched the proceedings at a distance of
about five yards ; but the crew, squatting on deck,

crowded close to the ropes, determined not to miss the advantage of the front row seats.

The ex-stoker opened the proceedings by making a bull-like rush at his antagonist. Broadmayne avoided the onslaught with comparative ease, but could not resist the temptation of delivering a left at the side of the other's head. Adroitly ducking, the man avoided the blow and retaliated with a jab intended for the Sub's ribs in the region of the heart. It was not a vicious blow. The ex-stoker, thinking he was bound to win, was loath to make an early finish. A spectacular display to delight his comrades was what he wanted. The knock-out, he decided, would come in the fifth round—not before.

Nevertheless, the jab jolted Broadmayne severely. It taught him a lesson. For the rest of the round he was strictly on the defensive, trusting to footwork to avoid further punishment.

The second round was much on the same principle. It ended with Broadmayne feeling none the worse, but the ex-stoker somewhat blown and perspiring freely. The spectators, disappointed at the tameness of the contest, blew off steam by shouting to their champion to get to work, and jeering at the Sub's wary and seemingly faint-hearted tactics.

Goaded by the exhortations of his messmates, the ex-stoker warmed to his work in the third round. More than once he drove Broadmayne against the ropes, where only by dexterity did he escape a disastrous " clinch." Once the Sub got home with a smashing blow between his antagonist's eyes. It would have knocked out any ordinary man, but the fellow, beyond recoiling, seemed none the worse. Quickly he had his revenge by delivering a straight left on Broadmayne's left cheek, which had the effect of sobering him completely for the rest of the round.

" Fourth round—seconds out of the ring ! "

Broadmayne left his corner feeling far from comfortable. The ex-stoker, with blood trickling from his nose, grinned disdainfully at him, then ducking, rushed headlong at his adversary.

For a brief instant the Sub stood his ground, then stepped nimbly aside. The ex-stoker's massive fist grazed his left ear, the impetus of the blow throwing the fellow forward. Before he could recover his balance, Broadmayne, putting every ounce into it, delivered a right, followed by a hook with his left.

Of what happened after that he had only a hazy idea. Like in a mist he saw the powerful figure of his antagonist collapse. He appeared to fall neither forward nor backward, but to subside as his knees gave way. To Broadmayne it seemed a full minute that this continued ; then, as his knees touched the steel deck the ex-stoker rolled over on his side.

" One . . . two . . . three . . ."

The man made an effort to rise. Broadmayne stepped forward, ready to finish the business ; but there was no need. Gasping like a stranded fish, the ex-stoker rolled over again.

" . . . Eight . . . nine . . . ten."

Down and out !

Still a bit dazed, Broadmayne went back to his

BRUTE STRENGTH 135

corner and leant heavily against his chum. The
men were cheering like mad. It dawned upon
him that they were cheering *him*. Tough, desperate ruffians they might be, but they were
sportsmen, members of a race that produces the
best winners and the best losers in the world.

Pengelly congratulated him; so did Barnard,
Marchant and most of the crew. But Captain
Cain held aloof. He was furious with himself
for having allowed the contest to take place. His
authority had been wrecked. The crew's attitude
towards his captives had undergone a complete
change. He bitterly regretted having taken them
on board.

Yet, short of committing murder, he could not
get rid of them. Had he been sure of his crew,
he might even have taken that step, although he
was loath to do so. He could not set them ashore :
they knew too much. Besides, he still hoped to
rake in a substantial sum for their ransom.

" Sail on the starboard bow, sir ! "

Instantly Captain Cain cast aside his train of
disturbing thoughts. Hurrying to the bridge he
levelled his binoculars.

" It's the Frenchman, my lads ! " he shouted.
" All hands to quarters ! She's ours, my
hearties ! "

CHAPTER XI

THE FIGHT WITH THE *SURCOUF*

THE *Surcouf*, for such she was, was approaching at twelve knots. She was a two-funnelled craft of about 3000 tons, painted black with white upperworks. Occasionally visible between the eddying clouds of smoke from her funnels fluttered the tricolour from her ensign-staff; while at her foremost truck was displayed a white diamond on a red ground, bearing the letters MM.

From the *Alerte's* bridge, Captain Cain scanned the horizon. There was no other vessel in sight. Even the upper part of the Casquets Lighthouse, now twelve miles away, was invisible. Everything seemed propitious for the coming venture.

Quickly the crew went to stations. All the slackness and resentment to discipline seemed to have gone by the board. Orders were carried out with the utmost alacrity, until—

" Wot you got there, Charlie ? " demanded one of the hands of a messmate who was making his way aft with a red, white and black flag under his arm.

" German ensign," replied the other. " Cap'n's orders."

" Blowed if I'll fight under that rag," declared the first speaker hotly. " I'm an Englishman, I am. Don't mind the French tricolour, mark you, but the Hun ensign—no, thank you. What say you, chum ? "

" I draws the line at that," replied the third man, and his protest was taken up by several of the others.

" What are you men jawing about ? " shouted Mr. Marchant, the gunner. " Look alive and get that ensign made up ready to break out."

To him the seamen voiced their protest. Even the gunner had his views upon the matter. He went to the captain and protested, stating that all hands were against using the German flag.

" Curse them ! " exclaimed Captain Cain angrily. " What does that matter ? "

" Matters a lot to them, sir," replied the gunner sturdily.

" All right then," conceded the pirate. " Hoist any flag you jolly well like. If this business is bungled, don't blame me. . . . Signalman, stand by to hoist the ' I. D.' . . . Gunner's mate, if I give the word to open fire, knock away her foremast. We'll have to stop her wirelessing at any cost if she won't give in tamely."

Throughout these preparations, Rollo Vyse and the Sub had been inactive. They point-blank refused to bear a hand, and the crew, now respecting their principles, let them severely alone. Captain Cain was quick to notice the change of attitude, and from fear of causing further discontent affected to be ignorant of the presence of the two chums.

The *Surcouf* had approached to within half a mile, when Captain Cain ordered the *Alerte* to be turned sixteen points to starboard. This had the effect of bringing her on a parallel course to that of the Frenchmen, although the distance between them when abreast was increased by the diameter of the pirate submarine's turning circle.

Up ran the two-flag hoist, the signal to heave to under penalty of being fired upon ; simultaneously, the six-inch quick-firer was unmasked and trained upon the *Surcouf*.

The next instant Captain Cain experienced one of the worst surprises in his life—and he had had a few in his time.

A livid flash leapt from under the *Surcouf's* bridge, followed almost immediately by a sharp report. Before any one on board the *Alerte* realised what had happened a seven-pounder shell burst against the dummy superstructure amidships, ripped a jagged hole in the funnel and cut away the mainstay, with the result that the mainmast, wrenching away the steel tabernacle, crashed heavily upon the poop.

Captain Cain was one of the first to grasp the situation. With all his faults, he was not lacking in courage when under fire. A sliver of metal had grazed his forehead, laying open the frontal bone; but in the excitement he did not heed the burning pain.

" Let 'em have it on the waterline, Gunner's mate," he shouted, countermanding his previous order to destroy the Frenchman's wireless gear.

Since he could not effect the capture of the *Surcouf* without resistance, he determined to sink her. It meant the loss of the expected booty, but the *Alerte* could not run the risk of a prolonged action. There was little danger of the hull of the submarine being perforated by the Frenchman's light quick-firer. Even if the outer skin were holed the inner plating would successfully impede the progress of the projectile. The dominating factor was the absence of any repairing base to which the *Alerte* could retire to heal her wounds. Whatever damage was received had to be made good on the high seas, and a badly battered craft would naturally be the object of interest if not of suspicion.

The gun's crew of the *Alerte's* quick-firer rose to the occasion. As fast as the breech-block could be open and snapped to, the powerful weapon spoke. Empty cartridge-shells clattering on the steel deck punctuated the sharp bark of the weapon, while shell after shell at point-blank range crashed into the *Surcouf's* hull.

But the Frenchman, in spite of the disproportionate odds in the matter of ordnance, maintained a steady fire, not only from the gun under the bridge, but from a similar weapon mounted aft. She then began to go astern, until the *Alerte's* quick-firer was masked by the stanchions of her bridge.

By this time the *Surcouf's* hull was holed in twenty places. A fire had broken out amidships, smoke was pouring in volumes from a dozen jagged apertures ; yet not a single shell had hit her 'twixt wind and water.

For nearly a minute the *Alerte* was raked aft without being able to reply. Two of the hands rushed towards the poop with the machine-gun. Before they reached their goal both were struck down by splinters of shell from a missile that had exploded against one of the cowls.

" Port eight, Quartermaster ! " shouted Captain Cain. " Now, lads, let her have it ! "

But even as the *Alerte* swung to starboard the *Surcouf* put her helm hard over. She was not " out " to sink a pirate, or be sunk herself. Her duty lay in saving her precious cargo.

A dense pall of smoke hid her from sight. Even Captain Cain was at first under the impression that she had sunk suddenly ; but when the thick cloud dispersed the *Surcouf* was sighted steaming away at full speed in the direction of Guernsey.

Pursuit was useless. To attempt to do so would only bring the pirate submarine closer to the French coast, and there were in all probability several torpedo boats at St. Malo. Certainly there were plenty at Brest and Cherbourg, and by following the *Surcouf* the *Alerte* would run the grave risk of being trapped in the deep bay between Cape de la Hague and Ushant, where the rocky and uneven bottom combined with violent currents made it a dangerous place for a submarine to rest on the bed of the sea.

The situation was a dangerous one. The *Surcouf* had got away. Already her wireless was sending out appeals for aid, and warnings that she had been fired upon by a mysterious craft.

Previously, the French authorities had been sceptical about the story of the *Cap Hoorn*. That craft had, in accordance to orders from their captors, proceeded lamely into Cherbourg, only to find that hostilities had not broken out between France and Germany. There was the evidence afforded by her shattered rudder-head, but the

French Admiralty officials, beyond disclaiming responsibility, declined to investigate the damage. Four hours later the *Cap Hoorn* left Cherbourg for Hamburg in tow of an ocean-going Dutch tug.

Nevertheless, the incident could not be entirely ignored. Some vessel had evidently run amok in the Channel. In consequence, the *Surcouf* was one of several merchantmen to be hurriedly armed against the aggressions of the mysterious filibuster. And now the *Surcouf* had reported the attack, and already the news had been transmitted, not only to the French naval bases, but to the British Admiralty. On both sides of the Channel and along the coast of Ireland swift destroyers were raising steam to engage in hunting down the modern pirate craft.

" Look alive, my lads ! " exclaimed Captain Cain. " If we're to get out of this with whole necks, we must waste no time. How many casualties, Mr. Pengelly ? "

" Seven, sir ; four serious, three light."

" Get 'em below," continued the skipper.

" They are already, sir," replied the second in command. " Parkins and Brown—the two who tried to get aft with the machine-gun—are the worst hit. Broadmayne and Vyse carried them below under fire."

" Did they ? " commented Captain Cain. Under his breath he muttered, " And a pity they hadn't lost the number of their mess." [1]

Quickly all available hands got to work. The

---

[1] To lose the number of one's mess, *i.e.*, to die, whether by violence or through natural causes.

dummy funnel was lowered and preparations made to patch the gaping rent and repaint the " smoke-stack " a different colour. The gashes in the upperworks were hidden by means of oval metal plates, one inside, one out, drawn together by a butterfly nut and thread. The tabernacle of the mainmast was rebedded and a new mainstay prepared ready to set the " stick " up again.

The while a most anxious and careful watch was kept on the horizon and on the sky, since it was quite possible that units of the French aviation service might co-operate in the search.

Three-quarters of an hour after breaking off the engagement with the *Surcouf* a liner appeared in sight, bound up-Channel. The *Alerte* could have avoided her by altering helm, but Captain Cain decided upon a bold display of bluff. He held on.

" Union Castle liner, Mr. Pengelly," he remarked. " We'll signal her."

" What for ? " demanded the astonished Pengelly. " Surely we've had enough for the present. Besides, she's British."

" Exactly," concurred the pirate skipper. " I'm going to ask her to take charge of our badly wounded cases. Signalman, hoist the NC."

The letters NC signify " In distress, need immediate assistance," are never purposely ignored. Corresponding to the wireless S.O.S., they would divert the largest liner or the humblest tramp.

Promptly the liner altered helm and slowed down. Passengers crowded to her side to look at the apparently battered tramp.

Standing upon the roof of the charthouse, the *Alerte's* signalman began to semaphore.

"*Alerte* of London, Grimsby for Corunna. Have been fired upon by vessel, nationality unknown, long. 3° 20' W., lat. 49° 50' N., at 10.30 a.m. to-day. Vessel disappeared steering W.S.W. Please report. Can you receive four badly wounded men ? "

To this the liner replied by semaphore that she would wireless the information, and that she would send a boat to transfer the *Alerte's* casualties.

" Many thanks," responded Captain Cain, through the medium of the semaphore. " No need to lower boat ; ours is available."

Captain Cain had already sent below to warn the wounded of his intentions. *They* were not sorry to be clear of the pirate submarine. Their chief anxiety was the thought that they might be deprived of their share of booty, but the wily captain reassured them on that point. He knew they would keep their mouths shut—at least for a period sufficiently long for his purpose. He was also ridding himself of the trouble of having useless men on board—men who would have to be fed and given a certain amount of attention and yet be totally unable to assist in working or fighting the ship.

By refusing the liner's offer to send a boat, Captain Cain had scored again. Not only did it prevent the mail boat's officer having a look round, but it obviated the risk of Broadmayne and his companion making a dash for freedom.

But the signal success of his ruse lay in the fact that the liner was already wirelessing the account of an imaginary attack upon the s.s. *Alerte*. The message was picked up by three destroyers from Cherbourg, which were then in a course that would bring them on the track of the fugitive. Immediately on receipt of this misleading report the French destroyers altered helm in the direction the mythical filibuster was stated to have taken.

The four wounded men were safely transhipped, the operation being performed under the fire of at least fifty cameras—much to Pengelly's disgust. He had no immediate ambition to figure in the limelight of the illustrated press; nor did Captain Cain show any enthusiasm, when through his binoculars he observed the liner's passengers taking snapshots of the *Alerte*. He wished he had set up the mainmast before meeting the liner. Should a photograph of the *Alerte* in her present condition reach the French authorities—as it was fairly certain to do—there would be a lot of explanation to prove that the *Surcouf's* assailant and the *Alerte* were not one and the same vessel.

" Do you want any further assistance ? " inquired the captain of the liner.

" No, sir," answered Pengelly from the boat alongside. " We're putting back to Falmouth for repairs. We can do the run under our own steam."

" Well, good luck to you," was the response, as the *Alerte's* boat pushed off.

Then, with a mutual dipping of ensigns, the liner and the tramp parted—the former to Southampton, the latter anywhere where she might obtain immunity from the pressing attentions of the swift, vengeful destroyers.

CHAPTER XII

HUNTED

"HERE'S a fine lash-up!" remarked Broadmayne to his chum. "We look like getting it in the neck. I won't give much for our chances if our destroyers take up the chase. Cain, or whatever his name is, may be a very clever and cunning rogue, but he's bitten off more then he can chew."

"It's rough luck on us," rejoined Vyse. "I don't hanker after the idea of being sent to Davy Jones's locker by a British destroyer."

"*Pro bono publico*," quoted the Sub. "However, we must make the best of things and trust to luck. Give me half a chance and my name's Johnny Walker as far as this hooker is concerned."

The chums were having a breather on deck before turning in. Seven miles to the nor'west the Wolf Light was sending out its red and white flashes. The *Alerte*, most of her scars patched, was making towards the Scillies; but whether Captain Cain intended to use one of the numerous and secluded channels between the islands as a hiding-place, was a matter for speculation as far as Broadmayne and his companion were concerned.

Gerald and Rollo had worked hard during the

day. That, no one could deny. During the action with the *Surcouf* they had remained passive spectators, taking refuge behind the conning-tower when the Frenchman's shells began to rip the *Alerte's* upper works. But when they saw the two men with the machine-gun topple head-long, they had made a simultaneous rush to the assistance of the badly-wounded men. This they did with a clear conscience. There was nothing in the act that could be construed as aiding and abetting the pirates in an unlawful act.

Nor did they hesitate to tend the other wounded members of the crew. Strangely enough, with all his elaborate preparations, Captain Cain had either neglected or purposely omitted to provide adequate surgical and medical stores, and in consequence the less severely wounded suffered terribly through lack of instruments and ether-chloroform. It was a painful business both to the wounded men and their unqualified surgeons to have to extract jagged slivers of metal without even the application of local anæsthetics. All the Sub and his companion could do was to cleanse the wounds with warm water and iodine, and bind them with rough-and-ready bandages that from an antiseptic point of view would have made a medical man shudder.

Broadmayne had completed his self-imposed task and was going on deck, when he encountered his late antagonist.

The ex-stoker's battered features wore a broad grin. Extending a huge hand, he greeted the Sub with a hearty shake.

" Put it there, chum ! " he exclaimed. " I was
whacked proper. I'd like to know where you
learnt that punch ! An' don't you forget it : if
ever you wants a friend, 'sides the one you've got
already, Jim Soames—Slogger Soames—is the man."

" We're getting on," observed Broadmayne,
when he related the incident to Vyse. " That
fellow isn't a bad sort. Wonder how he came to
row on this galley. And several of the crew seem
quite well disposed towards us. We might work
it."

" Work what ? " asked Rollo.

" Induce some of them to put us ashore,"
replied the Sub.

" Bit risky," observed his chum. " Not on our
account," he added. " That I don't mind. It
would be hard on those fellows if they were found
out. Cain seems a bit of a tartar."

" He may be," admitted Broadmayne. " But
he hasn't much of a hold over his men. And I
fancy, although I'm not sure, that Pengelly and
he are parting brass rags. That conversation we
overheard—about the cave behind a kitchen somewhere—struck me as if Cain and his lieutenant
don't hit it off together."

" Well, Cain won't truss us up for a flogging
after the licking you gave Soames," remarked
Vyse. · " I don't mind admitting I felt a bit on
the scared-stiff side when the bo'sun began
playing with his cat-o'-nine-tails. And Cain
hasn't turned us into pirates yet."

" And never will," added the Sub. " Hello,
we're altering course. What's the game now ? "

The *Alerte* was no longer heading towards the Scillies. She had ported helm and was now making in the direction of Land's End. She was showing her proper navigation lights and was fussing along just like any tramp bound up-Channel.

It was a dark and clear night. Although the sky was overcast and no stars were visible, there was a total absence of fog. It was easy to pick up the numerous lights marking the " Chops of the Channel." Even the flash of the Lizard—thirty miles away—could be observed, although under ordinary conditions its visibility extends over a radius of twenty-one miles only.

" There'll be a gale before very long," declared the Sub. " The excessive clearness of the lower atmosphere is a sure sign of that. The *Alerte* will have to seek shelter somewhere. . . . How about turning-in ? I'm dog-tired. It's no use remaining on deck."

To this suggestion Vyse readily agreed. He, too, was very sleepy. Not since they left Fowey had they had a good night's rest.

On the bridge were Captain Cain, Pengelly, and a couple of hands. Another was at the wheel, while the customary look-out was stationed for'ard. All the rest of the crew were below.

Both the captain and his lieutenant were well conversant with this part of the dangerous Cornish coast. In fact, although there was a chart on the chart-room table, neither of the two officers took the trouble to consult it.

Presently Captain Cain turned to one of the

hands and ordered him to lower the masthead lamp. It was the pirate skipper's intention to take the narrow, intricate channel between Land's End and the Longships; the absence of the mast-head lamp would give the lighthouse-keeper the impression that the *Alerte* was a small sailing craft. Thus he hoped to weather Cape Cornwall and seek refuge on the bed of St. Ives Bay until the threatened gale had blown itself out.

Giving the dangerous Brisons a wide berth, the *Alerte* opened out Pendeen Light. So far so good. It was now close on low water and no vessel would be entering or leaving St. Ives harbour for the next four hours.

" Vessel dead ahead, sir ! " reported the look-out.

Captain Cain uttered an oath. He wanted to arrive at the desired position he had chosen for purposes of submersion without meeting craft of any description. Here were the red, white and green lights of a steam vessel almost bows on to the *Alerte.*

He ported his helm. The other vessel did like-wise. Each now showed the other her red and white navigation lamps, for on rounding Cape Cornwall the *Alerte* had rehoisted hers. There was no danger of collision, but the two would pass far too close to Captain Cain's liking.

Suddenly the dazzling beam of a searchlight leapt from the stranger's bridge. For fifteen seconds—no more—it played upon the *Alerte,* throwing masts, funnel and upperworks into strong relief. Then it vanished.

"Destroyer!" exclaimed Pengelly.

"Let's hope she's satisfied," rejoined Captain Cain grimly, as he blinked at the sudden transition from the brilliant electric light to the darkness of the night. "No, curse her! She's turning."

A flashing-lamp began its preparatory blinks from the destroyer's bridge.

"What ship is that?" it inquired.

"Reply *Memnon* of Bristol," ordered Cain, addressing the signalman, who with ready presence of mind had fetched the Aldis flashing lamp from the chart-room.

The destroyer's response was a curt invitation to stop. "I'll send a boat to examine your papers," added the message.

"By thunder you won't!" muttered Captain Cain, ringing the engine-room telegraph for "Stop." "All hands below as sharp as greased lightning," he ordered. "Mr. Pengelly, warn the duty men to prepare for diving stations. I'll be with you in a brace of shakes."

Both the destroyer and the supposed tramp were losing way; the former, owing to her heavier displacement and narrow beam, having to reverse her engines in order to prevent herself overrunning the *Alerte*.

Captain Cain could hear the squeaking of blocks as the destroyer's boat was being lowered. He was rather dubious about the step he proposed taking. He estimated, although he had not taken soundings, that the *Alerte* was in eleven fathoms, with a sandy bottom. In the absence of electrically propelled motors, the submarine had either to go up or go down. She could not maintain a midway depth, for although fitted with compensating tanks, these alone, without the assistance of the horizontal rudders—which were useless unless the submarine were making way—would fail to keep her at a constant depth. Should the soundings prove much greater than he expected, the *Alerte's* hull might be unable to withstand the enormous pressure of water. If, on the other hand, the depth were considerably less, then the *Alerte's* mastheads would show above the surface, since there was no time to lower them before submerging.

The creaking of oars announced that the destroyer's boat had pushed off and was heading for the supposed *Memnon*. Again the dazzling searchlight was unscreened. There was no time to be lost.

Descending the bridge at breakneck speed, Captain Cain ran to the after-end of the conning-tower. Here, stowed in an air-tight box, was the smoke-producing apparatus used in conjunction with the dummy funnel to give the effect of a vessel with steam-propelled engines. In the same compartment were several explosive rockets.

Disconnecting the pipe that conveyed the smoke to the base of the funnel the pirate captain laid the nozzle on the deck. Then, hastily securing one of the rockets to a stanchion, he ignited the touch-paper.

The moment the detonator exploded, Captain Cain released the smoke cloud, descended the hatchway, and closed the water-tight cover.

" Flood ballast tanks ! " he shouted.

Three minutes later, the *Alerte* sank on practically an even keel to the bed of St. Ives Bay. The depth gauge registered eleven and a quarter fathoms, which meant that at high tide she would be lying in eighty-seven feet—sufficient to immerse the trucks of the masts to a depth of twenty-eight feet.

" That's done them ! " exclaimed Captain Cain exultantly to his second in command.

" Unless they depth-charge us," added Pengelly gloomily.

" They won't—why should they ? " rejoined the skipper. " They don't know but that we blew a hole in the old hooker and sank her for good and all."

" Perhaps they'll send a diver down to report."

" Not before daylight," declared Cain. " And then, if I am any judge of the weather, it'll be too choppy for that."

For some minutes every one kept silent. Although the watch below were almost overwhelmed with curiosity to know what had occurred, the captain gave strict orders that no conversation was to be permitted.

He was confident enough : Pengelly was showing signs of nervousness. Submarine work was not in his line. He was good enough for surface work —in fact, he was a good seaman—but he lacked the cold, calculating and resourceful courage of his chief.

" What's that ? " he ejaculated, as a dull rasping sound penetrated the hull of the submarine. " They're sweeping for us."

" Shut up ! " exclaimed Captain Cain sternly.

The grinding noise continued for fifteen long-drawn-out seconds. Then it ceased as abruptly as it had commenced. Shortly afterwards, the muffled thud of the destroyer's engines were heard, loud at first then gradually diminishing.

" She's off," declared Captain Cain. " What we heard just now was the sinker [1] of a mark-buoy. She's probably making for Falmouth for shelter —or else under the lee of Lundy. They've done us out of a comfortable berth, Pengelly ; we've got to shift."

" Now ? " asked Pengelly dubiously.

" Not until an hour before high water," decided the other. " We'll break surface and drift, using our engines only if absolutely necessary. With the set of the flood tide we ought to be swept through the Sound midway between Godrevy Island and the Stones. There's a minimum of fifty feet at high water."

" How about the lighthouse - keepers ? " objected Pengelly. " Ten to one they've been warned."

" Any more objections ? " asked Captain Cain, losing his temper. " Stow it, man. Why didn't you go in for gardening ? That's more in your line, I think."

With that Captain Cain went to his cabin, and, after warning one of the men to call him at six bells (3 a.m.), calmly went to sleep.

At the appointed hour the skipper was roused.

---

[1] Sinker—A lump of iron to which is attached the buoy-rope, and which serves to anchor the buoy to the bed of the sea.

Fresh as paint, he began preparations for bringing the *Alerte* to the surface.

Absolute caution was essential. The destroyer might not have gone : she might be anchored in the bay. The atmosphere might be still clear, the stars might be shining brightly. Until the submarine broke surface, there were no means of ascertaining what the above-water conditions were. And even with the periscope extended to its greatest height, the masts would be well above the surface before the eye-piece gave any indication of what was in the vicinity.

At length the *Alerte*, shedding tons of water through the scuppers in the superstructure, broke surface. Eagerly the captain threw open the hatch and came on deck. It was raining heavily. There was little or no wind. A heavy ground swell was setting in from the Atlantic. All these conditions supported Cain's declaration that there was a severe storm approaching.

Shouting to the watch on deck to turn out, the captain hurried to the bridge and took rapid bearings by the standard compass. To the south-'ard the harbour lights of Hayle bore S. 22 W.; St. Ives red light, S. 70 W., while Godrevy lighthouse was on a bearing S. 88 E. Transferring these data to the chart, Cain found the *Alerte's* position to be favourable for his project—to allow her to drift through the narrow passage known as the Sound into deeper water under the lee of an extensive shoal of half-tide rocks known as the Stones.

A sailor dashed up the bridge-ladder.

" We've brought up a mark-buoy with us, sir," he reported. " What are we to do with it ? "

There was no hesitation in the skipper's reply. In a trice he had considered and decided upon what was to be done. If the buoy were thrown overboard, it would serve as a guide to the destroyer's operations for examining the supposed wreck. If it were not there, then a vast area of the bay would have to be swept before the naval officers discovered that the " wreck " was no longer in the bay. The longer they took to make this discovery, the better the chances of the *Alerte* getting safely away.

" Cut the rope and unstrand the ends," he ordered, " then heave the buoy overboard."

By so doing, it would give the impression that the buoy rope had parted in rough weather. In all probability the coast watchers would find the buoy pounding against the rocks off Godrevy Point.

Almost imperceptibly the *Alerte* continued to drift. Every half-minute Captain Cain took angles with his sextant, while Pengelly attended to the compass bearings. Although the shore lights were visible, it was an impossible matter to distinguish the outlines of the coast. Conversely, no one ashore—not even the lightkeepers of Godrevy lighthouse—could discern the black hull of the *Alerte* as she was borne with all lights extinguished towards the gateway to safety. Even at a hundred yards the steady downpour of rain was sufficient to obliterate her from watching eyes.

Presently, the *Alerte* entered the red sector of the lower Godrevy Light. She was now in the danger zone. There was quite a nasty tide-rip, while the thunder of the breakers across the Stones on one hand and upon the rock-bound Godrevy Island on the other, were indications that spelt disaster to any vessel that missed the passage of the Sound.

It was an anxious time. More than once Captain Cain grasped the handle of the engine-room telegraph, fearing that the ship was drifting too close to the breakers. Then with remarkable suddenness the *Alerte* passed beyond the warning red sector.

" All clear, Pengelly ! " exclaimed the skipper. " We're through. Pass the word to the hands to lower masts and funnel and make all snug. Smartly, but with no unnecessary noise. Keep the lead going, there."

In ten minutes the work of snugging down was completed. The soundings gave a depth of ten fathoms.

Captain Cain descended from the bridge—slowly this time.

" Hands to diving stations ! " he ordered.

For the second time that night the buoyancy tanks were flooded. The *Alerte*, two and a half miles E. by N. of her previous and enforced resting place, lay snug and sound to await the passing of the threatened storm.

CHAPTER XIII

A BAFFLED QUEST

LIEUTENANT - COMMANDER RALPH RAXWORTHY, D.S.O., officer commanding H.M. Destroyer *Windrush*, leant over the after end of the bridge stanchion-rails to give final instructions to his sub-lieutenant.

" She's the one we want," he shouted, in order to make himself heard above the hiss of escaping steam. " Mind how you close her. Examine her papers, and if you find anything of the slightest suspicious nature, put her under arrest."

" Very good, sir," replied Sub-Lieutenant Allerton, instinctively patting his revolver-holster before dropping into the waiting boat. " Shove off for'ard. Give way, lads ! "

The boat, with the armed boarding-party, was soon speeding through the black water in the direction of the supposed *Memnon*, which lay rolling sluggishly in the full glare of the destroyer's searchlight.

Allerton, too, had his suspicions. Expecting to find a crowd of curious and perhaps amused seamen peering at the *Windrush's* boat, he was considerably puzzled to see only one man on the tramp's bridge and her deck absolutely deserted.

Even as he looked, a flash, followed by a roar, came from the *Memnon's* deck. A cloud of black smoke, its edges tinted with silver and the rays of the searchlight, rose sullenly in the faint breeze.

For some moments Allerton was undecided what to do. At first, under the impression that the mysterious vessel had opened fire, he altered helm in order to prevent the boat masking the destroyer's reply. Even as he did so, he noticed that the tramp was much lower in the water.

" The blighters have scuttled her, by Jove ! " he exclaimed. " Lay on your oars, lads. We don't want to be carried down with her."

Without the faintest doubt, the would-be prize was sinking fast. That was undeniable evidence of her guilt. No law-abiding merchant vessel would voluntarily destroy herself simply because she was about to be boarded by a party from a British man-of-war.

With great rapidity the *Memnon* sank. She did not heel or even roll. She disappeared amid a smother of foam, throwing out a swell that tossed the *Windrush's* boat like a cork. An oval patch of silvery light from the destroyer's searchlight marked the spot where the mysterious vessel had plunged to the bed of St. Ives Bay.

" Give way, lads ! " ordered Allerton. " We may find some of them in the ditch."

For a quarter of an hour the boat hovered around the spot. There were no signs of survivors —not even of débris. A little oil, floating in iridescent patches, alone marked the place, and even that was drifting sullenly with the weak tidal current.

At dead slow ahead the *Windrush* closed her boat. A mark-buoy and sinker were dropped overboard, the searchlight was switched off and the boat hoisted up and swung inboard.

" Good enough," declared the lieutenant-commander as his sub gained the bridge and reported. " We haven't made a capture, worse luck ; but we've done the next best thing. We've scuppered this pirate-johnny, whoever he may be. Right-o, Sub, carry on, please, while I write out my report."

The *Windrush* had that morning left Devonport under orders to patrol the coast between Hartland and Pendeen Points. Another destroyer was assigned a beat between Hartland and Worms Head, while a third cruised between Swansea Bay and Milford Haven. All outward and homeward bound shipping were to be spoken, and, in the event of any suspicion, to be boarded and have the papers examined.

This was in execution of a general Admiralty order embracing the whole of the West and South Coast of England and the South Coast of Ireland, but it was hardly expected that the mysterious pirate would be found in the approach to the Bristol Channel.

It was a piece of sheer good luck that had caused the *Windrush* to intercept the self-styled *Memnon*. Had the latter been half an hour or even twenty minutes later in rounding Pendeen Head, the destroyer would have turned and been on her way back to Hartland.

Two hours later, the Commander-in-Chief at Devonport was awakened by his secretary.

" They've got her, sir ! " exclaimed the latter, brandishing a signal-pad.

" Got who ? " demanded the still drowsy admiral.

" The pirate, sir ; a message has just come through from the *Windrush*."

The Commander-in-Chief took the pad and read :

" O.C. *Windrush* to C.-in-C., Devonport.   Radio No. 445.   Have honour to report that at midnight *Windrush* spoke vessel 2 miles W. 6 N. Godrevy Light.   Vessel reported herself *Memnon* of Bristol. Ordered her to close and sent boat to make examination.   Before boat could board *Memnon* sank, apparently result of internal explosion.   No survivors.   Have marked wreck.   In view of bad weather, request permission to return Devonport.— R. RAXWORTHY, Lieut.-Commdr."

" That looks like business, sir," remarked the secretary.   " I suppose she is the same craft that held up the *Cap Hoorn* and got a mauling from the *Surcouf* ? "

" She hasn't lost much time in going round the Land," rejoined the Commander-in-Chief.   " I wonder what in the name of blazes she was doing over this side ?   All right, Symington.   Transmit the signal to the Admiralty, please ; and reply to *Windrush*.   She's to put into Milford Haven until the weather moderates.   We'll send a dockyard tug and a couple of lighters with a diving party round as soon as practicable.   That's all ; good-night."

The Admiralty report was made public at 4.0 p.m. of the same day, but two hours earlier the London

evening papers brought out special editions with
double-headed headlines announcing the destruction of the pirate vessel that had commenced to
play havoc on the French side of the Channel.
Every newspaper brought out a different account.
For the most part, what they lacked in actual
detail they made up for by drawing upon their
imagination.

One, very wide of the mark, reported that the
pirate had been sunk off Cherbourg, in action with a
French cruiser ; another declared that the filibuster
had been rammed and sunk by a British light
cruiser off Beachy Head.   A third, that the mysterious vessel had been driven ashore in Mounts Bay
and that the crew had been taken prisoners and
were already on their way to London.   A fourth,
much nearer the mark, had contrived to obtain
information from St. Ives to the effect that the
destroyer *Windrush* had sunk the pirate vessel
Memnon off Trevose Head.   Not one in half a
dozen separate reports mentioned the important
fact that the corsair had sunk herself.

That same afternoon a westerly gale of force
ten—or with a velocity of sixty-five miles an hour—
was blowing in the English Channel and off the
north coast of Cornwall.   At Tresco, Scilly, the
anemometer even registered one hundred and
twenty miles.   For three days it blew with un-
abated violence, finally veering to the N.N.W.,
leaving in its wake a trail of disaster.   For nearly
a week after, a heavy tumbling sea was sweeping
in from the Atlantic, rendering investigation of the
wreck of the *Memnon* impracticable.

At length the sea moderated sufficiently to enable the dockyard tug and the two lighters to leave Plymouth Sound. They had not cleared the breakwater more than an hour when the Devonport wireless station received the following startling message :

" S.S. *Broadstone* making for Falmouth, towing Spanish oil-tanker *Mendez Nunez*, attacked, pillaged and disabled by vessel, nationality unknown, in Lat. 47° 20′ N., long. 9° 15′ W."

" Then there must have been a pair of 'em," exclaimed the Commander-in-Chief.

" Unless the original one got away," suggested his flag-lieutenant.

" What do you mean ? " demanded the admiral. " Didn't the *Windrush* report her sunk ? "

" Strange things happen at sea, sir," remarked the admiral's secretary.

" But there are limits," rejoined the Commander-in-Chief. " Well, the diving-party will get to work early to-morrow if the weather holds. I'm willing to bet a bottle of '14 Champagne to a Corona Corona that they'll find the wreck of the *Memnon* within three working days."

" Done, sir ! " replied the secretary promptly.

The admiral lost. In calm weather, divers descended and discovered the sinker of the buoy dropped by the *Windrush*. A couple of drifters swept a wide area without encountering any obstruction resembling wreckage. A naval seaplane assisted in the search, but without success. Reluctantly the authorities had to admit that the operation was a complete failure. The sunken *Memnon* had vanished as completely as if she had been swallowed up by a fathomless quicksand. But since no quicksand existed in the neighbourhood of St. Ives Bay, that theory was knocked on the head. Remained the question: What had happened to her?

CHAPTER XIV

A BROKEN REED

THROUGHOUT the three days during which the sea was raging furiously in the grip of the terrific gale, the *Alerte* remained submerged. Occasionally the giant seas sweeping over the Stones rocked her ever so slightly. The noise of shingle carried over the rocky ledge to wind'ard could be distinctly heard like a continuous roll of distant thunder, but as far as actual danger went the *Alerte* was as safe as if she had been lying at heavy moorings in the most sheltered berth in Falmouth harbour.

The difficulty of maintaining a constant supply of pure air was overcome by means of chemicals; so much so, that there was a slight excess of oxygen that had a peculiarly exhilarating effect upon the crew. Even the usually morbid and pessimistic Pengelly began by attempting feeble jokes. He next became boisterous and excitable, while on the third day even the light-hearted crew looked askance at him, so erratic was his behaviour.

Several of the hands showed signs of excessive excitability. The epidemic was spreading. Had the *Alerte* remained submerged very much longer,

all hands might have gone mad under the influence
of the super-oxygen charged atmosphere.

Fortunately for them, Captain Cain noticed the
symptoms. He decided to break surface and
remain with the hatchways open for at least an
hour, even at the risk of the heavy seas pouring
inboard.

At two in the morning of the fourth day the
Alerte was brought to the surface. Greatly to
her skipper's surprise—for the glass had risen far
too rapidly to prognosticate fine weather—the
storm had blown itself out. Crested waves were
surging over the Stones and thundering upon
Godrevy Island, but the pirate submarine was in
comparatively sheltered water, rolling sluggishly
to the long Atlantic swell.

Captain Cain's chief anxiety was now on account
of the oil fuel. The gauges showed that there was
only one ton left in the tank. By some means he
must get into communication with Captain Silas
Porthoustoc and arrange for the *Fairy* to proceed to a rendezvous with a cargo of liquid
fuel.

For the present the *Alerte* rode to a single
anchor, double watches being set to give the
alarm should a vessel be sighted, although the
position of the pirate submarine was well out of
the way of traffic, owing to the proximity of the
reef known as the Stones. At a few seconds' notice
the *Alerte* could submerge. Meanwhile, the hull
of the submarine was being swept by a current of
pure, ozone-laden air.

" Mr. Pengelly ! " shouted the skipper.

The second in command hurried along the alley-way, performing a fantastic two-step.

"Pull yourself together, man," exclaimed Captain Cain sternly. "We're in a bit of a fix."

Pengelly's light-hearted demeanour fell from him like a shedded garment.

"What is it now, sir ? " he inquired anxiously.

"Precious little oil-fuel left," replied the captain. "Look here : do you know Portreath ? What sort of a harbour is it ? "

"Not enough water for us," replied Pengelly. "You're surely not going to take the ship into port ? "

"No fear," responded Cain grimly. "But I want to send a boat ashore. You'd better take her. We must arrange with Porthoustoc to supply us with oil. While you are ashore, you might get hold of a batch of newspapers. We don't appear to be getting much information by wireless."

"There'll be a heavy breaking sea across the mouth of Portreath harbour," objected Pengelly.

"A chance for you to display your seamanship," added Cain, with grim humour. "We'll run up along before daybreak and then retrace our course. People ashore will think we're outward-bound. Pick your crew. I'll write a letter to Old Silas, giving him instructions."

Just before dawn the *Alerte* brought St. Agnes' Head broad on the starboard beam. Then she turned and ran leisurely down the coast, bringing up off the little harbour of Portreath just as the sun appeared above the gaunt and rugged Cornish hills.

To the coast-watching station she made a signal announcing herself as the s.s. *Eldorado* of Sunderland from Bristol to Whitby, following up with a request to know whether it was practicable to send a boat ashore.

Portreath station replied that it could be done, but care was necessary on account of the disturbed state of the bar.

" Carry on, Mr. Pengelly," ordered the inexorable Captain Cain.

The boat made the harbour safely. Pengelly, on stepping ashore, was met by one of the Customs men.

" Hello ! " remarked the latter. " Rather unusual you coming in here, isn't it ? "

" I have to post important letters," replied Pengelly.

" Lucky you didn't bring up off here a week or so ago," commented the official. " We'd have to have searched you."

" What for ? " asked the *Alerte*'s second in command, with well-feigned innocence.

" 'Cause of that pirate what was knocking about. Well, she's gone, thank goodness ! I wasn't none too keen myself, putting off to a vessel that might have been manned by cutthroats."

" We heard something about it," remarked Pengelly. " Rumours, of course. What did happen ? "

" She blew herself up over t'other side of

Godrevy Island," announced the man, with a sweep of his hand in the direction of St. Ives Bay. "Just as the *Windrush*—destroyer, she be —was about to nab her. They'll be starting salvage operations when the swell settles—maybe to-morrow."

"That's something to be thankful for," said Pengelly sententiously. "Not that they'd have got much out of the old *Eldorado* out yonder. There are enough risks at sea without the chance of being scuppered by a bloomin' pirate. . . . Where's the post office, mate ? "

The Customs man gave the required information. Pengelly walked away, posted Silas Porthoustoc's instructions and purchased a quantity of provisions and a big budget of newspapers.

He returned to the harbour and found that none of the boat's crew had deserted. He would not have been greatly surprised if some of them had made themselves scarce. He himself felt tempted to clear out, when his feet touched honest Cornish soil. It would be an easy matter to make his way to Penzance and arrange with Old Silas to share the plunder. But there were difficulties. He might betray Cain and obtain King's pardon, but what would happen to the booty then ? Its secret hiding-place would be divulged. He would not be a penny the better. And, if Cain evaded capture, his—Pengelly's—life would not be worth a moment's purchase. Possibly, similar fears had exercised a restraining influence on the boat's crew. Once "in the swim" it was a difficult matter to escape the whirlpool.

"Better look alive," cautioned the Customs man, looking down from the lofty quay-side. "There's a nasty sea-fog banking up."

The boat shipped a considerable amount of water in clearing the harbour, and by the time she ran alongside the *Alerte* the fog was so thick that the shore was entirely blotted out.

"Well, what's the news ? " demanded Captain Cain.

"Haven't looked, sir," replied Pengelly, tossing the bundle from the boat to the deck of the *Alerte*. "From what I've heard, they think us properly scuppered."

The boat was hoisted up and secured. At slow speed the pirate submarine nosed her way through the fog, intending to make for a certain secluded "sound " in the Scillies, there to await the arrival of the *Fairy* with the oil.

Having given the quartermaster the course, Cain selected a couple of newspapers and told the bo's'un to pass a number of them for'ard for the hands not on duty.

One of the newspapers was the *Western Gazette*. This the captain handed to Pengelly, knowing that the latter would derive interesting local information from it. The *Times* Cain retained and figuratively proceeded to devour with the avidity of a man who has for days been cut off from all accounts of the world's doings.

"Hello, Pengelly ! " he exclaimed, "we're fugitives from justice."

"I know that," rejoined Pengelly, with a show of asperity.

" 'Tany rate," resumed Cain, " there's a
warrant out for the arrest of Thomas Trevorrick
and Paul Pengelly for fraud in connection with
the Polkyll Shipbreaking Company. We're assumed to have absconded and to be hiding on
the Continent. There's two hundred pounds
reward."

Both men smiled grimly at each other. Evidently there was no connection in the minds of
the authorities between Trevorrick and the pirate
Captain Cain.

" And the *Memnon* is officially reported as being
destroyed," continued Captain Cain. " The
Admiralty state emphatically that she is the
vessel that attacked the *Cap Hoorn*. They weren't
far out there, Pengelly, but listen ! This is a
gem ! ' In consequence of the destruction of the
Memnon, all danger to shipping through piratical
action is now considered at an end. Accordingly
orders have been issued to the naval patrols
engaged in hunting down the pirate to return to
their respective bases.' Well, that's given us a
new lease of life. Wait till we replenish our fuel
tanks and we'll give My Lords a nasty eye-opener."

This time both men laughed boisterously.
Fickle Fortune was treating them with lavish
favour.

For some minutes there was silence, each reader
deep in his paper.

" By Jove ! " suddenly ejaculated Pengelly.
" Listen to this, sir : ' An inquest was held——' "

" Don't want to hear about inquests," interrupted Captain Cain. " Don't suppose mine will

worry me. Why should I trouble about other people's ? "

" You will about this one," persisted Pengelly doggedly. " It's Silas Porthoustoc. He was found dead in his garden. Heart disease, they say. The inquest was held in the Keigwin Arms last Monday."

" Confound the fellow ! " almost shouted Captain Cain angrily. " What possessed him to shuffle off this mortal coil at this time above all others, and to leave us in the lurch ? Ten thousand thunders ! Think of the oil-fuel we'll have to whistle for ! "

" And I've only just posted his orders," added Pengelly. " What did you tell him ? Will that give us away ? "

" No, it won't," declared the skipper. " It will convey nothing to outsiders. ' Scilly blooms ' and ' Jersey potatoes ' won't give them a clue. Trust me for that. All the same, it's infernally annoying."

" It is," agreed Pengelly.

Both men relapsed into silence.

" I hope Porthoustoc got that Abrahams fellow down from London to dispose of the booty before he turned up his toes ? " mused Cain.

" Wonder if Silas hid the stuff where I told him to ? " soliloquised Pengelly. " Well, it's all or nothing as far as I am concerned."

CHAPTER XV

THE OIL-TANKER

FOR two hours more the *Alerte* held on a westerly course through a blinding fog before Captain Cain resolved upon a plan of action. Generally capable of forming a swift and workable decision, he was now beset with so many perplexities that for once at least his ready resource failed him.

Against one outstanding asset—the Admiralty declaration that the patrolling destroyers had been withdrawn—was a more than counterbalancing debit. Cap'n Silas Porthoustoc's sudden demise had not only deprived the pirate of a necessary confederate—it had handicapped him severely in the important matter of refilling the almost empty fuel tanks.

It was impossible for the *Alerte* to enter any commercial harbour and obtain oil from the storage tanks without certain detection. Equally impossible was it for the same reason to receive supplies from an oil-tanker on the high seas, unless the pirate resorted to force. British vessels he had resolved to leave severely alone. There were Yankee tankers to be met with, but Captain Cain was chary in that respect. Although he had no love for citizens of " the greatest republic on earth," he had a wholesome regard for the physical and mental powers of the officers and crews of ships flying the Stars and Stripes. Men of the Latin races were excitable and easily intimidated, according to his estimation. A German could be bluffed, provided he could be made to realise the argument of brute force. But a Yankee strongly resembled a Briton, both in courage, resource and stubbornness.

No, United States tankers were not to be meddled with, he decided. Apparently the only course open to him was to operate on the French side of the Channel upon any likely craft using liquid fuel —and during the last few years King Coal was being seriously threatened by King Oil in the mercantile fleet, both of the Old and New Worlds.

Porthoustoc's death had affected the situation in another way. The *Alerte* had no means of sending her unlawful booty to England. In future she must be her own store-carrier, unless she found a secluded and safe base of operations. It was too hazardous an enterprise to attempt to approach any of the little frequented Cornish coves under cover of night and land the spoil by means of boats. Besides, the moment the news reached the Admiralty that the same or another pirate ship was " out," all the previous destroyer activities would be resumed with increasing zest. It was more than likely that orders would be given to depth-charge the pirate vessel if she sank herself under similar circumstances to that of the *Memnon* in St. Ives Bay. Captain Cain had a wholesome respect for the British Navy and its methods in dealing with submarine operations.

The only solution Captain Cain could find, lay in deserting home waters for less frequented seas. There were safe hiding-places off the African coast, ideal spots for burying the pirate's booty, until such times as the master villain could remove the spoil and cheat his partners in crime. But there again cropped up the baffling problem. Without sufficient oil-fuel, how was the *Alerte* to cover the sixteen hundred odd miles between Land's End and the African coast ? Was it possible to intercept the first oil-burning vessel they met, British or otherwise, and help themselves to the precious commodity ? Would a monetary payment in the case of a vessel flying the red ensign smooth over matters and at the same time absolve Cain from his promise to his crew and also remove their scruples ?

Picking up the copy of the *Times*, Captain Cain looked through the list of shipping as reported by Lloyds. Suddenly he gave a chuckle of satisfaction. Amongst the names appeared that of the s.s. *Mendez Nunez*, owned by the Bilboa Oil Company, which left Cadiz on the 9th instant bound for Swansea.

Hurrying to the chart-room, Captain Cain found and unrolled a chart of the west coast of Europe from Finisterre to Cape Clear. Assuming the speed of the Spanish tanker to be eleven knots, he arrived at the conclusion that the *Alerte* ought to fall in with her within twenty-four hours at about fifty miles S.S.W. of the Bishop Rock.

It was a daring proposition. Apart from the

risk of missing the Spanish tanker altogether, the position given was not far from the junction of the traffic routes for shipping to and from the Straits and the West Coast of Africa bound to and from the English and Bristol Channel ports. the Bishop Light being the first one sighted by homeward-bound vessels approaching Land's End. In the event of the *Mendez Nunez* being sighted, could the capture be effected without the risk of other vessels coming to the Spaniard's aid ?

Leaving Pengelly in charge of the bridge, Captain Cain called the gunner and the bo'sun to his cabin and put the case before them. He meant to ignore Pengelly altogether in the matter. Instinctively he knew that his second in command would strongly protest against the idea of an African base. Pengelly was all right up to a certain point in home waters, but not once but many times had he expressed his fears about proceeding far from his native Cornwall.

Both Barnard and Marchant fell in with the captain's suggestion. Already had they come to the conclusion that piracy, even with the assistance of a submarine craft, was too risky a game to be prosecuted for any length of time in British and French waters.

" You see the idea ? " said Cain. " A couple of good hauls of shipping homeward-bound from Senegal, the Congo, and other French and Belgian colonies, and our fortunes are made. We'll cache the booty, make our way home, charter a vessel all above-board, recover the stuff, and there you are. It's as simple as A B C. Our first business is with the Spanish tanker. Pass the word for'ard, Mr. Barnard. There's a double share to the first man who sights the *Mendez Nunez*."

Ten miles to the west of the Scillies, the *Alerte* ran out of the bank of fog into a clear expanse of water under a cloudless sky. The sea had moderated considerably, although there was a long, sullen swell that caused the pirate vessel to roll until her scuppers were under water. In these circumstances, should the *Mendez Nunez* be captured, making fast alongside the prize would be a manœuvre fraught with danger.

Captain Cain had made a correct guess with reference to the sighting of the Spanish tanker. A wisp of smoke away to the S.S.W. indicated the presence of a vessel. Half an hour later, two masts and funnel showed above the horizon.

Glass in hand, the captain went aloft. From his elevated perch he quickly ascertained that the on-coming craft was a tanker. Although end on, the vessel's build and rig confirmed his surmise. She was long, low-lying, with a funnel right aft. The only break between the funnel and the bows was a small structure crowned by the bridge and chart-house. She was flying no colours, but the yellow and red bands round her funnel were sufficient to proclaim her nationality.

Rapidly the distance between the two vessels decreased. Giving a rapid glance to reassure himself that there were no other craft in sight, Captain Cain descended from the cross-trees to the deck and thence to the bridge.

" Port a bit ! " he ordered.

By so doing the *Alerte* was merely conforming to the usual custom by which vessels meeting nearly end on ported helm. The action served its purpose. Quite in ignorance of the danger that menaced her, the *Mendez Nunez* followed suit, intending to pass the supposed tramp at not less than two cables' distance.

Already the *Alerte's* quick-firer was cleared for action, but was hidden from the Spaniard by the rise of the former's fo'c'sle. The moment the pirate vessel was in a position to enable the gun to bear, a shell was fired across the tanker's bows, instantly followed by the signal to heave to.

Signs were not lacking that this peremptory action had thrown the Spaniards into a state of panic. Apart from the threat of being sunk, they realised what the dire result would be of a shell exploding the highly inflammable cargo. Some of the crew rushed to lower the boats. The captain and some of his officers on the tanker's bridge were beside themselves with terror.

" Stop instantly," signalled the pirate.

Some one on board the *Mendez Nunez*—certainly it was not the captain—rang down for the engines to be reversed. The tanker soon lost way, and was presently lying head to wind in the long Atlantic swell.

With her machine-gun mounted on the bridge and trained upon the Spaniard, and with every available man conspicuously displaying his automatic pistol, the *Alerte* was cautiously manœuvred to come alongside the prize. There was very little risk to the submarine's hull. Her false upperworks might be stove in. The danger lay in the fact that the *Alerte* might fracture the light steel hull-plates of the tanker, in which case the former would have to do without the precious oil.

" Get your fenders out ! " shouted Captain Cain to the still dumbfounded crew of the *Mendez Nunez*.

Apparently some of the Spaniards understood English, or else they realised the intentions of the approaching *Alerte*. Three large fenders made of faggots bound with wire rope were lowered over the starboard side.

With a heavy jar, the pirate craft and the *Mendez Nunez* came together. One of the fenders nipped as the two craft ground each other's sides and was flattened like a pancake. Another carried away. The partially lowered boat was crushed to matchwood. Rolling a full fifteen degrees, the huge tanker stove in ten feet of the *Alerte's* bulwarks and buckled the stanchions at one end of her bridge.

" An hour of this and we won't have a shred of upperworks left," expostulated Pengelly. " Sheer off, sir, while we have the chance."

For a wonder, Captain Cain concurred. With her port screw going full astern, the *Alerte* drew clear of her prey.

It was no intention on the part of the pirate captain to abandon the attempt. Easing down a cable's length to leeward, he signalled HNT— " Smooth sea by pouring oil on it."

In a few minutes the pumps of the *Mendez Nunez* got to work. Volumes of crude oil were released, spreading in vast iridescent patches to lee'ard of the tanker. Although the swell still continued, it lost its dangerous aspect.

"That's the ticket!" exclaimed Captain Cain to his second in command. "Well, it's their oil they're using, not mine. . . . Steady on your helm . . . port a bit . . . meet her at that."

Again the *Alerte* closed her prey, this time on the port side. Held by hawsers and springs fore and aft, the two vessels no longer ground against each other with any danger of violence.

At the head of fifteen armed men, Captain Cain boarded the prize. No resistance was offered. The Spanish captain and all his officers, with the exception of two engineers, were ordered for'ard and locked in the forepeak with the rest of the crew. Two of the tanker's ejector pumps were led to the *Alerte's* tanks and the work of refuelling the pirate submarine began.

While this business was in progress, the boarding party were by no means idle. A systematic search of the officers' quarters yielded a little booty. The ship's stores and provision rooms were pillaged, and anything likely to be of service to the pirates removed.

Then the wireless gear was rendered useless, the operator of the *Mendez Nunez* having previously been ordered to produce a record of messages sent and received during the last four hours. None had been sent since the *Alerte* fired a warning shot across the tanker's bows, the operator having deserted his post in the general panic that ensued.

Meanwhile, Marchant the gunner, with a couple of hands, went below to the tanker's engine-room. Breaking open the tunnel of the main shaft, they fractured the propeller shaft by means of a slab of gun cotton. Within the space of fifty minutes Captain Cain had accomplished his task. He had replenished the *Alerte's* fuel supply, plundered the tanker, and had left her helpless in the Atlantic, with no means of summoning assistance other than by visual signalling.

" Recall the hands, Mr. Marchant," ordered Captain Cain, when the gunner returned on deck and reported the fracturing of the propeller shaft.

A shrill whistle had the immediate effect of bringing the boarding-party to the side.

" All correct, sir," reported the gunner, after the men had numbered off. " How about those chaps, sir ? " he added, pointing in the direction of the forepeak. " Do we let 'em out ? "

" No," replied Cain, with a sardonic smile. " Let 'em batter the hatch down when they find we're gone. A little extra damage won't signify."

Returning to the *Alerte*, the pirate captain signed to the two engineers of the tanker to cast off the hawsers ; then, backing clear of the *Mendez Nunez*, the *Alerte* made off at full speed in a nor'easterly direction, towards the Irish coast.

Forty-five minutes later, having dropped the tanker beneath the horizon, the pirate submarine altered her course for the distant African shore, secure in the knowledge that when assistance did come to the disabled tanker, the Spaniards would declare that their attacker was making in a direction far different to the course she eventually took.

Just before eight bells in the first dog watch, the bo'sun came up to Pengelly, who was in charge of the bridge.

" Two men missing, sir," he reported.

" Who are they ? "

" Broadmayne and Vyse, sir."

" Then make a search for them. They didn't smuggle themselves on board yon tanker by any chance ? "

" Oh no, sir," declared Barnard. " They were seen some time after we sheered off."

But the bo'sun had made a genuine mistake. At that precise moment Broadmayne and his chum were having a very lively time on board the Spanish tanker *Mendez Nunez*.

CHAPTER XVI

THE STOWAWAYS

" LOOK here ! " exclaimed Broadmayne, in a low voice, " are you game ? Now's our chance."

He pointed to the *Mendez Nunez*.

" Steady on," replied Vyse cautiously. " Supposing we get on board without being spotted ; what then ? Can you speak Spanish ; I can't. The blighters will take us for pirates—I don't blame them if they do—and there'd be a deuce of a rumpus before we could explain. They'd probably knife us out of hand."

The two chums were standing close to the poopladder while the plundering of the tanker was in progress. Their " passive resistance " was now tolerated without any interference on the part of the pirate captain. Provided they stood their trick in the ordinary work of the ship, they were not called upon to take any part in actual acts of piracy. They certainly earned their keep. Captain Cain had not to pay them. On the other hand, he still hoped to get a substantial sum for their ransom. On that account, coupled with the fact that already they knew too much to be released, they were retained on board the *Alerte*.

" Risk that," rejoined the Sub laconically.
" It's better than being sent to the bottom for good
and all, and that's what will happen if we don't
clear out."

" Right-o," agreed Rollo Vyse. " Wait till old
Pengelly's looking the other way and then shift like
greased lightning."

" And get spotted directly we gain her deck,"
objected the Sub. " No ; our best way is to drop
overboard, swim round under her stern, and hang
on to the falls of the boat they tried to lower. As
soon as the *Alerte* backs clear, then up we shin."

" Beastly dirty job," remarked Vyse, objecting
in turn, as he glanced at the oil-smothered water.
" All right. Lead on, Macduff ! "

Awaiting their opportunity, for Pengelly was
kept fairly busy in shouting orders to the men
tending the warps and transferring the plunder to
the *Alerte*, the chums made their way under the
bridge. Here, secure from observation, unless
any of the crew of the quick-firer came aft, they
clambered through the gap in the stove-in bulwarks
and dropped into the sea.

For the first time they realised the extreme
difficulty in swimming in oil-covered water. It
was a hard struggle to keep their heads above the
surface, and quite a strenuous effort to make
progress. To add to the peril, they were liable to
be crushed by the hull of the ship as she drifted to
lee'ard, while when they reached the wind'ard side
they might find that the drift was so considerable
that they would be unable to keep pace with it.

" Dog-stroke," gasped Broadmayne. " Better

than breast - stroke in this muck. We're all
right."

It seemed a fearfully long time swimming under
the tanker's squat counter. Then foot by foot
they struggled along the Spanish vessel's starboard
quarter to where the jagged timbers of the crushed
boat still hung from the for'ard falls.

With a gasp of relief the Sub stretched out his
hand and grasped the débris. He waited until
Vyse had obtained a hand-fast and then cautiously
hoisted himself out of the water and gained a
temporary refuge by sitting on the edge of the
boat's bow-thwart, where his chum soon joined
him.

So far so good. They were roughly fifteen feet
below the tanker's stanchion-rail. The boat's
bows were practically intact as far as the second
thwart, and hanging in a vertical position formed a
screen from the sight of any one who happened to
look over the tanker's side. But their plight was
far from enviable. Owing to the swell, the wreckage of the boat was thudding steadily against the
tanker's side and turning dizzily as the falls twisted
and untwisted. The chums were smothered with
black oil from head to foot. Some of the vile stuff
had found its way into Rollo's eyes, making them
smart exceedingly. Yet in spite of the various
discomforts he could not refrain from remarking
that they looked like a pair of blackbirds in a cage.

"There's the recall," exclaimed the Sub, as
above the hiss of escaping vapour from the *Mendez
Nunez's* steam-pipe came the shrill notes of a
whistle.

For a few minutes longer the chums listened intently. They could hear nothing more to indicate that the pirate submarine had parted company with her prize.

" Don't move," cautioned Vyse suddenly. " Look ! "

The stern of the *Alerte* was beginning to be visible as the vessel backed. If she carried sternway much farther, the fragments of the boat with the two fugitives clinging to it would be exposed to the view of the pirate crew.

More and more of the after-part of the pirate submarine's hull showed until the end of the main-mast derricks came into view. Then, at first almost imperceptibly, the sternway movement diminished. A smother of oily foam from the *Alerte's* twin propellers was flung astern. Her engines were going ahead. For a brief instant the relative position of the pirate craft and her prize remained un-changed ; then, gathering way, the *Alerte* forged ahead and disappeared from the view of the two chums.

" Think she'll be put about if we're missed ? " asked Vyse anxiously.

" Might," admitted Broadmayne. " Perhaps they're so taken up with their success that they've forgotten all about us. 'T any rate, up we go. We'll lie doggo as long as we possibly can, in case Cain has a fancy to renew our acquaintance."

It was no easy matter to swarm up that fifteen feet or so of trebled, twisted rope. Their hands, smothered in thick oil, had great difficulty to obtain a steady grip, while, to make matters worse, the tanker was again rolling badly. With every roll the falls with their human burdens bumped heavily against the ship's side.

At last the Sub reached the stanchion-rail. Crouching, he edged sideways to enable his companion to gain a place of safety. Then he gave a quick glance along the tanker's deck.

It was deserted. The two engineers, having completed their forced task of casting off the *Alerte's* warps, had gone below to obtain tools to effect the release of the rest of the crew, who, knowing that the pirate had sheered off, were clamouring loudly for help. Doubtless they were under the mistaken though by no means unfounded idea that their vessel was being scuttled, and that they were in peril of being drowned like rats in a trap.

Broadmayne's next thought was for the *Alerte*. A roll of the tanker raised the side sufficiently to enable the Sub to see right across her deck to the expanse of sea beyond. There was the pirate submarine, stern-on, legging it as hard as she could go in a northerly direction. Already she was between a mile and a half and two miles away and momentarily increasing the distance at the rate of a mile every four minutes.

" All clear," reported the Sub. " Keep down as much as you can in case Cain and Co. are using their binoculars. Now then, we've got to find a place to stow ourselves."

" Not in these trousers," rejoined his chum. " We're shedding a trail of oil. Deck isn't any too clean, I admit, but look there! A wash and brush up and a change of clothing is what we want."

"And likely to want," added Broadmayne. "Look alive; let's go aft and see what we can find. I agree as to the clothes. They're not respectable and are decidedly uncomfortable."

The engine-room and officers' cabins on board the *Mendez Nunez* were right aft under the poop, which, in her case, was flush with the part corresponding to the waist, except for the deck-house abaft the funnel.

A glance down the engine-room hatchway in passing revealed the fact that the place was deserted. Down the companion-ladder Broadmayne crept, his chum close at his heels, their progress marked by a double trail of oil.

"No one at home," remarked Vyse, stopping outside the open door of a cabin marked with a brass plate "El Capitaño." "Looks as if our late shipmates have been here before us."

"So much the better as far as we are concerned," added the Sub. "We'll borrow from the Old Man's wardrobe. Quick! Off with your gear. We can sling our discarded rags through the scuttle."

They stripped, "borrowed" the curtains over the scuttles to remove as much as possible of their coating of oil and then rummaged amongst the lockers under the bunk.

Vyse had spoken truly when he remarked that some one had been there before them, but apparently the pirates were sufficiently well found in the matter of clothing to trouble to steal the Spanish skipper's wardrobe.

In a few minutes the two chums were " arrayed " in garments of sufficient girth, but sadly lacking in length. Evidently El Capitaño was a short and very fat individual, for the Sub found himself wearing a pair of trousers that reached half-way between his ankles and his knees, displaying an expanse of pale blue shirt between the top of the " bags " and the hem of a coat somewhat resembling a monkey-jacket.

Nor was Vyse much better off. He had to content himself with a ridiculously short pair of knee-breeches—part of the Spanish captain's shore-going " plain clothes "—and a blue dressing-gown edged with scarlet silk.

" Look alive ! " exclaimed Broadmayne. " They are let loose for'ard. This way ! "

Stopping at what was obviously the officers' pantry and picking up a couple of small-sized loaves from a few that the pirates had considered beneath their notice, the Sub led the way to a narrow hatchway whence a steep iron ladder gave access to the steerage flats.

It was Broadmayne's intention to seek shelter in the triangular space traversed by the propeller shaft, but as he lifted the steel flap a waft of acrid-smelling smoke drifted up.

" No place for us," he exclaimed.

" Have the blighters started a fire ? " asked Rollo.

" No.   At least, I think not," replied the Sub ; " they have probably been monkeying with the shaft.   Hist ! "

They listened. Footsteps sounded overhead. The stowaways' retreat was cut off.

The compartment was in semi-darkness. A very subdued light filtered through the still-open hatchway. The floor was either level with or just below the waterline, while the walls forming part of the " run-aft " of the ship were unpierced by scuttles.

Groping, Broadmayne discovered that at one side was a large tank. It was rectangular and not shaped to fit the wing-plates, consequently there was a fair space between it and the curved side sufficient for several people to squeeze into.

It was a freshwater tank. The Sub could make out a couple of pipes leading upwards—one for filling, the other communicating with a pump in the officers' pantry.

The trap-hatch fell with a loud clang. The Spaniard who had come aft had narrowly escaped falling through the aperture. Without troubling to look down he had merely slammed the metal plate into position.

" That's good," said Vyse, in a low tone. " Cuts off most sounds. We can talk if we want to."

" So we can," added a husky voice, coming from behind the water-tank. " It's all right, chums ; it's only me—Slogger Soames."

" Bless my soul, Soames ! " ejaculated Broadmayne, " what are you doing here ? "

" Thought it about time I 'opped it," explained the ex-stoker. " Things were goin' a bit too strong on board the old hooker, even for me. I spotted you two slippin' over the side an' swimming round this 'ere vessel's stern. Says I to myself sudden-like, ' Well, 'ere goes. They'll want some one to bear a hand afore they're out of this 'ere mess.' An' I knows you won't give me away when we gets on the beach. Plymouth gasworks 'll suit me down to the ground after this little spree, I give you my word."

" How did you get aboard ? " asked the Sub.

" I was givin' a hand shiftin' cargo, in a manner o' speaking," replied Soames. " In plain English, we wur pinchin' the bloomin' Dagoes' duds. Then Marchant yells out for a sledge-'ammer. I fetches it aft, gives a look over the side to see you wur all right—you didn't spot me, but I saw you a-hangin' on to the nose of that there boat—and then I nips down 'ere. An' 'ere I be."

There were now sounds of great activity all over the ship. Judging by the tone of their voices, the officers were rapidly becoming acquainted with the disordered state of their looted cabins. From the engine-room came indications that the staff were preparing to get the machinery in motion.

A bell clanged loudly. A few seconds later the pistons began to move. The engines raced madly, while a disconcerting, rasping, groaning sound immediately underneath the fugitives' hiding-place told its own tale.

" Cain fractured the shaft before he left," declared Broadmayne. " I had an idea that's what it was."

For some minutes the terrific clatter continued, the deck-officers being unaware that anything was wrong, until they noticed that the ship was not

gathering way. Then a renewed outburst with
the engine-room telegraph gong was followed by
the engineers shutting off steam. The discordant
metallic clamour ceased, but a babel of excited
voices all shouting at once arose in its place.

Crouching behind the water-tank, the three
stowaways waited. They had not long to wait.
The hatch was thrown open and a couple of
dungaree-clad men carrying electric inspection-
lamps descended the ladder. The dazzling glare
seemed to penetrate every recess of that confined
space, especially while the newcomers were still
on the upper rungs of the ladder. But the Spanish
engineers did not waste time. They both disappeared through the manhole in the floor, a pair
of wavering intermittent beams of light flung
upwards through the aperture as they scrambled
over the tunnel of the shaft.

Presently, talking rapidly and angrily, the two
Spaniards retraced their way. Nothing could be
done with the shaft until the *Mendez Nunez* was
dry-docked. Meanwhile the tanker was drifting
helplessly, unable to send out a wireless call for
assistance.

For the three men hiding in the steerage-flat
the time passed very slowly indeed. They could
talk in low tones; they were able to leave their
cramped quarters behind the tank and stretch
their benumbed limbs. They had food of a kind;
for liquid refreshment they had to content themselves with the steady drip from a leaky joint, the
tank being covered in with a steel lid that could
only be removed by the aid of a spanner. They

were in Cimmerian darkness, for with the closing
of the overhead hatch even the subdued light that
had previously been filtering in was entirely cut
off. The air, too, was none too pure, mingled as it
was with the stench from the bilges, the still present
odour of burnt gun-cotton, and a penetrating reek
of garlic.

Broadmayne and his companions had no idea
of the time. Their watches had long since disappeared. Occasionally they heard the bells
struck, but the Spaniards' method of keeping ship's
time appeared to differ radically with that of
British-owned vessels. And since the flat was in
utter darkness, the fugitives were at a loss to know
whether it were day or night.

" Think it's safe to go on deck ? " inquired Vyse

" No, I don't," replied Broadmayne, emphatically. " The Dagoes have quieted down a bit ;
but the sight of us would probably be like that o
a red rag to a bull. We couldn't explain ; they
wouldn't listen, if we could. No ; we must stick
it. The tanker's bound to be picked up and towed
into port, and from her position it's an eighty per
cent. chance in favour of a British port."

Not very long after there were unmistakable
signs that the *Mendez Nunez* was being taken in
tow. The sluggish rolling motion gave place to a
succession of jerks. The water no longer splashed
against the hull plating. It gurgled as it ran past
the rudder, while the clanking of the steam-steering
gear announced that the tanker was again using her
helm.

" That's   good ! "   commented   Broadmayne.

" Who's for a caulk ?   I'll keep watch if you would
like to have a snooze."

This suggestion was acted upon, Soames relieving the Sub at the end of about two hours, as
nearly as he was able to guess the passing of time.
Then Vyse took on, and at the end of his trick all
three finished up the remains of the last loaf.

They were feeling ravenous again when they
felt the tanker's hull bump against something, and
heard the crew running along the deck and the dull
thud of wire-hawsers being brought to the winches.

" We're alongside," exclaimed Broadmayne.
" Listen ! "

Placing their ears to the hull plating, they could
hear the sound of an engine shunting trucks, then
—to their unbounded satisfaction—a voice shouting :

" All fast !   Look alive with that brow, lads ! "

" Time we shifted," declared Broadmayne, kicking out to work the muscles of his cramped legs.
" We've got to slip ashore quietly and without any
of the crew spotting us."

Mounting a few rungs of the ladder, the Sub
with a powerful thrust threw back the hatch-
cover.   There was no one in the alleyway.   A
cloud of steam issuing through the engine-room
fidley cut off the view of the deck ; but it was
sunlight, not artificial light, that played upon the
oil-reeking vapour.

Keeping together, the trio made their way
for'ard.   Just abaft the mainmast they could see
the inboard end of a brow inclined at a steep angle
Close to it stood two of the Spanish officers and a

13

couple of civilians. Several of the crew were at the guard-rails looking down at the crowd of sight-seers on the quay-side.

" Now ! " whispered Broadmayne.

The three made a mad rush for the gangway. One of the Spanish officers started when he saw two weirdly-garbed men followed by a third in strange rig making for the brow. Too astonished to attempt to bar their way, he could only shout and gesticulate to the Spanish seamen standing by.

One of the latter did endeavour to stop the fugitives. Broadmayne charged him, sending him crashing against a second Spaniard. In a trice the three Englishmen were running down the steeply-inclined brow.

" Hi—there ! " shouted one of the two civilians who were conferring with the Spanish captain. " Stop those men ! "

None of the crowd showed any inclination to obey the peremptory request of the individual who, Broadmayne subsequently discovered, was one of the Spanish Consulate staff. It was not on account of the powerful physique of the three fugitives that the crowd made way. Perhaps they guessed that the hurrying trio were in some way connected with the pirate crew who had held up the Spanish tanker. At all events, the sympathies of the on-lookers were with the fugitives, not the foreigners. Had Broadmayne and his companions wished, they could have got clean away.

But this was not their intention. Apart from cutting ridiculous figures by careering through the streets in garments that, like parallel lines, would

never meet on their bulky frames, Broadmayne
and Vyse had no cause for flight or concealment now
that they were safely on British soil.

" It's quite all right," shouted the Sub reassuringly. " We are not going to take to our heels. Is
there a policeman about ? Will some one please
fetch a taxi ? "

He had no occasion to ask what port they had
arrived at. He knew the place well. It was
Falmouth. The *Mendez Nunez* was berthed alongside the quay, almost under the shadow of Pendennis Castle.

A policeman hurried up and produced a notebook.

" What's all this ? " he demanded, looking askance at the nondescript pair.

" Pirates ! That's what they are ! " shouted the
consular official from the tanker's gangway.

The policeman put away his notebook and
measured the bulk of the two oddly-attired men
with his own size. He was a stalwart specimen of
the Force, but not to be compared in height and
weight with his would-be prisoners.

" In the name of the law ! " he exclaimed. " I
warn you. Any statement you may make will
be used in evidence against you. Now, are you
coming quietly ? "

" Yes," replied Broadmayne. " In a taxi ? "

He looked round to see where the ex-stoker was,
but saw him not. Slogger Soames had quietly
walked off and was well on his way towards the
town—the first stage of his journey back to his
native Plymouth.

CHAPTER XVII

GETTING TO WIND'ARD OF PENGELLY

AT four o'clock in the afternoon of the same day on which the *Mendez Nunez* was towed into Falmouth harbour, Gerald Broadmayne, " clothed and in his right mind " (to be precise, he had bathed, shaved and shifted into naval uniform) passed through the wicket-gate of Devonport Dockyard on his way to interview the Commander-in-Chief.

Rollo Vyse had gone home to assure his parents that he was not drowned, and that, if Mr. Vyse had ignored Captain Cain's demands for ransom, he might with perfect confidence continue to do so.

The chums' detention had been of short duration. At the police-station they had asked the inspector to send for two local residents whom they knew well, and who were ready to give their assurances that the two suspects could with safety be released. In the interval, ready-made and ill-fitting suits were sent to the station to replace the borrowed garments belonging to El Capitaño José Lopez.

A powerful car was hired and brought round to the police-station. To it Broadmayne and Vyse were escorted between crowds of curious spectators and followed by a knot of eager pressmen, who vainly sought an interview with either or both of the Englishmen who had come ashore from the Spanish tanker.

At Fowey the chums parted, Rollo to his home, the Sub to his, whence after a bath, a change into the uniform of a sub-lieutenant, and a square meal, Broadmayne resumed his car journey to Devonport Dockyard.

With mixed emotions the Sub traversed the familiar cobblestones of the dockyard, past the gigantic figureheads that served in a measure to remind the New Navy of the deeds of the Old, and ascended the steps of the Georgian portico of the admiral's official residence.

It was hard for the Sub to realise all that had occurred during the comparatively brief interval from the time the luckless *Ibex* left Fowey harbour. He was in a rather unenviable position. Captain Cain had undoubtedly saved his life and that of his companion. That, in Broadmayne's opinion, outweighed the pirate's cavalier treatment of his involuntary guests. In spite of his threats, Cain had respected their scruples and had not compelled them to perform any act amounting to piracy. And, with reference to the threatened flogging, the Sub was none too sure that the pirate captain would have proceeded to extremes.

And now Broadmayne had been officially called upon to give evidence against Captain Cain and his rascally crew. Ought he, he wondered, to reveal everything, even the secret of Cain's former association with the Senior Service as a commissioned officer ?

Cain was a pirate, a freebooter, an absconding swindler; but there was this in his favour—he had never molested a British ship, and he had not been guilty of murder, for even in the engagement with the *Surcouf* he had given directions controlling the fire, so that although the Frenchman had been badly mauled, none of her crew had been slain, the casualties, as subsequently given out, amounting to five men wounded.

It was a perplexing problem for Sub-Lieutenant Broadmayne. More than likely, from his intimate knowledge of the *Alerte*, he would be appointed to some vessel detailed to accomplish either her capture or her destruction. He did not hanker after the job; but he decided, if it were to be his mission, he would do his utmost to carry it to a successful conclusion. With Broadmayne, Duty, spelt with a capital D, was the one object of his life as far as the Service was concerned.

Then his thoughts turned to Pengelly. It did not take long to dismiss him. Pengelly, he decided, was a mealy-mouthed, double-faced blighter, hand in glove with Cain, speaking fair to his face and yet never scrupling to cheat him out of his ill-gotten gains behind his back. No, he had not the faintest sympathy for Paul Pengelly.

There was that other character, Silas Something. Broadmayne did not remember his surname, but he knew the number and name of his lugger. So did Vyse, who had overheard the plotting conversation between Silas and Pengelly. Very well, then; Rollo Vyse could tackle that part of the business. It would be something for him to do.

Broadmayne had not the detective instinct; Vyse had.

Giving his name to a messenger, Broadmayne was taken with little delay into the Commander-in-Chief's private office. Here, in addition to the admiral, his secretary and flag-lieutenant, were several lieutenant - commanders, including Rax-worthy, of the destroyer *Windrush*. A couple of civilian shorthand writers completed the gathering.

" Now, Mr. Broadmayne," said the admiral, after a few preliminaries, " we want your story. Take your time and don't omit details. They may seem unimportant, but in the long-run they may be of great service. Now, fire away."

The Sub did so, keeping nothing back, with the exception of his knowledge of Captain Cain's previous history. By the time he had finished, both the shorthand writers, although they worked in relays, were visibly fatigued; but the naval officers showed no signs other than those of intense interest.

Broadmayne was then subjected to a lengthy string of questions. Charts were produced and studied, plans of condemned submarines, and lists of when and where they were sold for breaking-up purposes were consulted. Notwithstanding the fact that the admiral usually dined at seven-thirty, it was nearly nine o'clock before the " levee " broke up, Broadmayne being " re-quested "—otherwise ordered—to report at the Commander-in-Chief's office at nine-thirty the following morning.

Broadmayne was putting on his greatcoat when

Raxworthy, breaking off a conversation with another officer, came across the vestibule to him.

" Where are you putting up ? " inquired the lieutenant-commander.

" At the Club, sir," replied the Sub.

" So am I," rejoined Raxworthy. " I'd like to have a pow-wow with you over this business."

" Very good, sir."

The two left the dockyard together, hired a taxi, and were soon bowling along Union Street to a residential club frequented by naval officers when sleeping ashore.

" You're dog-tired," remarked Raxworthy, noting the strained look in the other's eyes. " We'll have a meal and then you had better turn in   We'll defer our private conference till the morning."

" Better get it over now, sir," said Gerald, with a laugh. " Probably I'll be as fat-headed as an owl in the morning. And I've to see the Commander-in-Chief."

" Well, look here," said Raxworthy, " this is a sort of private tip ; the admiral's going to have you appointed to one of the destroyers told off to hunt the *Alerte*. Any objection if I apply for you ? "

" No, sir," replied Broadmayne. Since he was to be one of the hunters, it did not matter which ship he was appointed to. " Only I'd like to point out that, with his previous experience, Cain isn't likely to be caught napping by a destroyer again."

" We'd fix him by directional wireless."

" I've never known him to send out a message,"

declared the Sub. "He'll receive them gladly if they gave him an indication of the approach of a possible prize."

"How about the co-operation of a seaplane or flying-boat."

"Might, if the water's clear enough," admitted Broadmayne. "But there's one wav—if I might suggest——"

"Carry on," urged Raxworthy.

"Do the old Q-boat stunt, sir. A tramp well armed with concealed Q.F.'s and disguised as a French or Belgian African cargo boat."

"By Jove, the very thing!" exclaimed the lieutenant-commander. "I'll mention the suggestion to the admiral, tell him that the credit of it belongs to you, and try and get him to give me command. He'll probably start with ticking me off and finish up with doing his level best to get me the appointment. Of course, you'll be willing to serve with me?"

"Well, sir," replied Broadmayne, "you did your level best to send me to Davy Jones. I'll return good for evil and try to help you pull off the little stunt. We want to capture her, I presume?" he added anxiously.

"To capture," confirmed the lieutenant-commander gravely. "It will probably mean a hanging job for Cain and Pengelly. The others would certainly get a term of penal servitude. Failing capture—that is, if we fall in with the *Alerte* —we'll have to destroy her."

At the appointed hour Broadmayne reported to the admiral. This time it was a fairly short interview, but none the less important. Not only did the Commander-in-Chief promise to apply to the Admiralty for the Sub's appointment, but he approved warmly of the suggestion that a disguised and armed tramp should be employed as a decoy ship.

" There's another matter I want to mention," said the Commander-in-Chief. " I think you stated that a Silas Somebody was acting as a sort of intermediary, and that he was going to hide part of the pirates' booty to the benefit of himself and—let me see, who is it ? " He broke off to refer to a type-written report of the previous evening's evidence. " Ah, Pengelly ; that's the man. You've no idea where the place is ? "

" My friend Vyse might be able to give you additional information, sir."

" Then I'll have a wire sent to him," decided the admiral. " Perhaps he would be able to assist us while you are on particular service afloat."

" I think he'd be delighted to do so, sir," replied Broadmayne.

" Very well, then. You can carry on with your leave for a few days, but I wish you to be present when Mr. Vyse is here. We have your address ? "

At two the same afternoon, Broadmayne was " rung up " from the dockyard, the message stating that Mr. Vyse had arranged to call at Admiralty House at three ; would Mr. Broadmayne be present ?

Rollo Vyse was able to give some important information, namely, the number of the *Fairy*— PZ 4452b. Communicating by telephone with the

Registrar of Shipping at Penzance, it was found
that the owner's name was Silas Porthoustoc, and
that he lived just outside the village of Mousehole.
The registrar also added the somewhat disconcerting information that the individual under discussion
was dead and buried, and that his house was to be
sold by public auction on the following Monday.

" But I don't suppose, sir," he concluded, " that
that will interest you."

" Won't it, by Jove ! " exclaimed the Commander-in-Chief, when Penzance exchange had
" rung off." " It will. It rather simplifies
matters. If we can lay our hands on the specie or
bullion without the public getting wind of it, so
much the better for us, and so much the worse for
that scoundrel Pengelly. By the bye, the Captain
Cain, as he calls himself ; do you know by any
chance what his name is ? Is it Trevorrick ? "

" I've never heard him called by the name, sir,"
replied Broadmayne, while Vyse replied in a similar
strain.

" Because," continued the admiral, " if it were
Trevorrick, then we've fixed the precious pair.
They ran a shipbreaking concern on the river Fal.
Of course, it is only a surmise. There are heaps of
Pengellys in the West Country. I know several,
and they are men of unimpeachable character.
Very well, Mr. Vyse ; if you'll be so kind as to put
your services at the Admiralty's disposal, I think
you'll see the end of the Porthoustoc business."

This was on a Wednesday. Since the sale of
Old Silas's cottage was fixed for the following
Monday, there was little time to be lost. The

matter of recovering the booty could, of course, be managed by the use of a search-warrant, but for certain reasons the Commander-in-Chief decided to deal with it without invoking the aid of the law. Once the booty were taken possession of, then the Admiralty Courts could take up the case and restore the plunder to its lawful owners—the Norddeutscher-Lloyd Company.

The complicated machinery of Whitehall was set in motion at high pressure, with the result that early on Friday morning the Commander-in-Chief at Devonport was given authority to purchase the cottage without a limit being placed upon the amount to be paid.

Two hours later the admiral sent for a retired boatswain named Primmer, an honest, reliable and discreet old man, who had previously served three commissions under the Commander-in-Chief before the latter attained Flag rank.

" Primmer," began the Admiral brusquely, " I want you to buy a house."

The ex-bo'sun looked considerably surprised.

" Very good, sir," he replied. " But I beg leave to state, sir, I've already a little house at Mutley."

" Buy a house at Mousehole, near Penzance, and live in it," continued the Commander-in-Chief. " But only for a month—perhaps less than that. You'll have all expenses paid and fifty pounds in addition. Change of air will do you a world of good, Primmer. Take the missus and a vanload of furniture and you'll have quite an interesting holiday."

" Very good, sir," said the pensioner again.

Then the admiral explained matters and introduced Rollo Vyse as a supposed paying-guest.

" You two can work together splendidly," declared the admiral. " If you require additional assistance, wire at once."

The sale by auction was at eleven. At two o'clock came a wire from Primmer addressed in a precautionary measure to a private address at Plymouth—that of one of the Commander-in-Chief's staff. The telegram was to the effect that Primmer had secured the house and had paid the necessary deposit to Messrs. Jeremiah Built & Co., Auctioneers and Surveyors, of Penzance.

Directly Primmer reported that his furniture had arrived and that his temporary abode was ready to receive his guest, Rollo Vyse took train to Penzance.

After making arrangements for his luggage to be sent on, Vyse set out to walk to Mousehole.

His rôle was that of an artist wishing to make seascapes under winter conditions. There were, he knew, swarms of artists in Newlyn and Mousehole, so that by making out that he was one of them, his presence amongst a strictly conservative body of fisherfolk would not attract so much attention as otherwise.

It was a pleasant walk. Although December was well advanced, the air was mild. The bay looked a perfect picture in the slanting rays of the sun.

" Wonder where Silas's former abode is ? " he asked himself as he rounded a bend in the cliff path and saw the secluded little harbour of Mousehole nestling under the cliffs. " I'll ask. It may save my having to retrace my steps."

The first man he met after the decision was a
tall bronzed man wearing fishèrman's rig, including
thigh boots.

"Up-along, Maaster," was the reply.   "You'm
see chimbly over atop o' yon wall."

Vyse thanked him and went on.

"I've seen that fellow before," he soliloquised.
"Where ? Dash it ! That's done it. He's the
mate of the *Fairy*. I thought he looked a bit
straight at me. If he's spotted who I am, then
there's trouble ahead."

The recognition had been mutual, and the former
mate of the lugger was considerably perturbed
at finding Vyse on his way to the cottage where
Porthoustoc lived.

"Wot be 'is game, us 'ud like to know ? " he
muttered.

Since Silas's death, the former mate had become
the master and owner of the lugger *Fairy*, his
share on the various nefarious transactions undertaken by Porthoustoc enabling him to find the
purchase-money. The new owner was hoping to
continue in the former skipper's business. Reticent
and apparently slow-witted, he had formed a
shrewd idea of the nature of the *Alerte's* activities ;
but the difficulty that confronted him lay in
the fact that he did not know the medium of
communication between Captain Cain and his
agent. He was willing to become Porthoustoc's
successor in the business ; Cain would have been
only too glad of his services. But the con-
necting link had snapped, hence a complete
deadlock.

" Welcome, sir, welcome ! " exclaimed Mr. Primmer, on Vyse's arrival.

" Well, how goes it ? " asked Rollo.

" Terrible queer place, this, sir," replied the ex-bo'sun. " People hereabouts tell you everything you don't want to know. If you do want to know anything they are as tight as the intercepted thread of the breech-block of a fifteen-inch gun, if you understan' my meanin'. I'm taboo— sort of leper amongst this little lot. They don't take to newcomers."

" Well, I hope we shan't be here long, Mr. Primmer," said Rollo. " I'd like to get away before Christmas."

" Same 'ere, sir," agreed the new tenant cordially. " We'll get to work soon as you like. I've got crowbar, picks and spades an' such-like. An' I brought a sack of cement up from Plymouth. Thought it 'ud make 'em think if I got it hereabouts."

" I'll change, and then we'll have a look at the kitchen," decided Rollo. " It'll make a bit of a mess, I fancy."

" My missus she don't mind," said Mr. Primmer reassuringly. " Fact is, we've been doin' all the cooking in the spare room—proper sort o' galley it makes."

Having completed the necessary change of clothing, Rollo, accompanied by his host, went to the room under discussion. It was about twenty feet in length and fifteen in breadth, stone walled and stone floored. A doorway gave direct access to the garden ; another into the living-room.

There were two narrow windows, which gave the place a look of perpetual gloom. One wall was blank, the kitchen having been partly let into the steep hillside at the back of the cottage.

" That's our task," declared Rollo, pointing to the blank wall.

" I've been a-lookin' at it, sir," said the ex-bo'sun. " Wall's made of stone set in cement. It don't look as if it's been touched come these fifty year—maybe longer."

" I'll get a torch," said Rollo. " It's too dark to see much without artificial light. We'll have to curtain those windows pretty heavily when we work at night. Any one coming along that path —it's a public one, I take it ?—can see right in if we don't screen the windows."

Throwing the rays of his electric torch upon the mass of masonry, Vyse saw that the ex-bo'sun had good reason for his statement. The stones were black with smoke, the cement as hard as iron. Further examination showed that there was a small rectangular aperture in the roof close to the wall. Evidently the former occupants were in the habit of kindling a fire on the open hearth adjoining the wall and allowing the smoke to escape through the hole in the roof.

" 'Fraid the Admiralty have made another bad bargain, sir," remarked Mr. Primmer.

" It looks like it," admitted Rollo, scraping the cement with the back of the blade of his pen-knife. " I suppose the cave does exist ? Wonder if the entrance is under these flag-stones ? "

" We'll soon find that out, sir," declared

he other. " I've a pick and a crowbar close
handy."

It was a long and difficult task chipping away
the mortar between the flagstones. As Rollo
toiled and sweated, he wondered what it would
be like having to loosen cement. Mortar was hard
enough.

At length, one stone was eased from its setting.
With the aid of the crowbar it was lifted. Underneath was soft soil mingled with rock. Obviously
that mixture would not hold over the mouth of a
cave.

" Done there," admitted Vyse. " I'll swear old
Porthoustoc said ' behind the kitchen,' not under
it ; but there's no reason why the entrance should
or should not be in the centre. We'll try at one
side and work right along."

Rollo had not been scraping more than five
minutes when he gave an exclamation of satisfaction.

" This is new cement, Mr. Primmer ! " he exclaimed. " Look : it's quite clean underneath
the surface. Silas has been doing a bit of camou-
flage ; rubbing soot over the joints. The stuff
hasn't penetrated the cement like it has elsewhere.
However, we've done enough for the present.
We'll start again to-morrow morning. I don't
think we'll have much difficulty now."

That night Rollo slept heavily. He had had a
strenuous day. Accustomed to plenty of fresh air,
he invariably slept with the bedroom window wide
open.

Suddenly he awoke with a start to find the

14

room full of moist vapour. A sea-fog, banking up after a warm, humid day, had swept inland.

It was not the fog that had aroused him. A curious horripilation, such as he had never before experience, gripped him. For some moments he lay with wide-open eyes fixed upon the dark grey rectangular patch of open window.

Something prompted him to get out of bed and go to the window. He did so. Above the fog-bank, which perhaps was less than fifty feet from the ground, the stars were shining. The fleecy pall of vapour was moving, curling, and alternately diminishing and increasing in volume as it was urged landwards by the faint breeze. The fog, catching at his throat, made him cough slightly. As he did so, he distinctly heard the sound of footsteps moving rapidly and stealthily away.

His bedroom window was less than ten feet from the ground, the house being low. On his left was the front of the kitchen—a one-storeyed building. It was from that direction that the sound of the mysterious footsteps came.

Rollo's first impulse was to drop to the ground and go in pursuit, but calmer counsel prevailed. He was at an obvious disadvantage. He was not at all acquainted with the ground surrounding the house. He was barefooted and in pyjamas. There was also the question of arousing Primmer and his wife, since if he jumped from the window he could not regain his room except by the door, which was barred and locked. Besides, by this time the intruder had gone a considerable distance, for his footsteps were no longer audible.

"Well, I think I scared him," he mused. "In future, while I'm here I think I'll have a bed made up in the old kitchen. Then, if any one tries to break in he'll feel sorry for himself."

Next morning Vyse related what had occurred. Examination of the kitchen door showed that no attempt had been made to force it. Apparently the nocturnal visitor had either been disturbed before he could get to work, or either he had contented himself with flashing a lantern through the window, which was too narrow even for a slim man to squeeze through.

The forenoon Rollo spent in "pottering around" the village and harbour with his easel and palette, simply to sustain his rôle of a painter. At the same time he kept a sharp look-out for the *Fairy's* new owner, but in this direction he was disappointed.

After the midday meal, Vyse and his assistant got to work. They were on the right track this time. Three hours' strenuous toil resulted in the removal of a couple of large stones set in very hard cement. Through the small aperture thus formed, they could discern a cavern of generous proportions.

It had taken Silas Porthoustoc half a day to build up the mouth of the cave, working single-handed. Eight hours intermittent toil on the part of Rollo and Primmer resulted in a hole big enough for them to crawl through.

Armed with a torch, Rollo led the way. It was

a matter of about a three-feet drop to the floor of the cave, the natural mouth of which was of oval section, seven feet in height and four in width. In length it went back nearly eighty yards, the width and height increasing at ten feet or so from the entrance.

There was the booty, packed as it was when it was transhipped from the *Alerte* to the *Fairy*, with the exception of one or two sacks which had been opened by Old Silas, either for present use purposes or else to enable him to satisfy himself of the nature of their contents.

Working at high pressure, Vyse and his companion removed all the booty from the cave and stored it in one of the rooms. They then proceeded to wall up the cave, carefully discolouring the cement in order to impart the appearance of age.

At the same time, the new owner and master of the lugger *Fairy* was composing an anonymous letter to the chief officer of the Water Guard at Penzance.

Rollo had another disturbed night. With an automatic pistol ready to hand, he slept on a camp-bed by the side of the large pile of booty; but although he kept waking and tiptoeing to the window, somewhat to his surprise there were no signs of the intruder of the previous evening. As soon as the post office opened, a telegram was dispatched to Devonport asking for a van to be sent to remove the " furniture " ; while to allay suspicion on the part of his neighbours, Primmer spread the yarn that his recently-acquired cottage was haunted, that his wife refused to remain there another night, and that he had arranged to clear out that very day.

Just before noon a motor pantechnicon bearing the name of a well-known firm of furniture removers, but driven by a naval artificer in mufti and accompanied by four stalwart marines in civilian clothes (unfortunately their soldierly bearing discounted their rôle of furniture-packers), arrived at the late Porthoustoc's former abode.

Primmer's goods and chattels, together with the carefully-covered boxes and sacks of bullion and specie, were stowed in the van. His wife had previously gone on to Penzance station. Vyse and the ex-bo'sun were taking a final look round before locking up the cottage when a policeman walked up to the door.

"You haven't made a long stay," he remarked, addressing Mr. Primmer. "Seems to me you're taking away a sight more stuff than ye brought in a day or so back. D'ye mind if I have a look at some of those boxes?"

The ex-bo'sun, taken aback, glanced appealingly at Rollo, who merely shrugged his shoulders. In his part of an artist he could not very well assume any responsibility without giving himself away.

"Sure I do mind," replied Primmer, at a loss to say anything else.

"Then," continued the representative of law and order, "it is my duty to——"

He broke off suddenly, possibly thinking that the odds were too great for him to tackle single-handed. He gave a sharp blast on his whistle. From behind the stone wall appeared half a dozen men in the uniform of His Majesty's Water Guard.

"Contraband!" exclaimed the policeman, waving his hand in the direction of the loaded pantechnicon. "Caught red-handed you be!"

CHAPTER XVIII

THE DESTROYER AND THE DESTROYED

EXACTLY three weeks after the capture of the *Mendez Nunez* the *Alerte* arrived off the mouth of the Wad-el-Abuam, a small river flowing into the Atlantic a few miles south of Cape Bojador.

The estuary formed an ideal base for Captain Cain's new sphere of operations. Nominally within the limits of Rio del Oro—Spain's extensive, unproductive and loosely-held dependency, stretching from Morocco on the north to French Senegal on the south—the Wad-el-Abuam was hardly ever visited by vessels, except Moorish coasters and fishing craft.

The entrance to the river was a difficult one, a bar on which the surf broke heavily, extending practically right across it, although well on the starboard hand was a narrow channel carrying twenty feet at high water and protected by a long, narrow rocky island that not only served as a breakwater, but also effectively screened the estuary when viewed from seaward.

Within the bar the depth increased to sixty feet, with a bottom of firm white sand. Farther up, the bed was composed of mud that became more

objectionable as the width of the river decreased.
The banks were almost destitute of vegetation,
consisting of sand with a few palms and a scanty
scrub that afforded meagre food for goats belonging
to the inhabitants.   There were four or five small
villages populated by a tribe of savages, half Arab,
half Negro, who had long resisted any attempt
at subjection on the part of the Spanish troops
stationed at Villa Cisnero and other fortified posts
of Rio del Oro.

Within two hundred miles lay the Canary Islands,
with Funchal, the favourite port of call for ships
running between Europe and the west and south
coasts of Africa.   Farther to the south'ard was
Teneriffe, with Las Palmas, another frequented
coaling-station.   Both these were within the
Alerte's wireless radius, so that the pirates hoped
to obtain a fairly complete report of all vessels
passing within striking distance of their proposed
base.

" I suppose we haven't made a mistake," remarked Pengelly, as the *Alerte* slowly approached
the land.   " I can't see any sign of an estuary."

" It must be there," replied Cain, after consulting the latest but far from reliable chart of this
part of the coast.   " We'll stand in a bit more.
If there's any doubt about it, we'll send a boat and
take soundings.   The sailing directions state that
the island is hardly distinguishable from the main-
land except at short distance."

He levelled his binoculars for the twentieth time
during the last hour.

" By thunder ! " he exclaimed.   " Hanged if

there isn't a sail coming round the point. Native craft, by the cut of her."

" That's awkward," remarked the second in command. " We don't want company of that sort. She's heading towards us."

" Let her," said Cain, with his characteristic grim smile. " Let her. Mr. Marchant, serve out the small arms. Get up the machine-gun, but keep it out of sight until it might be wanted. We'll nab that fellow and make the crew pilot us in."

Little guessing what reception awaited her, the boat approached. She was a roughly-built craft of about thirty feet in length, bluff bowed and with a high, ungainly stern. Her rig resembled that of a felucca, but with a boom in place of the loose-furled sail usually affected by craft of the type to be met with in the Mediterranean. It could be seen that there were three men on board. One, dressed in a loose garment of white, including a burnous, was at the long, curved tiller. The others, darker skinned, wore loincloths only.

While the *Alerte* was yet a quarter of a mile from her, the felucca ported helm, close-hauled, and stood off in a nor' nor'-westerly direction.

" What's her little game, I wonder ? " remarked Pengelly. " I thought she was coming off to us."

" So did I," agreed Captain Cain. " But now I think she's a Moorish fishing vessel homeward bound. She had to stand out towards us to avoid running on the shoals. We'll collar her, Pengelly. If the old boy in the cotton nightgown is reasonable we'll pay him and let him go when he's piloted us in."

In obedience to an order from the bridge, the
Alerte's Diesel engines slowed down, till at a modest
three and a half knots the pirate submarine gained
a position between the felucca and the shore.
Having thus cut off the latter's retreat, the *Alerte*
starboarded helm and, working up to twelve knots,
began to overhaul the native craft with ease.

A cast of the lead gave nine fathoms, and since
the chart showed that the soundings were remarkably even on this course, Captain Cain had no
apprehensions of running his vessel aground.

The crew of the felucca seemed quite apathetic
when they saw the *Alerte* in pursuit. At a sign
from the white-robed Moor the two blacks lowered
the sails, one of them standing by to heave a line.

Declutching her propellers, the pirate submarine
gradually lost way, coming to a dead stop alongside the felucca.

By means of a conversation conducted chiefly
by signs, Captain Cain imparted his request for
a pilot, and without the faintest display of hesitancy
the Moor scrambled on board the *Alerte*, leaving
his two men to drop the felucca astern. Nor did
he betray any sign of fear when he saw the pirate
crew armed with automatic pistols. Calmly, and
in a dignified manner, he proceeded to find out
the draught of the ship. This he did by producing
a piece of cord about a yard in length and then
drawing the rough profile of a steam vessel. With
a much smaller piece of string he then measured
off the draught on his plan, and then pointing first
to the longer cord and then to the *Alerte* he
managed to make his meaning clear.

Captain Cain replied by indicating the longer cord and then holding up six fingers. The Moor nodded gravely and motioned to the pirate skipper to order the ship to forge ahead.

Slowly the *Alerte* made her way inside the island, and thence through the channel over the bar. The while the lead was kept going, Pengelly and the bo'sun taking bearings and noting how the channel bore for future occasions.

" Stand by and let go ! " roared Cain as the *Alerte* arrived at her anchorage. " Is the buoy streamed, Mr. Barnard ? "

" Ay, ay, sir ! " replied the bo'sun.

" Then let go ! "

With the rattle of chain tearing through the hawsepipe, the anchor plunged to the bed of the Wad-el-Abuam.

Pengelly turned to his captain.

" Snug little crib, this, sir," he remarked. " What about our pilot ? Are we going to over-haul his boat in case there's anything useful ? The blighter might have been pearling. One never knows."

" Certainly not," replied Cain, with a deep frown of disgust. " The fellow did us a good turn. Only an ungrateful, low-down swine would suggest such a thing."

Turning to the Moor, who was standing a couple of paces off, the pirate captain handed him a gold coin.

The pilot took the piece of money, made an elaborate salaam, and went to the side, the felucca having been brought to the gangway. Already the two negroes were hoisting sail. With another salaam, the Moor boarded his own craft, the ropes were cast off, and the felucca headed for the open sea.

Directly the intervening island hid the anchorage, the hitherto grave features of the pilot were suffused with a broad grin.

" Start up the motor, Tom ! " he exclaimed in English. " George, send the aerial aloft. By Jove ! I had the wind up when that pirate bloke suggested overhauling the boat ! "

In quick time the aerial was spread between the two masts and the " lead-in " connected to a powerful wireless set concealed between double bulkheads at the after end of the little fo'c'sle. A message was then dispatched in code to the Officer Commanding H.M.S. *Canvey*, giving the position of the pirate submarine's new base.

It was a smart bit of work. The *Canvey*, formerly a tramp steamer, had been fitted out by the Admiralty as a decoy-ship, disguised as the Belgian passenger and cargo boat *Candide* and supposed to be running between Borna, in Belgian Congo and Antwerp. Commanded by Lieutenant-Commander Ralph Raxworthy, D.S.O., she was armed with six six-inch guns and two submeged torpedo tubes, while for scouting purposes she carried in her hold two of the latest type of small flying boats fitted with folding wings. These aircraft could be hoisted out and ready to ascend within the space of twelve minutes.

But in order to locate the *Alerte's* base without exciting suspicion or giving any indication of her presence in the offing, Raxworthy had applied for seven boats of a type in use on this part of the coast. Each of these was fitted with a paraffin motor and a wireless installation, and was placed in charge of either a junior commissioned officer or else a warrant officer. For crew, West Indian negroes with a good knowledge of being able to manage a boat under sail, were enlisted for temporary service, two or three being told off to each boat.

It was a job that Sub-Lieutenant Gerald Broadmayne would have given much to have undertaken ; but in his case the risk was too great. Not on account of possible personal danger was he turned down. In spite of a skilful disguise he might be recognised by Captain Cain, should the two meet. In that case the pirate would realise that a British warship was hard on his heels and would take precautions accordingly.

Well before sunset the seven tenders, recalled by wireless, returned to their parent ship. Almost the first to arrive was the boat commanded by Sub-Lieutenant Allerton, who had served under Raxworthy in the *Windrush* when she claimed to have sunk the *Alerte* in St. Ives' Bay.

Allerton was in high feather. It was he who had " trailed the tail of his coat " across the path of the pirate submarine and had piloted her into the estuary of the Wad-el-Abuam.

" Cain, as he calls himself, is rather a sport," he declared to his rather envious brother-officers. " But that fellow Pengelly is an out-and-out rotter — a cross between a broken-down

mummer and pickpocket. You know the type
I mean."

" How is Cain a sport ? " inquired the torpedo
lieutenant.

" He ticked the mealy-mouthed blighter off
when he suggested helping himself to whatever he
could find in the boat," replied Allerton. " Cain
jumped on him properly, and gave me a German
ten-mark gold-piece as a sort of backsheesh. He'd
probably pinched it. I didn't ask questions. I'll
have the thing made into a brooch when we get
home."

Lieutenant - Commander Raxworthy did not
receive the information of the pirate submarine's
base with any degree of enthusiasm. In fact, he
was rather down in the mouth about it. He had
hoped that the *Alerte* would seek shelter in an
obscure port in Morocco. Then the *Canvey* could
go in and settle with her. The fact that the Wad-
el-Abuam was in Spanish territory, however loosely
held, complicated matters considerably. Without violating international law he could do nothing
unless the Spanish Government agreed to allow
the British warship a free hand.

Accordingly, the *Canvey* put into Teneriffe and
reported to the Admiralty by cable lest a lengthy
dispatch by wireless, even though it were in code,
should alarm the pirates and prompt them to
change their base.

For the next few days the decoy ship steamed to
and fro between the Canaries and St. Vincent
sending out fictitious messages *en clair* in the hope
that the *Alerte* would emerge from her retreat and

come outside the three-mile limit in order to seize a likely prey. But no *Alerte* put in an appearance.

Meanwhile, the Spanish Government had refused to accede to the British Admiralty's request. Since the pirate vessel had made use of a harbour in a Spanish colony, it was "up" to Spain to avenge the insult to her national dignity. Accordingly the destroyer *Villamil* was ordered to leave Cartagena and proceed to Wad-el-Abuam to destroy the *Alerte*.

The *Villamil* was an old vessel of three hundred and sixty tons, with a speed of twenty-eight knots. Her armament consisted of five six-pounders, of which three could fire ahead and three on the beam. In addition, she carried two torpedo tubes.

While the Spanish destroyer was speeding south, the *Alerte* remained riding to her anchors in Wad-el-Abuam. It was not owing to inclination on the part of Captain Cain that she did not put to sea. Wireless messages were frequently being intercepted from vessels bound to and from the French and Belgian colonies on the west coast of Africa. Tempting prizes they appeared to be. But the *Alerte* had developed a leak where the post of the vertical rudder passes through the trunk. A gland had given out. It would have been a fairly simple business to effect repairs could the submarine be dry-docked. In present circumstances it was a tedious and difficult process, and until it were completed the *Alerte* would be unable to submerge without the almost certain result of being flooded. While on the surface the leak could be kept under control; but at any great depth the hydrostatic pressure would be irresistible.

While this work was in progress, Captain Cain had not allowed other matters to slide. One of his first steps was to establish a signal station on the rocky island guarding and screening the *Alerte's* anchorage. Day and night armed men were on watch at the station, ready to signal to the pirate vessel the moment any sail appeared over the horizon.

Just before noon one morning, Captain Cain was informed that a craft looking like a destroyer was approaching from the nor'ard and steaming a course parallel to the coast.

Although fully conscious of the danger the *Alerte* was incurring by being caught in a disabled state, Captain Cain showed no sign of panic. He was trapped. He knew it. Unable to submerge, unable to ascend the river more than a few miles with a draught that considerably exceeded that of a destroyer, he realised that the only thing to be done short of scuttling the *Alerte* and chancing a doubtful refuge ashore in a barren country inhabited by fierce natives, was to fight it out.

In hot haste six men with the machine-gun were sent off in a boat to the island with instructions to keep under cover and not to open fire until the approaching destroyer came within a hundred yards of the rock, which she must do by reason of the tortuous course of the deep-water channel.

The *Alerte* was swung athwart the river to enable her six-inch quick-firer to bear. With the exception of the captain, Mr. Marchant and the gun's crew, all the rest of the hands were ordered below to be ready to replace casualties amongst the men working the quick-firer.

Presently a signal came through from the island : " Destroyer holding on. Is flying Spanish colours."

" In that case we needn't worry much, my lads, exclaimed Cain. " She's probably going down the coast. If she isn't, then we're more than her match. There's not a single destroyer belonging to the Spanish Navy with a gun anything approaching our six-inch. We'll give it her in the neck if she tries conclusions with us."

After a brief interval, another message came through : " Destroyer turned eight point to port and is making for the bar."

" Good enough, my hearties ! " declared Cain in his ringing, convincing voice. " Let her have it directly she pokes her nose round the bluff. What's the opening range, Mr. Marchant ? "

" Two thousand yards, sir," replied the gunner.

Under the captain's orders one of the crew ran off with a bundle under his arm. Presently a flag was hoisted at the ensign staff. For the first time the *Alerte* was showing her true colours—the " Jolly Roger."

Alone on the bridge, Cain stood calm and confident. There was not the slightest tremor in his large, powerful hands as he grapsed his binoculars ready to bring them to bear upon the as yet invisible enemy.

From his elevated position he gave a rapid glance
15

at the gun's crew. The men had closed up round
their weapon, the gunlayer bending as he peered
through the sights. In the rear crouched the load-
ing-party, each with his hands on a hundred-pound
projectile, ready the moment the breech-block
was opened to thrust the shell into the still smoking
breech. And somehow Cain's thoughts flew back
to a similar scene in the presence of an enemy.
Then, he was fighting for a just cause under the
glorious white ensign. Now, he was fighting for
no cause but his own, his hand against every man's,
and under the shadow of that emblem of dishonour
—the skull and cross-bones.

Round the precipitous face of the island appeared
the lean bows of the Spanish destroyer. Then her
round bridge, mast and funnels came into view.
Through his glasses Cain saw that her fo'c'sle gun
was manned by a crew of white-clad, swarthy-faced
men. . . . There was a deafening crash as the
Alerte's six-inch sent the hundred-pound projectile
hurtling on its way. . . . Even as he looked, Cain
saw a vivid flash immediately in front of the
destroyer's bridge . . . a cloud of smoke torn by
diverging blasts of air. . . . The smoke dispersed,
or rather the destroyer's speed carried her through
it. . . . The crew of her fo'c'sle six-pounder had
dispersed, too ; with them the gun and its mounting. . . . The bridge didn't look the same as it had
a few seconds previously—a bit lopsided. Flames
were pouring from a heap of débris in the wake of
the foremast.

At two thousand yards the appalling noise caused
by the explosion of the *Alerte's* first shell was in-

audible to the solitary watcher on her bridge. The scene brought within a very short distance through the lenses of the powerful binoculars resembled a " close-up " picture on the cinematograph—unrealistic by reason of the absence of sound.

Two vivid flashes leapt from the Spanish destroyer's deck, one on the port side, the other to starboard. They were her reply to the destructive " sighting shot " from the pirate submarine.

The *Villamil* had received a rough awakening. Her crew, not one of whom had previously been under fire, were lacking in that courage and tenacity that marks the Anglo-Saxon race. Appalled by the havoc wrought on the fo'c'sle, the gunlayers of the remaining weapons that could be brought to bear certainly did make reply. Their aim was bad. One shell whizzed high above the *Alerte's* masts, shrieking as it sped to bury itself harmlessly in the sand three miles away. The other, striking the water a hundred yards short of its objective, ricochetted and hurtled through the air full fifty yards astern.

Cain paid no attention to either. His interest was centred upon his attacker. He could hear the rapid crashes of the *Alerte's* quick-firer. He could see the results by the frequent lurid bursts of flame and the showers of débris as shell after shell struck the luckless Spaniard.

Still she came on, leaving an eddying trail of smoke. One of her six-pounders was firing spasmodically. She was reeling like a drunken man.

Suddenly Cain put aside his glasses and made a spring for the telegraph indicator, moving the

starboard lever to " full ahead." His quick eye
had discerned a glistening object curving over the
Villamil's side. A torpedo was already on its way,
travelling at the speed of a train in the direction
of the pirate submarine.

Well before the action the *Alerte's* oil-engines
had been started with the clutches in neutral
position. It was a precaution that was justified
in its results. Under the action of one propeller
only the *Alerte* forged ahead, her stern swinging
round as she overran her anchors.

Cain had no occasion now to use his binoculars.
The double diverging wake of the submerged
locomotive torpedo was plainly visible to the
naked eye. It was approaching very rapidly ;
the ship was swinging very slowly—too slowly, it
seemed.

For ten seconds the captain held his breath.
Looking aft, the rise of the poop intercepted the
wake of the torpedo. It seemed as if the *Alerte*
was doomed.

But no explosion tore her asunder. By less
than a couple of yards the deadly missile cleared
her stern, to detonate harmlessly against the steep
bank of the river half a mile away.

The *Alerte's* quick-firer was now silent. The
manœuvre that had saved her from the torpedo
had brought her almost bows-on to the *Villamil,*
with the result that the former's fo'c'sle masked
her line of fire.

By this time the Spanish destroyer had closed
to about a thousand yards. She was yawing
badly. Possibly her steam-steering gear had been

demolished and she was being conned from aft. Nevertheless, she was keeping to the channel which at this particular time brought her almost abeam. Her decks were a shambles, two of her funnels had disappeared. The rest of the bridge that had survived the *Alerte's* first shell had collapsed. One gun well aft alone was spitting defiance. Either she meant to ram her anchored opponent, or else she was manœuvring for a position favourable for the release of a second torpedo.

Again the *Alerte's* engine-room telegraph bell clanged. With the port propeller going hard astern, and her cables tautened like harp-strings, she began to swing into her former position.

For the first time since the action commenced Captain Cain spoke. Leaning over the bridge-rail he shouted to the gunlayer to aim for the Spaniard's aft torpedo-tube.

The *Villamil* was well down by the head and had a pronounced list to starboard. Her speed had appreciably fallen off. The menace of being rammed was now hardly worth taking into account ; but the torpedo—— At that range, if the Spanish torpedo-gunner knew his job, it was almost a matter of impossibility to miss.

Cain could see four or five grimy figures bringing the loading cage to the after-end of the tube. The torpedo was launched home. . . . He could see the convex metal cover swing into the closing position . . . the torpedo coxswain was getting astride the tube . . . in another three or four seconds . . .

A deafening crash told the anxious skipper of the *Alerte* that the six-inch was again at work. At a range of six hundred yards the shell got home. A terrific flash—it was far too vivid for the explosion of a shell—leapt from the destroyer. An enormous cloud of smoke was hurled skywards, completely obliterating the *Villamil* from Cain's vision. A blast of hot air swept over the superstructure of the submarine. Pieces of metal tinkled on her steel deck. Heavier pieces were falling with a succession of splashes into the smoke-enshrouded water.

Slowly the pall of acrid-smelling vapour dispersed. Where the destroyer had been was an expanse of agitated water surrounding a broad and steadily-growing patch of black oil. Of the eighty men who formed her crew, not one survived.

The only casualty on board the *Alerte* was No. 8 of the gun's crew, and he had been knocked out only after the *Villamil* had been destroyed. A fragment of steel descending with terrific force had struck him on the head, killing him instantly.

The action over, Captain Cain brought the rest of the hands on deck.

" My lads ! " he exclaimed, " if we were out for glory, we've got it. It wasn't of our seeking. It's riches, not glory, we're after. Now, lads, although there's no one of our opponents left to tell the tale, we'll have to get a move on. One more good capture and we pay off. With luck we'll finish repairs by nightfall. To-morrow I hope our aims will be realised. There's a Belgian vessel due to leave St. Vincent at dawn to-morrow.

She's ours for the asking.   I propose to capture her and bring her in here until we can unload everything of value.   All then that remains to be done is to hide the booty, make our way home and come out again as quite above-board West Coast traders.   That's all I have to say, lads. No hanging on to the slack, but plenty of beef into your work for the next few hours and everything will be plain sailing.   Pipe down ! "

CHAPTER XIX

RECALLED

THE decoy-ship *Canvey* lay at anchor off
St. Vincent, whither she had gone to
replenish her oil-fuel tanks. Both officers and
men were growing tired of the seemingly inter-
minable stunt of steaming to and fro between
the Cape Verde Islands and Teneriffe, vainly
inviting Captain Cain to " tread on the tail of my
coat." They wanted to cut into Wad-el-Abuam
and settle the matter once and for all. It was
galling to have to keep in the offing, while the
Spanish destroyer *Villamil* was at liberty to enter
the estuary and destroy the pirates' lair.

Day after day passed without untoward incident. Although the Spanish Government had
expressed its intention of keeping the British
Admiralty well informed as to the progress of
operations, no message was received by the
Canvey from London, or in fact from anywhere
that had any bearing upon the all-important
subject of the destruction of the pirate submarine.

And for a very good reason. No wireless
message from the *Villamil* was received by the

Spanish naval authorities after a brief report that the destroyer was about to enter the Wad-el-Abuam to attack the *Alerte*. From that time the movements of the destroyer were shrouded in mystery.

Presently it occurred to the Spanish Admiralty that all was not well with the *Villamil*. There was something decidedly ominous about the prolonged silence. The weather had been unusually quiet, so her disappearance could not be attributed to a sudden tempest. It seemed incredible that a unit of Spain's navy had been vanquished by a contemptible pirate ship. But at last that supposition had to be regarded as a fact.

About that time serious riots broke out in Barcelona. Every available Spanish destroyer was dispatched to that port to assist in quelling the disorder. Unable to police her territorial waters of the Rio del Oro, the Spanish Government, putting its pride in its pocket, made a request to the British Admiralty that the destruction of the pirate submarine should be undertaken by the British Navy.

The *Canvey* received her wireless instructions to this effect at noon. Without delay the awnings were furled, steam raised for seventeen knots, and the anchor weighed. The knowledge that the destroyers *Complex* and *Calyx* were under orders to leave Gibraltar for the Rio del Oro coast was no small factor in determining the *Canvey's* hurried departure.

No longer need she to steam slowly, with a red ensign fluttering aft, and her officers and crew rigged out like members of the humble but all-important Mercantile Marine. With her hitherto concealed guns showing their teeth and the white ensign streaming proudly to the breeze, she could dash into the estuary of the Wad-el-Abuam, summon the *Alerte* to surrender, and in default send her to the bottom for all time. But she must be first upon the scene. Should her friendly rivals, the heavily-armed *Complex* and *Calyx*, forestall her, then the *Canvey*'s motto would be the single word, Ichabod.

Two hours after leaving St. Vincent, Lieutenant-Commander Raxworthy was conferring with Broadmayne, who happened to be officer of the watch, when the leading telegraphist approached, saluted, and tendered a signal-pad.

The owner read the message. The corners of his mouth dropped.

" We're done out of a job, Broadmayne," he remarked. " The *Alerte's* settled with."

" Our destroyers, sir ? "

Raxworthy shook his head.

" Not an Andrew job this time," he replied. " Read this."

The message was a wireless signal *en clair* as follows :

" From s.s. *Bronx City* of Boston, Mass., from Accra to Lisbon. Encountered pirate vessel *Alerte* in lat. 19° 17′ N., long. 18° 23′ W. *Alerte* fired three rounds and attempted to close. *Bronx City* ported helm, striking *Alerte* amidships. *Alerte* sank in three minutes. Four survivors. Am proceeding.—ADAMS, Master."

" That Yankee's in luck," observed Lieutenant
Commander Raxworthy. " He stands to rake in
thirty thousand pounds. Carry on," he added,
addressing the leading telegraphist. " Copies to
ward-room, gun-room, and mess-deck."

In a few minutes the " buzz " was all over the
ship. The feeling of disappointment had a con-
soling feature. The *Canvey* would be ordered
home to be put out of commission, and that meant
the bluejackets' highly-prized privilege—paying
off leave, or " leaf " as the " matloe " insists on
calling it.

To settle the matter, an Admiralty wireless was
received announcing that operations against the
pirate submarine were to cease forthwith : vessels
concerned were to proceed to their respective
bases.

CHAPTER XX

THE AFFAIR OF THE *BRONX CITY*

"THERE'S that *Candide* asking for trouble, sir," replied Pengelly, as he entered the captain's cabin. "We've just intercepted a message saying she's leaving St. Vincent to-day."

"She's been reporting her movements long enough," said Captain Cain. "We'll see what we can do. We'll have to shift from here in any case. We'll find a suitable cubby-hole somewhere down the coast, even if we have to try the Nigerian backwater. One good haul, Pengelly, and we'll pack up and share the proceeds."

"We've done nothing much to write home about since we came south," grumbled the second in command. "Sending a Dago destroyer to the bottom doesn't put shot in our locker."

"Quite so," agreed Cain. "That's why I'm anxious to nab the *Candide*. Pass the word to Mr. Barnard that I want to be under way in an hour's time—just before high water."

When Cain came on deck all preparations were complete, except for breaking out the anchor. The *Alerte* was riding to the flood tide. The mud flats on either side of the estuary were covered. The air was hot, sultry and still. Outside, the surf thundered heavily on the bar.

At five knots the *Alerte* headed seawards, scraping past the submerged wreckage of the *Villamil* to starboard and the island to port, where the now-abandoned signal-station alone remained as a visible reminder of the pirate submarine's brief and financially disappointing sojourn in the estuary of the Wad-el-Abuam.

Just before two bells in the afternoon watch, smoke was observed on the southern horizon. Twenty minutes later the dark grey hull of a fairly big steamer emerged from the patches of haze.

" She's the *Candide* right enough," declared Cain. " Clear away the gun, my lads. One more hooker and our job's done. . . . No colours yet, Mr. Barnard. We'll let 'em have a good sight of the Jolly Roger in a brace of shakes. Pick your boarding-party, Mr. Pengelly. See that everything's ready in the boat."

The two vessels were approaching on their respective courses which, if adhered to, would enable the stranger to pass a good half-mile on the *Alerte's* port side. The pirate submarine held on in order to avoid arousing suspicion on the part of the stranger.

Suddenly Pengelly, who had been keeping the approaching craft under observation through a pair of powerful binoculars, turned to his superior.

" She's a Yankee, by Jove ! " he exclaimed. " She's flying the Stars and Stripes."

" Ay," agreed Cain, with a grin. " And there's the name *Bronx City* on her bows as large as life. Yankee colours and Yankee name don't turn a Belgian tramp into a United States hooker. I'm too old a bird to be caught with chaff. . . . Starboard a bit, Quartermaster . . . at that ! "

The eyes of the signalman, the gun's crew and the seamen standing aft with the rolled-up skull and cross-bones already toggled to the halyards, were all fixed expectantly upon the skipper of the pirate submarine as he stood at the extreme end of the port side of the bridge.

Captain Cain raised his right hand. At the signal the black flag was broken out, the International ID hoisted at the fore, while an instant later a shot whizzed across the stranger's bows.

The warning was promptly acted upon. The intercepted craft reversed engines, lost way and then came to a stop. The Stars and Stripes remained fluttering in the faint breeze.

Promptly Pengelly and his men pushed off to the prize, under cover of the *Alerte's* six-inch gun. Before the boat ran alongside the stranger, the latter's accommodation-ladder had been lowered.

Pistol in hand, Pengelly, followed by his men, swarmed up the swaying ladder. At the gangway, supported by several officers and crew stood a tall, hatchet-faced man in white drill uniform and with his peaked cap tilted well over his left eye.

" What in the name of tarnation thunder do you want ? " he demanded. " Cocktails, lime-juice or milk ? If you do, you won't get—so quit."

Pengelly realised that Cain had made a mistake. The vessel was not the *Candide* disguised, but the *Bronx City*, registered and owned in the United States. But having boarded her, Pengelly had no intention of returning ignominiously to the *Alerte*.

"No quitting this time, skipper," he replied firmly. "I'm not here to argue—this is my persuader."

He touched the barrel of his automatic with his left hand and then pointed to the *Alerte*, which was still closing the prize.

"Guess you'll swing for this," exclaimed the captain of the *Bronx City*.

"More ways than one of killing a cat," retorted Pengelly. "Now, you—officers and men—for'ard you go and keep quiet, or it'll be the worse for you."

Shepherded by half a dozen of the *Alerte's* armed boarding-party, the crew of the Yankee were made to go for'ard. Pengelly turned to the Old Man.

"I don't know your tally," he remarked.

"Cap'n Hiram Adams is my name," replied the skipper of the *Bronx City*. "Guess people know me from Quebec round the Horn and up to Seattle and on this side of the herring-pond, too, I reckon. Hope you're wiser."

"I am," rejoined Pengelly curtly. "Now let me see your papers."

Accompanied by the prize-master and followed by two of the *Alerte's* hands, Captain Adams went to his cabin, unlocked a safe and produced the necessary documents.

Pengelly's eyes opened with astonished satisfaction. The *Bronx City*, a twin-screw boat, had a rich cargo. She had come from Beira with a heavy consignment of gold from Lisbon. At Accra she had picked up a thousand barrels of palm oil. Amongst other articles enumerated on her manifest were ivory and ostrich feathers. In addition to her cargo, she carried nine Portuguese passengers—residents of Beira and Quilimane—on their way to Lisbon.

Unable tc decide what was to be done, Pengelly ordered one of the hands to semaphore the *Alerte* and inform Captain Cain of the identity of the prize and the nature of her cargo.

Back came the reply : " Stand fast. Am coming on board."

Cain lost no time in so doing. He was far more perturbed than was his second in command. He had gone against his resolution not to molest a United States ship. He had done so in all good faith—if such a term can be applied to rank piracy—but the fact remained that he had fired upon a vessel flying the Stars and Stripes.

Long before the *Alerte's* second cutter came alongside the *Bronx City*, Cain had made up his mind as to the course to pursue.

Ascending the accommodation-ladder, he made his way to the bridge where Captain Hiram Adams was standing under guard.

" I am sorry, Cap'n Adams," said Cain, after he had requested Pengelly to introduce him; " there's been a mistake on my part."

" Sure thing," replied the Yankee skipper. " But I calculate there ain't no darned mistake about that."

He pointed to the skull and cross-bones flying from the *Alerte's* ensign-staff.

" There isn't," agreed Cain, with a disarming

smile. " The mistake was entirely upon my part.
I took you for the *Candide*. S'pose you haven't
spoken her ? "

" Nope."

" She's doubtless skulking at St. Vincent,
scared stiff and afraid to meet me," continued the
pirate. " Well, Cap'n Adams, I'm not going to
do you any harm. I'm not going to touch an
ounce of your cargo———"

" But, sir," interrupted Pengelly, holding out
the ship's papers. " Look here."

Cain gave a quick glance through their contents.
Most of the cargo, including the gold, was
Portuguese property. It was a great temptation.

" I know my business, Mr. Pengelly," he said
sternly. " Now, Cap'n Adams, to resume. You'll
be free to resume your voyage in a few days.
In my own interests I am reluctantly compelled
to employ you for my own protection. If you give
no trouble you'll receive none. Is that clear ? "

Captain Hiram Adams nodded. A grim smile
spread over his lean features. After all, he was
coming out lightly. His ship was not to be sunk ;
his cargo was to remain intact.

" Guess it's your funeral—not mine," he replied.
" Get busy ! "

Cain proceeded to get busy. His first step was
to send for the *Bronx City's* wireless operator.

As soon as the fictitious message announcing
the ramming and sinking of the *Alerte* had been
sent out, Cain ordered the operator below, locked
the door of the wireless cabin, and placed an
armed guard outside.

16

" Gee ! Guess you're some lineal descendant of Ananias, Cap'n ! " exclaimed the master of the *Bronx City* admiringly. " Reckon you'd make a pile in Wall Street in next to no time."

Cain's next step was to place Pengelly with five men in charge of the *Bronx City*, and to order the chief and second officers of the latter on board the *Alerte*.

" Just as a matter of form, Cap'n Adams," he remarked ; " it will save a heavy strain on your steward's department. . . . Now, Mr. Pengelly, keep station four cables astern of me, if you please ; speed twelve knots. Under no consideration, should we sight another craft, will the *Bronx City* communicate."

The pirate captain returned to the *Alerte*. If the misleading wireless message " went down," then the *Alerte* had yet another lease of life and activity. The possible presence of British and foreign warships off the Rio del Oro was a danger which he fully appreciated. Once the coast was clear of that type of craft he could prey on merchantmen during the next few weeks with comparative impunity. He was very keen to snap up the hitherto much-advertised *Candide*.

He felt considerably elated over the *Bronx City* affair. His magnanimity would be an asset in his favour. His discrimination in refusing to plunder a cargo carried under the Stars and Stripes would show that he was not a wild dog at large. Altogether, he was very pleased with himself.

For the rest of the day the *Alerte*, with the

Bronx City keeping demurely in her wake, kept a southerly course. As night fell she stood in towards the coast, sighting land soon after dawn. Ahead lay the Bahia Arenas, an enclosed anchorage nearly ten miles in length and averaging one in breadth, with an extreme depth of fourteen fathoms. Separated from the Atlantic by a long low, sandy island, it received the Faltuba River, a fairly deep stream meandering between banks of mangroves and bounded for miles by miasmic swamps.

Years ago the Portuguese had attempted to convert Bahia Arenas into a commercial port. They built a stone fort, wharves and huts. The experiment was a failure. They had reckoned without the deadly climate. It was healthy enough for vessels lying at anchor in the sandy bay, but no European could for any length of time withstand the pestilential air that rose from the mangroves. The fort fell into decay, the wharves rotted. When in course of time the French took over the country between Cape Blanco and British Gambia, they sedulously avoided any scheme to open out the Faltuba River, and consequently no shipping had occasion to use Bahia Arenas for commercial purposes.

The entrance was an easy one. Even at low springs there were eighteen feet of water on the bar, with an additional height of twelve feet at high water.

Once inside, the *Alerte* signalled to the *Bronx City* to heave to. Captain Cain boarded the American and took charge of the bridge.

" I am going to run your ship aground, Cap'n," he announced to the Yankee skipper. " You'll come to no harm. The mud's soft. You'll come off before next springs—say in a week's time. By then, we shall be miles away."

Captain Hiram Adams made no audible comment. He merely put his tongue in his cheek.

Two miles up the river and hidden from the sea by a spur of high ground thickly covered with coco-palms, Captain Cain ordered the quartermaster of the *Bronx City* to put her helm hard-a-port.

At a speed of about five knots, the ship ran aground on the starboard side of the river, ploughing through the soft mud for quite her own length before coming to a dead stop. There she lay, on an even keel, with her bows within a hundred yards of the bluff of hard ground.

" You're lying nicely, Cap'n," observed Cain, as he prepared to withdraw the prize-crew. " I've taken the liberty to remove certain essentials of your wireless ; but I'll do my level best to send the stuff along to your nearest agents."

Returning on board the *Alerte*, Cain's first act was to send for her wireless operator.

" Any signals from the *Candide* ? " he inquired.

" None, sir," was the reply. " I've had the 'phones on almost continuous-like since midnight."

" Well, carry on," rejoined the captain, paying no heed to the man's carefully-worded complaint.

" Unfeeling swine ! " muttered the operator, as he made his way back to the wireless cabin. " Me carry on after sixteen hours' trick ? Not much."

CHAPTER XXI

MUTINY

"SHE'S safe enough, Pengelly," remarked Cain, indicating the stranded *Bronx City*. "Any trouble?"

"None whatever, sir," replied his subordinate. "Old Adams was as good as gold after you had explained matters."

"'Fraid we've missed the *Candide*, curse her," said the pirate captain. "We'll have to keep a look-out for something else. I've warned the operator. Well, take over now, Pengelly. I'm going to have a few hours' sleep. Call me if anything occurs."

"Ay, ay, sir," replied Pengelly.

Cain went to his cabin, locked the door, and with the exception of kicking off his shoes, turned in "all standing."

He had had a fairly strenuous time of late. He did not spare his crew, nor did he spare himself, but he forgot the important fact that he could go for long periods without rest and sleep, whereas most of the hands could not.

In less than a minute he was sound asleep.

A quarter of an hour later, Pengelly, accompanied by a couple of men, tiptoed to the door. He listened. Cain was breathing heavily in a sound slumber. The second in command bent down and peered through the keyhole. The electric light was burning. He could see nothing of the captain, since his range of vision was limited by the smallness of the keyhole. Above the door was a lowered ventilator. Cautiously, Pengelly stopped the opening with a damp cloth. Then he signed to one of the men.

The fellow applied a rubber tube to the keyhole. At the other end of the tube was a bag containing chloroform. For several minutes the suffocating fumes were being pumped into the cabin.

" 'Nough, if you don't want to snuff him out," declared the man.

" Sure he's insensible ? " asked Pengelly anxiously.

" Like a noo-born babby," replied the fellow confidently.

" Good enough," was the response. " Down with the door. Got lashings ready ? "

The two seamen put their shoulders to the steel panel. It gave slightly, but the lock held in spite of reiterated efforts.

" Get a sledge-hammer," ordered Pengelly impatiently, as he toyed with a belaying-pin.

A few blows with the heavy hammer shattered the lock. Pengelly, followed by more of the crew, rushed in. Cain, with a dazed look on his face, and making a gurgling sound as he strove for breath, was sitting up in his bunk with an automatic in his hand.

Without a word the captain levelled the weapon

and pressed the trigger. There was a deafening
report. The bullet, missing Pengelly's head by an
inch, flattened itself against the steel bulkhead.

Before Cain could fire again, Pengelly sprang
forward and brought the belaying-pin down upon
the pirate captain's skull.

" Turn on the ventilating fan, one of you,"
ordered the chief mutineer. " Place reeks like a
slaughter-house. Carry him on deck. He's not
dead. He'll be more useful to us alive. Pass a
lashing round his ankles, and when he comes to, see
that he's properly lashed-up."

They bore the body of the unconscious Cain on
deck, where the rest of the crew were assembled.

Of the two men—Cain and Pengelly—the hands
preferred Cain. He possessed certain qualities
that appealed to the crowd of lawless rascals.
Pengelly did not. But it was the affair of the
Bronx City that had enabled Pengelly to prevail
upon the crew to mutiny. They could not understand why Cain refrained from looting her valuable
cargo—why he should waste precious time in
bringing the prize into Bahia Arenas when the
Candide was somewhere south of Las Palmas and
likely to fall an easy prey to the *Alerte*. The chance
of capturing the *Candide* had gone, they decided.
The *Bronx City* remained.

" We'll have the gold," declared Pengelly to the
mustered crew. " We'll take it up the river and
bury it. Then all that remains to be done is to
take the *Alerte* to within a few miles of St. Louis—
or Bathurst, if more are in favour of it—scuttle her
and take to the boats. We'll have to pitch a

plausible yarn and get sent home as shipwrecked mariners. Then, in due course, we recover the gold and share out."

"How about the ransom for that Admiralty inspector bloke we kidnapped?" demanded one of the crew.

"And the *Cap Hoorn* loot?" added another.

Pengelly assured them that they would all have equal shares in the plunder. In his own mind he felt certain that they would not. Already he counted upon getting hold of the booty entrusted to the late Captain Silas Porthoustoc. He wasn't altogether too sure about Jasper Chamfer's ransom. For a considerable time he had harboured a suspicion that Cain was feathering his own nest with the money.

"Man and arm boats," he ordered. "We'll want every available hand for this job. We've got to gut the Yankee hooker and bury the stuff before dawn."

Into the boats tumbled the swarm of ruffians. Discipline had gone by the board. During Cain's régime every evolution had been performed with man-of-war smartness. Now Jack was as good as his master.

Alongside the stranded *Bronx City* ran the boats. Armed men, cursing and frantically brandishing their automatic pistols, swarmed up her sides. Without any ceremony, Captain Hiram Adams was made to hand over the keys of the strong-room. The American crew were driven for'ard and secured in the forepeak. Then the work of looting began. There was no method about the procedure. The pirates rifled indiscriminately. The strong-room door was forced and the gold-dust taken on deck, but not before a large quantity of the precious metal had found its way into the pockets of individual members of the *Alerte's* crew. The ivory being in bulk and too large to be conveniently hidden by the finders, was dumped into the boats. The American officers' quarters were invaded and their belongings either stolen or strewn all over the deck. The passengers were insulted, threatened and robbed ; while, to make matters worse, the pirates broached several casks of rum, and having drunk as much as they could carry—and more—they wantonly allowed the rest of the spirit to run to waste.

" Best batten the Yanks down and fire the ship," suggested one drunken rascal. " Dead men tell no tales. How about it, Cap'n Pengelly ? "

Pengelly objected. He shrank from work of that kind, not because he possessed any strong degrees of humanity, but because he feared the consequences.

" They gave us no trouble," he said. " The ship's hard and fast aground. She can't signal to any vessel in the offing. Let her alone. We'll get the stuff up the river and hide it."

Unsteadily, the besotted pirates dropped into the two deeply-laden boats and rowed back to the *Alerte*.

Cain, who had been left in charge of Barnard and a couple of hands, had recovered consciousness. Pengelly, after giving one furtive glance at his former partner, ascended the bridge ladder.

" Look alive, lads ! " he shouted. " Get the booty aboard ! "

" What for ? " bawled one of the crew. " If we've got to land the swag what's the use of unloading the boats and loading 'em up again ? Useless work, I calls it."

Instead of insisting upon his orders being carried out, Pengelly began to explain the reason.

" Don't you see that the people of the *Bronx City* are watching us ? " he replied. " If they see that we are towing the loaded boats up the river, they'll guess we're hiding the plunder ashore. Whip it aboard. It's worth the extra work."

" Then do it yourself," retorted the mutineer. " We've had enough back-breaking jobs lately. 'Sides, what odds if the Yanks do spot us ? "

His protest was upheld by several others. Marchant and half a dozen of the hands who were not so drunk as the rest tried to convince them of the soundness of Pengelly's order.

For some moments the dispute threatened to develop into a free fight, until Pengelly, fearful lest the objectors should gain the upper hand in a physical contest, bade the gunner pass the boats astern to be taken in tow.

The anchor was weighed and at four knots— more speed would have resulted in the swamping of the heavily-laden boats—the *Alerte* ascended the river.

Almost as soon as the pirate submarine had disappeared from view, the imprisoned officers and crew of the *Bronx City* were released by the Portuguese passengers.

Captain Hiram Adams' first step was to assure
himself that his ship had not been crippled beyond
being run aground. To his delight he found that
beyond the damage caused by the looters in their
work of plunder and the removal of certain wireless essentials, the *Bronx City* was unharmed. He
had given a shrewd and correct guess as to the
reason of the pirates' return visit. He had
summed up Cain as a man of his word, who was
in consequence not responsible for the orgy of
plunder. Therefore, he concluded, that there had
been an " almighty bust-up," and that Cain had
been supplanted by the loose-lipped, spineless
Pengelly.

Captain Adams had made several trips up the
Mississippi as far as Memphis. He had had many
experiences of running aground the soft mud-
banks that fringe the frequently-shifting channel
of that enormous waterway. He was now going
to put that knowledge to practical use.

" Say, how long will it take for a full head of
steam ? " he inquired of the chief engineer.

" I guess an hour," replied that worthy, knowing
that the fires had not been drawn when the ship
took the ground.   " Mebbe less."

" Then get busy," rejoined the Yankee skipper.

The chief went below with his assistant and
firemen.   Presently volumes of smoke poured from
the *Bronx's City* smoke-stack.

While steam was being raised, Captain Hiram
Adams ordered a kedge-anchor to be laid out in
the stream, and the stout wire hawser attached
to it to be led aft, so that the angle made by the

keel of the ship and the wire was roughly forty-five degrees.

As soon as the chief engineer reported that the pressure gauges registered a sufficient head of steam, the skipper telegraphed for full-speed ahead with the port engine.

Completely mystified, the chief obeyed, wondering what possessed the Old Man to go full ahead with one engine that would tend to drive the ship farther into the mud-bank.

Nor was the chief the only one puzzled. In fact, some of the crew wondered whether recent events had not touched the skipper's brain. And their wonderment increased when Captain Hiram Adams, with a huge cigar jutting at an acute angle from the corner of his mouth, descended from the bridge.

" Guess those darned cargo-lifters won't be comin' down before morning, Mr. Kelly," he remarked to his chief officer. " We'll be quit before then. Set an anchor-watch and inform me if anything happens."

" And the engines ? " inquired Mr. Kelly.

" Full ahead all the time," replied the skipper, and without offering any explanation, he went to his cabin to snatch a few hours' sleep.

All the rest of that day and throughout the night the port engine kept up its tireless task. The massive propeller in going ahead was constantly throwing aft volumes of water with quantities of mud held in suspension. Slowly but surely the soft slime was being sucked away from the vessel's port bilge, thus making a trench into which, when the time came, the *Bronx City* would slide sideways.

Just before the first streaks of the brief tropical dawn appeared over the dark outlines of the mangroves, Captain Hiram Adams appeared on deck.

It was now close on high water. Although the tide was still making, there was a considerable quantity of turgid fresh water coming downstream.

Giving instructions to the chief officer to bring a strain upon the wire hawser, the skipper telegraphed for the port engines to stop and the starboard for " Full Astern." The hull of the *Bronx City* quivered. For a brief, anxious period her fate hung in the balance. Then, with a squelching sound as tons of slimy black mud were shifted bodily, the vessel slithered into the trench and began to gather sternway in midstream, held only by the stern kedge.

With the least possible delay the wire hawser was hove taut and the kedge broken out. Then, at " Easy ahead," the *Bronx City* made for the open sea.

Meanwhile the *Alerte* had gone upstream, arriving well before nightfall at an anchorage five miles above the spot where she had left her latest capture. Here Pengelly, accompanied by two of the hands, went ashore, the new captain taking with him a prismatic compass.

Selecting a suitable spot, he took bearings on three conspicuous objects, making the necessary data in his pocket-book. His assistants watched the operation with semi-torpid interest. They had a vague idea of what he was about, which was what Pengelly wanted.

Returning on board, he mustered the crew. They crowded round in a disorderly mob—a striking contrast to the orderly way in which they fell in under Captain Cain's orders.

" I've fixed the spot for burying the booty, my lads ! " he announced. " The sooner we get to work the quicker we'll be able to make ourselves scarce. In a week the place will be overgrown——"

" Then 'ow the blazes are we to find it again ? " interrupted one of the audience.

" Quite a natural, intelligent question," rejoined Pengelly. " I've taken a three-point bearing. With either a sextant or a compass it will be as easy as winking to fix the spot to a yard. This is a mutual concern, my lads, so I'll chalk up the angles so that you can make a note of them in case anything happens to me. That's fair enough, isn't it ? Now, fall in half a dozen of you with spades, nip ashore and begin digging like Hades. Yes, the ivory won't hurt if it's well covered with canvas."

The digging party landed, while others, still under the effect of the rum, proceeded to unload the booty from the boats. While the operation was in progress, Pengelly chalked the required information on the bulkhead of the dummy fo'c'sle —only the bearings he wrote down for the information of the crew differed materially from those he had noted in his pocket-book.

Then he went ashore to watch the progress of the work of burying the loot.

" Wot abaht these 'ere austridge feathers ? " inquired one of the men, holding up a bunch for inspection.

" Share them out," replied Pengelly. " When we make port they'll fetch a tidy price. They won't keep here. . . . Pile the earth up, men. It's bound to sink a bit. Look alive. It's not healthy to be hanging about ashore with this mist rising."

While the new captain was superintending operations on the river bank, Barnard, who with two men had been detailed to keep an eye on the deposed skipper, came across to where Cain was lying on deck under the bridge.

" I wouldn't that this happened for worlds, sir," he remarked to his former chief. " I couldn't warn you. They'd have let daylight into me if I had. And these two men—Davidge and Cross— they are proper jonnick. If we've the rope's end of a chance to get you out of this mess, sir, we'll do it."

Cain smiled grimly. The effects of the chloroform, never very heavy, had worn off, but the blow with the belaying-pin had weakened him considerably.

" I see they've looted the *Bronx City*," he remarked bitterly. " That's the limit as far as they are concerned. Look here, Barnard. Do you think you three can get me into a boat to-night and row down to the *Bronx City*? I'd give myself up if only to turn the tables on that double-faced Pengelly."

The bo'sun shook his head.

" Can't be done, sir," he replied. " Ten to one Pengelly would search her, and where would we be then ? 'Sides, I've no liking to run the risk of shoving my head through a noose when there's a chance of steering clear of it. Never fear, sir ; the hands'll be wanting you back in command afore long. Pengelly, he's got no hold on them. 'Sides, he's no deep-sea navigator. He's all right in home waters, I'll allow, but here——"

Mr. Barnard concluded his opinion with an expressive gesture.

" And he knows little or nothing about submarine work," added Cain.

" He thinks he does, sir," said the bo'sun. " To hear him talk about what he can do with the *Alerte* submerged, you'd think he'd been at it nearly all his life."

" I wouldn't care to trust him to take the *Alerte* down," declared Cain. "And I doubt whether there are others on board who would."

" Must be moving, sir," interrupted the bo'sun. " The boats are coming off from the beach. I'll sound some of the hands. There ought to be enough of us to scupper that skunk Pengelly, but it's no use trying to talk sense to them while they're three sheets in the wind."

As soon as the new pirate captain came over the side, he gave orders for the boats to be hoisted and watches set for the night, explaining that the latter precaution was necessary owing to the possibility of the ship swinging on to the mud when the tide changed. He then had Cain taken below and

placed in the compartment previously occupied by
Jasper Chamfer. The ex-skipper's bonds were
removed, food and drink were placed in his cell,
together with a mattress and bedding.

Pengelly was considerably anxious concerning
his treatment of Cain. He feared him even though
the late skipper was safely under lock and key.
There was always a chance of the hands turning
against him, Pengelly, and demanding that Cain
should again assume command. While the decid-
ing factor that prompted Pengelly to keep his
captive on board was the fact that Cain alone knew
how to control the *Alerte* when submerged.

At dawn the hands were turned out and piped
to breakfast. Most of them had slept off the
brutish effect of unlimited quantities of rum. One
or two were in a happy state, others inclined to be
quarrelsome and pugnacious. But on the whole
they were in fair possession of their faculties and
were only too ready to get under way.

As soon as the motors were started up and the
anchor out, the *Alerte* was headed down-stream,
Pengelly being on the bridge and Marchant, the
gunner, conning the ship from the bows as she
threaded her way down the intricate and tortuous
channel.

Presently Pengelly leant over the bridge-rails.

" Mr. Barnard," he exclaimed, loud enough for
the watch on deck to hear. " Bring up the
prisoner, and place him under the poop in charge of
a couple of hands. Take all precautions. I hold
you responsible for his safe custody."

Taking Davidge and Cross, the men who had

17

signified their readiness to stand-by the ex-captain,
the bo'sun went below and unlocked the door of
Cain's cell.

" My orders are to take you on deck, Cap'n Cain,"
he announced. " S'pose you don't want to jump
overboard ? "

" Not under present conditions," replied the
pirate.

" Nor to give any trouble ? "

" There'll be enough before long, without my
having to cause any," rejoined Cain grimly.
" Why do you ask ? "

" Pengelly's orders were that I'm responsible
for you," replied Barnard. " I must lash your
hands, sir. A mere matter of form. I won't give
your wrists a tight nip, and if anything happens
as renders it necessary, sir, I'll set you free in a
brace o' shakes."

" That's all right, Barnard," said the ex-captain
reassuringly. " I won't kick : for the present
I'll knuckle under."

Meekly he submitted to have his wrists secured
behind his back, then preceded by Davidge and
followed by Cross, with the bo'sun bringing up the
rear, Cain made his way to the conning-tower
hatchway.

Pengelly watched him furtively. Cain gave no
glance in the direction of the bridge. Several of
the men on deck stood to attention, a compliment
that Pengelly did not fail to notice. None of the
hands paid that mark of deference to him, he
recalled.

At that moment the *Alerte* was rounding the last

bend in the river between her and the spot where
the *Bronx City* had been run aground.

Suddenly Marchant shouted:

" She's sheered off, by thunder ! "

A few seconds later Pengelly had an uninterrupted view of the next reach. Only too true
was the gunner's announcement. Not only had
the *Bronx City* got afloat; she was no longer
in the river, nor in the spacious Bahia Arenas.

" That's kippered the contract," growled
Marchant, who had abandoned his post for'ard
and had gained the bridge. " We ought to have
scuppered her. She'll report us and there'll be a
swarm of light cruisers and destroyers after us in
less than no time."

" She can't use her wireless," said Pengelly.

" Never said she could," retorted the gunner.
" She'll speak the first ship she meets and get her
to use her wireless. There'll be French cruisers
waitin' for us off the Senegal and the south'ard, an'
Spaniards up the coast—British destroyers, too,
I guess. An' we can't bust across to South
America—we ain't got enough oil."

" What do you propose, then ? " asked Pengelly
helplessly.

" Propose ? " echoed the gunner contemptuously. " Propose—ain't you supposed to be the
skipper ? If you don't know what's to be done,
who does ? Cain, of course; you'd best ask
him."

The ex-captain on his way aft heard the dialogue.
He shrugged his shoulders and looked meaningly
at the bo'sun.

" Pengelly 'll part brass rags with every one on board afore very long, sir," whispered Barnard.

The *Alerte* was now ploughing across the bay. The sandy island enclosing the mouth of the anchorage effectually concealed the open sea from sight, although in a short time the entrance would afford an almost interrupted view of the offing. Still, Pengelly gave no indication of the course he proposed to pursue.

Descending from the bridge, the gunner gathered several of the hands round him. Ignoring the new captain entirely, Marchant pointed out the additional risks they were running by reason of the escape of the *Bronx City*.

" Cap'n Cain's our man," declared one of the hands.

" No, he isn't," retorted the gunner. " He ought to be, I admit. That horse-marine on the bridge there ain't good for nothin'. But if Cain gets the upper hand, then some of us are in for a rough time. No, our best plan is to go in chase of the *Bronx City* and overhaul her afore she gets a chance to speak another craft."

" And then——? " asked one of the men.

" Then," continued the gunner, " we'll nab her, take all necessary precautions with her crew, abandon the *Alerte* and carry the *Bronx City* across to Brazil. There's no need to bring her into port. We'll scuttle her and take to the boats, pitch a yarn to the British Consul an' get sent home as shipwrecked mariners. How's that? "

The suggestion met with acclamation. Marchant reascended the bridge ladder.

" This ain't a one-man show, Mr. Pengelly," he said meaningly. " It's the wish of the hands that we recapture the *Bronx City* afore she lets the cat out of the bag."

" Very good," agreed Pengelly.

CHAPTER XXII

A STERN CHASE

"DEAR BROADMAYNE,—I suppose by the time you receive this you will have had a hand in sending the *Alerte* to her long, last home. Really, I don't envy your job, but it will be interesting to hear how it happened when you return home, which I suppose will be before very long.

"We—old Primmer and I—had quite an exciting time at Mousehole. We found Porthoustoc's swag, but hanged if the Customs and police didn't butt in, and we spent a night in the cells at Penzance before the admiral at Devonport got us released! I'll tell you all about it in due course.

"I've received the insurance money for the poor old *Ibex*, and I'm in treaty with a fellow at Burnham for the purchase of a smart little motor-cruiser—paraffin engines this time, so perhaps you'll find an opportunity and help me bring her round.—Cheerio, yours ever,

"ROLLO VYSE."

Sub-Lieutenant Broadmayne smiled as he replaced this missive in his pocket. The *Alerte* affair had already seen Rollo twice under arrest. . . . Perhaps old Vyse would have a third similar experience in connection with the pirate. . . .

Hardly likely, though. The *Alerte* was finished and done with. His chum was wrong in his surmise. The unenviable job had been carried out without any direct action on the part of H.M.S. *Canvey*.

The decoy-ship was homeward bound. She had put into the Canaries to pick up her mails and had proceeded. Already the famous Peak of Teneriffe was dipping beneath the southern horizon. Broadmayne, leaning over the taffrail, was in a pensive mood as he watched the water froth in the ship's wake.

Even as he looked, the ship began to circle to starboard. There was nothing very unusual about that. Possibly she was giving way to an approaching craft. But when the turning movement continued, the Sub began to show an interest in the matter. Still more did he—as did a hundred others—when the *Canvey*, having turned sixteen points, steadied on her helm and began to retrace her course to the south'ard.

Leaving the deserted poop, Broadmayne went for'ard. Groups of curious ratings were discussing the seemingly unaccountable turn. Several of the officers off duty, who were smoking on deck after " seven-bell tea," were also in a state of perplexity over the business.

It was not long before the secret was out and had spread the length and breadth of the ship.

A wireless message had just been received, stating that, since nothing had been reported of the s.s. *Bronx City* following her account of the destruction of the *Alerte*, the *Canvey* was to proceed in search of the American vessel, keeping a sharp look-out on the coast as far south as the fifteenth parallel.

"Rotten stunt," grumbled the engineer-lieutenant, who was eagerly looking forward to the *Canvey's* return to Devonport—to an event that would result in, amongst other things, the hoisting of a garland between the ship's masts. "We were sent out here to chase a pirate, not to act as nurse to a Yankee tramp."

"Well, why didn't she show up at Teneriffe or Funchal?" demanded Allerton. "'Sides, something must have happened to her, or she'd have wirelessed again."

"Bows stove in by the collision," suggested the paymaster-lieutenant.

"But she reported she was proceeding," rejoined the engineer officer. "Proceeding where? That's what I want to know."

"You'll probably find out, if we're here long enough," said Broadmayne chaffingly. "It'll take six months or more to carry out orders. We can't examine the coast in the dark. That means we'll have to stand off every night and close the land at the same spot at daybreak. 'Sides, there are hundreds of little harbours we'll have to explore——"

"Oh, shut up, do!" interrupted the exasperated engineer-lieutenant.

For three days and nights the *Canvey* ran south, speaking several vessels, none of which could give any information concerning the sought-for *Bronx City.*

During the morning of the fourth day, Broadmayne, who was officer of the forenoon watch,
received a report that a vessel's smoke was to be
seen on the port bow.

This was somewhat unusual, for off this part
of the African coast shipping gave the land a wide
berth on account of the dangerous and unlighted
Lazarus Shoal.   The *Canvey* was, in point of fact,
standing in closer than prudence demanded,
although in order to carry out her instructions
to watch the coast in the event of the *Bronx City*
having run aground, she had to run a certain
amount of risk.

" What do you make of her ? " asked Broadmayne of the yeoman of signals, as the stranger's
hull drew above the horizon.

" Flying Yankee colours, sir," replied the petty
officer, after a prolonged look through his telescope.   " There's a double-barrelled tally on her
bows, though I can't make it out yet.   She ain't
'arf 'opping it."

A few minutes later, for the two vessels were
approaching each other at an aggregate speed
of twenty-eight knots, the yeoman of signals
exclaimed :

" Crikey, sir !   She's the *Bronx City* ! "

Dispatching a messenger to inform the captain,
Broadmayne levelled his binoculars upon the
approaching vessel.   As far as he could make out,
there was nothing wrong with her outward appearance.   Her bows were certainly not stove-in ;
which, considering she had claimed to have
rammed and sunk the *Alerte*, was what the Sub

had a right to expect. Her wireless aerials were in position.

Just as Lieutenant - Commander Raxworthy gained the bridge, a three-flag hoist rose to the foremast head of the *Bronx City* : INM—Chased by a privateer. Then, before the *Canvey* could display the answering pennant, the code flag over the letter E, signifying that the following words were in plain spelling, fluttered in the breeze.

" ALE———"

There was no need to complete the name.

" Sound off ' Action stations ' ! " ordered the owner.

Raxworthy formed a shrewd idea of what had occurred, but he was too wary a skipper to leave much to chance. The approaching vessel bore the name *Bronx City*. It might or might not be her rightful tally. If, as might possibly be the case, the *Alerte* had captured the Yankee vessel, it was quite likely that the pirate submarine had turned over her crew and armament to her prize. Or the *Bronx City* might be the *Alerte* disguised.

On the latter point Broadmayne was able to inform his skipper that such was not the case. The *Alerte*, however cleverly camouflaged, could not assume the length and lofty superstructure of the approaching craft.

In double-quick time the *Canvey* was cleared for action. The guns were unmasked and trained upon the *Bronx City*. " Present use " ammunition was brought up on deck and placed beside the quick-firers, while the torpedo-tubes on the port side were charged with their deadly missiles,

ready at the first sign of aggression to deliver a
mortal blow at the huge target presented by the
stranger's hull.

The *Bronx City* was still a mile off when a
second vessel was sighted a good five miles astern
of her. Although she, too, was evidently travelling
fast, there was a noticeable absence of smoke from
her funnel.

Borrowing the signalman's telescope, Broadmayne had a good look at her. He was bound
to admit that the second stranger resembled the
pirate submarine. There were a few trifling
alterations in her appearance since the Sub had
last seen her.

" She's the *Alerte*, sir," he declared confidently.

Lieutenant-Commander Raxworthy was on the
horns of a dilemma. Should the *Bronx City* prove
to be manned by a piratical crew and he allowed
her to go on her way while he headed off her
supposed pursuer, the opportunity of laying the
former vessel by the heels would be lost. On the
other hand, if he stopped to examine the craft
flying American colours, the presumed *Alerte*
would seize the opportunity of turning tail and
disappearing. Again, he was not justified in
ordering a United States ship to heave to, for it
might result in an unpleasant international
incident between the Government of Great
Britain and that sitting at Washington. Having
been once tricked completely by the *Alerte*, he was
doubly cautious lest there be a repetition of the
ruse that had succeeded almost beyond belief.

At the captain's orders, a signalman taking up a

conspicuous position on the roof of the chart-house semaphored to the *Bronx City*, suggesting that for her protection the American vessel should turn sixteen points to port and follow the *Canvey* at a distance of ten cables astern.

To this the *Bronx City* replied by the single word " Sure."

The two ships were now abeam of each other. The stranger in the offing had turned and was retracing her course—additional evidence that she was not an honest craft.

The lieutenant-commander of the *Canvey* immediately rang down for full speed. The chase —a stern one—had commenced.

" *Bronx City* turning to port, sir," reported the officer of the watch.

" Good ! " ejaculated the skipper. " We'll drop her, of course, but it shows she's jonnick. Ask her what she's been doing, Mr. Broadmayne."

The Sub told off a signalman to semaphore the *Bronx City*, which, having completed her turning movement, was dead in the *Canvey's* wake. For nearly half an hour the exchange of messages was maintained at high pressure. Captain Adams told briefly all that was necessary—the capture of the *Bronx City* by the *Alerte*, and Cain's considerate treatment ; the detention in Bahia Arenas and the *Alerte's* broken promise in plundering the ship.

" Was Cain in command ? " inquired Broadmayne, through the medium of the hand-flags.

" Guess not," replied the Yankee skipper. " A mutiny, possibly. Pengelly was in command when we were ransacked."

The Sub returned to the bridge and reported events.   By this time the *Alerte* was less than three miles away, thanks to the superior speed of the *Canvey*; while, on the other hand, the *Bronx City*, unable to keep station, had dropped nearly that distance astern of the British decoy-ship.

Raxworthy could have sunk the pirate sub-marine by gunfire with the greatest ease, but he refrained.   He wanted to head her into shallow water before delivering the *coup de grâce*—unless she surrendered first.   He therefore ordered speed to be reduced to that of the chase, the guns to be secured, and piped all hands to dinner.

Two bells in the afternoon watch found the relative positions of the *Canvey* and her chase un-changed.   The *Bronx City*, in spite of the *Canvey's* reduced speed, was still dropping astern.

Realising that no useful purpose would be served by the Yankee ship attempting to keep in company, the *Canvey* signalled for her to resume her former course, with the additional intimation that as the *Bronx City's* wireless was disabled, the *Canvey* would report her position to Teneriffe station.

Almost immediately upon receipt of the signal, the *Bronx City* starboarded helm and dipped her ensign.   Twenty minutes later she was hull down away to the nor'ard.

The *Canvey* now increased speed.   There was no need for disguise.   Bravely her battle-ensigns streamed in the breeze, while her guns were again manned and trained as far ahead as possible, ready, if need be, to hurl their deadly and destructive missiles upon the already doomed pirate submarine.

It was now a foregone conclusion that the *Alerte* was doubling back to her former anchorage in Bahia Arenas. She could not submerge outside without going to the bottom, and since the depth without the bar is everywhere not less than sixty fathoms, such a manœuvre would result in the submarine being crushed like an eggshell under the terrific pressure of water. It was extremely doubtful whether she would fight. Her solitary six-inch gun would be hopelessly outmatched against the superior ordnance of her pursuer. Short of taking to the boats and scuttling the *Alerte*, the pirates had no alternative but to endeavour to reach the sandy bay and evade detection by submerging.

Raxworthy was playing his own game. Apart from destroying the *Alerte* by gunfire or torpedo, he could have headed her off-shore by reason of the *Canvey's* superior speed and carried her in the good old-fashioned way by boarding. Such a measure, involving a certain risk of casualties amongst the *Canvey's* ship's company, would have appealed to most of the men ; but the lieutenant-commander had other plans. He meant to compel the *Alerte* to surrender if it were possible. In any case, he wanted to take as many of the pirates as possible prisoners. To slay ruthlessly was against his principles. Prisoners, even if they were pirates captured red-handed, were entitled to a fair trial, and in that event the onus of dealing with them was removed from Raxworthy's shoulders.

At seven bells (3.30 p.m.) the *Canvey* gained sufficiently to enable one of her guns to fire a few yards wide of the chase. Simultaneously, she hoisted a signal summoning the *Alerte* to surrender.

By the aid of glasses it was easy for the *Canvey's* officers to see most of what was going on on the deck of the pirate submarine. Pengelly and the gunner could be discerned crouching on the bridge. On the poop were several of the crew clamouring and arguing. Some of them were evidently advocating taking to the boats. Most of them had brought their personal belongings on deck, so that it looked as if they had no intention of offering resistance.

At length the *Alerte* starboarded helm in order to take the deep and narrow passage over the bar. As she did so, Broadmayne noticed a tall burly figure ascend the bridge, grasp the cowering Pengelly and literally boot him down the ladder.

" Now, we'll have a run for our money, sir," remarked Broadmayne, to the lieutenant-commander. " Cain's got his spoke in again ! "

CHAPTER XXIII

CAIN RESUMES COMMAND

"UP aloft, one of you!" shouted Marchant. "See if the swine's in sight."

The *Alerte* was pitching as she faced the long Atlantic swell after crossing the bar in pursuit of the *Bronx City*. A few—a very few—of the crew were sober; the majority were befuddled in the transition stage between drunkenness and sobriety; while four or five, helplessly intoxicated, lay rolling in the scuppers.

One of the hands, pot-valiant, made an attempt to go aloft. Before he had ascended half a dozen ratlins he slipped. Luckily for him, the *Alerte* was at the limit of her roll. Instead of dropping into the sea he slithered helplessly round the after-shroud and subsided heavily upon the gunner. The pair fell in a heap on deck. The drunken seaman, none the worse for his involuntary descent, sat up and looked around as if seeking applause. Marchant staggered to his feet, his right shoulder dislocated.

Pengelly, from the bridge, saw the incident. It cheered him considerably, for with Marchant rendered *hors de combat* he was able to reassert his lax authority on the undisciplined crew.

A seaman, less drunk than his predecessor, went aloft. Before he reached the cross-trees he shouted, " There she lies—a point on our port bow."

" Sure she's the *Bronx City* ? " inquired Pengelly anxiously.

" Do you call me a liar ? " shouted the look-out man in reply. " If I says she's the *Bronx*, then she is. That's all about it."

With the oil-engines running " all out," the *Alerte* stood in pursuit of the fugitive. A couple of hours enabled her to gain on the *Bronx City* to such an extent that the latter was barely six miles ahead. At that rate, another hour and a half would enable the pirate submarine to overhaul her prey.

Although Pengelly had no liking for Marchant, he was forced to admit that the gunner's proposal to abandon the *Alerte* and take the *Bronx City* over to some obscure South American port was a sound one. The question of fuel largely influenced his decision. The *Alerte's* tanks were seriously depleted ; the *Bronx City's* coal bunkers were three-quarters full. It was on that account that Pengelly refrained from opening fire upon the Yankee vessel, otherwise he could have ended the chase half an hour ago.

At intervals, Pengelly raised his binoculars and watched the chase. It was on one of these occasions that he noticed a faint blur of smoke on the horizon at less than a degree to the left of the *Bronx City*.

Cursing under his breath, the pirate called to

18

the gunner to come on the bridge. Marchant, his right shoulder swathed in bandages, complied, grumbling and wincing as every step shot a sharp pain through the injured part.

" There's another vessel," announced Pengelly. " She's coming this way, I think. What's to be done ? "

" Done ? " repeated the gunner. " Why, collar the pair of 'em. We'll make a fine haul, I'll swear."

" But if she's a warship ? " objected the other.

" Is it likely ? " rejoined Marchant. " What would a warship be doing on this part of the coast ? Seein' as Cain reported us sunk—say what you like, that chap's got a head on 'im—there'll be none lookin' for us. Where's that glass of yours ? "

Steadying the telescope on the bridge-rail, the gunner, groaning with the effort, bent his head and applied his eye to the instrument.

" Tramp of sorts," he announced. " She's flying no colours. Odds are the *Bronx City* 'll tip her the wink. That being so, we'll have to send her to the bottom. . . . Yes, hang me, if she ain't closing."

For the next minute or so the gunner kept his eye glued to the telescope. Suddenly he dropped the glass and sprang to his feet.

" She's a British cruiser, blast her ! " he shouted. " Put about and leg it, Pengelly. If she spots us, it's all UP ! "

Without waiting for Pengelly to give the order, the quartermaster put the wheel hard down.

Round swept the *Alerte*, listing heavily to port as she swung to starboard.

The hands on deck, surprised by the sudden change of course, were clamouring to know why the pursuit had been abandoned.

" Why ? " shouted the gunner. " 'Cause we're being chased. No blessed Dago destroyer this time, but a British cruiser. We'll have to be mighty smart to dodge the white ensign."

" She's spotted us ! " exclaimed Pengelly, in a high-pitched voice. " The *Bronx City* is slewing round, too. Counfound Cain ! If he'd crippled the *Bronx City* instead of just running her gently on the mud, there'd have been none of this business."

" We'll be glad to have Cain on board before long," said the bo'sun, who had joined Pengelly and the gunner on the bridge. " I reckon our only chance is to submerge. Without Cain, how's it to be done ? You couldn't take her down, nor can I."

" Soundings are too deep for diving in any case," declared Pengelly. " Seems to me we're holding her, even if we aren't gaining. What's the time ? "

" Close on one bell," replied the bo'sun.

" Time to make Bahia Arenas well before dark then," continued Pengelly. " See here, Mr. Barnard, go aft and sound that swine Cain. Don't tell him I sent you, but ask him if he'll take charge of the ship for submerging."

The bo'sun departed on his errand. Presently he returned.

"Cap'n Cain says he'll consider the matter if you go and ask him yourself," he announced.

"Then you'd better go," added Marchant.

"Not I," said Pengelly.

While the *Alerte* held her own, Pengelly adhered to his resolution not to eat humble pie. But when, in the course of the afternoon, the pursuing vessel began to gain rapidly, he yielded to the importunities of the gunner, the bo'sun, and the majority of the crew.

"Look here, Trevorrick," he began, addressing his former partner and skipper by the name by which he was known at Polkyll Creek; "'spose we let bygones be bygones? Will you take charge of the ship and submerge her when we make Bahia Arenas?"

Cain looked him straight in the face. Pengelly could not bear the other's gaze. Unsteadily he averted his eyes.

"I'll submerge when I'm captain of the *Alerte* again, not before," replied Cain.

"Three cheers for Cap'n Cain!" shouted one of the hands, several of whom had followed the deputation aft.

At that moment a plugged shell shrieked past the pirate submarine, throwing up a huge column of spray as it ricochetted to strike the surface of the water a good five hundred yards ahead of the ship.

Pengelly made no protest to the demonstration in favour of the ex-captain. Followed by Marchant he returned to the bridge.

"Carry on, sir!" shouted half a dozen of the pirates.

Some one cast off the lashings that secured Cain's wrists. The bo'sun slipped an automatic into his hand. With a grim smile, Cain went forward and ascended the bridge ladder.

"Now then!" he exclaimed, sternly addressing the trembling Pengelly. "Who's skipper now!"

"You are," admitted the thoroughly scared man. "For heaven's sake, don't shoot!"

"Good lead is too precious to waste on rats," retorted Cain, thrusting the automatic into his pocket. "Get down, you treacherous swab!"

Pengelly began to descend the bridge-ladder, his progress materially assisted by the application of the reinstated captain's boot. The crew, notwithstanding their imminent peril, applauded lustily.

"Avast there!" shouted Captain Cain. "Shout when you're out of the wood—not before. Strike and secure masts! Look lively, there!"

While most of the crew were engaged upon this task, Cain beckoned to the bo'sun.

"Look here, Barnard!" he exclaimed in a low voice; "remove the rapid-flooding valves from all the boats. Take one below; heave the others overboard."

This the bo'sun did, unshipping a hinged plate that when secured by two butterfly nuts rendered each boat watertight. When open, the valves allowed the boats to take in water rapidly, so that their natural buoyancy was destroyed and did not hinder the submergence of the submarine. The solitary valve that was not thrown overboard was placed below, under the conning-tower hatch-way ladder.

"Well done, Mr. Barnard!" said Cain approvingly. "Now, tell Cross and Davidge to go below and secure both the for'ard and after hatches on the inside. Also tell Cross to inform the engine-room staff from me that as soon as I ring down for 'Stop' they are to come on deck through the conning-tower hatchway with all possible speed. Is that clear?"

The bo'sun repeated his instructions and went off to see that they were carried out. By the time he returned the crew had lowered and secured the masts and funnel for diving and were standing by, anxiously dividing their attention between the pursuing *Canvey* and their reinstated skipper's next order.

"All hands fall in in the waist!" shouted Cain.

The deck hands trooped to the place indicated, with the exception of Davidge and Cross, who, acting under orders, were standing by the valve actuating gear of the ballast tanks.

Deliberately, Cain thrust the telegraph indicators to stop, gave one quick glance at the vessel in pursuit and descended from the bridge.

By this time the *Alerte* was over the bar and about half a mile from the land-locked shore. The *Canvey*, none too sure of the entrance, had slowed down, the leadsman sounding as she cautiously smelt her way in.

As soon as the men whose duty lay in the engine-room came on deck, Cain made a slight imperceptible movement with his hand. Unconcernedly, the bo'sun stepped to the wake of the conning-tower and took three steps down the ladder. There he waited.

"Now, you treacherous, mutineering swine!" thundered Cain. "I'll give you one minute to get your lifebelts. You're to choose between being eaten by sharks or hanging by your necks in a British prison."

Before the astounded men could realise the significance of their captain's words, Cain made for the only open hatchway. There he stopped, his eyes roving whimsically over the dumbfoundered men, a supercilious smile lurking in his heavy bulldog features.

Marchant fumbled for his automatic. But for his injured shoulder he might have achieved his object. The pistol cracked, the bullet mushrooming on the armour-plated conning tower.

"Forty-five seconds more!" announced Cain, in cold, level tones.

The next instant Captain Cain disappeared from view. The conning-tower hatch descended with a metallic clang.

With the closing of the last means of entering the hull of the submarine the spell was broken. The crew, realising the fate that awaited them, were seized with panic. Some began to struggle into their cork lifebelts, others made a mad rush for the davit-boats, to find to their consternation that they were no longer capable of floating.

A shell, evidently of light calibre, struck the *Alerte* a few feet abaft the bows, demolishing the dummy fo'c'sle like a pack of cards. It was fortunate for the men that they were either in the waist or on the poop, for no one was hit ; but the exploding missile warned them that their pursuer was getting to work in earnest.

" Lower that cursed rag ! " shrieked Pengelly, pointing to the skull and cross-bones which, on the masts being lowered, the gunner in reckless bravado had hoisted at the end of a boathook. " Has anybody got anything that'll do for a white flag ? No ? Then, for heaven's sake, some of you in the poop hold your hands up, or she'll blow us to bits."

Several of the hands did so, while the signalman, clambering on the bridge, frantically semaphored that the ship had surrendered.

Even as the message was being signalled, the *Alerte* began to settle. In less than half a minute she disappeared beneath the surface, leaving the agitated water of the Bahia Arenas dotted with the heads of her mutinous crew.

The pirate submarine *Alerte* had made her final plunge.

CHAPTER XXIV

THE FATE OF THE PIRATE SUBMARINE

"BY the mark seven . . . Less a quarter . . .
By the deep six!" chanted the leadsman,
as the *Canvey* approached the bar.

"Starboard! Meet her at that!" ordered the
lieutenant-commander, telegraphing for speed to
be still further reduced. "Any signs of armed
resistance?"

"No, sir," replied Broadmayne; for now that the
Alerte had swung through eight points, her quick-
firer could be seen from the bridge of the *Canvey*.
"The poor bounders have got the wind up badly,"
he added.

"They'll get it worse, if they don't chuck up the
sponge," rejoined Raxworthy. "By Jove! If
they don't strike that Jolly Roger there'll be
trouble. For'ard starboard gun, there! One
round at the enemy's bows!"

The shell, a seven-pounder, shrieked as it sped
on its errand of destruction. A flash, a cloud of
black smoke and a shower of pieces of metal announced that the missile had accomplished its work.
Practically the whole of the for'ard superstructure
of the pirate submarine had vanished.

" Black flag's struck, sir ! " announced the gunnery-lieutenant.

" They're doing the ' arms up ' stunt," supplemented another of the group of officers on the Canvey's bridge.

The Alerte was losing way rapidly. A solitary figure appeared on the hitherto deserted bridge.

" We—surrender," came the semaphored message.

" Wise men," commented Raxworthy, as he faced aft to order away the boats containing the prize-crew.

" She's submerging, sir ! " exclaimed Broadmayne.

The lieutenant-commander turned abruptly. He was about to order every gun able to bear upon the pirate submarine to open fire, when he observed that men were leaping overboard in a state of uncontrollable panic. That altered matters. Had the crew of the Alerte been at diving stations, he would not have hesitated to hasten her departure by means of half a dozen high-explosive shells. The fact that the pirates were swimming for dear life in a shark-infested sea, compelled him to stay his hand.

" Away lifeboat's crews ! "

To the shrill trill of the bo'sun's mate's whistle the bluejackets rushed to man the boats. The excitement of the chase had vanished ; in its place was the whole-hearted eagerness to save life.

The Alerte disappeared with very little noise or commotion. Although the water was considerably disturbed, there was hardly any suction

he swimmers, although impeded by their cumber-
ome cork lifebelts, had little difficulty in getting
lear of her as she submerged.

" What's young Maynebrace doing ? " asked the
eutenant-commander as the loud report of a
evolver rang out, followed by three shots in rapid
uccession.

Broadmayne, also attracted by the reports, saw
he midshipman in charge of the second cutter
tanding up in the stern-sheets and firing appar-
ntly at some of the swimmers. Apparently
everal of the pirates thought that they were
bout to be shot as they swam, for they turned
nd began to strike out away from the rescuing
oats.

There was a wild, almost unearthly shriek. One
f the wretched men threw up his arms and dis-
ppeared. A patch of blood appeared on the
urface over the spot where he had vanished.
gain Midshipman Maynebrace fired, his objective
eing the head of an enormous shark, just as the
onster turned on its back to seize another victim.

Right amidst the straggling crowd of swimmers
ashed the two boats, their crews engaged between
ealing spanking blows with the blades of their
ars upon the water, and hauling the terrified
irates over the gunwales.

Cain had revenged himself upon his mutinous
ew. Only fifteen escaped the jaws of the
rocious tigers of the deep, and these were almost
ad with the horror of the scene.

Among those who fell victims to the sharks was
archant the gunner. Pengelly, wearing only a

shirt and trousers, was one of the survivors. His
hair had turned white during his desperate
swim.

The late second in command of the *Alerte* hardly
hoped to pass himself off as one of the ratings o
the pirate submarine. He realised that he wa:
far from being popular with the crew. Sooner o:
later they would " give him away." But the
attempt was worth trying.

As he came over the side of the *Canvey* he wa
interrogated by a stern-faced lieutenant, who de
manded his name and rating.

" Smith, Tom—deck-hand," he replied.

The *Canvey's* officer noted the particulars with
out comment. Pengelly went for'ard under arrest
ignorant of the fact that Sub-Lieutenant Geral
Broadmayne was watching him from the bridge.

" There's no sign of Cain, sir," remarked th
Sub to the owner. " That fellow just gon
for'ard is Pengelly. Marchant the gunner an
Barnard the bo'sun don't appear to be present."

" Hang it all ! " ejaculated Raxworthy, " yo
don't suggest that three of the pirate officer:
including the ringleader, are still on board th
submarine ? Pass the word to Mr. Hamley t
send Pengelly to the quarter-deck under an arme
guard."

The lieutenant on the gangway received the
message. Consulting the list he had made, h
found that no one answering to that name ha
been received on board. He sent a message t
that effect to the captain.

After considerable delay, Pengelly was foun

and brought aft. The moment he saw Broad-mayne standing behind the lieutenant-commander, he knew that the game was up as far as concealing his identity was concerned.

" Where's Cain ? " demanded Raxworthy, without any preliminaries.

Pengelly explained what had occurred, spinning an elaborate yarn that he had done his utmost to persuade Captain Cain to surrender, and trying to excuse himself for having ever set foot on board the *Alerte*.

The lieutenant-commander brought him up with a round turn.

" Enough of that ! " he said sternly. " Where is the gunner of the *Alerte* ? "

Pengelly shook his head. That was a question that he could not answer. He was still unaware of the fate of Mr. Marchant.

" And the bo'sun—Barnard, I believe, is his name ? " continued Raxworthy.

Again Pengelly let his tongue run riot, dwelling on Barnard's action in siding with Cain and going below with him.

" For what reason ? " asked the lieutenant-commander.

" Cain will probably try to bring the *Alerte* to the surface when he thinks the coast is clear," replied Pengelly readily enough.

" Two men cannot do that," interrupted Raxworthy.

" There may be more," rejoined the pirate. " I remember two hands at least going below. I did not see them come on deck again. Please remember, sir, I've done my best to answer your questions. I deeply regret——"

"Remove the prisoner," said Raxworthy sternly.

He waited until Pengelly had been taken for'ard, then he turned to Broadmayne.

"I suppose you are quite certain that the *Alerte* hasn't electrical propelling machinery ?" he asked.

"There was none when I was on board, sir," replied the Sub.

"I don't suppose four men will be able to disconnect the clutches and turn the propellers sufficiently to make the submarine move," remarked Raxworthy, half-seriously, half-jokingly. "She's there right enough. Well, I've given Cain a fair chance ; he wouldn't accept it. What happens now is his funeral, not mine."

Raxworthy returned to the bridge. It was now about an hour before sunset. The sheltered bay was as smooth as a millpond. There was nothing to indicate that the elusive pirate submarine lay ten fathoms deep except a small mark-buoy that had been placed over the spot where the *Alerte* had disappeared.

His orders were plain enough—to capture or destroy. He had done his best to carry out the first part of his instructions. Cain had foiled him in that direction by submerging. Short of powerful salvage craft and plant there was no means of bringing the submarine to the surface and then effecting her capture. The *Canvey* could wireless to Gibraltar dockyard for the necessary gear, but days—weeks perhaps—would elapse before the cumbersome salvage lighters could be towed to Bahia Arenas. There was no help for it but to act upon the second alternative —to destroy.

"There's one consolation," soliloquised the lieutenant-commander, "the poor brutes won't know much about it. It's a quick end."

Slowly the *Canvey* turned until her bows pointed nearly end-on to the mark-buoy. On the starboard side of the poop was a squat-looking object somewhat resembling the old-time siege mortar, its wide muzzle grinning upwards at an elevation of forty-five degrees. The weapon—a depth-charge projector—was loaded with a missile set to explode at sixty feet beneath the surface.

"All ready, Mr. Garnett?" sang out the lieutenant-commander to the gunner who was in charge of the apparatus.

"Ay, ay, sir!"

The engine-room telegraph bell clanged. Almost immediately the *Canvey* increased speed. The mark-buoy bore abeam, a cable's length to starboard.

Crash! went the propelling charge.

Like a gigantic salmon-tin, the missile described its parabolic flight—so slowly that observers on the bridge could see the huge canister turning over and over in mid-air.

It struck the water with a resounding thud, flinging up a shower of spray. Already the *Canvey* under fifteen degrees of starboard helm was rapidly increasing her distance from the mark-buoy.

Slowly the intervening seconds passed; so slowly that Broadmayne began to think the fuse of the depth-charge had proved defective.

Then came a truly stupendous roar. A slender column of water was hurled quite two hundred feet in the air. The hull of the *Canvey* shook under the terrific blast of displaced air. The tranquil waters of the bay were transformed into a mass of agitated waves.

The column of upheaved water fell with a loud hissing noise. For nearly half a minute the turmoil continued. Then, in the midst of the maelstrom, appeared a patch of calm, iridescent oil spreading steadily in all directions, while multitudes of fish, killed or stunned by the detonation, floated belly-upwards upon the surface.

" Away, diving-party," ordered Captain Raxworthy.

" With your permission, sir, I would like to accompany the divers, sir," said Broadmayne.

" Are you qualified ? " asked the lieutenant-commander.

" Yes, sir," replied the Sub. " I did a diving-course at Whaley when I paid off from the *Arcturus*, and I've been down to fourteen fathoms."

" Very good," was the rejoinder.

Broadmayne saluted and went off to make the necessary preparations.

The *Canvey* was equipped with two types of diving dresses, both designed and made by the firm of Siebe, Gorman & Co. One was of the common variety, in which the air is pumped

through a pipe from a pump above the surface of
the sea. The other was of the self-contained type ;
the air supply, judiciously combined with oxygen,
is contained in cylinders strapped to the back of
the diver. Thus he is independent of air-tubes,
life-lines and other contrivances likely to impede
his movements.

The Sub chose the latter type of dress. The
depth in which the *Alerte* had sunk was between
fifty and sixty feet at low water, the maximum
distance below the surface at which the self-
contained diving-suit can be used without undue
risk.

One of the seaman-divers was already being
garbed in a similar suit by his attendants ; the
other man was preparing to don a dress with life-
line and air-tube, the helmet being provided with
a telephone by means of which he could engage
in conversation with the above-water party in the
boat.

The descent was to be made as speedily as
possible before more sharks appeared upon the
scene of the wreck to feast on the bodies of their
less fortunate kind who had been killed by the
explosion. Nevertheless, Broadmayne and his
companions were warned to keep a sharp look-out
while under the surface. As a rule, a shark will
hesitate to attack a diver, but there have been
instances in which a terrible submarine struggle
has taken place between a diver and the tigers of
the deep.

The diving-boats pushed off and anchored fore
and aft as close as desirable to the wreck. The

10

diver with the air-tube type of dress was the first to descend, sliding at a steady pace down the shot-rope.

A tug on the life-line gave the attendants warning that the man had reached the bottom.

" Ready, sir ? " asked a petty officer.

" Right," replied Broadmayne.

The glass plate in the front of his helmet was screwed home. He was now cut off from the outside world as far as the air supply was concerned, and the sensation was not a pleasant one.

Unlike the first man to descend, whose helmet had been closed only when he was waist-deep in water, the Sub had to be finally equipped while in the boat. Assisted by the attendants—for his movements were hampered by the weight of his helmet, chemical - containers, chest and back weights, and leaden-soled boots, the whole amounting to 190 lb. — Broadmayne scrambled awkwardly and ponderously over the gunwale, grasped the shot-line used by his predecessor and began the descent.

In spite of the weight of the dress in air, it now had so little weight in water that the Sub had no difficulty in retarding the downward movement. Even the inconvenience caused by the unaccustomed air supply passed away after a few seconds.

Presently his leaden-soled feet touched the bed of the Bahia Arenas so lightly that he could hardly credit that he was standing on a floor of hard sand. So transparent was the water that he had no difficulty in seeing objects five or six yards off, all grotesquely distorted and exaggerated.

Grasping the second of the three distance lines, the Sub commenced his submarine walk, following the cord that the first diver had paid out. Evidently the man had not erred in his sense of direction, for the line lay motionless on the sandy floor. All around were pieces of jagged steel-plating, copper pipes and other débris from the ill-fated *Alerte*.

Presently an enormous dark grey mass loomed up in front. It was the hull of the pirate submarine. The seaman-diver, with bubbles rising from his helmet, was standing by. His job lay outside the hull; Broadmayne's and that of the third diver, inside.

In less than two minutes the third member of the party appeared. The first man, turning to reassure himself that his air-tube and life-line were clear of the jagged plates, worked round towards the stern. It was here that the full force of the powerful depth - charge had expended itself. Thirty feet or more of the after-portion of the submarine had been completely blown apart, together with most of the propelling machinery. There was not the slightest doubt about the destruction of the after-part of the submarine. It remained to be seen whether the water-tight bulkhead separating the motor-room from the 'midship and fore compartment had withstood the strain.

Signing to his similarly-equipped companion to follow him, Broadmayne clambered up the sloping side of the considerably-listing vessel. The ease with which he performed this feat rather surprised him.

Once again the Sub trod the deck—or, rather, what remained of the deck of the *Alerte*. The bridge had disappeared and the whole of the bulwarks and deck aft, leaving bare a full fifty feet of the massively-built submarine hull to where it terminated abruptly in a jagged edge of twisted steel. Most of the raised fo'c'sle had been blown away by shell-fire before the *Alerte* submerged, but between the rise of the fo'c'sle and the conning-tower, which was practically intact, the false deck was still in position.

Making his way to the forehatch—it was originally the torpedo-hatch—Broadmayne tried to open it. Being secured from below, the metal cover resisted his efforts. Foiled in that direction, the Sub retraced his steps to the conning-tower hatchway. As he did so, a dark object above the rail attracted his attention. It was Cain's ensign—the skull and cross-bones—still lashed to a boathook. When the *Alerte* submerged, the natural tendency of the ash stave was to float, but the metal hook engaging in one of the shrouds of the housed foremast had held it down. Even the explosion of the depth-charge had failed to dislodge it.

Drawing his knife, Broadmayne cut the emblem of piracy adrift and secured it to his belt. Then he resumed his investigations.

The conning-tower was also secured and clipped from the inside. Was it possible, he wondered, that Cain and his companions were still alive in the apparently intact and air-tight for'ard compartment of the hull?

Going aft, the Sub lowered himself cautiously over the riven edge of the hull-plating, lest a sharp projection should penetrate his inflated dress. Then, signing to his fellow-diver to remain, he switched on his submarine electric lamp and crept forward inside the hull.

The first twenty feet or so was greatly encumbered with wreckage, but on passing through the transverse bulkhead, the watertight door of which had been blown inwards, Broadmayne found that there was little damage done to the 'midships section.

As a matter of precaution and to save negotiating the débris-strewn motor-room again, the Sub unclipped and threw open the conning-tower hatch. Then proceeding for'ard he found that the door between the 'midships section and the bow compartment was wide open. It swung freely on its hinges, although the straining the hull had received made it impossible for the usually close-fitting door to close.

In the bow compartment, Broadmayne searched diligently for the bodies of Cain and his companions, but without success. Then he came to the door of the air-lock, by which a man in a diving suit could leave the submarine when the vessel was lying on the bottom. The door was shut. Usually six diving suits and twenty-four life-saving helmets were ranged along the bulkhead. The latter were there, jammed against the curved roof under the deck, but four of the self-contained diving-dresses were absent.

Prising back the locking-gear of the door of the

air-lock the Sub entered the compartment.   It
was, as he expected, empty, but the hinged flap
on the outside hull-plating was open.

Captain Cain had made a bid for life and freedom.
Whether he had succeeded or had been caught by
the explosion before he had got well clear of the
ship remains an unsolved problem.

There was no need for further investigation.
Broadmayne returned to his companions by means
of the conning-tower hatchway. Together they
dropped over the side and found the other diver
waiting by the distance cords.

In single file, the man with the air-tube leading
as the attendants in the boat slowly heaved in his
air-tube and life-line, the three made their way to
the shot-rope.

Then came the tedious ascent. To go up
quickly and without a pause was not to be thought
of. The great risk of being killed by excessive
blood-pressure on the brain had to be guarded
against. Slowly Broadmayne was hoisted, kept
hanging for several minutes and then hoisted a few
feet more, until at length he felt himself being
grasped under the arms and assisted into the boat.
Then his helmet glass removed, he sat and gasped,
gratefully inhaling copious draughts of fresh air.

As soon as the other divers were in the boat the
anchors were weighed and a course shaped for the
Canvey, which was steaming slowly in wide circles
round the scene of the wreck.

" Satisfactory   job ? "   inquired   Raxworthy
laconically.

" After-part blown clean away, sir," replied

Broadmayne. " All the other compartments are full of water."

" Any signs of bodies ? "

" No, sir."

" Did you see any ? " inquired the lieutenant-commander, turning to the seamen-divers.

" No, sir," answered the man who used the air-tube pattern dress. " I went right round the wreck on the outside—starboard side first and then port to the full extent of my life-line. No doubt, sir, the men in her were blown to bits. There was a plate torn right out close to her bows, I noticed. That shows how strong the force of the explosion was."

Captain Raxworthy nodded.

" Then there's no possible doubt about it," he remarked to the officers standing by. " Well, our work's done. The *Alerte's* destroyed." He paused and glanced over the side across the tranquil waters of the bay. " I'm rather sorry for that chap Cain," he continued. " He evidently was a bit of a sport. I'd like to have met him."

Before sunset, H.M.S. *Canvey* was steaming to the nor'ard, homeward bound.

.   .   .   .

Pengelly was found guilty and sentenced to a long term of penal servitude. The surviving members of the *Alerte's* ship's company received lighter sentences, but of sufficient severity to deter others who might wish to emulate the misdeeds of the captain and crew of the pirate submarine.

Gerald Broadmayne, lately promoted to lieutenant in consideration of his services in the operations against the *Alerte*, had to give evidence at the trial. But there were two points upon which he was silent : Cain's real name and former rank in the Royal Navy was one ; the other was the incident of the air-lock.

Often Broadmayne thought of that air-lock, especially when he gazed at the skull and crossbones bedecked relic of the *Alerte*. It was to him a fascinating and yet unsolved mystery. Did Cain succeed in his desperate effort to escape ? Or did the bed of the land-locked Bahia Arenas hold the secret of the fate of the captain of the pirate submarine until the sea gives up its dead ?

CAPTAIN CAIN

CONTENTS

CONTENTS

CAPTAIN CAIN

CHAPTER I

CAPTAIN CAIN REAPPEARS

" NOW, you treacherous mutineers!" thundered Captain Cain, of the pirate submarine *Alerte*, "I'll give you one minute to get your lifebelts. You're to choose between being eaten by sharks or hanging by your necks in a British prison!"

Before the astounded men, who had so basely turned against their skipper, could realise the significance of the pirate captain's words, Cain made for the only open hatchway. There he stopped, his eyes roving whimsically over the dumbfounded men, a supercilious smile lurking in his heavy bull-dog features.

"Forty-five seconds more!" announced Cain in cold, level tones.

The next instant Captain Cain disappeared from the view of the demoralised pirate crew. The conning-tower hatch descended with a metallic clang.

In the electrically lit interior he noticed that Barnard, the faithful boatswain, was at the wheels actuating the valves of the ballast tanks. Close to him stood the other loyal men, Davidge and Cross.

" Stand by ! " ordered Cain, glancing at his wristlet watch.

" Ay, ay, sir," replied the bo'sun, tentatively easing one of the valves a fraction of an inch.

Overhead came a terrific crash that shook the vessel from end to end.

Captain Cain raised one eyebrow—a favourite trick of his. He knew the significance of that detonation. The avenging cruiser *Canvey* had commenced to shell her victim. On the metallic deck overhead the shuffle of many boots told clearly enough that the miserable remnant of the mutineering crew was in a state of panic.

Again the pirate captain glanced at the watch, nodded curtly.

" Submerge : all tanks ! " he ordered.

During the brief period between the giving of the order and the settling of the submarine on the bed of Bahia Arenas, Captain Cain remained as still and silent as a statue. His active mind was reviewing not only the present situation but practically the whole of the career of the vessel that was even now doomed to destruction.

He recalled the circumstances under which the scrapped submarine R 81 was converted into a vessel, the *Alerte*, that looked like a tramp, but was actually an armed craft still retaining her diving capabilities. There was Pengelly, his second in command, that treacherous, incapable babbler who for a time had supplanted Cain as skipper of the *Alerte* to give place meekly to the indomitable captain when he found himself in a tight corner. . . . Then his mind dwelt upon the unexpected arrival of those two bright lads, Broadmayne and Vyse. They were, he remembered, a pretty tough proposition. His estimation of them was none the less on that account. . . . The *Alerte's* successive scraps with the *Cap Hoorn*, the *Surcouf* and the *Villamel*, whereby Cain had aroused the ire of Germans, Frenchmen and Spaniards ; the courteous treatment he had accorded to the Yankee *Bronx City*, and finally the mutiny and the pursuit by the British warship *Canvey* brought his hurried reminiscences down to the present moment.

In the back of his mind Captain Cain felt a slight resentment against the *Canvey*. In all his unlawful dealings he had studiously avoided any act of aggression that would affect British ships and shipping ; and it seemed hardly poetic justice that the *Alerte* should be destroyed by the action of a vessel flying the white ensign. On the other hand, he realised that as a pirate every man's hand was 'gainst his ; he was a fugitive, an outlaw either on the face of the waters or beneath the surface. In short, he was being treated as vermin to be exterminated without compunction.

A dull thud as the *Alerte* grounded upon the sandy bottom of the West African lagoon coincided with the conclusion of the pirate captain's train of thought. Although trapped in a steel cage, he was not " going out " without a desperate effort to save himself and the lives of the three loyal men who had risked everything on his behalf.

It was a decidedly lucky circumstance, whatever the cause, that the avenging cruiser had not continued to shell the *Alerte* as she submerged. Possibly, he decided, the white-livered mutineers had shown the white flag.

" You've got the rapid-flooding valve-plate, Barnard ? " he inquired of the bo'sun. " Good, now listen ; it's no use thinking that by lying doggo the cruiser will give us a miss ; she won't. In a few minutes she'll start depth-charging us ; so get busy. Now, all hands will don diving-dresses, and proceed through the air-lock. On gaining the bottom you will proceed to the starboard whaler, disconnect the release-gear and man-handle her along. With decent luck we ought to be well outside the radius of action of a depth-charge before they start operations. Yes, take your automatics and fifty rounds. Look lively, there ! "

In record time the four men had put on their self-contained diving-dresses, adjusted the helmets and satisfied themselves that the air-supply contained in reservoirs strapped to their backs was in working order.

Communication save by signs and tapping the metal head-gear was now out of the question. One after another the four entered the air-lock in which only a feeble electric lamp was burning. The water-tight door was closed. There was no need to secure it, for the pressure of the admitted water would quickly jamb it immovably against the bulkhead.

Then Cain opened a valve, admitting a steady flow of sea-water at high pressure. In less than a minute the pirate captain and his companions were immersed, the water thrusting strongly against their rubbered canvas suits and at the same time relieving the wearers of the hitherto handicapping weight of their leaden-soled boots and of the lumps of metal suspended from their corselets.

The light went out, apparently by the pressure of the water against the comparatively fragile bulb. For a few moments Cain fumbled for the locking gear that held the exterior door in position ; found it and wrestled with the recalcitrant door. At last it swung open, revealing a greenish haze— the sunlit water at ten fathoms beneath the surface.

One by one the men made their way through the open door in the hull of the *Alerte*, the pirate captain being the last to leave his ship, and trod on the hard, sandy bottom of the bay. Their first instinct was to put as great a distance as possible between them and the doomed sub-marine in the least possible time, for at any moment might come a tremendous explosion that would destroy them in an instant. It required all the will - power at their command to follow their captain as he felt his way along the bilge-keel of the submerged vessel. To increase their alarm the water overhead was continually darkened by swiftly-moving objects, while occasionally hide-ously dismembered portions of what had once been their comrades sank slowly, to be followed

in their descent by enormous sharks. Captain
Cain and his companions had little difficulty in
guessing at the fate of several of the mutineers.

At length the four survivors arrived at the
starboard quarter of the *Alerte*. Twenty feet
above their heads they could discern the outlines of the whaler—a steel-built boat from which
a plate with the quick-flooding device had
been surreptitiously removed and retained by
the bo'sun just previous to the *Alerte's* last
submergence.

A wire rope trailed overside, its flake resting on
the bottom. Seizing it, one of the men swarmed
up with surprising ease, clambered over the gunwale and tripped the releasing gear. The whaler
with the man in it dropped gently to the floor of
the lagoon.

The boat was eighteen feet in length, built of
pressed galvanised steel sheets, and provided with
hermetically-sealed air-chambers that, although
insufficient to impart buoyancy, reduced the dead
weight of the submerged craft to about forty
pounds. This provision had been made in order
to maintain as nearly as possible the *Alerte's*
metacentric height whether submerged or otherwise; and Captain Cain thanked his lucky stars
for the foresight that was now reaping its reward,
but in a different manner to that originally
intended.

Davidge and Cross lifted one end of the whaler,
one on either side of the bow thwart; Captain
Cain and the bo'sun took the almost negligible
weight of the after-end, and as quickly as their

somewhat impeded movement would allow the four set off towards the shore—a distance of about half a mile.

The firm sandy bottom made good going. It was not uniformly shelving. In places there were depressions, in others submarine mounds that approached within three fathoms of the surface. Cain, as he occasionally checked his course by means of a luminous compass, realised that if the British cruiser had carried a seaplane, their chances of escape would have been minimised almost if not quite to zero. In places there were dense patches of weed and kelp which had to be avoided. Fortunately these grew in comparatively small and isolated groups, but had they stretched in long lines parallel with the beach it would have entailed long and possibly fruitless efforts to attempt to hack a way through the barrier of tenacious marine growth.

On and on the four plodded with their burden, expecting every moment to hear the terrific explosion that was to give the *Alerte* her *coup de grâce*, and perhaps to be hurled on their faces by the surge of violently displaced water. According to Cain's calculation they were already beyond the effective limit of the expected depth-charge, but the possibility of being severely shaken was still to be taken into account.

Almost at every step fishes of weird aspect darted frantically away at the approach of the unusual apparition. Gigantic crab, pausing at first to contemplate an onslaught or a possible victim, scuttled sideways for safety, leaving behind them a trail of stirred-up sand. Eels too, distorted by the water, glided to and fro, showing more daring than the rest of the submarine denizens of the lagoon.

Yet there was a noticeable absence of sharks. Although these fearsome creatures will hesitate to attack a diver, possibly on account of the huge and distorted appearance of the man in his copper helmet, they have been known to put up a terrible fight. The four men were thankful that no sharks did appear ; but they knew that not so very far behind them a ghastly tragedy was being enacted in which easily-gotten food was the factor that had relieved them of the monster's presence.

The bed was now shelving rapidly. The depth had decreased to a maximum of three fathoms. Only a short distance separated the fugitives from the beach, and up till now no explosion had taken place.

A fresh situation was thereby created. It wanted but an hour to sunset, but the rays of the setting orb were shining straight on to the shore, while the avenging cruiser would be silhouetted against the light. It was, consequently, a highly risky business for Captain Cain and his companions to emerge from the water. As likely as not their burnished copper helmets would be detected from the ship the moment they broke surface. Their only chance, short of remaining submerged until after sunset, was to attempt to find the mouth of a small river which Cain had previously noted. It flowed into the lagoon by means of a right-angled channel, the seaward side of which was screened by a ledge of rocks covered with reeds ; but in the circumstances this shelter required some finding. They might easily miss it and perhaps skirt the coast in the opposite direction in a vain attempt to strike the bed of the stream.

At last the depth decreased to one and a half fathoms. It was inadvisable to proceed nearer inshore. Cain decided that if direction had been fairly maintained during the submarine walk, the mouth of the river ought to be to the right.

It would have been a simple matter to wait until dark. There was an ample reserve of air in each of the reservoirs. But to Captain Cain inaction was almost unbearable. He was always fretting to be up and doing. Possessed of superabundant energy, the ability to do without sleep for sixty hours at a stretch and to feel no ill-effect from it, and a restless disposition, he refused to take the simple path and wait. He wanted, if possible, to witness the destruction of the submarine upon which he had built his hopes of untold wealth—hopes that had crumpled to dust leaving him worse off than before.

A shipless, homeless fugitive, possessing nothing of material value but the diving-dress and the few things in his possession, Cain might well be forgiven if he had chucked up the sponge. The pirate captain had been cast in a stern mould. He realised that he was alive when almost every one else would consider him to be as dead as mutton. Not only alive ; he stood a fair chance of going on living ; and that qualification he considered to be half the battle. He meant by sheer grit and determina-

2

tion to win through and retrieve the disaster of his previous venture.

Although by no means a vindictive man, he smiled grimly when he thought of the fate of his partner, Paul Pengelly. He had distrusted the man from the very first.

" Hang it all ! " he soliloquised. " Give me a fellow who can smile decently and not have a perpetual grin on his face like a sea-sick monkey. Well, Pengelly's goose is cooked anyway. Either he's food for shark or else he's in the cells. There's one satisfaction, I shan't have to wring his neck, the double-faced swine ! "

Signing to his companions to slue the boat round, Captain Cain shaped a fresh course parallel, as he hoped, to the beach. Before the party had traversed a hundred yards they found the sand giving place to black slime. By this time the sun's rays were so oblique that the bed of the lagoon was almost in darkness.

Davidge and Cross hesitated. They had struck the soft patch before the skipper and the bo'sun. Finding themselves in danger of becoming stuck in the ooze they dropped their burden.

The captain signed to his " opposite number " to stand easy, and made his way to where the two seamen were held up. He, too, went ankle-deep in the tenacious mud, but the discovery did not in the least cause him any anxiety. On the contrary, it indicated that he had found the object of his quest—the mouth of the stream.

Signing to Cross to take his place aft, Cain grasped the bow gunwale, and as soon as the others had taken up their share of the burden the party set off keeping to the edge of the well-defined mud.   In another five minutes the captain found his helmet was only a few inches below the surface and that the sun was right in front of him instead of behind as hitherto.   They were safely inside the mouth of the river.

Still exercising the strictest caution the men emerged, dragging the whaler until its snout was out of water.   Then, standing in a ring, each diver unscrewed the observation window in the other's head-dress and removed the helmet.

On taking his bearings, Cain found that the party was screened from observation by the ridge of rocks which rose nearly twenty feet above the surface of the lagoon on one side and the muddy river on the other.   Smartly he was divested of his diving-dress, and without waiting for the others climbed stiffly up the irregular wall of rock.   Quick to take advantage of cover he made no attempt to stand, but, throwing himself flat upon the summit of the ridge, carefully parted the tall grass and reeds that obstructed his outlook.

What he saw did not surprise him, although it caused intense interest.   The cruiser *Canvey* was under way, but instead of making seawards—which she would almost certainly do had her mission been accomplished—she was steaming slowly and almost bows on to the spot where the fugitives had taken refuge.   At about a cable's length from her bows (although from Captain Cain's point of view it was difficult to estimate the distance correctly) floated a barrel on which

was a staff with a square of bunting that hung
listlessly in the motionless air.   The pirate captain
knew that the buoy marked the resting-place of
the *Alerte*.

" She's not done in yet, sir," remarked Barnard,
who had taken off his diving-suit and had just taken
up a position a few feet from his captain.

" No," replied Cain shortly.   " And don't
flatten the grass down like that.   We'll be spotted
if you aren't careful."

" Very good, sir," replied the bo'sun, and relapsed into silence.

Standing out boldly and darkly against the
setting sun, the *Canvey* approached yet nearer to
her unseen victim and increased speed.   A heavy
object leapt from her poop and struck the water,
throwing up a shower of foam.   The cruiser, star-
boarding helm, was rapidly turning to port when
a tremendous upheaval of water was followed by
the vibrating roar of the explosion of the depth-
charge.   The hitherto placid waters of the lagoon
were violently agitated, miniature rollers breaking on the beach almost at the foot of the captain
of the destroyed pirate submarine as if to bear
tidings of the loss to the redoubtable Cain.   Even
the reeds swayed in the rush of displaced air
following the concussion.

Barnard gave a sidelong glance at his superior
officer.   Not a muscle of Captain Cain's face
twitched.   With set jaw and unflickering eyelids
he remained motionless—thinking, scheming.

A minute or so later the pirate skipper broke
the silence.

" They're not wasting much time," he observed.
" Apparently they're sending down a diver to
make certain. . . . Well, Barnard, they won't find
pieces of us."

The bo'sun nodded soberly.

" Think they'll send ashore to have a look round,
sir ? " he inquired.

" Might," admitted the captain.   " If so, we'll
have to make ourselves scarce and leave no tracks.
But I fancy they're in a bit of a hurry. . . . Now,
you men !   Be careful.   The light's playing right
on us."

They waited and watched ; saw the diving-
party descend, reappear.   Then the boats were
hoisted up and turned in, and the *Canvey*, gathering
way, swung about and headed for the entrance to
the lagoon.   A quarter of an hour later she was
swallowed up in the rapidly growing darkness.

CHAPTER II

THE FUGITIVES

"NOW, my lads!" exclaimed Captain Cain briskly. "We're a quiet little party all alone. There's no reason why we shouldn't make ourselves comfortable."

He sprang easily to his feet. The others, stiff with the prolonged spell of inaction following their strenuous efforts, got up slowly and fell to chafing their numbed limbs. They felt down and out. The exciting events of the last few days culminating in a dare-devil dash for safety from the doomed submarine had left them limp and disheartened. They were without food, without shelter, outcasts on a strange, inhospitable shore.

Cain's energetic spirit never failed him. He knew only too well that in the present circumstances activity would be the only antidote to the poison of despair that was consuming the minds of his companions.

"Look lively, lads!" he said encouragingly. "We'll get the boat up above high-water mark, and we'll have a roof over our heads at all events. Has any one any 'bacca?"

Davidge produced about an ounce of dark twist

in a disreputable-looking pouch. The others had
to admit that they were without any of the fragrant
and comforting weed.

" Too much of a lash up at the finish to think
of that, sir," added Cross.

" Then 'tis as well I thought for you," rejoined
the captain, with a laugh. " I took the precaution
of putting a couple of pounds of flake in one of my
pockets—and matches in a damp-proof case. So
up with the boat, my lads, and then spell-ho and a
quiet smoke."

It was an easy though somewhat lengthy task
to get the boat up the beach. Thanks to the fact
that the valve-plate had been removed, the men
were spared the irksome business of baling. As
they dragged the boat a foot at a time up the
shelving beach, the water ran away rapidly, and
by the time the whaler's heel was clear of the river,
she had drained herself. Then, as a matter of precaution, the valve-plate was bolted in position so
that the boat would be ready for use when required.
She was then turned bottom up and supported
with her gunwale about a couple of feet from the
ground by means of piled-up stones.

Tobacco was then served out, and all hands
had a much-needed " stand-easy." They smoked
almost in silence, except for an occasional comment
that for the most part failed to elicit a response.

Although he was impatient to disclose his
immediate plans, Captain Cain wisely forbore to
put the case before his men at this stage of the
proceedings. He was content with the knowledge
that they were in a better frame of mind, thanks

to the soothing influence of the tobacco. Day-light, and with it food (for he was confident that although they were now hungry there was no prospect of starvation), would put a different complexion on things, especially after a night's rest.

" Now to sleep, lads ! " he announced, when the glowing bowls were extinguished. " I'm going to keep watch."

" But——" protested the bo'sun.

" I'm keeping watch," reiterated the skipper firmly. " If you like to relieve me at two bells (5 a.m.) for a couple of hours, Barnard, that's all I'll want."

The two seamen also expressed their readiness to stand a trick, but Cain would have none of it. It was an easy sacrifice on his part, and daylight would bring its reward in the form of a tolerant and easily persuaded audience.

With his loaded automatic in the right-hand pocket of his coat, Cain crawled from underneath the whaler and began to pace to and fro. It was a sultry night, and in the captain's opinion it was infinitely preferable to patrol the stretch of firm level sand to being cooped up underneath the up-turned boat.

Overhead the stars shone brilliantly with the customary splendour of tropic climes. Not a breath of wind disturbed the palm trees, not a ripple lapped the edge of the lagoon, although the surf boomed sullenly against the outlying reef. A faint sickly smell from the mangroves hung in the still air. The only sound of life was the stertorous breathing of the now sleeping men and the *ping* of the deadly mosquitoes.

In his silent beat Cain was thinking deeply. He summed up the present situation with merciless accuracy. Here he was with three companions of a different social standing. They were practically stranded on a deserted stretch of coast miles from the nearest British stations on the Gambia. Nearer, of course, were the French outposts on either side of Cape Verde, but Cain meant to give them a wide berth.

He made a mental stocktaking. The sole assets of the fugitives were the clothes they stood up in, four diving-suits, now not likely to be required, automatic pistols and ammunition, a couple of knives, a few personal effects of little value, and the boat with her equipment—oars, crutches, baler and compass—all of which had been secured to prevent loss when the *Alerte* submerged.

Within a few miles was the spot where Pengelly had buried a quantity of loot from the captured Yankee ship, *Bronx City*. Amongst the plunder there might be something of practical use. Cain decided to burke his scruples concerning American-owned booty. After all, he decided, he didn't plunder the vessel: that was the work of his treacherous partner. It was now a case of needs must, as far as Cain was concerned.

Then the pirate captain's thoughts turned to the future. He was an outlaw. He could never return to England. Officially, he supposed, he was dead. That gave him a new lease of life, a suggestion that seemed somewhat a paradox. He

had—or he hoped he had—money safely invested
in South America. Could he but lay hands on it
he would be content to settle down to a relatively
quiet life in a foreign land. Then there were the
men who had stuck to him through thick and thin
and who, he confidently expected, would continue
to do so. Well, he wasn't going to let them
down ; his perverted code of honour was sufficiently
straight to urge him to see that, to the best of
his power, they should receive a fitting reward for
their loyalty and devotion.

A mosquito settled on the captain's cheek
He caught and ground it between his powerful
fingers because it irritated him. Although fully
aware of the risk of malaria communicated by
these tropical pests, it was not fear that prompted
the action. Cain thought himself immune—he
had been salted years before. To him the atten
tion of the mosquito was symbolic of a difficulty
to be brushed aside firmly and resolutely.

Suddenly the steadily-flowing river was rippled
by something that attracted the captain's atten
tion. An ordinary person might not have noticed
the diverging wake under the starlit sky. He
paused and regarded the movement intently ; his
hand fingered the butt of his automatic.

Then, above the surface, emerged a long dark
object—something endowed with life. It was an
enormous crocodile. Slowly it drew itself clear
appeared to sniff the miasmic air appreciatively
and proceeded to make its way towards the whaler
and the men sleeping soundly beneath its shelter.

Cain might have aroused his men, but that

would disturb their well-earned rest; the same
objection applied to the use of the automatic, a
relatively feeble weapon of offence against the
armour-plated brute. Besides, he was loth to make
use of firearms lest there be any human inhabitants,
and he had no wish to attract the attention of
any one to the refugees on the beach of Bahia
Arenas.

With a quick, decisive movement Cain withdrew
his hand from his pocket, stooped and picked up
a couple of pebbles, each nearly as large as his
fist. Coolly and deliberately, as if he were driving
off an inquisitive dog, Cain strode to meet the
saurian. The brute halted and raised its scaly
head. Cain could see its small beady eyes blinking
in the starlight. Then, resuming its struggling
motion, the brute advanced with wide-open jaws.
Cain also maintained his forward movement and
hurled one of the stones at the crocodile's mouth.
Ere the missile struck, the brute had snapped its
jaws. The stone clattered and glanced harmlessly
from the protective plating over the skull. It
stopped; then prepared to close.

At less than three yards distance Cain, with all
the force of his muscular arm, sent the second
stone hurling through the air. This time the
missile hit the brute fairly on the point of the
lower jaw. So severe was the impact that the
thrower had good reason to believe that it was
one of the crocodile's teeth that had " carried
away."

The reptile had had enough. Lashing its tail
furiously as a defence against a rear attack, it

turned and made for the river. Not content with his success, Cain followed, picking up stones as he went and hurling them at the discomfited brute until with a tremendous succession of splashes it took refuge in the water.

Captain Cain's act of deliberate audacity had not passed unnoticed, although he was in absolute ignorance of the fact.

Barnard, the bo'sun, roused from his sleep, had seen his skipper secure his missiles. Realising that there was something of a dangerous nature on hand, the bo'sun crawled from under the whaler and quietly followed in Cain's tracks. He saw the crocodile. His hand flew to the butt of his automatic. But when the pirate captain advanced with the utmost intrepidity, Barnard brought up all standing, but ready at the critical moment to rush to the other's aid.

When the saurian turned and retreated, pursued by a steady discharge of stones, the bo'sun promptly returned to his bed of sand.

" 'Strewth," he muttered, " that chap's got nerves of iron ! He's the horse for my money I'd follow him from now till the crows come home."

The pirate captain resumed his beat. For more than an hour nothing occurred to disturb the train of his thoughts. He was beginning to feel tired—a sensation of lassitude confined solely to his legs, although his brain was as active as ever. He missed the " give " of a deck ; even the firm sand seemed hard and unyielding compared with the limited promenade afforded by the *Alerte's* bridge.

Another dark object attracted his attention—
this time on the seaward side of the tongue of
land.   At the sight of it, Cain's eyes glinted with
satisfaction, for the inverted dish-like creature was
a turtle—and turtle meant nourishing food.

He stopped, turned and stole softly to the whaler,
and without disturbing the sleepers secured one of
the stout ash oars.   Armed with this, he made
straight for the water's edge.   The turtle was then
about fifty yards away and crawling awkwardly
up the belt of sand.

Cain waited patiently until he knew he was
certain to cut off the animal's retreat ; then he
dashed straight for it.   Thrusting the loom of the
oar underneath the turtle, the captain levered his
prize over on its back.   In that position it was
helpless, its head and flippers floundering in the
air in a vain endeavour to right itself.   With one
blow of his knife, Cain severed the turtle's vertebra,
cleaned and folded the blade, and resumed his
vigil.

Once only during the long night did he consult
his watch.   He was not far out in his estimate.
It was a quarter to five.

At the hour he roused Barnard by a firm pressure
on the man's hand—a sure way to awake a sleeper
without causing him to start or call out.

" Two bells ! " whispered Cain, and backed out
to await the bo'sun's appearance.

" You may have a bit of a bother with crocodiles,
Barnard," he remarked.   " On the other hand, you
may not.   If you do, don't shoot on any account.
Unless you hit the brute in the eye or throat you'd

merely irritate the thing. In any case, I don't want any firing, but call me. You understand ? "

" Ay, ay, sir," replied Barnard.

" Have you a watch ? " asked Cain.

" I have, sir," answered the bo'sun, " but something's gone wrong with it since we left the ship."

" Then take this one," rejoined the captain. " Call all hands, myself included, at six bells."

Thirty seconds later, Cain was in a sound, dreamless sleep, as if he had not a care or a worry in the wide world ; nor did he stir until the bo'sun's time-honoured call of " Show a leg, there ! " brought him back to wakefulness, refreshed in mind and body to assume the responsibilities of another day.

" Now, grub, lads ! " he announced. " Davidge, you start a fire ; boil some of the turtle in the baler, and try your hand at frying turtle steaks. Cross will bear a hand. Mr. Barnard, I want you to come with me. Unless I'm much mistaken, we'll find some corn-stuff over there."

The bo'sun chuckled to himself.

" The Old Man's finding his feet again," he soliloquised. " He's started to call me ' Mister ' again."

Cain's surmise proved to be correct, for on a fairly open patch of ground that extended a long way into the forest he found plenty of wild maize, and in the forest itself a species of tree bearing something that had a close resemblance to the bread-fruit of the Pacific Islands.

" Think it's safe to eat it, sir ? " queried Barnard doubtfully.

" I'll start on it, anyway," decided the skipper.

" If it don't turn me up within the next twelve hours, I think you need have no fear about eating it."

They came back laden with the fruit and sheaves of ripe maize, to find that the cooks were well advanced with their task. The savoury smell greeted their nostrils a good fifty yards away.

" This is what I calls all right, sir," said Davidge, with a grin. " I could stick this out for a month of Sundays."

" That's good, then," rejoined the captain, although he was quite aware that turtle as an article of food for any continuous length of time speedily becomes objectionable. He remembered that there have been instances in which crews have mutinied on account of their being supplied with turtle instead of beef. But the principal business at the present moment was to give the men a satisfying and appetising meal—the surest method of getting the men to fall in with his plans for the immediate future.

CHAPTER III

VANISHED PLUNDER

"NOW, lads!" began Captain Cain briskly, as the men, their hunger appeased, were once more indulging in the luxury known to blue-jackets as "three draws and a spit." "We'll hold a council of war. I said ' council of war ' purposely, because, as you are aware, we're at war with mankind. We're fugitives on the face of the earth. The wilds of Australia or the backwoods of Canada are as dangerous to us as the heart of London—perhaps more so, since the world is small when one doesn't want it to be. The general presumption is that we're dead, lying six fathoms deep out there ; but that doesn't justify our going home quietly and turning over a new leaf. In short, we're forced to live on our wits, and if necessary use brute strength to obtain the direst necessaries of life.

"Now, then, I've been thinking things out. As you know, that rogue, Pengelly, cached a lot of booty taken from the *Bronx City*. The spot is within six miles of here. I mean to find the stuff, which will, I hope, provide sufficient for our immediate needs. There's gold dust, I believe, although I didn't actually see it."

" Quite right, sir," agreed Cross; " I seed Pengelly and a party hide the loot. Afterwards 'e gave every man a chance to make a note of the bearings in case of accident."

" And probably gave the wrong bearings," added Cain. "However, he's not likely to be hanging around over Tom Tiddler's ground—something will be hanging round his neck before very long, unless I'm very much mistaken. But to proceed. We've a boat in which we ought to be able to make our way to within a few miles of the Gambia. There we ought with luck to be able to be picked up by a vessel bound for South America. We must decide what yarn to pitch into them later on. Once in South America there'll be heaps of opportunities of making a fortune in a very little while. How ? you ask. Wait for the first revolution that crops up. You won't have to wait very long. Then seize opportunity with both hands, especially if opportunity is ballasted with gold.

" In any case, you stick to me, and I'll stick to you, and pull you through. You've all been proper jonnick in the past, and I won't forget it. You know I'm a man of my word. Now it's close on dead low water. In half an hour the young flood will be setting up the Faltuba River, so let's get a move on."

The boat was righted and launched. A quantity of maize was placed in the after-locker and a plentiful supply of turtle flesh hung up to dry in the now powerful rays of the sun. Each man examined and cleaned his pistol so as to be pre-

3

pared for any emergency that might involve the use of the weapons.

By this time the tide had changed. All along the shore the sand was discoloured by a dark line —oil from the depth-charged submarine that had drifted ashore during the night. A hundred yards or so away was a barrel with a sodden, smoke-begrimed piece of bunting hanging disconsolately from a staff passing through the bung. It was the mark-buoy the *Canvey* had laid down to indicate the position of the submerged *Alerte*. Of other flotsam there was no sign.

It required quite a tough tussle with the oars to take the whaler out of the mouth of the little river, but once on the lagoon progress was easy, especially as the estuary of the Faltuba was reached. Every one, Cain included, took a turn at the oars, and although no great amount of energy was displayed, the task soon became decidedly exhausting.

The sun beat down with terrific violence, and the only protection for the men's heads was the red woollen caps they had hastily put on when they made their hurried exit from the doomed submarine. Their feet, too, were bare, the men having discarded their ordinary foot-gear when they put on their diving-suits.

Not only were the direct rays of the sun unpleasantly hot. The reflected glare from the mirror-like surface of the water was almost as fierce. The metal-work of the boat was so hot that to touch it with the bare hand would result in a painful blister.

Presently the sandy shores of the lagoon gave place to the mud-banked, mangrove-bounded river. Here the conditions were worse, for added to the heat in the sickly miasmic mist that ascended in dense columns from the now turgid water, to disperse before it rose high enough to form a screen to the rays of the sun.

The river had afforded a depressing aspect when viewed from the *Alerte*; now viewed but a few feet from the water's edge it looked the absolute limit of desolation and discomfort.

"Nearly there, sir," announced Barnard. The bo'sun was rowing stroke. He had wiped the perspiration from his eyes by the simple expedient of rubbing them with the moist sleeve of his shirt. For the last quarter of an hour he had been rowing blindly, for the sweat was pouring down his face. "Just round that bend. A couple o' hundred yards, or three, maybe."

Cain grunted. In spite of the physical strength and grim determination he was feeling the effect of the hothouse-like conditions; but realising that he could stand it far better than either Davidge or Cross, he was voluntarily extending his spell at the heavy ash oar.

The bend negotiated, the landing-place appeared in sight, but now an unexpected hitch occurred. The booty had been taken ashore from the *Alerte* at about high-water. It was now only the second hour of the flood, and a hundred yards of soft, vilely-smelling mud separated the water from the river-bank. To attempt to traverse that distance even by the aid of boards was impossible. The slime was so soft that an oar thrust blade downwards as far as the loom met with little resistance and failed to find hard bottom.

There was nothing for it but to wait until the tide rose sufficiently to float the whaler over the mud. That meant at least three hours of tedious inaction in the miasmic air.

Thrusting an oar into the mud and bending the painter to it the men let the whaler swing to the strong flood-tide, hoping fervently that this flimsy mooring would hold. Then they prepared to endure the discomforts as best they might.

At the captain's suggestion they stretched their diving-suits from gunwale to gunwale to form some sort of protection from the sun, as the men lay in the bottom-boards. The rubbered canvas *did* serve as a shade, but underneath the air was stifling. Myriads of flies appeared and added to the general discomfort. They settled on hands, feet and faces until the sun-scorched flesh was black with the troublesome insects. It was almost useless to attempt to brush them away, for the next instant the flies swarmed again to the attack. To make matters worse, the sun-dried turtle flesh turned putrid and added its quota to the variety of offensive odours. The meat was promptly ditched.

In vain the men tried to smoke. Flies hovered over the glowing pipe-bowls, collapsing in dozens upon the hot tobacco. Even Davidge, who in times of shortage had been known to smoke a weird mixture of tea-leaves and rope-yarn, drew the line at flies in his pipe.

Hardly a word was spoken. With parched

mouths and swollen tongues the men sat in silence,
looking from time to time with blood-shot eyes
at the slowly rising level of the water and at the
tardy retreat of that expanse of mud which
separated them from the key that was to open
for them the gate of fresh adventure and good
fortune.

" 'S'pose tide 'll make high enough, sir ? "
hazarded the bo'sun.

Cain nodded.

" Bound to," he replied shortly.   " New moon
was the day before yesterday."

In any case, he mused, they would have to be
mighty smart in recovering the booty, if they
didn't want the whaler left high and dry for
another ten hours.

" Ditch-crawling isn't in my line," he concluded.
" Give me the open sea any day of the week.   Confound the mud ! "

At an hour before the expected time of high-
water, Cain roused himself.   The flood-tide had
eased off considerably, although there was a distinct
strain on the painter.   The loom of the oar was
six feet beneath the surface.

" We can do it now, men ! " he declared.

The others bestirred themselves.   The oar was
recovered and the boat urged shorewards.   Thirty
feet from the bank she smelt the mud.

" Keep going ! " shouted the captain, and leaning forward he lent his weight to the stroke oar.
Finally the whaler lost way ten feet from the shore
with a bank of liquid mud of her own making
showing up on either side.

" Try with an oar for'ard ! " ordered Cain.

The blade struck hard bottom at eighteen inches.

" Good enough ! " declared the captain, and using the oar as a jumping-pole he cleared the remaining expanse of slime, landing cleanly on the hard ground. Davidge followed, and having thrown the slack of the painter ashore, Cross rejoined his chum. The bo'sun was the last to essay the feat, landing on all-fours in six inches of particularly obnoxious slime.

The painter having been secured to a snag, the whole party hurried to the spot where Pengelly had buried the booty. Barnard had not the slightest doubt that he would be able to recognise the spot without the aid of cross-bearings.

" There it is, sir ! " he exclaimed. " In that hollow."

Notwithstanding the heat, the party broke into a run. Cain was the first to reach the much-desired site. When he did, he stopped dead.

So did the others. The soil had only recently been disturbed, but disturbed it had been. Instead of an almost imperceptible mound already covered with coarse vegetation, a yawning cavity was exposed to view, but of the eagerly-wished-for plunder not a sign !

For full thirty seconds no one spoke. The eyes of the other three travelled first from the rifled hiding-place to the impassive features of the captain and then back to the scene of their shattered hopes. After all their endeavours, their

discomforts and their sanguine expectations was
this to be their reward ?

" Some one's been 'ere afore us ! " exclaimed
Cross.

" Quite a logical statement supported by cir-
cumstantial evidence," rejoined Captain Cain
dryly.

" Eh, what, sir ? " asked the man.   " I don't
quite ketch wot you mean, sir."

" Merely that I agree with your remark,"
replied the captain.

" Who could it have been ? " queried the bo'sun.
" 'Tain't Pengelly or any of the others : that's a
dead cert. Do you think, sir, that some of them
blabbed to the skipper of the cruiser and he sent
a boat back after dark ? "

" No, I do not," declared Cain.   " The *Canvey*
cleared right off. I was keeping watch all night.
It was bright starlight. Nothing could have
crossed the lagoon without being sighted. It's
the natives who have collared the loot. Ten to
one they were watching everything that occurred
and had the stuff up the moment the *Alerte* went
downstream.   For all we know, they may be
keeping us under observation at the present
moment."

" An' larfin' fit to bust their sides," added
Cross. " That is if a blessed savage can enjoy a
joke. I'd like to ketch 'em at it ; that's all."

" Well, it's no use hanging on to the slack,
men," decided Cain briskly. " Success never
comes by giving way before difficulties. We've
got to surmount them. If we stand here kagging

much longer the tide will leave the boat high and dry. Our best plan is to get out of this cursed river as quickly as we can. Then we can make a fresh start on another tack. If we don't succeed, then my name's not—what it is."

CHAPTER IV

CAIN AND THE SCHOONER

IT was not yet high tide, but already the fresh water descending the river was stronger than the sea water carried up on the flood. In consequence, the boat made steady progress, the rowers sticking gamely to their task in spite of the heat. They realised that the sooner they gained the shore of the lagoon the better, since they would be free to rest without stifling in a miasmic hothouse.

Although bitterly disappointed at the knowledge that all their discomforts were in vain, they were buoyed up by their captain's optimism. One word of dismay from his lips would have figuratively " knocked the bottom out of everything." Only the coolness and seeming indifference to the stroke of ill-luck had kept his men from the depths of despair. More than that, he had encouraged them to expect success in the next enterprise, whatever that might be.

At length the whaler was grounded at the resting - place of the previous night. Removing the gear, the men hauled her up above high-water mark and turned her keel uppermost.

" There's one blessing, sir," remarked Barnard. " Built of steel, she won't split open in the heat same as if she'd been built of wood ; but I reckon it'll be pretty baking underneath her."

" I don't advise you to try it," replied Cain. " At least, not until the sun goes down. We'll have to stick it till then, but there is no reason why we shouldn't knock together some sort of shelter and roof it with palm leaves."

It was not until late in the afternoon that the men bestirred themselves to gather more maize and procure water that might by courtesy be termed fresh, although it was warm and brackish.

" Happen we might get another turtle to-night," suggested the bo'sun. " If we're lucky, I'll salt some of it down. There is a dip in the rocks over there where there's a tidy lot of salt. You were saying something about a voyage in the boat, sir. I've been thinking : how about fresh water ? The balerful won't last long, especially if the sun starts drying it up."

" Do you know what a gourd is, Mr. Barnard ? " asked Cain. " A husk enclosing a vegetable some-what resembling a cucumber. There are hundreds on the edge of the maize-patch. They'll make excellent water-carriers. Now, listen : we'll have the next twenty-four hours to rest, sleep and obtain food and water sufficient to provision the boat for a week. At this time to-morrow, if the weather holds fair, we'll start. I'm not keen on putting into Gambia, especially if people there are still discussing the *Alerte*. They might ask awkward questions. We'll stand off the land a

bit and trust to luck to sight a vessel bound south
—a sailing-craft for preference, or, next to that,
a small tramp, provided she's not British.   There
are craft constantly running up and down between
European ports and The Coast.   We'll be distressed mariners.   The yarn will serve if we all
pitch it right.   If they treat us decently, well and
good ; if not—well, there'll be considerable trouble
to those who ask for it."

As soon as the sun had set, Cain turned in, after
giving instructions that he was to be roused at
midnight to take Middle Watch, Davidge and
Cross being " on " till eight bells (12 o'clock)
and Barnard to relieve the captain at 4 a.m.

The night passed practically without incident,
except that the bo'sun succeeded in intercepting
and capturing a turtle.

The greater part of the next day was spent
under cover, the rough-and-ready screens of palm
leaves affording a much-needed protection against
the rays of the sun.

At five o'clock in the afternoon the whaler was
launched, twenty gallons of fresh water in gourds
being placed on board, together with turtle flesh,
maize and a quantity of the supposed bread-fruit,
which the men could eat without fear of poisoning,
since Cain's experiment had not resulted in any
ill-effects.

As soon as this task was completed the adventurers pushed off under oars.   A light off-shore
wind was blowing, and in consequence the absence
of a mast and sail was greatly deplored.

Half-way across the lagoon, the diving-dresses

were thrown over the side. Weighted by copper helmets and leaden-soled boots they sank at once.

"Chucking money away, sir," remarked the bo'sun. "They'd fetch no end of dollars at any port in South America."

"Quite," agreed Cain. "But it's evidence that's best got rid of. It would require a very smart man to explain to the biggest blockhead that ever held command of a ship how wrecked boat's crew come to be shipmates with four diving-dresses."

"Ay, ay, sir; of course," rejoined Barnard. "But if it comes to that, how do we explain away the whaler? Steel boats with flooding valves aren't the general run in ships."

"They're pretty common on The Coast," said Cain.

"Yes, sir; but supposin' we're picked up by a vessel bound for Accra or Cape Coast Castle? Like as not we'll be delayed there long enough for inquiries to be made."

"There I agree again," replied the captain. "I had hoped that the boat would pay for our passage. As it is, we'll have to sink her just before we're picked up."

The whaler had hardly crossed the bar and begun to lift to the long Atlantic rollers when darkness set in. It was a bright starlit night, and since a strictly accurate course was not essential the compass was dispensed with as an aid to direction. Instead of peering into the unlighted bowl the captain steered by the stars, keeping a course approximately due west.

He knew that there was little chance of being sighted by a large vessel. These invariably kept far off the ill-lighted coast. Even small craft, sailing-vessels especially, rarely approached within twenty miles until they were abreast of the ports to which they were bound.

Cain counted on falling in with a sailing-craft once he was clear of the belt of water where baffling wind alternating with prolonged calms were the order of things. He had no intention of finding himself on board a vessel equipped with wireless with the ultimate prospect of finding the police awaiting him on the quayside. By this time the news of the destruction of the *Alerte* and the conjectured death of the pirate captain and three of the crew would be wirelessed all over the world ; and it would be a difficult business to have to explain to the master of a vessel possessing that information how four men picked up in the vicinity of Bahia Arenas had no connection with the destroyed pirate submarine.

At dawn, Cain calculated that they were between thirty-five and forty miles from the coast. The weather continued fine, but there were heavy rollers that presaged a severe blow before very long. The red sky just before the sun rose above the horizon told the experienced men that ere long dirty weather would set in as clearly as if they had been provided with the most delicate barometric appliances.

Not a vessel was in sight. Sea and sky met in an unbroken circular horizon.

The three men looked decidedly uneasy. They

knew that there was bad weather not far ahead. They were aware that even if they attempted to retrace their course the heavy swell would make it impossible for the whaler to effect a landing. She would be capsized before she got within half a mile of the beach, and the sharks would quickly put an end to any attempt at swimming on the part of the crew.

" It's all right, men," said Cain, noting the expressions on their faces. " We're in for a blow, I admit ; but we'll be picked up before then."

A couple of hours later the captain's prophecy looked like fulfilment. Away to the nor'ard a sail showed on the horizon. Half an hour more and the sail resolved itself into a topsail schooner close hauled on the starboard tack, for shortly after sunrise the wind had veered round and now blew sou'west. Provided the schooner held on her course, which was extremely likely, she would pass within a mile to wind'ard of the boat.

" She'll sight us in half a shake," declared the bo'sun.

" Then ditch all the grub," ordered Cain. " We don't need to explain how we've got a collection of West African vegetables on board. Fill the baler with water and throw the gourds overboard. . . . No, not yet . . . wait till we're in the trough of the sea. They might have a glass bearing on us."

Taking advantage of the schooner being regularly hidden by the crest of a huge roller, the men in the whaler threw overboard everything that would be likely to contradict their statement that they were the survivors of the s.s. *Teglease*, of Cardiff, for Cape Coast Castle, which had foundered after collision with an unknown vessel fifty miles off Cape Verde. Then, hoisting a shirt at the end of the boat-hook, they awaited developments.

" She's sighted us, lads ! " exclaimed Cain.

The schooner was taking in her topsails, at the same time altering helm to pass slightly to lee'ard of the whaler.

When less than a cable's length away she hove-to, and a picturesquely-garbed, bearded fellow waved to the boat to close.

" We're in luck ! " exclaimed Cain. " She's a Greek, or I'm a Dutchman. Smartly there with that valve when I give the sign."

Cain was at the helm, Barnard pulling stroke and Davidge bow. Cross was standing by to receive a line from the schooner.

Then came a neat little piece of deception. Awaiting his opportunity as the schooner rolled towards the boat, Cain put the helm over. The whaler ran alongside under the schooner's main chain-plates, which as she rolled gave the boat's gunwale a sharp blow. Immediately the bo'sun bent forward and opened the flooding valve.

" Jump for it, lads ! " shouted Cain in well-feigned alarm. " She's stove in ! "

The men made a frantic leap for the rail, Cain, being the last to leave, grasping the channel irons of the schooner as she began to recover from her roll. Even as he hoisted himself on to the chain-plates the whaler disappeared beneath the surface.

"Pigs!" howled the Greek skipper, furious at the loss of what appeared to be a serviceable boat which he could have had hoisted in and subsequently sold for a good sum at the first port he touched. "You losa good boata! Ver' much money alla gone. 'Oo you? Vere you froma come?"

"Run down the night before last," replied Cain, swallowing the insult of the epithet.

"Run down, ah! You wanta me give you passage. 'Ow mucha you pay?"

"We haven't a red cent between the lot of us," declared the late captain of the *Alerte*.

The Greek shrugged his shoulders. He could not refuse to take the supposed shipwrecked mariners on board. Presumably the owners of the lost vessel would pay for the men's food and other items, but his owners, Papedouloukos Frères of the Piræus, would stick to any money paid on that account. He, Captain Georgeos Sepotos of the schooner *Nike*, did not feel at all anxious to increase the coffers of his employer over that business, however much he wanted to fill his own. The loss of a good boat, too, had shattered his dream of making a bit on his own account; while, to put the lid on everything, the men he was about to succour were, according to their own declaration, penniless.

"Verra good!" exclaimed Captain Georgeos Sepotos. "You maka work ze ship, you know anyting abouta machinery? We hef no engineer of much use. Motor it no maka move."

"I'll see what I can do, Cap'n," said Cain very

mildly. "Of course you don't want to use it in a steady breeze like this."

"No, but I wanta fit to go ready when no breeze is," rejoined Sepotos. "Go for'ard an' getta food. Den you will work."

Cain and his companions went for'ard, where they were given a meal consisting chiefly of goats' flesh, biscuit and olives. Of the seven hands berthed before the mast only one had a slight smattering of English, and, judging by the appearance of the crew, they were a pretty villainous lot. On the other hand, Cain and his companions in misfortune might well be taken for what they actually were—pirates. A stubby beard of four days' growth, features tanned by salt spray and sun to the colour of rich mahogany, clothes dirty and ragged, their red worsted caps, all combined to make them look almost as villainous as the motley-garbed Levantines.

It puzzled Captain Cain considerably to know why a small topsail schooner hailing from the Piræus should be so far down the West African coast. Usually Grecian sailing-craft confine their activities, legitimate or otherwise, to the Mediterranean. He made up his mind to find out. Incidentally he had already decided to make the Greek skipper " sit up " before very long.

After the sorry meal, which was served in an appallingly squalid fo'c'sle, Cain was told to go below to the motor-room, while Barnard was ordered to take a trick at the helm, and the other two told off to assist in working the ship.

It did not take Cain long to discover what was

4

wrong with the engine—a decrepit four-cylinder motor of an obsolete French pattern. The so-called engineer previously responsible for the running or non-running of the outfit had cherished the totally mistaken theory that timing-gear should be liberally lubricated. In a few minutes Cain, with the aid of petrol and rag, had cleaned out the ignition system and had succeeded in getting the motor to fire. This done, he deliberately altered the timing, as he felt certain that this slight derangement would be quite beyond the skill of the Greek engineer to rectify.

He then reported to Captain Sepotos that the motor was fit to run, inquired where the *Nike* was bound, and was told to ask no questions, but to go for'ard.

Cain did so. For the present it was quite in the scheme of things for him to knuckle under. Rather grimly he wondered what the Greek would think if he knew that four of the crew of the pirate submarine was aboard, and that each possessed a deadly automatic pistol.

For the next three days nothing of consequence occurred. The wind increased to gale force, but the *Nike* carried on under close-reefed fore-and-aft canvas and made fairly good weather of it. Amongst other things that Cain discovered by casual conversation with the English-speaking Greek in the fo'c'sle was that the *Nike* was laden with cheap and inferior whisky to be surreptitiously sold to the natives of Belgian Congo ; and with obsolete rifles of Russian manufacture for the same sort of customers—the sale of both articles to blacks being strictly prohibited. Nevertheless, the trade could be carried on with slight risk and at an enormous profit.

It soon became evident that Captain Georgeos Sepotos was continually going out of his way to insult the Englishmen. Not only did he curse them without stint ; he made a point of compelling them to undertake the most unnecessary and degrading tasks he could think of; testing Cain's forbearance almost to breaking-point by making remarks in Greek to various members of the crew, and holding up the British nation and Cain and his companions in particular to derision. Although none of the four understood Greek, it was not a matter of impossibility to realise the nature of Captain Sepotos' remarks.

Cain still held himself under control.

The climax came on the fourth day after the rescue. The *Nike* was then within eighty miles of Sierra Leone. The gale had blown itself out, and the schooner was crawling along at a couple of knots under every stitch of canvas she could possibly set.

Davidge had been sent with others to the topsail yard. Although a seaman, he had never served in a sailing-craft, and a knowledge of " masts and yards " was a mystery to him. Nevertheless, he went aloft, bungled badly, and received a torrent of abuse from the Greek skipper.

On the principle that " hard words break no bones," Davidge ignored the outburst, merely replying with what in naval and military description is known as " dumb insolence."

As the Englishman turned to go for'ard, Sepotos dealt him a heavy kick that almost sent him on his face. Cain, standing by, gave one glance at Barnard—a glance that meant volumes; then striding up to the Greek skipper he struck him fairly and squarely upon the point of the jaw.

Too late did Sepotos' hand jumble for the hilt of his ready knife. Lifted clean off his feet by the force of the blow, he traversed a good three yards in a beautiful parabola before his oily head came in violent contact with the trunk of a pump. There he lay down and out with the blood oozing from his mouth and nose.

Those of the crew on deck were too dumbfounded to speak or move. Long before they recovered their senses the four Englishmen, shoulder to shoulder, had the foreigners covered by the sinister muzzles of their automatics.

" Hands up ! " roared Cain.

The meaning was plain enough, even though the Greeks, with one exception, were ignorant of English.

At a word from the pirate captain, Davidge made a tour round the deck, relieving each Greek of his sheath-knife and tossing it overboard. This done, Davidge was posted at the helm, the man whose place he had taken being ordered for'ard with the others.

" We've done it ! " declared Cain. " They've been jolly well asking for it ever since we came aboard—and now they've got it ! Cross ! "

" Ay, ay, sir ! "

" Throw a bucket of water over that carrion,"

ordered Cain, pointing to the still prostrate
Captain Sepotos. " He can very well do with a
wash. Inform me when he recovers."

" That was some hit, that, sir," exclaimed Cross
admiringly. " Fair on the point it was, pretty as
you'd see anywhere. Guess you've done him in,
sir."

" Nonsense," replied Cain. " If I had hit him
hard, then—— Bring him round, Cross. I want
to get the job squared up."

In about a quarter of an hour, during which
time the Greek crew were huddled for'ard like
sheep, Sepotos sat up and took notice. He did
not seem at all satisfied with the result of his
investigations. He was cowed utterly.

" Now, you bundle of vermin ! " exclaimed
Cain. " In ten minutes you will be over the side
—understand ? "

" Mercy, sah ! " almost shrieked the terror-
stricken Greek. " Do not murder——"

" Who said anything about murder," interrupted the pirate captain. " Hold your jaw and
listen. You and your scum will be put into a boat.
You can provision her and take in sufficient fresh
water for four days. Freetown's a matter of
ninety miles to the nor'east ; you'll make it in
three days, if you get busy. We're taking possession of the schooner. As far as you're concerned she's lost. You can pitch your own yarn
about that, but I don't advise you to tell the truth.
You're a spirit smuggler and gun-runner. If the
British authorities find that out it's a stiff term of
imprisonment you'll get. Savvy ? "

Sepotos nodded feebly. He quite understood. He was like a toad under a harrow. If he denounced Cain and a British cruiser were sent to put the *Nike* under arrest, he would have to appear as a witness. In that case the whole story of his illicit practices would come out. The schooner would be seized and the cargo confiscated, and he would get a long term of penal servitude. In any case the *Nike* was lost to him. Better, he decided, to announce that she had been sunk, than to risk imprisonment in addition to the loss of the ship.

" I onnerstanda," muttered the Greek.

" I knew you would," rejoined Cain grimly. " Take my advice and make your men stick to the same yarn, or you'll find yourself in prison within a week. Now, then, order your men to lower the longboat, and send a couple of hands below to serve out four days' provisions. I'll give you ten minutes."

With greater alacrity than they had previously displayed, the Greeks swung out and lowered the boat. Into her was handed a compass, mast and sail, in addition to the provisions. Each man was told that he might take with him what money he happened to possess, but about forty pounds in various currencies belonging to the owners Cain detained. He also refused permission for the ship's papers to be taken away by the captain.

" D'ye think we've hands enough to work the ship, sir ? " asked Barnard. " Supposing we keep back that fellow ; he speaks English of sorts."

Cain considered the suggestion. He was not at

all prejudiced in favour of it. He never had a high opinion of the modern Greek, however much he admired the Greece of old, when it was a mighty empire that produced *men*. There arose in his mind the problem of what to do with the fellow on the termination of the voyage, wherever it might be. He might inform the authorities at the first port they made, since he was not implicated in the drink and arms-running business to the same extent as the cowardly Captain Georgeos Sepotos. On the other hand, he might—and probably would —be coerced into discreet silence. Four hands were, after all, few enough for the task of working the schooner.

" Very good," he replied. " Tell him to fall out, Mr. Barnard."

The Greek did so without the slightest hesitation. To him the bo'sun explained that he would be required to assist in working the ship, and provided he gave no trouble, he would receive none, adding that if he carried out his duties well he would be paid considerably more than if he had remained on board under the orders of Captain Sepotos.

" And what's your tally—your name ? " concluded Barnard.

" Basil Zaros, sah," replied the man. " Me all righta. Spik Englis'. Me been in Englis' ship vourteen mont's."

As soon as Captain Sepotos went over the side the boat pushed off. The Greek skipper was feeling too dazed from the effects of the blow to openly display the state of his feelings ; nor was

Cain a man to crow over a beaten foe, however mean and despicable.

In less than an hour the boat, under sail, was out of sight, while the *Nike*, under her new masters, was bowling along towards the distant South American coast.

CHAPTER V

ACROSS THE ATLANTIC

IT was a bold project taking the little craft across the wide Atlantic, but there were good prospects of the satisfactory realisation of Captain Cain's plans. For one thing, the *Nike* was a stoutly-built and weatherly craft, although lacking the efficient upkeep that is generally bestowed upon vessels flying the red ensign. With her reduced complement there was fresh water more than sufficient for the needs of the crew. The provisions, although of a nature that a British crew would jib at, were enough to last a month. There was little fear of the voyage being unduly protracted by calms, since there was a motor on board which might reasonably be expected to take the vessel along at a steady four knots ; while it was a matter of a few hundred miles before the *Nike* picked up the favourable south-east Trades.

On the other side of the picture they were un-questionably short-handed. It meant long watches and the mustering of all hands whenever it became necessary to trim or take-in sail.

Almost the first thing Cain did, as soon as the boat was out of sight, was to stow the square topsails and send the yards down, thus virtually converting the vessel into a fore-and-aft schooner. That alone saved a considerable amount of labour in the subsequent management of the ship, although in light and favourable winds her speed would suffer in consequence.

"Better to jog along steadily than to risk losing your sticks over the side, Mr. Barnard," he observed. "I'm not keen on sending any one aloft on a dark night to take in topsails. And there's another thing; hanged if I like all that booze aboard. It may cause a racket when we get across to the other side. We'll start the lot."

"Not keep any, sir?" asked the bo'sun dubiously.

"No, not a drop," rejoined Cain. "This is going to be a long ship—a very long ship. The rifles? We'll hang on to them. We might strike some place where there's a revolution on. This is not at all an unlikely proposition. If so, they'll come in handy. Just before we left England, you may remember, there was a revolution in Paraquil del Norte. It might still be on. If it isn't, it's ten to one the counter-revolution is in full blast. Hang it all! I may yet become a second Cochrane, or another O'Higgins."

"Who might they be, sir?" inquired Barnard.

Cain explained.

"And you, Barnard, might rise to the rank of general in the Paraquil del Norte Republican Army," he added. "How would that suit?"

"It depends a lot on the dibs, sir," replied the

bo'sun. "Wearing a cocked hat and gold lace isn't much of a catch unless there's plenty of rhino to go along with it."

"We'll get plenty, never fear," rejoined Cain confidentially. "Now pipe hands to dinner. After that we'll whip those casks out of the hold and ditch them."

It was not because Cain was a teetotal fanatic that he ordered the spirits to be thrown overboard. On the contrary, he was fond of a whisky-and-soda, but he was willing to deny himself that—even though the whisky was pretty inferior stuff of the fire-water brand—rather than risk the possible ill-effects of potent spirit as far as his men were concerned.

There was no open hesitation on the part of either Davidge or Cross at the curt order to "up-casks and overboard." They knew their skipper pretty well by this time, and were well content to abide by his judgment. Incidentally they realised that it was not well to trifle with the savage temper which Cain himself had often a severe struggle to keep under control.

Zaros, although he had good cause to fear the new skipper, cherished an idea that he might circumvent him by guile. During the task of throwing overboard the casks he contrived to secrete a bottle in his jumper and afterwards to transfer it to his locker.

For the next week all went well. The wind held fair and steady, enabling the *Nike* to reel off mile after mile with the regularity of clockwork. No inquisitive warship, sent in pursuit by an out-

raged Government, appeared in sight. It was safe
to conclude, therefore, that the Greek ex-skipper
of the *Nike* had deemed discretion the better part
of valour and had preferred to utter futile maledictions upon the Englishmen who had got to
wind'ard of him than to risk penal servitude at
the price of revenge.

Zaros appeared to shape so well that Cain
decided to let him take a trick at the helm without
keeping him under constant supervision, and for
five days following this innovation the Greek
carried out his duties faithfully.

One evening Zaros stood the First Watch. At
four bells Cain and Davidge were turned in;
Barnard and Cross were standing by to take the
Middle Watch. It was a bright moonlight night
with a fairly calm sea. The *Nike*, close-hauled
in the port-tack, was making about three and a
half knots.

Suddenly a rasping sound was heard, followed
by a shriek and a heavy splash. In a trice the
bo'sun dashed on deck, followed by Cross. Even
in the short time that elapsed between the noise
and Barnard gaining the deck the schooner had
run up into the wind with her fore-and-aft canvas
shaking violently.

Bounding aft, the bo'sun gripped the wheel
and put the helm hard-a-port. Fortunately the
schooner had not lost way, and being easy in her
helm was now under control, but not before Cain
and Davidge appeared from below.

" Man overboard ! " roared Barnard.

" I see him ! " announced Cross, pointing to a

small dark object a couple of hundred yards on the *Nike*'s starboard quarter.

"'Bout ship!" ordered Cain. "Stand by the head-sheets."

"Helm's a-lee, sir!"

The schooner went about without hesitation. Well it was that Cain had long before decided to dispense with the square topsails.

"I'll take her," said the pirate captain, placing his hand on the wheel. "Stand by, Mr. Barnard, to pick up the man. See that you've bowlines handy."

"Ay, ay, sir," replied the bo'sun, and went for'ard to carry out the skipper's orders.

His worst enemy—and he had many—could not deny that Cain knew how to handle a craft whether under steam or sail. Gauging his distance to a nicety, he first bore away and then put the helm down gently until the *Nike* lost way with her forefoot within an oar's length of the man in the ditch.

Barnard heaved a bowline. The Greek clutched at it wildly.

"Slip it round you, you lubber!" roared the bo'sun.

Zaros made no attempt to carry out the instructions. Already the schooner was gathering sternway and tending to fall off the wind.

"Clap on, you!" exclaimed Barnard, throwing the slack of another line to Davidge and Cross. Then passing the loop round his waist the bo'sun leapt overboard, made a hitch round the still floundering Greek and shouted to the men to haul away roundly.

Thirty seconds later Barnard was contemplating the shivering, cowering figure of the man he had rescued as the Greek crouched on the deck.

"Drunk as a lord!" he muttered, and, grasping Zaros by the legs, hauled him aft without ceremony and dumped him at the feet of Captain Cain.

"Yes; I know," remarked Cain calmly. "The poop reeks with spirit. Get him below and shove him in his bunk. I'll deal with him in the morning."

It was not until six bells in the Forenoon Watch that the wretched Greek had recovered from the debauch that had not only nearly cost him his life but had imperilled the safety of the ship.

With perfect fairness Cain had deferred judgment until Zaros was able to give a coherent explanation of his actions. There was evidence in plenty to prove that the man was hopelessly intoxicated. A broken bottle found at the foot of the binnacle was produced, bearing a label that showed it had been pilfered from the hold.

The Greek admitted his guilt and begged for mercy.

"Mercy you have received," said Cain sternly. "Your life has been spared. You have to thank Mr. Barnard that you're not food for sharks. Now the sentence is this: for secreting liquor contrary to orders you will receive a dozen lashes. For being drunk on duty another dozen, and for neglect you will be awarded yet another dozen, with the understanding that if you give no further trouble until the end of the voyage they will be remitted. Trice him up, lads!"

The Greek, howling in anticipation, was secured

by wrist and ankles to the belaying-pins round the mainmast. Then, armed with an unstranded piece of tarred rope, Barnard proceeded to execute the sentence.

At the twenty-fourth lash the Greek, too exhausted to continue his wild shrieks, was cast loose, water and vinegar was applied to the raw weals, and he was told to take to the hammock until further orders.

A week later the rugged coastline of the Republic of Paraquil del Norte hove in sight.

Now came a doubly anxious time. The *Nike's* charts did not embrace the South American coast; the harbour of Bomanares, for which Cain was making, had an intricate entrance; and, moreover, the pirate captain was not at all sure of the welcome he would receive when he brought a schooner with a cargo of small arms into port.

As it was too late in the day to hope to gain the harbour before darkness set in, the *Nike* was hove-to, but with the first streaks of dawn she approached the land.

There was not a breath of wind to ruffle the placid surface of the sea. From shorewards came the dull rumble of heavy gunfire, while away to the nor'ard three or four vessels, having an appearance of warships, were steaming slowly as if they were conducting blockading operations.

" Hanged if I like the look of things ! " said Cain to the bo'sun. " I wanted a revolution, but this is a bit too premature. Until we see how the land lies, we'd better go slow. I'll start up the motor."

He went below, taking Davidge with him. Although the man had had no experience of marine engines, whether internal combustion or otherwise, he could be relied upon to work the throttle and reverse gear.

As soon as Cain got the motor to start, and to be thoroughly warmed up, he went on deck, called out for " full ahead," and steadied the schooner on her course.

Nearer and nearer grew the entrance to the harbour. On the hills on the southern side field-guns were shelling the town, while the batteries protecting Bomanares were as vigorously replying.

" Now we're here we'll carry on," decided Cain. " We haven't crossed the Atlantic to be scared stiff by a few seven-pounder shells. There's one blessing, those gunboats don't seem to be interfering with us."

A quarter of an hour later the warships were hidden in a faint haze, but Cain gave an exclamation of annoyance when he noticed a motor-launch flying a green, yellow and black ensign approaching straight for the *Nike*.

" What rag's that, sir ? " asked Barnard, who had been studying the launch through a pair of powerful binoculars, late the property of Captain Georgeos Sepotos.

" The Republic of Ouro Preto," was the answer. " What Ouro Preto's doing in this concern beats me."

" She's chock-a-block with cocked hats an' gold lace, sir," reported the bo'sun.

Cain nodded. His aggressive jaw was thrust forward—a characteristic feature when he was faced with a tough proposition.

" They mean to board us," he declared. " It'll take more than a dozen gilded popinjays of a tenth-rate South American Republic to stop us going into Bomanares, Mr. Barnard. 'S'pose it's a natural curiosity since we show no colours. Pity there isn't a red ensign on board, but I'm hanged if I'll sail under Greek colours. Get Cross aft, Mr. Barnard. Place Zaros at the helm. You might bring a tin of petrol on deck, loosen the stopper and place it at the gangway. We may be able to part on amicable terms. If we don't, then I feel sorry for those gim-crack flatfeet in yonder launch."

A minute later Cain gave the order for the motor to be declutched. He was too wily to enter the limits of territorial waters. Evidently the Ouro Pretoan launch thought so too, for she slowed down and circled to starboard until such time as the schooner was imprudent enough to approach within the line of territorial waters.

" Enough of this fooling," muttered Cain angrily, and signalled to the launch to close.

There was some delay, during which a hurried consultation took place between the coffee-coloured officers in the stern-sheets. Then the launch gathered way, and finally ranged up alongside the *Nike's* starboard quarter.

" What ship is this ? " hailed a voice in Spanish. ' Where are you bound ? "

" Inglis ! " replied Cain briefly.

5

" Ah ! you Inglis den ? " rejoined a voice in broken English. " Vy you no show colours ? "

" Lost them in a gale of wind," said Cain mendaciously. " We're bound for Bomanares with a general cargo."

" It is forbidden, señor capitan," declared the spokesman. " Der is guar—how you call it ?—var——"

" War," prompted the pirate captain.

" *Si*, dat is so," agreed the other, purposely avoiding another attempt to pronounce the word that had proved such a stumbling-block. " It declared is by the Republics of Ouro Preto an' Banda Rica against the Republic of Paraquil del Norte."

" And who's winning so far ? " asked Cain.

" Ouro Preto an' her ally, Banda Rica," declared the Spanish-speaking officer proudly.

" Then my money's on Paraquil," remarked Cain in an aside. " Who says we cannot enter the port ? "

" By de authority of dis," replied the officer, brandishing a paper with an enormous seal. " It is de order, señor, dat you follow me to Olivenca for de examination. You suspect are. Señor, I regret, but you are under arrest."

CHAPTER VI

RUNNING THE BLOCKADE

AT a word of command two men armed with rifles and sword-bayonets clambered awkwardly over the schooner's side. The English-speaking Ouro Pretoan followed, giving a curious glance at the meagre crew of the *Nike* as he did so.

As far as Captain Cain was concerned, it did not matter very much whether he offered his services to Ouro Preto or to her antagonist, Paraquil del Norte. It was the high-handed proceeding on the part of the representatives of the former Republic that " got his back up " and strengthened his resolution to throw in his lot with the weaker side. Of the matter in dispute he knew nothing and cared less. Adventure, with the prospect of a monetary reward, was his choice, and on the face of things he looked like getting the former, although just at present the pecuniary possibilities were none too rosy.

Already his quick wit was planning out a scheme for immediate action. He had not the slightest doubt but that he could get the upper hand of the bilious-looking warriors in the launch. It was the gunboats that had to be taken into consideration.

Would it be possible, he asked himself, to over-power the boarding party and motor right into the harbour before the warships could be upon the scene ? Had he still been in possession of the *Alerte* he would not have hesitated to engage the whole of the Ouro Preto flotilla ; the pirate sub-marine's six-inch quick-firer would be more than a match for the gunboats' ill-served ordnance. But, he reflected, the *Nike* was not the *Alerte*.

He turned on his heel, strode away from the side and made as if to go to the wheel. The three Ouro Pretoan soldiers followed.

The moment they were hidden by the bulwark from their comrades in the launch, Cain swung round and levelled his automatic at the officer's head. Simultaneously Barnard and Cross covered the armed guard, while the Greek stepped up to each man and deprived him of his weapons.

It was all done in a few moments and without a word being spoken or a sound likely to arouse suspicion being made.

As soon as the Republicans were disarmed, Cain pointed significantly to the fo'c'sle hatchway. The men, still covered by the bo'sun, marched off without resistance.

Cain stepped to the side again and gave a quick glance at the launch alongside. Evidently her crew thought they had an easy task, for they were for the most part sitting down and smoking enormous cigars. The launch had been made fast fore and aft, but the bowman had rejoined his companions in the large open cockpit.

Before the Republican soldiers knew what was

happening, Cain heaved the open petrol can upon the fore-deck of the launch and flung a lighted box of matches previously dipped in petrol after it. In an instant the bow part of the boat was enveloped in flames that rose so high as to threaten the schooner with destruction. In fact, Cain realised that he had rather overdone matters.

Yelling in terror, the remaining Ouro Pretoans, dropping swords and rifles, made a frantic rush for the only sanctuary available—the deck of the *Nike*. There, covered by the automatics of Cross and the captain, they divided their attention between keeping their hands up and clapping them to various parts of their gilt-braided uniform to stifle smouldering cloth that for the most part smouldered only in their heated imagination.

With blows of an axe Cain severed the warps that held the launch alongside, rushed to the wheel and gave orders for " full ahead." The *Nike* gathered way only just in time, for already her dry and lavishly-tarred bulwarks were burning —a calamity which Zaros, with commendable presence of mind, averted by means of buckets of water.

By the time the prisoners were safely under hatches the *Nike* was well inside the three-mile limit. There lay the harbour. Three miles on her starboard quarter appeared the light-grey hull of one of the hostile gunboats.

Her skipper was obviously puzzled. He was undecided whether to make for the still fiercely-burning launch and rescue possible survivors or to stand in pursuit of the schooner. In his indecision he shaped a course that would bring him approximately midway between the launch and the present position of the *Nike*.

A flash leapt from the gunboat's bows and a projectile whizzing a good hundred yards from the schooner's starboard bow knocked up a shower of spray a full quarter of a mile beyond her.

" You've got to do better than that, old son, if you want a coco-nut or a fat cigar," exclaimed Cain.

Another shell followed. This time it fell short, ricochetted and passed a cable's length astern.

The Englishmen cheered ironically. Zaros, at the first shot, had made himself scarce. After all, the fight was none of his seeking, but how he hoped to find protection from a high-explosive shell behind the two-inch planking of the schooner remained an unsolved problem.

If the Greek " had the wind up," the prisoners were stricken by a perfect tornado of blue funk. They shrieked, cursed, shouted and hammered frantically upon the strongly - secured hatch in their frenzied efforts to escape being pulverised by the shells of their compatriot or being drowned like rats in a trap.

" We're more than holding her," commented the bo'sun. " She's not doing more than five knots, the old tin kettle."

Cain nodded. He realised that Barnard's estimate was over-sanguine, but even at the rate of the pursuing craft the *Nike* would be inside the harbour before her pursuer had a chance to overhaul her.

Shell after shell hurtled through the air, all hopelessly wide of the mark, until the crew of the schooner found the effort of raising cheers for the gunboat's erratic aim was too monotonous. But when one missile whizzed fairly between fore and main masts and severed the triatic-stay, even Cain realised that a lot of damage might be done by another fluke.

Then, without warning, the motor stopped. That was a calamity that might have been expected owing to the wheezy state of the antiquated engine.

Shouting to Barnard to take the helm, Cain dived down the ladder leading to the motor-room, pushed Davidge aside and adjusted throttle and ignition. All to no purpose. The motor obstinately refused to function.

Finding his efforts unavailing, the pirate captain returned to the deck. In the circumstances he was in a helpless position. There was no wind. Even had there been, the gunboat would be alongside before the canvas could be set. The *Nike* was a mile from shore, and the pursuing craft now only a mile and a half astern.

" We're all right, sir ! " exclaimed the bo'sun, pointing overhead. " She's hooking it ! "

Looking skyward, Cain saw a large biplane passing overhead. In less than a minute she was over the gunboat, that had changed from pursuer to fugitive, and was plastering the water all around with bombs. From a destructive point of view these missiles were as harmless as the gunboat's shells. The biplane was far too high for precision.

Apparently her crew were reluctant to descend to effective bombing elevation, and showed as great a lack of initiative as their opponents had shown in their gunnery.

But the intervention had saved the *Nike*. By the time the biplane was on her way back from her ineffectual attempt to destroy the gunboat a steady on-shore breeze had sprung up.

Under foresail and headsails only the schooner was steered for the entrance of the harbour. Shells flew fairly close to her from the Banda Rican field-guns as she forged slowly ahead across the sheltered waters of the harbour, but after a while the artillery duel was resumed between the rival Republican forces, and the *Nike* was allowed to bring up unmolested alongside a jetty.

As soon as the warps were secured, a party of Paraquilan officers, whose uniforms vied in colour and brilliancy with those of their opponents, came aboard.

" Are you the schooner we are expecting ? " inquired one of them in excellent English.

" Rather—of course," replied Cain.

" From New York ? "

" No, from Liverpool."

" But, señor capitan, I do not understand," rejoined the perplexed general. " We know of no English vessel expected here. We are awaiting a cargo of high explosives from New England."

" 'Fraid we're not that," said Cain. " We've a nice cargo of small-arms and——"

" And what, señor capitan ? "

" What do you do with the prisoners that fall into your hands ? " asked Cain bluntly.

" Shoot them — as a general rule," was the reply, in tones that expressed surprise that such a question should require such a simple answer.

" Well, then," rejoined the pirate captain, " I've a nice little bunch of generals and privates in my fore-peak. I had hoped to make you a present of the whole crowd of them ; but I won't. They are under the protection of the British flag, only unfortunately we haven't a British ensign on board. That's a bit of a nuisance, because I wanted to give you a hand with your little scrap. As it is, I must remain on board and keep an eye on my prisoners."

" And if I do not give you permission to depart : what then ? "

" It would take a jolly sight better man than you to stop me," retorted Cain, his hitherto unruffled features developing a scowl that was generally a sign for an opponent to draw in his horns.

The general's demeanour underwent a quick change.

" It was but a jest, my friend," he replied in a conciliatory voice. " The prisoners, when you hand them over, will be given fair treatment. I swear it by the Virgin ! . . . And now, concerning those rifles——"

" Come aboard ! " urged Cain.

The rest of the conversation was of a purely commercial nature, involving a lot of unnecessary haggling, since the pirate captain refused to make any reduction of terms and the Paraquilan general was anxious to obtain the arms and munitions at almost any price.

In twenty minutes General Leon y Poseda, Minister of War for the Republic of Paraquil, went ashore.

"It's all right so far, Mr. Barnard," announced Cain, loud enough for the crew to overhear. "I've sold the goods for fifty thousand dollars. They're bringing the money down in an hour's time. Of that sum I'll stick to ten shares, you'll have five, Davidge and Cross two each and the Greek one."

"And how much is a share, sir?" asked the bo'sun anxiously. "I never was much of a hand at figures."

"Two thousand five hundred dollars, Mr. Barnard. Roughly, a Paraquil dollar is worth three shillings and sixpence."

"Then I reckon my fortune's made, sir."

"It's only a step in that direction, Mr. Barnard. You wait till we've carried out our plans. You'll be a millionaire in whatever part of South America you decide to settle down."

"I'd rather have a couple o' thousand quid and be able to settle down in England," rejoined the bo'sun, yearning for the homeland from which he had voluntarily exiled himself. "But say, sir, how are we going to get away with the coin? This one-hoss Republic's blockaded by land and sea, as far as I can make out."

"Precisely," agreed Cain; "but trust me to

find a way out of that difficulty. Now, Mr. Barnard," he added briskly, " get the hands to work to clear hatches. We've got to deliver the goods before we handle the rhino, so look lively ! "

CHAPTER VII

THE PROBLEM

BY this time firing had ceased on both sides.
The war between Paraquil and the allied
Republics of Ouro Preto and Banda Rica was being
waged in a desultory fashion. Bloodthirsty in
sentiment, the rival armies showed no great desire
to engage in a pitched battle. The Paraquil Navy,
consisting of three old armed river steamers, had
sought refuge in Bomanares Harbour, after de-
clining an engagement with the numerically
superior but antiquated gunboats of Ouro Preto.
Already Paraquil was invested by land and sea,
and only the necessity of having to coal had
temporarily caused the withdrawal of the gunboats,
thereby enabling the *Nike* to run the blockade.
Every morning the artillery duel took place
between the opposing forces, until having exhausted
their respective quotas of ammunition the guns
remained silent until the following day. Generally speaking, very little damage had been done
owing to the defective nature of the shells and the
inefficiency of the artillery-men. Whenever a clash
did occur, and prisoners were made, the latter were
afterwards shot in batches.

Cain was determined to obtain guarantees for the safety of his captives. Although General Leon y Poseda had sworn to spare their lives, the pirate captain regarded the man with distrust. For one thing, had the General authority, in the name of the President of Paraquil, to accede to Cain's demands ? That he would have to find out. Meanwhile the captive officers and men would be kept on board the *Nike*.

So far the pirates had done remarkably well from a monetary point of view. Davidge and Cross could hardly realise their good fortune, and were already planning how, when and where they could go ashore and spend some of their newly-acquired wealth. Zaros, too, was almost beside himself with joy. He never expected to share in the plunder, and, coupled with the fact that the third dozen lashes had been remitted, he was ready to do anything for his new skipper, who was, he decided, a thousand times better than the crafty Captain Georgeos Sepotos.

As soon as the hatches were removed and the tackle rove for getting out the bulky cases of arms and ammunition, Cain ordered the men to knock off and held a council of war. He pointed out the possibilities of adventure and profit by taking an active part in the present war.

" Englishmen and Irishmen have gained honour, riches and renown in wars between various South American Republics," he told them. " Similar opportunities await you. You might even have your portraits on the postage-stamps of Paraquil and go down to posterity as national heroes ! It is a sound proposition, lads, and take it from me a thundering good chance to coin money if we go the right way to work. I've already sounded that gold-braided blighter who was on board just now, and he's bringing the Admiral of the Paraquilan Navy down to have a yarn. I haven't seen their navy yet, and don't expect it's up to much ; but there's no reason why we should accept billets afloat if there are more attractive ones ashore. Hello ! Here they come ! "

The crowd of curious sightseers, comprising soldiers, negroes, mulattoes and Indians, women of varying degrees of colour and a swarm of, for the most part, almost naked children, had lined the quayside ever since the *Nike* entered the harbour. They parted, leaving a narrow lane through which the Republican officers made their way.

At the head of the party shuffled a stoutly-built individual with features so frequently encountered amongst South Americans of Semitic-Spanish descent—full, red lips, dark brown eyes and a mop of crisp curly hair. His head, instead of being erect upon his shoulders, appeared to be permanently jutting forward, so that his chin was lower than his hunched torso. There was a shifty, furtive look about his eyes, for which perhaps there was good reason, for he was Presidente Lippo Bramo, whose life had been attempted six times during the three months following his election as head of the Republic of Paraquil.

One step behind and slightly to the President's left stalked Cain's former visitor, General Leon y Poseda ; while at a similar distance on the left

was another of the " comic stunt-merchants " (as
Cain contemptuously called them) of the Republic.

This was Almirante Mondez Gimletto, head of
the decrepit collection of coffin-ships that comprised the Paraquilan Navy. He was slightly
above middle height, with heavy, flabby features,
on which sat a peculiarly irritating grin. His
lips were full, the upper one overhanging the
lower, while his receding chin and parrot-like
beak gave the casual observer the impression that
Nature had been careless in the proportions, and
had slapped on to Mondez Gimletto's nose flesh
and bone that might with advantage have gone
to build up a decent chin.

On his head was perched a yachting cap, beneath
which the well-oiled hair descended to such an
extent as to suggest that months must have
elapsed since last he was attended by a hairdresser.
His " naval " uniform consisted of a double-
breasted blue cloth coat with gilt buttons, to the
cuff-sleeves of which had been sewn the shoulder-
straps from a British Flag Officer's full-dress
uniform. Grey flannel trousers tucked into high
rubber boots completed this remarkable " get-up."
For weapons he sorted a cavalryman's sabre and
a huge revolver in a holster strapper and a waist-
belt.

" If that," soliloquised Cain scornfully, " if that
is the blighter who expects to give me orders, the
Paraquil Navy is a ' wash-out ' as far as I'm concerned. Faugh! That sickly smile reminds me
too much of that swab Pengelly. That merchant
reminds me of a certain type of amateur yachts-

man at home—the display of so-called uniform is in inverse ratio to their knowledge of the sea. No ! No Paraquil Navy stunts for me ! "

In the wake of the star trio trailed lesser luminaries of the troupe, attended by soldiers of the President's guard—coffee-coloured, knock-kneed specimens, clad in scarlet coats, dirty white trousers and kepis and armed with antiquated breech - loaders and long triangular bayonets. Almost without exception the guard were barefooted.

Following the guard came mules laden with strong-boxes and escorted by more troops whose uniforms consisted principally of broad-brimmed, high-crowned hats, cotton shirts and trousers, and armed with machetes, revolvers and rifles of various patterns.

The President, General Poseda and Almirante Gimletto boarded the *Nike* and were duly received by Captain Cain, who was too astute a man to betray the desire to " choke off " his distinguished guests, since there was a possibility of putting them to good use.

With Poseda as interpreter, a lively conversation was maintained between Captain Cain and his garlic-scented visitors, during which Barnard was methodically opening the strong-boxes and examining the contents.

" Bit clipped, some of that boodle, sir," he announced. " But they're dollars, right enough ; not chucks of lead same as a Chink tried to do it on me out in Shanghai."

The coin having been counted and stowed

away aft, a gang of negroes set to work to clear the hold of the cargo and ammunition, but not before Cain had considerably startled the ebony-featured mob by making them throw away the almost inevitable cigar that each man was smoking.

" Ver' good! " exclaimed General Poseda admiringly. " You know how to order men. I do not think they would obey me in that."

" If I don't know how to handle men no one does," rejoined Cain grimly. " If you've no objection to be blown sky-high through some careless blighter dropping a lighted cigar on a defective keg of cordite, I have ! "

The General nodded, and, turning to Almirante Mondez, Gimletto engaged in rapid conversation.

" My friend here," he said, switching back to Captain Cain and indicating the inanely-grinning head of the Paraquilan Navy—" my friend here is desirous to know whether you would accept a post as capitan of one of our warships. It would also be possible to offer commissions to these gentlemen," indicating Barnard and the three hands.

" The Almirante is very kind," replied Cain, " but the matter requires consideration. I must place your proposition before my companions, although no doubt they, even as I, would be ready to devote their experiences and venture their lives for the well-being of the Republic, subject, of course, to suitable remuneration. But that reminds me, General. I'm rather anxious to have that money I've just received handed over to my

6

agents, the firm of Señor Paquita of Copiapo, Chile. As you will realise, if my services are required it would not do to leave thousands of dollars aboard the schooner."

General Leon y Poseda nodded sympathetically. A similar problem had been worrying him for a considerable time. As General of the Republican Army he had well feathered his own nest, but there was little sense in doing that if the blockading force were victorious. He might escape with his life, but he could not take his ill-gotten hoard with him. He had contemplated putting his riches on board the best of the ill-conditioned vessels comprising the Republican Navy and attempting to run the blockade.

A similar idea had occurred to Captain Cain. To carry it out he would be willing to accept service of a very temporary nature under Almirante Mondez Gimletto ; he would be ready to risk long odds in an encounter with the fleets of the allied enemy—until he realised that there was a hundred-to-one chance against him. He doubted whether the old tub could maintain a speed of five knots for four consecutive hours ; and, doubting, abandoned the idea.

Presently General Poseda pointed towards the mouth of the harbour. Cain looked in the same direction, but could see nothing worthy of note.

" Keep on looking," said the general. " Pretend we are discussing the defences in case the Almirante is suspicious. We are supposed to be friends, but Madre di Dios ! " A shrug of the shoulders expressed volumes of thought concerning Poseda's

opinion of Mondez Gimletto. " I have a plan to
our mutual advantage. Arrange to call at my
quarters, in the Calle Olivier, at eight to-night,
and we will go further into the matter."

Cain assented. Here was another possible chance
of spoiling the Egyptian to his own advantage;
and that, after all was said and done, was what
he came to Paraquil for.

When the President and his staff had taken
their departure and the last case of small-arms
had been removed to the arsenal, Cain broached
the subject of entering into the service of the
Republican Navy. He did not put the proposition in an attractive light, and he was not at all
surprised when the bo'sun " turned it down."
Davidge and Cross were of the same opinion
They didn't mind fighting with the prospect of
adding to their newly-acquired riches; but they
drew the line at sacrificing themselves to the guns
of a numerically superior and far more formidably-
armed foe, the promised guerdon of commissioned
rank in its Republican Navy notwithstanding.

Then, to the surprise of the rest, Basil Zaros
lifted up his voice. The idea, he explained,
appealed to him. The prospect of strutting about
on the quarter-deck of an ex-Hudson River
passenger steamer, and to be rigged out in gold
lace with a cocked hat and a sword, touched his
vanity, although he had already promised himself
that no vessel under his command would leave
Bomanares Harbour while the enemy warships
cruised about outside. Then, at the end of the
war, he could return to his native country and

buy a farm on the slopes of Mount Hymettus, and thus fulfil the dream of his life.

"Quite a good scheme," remarked Cain, who realised that this was an easy way out of the difficulty of how to rid himself of the presence of the oily little Greek. "I'll see that Almirante is informed of your decision as soon as possible."

A fair division of the dollars followed the breaking up of the meeting. Cain, who would have rooked without compunction any one whom he had occasion to distrust, was absolutely straight in his dealings with his subordinates who had so loyally stood by him when fortune had temporarily deserted him.

To them he broached the subject of how to get the money away into safe keeping. He mentioned Copiapo, pointing out that Chile was on the other side of the South American continent.

"Haven't these chaps an aeroplane, sir?" suggested the bo'sun. "Couldn't we get the general to run the boodle out of the country?"

"And let the airmen rook us, eh?" rejoined Cain. "I wouldn't trust a Paraquilan with half a dollar of mine, let alone fifty thousand."

Nevertheless, Barnard's remark caused Captain Cain furiously to think.

CHAPTER VIII

GENERAL POSEDA'S SCHEMES

LATE in the afternoon the prisoners taken
from the Ouro Preto blockade-launch were
removed from the *Nike's* fore-peak and handed over
to the armed guard from the citadel of Bomanares.

In spite of General Leon y Poseda's assurances
that they would be treated as prisoners of war,
the attitude of the crowd of spectators on the
quay did not convince Cain of the general's ability
to carry out his pledge. Even the troops sent to
escort the captives preserved an air of detachment as if they wouldn't mind in the least if the
rabble saved them the trouble of performing what
appeared to them to be a totally unnecessary
routine. Why bother to have to look after and
feed a few Ouro Pretoan enemies when the matter
could be easily and spectacularly settled by lining
them up against a blank wall and expending a
few rounds of ammunition ?

" Wot do yon niggers mean by yellin' out ' more
tay,' Jim ? " inquired Davidge of his pal Cross.

" Don't yer know ? " was the rejoinder. " It's
a way they've got in these parts ; when they
don't like a bloke they give 'im ' more tea.' That

usually polishes 'im off proper-like. Hullo, wot's our skipper up to ? "

Cain had taken in the situation at a glance. He felt himself morally responsible for the safety of the men who had fallen victims to his daring.

" Carry on here, Mr. Barnard ! " he exclaimed, and beckoning to Davidge and Cross he leapt from the schooner's bulwarks down to the quay, forced his way through the mob and planted himself in front of the irresolute guards.

He gave three commands in English. On the parade ground at Whale Island hundreds of superbly disciplined blue-jackets had suffered themselves to be manœuvred with the ease of a well-oiled machine at the sound of that far-reaching imperious voice.

There was no mistaking the significance or the vehemence of the Englishman's orders to the ill-assorted squad of Paraquilan guards. They literally " jumped to it," bringing their rifle butts down with such vigour and irregularity that Cain had all his work cut out to refrain from the curt, scathing command, " As you were ! "

The mob of half-castes and negroes gave back a few yards, then urged on by a gigantic mulatto they bore down upon the escort ; even grasped the rifles and tried to wrench them from the again wavering soldiers.

Cain had his automatic. It remained in his pocket. Without another word he took two paces forward and kicked. Long experience had taught him how to handle white men ; it had also taught him the futility of using his fist against

the armour-plated skull of a nigger. He knew
that the best way to deal promptly and effectively
with a " son of Ham " was to tackle him in a
weak spot—his shins.

The mulatto dropped, screaming with agony.
In a twinkling of an eye Cain followed up his
advantage. Gripping the terrified wretch by the
arms he hurled him into the press. Half a dozen
of the mob went down before the human missile ;
the rest took to their heels.

Again Cain faced the escort.

" Party—'shun ! . . . By the right ! . . . Quick
—march ! "

They stepped out—smartly, taking into consideration what they were. Cain marched by the
side of the incompetent captain whose lax authority
he had superseded, while Davidge and Cross took
up a position behind the rear rank, enjoining the
considerably astonished men to " Pick it up,
there ! Right, left ; right, left ! "

Secure from further molestation, the prisoners
were escorted to their quarters, where Cain, having
satisfied himself that the governor of the citadel
knew his orders, left them, but not before they
had expressed their gratitude to the man to whom
they owed their plight.

Accompanied by his two men, Cain strode back
to the schooner, contemptuously ignoring the
scowls that were directed towards him by the
scum of the town, although he was quite aware
that many of them would have thrust a knife
between his shoulder-blades—if they dared.

Already Cain had gathered a fairly compre-

hensive and impartial idea of the state of the
unhappy country in which he found himself. It
was, he decided, not the fault of the people, but
of the rulers, that the Republic of Paraquil del
Norte had come perilously close to a cropper.
That the place had possibilities he had no doubt.
It was mainly an agricultural and grazing country,
with a fair amount of mineral wealth. The
climate, although hot, was not so enervating as
that of several South American States that had
" made good " during the last fifty years. The
people, apart from the peons, seemed to be inclined
to be industrious and law-abiding; but to what
purpose, Cain asked himself, when they were
governed by such absolute misfits as President
Lippo Bramo.

It was solely owing to the latter's ignorance
and vaingloriousness that Paraquil del Norte
found herself at daggers-drawn with the Republics
that bounded her territory north, south and west.
Both Banda Rica and Ouro Preto were striving
to be progressive in face of the usual difficulties
with which young Republics have to contend.
They had made overtures to President Bramo for
the formation of a Confederate State in order that
the territory might be developed and trade fostered
under mutual and expansive terms.

President Bramo would have none of it. What
he wanted was military power—to be a sort of
Napoleon at whose slightest whim both Banda
Rica and Ouro Preto would tremble. In his
dictatorial manner he forced his country into war,
firmly convinced that he could fall upon and crush

Banda Rica before her ally was ready and then proceed to effect the conquest of Ouro Preto.

Unfortunately he forgot one thing ; he lacked the support of the people over whom he had been placed in power by a " graft " election. His army, never very enthusiastic, was beaten almost at the outset in a battle that could only be described as a series of manœuvres between two opposing forces at long range. From that moment President Bramo was on the defensive, his troops giving way before the double invasion of the aggressive Republics. His generals, showing far more concern for their personal safety and for the opportunity afforded in the amassing of ill-gotten wealth than for the defence of the country, were already plotting to overthrow the dictator and to secure favourable terms with the invaders in so far as it affected them. Of what happened to Paraquil del Norte they knew little and cared less.

To Captain Cain, with his iron nerve, unquestionable courage and indomitable resolution, the problem was an enthralling one.

" By Jove ! " he exclaimed, " isn't this an opportunity for a MAN ! To put the hostile Republics in their place, to straighten out internal complications, to set up a high standard of law and order, was not an impossible task even to one who had been, and still was as far as he knew, a proscribed pirate."

Yet it was a hard task. To sweep aside the rotten system that was responsible for the internal disorders, to remodel the fighting forces, to secure permanent peace, both within and without, was

truly an Augean task. And what then ? Suppose
he attempted and succeeded ? Would all his
efforts be in vain by reason of his inglorious
past ?

By the time he returned to the *Nike* he had
thrashed out the question pretty thoroughly,
decided to go slow for the present, and see how
the land lay. Meanwhile another matter required
immediate attention—that of the problem of how
the fifty thousand silver dollars was to be removed
from the threatened city to a place of safety.

It was nearly sunset when he went ashore again,
this time to visit General Leon y Poseda. Judging
by the aspect of Bomanares, there was little to
suggest that " there was a war on." Hostilities
by mutual consent ceased at midday. There
were troops stationed in the outlying posts and
in the sandbagged trenches, but not a rifle shot
disturbed the stillness of the evening. In the
plaza the tinkle of mandolines and guitars and
the chatter of mantilla-wearing women and
sombreroed men testified to the non-eradicable
customs and traditions of Old Spain. The air
was filled with the aroma of good cigars. Food
might be scarce, but what mattered if the soothing
properties of the fragrant weed were not to be
denied to the easy-going populace of Bomanares ?

Cain had little difficulty in finding the general's
house. Under the portico stood two soldiers—
negroes with flat chests, protruding paunches and
permanently bent knees. Both were smoking the
inevitable cigar. Their rifles, with fixed bayonets,
reclined against the wall.

At the sight of the Englishman they grabbed their rifles and stood awkwardly to the salute—one with his *kepi* over his nose, the other with his headgear on the back of his woolly skull. Having rendered the perfunctory tribute, one of the men prodded a gong with the butt-end of his rifle, and in answer to the summons a white-haired mulatto in a scarlet coat appeared and signed to the visitor to enter.

" Welcome, Captain——" exclaimed General Poseda, pausing interrogatively. " I have not yet learn your name."

Without hesitation Cain replied. He had been expecting this. Obviously he could not announce himself as the supposed defunct Captain Cain of the pirate submarine *Alerte*, for it was reasonable to suppose that the news of his former exploits had already reached this South American port. Equally unwise would it be to give the name of Trevorrick under which he had in partnership with Paul Pengelly run the ill-starred ship-breaking yard at Polkyll. There was such a thing as an extradition warrant for fraudulent directors, he remembered. Still more emphatic were the reasons why he should not reveal himself under his true name when not so very long ago he held a commission in his Britannic Majesty's Royal Navy.

" Trevor is my name, General," he replied, using the first two syllables of one of his *noms-de-guerre*, " Aubrey Trevor."

" English naval officer, of course ? " suggested his questioner.

" During the Great War—yes," was the reply.

"But, General, it is not with the past that we are concerned but the present—and future."

Poseda bowed. Whatever his character might be, he was not deficient in true Castilian politeness.

"Exactly," he agreed. "Pray take a chair. A cigar ? A glass of real Scotch whisky ? "

Cain accepted the cigar but declined the spirit. He was one of that type of men who cannot "carry a lot" with impunity, although he was partial to Hieland dew. And now he had to make good use of a clear brain ; besides, he decided, he didn't want Barnard and the hands to think that he had been drinking when he had denied them any indulgence in intoxicants.

The general opened negotiations in the usual Paraquilan fashion, namely, by elaborate and prolonged preliminaries before coming to the point. Cain let him wander, although it went against the grain to have to listen to a long and totally unnecessary preamble, realising that perhaps in a ton of chaff he might pick out a grain of wisdom.

"As I mentioned at our last meeting, Capitan Trevor," resumed Poseda, "it is the difficult matter concerning the removal of certain money from this city. Do you know anything about the management of airships ? "

Cain controlled his surprise. He had not the faintest idea that the Paraquilan Republic possessed any air-fleet beyond a couple of antiquated biplanes. To a man the greater part of whose life had been spent in navigating all kinds of surface and submarine craft often without any knowledge of their distinctive peculiarities, the problem of having to deal with a lighter-than-air vessel ought not to present unsurmountable difficulties.

" Of course," he replied, which was literally true ; although he had never been in the air he had seen Blimps landing, manœuvring and returning to their bases.

" Excellent ! " exclaimed Poseda. " There is an airship available. We bought it from the Brazilian Government a few months ago. They had acquired it from the United States. We have plenty of petrol, but, most unfortunately, very little hydrogen, sufficient only to take the ship a distance of a thousand of your English miles— perhaps less."

" Hardly enough to make Copiapo," remarked his listener.

Poseda elevated his bushy eyebrows.

" Why Copiapo ? " he asked.

" I have already explained why," rejoined Cain.

" For your benefit—not mine."

" For yours and mine," said the pirate firmly. " I'll undertake the voyage. Have you any trained airmen available ? "

" Two," was the reply. " One is a compatriot of yours—the pilot of the biplane that came to the rescue of your schooner."

This was more news. Cain wondered who he might be, and whether he had ever come across the fellow in happier times. He hoped not. Nor did he feel inclined to take kindly to the man. In his opinion he lacked the dash that characterises the British airman, or else why did he hesitate to plane down and bomb the Ouro Pretoan gunboat at effective altitude instead of hovering absurdly high over his objective ?

" What is the English airman's name, General ? " he inquired.

" Kayburn—at least that is the name he gave," replied Poseda, with a scarcely-concealed sneer. " It matters little to us—the name."

" Naturally," agreed Cain dryly. " I thought, perhaps, that I might have met him. I don't think I have."

" Then that pleasure is still in store for you," added the general. " And now, Capitan Trevor, I think we might arrange details. To-morrow you will be appointed a full colonel in the air-fleet of Paraquil del Norte——"

" And my men ? "

" Will take service under you. I presume that will be agreeable ? To-morrow, then, I will take you out by motor to see the airship, unless you object to being under shell-fire ? "

" I'd rather be under shell-fire than under your orders, you swab," thought Cain, as he settled down to hear the general's plans to get away with his ill-gotten wealth.

CHAPTER IX

PENGELLY ESCAPES

THE grey mists that throughout the morning had been lurking in the narrow, rocky valleys with which the dreary plateau of Dartmoor is intersected began slowly and unobtrusively to creep towards the quarries and the gaunt stone prison buildings of Princetown.

Almost the first intimation of the dreaded fog by the alert warders was the signal given from the prison for the gangs to reassemble and to be marched back to their gloomy quarters—a signal that adds tremendously to the burden of responsibility thrown upon the broad shoulders of the armed custodians of the convict-parties.

"Knock off, there, and fall in!" was the stern command to a group of grotesquely-garbed, close-cropped prisoners engaged in loading up huge slabs of dressed granite on a number of trollies by means of a crane

One of the convicts addressed straightened his back and sniffed appreciatively at the moist air. To him it smelt reminiscently of the sea, bringing back memories of the seemingly distant days when he trod the planks of a ship—a free man.

He was short of stature, being about five feet seven in height, but broad of chest and shoulder. He had sallow features and a close crop of snow-white hair that once, not so very long ago, was raven-hued and curly. His face was burnt to a deep bronze colour and creased with innumerable wrinkles. His hands were broad, with stumpy fingers covered both with partly healed and open cuts as a result of his enforced labour at the quarries. Although, according to the prison records, his age was given as thirty-four he looked ten years older. His name—which he had dropped in order to answer to No. 123—was, according to the same authority, Paul Pengelly, and his sentence, on conviction on a charge of piracy on the high seas, was penal servitude for life.

Grumblingly No. 123 fell in with the rest of his companions in crime. He was not in a pleasant state of mind. Apart from the constant resentment of having to look forward to over twenty years of unremunerative forced labour, he had been " ticked off " twice that morning by a stern-faced warder ; while to end a far from perfect day the advent of the fog had curtailed the only privilege he valued—that of being in the open air —and had threatened to substitute the four grim walls of his dreary cell.

The gang marched off. Already the warders at the head of the woebegone procession were invisible from No. 123's place in the column. Armed warders on either side gripped their rifles tighter and cast keen, alert glances at their charges. They had no desire to have to engage in a manhunt, often finding themselves belt-deep in mud and water, amongst the bogs and hills of Dartmoor.

Suddenly a dull rumble reached the ears of the party—a rumble that steadily increased in volume. A convict belonging to another gang had, probably through sheer devilment or possibly by accident, released the shoes that " scotched " the wheels of a number of granite-laden trucks. Gathering momentum every instant the trucks were tearing down the incline in the wake of the gang.

" Right incline, there ! " shouted the warder in charge of the party. " Look lively there ! "

The convicts executed the manœuvre quickly enough, although not with a precision that would have won admiration from a regimental sergeant-major. The now irregular column halted, the men, interested at even such a common occurrence, turning their lean faces in the direction of the now rapidly approaching line of trucks, which, distorted grotesquely by the fog, looked like a row of gigantic pantechnicons.

Without warning, and possibly acting upon a sudden and unpremeditated impulse, two of the convicts broke away and with hunched backs and lowered heads made a dash for the boulder-strewn ground.

" Halt ! " shouted an authoritative voice.

Already the two men were almost swallowed up by the pall of white fog.

" Fire ! " ordered the same level tones.

Three rifles cracked as one, sending spurts of yellow flame stabbing the watery, clammy vapour. Followed a hideous, blood-curdling yell.

7

" That's settled one of 'em ! " declared the warder in charge coolly. " See who it is, Johnson."

The warder addressed threw his rifle on the crook of his arm and strode in the direction from whence the cry of pain had come. He searched amongst the gorse, found unmistakable tracks of the fugitives in the moisture-laden grass, but the convicts had got away. There was no sign of blood.

" Old trick," muttered the warder angrily. " Made out he was scuppered. Well, it's worked so far, confound it ! "

By this time whistles were being blown in all directions. Additional warders, alarmed by the noise of the firing, came stumbling through the fog along the road from the prison to take up the pursuit. Once again the close column of convicts got moving until they entered the gloomy portals of the prison.

The muster-roll soon made it clear that three men were missing : Nos. 72, 81 and 123.

To Pengelly the whole business seemed a sort of confused dream. He had long ago made up his mind to seize the first opportunity that offered to attempt his escape. There is far more inducement for a life-sentence man to try and break bounds than one serving a shorter term of imprisonment. The latter realises the folly of losing his " remission " in the event of his being captured. The former, with perhaps fifteen or twenty years of imprisonment ahead of him, does not value the privilege of having part of his sentence reduced for good conduct.

But No. 123 was quite unprepared for what was about to take place, and possibly on that account fortune favoured him. At any rate, he was a spectator of the flight of two of his gang-mates, saw the flashes and heard the reports of the warders' rifles, and the rapt attention that gripped his companions in crime.

Even then he hardly knew what he was doing. A sudden, erratic impulse seized him. Steadily and softly he stepped back a couple of paces, realised that every one, warders and prisoners both, were intently looking in the direction the two fugitives had taken, turned and glided like an eel into the mist.

He felt no elation at this stage of the proceedings ; elation would follow the realisation of his efforts. At present he hardly realised that for a few moments at least he was a free man—free to breathe, to move, to see, to listen with these senses unhampered by the presence of those human personifications of the Law—the grim-visaged warders.

Of the five senses one was yet denied him—that of sound. Utter silence was imperative as far as he was concerned. He crept cautiously from boulder to boulder, listening to the clamour in which he dared not participate. The gruff shouts of the convicts who, heedless of the wrath of their warders, yelled encouragement to their companions who had made a bid for freedom.

Through the fog came, too, the echoing blasts of the searchers' whistles, their anxious inquiries of one another as they temporarily lost touch in that baffling mist. More than once, deceived by

the acoustic properties of that heavily vapour-
charged atmosphere, Pengelly felt certain that the
hunters were coming his way.

He bent his head and ran like a hound.

Sound in wind and limb, the escaped convict
held on more or less blindly. He could hardly
see a couple of yards ahead of him, but with the
innate sense of direction possessed by those who
go down to the sea in ships, he did not make the
fatal error of running round in a vast circle. He
noted the direction of the light wind. As long as
he kept the breeze playing on the back of his left
ear he knew he was pursuing a northerly direction.
Fainter and fainter grew the noises of his or some
one else's trackers : he had shaken off the hunters.

Yet the man was not content to sit down and
rest. The situation was gradually dawning upon
him in all its significance. He was free of the
dread prison, alone on the wild, trackless, morass-
dotted moor ; without money, without friends,
without shelter save that afforded by Nature,
without clothes other than the hideous garments
liberally stamped with that odious device, the
Broad Arrow.

As he made his way, with every sense on the
alert, he began to formulate a plan of action. Not
that he was likely to stick to it ; his vacillating
nature—which had to a great extent been responsible for the numerous failures of his career
—was too deep set to be uprooted, but in the back
of his mind it occurred to him that some sort of
programme was necessary.

He was crafty enough to avoid the pitfall into

which so many escaping prisoners have fallen—
to make in the direction of his home. 'Twixt
Lizard and Land's End, where almost every yard
of the coast and the plateau bounded by it was
familiar ground, there were snug and secure
hiding-places in hundreds. The temptation to
attempt to reach the western part of the Delectable
Duchy was great, but he knew the risks to which
he would be exposed if he dared to travel in that
direction. Thanks to the telegraph, and still more
so to wireless broadcasting, thousands of Devon
and Cornish folk would be keeping their eyes open
for a stranger slinking westward in the darkness
of the night.

The two men whose attempt had prompted him
to essay his dash for freedom had gone in the
direction of the setting sun. That was an additional
reason why he should not do so. He would keep
going north—north because that was not the way
either to his home or to that most secure lair of
the escaped criminal, the Metropolis.

He held on, alternately running about fifty
yards, halting to detect the possibility of hearing
suspicious sounds, and then walking another fifty
yards, thus maintaining a pace of close on six
miles an hour. Avoiding the gradient that he
knew would lead to the summits of the tors,
steering clear of the valleys, he covered mile after
mile. It was a triumph of cunning over instinct.
Instinct prompts a man uncertain of his surroundings to make for the high ground ; it was
also a strenuous struggle against the pangs of
hunger. In the valleys there would be home-

steads, but homesteads meant vigilant owners and keen-scented watch-dogs. It was a thousand-to-one chance against the probability of enlisting the sympathies of any of the inhabitants of Dartmoor. They might give him food ; they might not. In any case, they would be certain to give information of the convict's presence.

More than once he plunged boldly into a swift-running mountain torrent, realising that if bloodhounds were to be employed in following his track the scent would be destroyed by walking through water. Again and again he was compelled to make detours to avoid bogs—pits for the unwary, but to him clearly indicated by the difference in colour and variety of the grass.

Almost unconsciously he had crossed the rough road that cuts the Moor from Ashburton to Tavistock. Great Mis Tor he passed on his left, the frowning heights unseen in the dank fog. Ahead lay a vast track of upland—barren, almost uninhabited and covered with rugged boulders, culminating in a bleak plateau whence rivers of Devon rise to flow in diametrically opposite directions to the English and the Bristol Channels. Beyond that the smiling fields of Devon, with villages and farms at almost every mile. Then his vigilance would have to be redoubled, but cross it he must if he were to gain the sea in the neighbourhood of Barnstaple Bay.

Then given an opportunity to steal a boat he, Pengelly, seafarer almost all his life and one-time second in command of the pirate submarine *Alerte*, would be on his natural element. It ought

to be an easy matter to hail an outward-bound
trader, pitch a yarn and find himself once more
" bound foreign."

But he was not there yet. The distant rumble
of a train warned him that he was on the northern
edge of " Dartymoor " and not far from the town
of Okehampton. It was now getting dusk.

Cautiously Pengelly descended the steep incline
and approached the railway. The fog showed
signs of lifting. Already, in spite of the waning
light, objects were discernible at a distance of
about twenty or thirty yards. The threatened
dispersal of the mist brought slight consolation
to the man. Fog at sea he loathed like any other
seaman. That meant a risk of collision or of
piling one's craft upon an invisible ledge of rocks.
Here on Dartmoor he regarded the blinding mist
as a direct gift of Nature to one of her badly-used
children.

He found himself confronted by a hedge ; hailed
it as a harbinger of good fortune. It was the first
hedge he had seen since he first entered the gloomy
portals of the great convict prison, and the sight
of it even in its restricted aspect was a pleasing
one after the rough stone walls that encompass
the sparse grazing lands of Dartmoor.

Beyond was a field of turnips. With more
recklessness than he had hitherto displayed,
Pengelly threw himself upon the raw vegetables,
gnawing ravenously at the pithy roots. Then
armed with some of the spoil for future consumption he plunged under the railway by means of a
narrow culvert and found himself in a patch of

gorse-covered ground with a high road only a few yards beyond—and a fairly frequented thoroughfare it was, judging by the hooting of horns by cautious motorists as they felt their way along the road.

Pengelly stopped short in his tracks and reasoned the position with himself. It was unlikely, he argued, that his pursuers would think that he had secreted himself so close to a made road, and with a railway only a few yards away. The ground looked as if it were rarely used, if at all. Except for fuel, there was nothing of value to be got out of that gorse-covered strip of land.

Already he had covered fifteen miles of difficult country, he estimated, perhaps more, taking into consideration the enforced detours. He was feeling tired in spite of his wiry frame and muscular limbs. It would be fairly safe to snatch a few hours' sleep and resume his flight in the very early morning.

Crawling into a cavity formed by the gnarled roots of a clump of gorse, Pengelly tried to fall asleep. Notwithstanding his bodily fatigue he could not, although he closed his eyes and stretched his limbs in sheer exhaustion.

He found himself thinking—thinking, not of the present, but of the future ; what he would do when permanent freedom was assured. Money was the first of many of the ideas that resolved themselves in his mind. There was plenty of it to be had ; he knew where he could lay hands on it if he dared. At old Silas Porthoustoc's cottage, for instance, where a goodly portion of the *Alerte's*

ill-gotten plunder had been secreted by the old
Cornish smuggler.   Well, Silas had lost the number
of his mess : Pengelly knew that.   As far as he
knew, the stuff was still in the case behind the
old man's kitchen.   But to go to Mousehole, where
he was well known, and to attempt to recover
the tempting prize, was out of the question.

Then there was the money Cain had sent out
to South America to be deposited in the joint
names of Trevorrick and Pengelly at Saldanha's
at Bahia.   Well, Cain was out of it, rotting in the
shattered hull of the *Alerte* on the bed of a West
African lagoon, and Bahia was not an ungetatable
port.   Scores of vessels left the Bristol Channel for
Bahia in the course of a year.   Then cropped up
the disconcerting question : how could he, Pengelly,
a convicted pirate, supposed to be serving a life
sentence, hope to establish his claim ?

Remained a third source of possible wealth : the
loot from the *Bronx City*, the Yankee ship the
Alerte had captured a few days only before her
destruction.   That ought to be where he had
buried it on the banks of the Faltuba River, and
with no one to dispute his presence there.   He
recalled the trail.   None of the crew of the *Alerte*
had given away the secret, or if they did it was
after they had been sentenced.   A fairly easy
matter, he decided, to ship aboard a " Coast
trader " and work his way up from Freetown to
Bahia Arenas.   In his waking dreams he chuckled
to think that he was scoring over his dead partner,
Captain Cain.

That Pengelly was a vindictive man was putting

the case mildly. Although he had every reason to believe that Cain, whom he had so treacherously treated, had been lost in the depth-charged submarine, death had not squared the account.

It has been said that a Yorkshireman will carry a stone in his pocket for ten years on the chance of getting even with the man who has grievously wronged him by hurling the missile at his head. With equal truth it may be added that in ninety-nine cases out of a hundred the Yorkshireman will, when he has his long-sought enemy at his mercy, surprise both himself and his aggressor by a spontaneous and generous forgiveness. But not so a Cornishman with Spanish blood in his veins, such as Pengelly was. He will pursue his vindictiveness relentlessly, and even if the object of his wrath escape by death he is not satisfied. Unable to have his enemy in the flesh, he will continue to revile his memory.

Pengelly was still anathematising his supposed deceased partner when he fell asleep. Once lost to the world his slumbers were so deep that hours passed before he awoke with a start and found the sunshine streaming obliquely through the gaps in the furze above his head.

For a few moments he could not realise where he was. The unexpected change of environment from the grim cell, the absence of the peremptory summons for the convicts to begin another day of hard, profitless toil, required some time for comprehension.

A wheezing cough brought Pengelly's tautened nerves " up all standing." His first instinct was

to take to his heels; his second to clench his
gnarled fist, and, if necessary, to smite the
discoverer of his hiding-place into a state of
insensibility.

Then, as he looked, he realised that he was in
no immediate danger. His retreat had not been
found.

Lying under a bush at less than five yards away,
was a man whose garb pronounced him to be of
the seafaring class. His face was turned in Pengelly's direction, but the convict was able to
reassure himself that those upturned eyes had not
seen him. The man was coughing violently, the
effort shaking his whole frame and causing beads
of perspiration to stand out on his mahogany-
coloured forehead. By his side was a bundle tied
up in a blue handkerchief, while a few feet away
was half a loaf.

Ravenously Pengelly eyed the bread and the
supposed owner; decided that it would be too
risky to attempt to filch the food from a man who
obviously was in a very weak condition. The
prolonged fit of coughing warned him that if
passers-by were attracted by the sound he would
run a risk of discovery.

Pengelly was meditating an unobtrusive retreat
when the fit of coughing passed.

The man began to mumble, incoherently at first,
but gradually the short and rapid sentences became
clear.

" That much for an extra master's ticket ! . . .
Fifteen years in command. . . . Eighteen months
on the beach, and now : a berth afore the mast,

an' they tell me I'm lucky to get that. . . . While
the jolly old War was on it was Merchant Jack
this an' Merchant Jack that. . . . Nothin' but
' what a brave fellow he is to bring us our food,
U-boats notwithstandin'. . . . And now——"

The voice trailed off into incoherent mumbling.

Pengelly, listening intently, forgot his troubles
in listening to those of the other man. In a way
there was a bond between them. Both had been
merchant service heroes of the war ; both were
" wash-outs." In Pengelly's case it was chiefly
the slackness of the shipping industry that had
forced him along the downward path of crime ;
in that of this waif of the sea the same cause had
hurled him from the quarter-deck to the unsym-
pathetic " beach," and apparently was now about
to pitch the old master-mariner into the fore-peak
of a tramp.

" Afore the mast on a twelve-hundred tonner,"
muttered the man. " And once I was in command of a twelve-thousand-ton vessel ! . . . Take
it or leave it, they told me. . . . What was a man
to do ? "

Another fit of coughing interrupted the ex-
master mariner's address to an unseen audience
consisting of one desperate convict.

" Jerusalem ! " ejaculated Pengelly. " He'll
never ship aboard another craft unless it's got a
flat lid and a flat bottom, an' a fathom in length
at that. Strikes me he's slipping his cable fast."

Rapidly the convict summed up the situation.
He was that type of man who possessed almost
every imaginable bad trait—a blackguard, ruffian,

confirmed liar and one who would not hesitate to
turn against and betray his closest chum. Yet
somewhere in this unsavoury cesspit lurked a
small, a very feeble, spark of sympathy towards
the human wreck but five yards from him.

The man was obviously very ill. Would it be
safe, Pengelly asked himself, to go to his assistance
without the almost absolute certainty of finding
himself behind prison bars again within the next
few hours.

The spot where the old merchant skipper lay
was screened from observation from the high road,
but the old man's coughing and now incoherent
muttering would be audible to any one passing
along.

For some moments Pengelly hesitated, then
decided to increase the distance between them.

" Like as not, some one will stumble across
him," he thought.   " But yet——"

A horrible rattle in the throat of the dying
man interrupted the convict's train of thoughts.
Raising himself on his hands the old sailor gasped
violently, then his extended arms gave way and
he sank face downwards upon the ground.

An uncanny silence followed.

Pengelly waited, half expecting to hear the
sounds of curious passers-by attracted by the
noise. For a full five minutes he remained on
the alert. Now that the man was undoubtedly
dead the convict's sympathy had vanished. He
could do nothing for the dead, but the dead
might be able to do something for him.

A quarter of an hour later, Pengelly took the

high road, clad in the clothes of the late mercantile seaman and carrying the handkerchief-covered bundle under his arm. The corpse on which the broad-arrowed clothing had been drawn, Pengelly had hidden under the gorse.

" Reckon he'll not be found for weeks," mused the ruffian. " When he is, it'll take more'n a Crowner to prove that it isn't Paul Pengelly."

CHAPTER X

A VENTURE FAILS

A GOOD - NATURED motorist noticing a
sturdy, white-haired mariner tramping along
the road, gave Pengelly a lift nearly into Taunton,
a distance of about thirty miles. This was a rare
slice of good luck in more senses than one. Not
only was the convict quickly and comfortably
carried over a long stretch of the distance between
him and Bristol, but it enabled him to escape
possible detection.

So firm a faith had Pengelly in his own coolness
that he had taken to the road unhesitatingly,
now that he wore the clothes of the deceased
ex-master mariner, and was ready to walk past a
policeman without turning a hair. But when the
car tore past a couple of warders who were questioning a yokel at a cross-roads the convict felt all
the former terrors return and thanked his good
fortune that the sleuths did not glance twice at
the owner of the car and his companion.

On the outskirts of Taunton, Pengelly was set
down, his benefactor giving him five shillings to
help him on his way, and wondering on the unusual reticence on the part of his passenger and

his ignorance of topical events displayed in the few scraps of conversation.

The ex-convict, too, was aware of this. Even a few months on Dartmoor take a lot of making up as far as being in touch with the outside world is concerned. He realised that he would have to " go slow " until he had picked up the train of events, and had been able to " pitch a yarn," and, what was more, stick to it.

He was too wary to attempt to seek a bed in a common lodging-house, but towards the end of the day he prevailed upon a good-natured farmer to allow him to sleep in his hay-loft with the sole proviso that no smoking was allowed.

" No smoking," rejoined Pengelly, " I wish I had something to smoke."

With which the farmer gave him half a packet of cigarettes and told him to smoke in the open, and then come to the back door for a glass of cider.

Left to himself, Pengelly took the opportunity to overhaul his possessions, although he had already made a brief examination of the contents of the dead man's pockets.

The examination showed that the old master mariner's name was Solomon Tuke and that, according to a letter found in a salt-stained pocket-book, he had been offered a berth as A.B. on the s.s. *Tombo*, which was due to leave Bristol on the following Saturday for Accra, calling at Bathurst, Freetown and Dixcove. It was apparent from the way in which the missive was written that the person obtaining the post for Solomon Tuke was unknown to him, but had taken pity on him through an appeal from the former master mariner.

The only other articles in the pockets were a knife, a faded photograph, certificates and sea-faring documents and a small bottle of capsules without a label. The last-named Pengelly threw away.

He next turned his attention to the bundle. It contained two blue-and-white checked shirts, a cholera belt, a pair of socks and an old silver watch without hands. This comprised Solomon Tuke's entire sea-going kit. In the toe of one of the socks, Pengelly found something wrapped up in a piece of tissue paper : a sixpence and a three-penny bit.

" He was on the rocks, right enough," commented the convict, as he transferred the coins to keep company with his five shillings.

The next night found the convict at Axbridge, and on the Friday evening he arrived at Bristol, where he was not at all flattered by the official description of Paul Pengelly that stared at him from almost every hoarding he encountered.

Hitherto Pengelly had not set foot in Bristol, nor had he even served in Bristol ships, yet he found himself wondering whether by chance any of the officers or hands of the s.s. *Tombo* might be known to him. That was a risk he must run, trusting to chance that his altered appearance, following the destruction of the *Alerte*, would be in his favour. Again, some of the crew might have served under Captain Solomon Tuke in his

8

palmy days, or have been shipmates with him in less favourable auspices.

Inquiring for the s.s. *Tombo*, he found she was not at Bristol but at Avonmouth, and that she was due to leave at tide-time, which happened to be at 4 a.m.

Pengelly took train for the five-mile journey, found the ship and went aboard ; reported to the bo'sun, and was asked why he hadn't reported earlier, the request being embellished with a few chosen specimens garnered from that officer's extensive vocabulary.

Ten minutes later Pengelly, having " stowed his duds," was fast asleep in a stuffy bunk in the tramp's fo'c'sle.

During her voyage out he managed to shape fairly well, although at first he had some difficulty in responding promptly to the name " Tuke " ; but his relief was great when he found that no one on board showed any signs of recognising him as late second in command of the pirate submarine *Alerte*.

As the *Tombo* neared the scene of the *Alerte's* last adventure, Pengelly began to devise some scheme to revisit Bahia Arenas, but without success. He could see the place on the port hand, its mangroves just discernible through the miasmic mists. But since there are no means of leaving a tramp doing a steady six knots except by jumping overboard and swimming—a feat he would have attempted with every prospect of success were it not for the presence of sharks, since, like most Cornishmen, he could swim for long distances—he had to stand and watch until the desired place faded away on the port quarter.

It was not until the *Tombo* brought up in the estuary of the Gambia River that a chance presented itself. The difficulty was to get clear of the ship, for as soon as he was missed the Old Man would inform the authorities at Bathurst and probably delay sailing while an exhaustive search was being made.

The idea suggested itself to him that he might try the very old trick of leaving his clothes on the beach and thus giving the impression that he had been drowned while bathing ; but he quickly dismissed that scheme. Unable to get other clothes without " giving himself away," Pengelly realised that the scanty garments worn by the natives would render him too conspicuous if he attempted to follow their example.

Before the ship weighed Pengelly had scored again. Contriving to get hold of a cartridge, he extracted the cordite and ate it. In a couple of hours he looked as if he had one foot in the grave. The Old Man, scared out of his wits lest the malady would spread to the rest of the crew, had him sent ashore and placed in hospital.

Twenty-four hours after the *Tombo* had sailed, the case-hardened malingerer was as fit as a fiddle.

His next step was to engage on board a small motor-launch, the owner of which did a fairly good trade—often of a highly illegal nature—with the natives along the coast. Being of a grasping nature, the owner listened to Pengelly's hints about treasure buried in the Faltuba River, and, convinced that there was something in it since his informant was anxious to visit the spot, agreed to work the claim on equal terms.

Ten days later the launch, having covered some two hundred and fifty miles of coastwise cruising, arrived at Bahia Arenas.

As he gazed at the familiar lagoon, Pengelly could not help thinking of the *Alerte*, whose shattered remains lay in the sandy bed fathoms beneath the launch's keel; thought, too, of his partner and rival who, as he was fully convinced, had found his tomb within the rusting hull of the pirate submarine; gloated over his prospects of laying his hands upon the booty, and regretted that he would have to hand over one-half of the find to the other beach-comber seated in the launch. Were it not for the four kroomen comprising the crew, Pengelly would not have hesitated to knock his temporary partner over the head. . . . Then, too, he remembered that there would be difficulties in explaining the man's disappearance, and still greater ones to give a convincing account of how he came to be in possession of so much wealth.

Still plotting, Pengelly headed the launch towards the mouth of the river. It was flood-tide, and the boat made good progress up stream between the mangroves. The air was moist and reeked with a nauseating odour resembling that of decaying marigolds; flies abounded, mosquitoes *pinging* in swarms about the ears of the two white men. The owner took considerable quantities of whisky, but Pengelly, from motives that had nothing to

do with virtue, refused the proffered bottle again
and again.

" How much farther, Tuke ? " asked the owner
irritably.

" Matter of a mile or so," replied Pengelly.
" We'll have the boodle within an hour, never you
fear. We must handle the stuff ourselves, an' not
give the niggers a chance to look in."

" 'Course ! " hiccoughed his companion. " Fair
does between pals, but we ain't here to—to—what's
that ? "

" Only a crocodile," replied Pengelly, glancing
in the direction to which the man's outstretched
and shaking hand pointed.

Crocodiles are common to rivers of tropical
Africa, and consequently the sight of one would
not cause unusual comment on the part of the
old " Coaster." The inference Pengelly deduced
was that his companion was not only drunk, but
that he " saw things." In this state he would be
certain to " give the show away " to the observant
Kroomen.

Presently Pengelly switched off the ignition, put
the helm hard-a-port, and allowed the launch to
run gently aground on the left bank of the river,
the tide being sufficiently high to enable him to
carry way over the mud.

It was about half a mile from the place where
he had previously landed with the looted spoil
from the *Bronx City*, but he calculated that the
unusual exertion of having to walk that distance
would steady his inebriated partner. Then, telling the head " boy " to take the launch higher

up stream, and run her ashore at a given signal,
Pengelly took the arm of his companion and urged
him along at a rapid pace.

" I shay——" expostulated the owner.

" Nearly there ! " interrupted Pengelly. " In a
few minutes you'll be a rich man."

" Of course, Tuke, of course," rejoined the other,
blinking in the hot sunshine. " Risch man—
nat'rally. Pay you half my price. That's fairish,
isn't it, Tuke ? Bet ten to one you didn't know
of it fairly. Shouldn't be 'tall surprished if you
was one of them pirates. Lemme shee : *Bronx
City*, wasn't it ? "

Hot rage surged in Pengelly's breast. In his
maudlin state the old beach-comber had revealed
both his plans and his suspicions. Evidently he
was convinced that " Tuke " was one of the
Alerte's crew, and that, trading upon this knowledge, he meant to blackmail him into parting with
the whole of the booty for a trifling sum in cash.

For some moments the launch owner's life hung
by a thread until Pengelly, realising the danger
that he might be accused of murder, thrust his
knife back into the sheath. He firmly meant to
put the fellow out of the way, but there must be
a neater way of doing it.

At length Pengelly, still urging his companion
along, reached the spot where the booty had been
so carefully hidden. Then he stood stock still,
gazing dully at the grass-grown cavity.

He was not the first to be disappointed over
the loot from the *Bronx City*, but his dejection
was none the less on that account.

" Where ish't ? " inquired the other thickly.

" Gone," replied Pengelly.

Expressing neither anger nor disappointment at the information, the beach-comber turned fishy eyes upon his companion.

" P'rapsh it's sunk a bit," he suggested. " Lemme see."

Rolling into the hole the man got on his knees and began scratching the soil with his hands.

Pengelly paid no attention to him. His whole thoughts were centred upon the problem that now confronted him. Deprived of the booty that he himself had hidden, threatened with vague hints of exposure, he was now stranded on a West Coast with little prospect of finding a ship. Doubtless the old beach-comber would be in a furious passion when he realised that he had been duped, and would probably denounce " Tuke " as a pirate— if he had the chance. The booty hidden in Silas Porthoustoc's cottage at Mousehole, the loot buried on the banks of the Faltuba—Pengelly had failed to lay his hands on either. Remained the money Cain had had transferred to Bahia. Saldanha, he recalled, was the name of the pirate captain's agent. Well, the next goal of Pengelly's efforts must be Bahia. . . .

Suddenly Pengelly's thoughts were interrupted by a grim chuckle from his intoxicated companion. He had unearthed a strip of green rot-proof canvas and was holding it up with both hands. Right across the fabric were stencilled in black letters the words, s.s. *Bronx City*.

" Didn't I shay, Tuke, as you were a pirate ? "

prattled the man. " Proves it, doesn't it, eh ?
Blood-monish to be earned, eh, Tuke ? . . . No,
no ! Mean no offensh, Tuke. Take it back.
You an' me's pals . . . pals most certainlysh."

With a swift movement Pengelly grasped the
tell-tale piece of canvas from the other's nerveless
fingers. The beach-comber, frightened at the
action, sat down on the side of the hole and, drawing
a flask from his pocket, drank deeply.

Pengelly let him drink ; then holding him by
the arm led him back to the bank, where he
signalled for the launch to run ashore.

Hauling the owner over the turtle-back deck,
Pengelly carried him up and made him sit down
on the deck in the space between the transom
and the cockpit, with his feet on the stern bench.

" Boss him drunk ! " he announced to the head
Krooman. " Start motor ! "

The negro grinned at the obvious information
and proceeded to crank the engine. Pengelly at
the helm put the reverse gear into action and the
launch backed away from the scene of the thwarted
enterprise.

In mid-stream, Pengelly thrust the lever into
the ahead position and shaped a course towards
the lagoon, glancing from time to time at his
inebriated companion, who was showing signs of
subsiding into a drunken slumber.

Suddenly one of the Kroomen gave a shout and
pointed to an object dead ahead. It was a large
floating log. Pengelly had already seen it.

At the warning he reversed, throttling down as
he did so. The launch lost way and gradually

began to go astern. He gave her full throttle, and, trembling under the pulsations of the four cylinders, the boat's speed rapidly increased.

Then with a deft movement and without attempting to throttle down, Pengelly put the reversing lever from hard astern to full ahead. With a violent jerk the launch checked her sternway and forged ahead. The change of momentum had the effect Pengelly had anticipated. There was a sullen splash, hardly audible above the roar of the exhaust. Without turning his head Pengelly knew that his would-be blackmailer had been jerked completely over the stern.

The launch travelled quite a hundred yards before Pengelly paid any heed to the shouts of the native crew, although he was fully aware of the cause of their excitement; but when he did look astern, his well-assumed anxiety to rescue his partner was calculated to disarm any suspicion.

He knew perfectly well that the surest method of picking up a man for a single-screw vessel is to keep the engines ahead, circling and approaching the person to be rescued bows-on and if possible head to wind, losing way when close alongside the drowning man. Deliberately Pengelly put the reverse gear on hard astern, with the result which he fully expected. Instead of being able to steer the boat as she gathered sternway, the use of the helm had hardly any effect. The launch made a wide sweep well clear of the struggling man.

One of the Krooboys threw a lifebuoy as the boat backed past, but it fell short, and by this time Pengelly's partner was too far gone to get to it.

Even as the ex-pirate attempted another purposely bungled manœuvre the luckless man disappeared beneath the chocolate-coloured waters of the Faltuba.

CHAPTER XI

DISILLUSIONED

" MAQUISHA ! " (Finished !) exclaimed the head Krooman with a terrific grin, as if his former master's death was something of the nature of a boon to his black crew. " You boss. Make lib for talk one-time. Den we can do, savvy ? "

Pengelly nodded. He understood that this was the Krooman's declaration of willingness to serve the new master.

His chief anxiety was to get across the Atlantic. Now that his would-be betrayer was out of the way it would be policy to return to Bathurst and tell a plausible story of his partner's disappearance. The natives would back him up, giving evidence in all good faith. On the other hand, if he failed to return to the Gambia the officials would " smell a rat," and probably a warrant would be issued for his arrest, and a description of him sent to almost every port in the civilised world. Pengelly did not want any more warrants issued for his apprehension ; he had had too many already, and perhaps he might not be so lucky next time.

When at length the launch returned to Bathurst

with only a gallon of petrol left in her tank, the news of the disappearance of Jimmy Rice (curiously enough, Pengelly had not previously heard the name of his partner) was accepted without much comment on the part of the white colony. Rice had a bad reputation as a " fire-water " smuggler, and was known to be a very hard drinker. There was an official inquiry, at which the Kroomen were all agreed that the affair was a pure accident, thereby clearing Pengelly of all suspicion ; and since the latter's plight was made public, " Solomon Tuke " was an object of sympathy, and a subscription list was opened on his behalf.

A week later, since the s.s. *Tombo* was not expected to call at Bathurst on the homeward voyage, Pengelly obtained a berth on board a petroleum carrier returning to the Mexican Gulf to fill up with another cargo of oil for " The Coast."

On the first day after clearing the Gambia, Pengelly was standing easy during the First Dog Watch when one of the hands remarked :

" Strikes me, Tuke, I've seen you afore. S'welp me ! I know the cut of your jib."

" More'n like," agreed Pengelly, concealing his annoyance. " Seein' I've bin afloat for twenty years off an' on, 'tain't nothin' out of the common. Where d'ye reckon you've seen me ? "

" Must a' been shipmates afore," rejoined the man. " Lemme see, I've served aboard the——"

He mentioned the names of nearly a score of vessels, finishing up with the s.s. *Pickfast*—the collier Cain had detained in order to tranship his first captive, the Admiralty agent, Chamter.

Pengelly gave an involuntary exclamation of surprise.

" No, you weren't aboard o' 'er," pursued the man. " 'Twas only last year. We were bound from Noocas'l to Kingston, Jamaiky, wi' coals. . . . Love a duck ! You weren't the brass-bound bloke wot brought off a cove to us to take along to the West Indies ? "

" Never was a brass-bound bloke," lied Pengelly. " What made you think I was ? Let's have the yarn."

" Well, it wur like this : we was standin' down Channel when we was signalled to 'eave-to. When we did, the vessel wot spoke us—I can't recall 'er name—sent a boat off to us. There was a orficer in charge of 'er an' 'e axed our Old Man to take a passenger—an undersized sort o' chap. That there orficer was summat like you—not exactly, though—an' had your sort o' voice."

" It weren't me," declared Pengelly, purposely imitating the speech of a " shell-back."

" Well, it ain't up ter me to contradict a mate to his very face," rejoined the man, with a deliberate wink. " But 'tain't the first time a man's shipped under a tally that ain't 'is own."

" Wot d'ye mean ? " demanded Pengelly.

" No offence, mate," replied the other. " Don't suppose it 'ud make a hap'orth o' difference if you was the chap I took you for—but I'm a bit curious."

This conversation shook Pengelly up considerably. There was no knowing what it might lead up to. The seaman might know more than he cared to reveal. He looked the sort of man. The ship was equipped with wireless. Once *that* got to business on his account, Pengelly realised that he would be hopelessly trapped, hauled back to prison, while there would be a good round sum as a reward to be shared between the persons responsible for his rearrest.

For the next week nothing occurred to cause Pengelly's fears to return. Although he kept closely on his guard, the man whom he distrusted never referred to the disquieting conversation, and gradually the pirate's state of mind grew calmer.

What he feared more than anything was the possibility of the news of his escape from Dartmoor reaching the ship; in which case the man who had challenged his identity might put two and two together and denounce him to the captain.

The ship was within two hundred miles of Cape San Roque when chance again intervened. A wireless message was received stating that in view of the fact that a state of hostilities existed between the Republic of Paraquil del Norte and the Allied States of Ouro Preto and Banda Rica, the ship was to put into Bahia and await further orders.

This information was received with enthusiasm by the officers and crew. It indicated that they were to be employed in running oils for one of the combatants, with the certainty of receiving extra pay as " war risks," and everything considered the danger was not great. Neither side had employed mines for sea defence; nor did they possess submarines. If the ship were captured that would entail a certain amount of hardship, but the pay of the hands would continue. On the top of everything, there was a spice of adventure that appealed to the roving natures as something above the ordinary everyday dangers that Merchant Jack regards on the principle that familiarity breeds contempt.

As for Pengelly, he would have liked to have danced a hornpipe out of sheer excitement and delight. Bahia ! That was the goal of his present endeavours. He was not going south to engage in blockade - running at sixty dollars a month. He would desert at Bahia and pay a visit to Dom Saldanha, and press his claim for the money deposited by Captain Cain in the name of Thomas Trevorrick—money that formed part of the ransom extorted from the passenger with the *Pickfast* under circumstances to which Pengelly's questioner had recently alluded.

Accordingly, Pengelly smuggled himself ashore within two hours of the ship's arrival at Bahia, bribed a Brazilian Jew to allow him to hide in his house and to supply him with clothes calculated to give him the appearance of a man of means. His next step was to induce the Jew to get a lawyer to draw up a false affidavit to the effect that Solomon Tuke was the next-of-kin of Thomas Trevorrick, deceased, and therefore entitled to the money deposited in Trevorrick's name with Saldanha's.

He knew perfectly well that such a procedure would not stand a ghost of a chance in England, but in Brazil things were worked differently. A little bluff backed up by forged documents, he decided, ought to effect the desired transfer of Captain Cain's and his own share of the plunder.

Failing that, he determined to risk revealing his identity as Paul Pengelly, since he had Cain's word for it that the money was deposited in their joint names with Saldanha's—and more than likely Dom Saldanha was a shady individual or Cain would not have placed his illegally-gotten wealth in the Brazilian's safe.

The tanker which had carried him across the Atlantic had hardly cleared the harbour when Pengelly emerged from his retreat and shaped a course down the Avenida 15 Mayo to the offices of Dom Saldanha. He was rigged out in alpaca coat, white waistcoat with scarlet cummerbund, full-cut trousers and brown leather shoes. Tilted rakishly on his head he wore a panama. His unkempt beard had been trimmed to " torpedo " shape, his white hair had been cut close and dyed to dark brown. Altogether, Pengelly fancied himself, and fondly imagined that his appearance, combined with his ready resource and his forged credentials, would be more than sufficient to enable him to carry out his coup.

He was shown into the private office of Dom Saldanha—a suave, well-set-up Brazilian of pure Portuguese descent, who spoke English fluently and with only a few mispronunciations.

As Pengelly began to state his case, Dom Saldanha was all attention and politeness, but when his visitor began to get down to what he considered hard and telling facts, the Brazilian's face assumed a puzzled and incredulous look.

" My dear Mr. Tuke ! " he protested. " I am afraid there must be some misunderstanding. The name of Thomas Trevorrick is an entire stranger to us. No one of that name has deposited in our vaults. More, I can safely assert that in the year you mention we transacted no business with any client in England."

" But surely this is a mistake," expostulated the bewildered Pengelly.

" Assuredly," agreed Dom Saldanha blandly. " A mistake on your part. To satisfy you, I will produce a list of persons who have deposited money and securities with us in the year you gave. Of course this is departing from our usual custom, but in the circumstances——"

He touched a bell.

" —Meanwhile, if you are contemplating entrusting us with any financial transactions, Mr. Tuke, you may rest assured that we will give the matter our closest attention."

The door opened and a clerk appeared. To him Dom Saldanha gave certain instructions in Portuguese. The man returned with a leather-bound volume and placed it in front of his employer. It was a list of names and addresses, with the respective ledger folios. Although Pengelly scanned the pages, not a single name of English origin occurred.

" That, I think, must satisfy you," remarked Dom Saldanha.

Pengelly nodded dazedly.

" And there is no further business ?   No ? "

The Brazilian placed his foot upon a knob

9

concealed under the carpet, with the result that the bell of his desk telephone rang peremptorily.

Dom Saldanha raised the receiver, listened to an imaginary request and turned to his visitor.

" I must wish you good morning," he said suavely. " A client has just telephoned for an interview."

Pengelly went out. As soon as he had gone, Saldanha shut the top right-hand drawer of his pedestal desk. In it, ready to hand, reposed a loaded automatic. More than once Saldanha had to be very drastic in dealing with desperate callers.

" I wonder what he did really want ? " mused the Brazilian as he locked the drawer. " *Gracias a Dios* ; he went quietly."

But Pengelly was raging furiously by the time he gained the street, cursing the memory of his partner for his perfidy, although he forgot his perfidy towards *him*.

Three times he had failed to lay his hands on various loot that had fallen into the clutches of the captain of the pirate submarine. And now, once more, he was stranded and practically penniless in a strange land, with the last hope of enriching himself on Cain's unlawful possession totally shattered.

Within two minutes of the time when Pengelly left the offices of Saldanha, Captain Cain entered them.

CHAPTER XII

KAYBURN, THE AIRMAN

ON the day following Cain's interview with General Leon y Poseda the bombardment of the town of Bomanares was resumed with more than its usual vigour ; so much so that when the general took the pirate captain in his car to visit the Air establishment, the road on the outskirts of the town was subjected to such a furious shelling that to proceed was too risky a procedure for the Paraquilan officer.

Cain, glancing at his companion, could see that Poseda had the wind up—badly. Nor was the driver in a better state. He was trembling like a leaf.

"It is frightful," commented Poseda. "They will smash the car."

"In that case, suppose we walk ? " suggested Cain coolly.

Poseda made no reply.

"I hope I'm not keeping you from your duties," continued Cain. "In view of the serious nature of the offensive, perhaps you ought to be with the troops."

"It is unnecessary," replied the general, failing

to note the thinly-veiled sarcasm. " My orders were sent to the troops two hours ago. *Dios !* The firing is fearful. The enemy must have got hold of some new kind of shell, and many of them."

Viewed from a hollow half-way up the side of a hill, the bombardment did not strike Cain as being intensive. The shells were of a high-explosive type, doing little damage—except where they actually hit, the force of the charge going for the most part straight up in the air. It was the deafening crashes that got on Poseda's nerves.

Presently through the glasses Cain noticed a strong force of hostile infantry issuing from the trenches with the evident intention of rushing a position on the slope of a hill. The position, of course, would give the enemy a chance to penetrate the cordon of forts on the landward side of the town.

The infantry advanced in open order, receiving little, if any, resistance from the Paraquilans holding the defences. Possibly the latter had been completely demoralised by the initial bombardment. At any rate, hardly a rifle-shot rang out, and the defending ordnance was silent.

" General," remarked Cain. " It looks as if you are wanted to stop that assault. Are there no reserves to be rushed up ? "

Poseda stirred uneasily. There was now no reason why the car should not proceed, for the shelling of the road had ceased.

Before he could frame a reply, the loud drone of an aeroplane was heard almost immediately overhead. On the underside of its lower main planes were the distinctive markings of the Paraquil del Norte Air Service. It was the same bus that had driven off the Ouro Preto gunboats in pursuit of the *Nike*.

The biplane attacked, but Cain noticed what he had previously commented upon before—the apparent reluctance of the airman to get within effective range. Maintaining a height of about three thousand feet, he dropped bomb after bomb, all of which fell wide of the now bunched up troops as they converged towards their objective.

Yet the airman turned the scale of battle. Caught in the open, the hostile troops bolted for their trenches. As far as Cain could see by means of his binoculars, no one appeared to be hit.

"Funny blighter, that airman," he mused. "Why on earth he doesn't plane down and machine-gun that mob beats me. He's simply throwing away a superb chance."

General Poseda clapped his hands in sheer delight.

"They are beaten!" he exclaimed. "That airman is your compatriot; the man we are going to see. He will be back at the aerodrome before us."

Poseda was correct in his surmise, for when at length the car drew up outside the aerodrome, it was met by a tall, slim, pleasant-faced man of not more than thirty years of age.

The general referred to Cain as "Commandante Trevor of the Paraquil del Norte Air Fleet" when

the airman was introduced to him, and followed
up by embracing and kissing the "hero of
the glorious victory," much to the "hero's"
embarrassment.

"Pleased to meet you, Kayburn!" exclaimed
Cain.

The two Englishmen gripped hands cordially.
Cain, on his part, took at once to the pleasant-
faced man, especially as he was able to reassure
himself at the first glance that he was an utter
stranger, and therefore not likely to know anything about the pirate captain's past. With that
sound judgment of his Cain realised, too, that the
faint-hearted stunts of the aviator were not due
to temerity. There was another reason : that he
meant to find out.

"We have come on a visit of inspection," declared Poseda pompously.

Cain could hardly refrain from smiling. The
whole business appeared to him to be a sort of
comic opera. Only in South and Central America
could petty Republics exist under such a display
of buffoonery. And the tragedy of it all was that
there were excellent material and splendid conditions being completely neglected, or rather
suppressed, through the incompetency of leaders
of the Poseda type.

It was an aerodrome! Even Kayburn positively blushed for shame when he pointed out
the two biplanes that represented the Republic's
heavier-than-air fleet. Cain had seen vastly
superior machines sold by the Disposal Board at
home for less than twenty pounds. It seemed a

miracle that either of them could leave the ground.

Cain made no comment. He could see that Kayburn did not require one. At any rate, these antiquated buses were useless for the purpose of transporting his fifty thousand dollars out of the Republic of Paraquil del Norte. Somewhat sceptically he inquired where the airship was housed.

The "shed" was about half a mile away. Considering the resources at his command, Kayburn had made rather a good show with it. A natural gorge or cañon formed the floor and sides, the rocky walls towering sheer to a height of nearly two hundred feet. The eighty-feet gap from brink to brink had been spanned by a heavy trellis-work of timber, which was boarded on with thick planks, on the top of which sandbags were placed sufficient to stop a direct hit from the heaviest projectile the hostile Republics possessed.

The airship was by no means a giant, measuring only four hundred feet in length, and with an extreme width of sixty-two feet. It was of the rigid type, and was propelled by four side propellers actuated by chain-drive to motors each of 600 horse-power. Originally it had been constructed in the United States for Polar exploration, but for some reason the project was abandoned and the airship was sold to Brazil for use in making a survey of the upper reaches of the Amazon. This scheme also failed to materialise, and the airship passed into the hands of her present owners, the Government of Paraquil del Norte.

"She's in fair condition," declared Kayburn,

" only you see, sir, we haven't a crew for her. And there's another difficulty—hydrogen gas. We've several thousand cubic feet stored away under pressure, but not enough for severe flying conditions."

Undoubtedly Kayburn would have liked to say more, but for the presence of General Poseda; and Cain quickly realised that the latter's company was a brake upon the wheel of mutual confidences.

" Look me up on board the *Nike*, Kayburn, " said Cain promptly.

" Thanks awfully, I will," replied the airman, with equal celerity.

Poseda scowled with annoyance. He realised that he had been circumvented. In his slow, pompous manner of speech he had been " left standing " by the rapidity of Cain's invitation and its acceptance. As matters stood at present he did not want any exchange of confidences between the two Englishmen.

" Why not dine with me, gentlemen ? " he asked, concealing his chagrin under the cloak of an oily smile.

" Sorry," replied Cain briefly; " I cannot leave the ship this evening."

At six in the afternoon Dick Kayburn came on board.

" You ticked that old bird off all right," he remarked. " I could see he was out to prevent our enjoying a chin-wag. My word, it's a blessing having an Englishmen to talk with in this forsaken hole."

" Then what made you come to it, might I

ask ? " inquired Cain, in a way that Kayburn could not possibly take offence.

" Luck—hard or otherwise," replied the airman. " To go back to the beginning of my flying career I was a flight lieutenant in the old R.F.C. They tell me I was pretty good at stunts, but a rotten pilot. In fact, one night I unloaded the goods on Dutch territory when I thought I was bombing Dusseldorf. In the R.A.F. I was kept pretty busy just over the lines—they wouldn't trust me on the long-distance bombing stunts after that. Then I was demobbed, and at a loose end, like hundreds of fellows in '19. Naturally I wanted a job. I found one. A bloke who claimed to be an ex-officer who had been blown up three times and gassed three times ' pitched the yarn ' and we started on a partnership show. He vanished, so did my two hundred pounds. Afterwards I found out that he never was in khaki, but had been munition-eering in a cushy show well beyond the air-raid area. No doubt he'd been blown up three times —by his foreman for being late, I take it ; and as for the gas—well he'd plenty of it left when I met him !

" That tore it. I was practically on the rocks when I got a billet out here as flying instructor to the Paraquil del Norte Commercial Aviation Company. They started with a dozen old buses, and in a month there were only three left. Then the bust up with Banda Rica came off, and the blighters sort of roped me in. I couldn't leave the place, I didn't want to starve, so I signed on. I take good care to go slow, though."

" So I have observed," agreed Cain. " Might I ask why ? "

" For one reason, I don't see why I should risk my neck for the sake of President Lippo Bramo and his underlings," explained Kayburn. " If I'd volunteered for the job it would have been a different matter. And there's another reason : I haven't any quarrel with the Republics of Ouro Preto and Banda Rica, and it's a rotten business blowing men to bits when they're not enemies of yours."

" It would be interesting to know whether they would entertain the same sentiments towards you if you fell into their hands," remarked Cain dryly. " 'Fraid I'm not so discriminating : I've just landed a few thousand rounds of small-arms ammunition and a tidy number of rifles."

" Poseda wanted me to bomb the capitals of the hostile Republics," continued Kayburn. " I told him I couldn't; said the old bus couldn't keep up for more than an hour. That's a fact, too. So I just potter around and drop a few eggs just to keep the other crowd from butting in too close."

" That will never end the war," declared Cain. " What's wanted is something to put the wind up the enemy. Scare 'em stiff ; force them to ask for terms."

" They'd do that were it not for old Bramo, Poseda and Gimletto," said Kayburn. " Those chaps are the stumbling-blocks. The country would forge ahead all right if they were out of it."

" So I think," agreed Cain. " I came here with the avowed intention of piling up dollars, but since then I've rather taken a liking to the place. It wants disinfecting and fumigating—meaning that the present Government should be pushed out of it, and then things will improve. I'm thinking of trying to improve matters."

"You are, sir?" asked Kayburn eagerly. "My word, what a topping idea! I'd like to give you a hand, if you'll let me."

"I think it can easily be arranged," replied Cain slowly. "Shifting President Lippo Bramo and staff, I mean. However, there's a matter that in my opinion takes precedence: that's what I want to consult you about. It concerns the root of all evil—money."

"'Fraid I've precious little of that, sir," declared Kayburn frankly.

"You never know your luck," rejoined Cain oracularly. "'Tany rate, I've fifty thousand dollars in silver on board at this present moment, part of which belongs to my men. Now I want to get that out of the country, and I fancy General Poseda is on the same lay, with this difference. I made mine honestly. He didn't."

The pirate captain spoke with conviction. According to his tenets, despoiling the Egyptian was honest work, and he had not the faintest scruples when it came to wresting Poseda's hoard from him.

"Now to come to the point," continued Cain. "This airship is, I understand, capable of flying, say, to Copiapo. That place is, as you're probably aware, on the Chilian coast."

"I wasn't," admitted Kayburn frankly. "It's all right for distance, but there's the Andes.

She'd never have enough lift to take her over them. 'Sides, there's the return journey."

Cain looked and felt disappointed.

"Can you suggest a place?" he inquired. "Somewhere in fairly stable country where there won't be a revolution, say, within the next six months? Somewhere where we can obtain hydrogen sufficient to give the airship an extended radius of action?"

"There's Ascuncion, in Paraguay——"

"No go," declared Cain. "Paraguay is more often than not in a state of insurrection. Somewhere in the north is what I want, since we can't get over the Andes."

"Sorbombo, then. There's plenty of fairly good coal-gas to be obtained there."

"Where is Sorbombo?" asked the pirate captain. "I've never heard of it."

"Fifty miles from Bahia," replied Kayburn. "That's the place where the airship was stationed when she belonged to the Brazilian Government. They'd supply the gas and won't ask too many questions if payment is promptly forthcoming. And, what's more, the airship shed is still standing."

Cain grunted with satisfaction. At Bahia was his old acquaintance Saldanha. He had not had any transactions with him in the *Alerte* affair, although, he recalled with a grim smile, he had gulled his skulking partner Pengelly into the belief that he had. At any rate, the fifty thousand dollars would be safe with Saldanha.

"I'll see she's navigated there," he declared

confidentially, " if you'll be responsible for her management. Your crew will be trustworthy, I hope ? "

" I think so," replied Kayburn. " At any rate, they're not jumpy. They'll keep their heads in a tight corner."

" Hope there won't be any tight corners," rejoined Cain grimly. " If I fall I like to fall a few inches. It's better to tumble off the bottom rung of a ladder than to come a cropper from the top. I'll take my men, of course. They'll be handy, being seamen."

" Excuse me, Mr. Trevor," remarked the airman, " but weren't you in the Navy ? "

" You haven't met me before, I suppose ? " countered Cain.

Kayburn shook his head.

" Not to my knowledge," he replied. " One met hundreds of fellows during the War, but only in a few cases is a face remembered. But you have the cut of a pukka naval officer."

" Lieutenant-Commander," announced Cain. " I retired in January '20. Well, that's settled. Now, how about shanghai-ing the President and his little mob ? That business will, I take it, be fairly simple. At any rate, leave details to me. What is more to the point, we can't leave Paraquil without some form of government."

" Exactly, sir," replied Kayburn, " but the present crush will take a lot of beating—for inefficiency."

" Is there any one you could suggest to act as provisional president ? " asked Cain. " He'll have to be some one fairly popular—but not too much so—with the populace, and a fellow who'll eat out of our hands when we return. Meanwhile, we must put the wind up the enemy, and that must be timed to take place an hour or so after Bramo & Co. are shanghaied."

It was eleven o'clock at night before Cain and his new ally, Dick Kayburn, parted company. They had carefully laid their plans; it remained to be seen whether deliberation and foresight would reap the reward.

CHAPTER XIII

SHANGHAI-ING THE PRESIDENTE

IN his most sanguine moments Captain Cain hardly expected that his scheme would go forward without a hitch; but he was quite unprepared for the startling development that occurred in the progress of the War.

The Greek, Basil Zaros, had been given the rank of Capitan-Commandante of the Paraquil del Norte Navy, and was under the direct orders of Almirante Mondez Gimletto. Cain had jestingly remarked that there was no need to shove a gimlet into the Paraquilan ships; they had dry-rot already.

However, Gimletto had an idea and, somewhat unusually for him, proceeded to carry it out. He had one of the steamers, the *Estramarella*, protected with boiler-plates and sandbags, mounted a six-inch gun on her fo'c'sle (which he did on the time-honoured principle of robbing Peter to pay Paul; or, in other words, he took the gun from one of the forts for naval use) and then ordered Zaros to take the *Estramarella* to sea and engage the two blockading gunboats.

The Greek was in a blue funk, but there was no

escape. If he refused he would be shot. Vainly he appealed to Cain to save him from the desperate task ; the only consolation he received was the remark that he'd joined the Paraquilan Navy by his own choice, and that he must make the best of it.

Accordingly, one dark night the *Estramarella* cast off from the quay and proceeded seawards. All lights in it were obscured, but the hiss of escaping steam from the badly-packed glands of her machinery could be heard for miles.

Trembling as he stood on the bridge of his first command, Zaros wished that he had never been born. His dreams of a farm on the slopes of Mount Hymettus were as hazy as the vapour from the *Estramarella's* steam-pipe. He debated whether he could not skirt the shore and escape, or else surrender tamely to the enemy, until he remembered that it was the practice of the hostile Republic not to give quarter. Better, he decided, to die fighting than to be propped up against a wall.

His crew were pretty determined men. They would shoot him where he stood rather than surrender. That was an additional inducement to the Greek to do his duty.

Fortifying himself with liberal doses of *meicol*— the Paraquilan equivalent to rum—Zaros held on until he was clear of the harbour. There was a strong easterly wind, and on that account the noise of the escaping steam would be inaudible to the blockading gunboats.

Putting his helm hard-a-starboard, Zaros steered northward, keeping close in-shore until he reckoned

that he was five miles from the enemy ships.
Ninety degrees of port-helm brought him back on
an easterly course. Then he held until the *Estramarella* was eleven miles from land.

By this time the Ouro Preto gunboats had
commenced to run their searchlights, keeping the
beams turned upon the entrance to the harbour.
At full speed—the *Estramarella* being forced up to
six knots at imminent risk of blowing out her
boilers—the Paraquilan vessel approached her
enemy from the quarter that an attack, if any,
was least expected.

A thousand yards . . . nine hundred . . . eight
. . . seven.

No sign came from the gunboats. Zaros, chock-
a-block with Dutch courage, stopped his engines
and waited until the relative positions of the
searchlights told him that the enemy ships were
about a cable's length apart on opposite and
parallel courses.

Then the *Estramarella's* six-inch quick-firer,
trained at fifteen feet below one of the search-
lights, opened the ball. At that range it was
almost impossible to miss. The shell exploded
well aft, completely wrecking the stearing-gear.
In the confusion both hostile gunboats put their
helms hard over. Each, being on the other's
turning circle and converging, realised that a
collision seemed inevitable ; and collide they
did, one of the gunboats ramming the other fairly
amidships.

Shouts and yells rent the air. The crews were
panic-stricken, those of the rammed craft struggling

10

to clamber on to the fo'c's'le of the vessel that had collided with her.   There was no attempt made to return the *Estramarella's* fire.

At this juncture Zaros ordered the *Estramarella's* searchlight to bear upon the enemy, and, taking in the situation, he promptly opened fire upon the ramming craft.

In five minutes the latter sank.   As she did so she left exposed the gaping rent in her consort's side that hitherto had been plugged by her bows. Amidst a roar of escaping steam and the shrieks of the crew, the second gunboat disappeared beneath the waves.

Two hours later the *Estramarella* returned to Bomanares.   Although it was well past midnight the town was *en fête*.   Zaros, now as drunk as a man can possibly be without losing complete control of his lower limbs, was met and embraced by Almirante Mondez Gimletto, and the President there and then presented him with the Order of the Legion of Paraquil del Norte—a reward which the Greek failed to appreciate when later on he found that no monetary award went with it.

The naval action, insignificant as it was in reality, added immensely to the Government's waning prestige.   The blockade was raised, it was declared ; victory was now assured.

Unfortunately for this optimism, the allied Republics were stung to renewed activity.   The bombardment became a twelve-hour business daily.   More troops were rushed up to strengthen the attacking forces ; while, to make matters worse for Paraquil, four gunboats appeared in the offing to replace the two that had been lost.

Against these intensified measures, General Poseda and Almirante Gimletto did little or nothing. In consequence, their shortlived popularity waned. There were demonstrations in the plazas, crowds, including many soldiers, parading with shouts of " Down with the Presidente ! "

It was shortly after one of these demonstrations that Kayburn suggested to Cain the name of a suitable candidate for the temporary presidency.

" Pedro Aquillo is the man we want," he declared. " He has a fair amount of popularity. I've sounded him, and he's willing to seek election and then to resign—for a consideration, of course."

" Naturally," replied Cain. " Who is he ? "

" Father's a Paraquilan ; mother, of mixed English and Portuguese descent."

" H'm ! Let's hope the British strain is well-nigh eliminated," remarked the pirate captain. " I never had much use for mongrels."

" If it comes to that," countered Kayburn, " is there a more mongrel nation than the British ? Saxon, Kelt, Dane, Norman and half a dozen other strains, and the result holds its own with any other nation on the face of the earth."

" Granted," acquiesced Cain, " but all the races you name originate from districts north of the 45th parallel, and as a rule the farther north the better the strain. No, what I kick against is the mongrel with negro or Indian blood in his veins —a Paraquilan, for example. Well, we'll give the fellow a run. Now then ; this little stunt con-

cerning the shanghai-ing of the Presidente, when
will you complete your arrangements ? "

" I'm ready any time," replied the airman. " I
suppose we'll make one trip do for both jobs :
the transfer of the silver and the abduction of
President Lippo Bramo ? "

" I made arrangements with Poseda to take
charge of his dollars," announced Cain, with a
laugh. " He's getting more and more jumpy every
hour : thinks the mob will do him in and seize
his cash. I say ' his ' with reservations. You say
your airship's ready for flight ? Good ; I'll bring
up my fifty thousand dollars this afternoon.
You'll see to issuing invitations to the President
and staff to witness the departure of the airship
on a bombing expedition ? "

" Rather," rejoined Kayburn, with a chuckle.

Accordingly the silver, escorted by Cain, Barnard, Davidge and Cross, was taken in waggons
to the aerodrome and safely deposited in one of
the gondolas of the airship. An hour later another
quantity of silver, aggregating 100,000 dollars, was
placed on board. It was General Poseda's ill-
acquired wealth, and to disarm suspicion it was
packed in canisters which bore inscriptions to the
effect that they contained " gas."

The flight, suggested by Kayburn and authorised
by General Poseda, was to commence half an hour
before sunset, and the occasion gave the inhabitants
of Bomanares an excuse for yet another fête,
which was to be attended by President Bramo,
General Poseda, Almirante Gimletto and other
heads of Government departments.

Poseda's statement concerning the projected flight—he had given out that it was for the purpose of bombing the capital of Ouro Preto—had the effect of causing another wave of popularity towards the Government. Instead of hisses and shouts of dissent, the President was greeted with enthusiastic *vivas* as in full uniform and attended by his staff he appeared to witness the airship's departure.

The crew of the airship consisted of Cain, a navigating officer in command, Kayburn as pilot and second in command, Barnard, Davidge, Cross and eleven Paraquilan airmen on whom Kayburn could rely. The huge vessel, her ballonettes charged to the fullest capacity, was hauled from its shed and " anchored " by means of ropes held by two hundred troops.

" You'll have to issue the invitation to the President," remarked Cain to Kayburn, as the two leant over the rail of the catwalk and surveyed the animated scene. " If I asked Poseda he might smell a rat. . . . I must learn the lingo. How long will it take, do you think ? "

" That depends," replied the airman guardedly. " If you know French and Latin that will help a lot, but it rests largely with the individual. Some pick up a knowledge of foreign languages very much quicker than others. You ought to be able to carry on a conversation in a couple of months. . . . Right-o: I'll go and have a pi-jaw with old Bramo."

It was soon evident that Kayburn had a very persuasive manner in dealing with the pompous

President.   Cain noticed that Poseda frowned and
shook his shoulders when Kayburn requested
Bramo to come on board and pay a state visit
of inspection ; but the President, grinning with
gratification, led the way, and the rest of the staff
had no option but to accompany him.

The gaudily uniformed crowd were shepherded
into the fore bomb-dropping compartment, and
were listening with the deepest gratification to
Kayburn's highly exaggerated description of the
powerful nature of the offensive armament, when
Cain gave the signal for the men grasping the
holding-down rope to let go.   The order was
obeyed promptly and without any suspicion on
the part of the Paraquilan officer in charge of the
" ground-party," possibly because he imagined
that the President had suddenly decided to experience a trial flight.

Up soared the airship under the lifting power of
her hydrogen-filled gas-bags—so gently that the
President and his companions had no idea that
the airship was free until the loud cheers of the
thousand spectators greeted the daring of the head
of the Republic, and the slight swaying movement
caused the visitors to gaze at each other with no
little apprehension.

A gong rang twice in quick succession—the
signal for the motor to be set going.

" What has happened ? " demanded Bramo,
addressing his guide.

" I'll see, your Excellency," replied Kayburn, and
slipping through the doorway he promptly slammed
the metal flap and bolted it on the outside.

" Scuppered the lot ! " he announced, as he rejoined Cain in the pilot-cabin. " Hear them ? They're in a blue funk already."

" They'll have the door down in half a shake," declared the pirate captain. " Go and tell them to stow their row or there'll be trouble."

This Kayburn did, informing the President that he and his companions were prisoners, and that if they gave any trouble he would release the gondola in which they were.

" And it is a long drop, señores," he added. " Already we are eight hundred metres above the ground."

" What is the meaning of this outrage ? " demanded the President in none too confident a voice.

" No outrage," replied Kayburn blandly. " It is a general deportation of the late Government of Paraquil carried out at the orders of the provisional President of the Republic. If you give no further trouble you will receive none, but I again warn you that resistance means death."

They were quiet after that. To be deposed was quite a common occurrence as far as the rulers of Paraquil were concerned. Usually death by shooting followed as a natural sequence, but now the procedure promised to be different.

For ten minutes the airship hovered over the northern section of the hostile lines. A few spasmodic rifle-shots greeted her, but in the absence of anti-aircraft guns she was immune from shrapnel.

By the aid of glasses Cain could make out the

results of the airship's appearance. Hitherto the besieging forces, although they knew of the fact that Paraquil possessed a huge lighter-than-air craft, were under the impression that either she was unfit to fly or else her crew lacked sufficient confidence and capability to take her up.

For the most part the Ouro Pretoan troops had taken cover, only a few remaining to fire at the airship. Between the lines men were bolting for whatever shelter that offered, even trusting to the flimsy adobe huts with palm-leaf thatch.

"We could win the war in a couple of hours," declared Cain. "A bomb or two would be an act of humanity."

"I vote we wait, sir," suggested Kayburn. "A little inoffensive demonstration will put the wind up 'em. Later on, if you've no objection, we'll issue an ultimatum, and then pay a visit to Cordoba-da-Fe. That's the most important town in Ouro Preto, although it isn't the capital. Well, sir, we've got the late Paraquilan Government on board; what do you propose to do with them?"

"Maroon 'em," replied Cain grimly. "Not on hostile territory. Much as I dislike these oily-featured individuals, I'm not going to leave them to the tender mercies of the enemy. No; we'll descend in a secluded spot. There's no wind, so there ought to be no risk worth considering. We'll turn them loose. They can't get back to Bomanares, and wouldn't if they could. It wouldn't be exactly healthy for the ex-President to show his face in that place again. Right-o, we've demonstrated enough for to-day."

Ringing for the motors to increase to economical cruising speed, Cain settled the airship on a northerly course, checking direction by reference to a fairly reliable map. In an hour and ten minutes she had traversed the whole length of Ouro Preto and was over the neutral Republic of Preyacal.

"How will that do?" inquired the pirate captain, pointing to an expanse of green surrounded on three sides by dense forests.

"Might," replied Kayburn, bringing his glasses to bear upon the spot. "It's difficult to realise what a temporary landing-ground is like from this height. It may be steeply-sloping ground, although at this altitude it appears to be as flat as a pancake."

"Take her down, then," rejoined Cain, stepping aside to let the airman take control. "If we don't like the look of things we can ascend. According to my reckoning the town of Hujas is only twenty miles away to the east'ard. A tramp of that distance will reduce Almirante Mondez Gimletto's fat considerably."

In practically still air the airship descended until Kayburn checked the descent at eighty feet from the ground. The spot was ideal for the landing, the coarse grass was not too high, while there were sun-dried cracks in the ground to offer excellent holding for the emergency grapnels.

Kayburn gave an order. A few seconds later powerful exhaust pumps began to reduce the quantity of hydrogen in the ballonettes and store it under pressure in gas-tight cylinders.

As soon as the gondolas bumped lightly on the

ground, six of the crew descended, holding on
until their weight was more than compensated
by the reduced " lift " of the hydrogen. Then,
planting the flukes of the grapnels in the ground,
they gave the signal for their comrades on board
to heave down on the four holding cables.

More gas was then pumped from the envelope
to neutralise the weight of the portly ex-members
of the Paraquilan Government ; for until this
was done the shanghaied men would not be set
ashore.

Ordering half a dozen of the crew to act as armed
guards, Cain, accompanied by Kayburn and
Barnard, went to the door of the gondola in
which ex-President Bramo and his companions
were secured.

" Listen carefully to what I have to say, General
Poseda ! " he exclaimed, addressing the only
English-speaking member of the party. " Bramo
and the others will come to no harm if they carry
out my orders. I suppose you are aware that
they were carried off under the orders of the
Provisional Government of Paraquil del Norte ?
You are not ? Well, you know now. First, tell
your companions to throw their firearms out of
the scuttle. They may retain their swords ; but
if I find any other weapon amongst you, look out
for squalls. You don't know what that means ?
Sorry, I'd forgotten you aren't a sailor. In other
words, do as you're told or there'll be trouble."

Poseda conveyed the gist of this order to his
companions, and presently a number of firearms
were projected through the open scuttle on to the

ground, where one of the airship's crew collected
them and placed them on board again.

The door was then unlocked and the prisoners
were told to come out at half-minute intervals.
Looking sullen and downcast they emerged until
Poseda alone was left. No doubt their feelings
were those of relief when they found their feet
touching solid ground, but they were still in the
dark as to where they were.

Cain asked Kayburn to explain. The airman
did so, adding that the town of Hujas was only
thirty kilometres away, and that if they stepped
out smartly they ought to be there by sunset.

" Belay there a minute, Kayburn ! " interrupted
Cain. " Sorry to butt in, but I can't see friend
Poseda. I'll fetch him along."

Going to the gondola, at the door of which
armed guards were still posted, the pirate captain
ordered Poseda to come out.

The general obeyed, grinning inanely.

" It's all right, Captain Trevor ! " he exclaimed
mysteriously. " It's a very smart piece of work
this coup of yours. Of course I know that to
allay suspicion you have to include me. I don't
mind. We are now able to resume our voyage
with our respective treasure."

" Are we ? " rejoined Cain in cold, cutting tones
that made Poseda recoil. " Are we ? Is that how
you obey my orders ? Line up with the rest this
instant ! "

" But, señor—— "

" This instant ! " thundered the pirate captain.

The wretched Poseda skipped to the ladder,

moving quicker than he had done for years, fell on his hands upon the ground, recovered himself and ran to take his place by the side of his companions in misfortune to the accompaniment of roars of laughter from the crew of the airship.

Cain held up his hand. The levity died away. Although the Paraquilan airmen were ignorant of English, the gesture of the pirate captain needed no interpreter.

" Now, Mr. Kayburn ! " he began. " I am about to deliver a short speech. If you will kindly translate for the benefit of the native crew, and General Poseda will do the same to enlighten the ex-President, I will begin.

" I came to Bomanares with the intention of helping Paraquil against her enemies. As a practical proof I brought a cargo of munitions, which the Minister of War was very pleased to receive. For the cargo I was paid fifty thousand dollars, part of which I apportioned amongst my crew. I will say nothing further concerning General Poseda's suggestion to me. Unless he reveals to his companions in roguery or they counsel him to do so, the matter ends by the officers and crew of this airship being the richer by a hundred thousand dollars.

" But what I particularly want to point out is the circumstances that compelled me to kidnap the Government of Paraquil, observing that the act was sanctioned by the provisional President, Pedro Aquillo. I discovered from reliable sources that it was the intention of these gentlemen (looking in the direction of Bramo and his companions) to let my men and me risk our lives for the Republic ; then, should Ouro Preto and Banda Rica be defeated, I was to be conveniently put out of the way, and the fifty thousand dollars would be taken by the President and his Ministers. That state of affairs I mean to alter. I hope to make, and I feel certain I shall succeed, the Republic of Paraquil del Norte a State fit for honest men. That is all. You are dismissed. Thank your lucky stars, ex-President Lippo Bramo & Co., that you've a white man to deal with."

Cain expected angry and indignant protests. There were none. The members of the late Government turned and hurried away.

"Now, this applies to all hands," announced the pirate captain after the shanghaied officials had disappeared. "The hundred thousand dollars forming part of the illegally obtained hoard of General Poseda will be distributed as follows, as soon as we are up again. I take twenty thousand ; a similar sum will be allotted to Mr. Kayburn. To Mr. Barnard will be handed ten thousand dollars. The remainder, fifty thousand dollars, will be divided equally between the hands, British and Paraquilan alike."

Checking a demonstration of joy on the part of Barnard, Davidge and Cross, the pirate captain requested Kayburn to translate. When he had done so the enthusiasm was unbounded.

Cain let the men give vent to their exuberance, then he gave orders for the airship to get under way again.

" Thanks awfully, Mr. Trevor ! " said Kayburn,

when at the first favourable moment the two were able to exchange words. "But, I say, aren't we helping ourselves rather—rather——"

He broke off, unable to frame the thought in his mind.

"Yes, we are, rather," added Cain. "But if you never have anything weightier on your conscience you're decidedly lucky, old son."

"It was rather a smart move, that of yours, sir," continued Kayburn—"finding out all about Bramo's intention to do you in and collar the money."

"'S'pose it was," agreed Cain. "As a matter of fact, it was pure guesswork on my part, and, judging by the way those greasy rogues took it, I wasn't far out."

CHAPTER XIV

" JUDAS ! "

WITHOUT any outstanding incidents the airship arrived at her destination, the sheds at Sorbombo. According to recently-passed regulations relating to the attitude of neutrals towards aircraft of nations at war, the Paraquilan airship was permitted to remain forty-eight hours on Brazilian territory and to take in what fuel and hydrogen she required to enable her to continue her flight. If, at the expiration of the period of grace, the airship could not or would not resume her voyage internment would follow automatically.

Already the silver dollars had been apportioned, and the task was to place them in safe keeping. Since Cain and Kayburn could not both leave the airship at the same time, the airman asked the pirate captain to deposit his share in a bank in Bahia.

Hiring a powerful motor and taking Barnard, Davidge and Cross as armed escort, Cain took the silver into Bahia and drove straight to Dom Saldanha's bank.

Years ago Cain had had transactions with the firm. That was when he was a junior-lieutenant on one of the ships of the British South American and West Indies squadron; and it was hardly likely that Saldanha would recognise his client as such.

The pirate captain acted perfectly honourably with his men. He saw that Barnard and the others deposited most of their shares and received the necessary receipt; carried out Kayburn's request as to the deposit of his twenty thousand dollars; and then he paid in practically the whole of the money he had retained for himself out of the proceeds of the *Nike's* cargo and of his share of Poseda's hoard.

This done, he requested to be shown into Dom Saldanha's private room.

" Good day, señor—— " exclaimed the Principal, glancing over his spectacles at a slip of paper on which Cain had written his present assumed name. " Ah! Dom Trevor. Remarkable! Only a matter of minutes since, an Englishman was inquiring for a Señor Trevorrick. Perchance he made a slight mistake in your name, and wished to arrange an interview ? "

This information caused Cain furiously to think. Evidently some one had a well-founded idea that the captain of the pirate submarine *Alerte* had not perished with his command; but who? Not for one moment did he imagine the person referred to to be Pengelly; he was serving a life-sentence. Nor could it very well be any of the crew for similar reasons. But on further consideration it might be some one sent out to Bahia on Pengelly's information, since Cain had stated that he was about to transfer a portion of his ill-gotten booty to the care of Dom Saldanha—a proposal that he had no idea of carrying out.

Keeping his features under perfect control, Cain shook his head.

" I am afraid the business that brought your late client here has nothing to do with me," he replied. " What was the person's name ? Or is it a breach of confidence to reveal that information ? "

" Not at all," answered Saldanha. " As a matter of fact, no business resulted. The caller gave the name of Captain Solomon Tuke."

" Never heard of him," declared Cain emphatically. " Now, señor, if you will be so kind as to favour me with your attention."

For the next twenty minutes the two men discussed the matter of investments, and having accepted Saldanha's proposals, Cain took his leave.

His next step was to order dinner for his companions, leaving them in a café while he went to an hotel which he knew to be rarely used by British visitors to this Brazilian port. He had no wish to fall across any one likely to recognise him, but he had a strange yearning to see an English newspaper.

A waiter handed him a couple of papers. They had been published in London three weeks previously. Scanning these, Cain could not help realising how hopelessly he had lost touch with events at home. References to things that had taken place and were familiar to millions of

II

Britons all over the world were baffling mysteries as far as he was concerned.

"I can understand old Rip Van Winkle's perplexity now, by Jove!" he exclaimed. "What wouldn't I give to have a holiday in London!"

Presently his interest quickened at the heading— "Echo of the *Alerte* case." It was a report of an inquest held at Okehampton on the decomposed body of a man in convict's clothes, and went on to say that the corpse had been identified as that of Paul Pengelly, late second in command of the pirate submarine *Alerte* who had effected his escape from Dartmoor a month ago while undergoing a life-sentence.

"I wonder," mused Cain. "That blighter was a cunning rogue. I wouldn't be satisfied that he's dead until I've seen him in his coffin. Now, if Pengelly has thrown off pursuit, he'll probably make for Bahia to get what he imagined to be his share of the cash. That being the case, and putting two and two together, I shouldn't be very much surprised to find that Pengelly and that chap Tuke are one and the same person. That's unfortunate. Supposing he spots me? But, after all, he can't do much. He daren't denounce me, because he must know that he'll be liable to extradition."

Leisurely completing his meal, Cain paid and tipped the waiter and strolled out into the plaza, where he found Barnard and the others waiting by the car.

"We've seen that sweep Pengelly, sir," announced the bo'sun.

Cain nodded.

" I had my suspicions he was here," he rejoined. " Did he see you ? "

" No, sir," replied Barnard. " We were sitting at a table and could overlook the street. Pengelly came along dressed up like a regular toff. He didn't look our way ; in fact, he was keeping his eyes on the ground and looking very much down in the mouth."

" Let's hope he was," said Cain, with a laugh. " We don't want to run across him if it can be avoided, although he'll be afraid to say anything. But, on the other hand, if he's still under the impression that we are down in Davy Jones's locker we'll let him carry on with it. Right-o, lads ! All aboard ! We'll get clear of Bahia as sharp as we can."

.   .   .   .

Meanwhile Pengelly, his hopes once again dashed to the ground, was pacing the streets of Bahia, and racking his brains over the problem of existence. He had yet to face the wrath of the Jew who had given him shelter, found him clothes and provided money to enable him to present himself to Señor Saldanha as a co-partner of the deceased Thomas Trevorrick. It was more than likely the Jew would prosecute him as a person guilty of obtaining goods by fraudulent misrepresentation, and Pengelly had no desire to make the acquaintance of another prison — and a Brazilian one at that. The obvious way out of the difficulty was to decamp ; but there again the problem arose : where could he go ? He had not sufficient money to pay for a long railway journey; he dare not attempt to find a berth on a British or a Yankee vessel, and he was most reluctant to ship aboard a craft officered and manned by non-English-speaking men.

In this downcast mood he passed within ten yards of Barnard and his two companions, and made his way to one of the quays.

Here, as luck would have it, a man, drawing the correct conclusion that here was a foreigner down on his luck, handed Pengelly a printed slip of paper. On it, in a weird jargon supposed to be English, was a call for volunteers for the Army of Paraquil del Norte now at war with Banda Rica and Ouro Preto.

" Ver fine chance for ze aventurer, señor," remarked the agent wheedlingly.

Pengelly considered the matter in his usual, indecisive manner, could not make up his mind to accept the invitation or to decline it. He was adventurous by nature, yet he hadn't any desire to be a target for hostile riflemen; he wanted money, wondered whether there was any chance of making it quickly as a foreign volunteer; decided that he could not make his way south with only ten milreis in his possession, and said so.

" That is of no deefeecultee, señor," prompted the agent, whose incentive was the Brazilian equivalent to ten English pounds for every likely recruit he obtained. He did not think it necessary to add that there was a thousand-to-one chance of anybody getting through the hostile lines around Bomanares; but Pengelly did, adding that he had been paid off from an oil-tanker that was under orders for Bomanares and that his skipper didn't place much hope on being able to run the blockade.

"Again there is no deefeecultee, señor," continued the plausible agent. "But a few minutes ago I speak wid a man who was motor-driver to de Paraquilan officers. He tell me Paraquil airsheep am ober at Sorbombo, an' officeers dey are 'ere in Bahia. Dy give you passage to Bomanares, see ? "

"Right-o, old son ! " replied Pengelly recklessly. "Where is the car ? "

"Von minute," exclaimed the man. "Der is formality to undertake. Come dis way an' sign papaire."

Pengelly followed him into a sort of office, carelessly put his assumed signature to a form without which the agent could not claim the capitation fee, and was directed to a certain plaza there to inquire for Manuel Paz, the chauffeur to the Paraquilan officers.

" 'Tany rate, if they give me a lift to Sorbombo, I'm well clear of that Jew," thought Pengelly, as he hurried in the direction of the plaza. "If I change my mind and get left behind, then I'm no worse off than I am at present, so here goes."

The approach to the square was through a narrow lane which ran into the north side of the plaza. Consequently Pengelly came out on the shady side of the place where a porticoed building cast a sombre shadow on the pavement. Right in the full glare of the sun was the only car to be seen.

Suddenly Pengelly " brought up all standing," with his eyes starting out of his head, for by the side of the vehicle were the men whom he had every reason to believe were rotting on the bed of Bahia Arenas—Davidge, Cross, Barnard the bo'sun and Captain Cain.

Recoiling, Pengelly took refuge behind a stone pillar. Hardly able to realise that his eyesight was not at fault, he waited and watched. He had made no mistake : there were his old ship-mates very much alive.

Presently the car moved away, leaving the would-be recruit for the Paraquil del Norte Army standing under the shady portico.

" I'll get even with him yet," muttered Pengelly, shaking his fist in the direction of the now out-of-sight Captain Cain. " It's no use my tackling him and getting him to pay up if I keep my mouth shut. He'd more than likely plug me with an automatic pistol bullet. Nasty customer to tackle is Cain ! No ; that's no go. Well, thank goodness he didn't spot me. . . . Ah ! I've an idea—a regular topping brain-wave ; so here goes."

A few minutes later Pengelly took a table at an open-air café, ordered writing material and a bottle of wine, then after brief deliberation he wrote as follows :

" BAHIA, BRAZIL.

" SIR,—I feel it my duty as a Briton and a patriot to inform you that Thomas Trevorrick, otherwise known as Captain Cain, late of the pirate submarine *Alerte*, is alive, as are three of his crew, namely, Barnard (boatswain of the ship), Davidge and Cross. I have just seen them in this city and have found out that they are in the service of the Army of Paraquil del Norte.

" When you act upon this information and cause the pirates to be handed over to the British Government, I request that the reward offered for their apprehension will be paid me, c/o Banqua Nacionale, Calle Balmaceda, Bahia.—I have the honour to be, Sir, your humble and respectful servant,   Solomon Tuke.

" To the Chief Commissioner of Police,
        Scotland Yard,
            London, England."

CHAPTER XV

CAIN'S ULTIMATUM

"THERE'S your scrap of paper, old bean," announced Cain cheerfully, as he handed Kayburn an official receipt for 19,500 dollars deposited with Dom Saldanha & Company. "A nice little nest-egg for a rainy day! With luck you ought to augment it considerably before this year's finished. How are things progressing?"

Kayburn took the receipt and placed it in his pocket-book.

"Thanks awfully, sir," he replied. "Things progressing? I've made it all right with the officer in charge, and we've taken in sufficient hydrogen for three months. We're all ready to get under way when you give the word, sir."

"We'll make a start at once, then," decided Cain. "I want to leave an ultimatum at Cordoba da Fe on our way south."

"Very good, sir," rejoined Kayburn. "I suppose you wouldn't care to stop at Hujas on our way south and inquire after the health of the ex-President of Paraquil del Norte?"

"I hope we've finished with that mealy-mouthed rascal," replied Cain. "It's curious how hard it is to shake off rogues of that kidney. Curiously enough there was a fellow in Bahia who played me a very dirty trick. I didn't see him, and he didn't see me, but three of my men spotted him. I shouldn't be surprised if I didn't fall foul of him before very long. If I do, by Jove, there'll be something for him to write home about."

Kayburn did not ask for further information, nor did Cain attempt to enlighten him.

"He's a jolly decent fellow," thought Dick Kayburn. "A thundering good sort; but I'm hanged if I'd like to rub him up the wrong way!"

Early next morning, when the airship was nearing the north-eastern frontier of Ouro Preto, Cain entered the pilot's cabin to relieve Kayburn.

"Let me know what you think of that?" he remarked, handing the younger man a sheet of paper.

It was Cain's ultimatum to the Republic of Ouro Preto, stating that on Thursday next the Parquilan airship would revisit Cordoba da Fe. At the hour of eleven she would take up a position two thousand feet above the citadel. At 11.15, if in the meanwhile the Republican colours were not struck and a white flag hoisted over the building, the citadel would be destroyed. At quarter of an hour intervals other public buildings would be bombed until the Ouro Pretoan Government agreed to terms of peace as follows :

(a) The blockade of Bomanares to be raised forthwith, and the troops of the Allied Republics were to be withdrawn across their respective frontiers.

(b) An indemnity, either in money, food-stuffs or raw material, to the value of 5,000,000 dollars, to be paid to the Government of Paraquil del Norte within three months of the signing of the peace treaty.

(c) Armaments of the Allied Republics to be restricted, and standing armies to be reduced to 5000 men.

(d) The armed forces of Paraquil del Norte are to be correspondingly reduced.

(e) No export or import duties are to be imposed on goods sold by Paraquil del Norte to Banda Rica and Ouro Preto, or *vice versa*.

" Think they'll knuckle under, sir ? " asked Kayburn.

" They will," replied the pirate captain confidently. " The terms are easy. Five million dollars isn't much, considering the resources of the place. It will be only a little more than the amount of damage done to Bomanares during the siege. Yes, I think they'll accept."

The appearance of the Paraquilan airship over the largest city of Ouro Preto was a signal for general consternation amongst the inhabitants. Before the vessel was over the outskirts of the straggling city the squares and streets were practically deserted. Here and there could be seen individuals whose curiosity or bravado was stronger than their desire to seek doubtful shelter on the ground floors of the large stone buildings, while one reckless man emptied his revolver in the direction of the airship that floated serenely a good thousand feet beyond the range of the relatively harmless weapon.

Unruffled, the airship maintained her stately progress—a fact that caused almost as much conjecture on the part of the inhabitants of Cordoba da Fe as the first glimpse of her had caused consternation. There was something decidedly uncanny in the way the Paraquilan vessel passed exactly over the citadel and yet failed to take advantage of her position to drop bombs upon the place.

Opening the chute of the bomb-dropping gadget, Cain released three small parachutes at five seconds' interval. Each parachute had a tin case containing a copy of the ultimatum.

" Hard-a-port ! " ordered the pirate captain. " Let's see what happens."

The airship executed a turn of sixteen degrees, slowed down and remained almost motionless over the ground, in the teeth of a twenty-miles-an-hour breeze.

One of the parachutes fell on the flat roof of a small building ; another dropped into a deserted street ; the third fell in the plaza in front of the cathedral. Here about half a dozen men were standing about, torn between curiosity to watch the airship and anxiety to take refuge in the sacred building.

As the parachute dropped they backed behind the pillars supporting the porch. Nothing happening, they mustered sufficient courage to look from a distance at the collapsed silken envelope. Finally one man, more daring than the rest, approached the parachute, holding one hand over his eyes as if that were sufficient protection from a possible explosion. Then gingerly detaching the tin case and carrying it at arm's length he proceeded to rejoin his companions, who took to their heels in a panic, leaving him standing in solitude in the centre of the plaza.

Quite five minutes elapsed before a priest came from the cathedral and inspected the case. Apparently the finder was unable to read, so the cleric announced the message written on the outside of the tin. Then, holding the case above his head, the man ran as hard as he could to the citadel.

"They've received that all right," declared Cain. "Bring her back on her former course, Kayburn. Now we'll see what our reception at Bomanares will be like."

Night had fallen when the airship approached her hangar. The arrival had been timed for an hour after sunset in order to avoid drawing the fire of the hostile batteries. On the landing-ground position-lights and powerful arcs announced that all preparations had been made for the arrival. A vast concourse of people, strangely silent, thronged the steeply - rising ground on each side.

But directly the holding - down ropes were thrown and the airship came to rest, shouts of "Where are the traitors ? What has become of that coward, Lippo Bramo ? " rent the night.

Cain held up his hand for silence, obtained it and then motioned to Kayburn to address the crowd. With almost perfect command of the hybrid Spanish-Indian language Kayburn "let himself go." He held the vast audience spellbound, save for hisses when the names of the members of the late Government were mentioned. Then, when he announced that on the following Thursday the city of Cordoba da Fe would be bombed unless the enemy accepted terms, enthusiasm ran riot. And no wonder : Paraquil had had almost enough war. She had been content to remain on the defensive, but when food supplies began to run low and starvation seemed only a matter of a few days ; when her more-or-less trusted rulers had apparently left her in the lurch—then the acute nature of the situation dawned upon the usually light-hearted inhabitant of the small extent of the Republic as yet not overrun by the armies of Ouro Preto and Banda Rica.

So far Cain's plans had gone well. The puppet candidate, Pedro Aquillo, had been successfully engineered into the Presidential chair ; a Spaniard who had served as an attaché on the Western Front in the Great War had been appointed Minister for War, and by his initiative had already succeeded in creating a vast improvement in the *morale* of the Paraquilan troops. In addition to all this, the knowledge that they now possessed an efficient airship which had already demonstrated its capability to menace the farthermost parts of the hostile Republics; and they had the Englishman's promise that within the next few days Paraquil del Norte would be at peace.

No wonder, then, that enthusiastic shouts of " Viva los Ingles " rent the air.

Cain lost no time in making preparations for the flight to Cordoba da Fe. Fully aware that amongst the motley population of Bomanares there would be several miscreants who were not above betraying the State to its enemies, he made no secret of the grim task he had set himself to perform should the Republic of Ouro Preto reject the ultimatum.

The unfilled bomb-cases were taken with much ostentation from the citadel to the flying-ground, where they were charged with 700 kilos of high explosives placed on board the airship. Four machine-guns with men to work them were mounted in various parts of the ship. Stores and provisions were replenished and the intricate machinery and actuating gear overhauled and tested. Finally, twenty soldiers were warned for duty on board to act as ceremonial guards should Cordoba da Fe surrender.

There was one person at least in Bomanares who viewed these preparations with apprehension. That was the Greek, Basil Zaros. Following upon the involuntary flight of Almirante Mondez Gimletto there were two aspirants to the post of Minister of Marine. One was a native of Paraquil who now held command of one of the armed steamers ; Zaros was the other. On account of his popularity over the successful engagement with the blockading gunboats, the Greek stood the better chance of the two. Apart from his well-concealed cowardice he was a good

organiser, and if he succeeded in becoming Minister
of Marine he would no longer have to take an
active part in naval fighting. Moreover, he would
be in a position to make money in certain crooked
ways in which Greeks excel.

But now this roseate prospect bid fair to be
overclouded. When the war was over there
would be no need for a Paraquilan Navy; the
Republic possessed no merchant shipping beyond
a few river steamers. Consequently Zaros would
be in that undesirable state known to seafarers
as being " on the beach." He would prefer that
the war went on indefinitely. He even contemplated the possibility of crippling or destroying
the airship; but lacking the nerve and fearing the
consequences of failure he contented himself by
uttering maledictions on the vessel, and on all
on board her, hoping fervently that something
would happen to make the attempt completely
unsuccessful.

Just before midnight on Wednesday the airship started on her errand of destruction or mercy;
that depended upon the sequence of events.
Throughout the two preceding days the batteries
of the investing forces had been silent. Cain
regarded this as a good omen. To him it proved
conclusively that the enemy were chary of pro-
voking the airship to acts of reprisal. Nevertheless, he decided not to run any risks of taking
the vessel up by daylight. Her previous ascent
was an entire surprise to the hostile gunners,
and before they could man their weapons the
airship was out of range. On this occasion the

day, if not the time, of her departure had been well advertised.

It was an anxious five minutes after the airship left her shed, as far as Cain was concerned. He realised that if the enemy showed any initiative they would have registered the range during daylight, and trusted to luck to shell the vessel as she was being hauled out into the open.

With hardly a sound and unaccompanied by the whine of enemy projectiles, the airship shot skywards as soon as the holding-down ropes were released. Not until she attained an altitude of eight thousand feet did Cain give orders for the motors to be started. Then, working up to a steady forty miles an hour, the airship headed for the distant city of Cordoba da Fe.

At daybreak, finding he was ahead of the scheduled time, Cain ordered the speed to be still further reduced; and, requesting Kayburn to have him awakened in two hours' time, went to his cabin to enjoy a well-earned repose.

At nine o'clock the hands, with the exception of those absolutely necessary for the navigation of the airship, piped to breakfast. An hour later, Cain " went the rounds " to satisfy himself that everything was in readiness, and that every one knew his orders. On no account was indiscriminate rifle-firing to be indulged in by the soldiers on board—a command that would be somewhat hard for a Paraquilan to carry out, since the general instinct of these men, whenever they have a loaded rifle in their hands, is to let it loose upon somebody or something.

The bells of the city were striking the hour of eleven when the Paraquilan airship, swooping down from the high stratum of clouds, hovered over the citadel at the previously-stated altitude of only two thousand feet.

No gunfire greeted her appearance. The national flags flew over the citadel, the barracks and most of the public buildings. The streets and plazas were almost empty, but on the hills to the north and west of the city great crowds of people were congregated.

" They mean to defy us," declared Kayburn, who was standing by the controls that actuated a rapid increase of hydrogen to the ballonettes— a precaution necessary in the event of the batteries opening fire, in which case the airship would have to ascend rapidly to a safe altitude.

" It's bluff, pure bluff," rejoined Cain. " I'll stake my bottom dollar that they'll strike those rags within thirty seconds of the quarter."

" Let's hope you're right, sir," remarked Kayburn.

Slowly the seconds ticked away into minutes until the clocks struck the quarter. Cain, giving a quizzical glance at his companion, swung round and pressed the switch communicating with the bomb-dropping device.

The airship gave a perceptible upward jerk as the heavy missile left the chute. From the scuttles of the pilot-house the course of the falling bomb was invisible until it had traversed five hundred feet of space. Then it appeared within the radius of vision, turning slowly on its vertical

12

axis in spite of the steadying fans, as it hurtled with terrific and ever-increasing rapidity towards its objective.

A vivid yellow flash, a deafening roar, and the deadly high explosive had done its work. The airship, caught in the wave of displaced air, rocked, lurched and pitched in the midst of the dense acrid-smelling cloud of smoke. Deafened by the stupendous roar, none on board realised that the vessel had just been lifted vertically through five hundred feet of space, and then had dropped twice that distance ere she drew clear of the nauseous fumes.

For quite five minutes Cain peered in vain through the dust and smoke to observe the results of his stern messenger; but when the veil was lifted he was no longer in doubt as to the accuracy of the missile and the havoc it had accomplished.

The citadel, a Spanish-built structure, quite capable of performing the duty it had been called upon to fulfil in the sanguinary war of independence in the early nineteenth century, was not proof against the powerful bomb, however much it had been against the smooth-bore muzzle-loaders of the days of Bolivar and O'Higgins.

The massive square tower had been completely demolished, a pyramid of still smoking stone and timber filling the greater part of the courtyard that had enclosed it.

From the buildings surrounding the outer wall —a feature that had prevented damage beyond the precincts of the citadel—hundreds of the terrified inhabitants, who had taken refuge in cellars, poured panic-stricken into the narrow streets, their sole object being to put as great a distance between them and the public buildings before the next quarter of an hour elapsed.

At precisely ten minutes from the time of releasing the first bomb, Cain gave orders for the airship to take up a position two thousand feet above the artillery barracks.

Suddenly Kayburn uttered an exclamation of satisfaction, and pointed to the flagstaff over the building. The national colours of Ouro Preto were being lowered, while a man stood by with a white flag ready to hoist.

"Thought so," remarked Cain. "Yes, the other ensigns are being struck. . . . Belay there, and secure the release gear, Mr. Barnard! It won't be wanted again."

The airship came to earth about a mile outside the city. Cain, accompanied by the men who had served under him from England and by the Paraquilan guard, made his way to the City Hall, where he was met by the Governor of the district, the Commandante of the fortress and the Mayor and other civic officials of Cordoba da Fe.

The Governor explained that he had received telegraphic instructions from the Presidente of Ouro Preto too late to prevent the release of the bomb.

"Were there any casualties?" asked Cain.

"No, Señor Capitan-general," replied the Governor. "The citadel had been previously evacuated."

"In that case the damage doesn't matter,"

rejoined Cain cheerfully. " The citadel won't be wanted again."

Waiting only to receive a formal acceptance of the peace terms, Cain returned to the airship, leaving the guard under the command of a captain to represent the Paraquilan Government until the terms were ratified and the indemnity paid.

" That's all shipshape and Bristol-fashion, Kayburn ! " he exclaimed, when he rejoined the English airman. " Now up we go. We'll wireless the good news and then we'll make for Bomanares to reap the reward of our labours."

CHAPTER XVI

IN THE HOUR OF HIS TRIUMPH

PAUL PENGELLY was in the depths of despair. Six months had elapsed since the day on which he wrote to Scotland Yard, betraying his one-time partner.

He had heard nothing in reply. Although he eagerly scanned the English newspapers, which were to be seen in the Bahia public libraries, not a word or a hint had been given to indicate that his startling information had been communicated to the Press. That, he decided, was not to be wondered at ; but he could not understand why the reward had not been sent out to him. Time enough had elapsed for Cain to have been extradited and brought back to England ; yet the authorities, both at home and in South America, seemed to be doing absolutely nothing in the matter.

Meanwhile Pengelly just managed to exist. He began almost to regret that he was not back in Dartmoor Prison. There, although the work was hard, he was sure of his food. In Bahia he was not. Fear of a chance meeting with a former seafaring acquaintance kept him away from the quays. He had tried his hand at various odd jobs, even that of a fireman on board a river steamer, a task almost invariably undertaken by members of the coloured population of Brazil. He had toiled under a blazing sum in the coffee plantations ; had driven a team of mules on a cotton-growing estate, and had been obliged to accept work that even a *peon* would refuse.

By this time his liabilities to the Jew who had posed as his benefactor had accumulated considerably. At first the man was inclined to believe Pengelly's story that, although he had been disappointed at being able to obtain money from Saldanha, there was a large sum shortly arriving for him from London. As time went on and the promised windfall did not materialise, the Jew took steps to recompense himself by other means.

One evening Pengelly returned to his squalid lodgings with 500 *reis*. On paper that looked a fair amount, but actually it represented a little more than a shilling.

Somewhat to his surprise he found that the Jew departed from his lately-acquired habit of reviling his unprofitable guest, and after supper offered Pengelly a bottle of wine.

" This to your good fortune, Señor Tuke," exclaimed the Jew. " In the market-place to-day a wise woman told my fortune. Gracias ! She was certain that within the next few days a foreigner would receive a fortune and that I would benefit by it. Drink to the glorious days that are to come. Señor Tuke ! "

Pengelly did drink. That was the last act he was conscious of for the next twelve hours.

He awoke with a terrific headache. His tongue was swollen and parched; his eyesight seemed blurred and distorted. He could not at first realise where he was, until the thud of a propeller and the erratic movement of the darkened hole in which he found himself announced the unpleasant truth that he had been drugged and placed on board a ship.

"That swine of a Portuguese Jew has made money out of me, after all," he thought grimly. "I wonder what he got for shanghai-ing me?"

His disjointed thoughts were interrupted by some one on deck shouting out an order. The words were in English.

Pengelly positively quaked. After his precarious existence in Bahia, he did not mind so much if he had been dumped on board a foreigner; but English!—more than likely the vessel was bound for a British port. In that case he would be very much out of the frying-pan and into the fire. He knew the patience and vigilance of the police when hunting for an escaped prisoner, although had he been aware that the body found near Okehampton had been buried as his, he might not have felt so apprehensive.

Presently another fit of drowsiness overcame him and he fell asleep, only to be roused by the door of the cuddy being thrown open and a lamp flashed on his face.

"Out you come, right now!" exclaimed a nasal voice.

" What d'ye mean, dash you ? " retorted Pengelly, with an effort to assert his position as a master mariner of the British Mercantile Marine. " What's the meaning of this outrage ? D'ye know who I am ? "

" Nope ! " replied the man curtly. " An' I guess I don't care. Git out of it, you dope-slugged son of a gun ! "

It was impossible to look dignified when huddled on a floor measuring four feet by three, and still under the influence of doped liquor into the bargain. Pengelly could now only blink like an owl and try to moisten his parched lips with a hot and dry tongue.

" Lay hold of his legs, Jake ! " continued the interrupter of his slumbers. " I'll learn him, sure ! "

The next instant Pengelly's knees were forced against his chin. With none too gentle a heave he was hauled over the metal coaming of the doorway and dumped in the alley-way. Nor was he allowed to remain and rest there. A powerful hand gripped him by the back of the neck. He was yanked to his feet and, aided by the application of the toe of a sea-boot, he was propelled into the sunlight.

" Here he is, Cap'n," announced the mate, who had superintended the new hand's progress from the cubby-hole.

Still blinking, Pengelly found himself confronted by a short, red-faced, broad-shouldered man in soiled white duck uniform and with a peaked cap resting on the back of his head.

" Say, what's your last ship ? " demanded the captain.

No answer.

" Chock-a-block with dope," declared the Old Man. " Take him for'ard, Mr. Mate, an' souse him some. Then put him into the port watch and see that he gets busy. If he don't, bring him along to me."

" Look here——" protested the victim.

The skipper took two steps forward and shook his fist in front of Pengelly's nose.

" Jumpin' Jerusalem ! " he shouted. " What d'ye mean by telling me to ' look here ' ? If you don't quit right now an' get busy you'll get more'n a look from me, you slab-sided hobo ! Skip, I tell ye."

Pengelly skipped so hurriedly that he fell and rolled into the scuppers. Being in a favourable position he was well soused with salt water by all the hands on that part of the deck, until, looking like a half-drowned rat, the miserable man was allowed to recover his feet.

" Can you splice ? " demanded the mate.

" Yes, sir," replied the chastened man.

" Then git an' cut out that nip in that there three-inch hawser," was the order. " If you ain't made a satisfactory job of it before eight bells you'll be feel darned sorry, I guess."

Pengelly went ; remembered that he had not a marline-spike ; borrowed one from a member of the crew who was engaged upon a similar task, and set to work.

Many years had passed since he had last done

any wire splicing. The hawser was of flexible
steel, and had been badly " nipped " as the ship
was warping out of her last berth. Although his
hands were rough with hard work, the sharp
ends of the wires made the blood flow from a score
of painful punctures, even before the preliminary
business of cutting out the " nip " by means of
a cold chisel was accomplished.

As he toiled, Pengelly sought to find out what
ship he was on. Already he knew that she was a
Yankee. The lifebuoys hanging from the guard-
rails of the forepart of the bridge settled that
problem. They bore the words " s.s. *Great Content,*
Boston."

" A floating lie from truck to keelson," thought
the unfortunate man. " Where's she bound, I
wonder ? "

It was now close on nine o'clock, and the sun,
although high in the sky, bore almost dead astern.
That informed him that the course was sou'-west.
So far, so good ; he was not homeward bound.

Just before the hands piped to dinner, the mate
strolled for'ard and inspected the new man's
work. Evidently he looked forward to giving
Pengelly a generous share of his extensive vocabulary, with the additional relish of applying his
ever-ready sea-boot ; but the task had been performed so well that the mate had not a chance
even to complain.

During the meal—it was the best one Pengelly
had tasted for months—the " darned Britisher "
came in for good-natured banter from the tough
New Englanders, and after trying to " pull his

leg " by telling him they were bound for Patagonia with a cargo of refrigerators, they informed him that the *Great Content* was putting into Bomanares Harbour *en route* for Valparaiso *via* Magellan Straits.

This information did not cause Pengelly any great anxiety. He was not at all anxious to come face to face with the man whom he had betrayed ; he had a hazy notion that Cain was somewhere in Paraquil del Norte ; or, now that hostilities were over and the Republic had no need for foreigners to stiffen the ranks of their fighting forces, the pirate captain might have transferred his activities elsewhere. It was Cain's blood-money Pengelly wanted—not the man. He could easily avoid all chance of meeting his former partner by remaining on board the *Great Content* during her brief stay at Bomanares.

Inquiries in another direction elicited the information that Pengelly's wages as an A.B. would be fifty dollars a month. That and his keep would be enough to enable him to save a fair sum by the end of the voyage, he decided. By that time the reward offered for Cain's apprehension (for although this was announced before the destruction of the *Alerte*, the declaration had never, as far as he was aware, been cancelled) might be forthcoming.

But there was another side to the picture— one of which Pengelly was as yet in ignorance. The Jew who had acted as a crimp and had placed the Englishman on board the *Great Content* had been paid the sum of eighty dollars ; this the

Old Man would deduct from Pengelly's pay, besides other charges for his kit which he drew from the ship's "slop chest." Consequently, if he completed the round voyage—a matter of three months—Pengelly would be fortunate if he came ashore with twenty dollars to his credit. If he deserted at Valparaiso he would be even worse off, for, owing to the frequent disappearances of seaman in South American ports, it had become the custom for only a small part of a man's wages to be paid him at the end of each month, the balance being made up at the end of the round trip.

On the third day out of Bahia, the *Good Content* ran into a hurricane. It was the worst known for three years. The seas ran " mountains high," huge masses of foam-flecked waves breaking continuously over the fo'c'sle and flooding the well-deck, carrying away bulwarks, starting the steel plating of the 'midship deckhouse and generally playing havoc. For thirty-six hours the ship battled with the gale, steaming head to wind and never making a mile in the whole of that time. Everything had to be battened down, the watch on deck could not be relieved, those below had to exist in the hot, unwholesome air 'tween decks, and were compelled to hang on with one hand while they conveyed their food to their mouths with the other.

Shortly after midnight the hurricane showed indications of abating, but its " last kick " did the damage. A terrific wave carried away the rudder. The mass of steel as it hung only by the lower pintle fell athwart the swiftly-moving propeller. According to the accepted theory, the impact should have ripped the blades from the boss. The engines began to race furiously. It was not the propeller that had suffered but the propeller shaft. Fractured thirty feet from the stern gland the shaft had sustained damage beyond the resource of the engineers on board to repair. The ship was as helpless as a tin can drifting on the surface of a duck-pond.

Her head fell off, she wallowed in the trough of the enormous seas, lying right over before the force of the wind.

To Pengelly, battened down in the stuffy fo'c'sle, it seemed as if this were the end. He had a momentary glimpse of a dozen hands slithering to lee'ard, accompanied by everything that had not been firmly secured. The lamps went out. In the darkness men cursed, shouted, struggled frantically to get out of the jumble of humanity and gear lying in the angle formed by the fo'c'sle floor and the lockers and bunks that occupied the curving side of the bows.

The ship recovered herself; rolled again, this time to wind'ard, receiving a tremendous beam sea that carried away her boats on the port side and staved-in the engine-room fidleys. After that she rolled again and again, but with less heel. The hurricane had blown itself out.

Presently the dog-weary men of the duty watch were relieved, and Pengelly with the rest of the port hold went " on." Beyond clearing away the raffle on deck, they could do little. The ship

was drifting helplessly towards the not so distant
Brazilian coast, while her wireless operator sent
out frantic S.O.S. calls for aid.

Just as dawn was breaking a medium-sized
liner appeared upon the scene. With a choking
sensation in his throat, Pengelly recognised her
as the *Bronx City*, which, having been withdrawn
from the West African route, was running between
New York, Rio de Janeiro and Buenos Aires.
Only too well Pengelly recalled the circumstances
under which she had been captured by the *Alerte*;
how, in spite of Captain Cain's assurances that she
would not be pillaged, he, Pengelly, had wantonly
broken the pledge, and had not only ransacked
the cargo, but had insulted the officers and men.

The one chance lay in the hope that Captain
Hiram Adams, the tough old skipper of the Yankee
Bronx City, no longer commanded her, and that
she now had a new crew; otherwise it seemed
impossible that sooner or later he would be recognised by some of his former victims.

Slowing down a couple of cables' length to
lee'ard of the *Great Content*, the *Bronx City*
signalled to the former to send off a hawser, and
that she would then tow the disabled vessel into
Bomanares Harbour.

The captain of the *Great Content* leant over
her bridge sails:

" Send away a boat, Mr. Sycamore ! " he shouted,
addressing the mate.

" Ay, ay, sir," was the reply. " Get busy,
lads. Dump that coil into the stern-sheets,
you ; and you guys, man that there boat."

" You guys " included Pengelly. He had no option but to take his place in the boat. The second mate steered, four men rowed, while Pengelly paid over the rope which was to establish communication between the two vessels.

Once more fickle fortune favoured him. Engaged in his task, he had to watch what he was doing, so that he could keep his face down and his head turned away from the *Bronx City*. As the boat ranged alongside the ship the captain hailed her. There was no mistaking that voice : it was that of Captain Hiram Adams.

At length, her task accomplished, the boat returned to the *Great Content*. To the end of the grass line a flexible steel hawser was secured and paid out until the disabled ship was ready to be taken in tow.

This business was an anxious one. There was still a good sea running, although in the almost total absence of wind the waves no longer maintained a crested, broken character. Rudderless, the *Great Content* steered like a dray—sheering erratically, straining at and overrunning the hawser every few minutes.

At six o'clock that evening both vessels were safely moored alongside the wharf at Bomanares. Both captains went ashore, the skipper of the *Great Content* to cable to her owners and to make arrangements for the necessary repairs to be effected ; the *Bronx City's* Old Man to obtain oil fuel, for the heavy consumption due to the towing operations had almost depleted the rescuing vessel's store of liquid fuel.

Both were doomed to disappointment. Boman-ares was *en fête*. The festivities had just started and would continue for two whole days, during which time no work would be undertaken.

" It is the fête of the election of the new Presidente, señores," announced the Paraquilan harbour-master. " To-morrow, if the caballero capitanos will order their ships to be hung with flags, the Government of Paraquil del Norte will appreciate the compliment. Most certainly, señores, you should see the grand procession when the Presidente proceeds in state to the Government House."

" Darn the President, say I," grumbled Captain Adams' companion, when the two skippers were returning to their respective commands. " Guess I'll not dress ship for a copper-coloured gold-bug of a tin-pot Republic. Nope ! Nuthin' doin' ! "

" Make it a deal," suggested the skipper of the *Bronx City*. " I calculate the Paraquilan crowd won't be over-anxious to oblige if we don't cotton on to their one-hoss Thanksgiving Day celebrations. An' mebbe the bunting will be all the better for an airing. Who is the President, d'ye know ? "

" Nope," replied the other. " An' wouldn't give a red cent to know."

As soon as the *Great Content's* Old Man returned on board, he was bearded by a deputation from the crew. As it was a national holiday, could they have an advance and a day ashore ?

" I guess I think on it, boys," he replied.

Five minutes later a burst of cheering came

from the *Bronx City*. Her crew had made a similar request and Captain Adams had given the required permission. After that the skipper of the *Great Content* could not well decline the men's demands.

Being Yankee ships, they were dry, and the men drier still with the prospect of unlimited beer and wine ashore. Those on the *Great Content* began to smarten themselves up in anticipation of a glorious spree.

" Ain't you gwine, Tuke ? " demanded one of the hands, noticing that Pengelly showed no signs of joining in the festivities.

Pengelly hesitated. He was most anxious to indulge in an evening in one of the cafés, but he feared to run the risk of being identified by any of the *Bronx City's* crew. On the other hand, they most likely had gone to the grand plaza, where the illuminations were brightest and the attractions numerous and varied. There might be a secluded wine-shop nearer the wharf.

In the end he went off arm in arm with a couple of exuberant Yankees. By midnight he was as drunk as his companions, and the three were " lost to the wide " in a wine-shop in one of the principal streets of Bomanares.

Just before eleven on the following morning Pengelly was roused from his drunken slumbers by the sound of a band, the frantic clamouring of the church bells, and a loud and prolonged fusillade of pistol-shots.

" What's on ? " he demanded thickly, addressing one of his boon companions of the previous night.

13

"Guess it's that fool procession," was the reply. "Let's see anyway. Come along right here."

The Yankee helped Pengelly to his feet and led him from the room on to a balcony overlooking the processional route. Feeling pleased with himself and everybody and everything in his maudlin state, Pengelly gripped the rail of the balcony and tolerantly surveyed the scene.

Both sides of the street were crowded with sightseers armed with flags, streamers, flowers and confetti. Many of the male spectators were displaying their enthusiasm by discharging their revolvers in the air. Almost all the houses had four or more balconies : these were fully occupied, while other enthusiasts leant over the parapets of the flat roofs of the houses.

As yet the procession was not in sight. In a neighbouring plaza a military band was playing "La Paloma" to the delight of a hundred whole-hearted tango dancers. In the distance came the crash of the opening bars of the Paraquilan national air, "Chuachinetto." At the same moment the guns of the citadel began to thunder out a salute.

A hush fell upon the multitude—a sort of spontaneous pause to enable it to recover its breath before giving vent to a roar of welcome to the new controller of the Republic's weal. The troops lining the route, who had hitherto been lolling about in the characteristic attitude of the indolent South American, threw away their cigar-butts and cigarette ends, pulled themselves together and awaited the order to pay military respect to the head of the State.

"Take care of yourself, Tuke!" cautioned his companion. "You'll be over that there rail in a shake."

Pengelly turned and grinned vacuously at the Yankee seaman. More than half-seas over, the preparations for the procession amused him in a childish sort of way, although he had entirely forgotten the real nature of the proceedings. He began to beat time to the music, found himself "out," and, abandoning his rôle of conductor, leant over the balcony again.

"Blessh me!" he exclaimed. "There's the Old Man just below us. Gi' him a cheer, lads!"

The suggestion was not carried out, but the American, following the direction of Pengelly's down-pointed hand, saw that his companion was right. In a balcony of the first floor stood Captain Adams and the skipper of the *Good Content*. In his befuddled state Pengelly did not appear to notice the presence of the man he had good reasons to avoid.

The band at the head of the procession passed, the musicians blaring for all they were worth. A number of horsemen on gaily-decked steeds followed. Next a detachment of the military and a strong force of civil guards.

Next came an open carriage drawn by eight white horses. In it sat a stern-faced, heavy-browed man in evening dress, with the broad pale blue-and-orange sash of the Order of San Custoval across his chest. With the faintest suspicion of

a smile he raised his hat to the crowds right and
left, while the troops lining the route presented
arms, and the spectators yelled themselves hoarse
with shouts of " Viva el Presidente ! "

Pengelly stared. His eyes opened wider and
wider, his jaw dropped. He could hardly believe
his senses, for the man seated in the state carriage
was none other than his former partner, Tom
Trevorrick, otherwise known as Captain Cain.

Still under the influence of cheap wine and
bad beer, Pengelly threw discretion to the winds.
Had he been sober he would have taken care
that Cain did not spot him ; being drunk, he did
not care if he did. In fact, he wanted to claim
acquaintanceship with the man on whose head
a price had been fixed—a reward that Pengelly
fondly hoped to receive.

" Tom, ahoy ! " he hailed, in stentorian tones,
and unconsciously relapsing into the Cornish
dialect. " Trevorrick, here ! Whar be tu, Tom ?
Three cheers for Cap'n Cain ! "

Cain glanced at him. The shouts of the inebriated man had been audible above the plaudits
of the spectators. Without a sign of recognition
the Presidente and pirate turned his head to
acknowledge the greetings of the crowds in the
footwalk on the opposite side of the street.

Others had heard Pengelly's shouts, amongst
them the two Yankee skippers in the balcony
below.

" Say ! " exclaimed the Old Man of the *Good
Content*, " I guess that's the Britisher we shipped
aboard at Bahia."

" Sure thing ! " rejoined Captain Hiram Adams. " Sure thing, again, he's a guy I've been longing to boot for a twelvemonth."

" Guess my chief mate's done that a'ready," declared his companion. " Why youse so gone on giving him your boot ? "

" I'll give him something worse when I get hold of him ! " ejaculated Captain Adams, leaning over the rail and looking up at the balcony above.

But no Pengelly was to be seen. Suddenly aware of his foolhardy display, he had sobered sufficiently to make a discreet retirement.

" See here ! " said the skipper of the *Bronx City*. " I've done you a good turn, haven't I ? "

" Sure," admitted the *Good Content's* Old Man. " An' I guess you'll not forget to ask a good pile of dollars for salvage."

" I'll not deny that," rejoined Captain Adams, " but your owners 'll cough that up. 'Tain't what I'm driving at. It's the Britisher ; he's one of your men, ain't he ? "

The skipper of the *Good Content* was understood to admit that he was.

" See here, then," continued his companion. " I'll take him off your hands. You can sort of lose him, and I'll give you two hundred dollars if you'll put him aboard the *Bronx City* as soon as he shows up."

" Mighty particular on a darned Britisher, ain't you ? " inquired the *Good Content's* Old Man. " A' right ; guess you're welcome to him right now for two hundred dollars. It's a deal ! "

CHAPTER XVII

A BOLT FROM THE BLUE

IN the hour of his triumph Cain had sustained a nasty shock.

His plans during the last six months had gone smoothly. Having secured what appeared to be a lasting peace for the Republic of Paraquil del Norte he had set about to gain the highest pinnacle of fame that that country offered. Already he had mastered the language—had won the admiration and devotion of her inhabitants by his firmness and discretion in the affairs that had arisen following the declaration of peace.

According to previous arrangements, Pedro Aquillo, the successor to the Presidential chair left vacant by the involuntary flight of Lippo Bramo, had announced his resignation in favour of Captain-General Trevor, as Cain was known to the inhabitants of Bomanares. Aquillo was wise in his generation. In accepting the arrangement he realised that the shorter his tenure of office the better. Provided he remained Presidente for three months he could retire with a pension of five thousand dollars a year, according to the law of the Republic. Incidentally he was the first Head of the State to take advantage of those terms. His predecessors had remained long enough in office either to fall victims to the bullets of political or personally actuated assassins, or else had been forced to flee the country.

And now Cain ruled as Presidente Trevor.

Already, as the master-mind behind the puppet Aquillo, he had set the country on the road to prosperity. His power for organisation, his indomitable courage and determination to get things done, had resulted in a stability of government and a national spirit of progress that had already borne fruit. Foreign trade flourished ; exports of raw material which grows abundantly on the rich soil of Paraquil rose by leaps and bounds. Internal communication had been enormously improved and developed, with the result that the warehouses and storehouses of the port of Bomanares were crowded with produce that found a ready sale in the old world.

Cain had not forgotten those compatriots of his who had helped him to the position he now held ; but he was too far-seeing to put them into high places of State lest the jealousy of the native ministers might be aroused.

Barnard, ex-bo'sun of the *Alerte*, was now owner of four small steam vessels engaged in a good coast-wise trade between Bomanares and the ports of Ouro Preto, Banda Rica and Uruguay ; Cain finding the necessary capital and handing it to him as a gift.

Davidge and Cross, also at their former captain's charges, were doing well on a ranch about twelve miles from the capital.

An exception to Cain's policy was made in the
case of Dick Kayburn, but this was on account
of the airman's service to the State. With the
full consent of the Senate, he had been appointed
Director of Postal and Telegraph Departments
at a salary that enabled him to entertain hopes
of returning home a rich man at no distant date.
On that account only Cain envied him; there
could be no honourable retirement in the old
country for a proscribed outlaw.

On the eve of his election Cain was informed
by the Minister of Foreign Affairs that a British
warship was on her way out to Bomanares.
This information was somewhat disquieting; he
had no desire to have to welcome a ship flying
the white ensign, although he reassured himself
by the knowledge that the report of his death
had been fully accepted by the British Government. As far as he was aware, no one, with the
exception of his three faithful followers, had the
slightest suspicion to the contrary.

" Why does a British warship want to come
here ? " he inquired of his informant.

" Because, Excellency, she is bringing out the
new British Consul - General for Paraquil del
Norte," replied the Minister for Foreign Affairs.
" See ; here is the announcement, cabled by
Reuter to-day."

It was to the effect that the British light cruiser
Jutland, Captain the Honourable Sir John Car-
dyke, R.N., had left Portsmouth on the 3rd
instant to relieve H.M.S. *Inconstant* on the South
American Station. She would call at Bomanares

en route for the purpose of landing the newly-appointed Consul-General to Paraquil, Sir Peter Muspratt, and presumably the captain of the cruiser would pay a ceremonial visit to the President of the Republic.

" I wish I had a current Navy List," thought Cain. " I could then find out if any of the officers on the *Jutland* were—hardly likely, but, hang it ! I shouldn't wonder if they didn't try to find out everything about me ; when and where I was born, who my parents were, how and when I cut my first tooth and all that balderdash. I'll have to draw another cheque on the Bank of Imagination."

He went to bed in a bad humour.

The sun was shining brightly when the Presidente-elect awoke. The misgivings of the previous evening had vanished. He felt as bright and high-spirited as he could have hoped. He was on the very threshold of success—an attainment he had reached by sheer force of character, aided by the whole-hearted efforts of his little band of compatriots. Out of the chaos of a disorganised Republic he had evolved order and prosperity. He still looked forward to seeing Paraquil del Norte one of the most progressive and well-organised States of the South American continent.

As he dressed—he scorned the assistance of a valet—he could hear the tinkle of stringed instruments, the blare of brass bands, the irregular reports of pistol-shots and the *vivas* of the multitude. Even at that early hour the inhabitants of Bomanares were displaying their enthusiasm for the new Head of the State.

At the prearranged hour, Cain entered the state carriage as the sole occupant. The resigning Presidente, Pedro Aquillo, was to follow in the next carriage with the heads of the Army, Navy and the Minister for the Interior.

"The bodyguard is ready, Excellency," announced the officer commanding the Presidente's personal troops, as he saluted and then tendered the hilt of his sword in token of fidelity.

"Let them precede the carriage," ordered Cain.

"But, your Excellency," protested the officer, "they are for your protection, and must needs shield you with their bodies from possible danger."

"I do not think that any one will hurl a bomb at me to-day," said Cain, with a whimsical smile. "Order the guards to ride in front of the carriage."

The ceremony that conferred the title of Presidente on Captain Cain proceeded without a hitch ; and then, amidst the plaudits of the crowds, the blaring of bands and the thunderous roar of the saluting guns, the Head of the Republic of Paraquil del Norte set out on his triumphal progress through the principal streets.

A bomb was hurled. It was not of a type employed by anarchists to remove the heads of authority, whether they be Emperors, Kings, Presidents or Governors. It was a raucous greeting from the lips of the renegade and traitor, Paul Pengelly.

Only by a supreme effort of self-control did Cain

keep his feelings under command. He realised that figuratively the cat was out of the bag. Amongst the crowds who must have heard that bellowing greeting, there would be some who understood its meaning. As likely as not Dick Kayburn, riding in the third carriage, must have heard and grasped the significance of the words. If the secret were to leak out—that the Presidente of Paraquil del Norte was the notorious captain of the pirate submarine *Alerte*—Cain's efforts to make good, all his strenuous endeavours of the past six months, would be undone.

He had to act, and that quickly.

At the end of the street, Cain ordered the carriage to stop. The guards proceeded for nearly fifty yards before they realised that the rest of the procession was held up.

Back cantered the officer commanding the bodyguard. The Presidente beckoned to him to come nearer.

" A man has shouted insulting words," he said.

" That is so, Excellency," replied the officer. " I myself heard him, but he spoke in a foreign tongue. I did not understand, or——"

He significantly tapped the holster of his revolver.

" Detach four of your men," ordered Cain. " Find the culprit and put him under close arrest. He is to communicate with no one. Report to me this evening as to where he is detained."

" Excellency, he is an Americano," protested the officer, who in common with most of the South American people regard citizens of the

United States as individuals with whom it is unwise to interfere. From Mexico to Patagonia, Yankees are generally termed " Americanos " by the Spanish-speaking population.

" He is no Americano," declared Cain. " Even if he were, no matter. He has committed a breach of the peace on the soil of Paraquil del Norte. Find him and place him under arrest."

The officer saluted and cantered back to his men. A quarter of an hour later, Pengelly, wishing fervently that he had not left the *Good Content,* was in solitary confinement in a cell in the citadel.

CHAPTER XVIII

CAIN'S DECISION

FOR the rest of that busy day the new Pre-sidente, although he was kept fully occupied by receiving congratulations, attending a cere-monial banquet and making and listening to speeches, could not banish the haunting doubts that followed upon his former partner's ribald greeting. So far the incident seemed to have attracted little attention, and no one commented upon it to Cain himself.

Satisfied that Pengelly was safely under lock and key, Cain decided to let him cool his heels in a cell for a day or two before the culprit was brought into his presence. Curiously enough the pirate captain felt no resentment towards his former comrade. All he wanted to do was to muzzle Pengelly effectually, not only for his own safety but for that of the ex-convict. Now that the man had escaped from Dartmoor, Cain had no wish to send him back to lifelong imprison-ment. Provided he gave an undertaking to hold his tongue and live in retirement in any other State but that of Paraquil del Norte, Pengelly would not suffer at Cain's hands, even if the hitherto well-preserved secret of the Presidente's identity were revealed.

Pengelly sober, he decided, would never have dared to utter a statement that would have implicated himself as well as his former partner. Pengelly drunk was a menace both to himself and others; therefore he must be protected against himself.

Next morning Cain received two nasty jars. It was Dick Kayburn who, innocently enough, gave the first.

" I say, sir ! " he exclaimed, holding out a newspaper. " Do you remember that pirate josser who played Old Harry in the Atlantic last year, and was supposed to have been drowned in the *Alerte* ? "

" I remember something about it," replied Cain, with well-feigned disinterestedness.

" Well, he isn't, apparently," continued Kayburn. " He is knocking about somewhere in South America. By Jove ! I'd like to meet that chap."

" And render a service to humanity by shooting him at sight, eh ? "

" Rather not, sir," protested Kayburn. " He's rather a good sport, I should imagine. 'Tany rate, he played a fairly clean game from all accounts."

Cain took the proffered paper, a copy of a London journal, that had only just reached Bomanares.

The paragraph under discussion was headed, " HAS CAIN COME TO LIFE ? " and went on to state that some one had raised a question in Parliament as to whether the British Government proposed taking any action in the report received from a Mr. Solomon Tuke stating that he had seen the notorious Captain Cain, late of the pirate submarine *Alerte*, in Bahia. The answer given was that His Majesty's Government had the matter under consideration, and, in the public interests, it was undesirable to make a statement at present.

" There's one thing certain," remarked the Presidente. " If Cain is in Paraquil he won't stay here very long if I have anything to do in the matter. You said you'd like to meet him, Kayburn. Well, if you do, you might let me know what you think after having made his acquaintance."

" 'Fraid I'll not get the chance, sir," said the other. " In fact, I'd rather not meet him if you're going to make it hot for him. He's a sportsman, that chap ! "

As soon as Kayburn left the Presidency, Cain had to attend a levee. This was just over when a servant handed the Presidente a visiting-card.

" The Caballero Capitan requests a private audience, Excellency," said the man.

Cain glanced at the card. It bore the words, " Captain Hiram Maddox Adams—s.s. *Bronx City*."

Resisting the impulse to refuse to see the Yankee skipper, Cain told his servant to show him in.

Outwardly cool and self-possessed, but with a dry sensation in his throat, Cain awaited the appearance of the man whose vessel he had once seized under conditions of flagrant piracy.

"I'm right pleased to see you, President," exclaimed Captain Adams. "Shake!"

The greeting, given in English, left Cain under no delusions as to the American's ignorance of the true nationality of the Head of the Republic of Paraquil del Norte.

He took the proffered hand.

"Well, sir," he remarked, "is there anything I can do for you? I presume you wish to see me on some private matter."

"I guess ye can, right now," replied Captain Adams. "Say, President, there's a man aboard the Ammurican ship *Good Content*, only he ain't aboard; he's in prison in this city."

"Really; and what is his name?"

"Tuke—Solomon Tuke."

This information came as a nasty shock. Tuke, then, was Pengelly's assumed name; it was also, according to the report in the newspaper, that of the man who had given information of Cain's presence in Bahia. Although he had seen Pengelly in that Brazilian city, he had been quite satisfied that the latter had not seen him. Now, apparently, he had. More, he had stooped to the lowest act of meanness. He had betrayed his former comrade for the sake of a miserable sum for blood-money.

"And supposing your statement is correct; that Solomon Tuke is under arrest in Bomanares?"

" I guess, President, I could do with him aboard the *Bronx City*."

" But I understand he belongs to the *Good Content*."

Captain Adams gave a deliberate wink.

" President, we've met before," he said. " I ain't kickin' at that. You're a white man, sir, and when you took the old *Bronx City*, you played the game an' kept your word. I've got no grouse against you. But that low-down hobo Tuke— if that's his name—he's the fellow I've got to deal with, sure. I guess he played it pretty low down with you, before he looted the *Bronx City*, didn't he ? "

Cain nodded.

" Wal, it's just this : hand him over to me, an' I guess he'll wish he'd never been born when he's aboard the *Bronx City* on the way to N'York and Sing Sing. Say, is it a deal ? "

With his usual rapidity for coming to a decision, Cain reviewed the proposition. On the face of it this seemed an excellent solution to the difficulty. Obviously Captain Adams was sincere in his regard for the man who had treated him so magnanimously when the *Bronx City* fell a prey to the *Alerte*. Adams was evidently tremendously anxious to get hold of Pengelly, convey him to the States and there have him put on trial for piracy, with the inevitable sentence of imprisonment for life in the State Penitentiary of Sing Sing. Once there, Pengelly would be in a living tomb.

" Sorry, Captain Adams," replied Cain, " but it can't be done."

14

" Can't be done, President ? " echoed the Yankee. " Say, why ? "

" It's not my usual custom to explain my decisions," declared Cain. " I'll make an exception. Tuke, as you call him, is on Paraquilan territory. There he will remain until I think fit to have him conveyed elsewhere. I appreciate your anxiety to get quits with him ; but, believe me, the injury he has done me is far greater than the matter of which you reminded me. So I maintain that I have a higher claim. Rest assured that I will deal faithfully with him."

The skipper of the *Bronx City* ruminated.

" Guess you're right," he remarked at length. " I always said that guy was a skunk, and that you are what you Britishers call a sportsman Shake on it ! "

A slight flush of pleasure suffused Cain's tanned and weather-beaten features. For the second time that morning he had been paid the highest tribute a man can secure—the compliment of being called a sportsman.

" Thanks ! " he replied, as he grasped the proffered hand.

" And," continued Captain Adams, with the suspicion of a wink, " you can take it from me that I'll be mum as a mollusc over the business. 'Tain't for me to talk about a man that's tried his hardest to make good. See here, President, if ever you want help, and I can be of service to you, don't forget Hiram Maddox Adams of lil' ol' N'York."

Left to himself, Cain pondered over the situa-

tion. There was much to be done, and very little
time in which to do it. Firstly, there was the
question of what to do with the traitor, Pengelly.
In the circumstances, Cain would be justified in
having him shot ; but he realised that that was
too simple a solution to the difficulty. Pengelly
dead, his troubles would be over. Alive, he would
simply exist in a torment of fear—a far greater
punishment than being brought to face the
muzzles of the rifles of a firing-party.

Cain excused himself by thinking, " The swab
isn't worth a bullet," but in his heart he did not
wish to have his former partner's blood on his
hands, although Pengelly would not have hesitated
to have Cain's blood-money in his.

Within twenty minutes of the termination of
his interview with the skipper of the *Bronx City*,
the Presidente alighted from his horse at the entrance to the citadel.

" I wish to interview the prisoner Tuke," he
said to the Governor of the citadel. " I will see
him alone."

" But, Excellency," expostulated the other,
"the man may be violent. In any case, let me
place an armed guard outside the cell."

" I will see him alone," reiterated the Presidente,
in a tone that the officials of the Republic had
already learned to know and obey.

The door of the cell swung back. Cain deliberately locked it and placed the heavy key in
his pocket. Then he turned and faced his former
comrade.

Pengelly, who had been seated moodily on a

bench, rose and backed into the farthermost corner of the apartment. All his bravado had oozed out of him. With drooping jaw and staring eyes he literally cowered beneath Cain's supercilious gaze.

"Hello, Pengelly!" exclaimed Cain. "You don't look as if you are particularly pleased to see me. Yesterday you greeted me in your old happy style. Why this change?"

"I didn't mean anything, Tom," replied the prisoner in a wheedling tone. "I was sort of taken aback at seeing you riding in state. And being under the influence——"

"Of course," interrupted his visitor cheerfully. "Of course! Bad habit that; and, in any case, you ought not to have shouted at the Presidente, even though he were your former partner. It's not done, even in Paraquil. However, we'll say no more about it."

"Thanks, Tom!" exclaimed the wretched man, "I won't do it again."

"You won't, because you will not have another chance to greet me as Presidente of Paraquil," remarked Cain. "But, as I said before, the incident is closed. That brings me to another matter. What made you assume the tally of Solomon Tuke?"

Pengelly explained. His former comrade listened patiently as the other related the incident of the escape from Dartmoor, and his chance meeting with the dying seaman whose name he took. At that point he decided that it was undesirable to continue the narrative.

"Rather an ingenious move, that," remarked Cain. "One would have thought that once you got clear of England you wouldn't want to get mixed up with piracy again."

"Nor have I, on my solemn oath!" declared Pengelly.

"Sorry to contradict you," declared Cain cheerfully. "I didn't imply that you dabbled in piracy by act. You harked back to it by communicating with Scotland Yard, didn't you? I believe I'm not betraying any confidence when I state that a certain individual informed me that Solomon Tuke wrote from Bahia to the effect that Captain Cain of the *Alerte* had been seen there."

Pengelly's oily features became positively green. Whimpering like a petulant child, he threw himself on the ground and grovelled at the feet of the man he had done his best to betray.

"Get up!" ordered Cain sternly.

"Mercy!" howled the wretched man.

"Get up!" repeated his accuser. "Pull yourself together, man! I haven't threatened you."

"N'more you have, Tom," agreed Pengelly.

"Then, listen," continued Cain. "First let me remind you of an order I gave you when we commissioned the *Alerte*. You were to address me as 'sir.' Apparently you have forgotten, although as far as I am aware you never 'signed off' as second in command of the submarine. That's that. Now for the other matter. You did your best to betray me and the three who remained faithful from the time when you tried to assume command of the *Alerte*, and made rather a mess of it. I think you'll agree with me on that point. As a result of your sneaking communication a British cruiser is on her way to Bomanares, ostensibly to dump a consul into the State, but actually, I presume, to get Paraquil to extradite us. By us, I include Barnard, Davidge, Cross and you. Did that ever occur to you when you penned that demand for blood-money ? On the face of things, it seems quite probable that within the next two months you'll be safe in Dartmoor again, and I fancy the authorities won't give you another chance to slip through their fingers."

Cain paused to let the dread significance of his words sink in.

" Why don't you have me shot ? " asked the terrified scoundrel. " Anything's better than being sent back to prison."

" I'm not going to that trouble," replied Cain. " Why should I end your wandering Jew existence ? I've made good out here ; you butt in and bring down my schemes like a pack of cards. The fact that you've buried yourself under the ruins doesn't concern me. That's your funeral. All I mean to do in your case is to keep you here until I'm collared. I don't mean to be arrested if I can help it ; but if I should be, you will be in the same boat. For the present, you're being kept out of further mischief, and provided you give no trouble you will receive none. We'll leave it at that."

Deliberately turning his back on his former comrade, although by so doing he recognised that Pengelly might deal him a blow with the stool,

Cain unlocked the door, went out and secured the bolts on the outside.

So far he felt satisfied with his interview. He had left the wretched Pengelly a prey to the deepest apprehensions—a far greater punishment to a coward than actual bodily pain.

On the following day Cain attended the first meeting of Congress under his Presidency. His speech is still quoted in Bomanares as a practical step towards an ideally constituted and governed Republic. He dealt amongst other matters with the reduction of armaments, and proposed that the sole fighting airship the Republic of Paraquil del Norte possessed should be sold by public auction, since it was constructionally unsuitable for conversion to commercial uses.

This suggestion he carried without a single dissentient. Cain left the Senate House at the termination of the proceedings with his tongue in his cheek.

His next move was to get in touch with his three faithful followers—his former shipmates in the *Alerte* and *Nike*. To them he revealed the precarious nature of the situation as it applied both to her and them.

" The British Government has acted upon that swab Pengelly's information," he announced. " If it came to the point, I firmly believe that Paraquil would stand by her present Presidente through thick and thin ; but I don't want to see the Republic embroiled in a row with Great Britain, so I mean to quit."

" And we'll go with you, sir," declared Barnard.

" As I expected," rejoined Cain. " It's rough luck on you fellows, especially as you're doing well with your respective enterprises. There'll still be time to dispose of your stock at a profit."

" When do you propose to do a bunk, sir ? " asked the ex-bo'sun.

" I do not propose to ' do a bunk,' Mr. Barnard," corrected his former captain, with a touch of hauteur. " When I go I will go decently : all fair and above board, so to speak. In about another ten days' time Paraquil will be electing another Presidente. Now, listen, Mr. Barnard. In a week the airship will be sold by public auction. I want you to bid for her, and, what's more, to outbid every one else. I'll transfer thirty thousand dollars to your credit ; but she won't fetch any-thing like that amount. If I'm mistaken and she does command a higher bid, carry on. We must have her at any price."

Barnard and the two hands had been gone barely a couple of minutes before Dick Kayburn blew in like a young tornado.

" Sorry to disturb you, sir," he began, " but I've just heard that the airship is to be sold. Is that a fact ? "

" 'Fraid it is," replied Cain.

" Pity," rejoined Kayburn wistfully. " We might have kept the jolly old thing just for old times' sake, and have a joy-ride occasionally. Although I'm stickin' my job—and it's a pretty dismal sort of business—I'm still keen on the air. I'm hoping to develop an aerial postal service."

" We studied the question pretty thoroughly," said Cain, " but after careful consideration it was decided to dispose of the airship, since it would not be wanted for military purposes and could not with advantage be converted to commercial uses. So she is to be put up for auction."

" Dashed if I don't make a bid for her," declared Kayburn. " I don't suppose she'll fetch much. I could rent the 'drome, couldn't I, sir ? Even if she didn't pay her way, I'd have an awful lot of fun out of her."

" Sorry to have to disappoint you," remarked the Presidente, " but she won't be knocked down to you. I'm backing a bidder."

" You, sir ? " exclaimed the airman in astonishment. " Then, of course, I'm out of it ; unless you have me to run the old thing for you."

Cain regretfully shook his head. He had taken a great liking for Kayburn, and the thought that he would have to say farewell, perhaps for ever, was a sad one.

" Look here, Kayburn," he said, " I'm going to confide in you. For the present I know you will maintain silence on what I am about to relate. After I've cleared out, that condition will be no longer binding."

" You're clearing out, sir ? "

" Yes ; resigning my office and leaving Paraquil del Norte for good. Circumstances over which I have no control compel me to take this step. You remember you mentioned that Captain Cain, late of the pirate submarine, is somewhere in South America ? "

" The blighter hasn't been doing you a rotten turn, has he, sir ? " inquired Kayburn anxiously.

" He has," declared the Presidente. " Have you ever met him by any chance ? "

" Never ! " replied Kayburn, with conviction.

" Think again ! "

" I'm certain I haven't."

" I wish you could be sure on that point, Kayburn," said Cain. " But you're mistaken. You've seen him scores of times. You are looking at him at the very moment ! "

For a brief instant Kayburn was astounded. Then he laughed light-heartedly.

" I'm glad to know that," he replied. " I always said Captain Cain was a topping sort of fellow. If you are he, sir, I'm——"

" Wait," interposed the elder man. " Wait till I've explained matters a bit. Remember, when I've done so, there's no one in the whole of South American who will know as much about my past as you will."

Briefly, yet without omitting any important feature, Cain outlined his career, his object in taking to piracy, his escape from the depth-charged submarine, his adventures on the Coast and across the Atlantic. Finally, he revealed the facts concerning Pengelly's treachery, and how the latter came to fall into the hands of his enemy and former partner.

" And," he concluded, " now that there's a British cruiser on her way out here, ostensibly to land a Consular Agent, but actually to get me extradited, I am leaving Paraquil ; not that I am afraid to remain, but because I do not want to cause complications. I am not running away. I am resigning deliberately and taking my departure by airship. That's why I instructed Barnard to bid for the vessel."

"Rough luck on you, sir."

"It is," admitted Cain gravely. "But it's the fortune of—well, one can hardly call it War. I'm not the only one of thousands who hoped to make good and outlive a somewhat dishonourable past. Rarely can it be done. The ghosts of one's former indiscretions follow a man as closely as his own shadow. I cannot even offer the lame excuse that I was young and inexperienced : I wasn't. I was old enough to know better, and now I must pay the penalty."

For some moments there was silence.

"My giddy aunt, sir ! " suddenly exclaimed Kayburn eagerly. "This is a bit of a tough proposition ; but can't I chip in ? Don't say ' no ' until you've heard me out. I'm a bit fed up with things here. Why shouldn't I go with you ? You've set me on my feet. If I don't do another stroke of work as long as I live I'll have enough to rub along with. I really couldn't stick it here under another Presidente of the Lippo Bramo type."

"I don't think Paraquil will ever have another of that sort," interposed Cain.

"Well, any one but you, then, sir. How will that do ? "

Cain considered the proposition. After all was said and done, Kayburn was a free agent. He was under no cloud ; nor did Cain intend to revert to his illegal though quixotic methods of raising the wind, and consequently Kayburn would not be called upon to incriminate himself.

"You may find it horribly dull if you throw in you lot with me," he said. " I've made up my mind to carry on running straight. I do not intend to dabble in the political affairs of whatever country affords me an asylum. I have achieved my aims in Paraquil del Norte and placed myself in the highest possible position in the State. With the record I am content. Henceforth my intention is to settle down quietly—or as quietly as the internal conditions of the country will permit—and dabble in some sort of hobby ; something, experimenting in aviation, mining or any old thing that takes my fancy. You'll find that pretty tedious."

"Not I, sir," replied Kayburn. "Aviation ? By Jove ! That would suit me down to the ground and up above the clouds, if it comes to that. Is it a deal, sir ? "

"It's a deal, Kayburn," replied Cain gravely.

CHAPTER XIX

THE *JUTLAND'S* MISSION

H. M. light cruiser *Jutland* was fighting her way down Channel in the teeth of a steadily increasing sou'westerly gale. Leaden seas topped with foaming wind-torn crests pounded against her knife-like bows and threw blinding showers of spray high over her bridge, riming the funnels with salt, and driving the oily smoke across the quarter-deck and far to lee'ard. Overhead dark grey clouds with ragged mares'-tails scudded across the dark sky. The wind howled dismally through the tautened shrouds, and shrieked over the top of the tightly-strained bridge-screens, behind which bent the oilskin-clad officers and men who cursed the atmospheric conditions in no uncertain voices. It was cold, bitterly cold, and even the prospect of sweltering in the Tropics within the next few days was no compensation as they envied their mess-mates in the watch below—the men " fugging " in the battened-down mess-deck, the officers foregathered comfortably round the ward-room table and enjoying their dinner.

But even in the cosily - furnished ward-room things were not altogether merry and bright. The King's health had been drunk by the seated members of the mess, and the port had commenced to circulate. There was no hurry to rise from the table. Bridge and other kindred amusements were out of the question with the ship rolling and pitching as she did. The fire in the polished brass stove was smoking abominably, the mess-man had not covered himself with glory in the serving up of the meal, although possibly the occupants of the ward-room had become critical epicures after their prolonged residence in the Naval Barracks; the newspapers were already twelve hours old; and most of the officers were correspondingly new to each other. In short, they hadn't shaken down yet, and were much in the same position as a crowd of new boys at school.

Presently a messenger entered the room and handed a slip of buff paper to the Mess President. Before many days passed, considerable interest would be shown in that scrap of paper—and interest that would increase with the length of the commission. As it now happened, hardly any one paid the slightest attention to it. It was the news bulletin received by the ship's wireless, and in all probability contained items dealing with events all too recent to arouse interest.

The Commander glanced at the paper, elevated his eyebrows in mild surprise and passed it on to the Paymaster-Commander.

" There's something that will stir your gouty

frame, Pay," he remarked. "*Tempus fugit.* It was five years ago ; or was it seven ? "

"By George, yes ! " ejaculated the accountant officer. "I always maintained there was a mystery about the affair. 'His Majesty the King has been graciously pleased to grant a free pardon to Ambrose Gregory Alhampton, formerly Lieutenant-Commander, Royal Navy, tried and sentenced by court-martial to eighteen months' imprisonment.' Well, well ! You know him, of course, Commander ? "

"In my term at Dartmouth," replied The Bloke. "I was away Chinaside in the old *Bellona* when the case cropped up. What was the mystery, Pay ? "

Already others seated round the board were literally sitting up and taking notice. The Pay-master-Commander, flattered by the attention he had attracted, sipped his port, smacked his lips and started his yarn :

"It was shortly after the War," he began. "I suppose things were a bit out of the usual in the sort of stagnation period following the Armistice. Alhampton was a Lieutenant-Commander, just appointed a promotion to the *Cerebos*—the 'Old Salt Cellar' she was called. He was a queer sort of chap, was Alhampton. Had a temper on him like a tiger ; never seemed to care a rap for any one or anything. But he could handle men. He'd picked up one or two decorations in the Submarine Service before he came to us ; but in a large vessel he seemed like a fish out of water.

" Then he got mixed up in the Devereux forged cheque affair ; in fact, he was the culprit, although I always had my doubts. He was put under arrest, and I had to act as Prisoner's Friend. Think I could be of any use ? Not a bit of it. He pleaded guilty. The Deputy-Judge Advocate refused to accept the plea, and ordered one of Not Guilty to be entered. Even then Alhampton hardly said a word. I couldn't get him to make any statement. He seemed to be utterly bored stiff with the whole proceedings ; but it's my belief he had some queer quixotic idea in the back of his head. 'Tany rate he got eighteen months, and was dismissed the Service with disgrace."

" Evidently some fresh evidence has come to light," remarked the Commander.

" Well, sir," announced the Navigator, " I came across Devereux at the United Services about a week ago—no, it must have been nearly a month ago. He mentioned that Gilderoy, the principal witness for the prosecution, had died that same morning. Devereux, you know, was always doubtful about Gilderoy's evidence. His theory—of course he hadn't any real grounds for it—was that Alhampton was tricked by Gilderoy into forging the cheque, and that Gilderoy had got Alhampton three sheets in the wind when the deed was done."

" Then it's quite possible that Gilderoy's death has had something to do with Alhampton's pardon," remarked the Paymaster-Commander. " Alhampton was that sort of chap. He wouldn't lift a little finger to clear himself if he had half of the silliest, rotten notion that he didn't want to. Where is he now, I wonder ? "

" I wonder ? " echoed the Commander. " I've asked several people who used to know him. He simply vanished when his time was up. Probably a down-and-outer in some back-block. It'll be interesting to see if he shows up again after the proclamation of a free pardon. It's my opinion he won't. He's too jolly stubborn—quixotic, you said, didn't you, Pay ? I'd call it pig-headedness."

Meanwhile an animated conversation on another subject had arisen at the lower end of the table. During a lull in the discourse the Engineer-Lieutenant-Commander appealed to the Commander to settle a point of dispute.

" Where, exactly, sir, was the *Alerte* sunk ? " he inquired.

" Don't know," replied The Bloke. " We were chasing her in the Channel, but she slipped between our fingers like an eel. She went south, I believe. You'd better ask Broadmayne. He was in at the death."

The lieutenant thus appealed to, Gerald Broadmayne, had been a keen but silent listener to the conversation between the senior officers of the Mess, a tall, strapping fellow of six feet two inches. He had been captured by Captain Cain and had been detained on board the pirate submarine for some time, when he eventually made his escape. Later on, as sub-lieutenant in H.M.S. *Canvey*, he had taken an active part

15

in the operations that led to the *Alerte's* destruction.

" At Bahia Arenas on the West Coast of Africa," he replied.

" What happened exactly ? " inquired the Commander. " I read the official report, but there were several details omitted that might have been most interesting. She was depth-charged, I believe, and a subsequent examination made of the wreck."

" I was one of the party who went down to search the wreck," said Broadmayne.

" And you found no signs of the pirate captain ? "

Broadmayne shook his head.

" She was knocked about considerably," he replied. " No one on board could have survived the effect of the depth-charge."

" And yet there was a rumour—it actually got into the Press—that Cain was seen somewhere in South America," remarked the Commander.

Broadmayne made no further comment. He, too, had seen the report, but he had not connected it with the *Jutland's* forthcoming visit to Bomanares. There were only three persons in the ship who knew that : the Consular Agent, who as a civilian was being given a passage ; the Captain of the ship and his secretary, the Paymaster-Lieutenant. All three had been given to understand that this was a highly confidential matter, and that the strictest reticence and reserve must be preserved in connection with the real nature of the light cruiser's mission.

And there was only one person on the ship
who knew that Lieutenant-Commander Ambrose
Alhampton and Captain Cain were one and the
same person ; and that was Lieutenant Gerald
Broadmayne. He had held the secret from the
first day of his enforced detention on board the
Alerte ; and now his silence on that point had
become a matter for self-congratulation, since
he had just heard that the " broken " officer
had, obviously for reasons that proclaimed his
innocence of a certain charge against him, been
granted a " free " pardon.

It was as yet unknown to him that Cain was
the present head of the Republic of Paraquil
del Norte. Nor did he know that it was on
account of his previous personal knowledge of
the pirate, Captain Cain, that the Admiralty had
appointed Gerald Broadmayne to the *Jutland,*
so that should opportunity arise he would be
able to offer conclusive evidence of identification
of the much-wanted criminal.

From the time he went down in a diver's dress
to examine the wreck of the *Alerte*, Broadmayne
had entertained the idea that Cain, courageous
and resourceful as he was, had contrived to make
his escape before the vessel was shattered by the
explosion of the depth-charge ; but he had kept
his theories to himself, not even letting drop a
hint when called upon to make a report to his
superior officer, the captain of the *Canvey.*

He realised that the situation, as far as Captain
Cain was concerned, was becoming still more
complicated. Assuming that the crime for which

he had been convicted had not been committed
by him, and that the Royal pardon had been
given on that account, how would Cain's subsequent piratical deeds bear upon the case?
Evidently the man had been driven by desperation, poverty and sheer ill-luck, as a result of his
conviction, to take to a career of lawlessness upon
the High Seas; and in Broadmayne's opinion
it seemed very hard lines that Cain should be
pardoned for one offence which, presumably,
he did not commit, and yet be liable to further
punishment for subsequent offences attributable
solely to his unmerited sentence.

Broadmayne debated with himself upon the
advisability or otherwise of communicating the
information he held upon the joint identity of
Alhampton and Cain. He realised that if the
knowledge would prove a factor in the man's
favour he ought to do so. Until he was satisfied
that it was to Cain's advantage, he decided to
keep the information to himself.

At midnight Broadmayne, clad in oilskins,
sou'wester and sea-boots in addition to his ordinary
rig, turned out to take his Middle Watch.

It was now blowing "great guns." He had to
grip the hand-rails of the bridge-ladder and hang
on with all his might to prevent himself being
carried away by the furious blast that whistled
between the steps of the unprotected means of
ascent.

It was a bitterly cold night. Hail and sleet
drove almost horizontally against the lieutenant's
head and shoulders as he sheltered as best he might

behind the bridge-screens. The icy pellets rattled against the board-hard painted canvas like the noise of a Maxim gun. It was almost impossible to hear any other sounds. Even the shriek of the gale was almost drowned by the continuous tattoo of the hail and the *swish-swish* of some showers of stinging salt spray.

"Wish you luck, old son," bawled the officer he was relieving. "We're doing eighteen knots, course two, two, five. The Owner is to be called at daybreak. That's all, I think. Cheerio!"

The late watchkeeping officer disappeared in the darkness to seek oblivion between the blankets of his bunk, leaving Broadmayne to accept responsibility for the safety of His Majesty's property to the value of a million pounds, and the lives of every soul on board.

Occasionally as the light-cruiser's bows plunged into the creamy froth of the crested waves, Broadmayne could distinguish the hunched figures of the two "look-outs" stationed in the eyes of the ship, silhouetted against the light grey background. The next instant the smother of water would break inboard, completely obliterating the forms of the two men until the vessel again dropped her bows to meet the shock of the succeeding "comber."

"Those poor blighters have a shaky job," thought the lieutenant. "Mine's a soft one by comparison. Goodness only knows what they're placed there for: they can't see half as well as on the bridge look-outs."

A little later on Broadmayne found his thoughts

reverting to the problem of Captain Cain. He could not dismiss the matter from his mind. Between the receiving of the reports concerning the condition of the steaming lights, periodical visits to the quartermaster at the steam steering-wheel, exchanging words with the engineer-commander with reference to the revolutions of the triple propellers and half a dozen other items in connection with the routine of a watch-keeping officer, the lieutenant's thoughts harked back to the case of the captain of the pirate submarine.

When he had been in Cain's power the pirate captain had not treated him any too well. In fact, he recalled grimly how Cain had threatened him with a " dose of the cat " ; but even taking that into consideration, Broadmayne could not help feeling a certain amount of admiration and sympathy for the ill-used man.

CHAPTER XX

THE PRESIDENTE RETIRES

IT was a glorious morning when the *Jutland* entered Bomanares Harbour, and, without exception, officers and men had their first glimpses of the capital of the Republic of Paraquil del Norte. Without the aid of local pilots she had found her way up the intricate channel, often with less than a fathom of water under her keel plates, and had brought up to one of the large mooring-buoys almost in the centre of the spacious harbour. She had saluted the flag of the Republic, and the shore battery had promptly replied, gun for gun; a fact that favourably impressed the *Jutland's* ship's company as indicating the smartness with which the little State was run.

" I remember back in 'nought twelve," remarked the Commander reminiscently, " we put into a certain South American port that shall be nameless. We gave them the usual expenditure of blank ammunition, and the fort replied with three guns ! 'Course our Owner got a bit rattled and sent ashore to know why his salute hadn't been returned properly. Hanged if half an hour later a crowd of gold-laced officials didn't put off to the ship, apologised profusely and explained that they'd used up all their saluting charges. Our skipper accepted the explanation, but added that international etiquette demanded the full return salute—gun for gun. The Republican officials were ' desolated '; so to take pity on them and to salve his *amour-propre*, our Owner sent ashore a seven-pounder and the requisite number of rounds to complete the salute. When the gun was returned to the ship the shore johnnies decorated it with flowers and sent off a thundering big barrel of wine. I got tight that evening," added The Bloke whimsically, " but I was only an ' acting-sub ' in those days."

" How long are we here for, sir ? " asked the Engineer-Lieutenant-Commander. " It seems quite a posh show. I'd like to go ashore and have a look round."

" Far as I know we're landing the Consul-bird and weighing at once," replied the Commander. " If we do stay a day or so the ship will be overrun with garlic-smelling shore-lubbers, and then ' good-bye ' to all my new paintwork ! "

The piping of the bo'sun's mate's whistle, followed by a hoarse order to hoist out the captain's gig and bring her alongside the accommodation ladder, was followed by preparations to " pipe the side," when the consular official left the ship to take up his new appointment.

" Seen the Commander's Order Book, old bird ? " inquired Davidson, one of the junior watchkeepers, addressing Broadmayne. " Your tally's in it."

The lieutenant hurried off to verify the statement. To his surprise he found that he had been detailed to attend upon the captain when the latter went to pay a ceremonial visit to the Presidente of the Republic of Paraquil del Norte.

Changing into the proscribed " rig " and buckling on his belt and sword, Broadmayne fell in on the quarter-deck to await the skipper's appearance. As soon as the captain had acknowledged the salute of the assembled officers, Broadmayne descended the ladder and stepped into the boat ; the Paymaster-Lieutenant-Commander in his capacity of captain's secretary and interpreter followed, the Owner being the last to step into the waiting craft. At the quayside the order of disembarkation was reversed, the officers standing rigidly at the salute on the quay while a military band played the British National Anthem, followed by the official " hymn " of the Republic.

Broadmayne was rather astonished at the smart appearance of the officers of the Paraquilan Army. They were well set up and alert, and looked very different to what he had been led to expect after hearing various stories of his brother officers' experiences in sundry South American ports.

" I regret, Señor Capitan, that there is no Presidente to welcome you," announced one of the officials. " Just at present the Republic is without a Head, and our late Presidente's successor will not be elected until next week. It is all the more to be regretted, Señor Capitan, since our late Presidente is British born."

Whatever disappointing thoughts entered the mind of the British naval captain, he kept his feelings under perfect control.

" Indeed ! " he rejoined. " I am afraid, then, that I am the loser. I should have liked to have met your former Presidente. Did he meet with an untimely end that you should have referred to him as ' late ' ? "

" Not at all, Señor Capitan," the deputy hastened to explain. " He retired from office with the best of wishes from his colleagues, after they had in vain attempted to persuade him to change his mind. It was solely on account of his health that he resigned—owing, undoubtedly, to malaria contracted in another country. Paraquil del Norte is, as you are probably aware, Excellency, one of the healthiest districts in South America. Yet, somehow, Presidente Trevor found that it did not suit him. So he went."

" To what country did he go ? " asked the skipper of the *Jutland*. " Pardon me, but the facts you relate have aroused my curiosity."

" He went north, Señor Capitan. No doubt we shall hear in due course the locality upon which his choice has fallen."

" And did he go alone ? "

" *Nombre de Dios !* Assuredly not, Excellency. Five of his compatriots accompanied him. Three I know not the names of, and little of them except that they came to Bomanares in a sailing-vessel called the *Nike*. She still lies in the harbour awaiting a purchaser. Another companion of the former Presidente was named Kayburn, who during

the war with Ouro Preto and Banda Rica was head
of our Air Service.   The fifth——"

The Paraquilan hesitated.

" The fifth——" prompted the captain of the
cruiser.

" Although I do not like to have to mention it,
Señor," explained the deputy, " the fifth was a
man with whom the Presidente did not appear to
be on very good terms.   Even an Englishman, I
notice, has his likes and dislikes towards others,
even as much as a Paraquilan.   I do not know
why there was a disagreement.   The man's name
was Duke or Tuke."

" Yes, that's it," supplemented one of the
deputy's companions.   " Tuke, Christian name
Solomaneos."

" Solomon Tuke," corrected the other.

By this time the British naval officer was feeling
sure of his ground.   He remembered that Solomon
Tuke was the name of the individual who had
given information to Scotland Yard concerning
the presence of Captain Cain in Bahia.   The
obvious inference was that the informer had come
south to Bomanares and had fallen into the power
of the man he had betrayed.

" A most interesting man, Presidente Trevor,"
remarked the *Jutland's* Owner.   " I should have
liked to have met him.   Do you happen to have
a photograph of him ? "

" Not a studio portrait, Excellency.   The Presidente was so modest in manner that he would
never consent to pose to a photographer.   There
are, of course, informal portraits—snapshots, I

think you call them in England. I will find some and show them to you. Meanwhile, Señores, pray partake of the humble hospitality at our command."

The Paraquilan, accompanied by several of the principal officials of Bomanares, escorted the British officers to the Presidency, where a lavish feast had been prepared in the latter's honour. Portraits of former Presidentes adorned the walls, even the oily, flabby, loose-jowled features of Lippo Bramo being included, although the artist had executed his subject with remorseless accuracy. The only portrait that did not appear was that of Presidente Trevor.

"I will now endeavour to fulfil my promise, Señor Capitan," remarked the deputy at the close of the repast. "There are several photographs in which our late Presidente appears."

He gave an order to a secretary. The man went out, returning presently with a large album.

"Here we are, Excellency," continued his host. "'The Presidente at the State Aerodrome,' 'the Presidente at the opening of the Chamber of Commerce,' 'the Presidente inspecting the 9th battery of Artillery'—these give quite a good idea of what our respected ex-Presidente is like."

The captain studied the prints intently, then he signed to Lieutenant Broadmayne.

"Have you seen this person by any chance?" he asked in English.

The lieutenant gave one quick look. It was quite sufficient.

" Captain Cain," he declared.

" Thank you," replied the skipper quietly, and resumed his studied perusal of the views depicting various incidents in the brief, meteoric and far from inglorious career of Presidente Trevor.

The gathering broke up after speeches on both sides, the Paraquilans welcoming the visit of the British warship, and expressing a hope that she would prolong her stay in order that her officers and men might learn something of the internal conditions of the progressive little Republic which owed so much to British initiative and determination.

On the other hand, the captain declared that he appreciated the hospitality of Paraquil del Norte, hoped that arrangements could be made for the vessel to remain for a few days at Bomanares, and stated that H.M.S. *Jutland* would be open to visitors for the next three afternoons from two till six p.m.

" That will make our commander tear his hair," he commented to his secretary. " I think I'd better give him three days' leave to go shooting up country. Broadmayne identified the ex-Presidente ; I feel rather sorry for the chap. He's evidently done some sterling work here, and has tried to live down his past. It's a rotten job having to track down a fellow like that."

On returning to the ship the skipper sent for Broadmayne to come to his private cabin.

The lieutenant did not feel at all elated over the business. He realised now that his appointment to the *Jutland* had been largely influenced by the fact that he had known the captain of the pirate submarine, and that he was now being called upon to act as a sort of informal witness for the prosecution.

" I must ask you to draft a report dealing with your identification of Presidente Trevor of Paraquil del Norte as Captain Cain, Mr. Broadmayne," began the skipper. " In confidence I don't mind admitting that I loathe the whole business ; but I have no option but to obey the instructions of My Lords."

" Very good, sir," replied the lieutenant quietly.

Already he was pondering over the new phase of the business. Now it began to occur to him that he might, without prejudice and perhaps with advantage, give information that he had for so many months kept to himself.

" Might I make a statement, sir ? " he asked.

" Certainly ; carry on."

" I have been able to identify Captain Cain, sir ; but there is another matter on which I may be able to give information. Perhaps, sir, you have seen the report on the Royal pardon being granted to Lieutenant-Commander Ambrose Alhampton."

" The commander called my attention to it," admitted the Owner. " Alhampton was, I am given to understand, an old shipmate of his. But I fail to see what parallel there is to the case of the pirate Cain. Alhampton was found guilty of a charge of forgery—a charge of which he has recently been declared innocent."

" Lieutenant-Commander Alhampton, Captain Cain and ex-Presidente Trevor are one and the same person, sir," announced Broadmayne.

The skipper gasped with astonishment.

" Is that a fact ? " he demanded. " Can you prove it ? "

" Certainly, sir. I tackled Captain Cain on his identity when I was his prisoner on board the *Alerte*. He admitted it. I remembered him as a two-and-a-half striper when I was a cadet at Dartmouth."

" Then why didn't you report it ? "

" From a Service point of view I ought to have done so, sir."

" Of course ; then why didn't you ? "

" I considered that Captain Cain was laying up quite enough trouble for himself without my raking up his past, sir. He seemed particularly raw on that subject."

" That is not to be wondered at," admitted the captain, dropping his official air, and talking as man to man over another's troubles. " After all's said and done, he played a straight game as far as British interests were concerned. He ought not to have run amok as he did, although with an unjust punishment and a stiff sentence worked out on that account he has some excuse. Apparently he realised his error after his escape from the *Alerte* (I'd like to know how he managed that, by Jove !) and has tried his utmost to run straight. Yes, Mr. Broadmayne, your disclosure complicates his case considerably."

" Do you think the fact that he has received

the Royal pardon will influence the Government's attitude, sir ? "

" H'm, 'fraid not. He's a pirate, when all's said and done."

" Officially he's reported as dead, sir."

" And, also officially, he's reported alive again," rejoined the skipper dryly. " I doubt whether the crime of piracy can be wiped out. In olden times things were different. Henry Morgan, the famous pirate and buccaneer, was pardoned and given the Governorship of Jamaica ; but I doubt whether any lawyer would dare quote that as a precedent. The only course I could suggest is that the Government be advised to drop the whole business and let Alhampton free to make a home in a foreign country. Fortunately the matter hasn't reached a demand for extradition yet. I hope it never will. However, you might let me have the report, Mr. Broadmayne, together with a statement embodying the facts you have just related. I'll use what little influence I happen to possess to urge My Lords to take a lenient view of the case. But, again, there are other countries involved : Germany over the *Cap Hoorn* incident ; France on the affair with the *Surcouf* ; Spain on the loss of the destroyer *Villamil* ; and Uncle Sam over the seizure of the *Bronx City*. All those Governments will be out for Cain's blood. Poor devil ! He chose an apt name when he adopted that of Cain : every man's hand against his."

" Not every man's, sir," remarked Broadmayne.

" Well, probably not," admitted the Owner.

CHAPTER XXI

TO THE RESCUE

DRAWING up the report dealing with Captain Cain's identity was one of the most distasteful tasks Broadmayne had ever been called upon to perform. He did it, since it was an order; but he would have given much for some one else to perform the task.

On the other hand, his skipper's sympathetic views upon the case gave the lieutenant hopes that even yet something might be done by the British Government to extend the terms of the pardon granted to Lieutenant-Commander Alhampton for a crime that he had not committed to cover one that he had. Even then, as the Owner of the *Jutland* had just reminded him, Broadmayne remembered that there were other plaintiffs in this international affair.

That same afternoon Broadmayne was " on " as Officer of the Watch, a duty which in harbour mainly consists of wearing a sword-belt without a sword, carrying a telescope and receiving sundry visitors.

" What vessel is that, signalman ? " he inquired, indicating a black-hulled craft with white top-

16

sides and deck-houses which was making her way up the tortuous channel to Bomanares Harbour.

"*Bronx City*, sir," replied the man. "She's flying Yankee colours."

"Very good," replied the O.W.

The *Bronx City* dipped her ensign as she passed the British light cruiser, a compliment which was punctiliously returned by the *Jutland*; then, easing down, she made fast to one of the wharves just below the Custom House.

That evening, as soon as his "trick" was done, Broadmayne went on the beach and, boarding the *Bronx City*, asked to see Captain Adams.

"Your servant, sir," exclaimed the bluff old Yankee, glancing from the piece of pasteboard in his hand to the bronzed, clear-cut features of his visitor. "What can I do for you?"

"I've seen you before, Captain Adams," said the lieutenant, "but only at a distance through a pair of binoculars."

"Guess I'm none the worse for that, Lieutenant Broadmayne," rejoined the other, with a laugh. "So you want to fix the cut of my jib close up, eh?"

"I was in the *Canvey* when you were chased by the *Alerte*," announced Broadmayne. "Naturally the incident interests me. I want to ask you for certain information concerning Captain Cain."

Hiram Adams shut up like an oyster.

"Guess you'll not get it," he remarked after a pause.

" That's unfortunate," continued Broadmayne cheerfully. " I had hoped that you'd be willing to say something in Captain Cain's favour."

" Reckon I'd do that," admitted Captain Adams. " He played a square deal with me. But why should I ? You Britishers have got a knack of turning things t'other way round like greased lightning."

" Captain Adams," said the lieutenant earnestly, " I want to do the man a good turn. He needs it badly enough, Heaven knows. I'll be perfectly open with you. It's no use being at cross-purposes. Cain was, as you are aware, Presidente of Paraquil."

" And that the Presidente of Paraquil is the pirate Cain ain't no secret," rejoined the Yankee. " Seein' as I heard the news yelled at him when he passed through the streets on the day of his election."

" Possibly that information hasn't gone very far," remarked Broadmayne. " For instance, I don't suppose you mentioned it to any one in New York."

" Nope," declared Captain Adams. " 'Tain't for me to blacken a man's character when he's trying to play the game. But why do you ask ? "

Broadmayne related the circumstances dealing with Cain's career as a British naval officer, of his false accusation, trial and sentence, and of the subsequent granting of a Royal pardon.

" He would have been quite safe and doing good work as Presidente Trevor of Paraquil if some one hadn't given him away," continued the lieutenant. "A miserable blighter of the name of Tuke gave information in Bahia, you know."

"Guess I can put you wise a bit more," declared Captain Adams. "Tuke was the name of the guy who shouted out at the Presidente. I don't suppose that's his right tally. 'Tall events, I spotted Mister Tuke as the greaser who bossed the show when the *Alerte* took the *Bronx City* into Bahia Arenac, Cain being sorter out of it. A kind of mutiny on the pirate ship it were. However, when I heard the guy spout, I looked. Sure enough I spotted him as the fellow I had a down on, and I fixed up then and there to have him shanghaied aboard the *Bronx City*. I wasn't just that slick, 'cause Cap'n Cain had him nabbed afore I could get to work."

Broadmayne heard the information with considerable satisfaction. He recognised the fact that Tuke the informer and Pengelly the second in command of the *Alerte* were one and the same, and that Cain had displayed his customary initiative in securing the person of the man who had so grievously betrayed him.

There was yet another point which could not at present be cleared up. Broadmayne had read of Pengelly's escape from Dartmoor, and how a dead body was identified as his.

"So you lost your chance to get even with the blighter," remarked the lieutenant.

"Sure thing," agreed the Yankee skipper. "Next day I called on the Presidente and asked him as a favour to hand the guy over to me.

Cain thanked me for calling, but said he wasn't going to; from which I calculate he'd got something fixed up right away for the skunk. I saw it was no use arguing with a fellow like Cain. Guess you know what he's like when he sets that jaw of his. So I saw he'd first claim on the boob, and let it go at that."

" So Cain's got his betrayer in his power ? "

" Sure thing ; an' by this time I guess Tuke— if that's his name—will be wishin' he never was born."

" Cain's a man who——"

" Cain's a man," interrupted Adams. " No need to say more. I hope he'll come out on top."

" Exactly," agreed Broadmayne heartily. " Only I'm afraid his difficulties are not yet over by a long way."

" And I as good as told him so," said the Yankee skipper. " Also I mentioned that if he did want a hand to help him out of a mess he'd only to send to me at N'York City. He played the game with me, and it's up to me to give him a square deal."

" I suppose you don't know where he is ? "

" Haven't an earthly," declared Captain Adams. " And if I did I wouldn't tell a soul—except you, Mr. Broadmayne. All I know is what you no doubt know already : that he cleared off in an airship with half a dozen of his pals—and Tuke. It's my belief they went north, but likely as not they'll get rid of their conveyance as soon as possible. An airship leaves too big a trail to be convenient, I guess."

On returning on board the *Jutland* the lieutenant reported to his skipper the conversation he had had with Captain Adams.

" If Adams is as good as his word, Cain won't have much to fear from the United States Government," commented the captain of the *Jutland*. " Apparently the only complaint lodged at Washington on account of the *Alerte* was the seizure of the *Bronx City* ; and on that occasion Pengelly was officer in command of the pirate submarine. Unfortunately the same conditions do not apply in the case of offences against the French, German and Spanish Governments. Once the facts concerning Cain's identity come to light there'll be a holy terror of a bother with the Foreign Office. All we can hope is that the British Government can be induced to drop these proceedings—between you and me, Broadmayne, I loathe this investigation business—and let Alhampton alone to settle down somewhere in the New World. Neither he nor the Government would have a moment's peace if certain foreign powers knew that he were in England."

On the following day a grand fête was to take place in honour of the British warship's visit. Sports and games were arranged to be held ashore, followed by a dinner to the officers and crew, the proceedings to terminate with a grand display of fireworks and an illumination of the city.

At six bells in the Forenoon Watch (11 a.m.) routine ceased for the day ; the men changed into No. 1 rig ; boats were hoisted out and steam raised in the steam-cutter and pinnace in order to land the guests.

At fifteen minutes past the hour the crew fell in by divisions on the quarter-deck ready for the captain's inspection before going ashore.

A bugle note rang out shrilly, as the Owner, accompanied by a group of officers in tropical uniform, appeared on the quarter-deck. The double rank of bluejackets and stokers sprang to attention with the knowledge that following a brief yet critical inspection they would be free for the rest of the day.

The silence, broken only by the trailing of scabbards across the deck as the captain's retinue followed the skipper up in front of the motionless ranks, was suddenly interrupted by the appearance of a signal-boy holding a buff " chit " in his hand.

The captain took the proffered paper, acknowledged the boy's salute and read the message. Then he turned and conferred with the Commander.

" Pipe down ! " came the unexpected order.

In forty seconds the quarter-deck was deserted save by the Captain, Commander, senior engineer officer and the Officer of the Watch. No explanation of the sudden alteration of plans had been made, nor was one expected ; but in an incredibly short space of time the " buzz " was all over the ship.

A negro revolt had broken out in British Noyada. The blacks, easily influenced by a negro agitator, had risen and were attacking the white planters and traders up-country.

Already several estates had been fired and Britons —men, women and children—foully murdered. The rebels, maddened by unlimited quantities of rum, were even threatening the coast towns, when the armed police and volunteers were barely sufficient to hold the infuriated negroes in check.

Wireless orders had just come through for the *Jutland* to proceed to British Noyada at full speed. Already the men were changing into working rig, boats were being hoisted in and steam raised for thirty-three knots. Semaphored messages to the Paraquilan authorities expressing regret that the proposed festivities must be cancelled were sent off, and within three-quarters of an hour of the time she received her wireless orders, H.M.S. *Jutland* was steaming north as hard as her triple screws could urge her and with a long trail of black smoke belching from her red-hot funnels.

From Bomanares to British Noyada is roughly three thousand nautical miles—ninety-one hours' steaming at thirty-three knots. Meanwhile the drink-maddened negroes were burning property, looting and murdering.

CHAPTER XXII

TEMPEST IN MID-AIR

"WHAT'S he going to do with me?" asked Pengelly.

Cross, temporary gaoler, eyed his former officer dispassionately.

"Ask me another," he replied. "'Ow d'ye expect me to answer a question like that?"

It was the second day of the airship's final flight from Bomanares to an unknown destination. Her crew consisted of Cain as captain, Dick Kayburn as second in command, Barnard, Davidge, Cross and three Paraquilan engineers who signed on upon the understanding that they would have their passage paid back to Bomanares on the termination of their month's agreement. Also, but not as one of the crew, was carried Paul Pengelly.

"Look here, Cross," continued the prisoner, "I never treated you badly, did I?"

"Don't see what odds that's got to do with the point," retorted Cross.

"But have I?"

"Since you ask, I might as well say 'yes' an' 'ave done with it."

" When did I ? "

" When you did the dirty on the cap'n, and peached to Scotland Yard," replied Cross. " That did the skipper out of a decent billet and put me an' my mate into a rotten hole just as we were gettin' along all shipshape an' Bristol-fashion, you dirty Jew ! "

" I'm not a Jew," declared Pengelly hotly.

Cross gave a steady glance at the full red lips of the prisoner.

" Pity you weren't, then," he replied bluntly. " I've no call to be down on a chap 'cause he's a Jew. In a manner o' speakin', a true Jew ain't a bad sort. It's the miserable blighters like yourself what won't own up to it that gets my goat. If there's one thing to be said in your favour 'tis that you haven't pinched a good Scottish name, an' set up as a finansewer. But the point is you're kippered this time. I reckon Cap'n Cain 'll have you sent back to England to serve the rest of your time."

" He promised he wouldn't do that," said Pengelly eagerly. " Does he mean to——"

" If I'd had any say in the matter," interrupted Cross, " I'd have you swingin' by your neck from this blessed airship. If the cap'n promised he'll keep his word. His name isn't Pengelly, nor Solomon Tuke neither."

" What is he going to do with me, then ? " asked Pengelly, reverting to his first question.

" Better ax him when you sees 'im," was the only reply.

Cross went out, locked the door after him and

left the prisoner to his not too comfortable reflections.

Pengelly was far from happy either bodily or mentally. Existence in a submarine had been a nightmare to him; a captive on an airship was even worse. He had a horror of heights, and although from his cell he had no ocular evidence that the airship was thousands of feet up, his imagination led him to conjure up appalling pictures of what might happen should the vessel meet with disaster.

Because he was not a man of his word and never hesitated to break a promise should it suit his purpose to do so, Pengelly was dubious of Cain's assurances that he would do his prisoner no bodily harm. Ever since the moment when " Presidente Trevor" had placed him under arrest, Pengelly was living in an agony of terror as to the uncertainty of the form of punishment that Cain was going to inflict.

Too late he realised that by his act of perfidy—his betrayal of his former partner—he had involved himself in the wreckage of Captain Cain's ambitions. Cain was still a free man and, judging by his standard of reckless courage, likely to remain so; whereas Pengelly had not only lost his liberty but all chance of gaining possession of the reward for the capture of the pirate captain as well.

Meanwhile Cain was revelling in the situation.

Bitter though the realisation was that he had been compelled to resign his position as head of the prosperous little Republic of Paraquil del

Norte, he realised that his career was far from being finished. With a small but thoroughly trustworthy band of compatriots there was no knowing what high endeavour lay before him.

He was now a fairly rich man. His wealth was judiciously invested in sound concerns in various South American cities. If he wanted adventure there was plenty to be had. With an airship at his disposal he would be welcomed by any other of the South or Central American Republics when trouble was brewing either internal or against a rival State. Even if no fighting were necessary there was a big future for commercial aviation ; while if necessary he could dispose of the airship to an aviation company and retire to a remote district where there need be no questions asked as to the past career of the stranger within its gates.

For the present Cain was in no great hurry. The airship was well equipped for a lengthy flight. Her offensive armament, with the exception of a pair of machine-guns and half a dozen rifles and automatics, had been removed. The weight thus saved was considerable, and had been replaced by additional cylinders of compressed hydrogen and supplementary petrol tanks. Without having to depend upon ground assistance the airship was capable of keeping up for at least three weeks, and in that time the whole length and breadth of South America could be flown over.

One thing Cain had firmly decided upon : there was to be no more piracy. Piracy, he felt convinced, did not pay ; and however circumspect he had been in choosing his victims, the result was not in his favour. Looking back, he realised that he was indeed lucky to be alive. It had been a mistake. He had tried, and was still trying, to remedy the errors of the past, but it took some doing.

He even regarded Pengelly's treachery with good-natured tolerance. There was little satisfaction in wreaking his vengeance upon a despicable man of that type. He meant to turn the fellow adrift in some district where he could do no further mischief, and let him live a prey to his uneasy conscience. He would be safe enough in any part of Latin America, provided he had the sense to keep his mouth shut concerning his unworthy past ; and provided he was willing to work, Pengelly would be in no danger of starvation.

Cain's reveries were interrupted by Kayburn entering the cabin.

" Have you noticed the glass, sir ? " inquired Dick. " It's falling like a hundred of bricks."

" I haven't," replied Cain. " What is it now ? "

" We're at five thousand feet, sir," reported Kayburn. " At that altitude the barometer ought to be in the neighbourhood of 25·6 inches. It's now at 22·4 inches and still falling."

Cain went to the aneroid fixed to the cabin bulkhead. The reading confirmed Kayburn's statement as to the behaviour of the barometer in the pilot's cabin.

" We're in for something, it seems," remarked Cain. " What do you propose to do ? I'd know

how to act if I were at sea ; but this business is a
bit beyond me."

" Run for it," replied Kayburn laconically.

" All right ; carry on," was the response.

Kayburn went back to the pilot's cabin. Presently he returned.

" We're in for it, sir," he announced. " Just
come and look."

It was an awe-inspiring sight that met the gaze
of the captain as he scanned the horizon. The
airship was forging steadily ahead in a wide belt
of sunlit air. North, south, east and west masses
of lead-coloured clouds edged with coppery hues
appeared to form an impenetrable barrier from
earth to an altitude far beyond the powers of the
airship to surmount.

Immediately beneath the vessel the earth was
hidden by wind-torn masses of clouds glistening
snow-white in the rays of the sun, but looking
vicious and dangerous as they swept over the
invisible ground.

To all intents and purposes the airship was
flying in a vast lidless box, the walls and floors of
which consisted of masses of highly electrified
clouds that threatened to close in and envelop
the flimsy gas-supported craft. In vain Kayburn
sought for an opening through which to drive the
airship. There was none.

" We'll have to chance our luck and climb," he
declared.

" Very good," replied Cain calmly.

Manipulating the valves that admitted additional
hydrogen to the gas-bags and adjusting both

horizontal and vertical rudders, Kayburn began to increase altitude. He had a space of roughly ten miles in which to manœuvre before coming in contact with the masses of cloud.

Apparently there was no help for it; the airship must force her way through some part of that wall of condensed vapour; but Kayburn hoped that at a high altitude the risk of being destroyed by lightning would be less than elsewhere.

Soon, however, it was evident that the airship was practically in the worst possible position: in the centre of the cyclonic storm. Overhead the sunlight faded as sheets of copper-coloured cloud shut off the rays of the orb of day. Denser and denser grew the pall of vapour until the airship was in an atmosphere resembling that of a moonless and starless night, save when vivid flashes of lightning swept athwart and astern of her track.

She was rolling heavily; pitching, bumping, and spinning in addition. To the crew it seemed as if the flimsy envelope was in the grip of a titanic hand that was doing its level best to shake the airship and crush it to fragments.

Under these conditions the propellers were doing more harm than good, for as the airship's nose dipped in spite of the pilot's frantic efforts to keep her on a level keel, the thrust of the screws tended to drive her earthwards. Conversely, as she squatted on her tail the propellers showed an inclination to keep her at an oblique angle.

Kayburn telegraphed for the motors to be

stopped. The airship, now nothing more than a cigar-shaped balloon, no longer behaved so erratically, although she rolled and spun at the mercy of the furious and contrary air-currents.

It was no longer dark. Flash succeeded flash, the electric fluid playing on the moisture-laden envelope. The roar and crash of the thunder were continuous, completely drowning all other sounds.

Iron-nerved though he was, Cain realised a sense of utter impotence. All he could do was to hang on and grip like grim death. He could see nothing. The glare of the lightning was so vivid that vision was paralysed. He could hear nothing. He was dimly conscious of the acrid fumes of petrol and hydrogen; realised dully that there was a leakage somewhere, and that it was a fortunate thing that the electrical ignition had been switched off. The while he recognised the fact that at any moment lightning might do its deadly work, and that the airship would then crash earthwards, a mass of fiercely-burning wreckage.

For how long this state of affairs continued Cain had not the slightest idea. He was in utter ignorance of what had happened to his companions. If Kayburn and Barnard were still in the pilot's cabin there were no indications of their presence. Of whether the airship was a hundred or ten thousand feet up he had not the faintest notion. He was barely conscious of hanging on with both hands while his feet slithered on the corrugated aluminium gratings as the storm-tossed craft described erratic curves in the midst of the thunder-clouds. With the knowledge that there was a leakage of hydrogen it was logical to conclude that the airship was losing altitude, but at what rate and to what extent remained an unanswered problem.

Gradually Cain became aware that the airship was growing steadier, that the flashes of lightning were neither so continuous nor so vivid, that the thunder, although heavy, was diminishing in deafening intensity. It seemed, too, that daylight was returning, although he was by no means sure on that point. To his sorely-tried optic nerves the light appeared much in the same way as it does to the eyes of a railway traveller as the train nears the exit to a tunnel.

Venturing to let go with one hand, Cain rubbed his eyes and peered into the dial of the altimeter. For some moments he saw nothing but a blur of violet hue, but presently he made out the needle of the dial. It indicated one thousand five hundred feet.

" She's dropping, sir ! " shouted a voice in his ear.

" That you, Kayburn ? " replied the captain. " Yes, by Jove ! she is. You all right ? Good : same here. There'll be an almighty crash, I'm afraid. Where's Barnard ? "

" Here I am, sir," replied that worthy.

Peering in the direction whence the voice came, the captain discovered that Barnard was sitting on the floor with legs and arms entwining the pedestal supporting the motor-room telegraph.

17

Bending to the voice-tube, Kayburn shouted orders for the two emergency ballonettes to be charged to maximum pressure.

There was no response.

" Will you carry on, please, sir ! " he exclaimed. " I must see what's wrong 'midships."

Groping his way along the cat-walk, Kayburn at length reached the motor-room. The Paraquilan mechanics were huddled in a corner, holding on to each other in mortal terror.

Finding that it was hopeless to get them to bestir themselves, the Englishman made a dash for the valve controls. A gentle hiss indicated the release of the emergency hydrogen. Waiting only to close the valves when the pressure gauges showed that the ballonettes were charged to their utmost capacity, Kayburn returned to the pilot's cabin.

" We're lifting," announced Cain.

" Thank Heaven ! " ejaculated Kayburn fervently.

A few seconds later the airship was bathed in brilliant sunshine. The clouds had either discharged their super-laden moisture or had drifted away. Less than three thousand feet below could be discerned a vast expanse of tropical forest, while dead to lee'ard rose a mountain-range faced by a precipitous line of cliffs, the summit of which towered high above the altitude of the drifting airship.

" We must start up the motors," declared Kayburn, as the fresh danger became evident.

" Belay there ! " cautioned Cain. " The whole

place reeks with petrol and hydrogen.   One spark
will blow us sky-high."

Calling to Davidge and Cross, Kayburn hastened
frantically to discover the leakage.   It did not
take long to find.   A petrol pipe had fractured
close to the union of the carburettor, while one of
the hydrogen cylinders had been wrenched from
its securing rods and by so doing had started the
supply pipe.

The petrol leakage was soon rectified ; in the
case of the hydrogen escape nothing need be done.
The cylinder was now empty and the fumes were
rapidly dispersing.

" I think it's safe to start up now," reported
Kayburn.

" And about time too," added Cain gravely, as
he pointed to the wall of rock now less than half
a mile away.

Followed another anxious moment as the motors
revived into a state of activity.   Then, gathering
way, the airship circled eight degrees to starboard,
skirted the spur of the menacing crags and, rising
slowly yet surely, steadied herself on her former
course.

CHAPTER XXIII

PORT BALLATOR'S S.O.S.

CONSIDERING the appalling nature of the ordeal through which the airship had passed, it was a matter for congratulation that she had escaped so lightly. Apart from the fracture of various pipes, a hole had been made completely through one of the main ballonettes. What caused the damage no one on board knew, but the fact remained that there was a clean rent on opposite sides of the compartment, as if a three-inch projectile had penetrated it without exploding on impact.

The loss of gas was a serious, though not dangerous matter, as it entailed drawing upon the reserve of hydrogen. Barnard undertook the repairs to the fabric, the airship being stopped for that purpose. At three thousand feet he was lowered over the side by means of a bo'sun's chair, and succeeded in making a gas-tight repair by the use of adhesive canvas.

Although the damage to the airship was but slight, the crew had been subjected to a terrific mental strain. Even Cain had to admit that he felt as limp as a wet rag, and Kayburn, the

enthusiastic young airman, frankly declared that
he "had the wind up," and wouldn't be sorry
to exchange the pilot's cabin of the airship for
the joy-stick and rudder-bar of a heavier-than-
air craft. Barnard, Davidge and Cross were
scared stiff, although their greatest anxiety
appeared to be that of concealing their state
of mind from each other. As for the Paraquilan
mechanics, they were "down and out." Kayburn, assisted by Davidge, had to undertake the
task of attending to the motors.

In the period of reaction following the terrific
electrical storm, Pengelly was forgotten. No
one paid any attention to him until Cross, going
to the prisoner's cabin, found the traitor lying
senseless upon the floor.

About sunset the mechanics recovered sufficiently to be trusted to remain at their posts,
and Kayburn was able to rejoin Cain in the pilot's
cabin.

"I wonder if the storm put our wireless out
of gear," remarked the captain.

"I'll test the set, sir," replied Kayburn.

"No immediate hurry," was the response.

"May as well do it now," rejoined Kayburn

His companion nodded.

"As you like," he said. "After all's said and
done, what's happening won't affect us very
much."

"But I don't like losing touch with what's
going on," declared Dick, as he went to the 'midships cabin, where the four-valve receiving set
was installed.

He had not been more than five minutes in the wireless room when he returned to the pilot's cabin.

" My aunt, sir ! " he exclaimed excitedly. " There's a jolly big bust up taking place in British Noyada — a nigger insurrection. The swine are playing hell from all accounts. Men-of-war are under orders to proceed to the scene at full speed. Port Ballator is isolated. A message states that the police and volunteers are running short of ammunition, and may not be able to hold out for more than twelve hours. And there are women and children——"

" Mr. Barnard ! " sang out the captain.

" Sir ? "

" Take the helm, please. Keep her as she is— north ten west."

" North ten west, it is, sir," replied Barnard, as he took the wheel which had been relinquished by his skipper.

Cain unfolded an aerial map and placed it on the table. For a minute or so he was busy with parallel rulers and dividers.

" We're roughly five hundred miles from Port Ballator, Kayburn," he announced. " Six hours hard going. Dash it all ! Why did we ditch our bombing-gear when we left Bomanares ? I don't know. It would have come in mighty handy. Drink-sodden niggers with razors lashed to canes, I know what that means."

" But there are warships rushing up," Kayburn reminded him.

" Yes ; but they may be too late. We'll

chip in for all we're worth, old son. If British bluejackets and marines have landed before we show up we can sheer off. Please stand by in the wireless room in case there are any other messages bearing upon the affair."

Already Cain's unusual fit of depression following the storm had vanished. He was his old self, alert, active in body and mind, his whole energies centred upon the task that confronted him.

Summoning Davidge and Cross, the captain explained the situation to the three men.

"Pity we didn't bring the bombs along with us, sir," remarked Davidge.

"That's what the cap'n said," declared Barnard, without shifting his gaze from the compass bowl.

"We've firearms," said Cain, "and, of course, the niggers won't count upon an airship butting in to upset their little game. It will be the moral effect that will count, I expect; but take it from me, my hearties, if there's a chance to send a few dozen of the swine to blue blazes, I'll take it. If we get over the brutes, we'll give 'em something to remember! Cross, you might collect every article of weight that we can spare. An ounce of metal dropped from a height of, say, four hundred feet, will knock a man's brains out. . . . And our pair of machine-guns!"

Night had now fallen. The airship had to depend solely upon stellar observations to correct her course, for the land, five thousand feet below consisted of dense vegetation and without any towns or villages that might be identified as aids to navigation. Kayburn, as he frankly admitted, was no pilot, in the sense that he could determine his position by observation of the altitude of certain celestial bodies. The whole responsibility in that respect had to be shouldered by Captain Cain.

Nevertheless, Cain found time to pay Pengelly a visit. It was the first he had made since his former partner had been placed on board the airship.

The prisoner had recovered his senses, although he was in a state bordering upon panic.

"Stow that!" interrupted Cain sternly, as Pengelly began to whine and grovel. "Pull yourself together and be a man—if you can. You were once. Now, listen; there's fighting to be done and I want you to bear a hand."

Pengelly raised his eyes. His full lips appeared to pout more than usual.

"Fighting?" he echoed. "What sort of fighting? The old game, eh?"

"No," replied Cain shortly.

His former partner looked disappointed. Pengelly was a man of strange moods. When he had a chance to "do his bit" in the Great War, he exhibited a craven eagerness to keep out of harm's way. Five times he figuratively crawled before a tribunal, and finally failing to get exemption contrived to avoid the danger of the firing-line for a safe job in a munition works in England. After the Armistice he announced himself as an ex-officer who had shed his blood for King and Country on three different occasions;

but very soon after he had entered into partnership with Cain in the Polkyll Shipbreaking Company the ex-naval officer saw through the shallow deceit of the recreant Pengelly.

Yet, on the other hand, Pengelly had proved himself to be a fighter. Even Cain was surprised at the manner in which he had played his part in the action between the *Alerte* and the Spanish destroyer *Villamil*; and it was in the hope that Pengelly would exhibit similar enthusiasm that he had invited the fellow's aid in the anticipated operations against the revolted negroes.

"There are women and children in peril," said Cain.

Pengelly shrugged his shoulders. Chivalry was not one of his strong points.

Cain started on another tack.

"I'm willing to pay for your assistance," he said. "Play the man; fight as you did at Wad-el-Abuam, when we scuppered the Spaniard, and we'll cry quits. I'll land you within easy distance of a town either in Brazil, Venezuela or Colombia, give you cash to carry on, and then, provided you don't trouble me, I'll not trouble you."

Pengelly pondered over the proposition.

"I suppose you'll give me away to Scotland Yard as an escaped convict?"

"I'm not in the habit of communicating with Scotland Yard," replied Cain, with thinly-veiled sarcasm.

"All right: it's a deal," agreed Pengelly.

Cain handed him an automatic.

"It's loaded," he said. "You'll find spare

ammunition for'ard. I want you to serve one
of the machine-guns with Davidge."

The captain turned his back upon his former
partner and strode out, leaving the door unlocked. Meekly Pengelly followed, his emotionless
features belying the thoughts that rioted in his
brain.

Shortly before midnight Kayburn picked up a
message to the effect that the insurgents had
effected an entry into the southern part of Port
Ballator and had fired several of the buildings.
The defenders, whose losses were heavy, were
still holding out, but were hemmed in on all sides.
The negroes had sunk several large barges on the
bar of the river, thus making any escape by water
impossible, and at the same time preventing any
armed boats from effecting a dash to the beleaguered town. As a matter of fact there were
no armed boats, for the simple reason that the
British warships were still a couple of hundred
miles away.

At one in the morning, Cain called his companions' attention to a lurid glare on the horizon
almost dead ahead. Other fires of lesser magni-
tude were also visible. The airship was approaching the frontiers of British Noyada.

A few minutes later Cain gave the order, " On
bow searchlight. Stand by, machine-gun party ! "

The commands were promptly executed.
Barnard and Cross manned one of the machine-
guns, the other being served by Davidge and
Pengelly. One of the Paraquilan mechanics
connected up the lead from the dynamo to the

for'ard searchlight, adjusted the carbons and directed the powerful beam at ten degrees below the horizontal.

" Look, sir! The altimeter! " suddenly exclaimed Kayburn warningly.

Cain glanced at the instrument. The needle was steadily going back. At the present moment it indicated eight hundred feet.

" What's wrong? " he demanded, and bending to the voice-tube ordered one of the mechanics in the motor-room to go to the gas-container chamber and release more hydrogen into the ballonettes.

For about two minutes the downward movement was checked. The airship even gained a thousand feet; then the earthbound drop began again.

" Give more gas! " shouted Cain.

" *Dios, capitan!* " replied the scared Paraquilan. " It is escaping as fast as it goes in! Four of the ballonettes are leaking."

Cain set his jaw tightly.

" More gas! " he ordered. " All of it, if necessary."

It was perfectly obvious that the airship's career as an airship was approaching the end. Realising this, Cain determined to keep up until the vessel was within a mile or so of Port Ballator. If he could not fight the insurgents from the air, he would do so on the ground. His chief fear was that the airship would make a forced landing too far from the scene of conflict, and all his energies were devoted to nursing her along towards the spot where the fiercely-burning fires indicated the presence of the infuriated negroes.

By this time the airship seemed to be going straight for a wall of red-and-orange flame, surmounted by a pall of dense black smoke that appeared to hang motionless in the still air.

Not a moment too soon did Cain telegraph for " Stop ! "

The motors ceased their steady drone. An uncanny silence followed as far as the interior of the craft was concerned. For without the crackling and roaring of the flames, the sharp fusillade of small-arms and the frenzied shouts of the rum-maddened negroes indicated that the British defenders of Port Ballator were still maintaining a desperate resistance.

" Stand by to jump clear when she makes contact, lads ! " roared Cain. " Stick to those machine-guns and keep together. We'll give the brutes a thundering hiding yet."

Thirty seconds later the airship bumped. She had dropped with her bows depressed, and although the compact was not severe the for'ard compartments were buckled and the reek of hydrogen filled the heated air.

All hands, armed to the teeth, leapt clear, the machine-gunners sticking gamely to their weighty charges. They had barely covered a hundred yards when the glare of the burning buildings paled into insignificance by a terrific flash. The remaining gas left in the ballonettes had exploded. The airship was a mass of fiercely-burning flames.

CHAPTER XXIV

EXIT PENGELLY

" KEEP in touch ! " shouted Cain. " One machine-gun on each flank."

The little band pressed on, guided by the shouts and reports of firearms. Apparently the negroes were so intent upon their work of murder and rapine that they had failed to notice the burning airship.

For the first quarter of a mile over which Cain's party made their way, the ground consisted of swamps covered with sugar-cane. Attempts had been made to burn the canes, either by the defenders in order to create an exposed arc of fire, or else by the attackers out of sheer love of destruction; but these efforts had met with little success.

Presently, on breasting a slight incline, Cain made out the figures of a mob of negroes silhouetted against the glare of the burning buildings. Almost at the same time bullets began to whine over the heads of the airship's crew.

" Lie down, men ! " ordered Cain.

He crawled forward a few yards and levelled his binoculars. Then he rejoined his men.

" All right so far," he reported. " The swine haven't spotted us. It's the defenders' bullets that are singing over our heads. Left incline ! Make for the lee of that building."

The building was a large store that was now well alight. It had evidently been plundered before being fired, for close to it lay the bodies of about a score of looters who had been shot down by the defenders before the latter were compelled to withdraw to the farther end of the town. The reek of charred flesh and burning spirits filled the air.

" Cheerful - looking specimens, what ? " remarked Kayburn, indicating a couple of corpses lying in the centre of the wide path, each grasping a razor lashed to a pole in his nerveless hand, and with a hideous grimace on his ebony features.

" They won't do no more 'arm, sir," added Cross.

" I don't know so much about that," declared Captain Cain, who had overheard the remark. " Ever heard of nigger playing ' possum ' ? Better make sure they're properly done in."

The party made another advance, slowly and cautiously. Ignorant of the lay of the land, Cain had to exercise the greatest discretion until he could obtain a fairly comprehensive idea of his objective. He planned to make a flank attack, but at the same time he had to make sure that he and his men would not be subjected to a flanking fire from the people he had come to attempt to rescue. Mistakes of that nature, he knew, had occurred before.

A huge negro, staggering under the weight of the loot he bore, appeared round the corner of one of the buildings and came straight for the spot where Cain's party stood. He was within twenty yards of them before he realised his danger.

Dropping his booty and yelling like a maniac, he turned and fled. Realising that if the negro were able to communicate the news of an armed party to his fellow-insurgents all chance of a surprise would be thrown away, Cain levelled his automatic.

By this time the fugitive had increased the distance to about sixty yards—an uncertain range for a pistol.

The sharp crack of the weapon was almost inaudible in the terrific din, but Cain's aim was none the less deadly on that account. The negro, hit fairly between the shoulder-blades, gave a convulsive spring in the air, with his arms outstretched. Then he fell face downwards, writhed for a matter of about ten seconds and lay still.

Advancing by a series of short rushes and taking advantage of the doubtful cover afforded by the smoking débris of a number of wooden huts, the airship's crew got within two hundred yards of a large body of negroes. The latter were either rallying after a repulse or were concentrating for an assault. Many of them were armed with rifles (an ominous business, that; it meant that they had managed to secure the weapons from some of the white men); others brandished machetes and their favourite close-quarters weapon, a razor lashed to a bamboo;

a few carried cans of petrol, while half a dozen black fiends were holding on to a baulk of timber with the obvious intention of using it as a battering-ram.

Although in full view of the defences they were not subjected to rifle-fire. Ammunition, as far as the British were concerned, had long since run low. All they could do was to reserve their fire until every shot told.

" Let 'em have it ! " exclaimed Cain. " Aim low and give plenty of traverse."

The machine - gunners set up their weapons—air-cooled and capable of firing 500 shots per minute. Belts of ·250 ammunition were brought up to the mechanism. The men bent over the sights.

" Let's hope they won't jam," thought Cain, as he gave the signal to open fire.

The rapid, sputtering explosions of the machine-guns outvoiced the frenzied shouts of the drink-maddened mob. A sheaf of bullets ricochetting from the sun-baked earth took toll of the insurgents. Men fell in heaps without having time to realise whence death came.

For the most part the negroes were too inflamed with rum to flee in terror. Quite a hundred of them, led by a gigantic brute wearing the white tropical helmet of an officer of the British Noyada police, attempted to charge the deadly machine-guns.

The attackers melted away before the death-dealing bullets, but it did not mean that the conflict was a one-sided business. Even in their

frenzy the negroes were cunning brutes, for in
a very short time they renewed the attack, supported by a rough-and-ready sort of armoured tank.

This consisted of a couple of large, cylindrical
iron boilers, urged onwards by a dozen stalwart
men, while fifty others followed under the lee of
the moving fortress. Although the curved surface
of the boilers was splayed with nickel, the machine-
gun bullets were futile against the thick metal
plating.

Cain realised that here was a factor that had
not entered into his calculations ; but he was too
wary a leader not to deal an effective counter-
stroke. During the advance he had noted the
lay of the land, against the possibility of having
to fall back against overwhelming numbers, and
in view of that contingency he remembered seeing
a stone building, almost the only one that had not
been set on fire.

The moment he saw that the machine-guns
were useless against the metal mobile shields, he
gave the order for retreat As soon as the negroes
were aware of the retirement of their foes, most
of them started in pursuit, firing erratic volleys
as they ran. The boilers they abandoned as unnecessary encumbrances.

" Stand fast, men ! " roared Cain. " Let 'em
have it ! "

The order was obeyed with alacrity. Even the
Paraquilan mechanics had sufficient confidence
in their leader to change their somewhat precipi-
tate retreat for a halt with their faces to the
foes.

18

Again the machine-guns spoke. Bereft of the shelter of their rolling defences the insurgents broke and fled, leaving the ground strewn with their dead and wounded.

Cain was quick to take advantage of the situation. No longer was there need to fall back upon the position he had originally intended. The boilers, standing deserted in the centre of the street, were his for the asking. If they had served as an efficient shelter to insurgents, they would serve an equal purpose for him.

" Forward, men ! " he ordered. " We'll have those boilers ! Mind as you advance, in case any of the wounded niggers slash at you with their knives."

The objective was reached without opposition, and Cain immediately took steps to consolidate the position. The boilers were shifted until they stood parallel to each other and at a distance of ten feet apart. At each end a machine-gun was posted so as to command an almost complete front. Stones were piled up at either end to form a low barricade and also to prevent any attempt on the part of the negroes to roll the cylinders together and thus crush the defender between the two masses of metal.

So far Cain had attained a considerable measure of success. Even if he had not driven off the rebels completely, he had created a diversion in favour of the sorely-pressed Europeans in Port Ballator. Yet he was unable to effect a juncture with the people he had come to aid. More than likely they were unaware of what had occurred,

and there were no feasible means of communicating
with the garrison. Until Cain could establish
his identity it would be gross folly to attempt
to make his way to the barricades protecting
Port Ballator. In the uncertain light, Cain and
his men would almost certainly be shot down by
those he had risked everything to rescue.

Undoubtedly he had committed the same error
that Britons have done and will do all over the
world; he had underrated his foe. He had
calculated upon the negroes taking to flight at
the first bark of the machine-guns. It was quite
possible that they might renew the attack; although, on the other hand, they would probably
abandon their designs upon Port Ballator after
daybreak. Even a drink-influenced black hesi-
tates to attempt by day what he would with the
utmost recklessness under the cover of night.

Another circumstance that had upset his calculations was the loss of the airship. Had she
remained up, her appearance would have struck
superstitious terror into the hearts of the insurgents, and once they had taken themselves
off, Cain would be at liberty to resume his Odyssey.
As it was, in the event of the siege being raised,
Cain and his companions would be stranded in
Port Ballator. It was quite possible that some
of the officers of the British warships hurrying to
the rescue might recognise the former captain of
the pirate submarine *Alerte*; and although they
would probably " look the other way," he had no
desire to come in contact with the service in which
he once held commissioned rank.

For the next hour or so things were relatively quiet. The rifle-firing had died away, and, although the blacks continued their blood-curdling yell, no renewal of the fighting was attempted.

"I shan't be sorry to see the dawn, Kayburn," remarked Cain. "If those blighters don't clear off, we'll have to make a dash for the town as soon as it's light."

"The warships ought to be there by that time," rejoined Kayburn, "if only——"

"Look out, sir !" shouted Barnard warningly. "The blighters are bunching up for a rush."

It was only too true. While hundreds of the insurgents were yelling themselves hoarse, others had crept quietly under the lee of a gentle rise of ground within a hundred yards of Cain's defences, and in practically the only position where they were not exposed to machine-gun fire without the weapon being open to a flanking fire from the ruined buildings on the left. Already bullets from that direction were either whizzing overhead or else pattering loudly upon the boiler-plates.

The assault was of brief duration, but not lacking in intensity. Kayburn had a disjointed impression of what occurred. He remembered emptying his automatic into the faces of a crowd of diabolical-looking negroes who attempted to clamber over the metal boiler ; noticed out of the corner of his eye that one of the machine-guns was silent with a cartridge jammed immovably in the breech ; saw Cain seize the remaining gun, leap upon the metal breastwork and splay bullets at point-blank range into the yelling, frenzied mob; felt something hit him like a blow of a sledge-hammer, and fell back into the darkened recess between the boilers, with a bullet through the shoulder.

For an ill-defined period Kayburn felt as sick as a dog. Then the mist cleared from his eyes. Cain was lying close to him, his head supported on Barnard's arm. The negroes had abandoned the attack.

"What's the matter with that fool?" suddenly exclaimed Davidge, pointing with a bandaged hand over the top of the defences.

Kayburn staggered to his feet and looked.

Right on the heels of the vanquished blacks ran Pengelly flourishing an automatic and shouting at the top of his voice. He made no attempt to fire the weapon. In the glare of the burning buildings his movements could be clearly seen. He looked like a dog chasing a crowd of terrified sheep.

A moment later and by some unaccountable impulse the rearmost of the fugitives stopped; turned and threw themselves upon the madman— for mad he undoubtedly was.

Knives and razors glittered in the firelight. Pengelly was down with a dozen bloodthirsty wretches hacking at his already lifeless body.

Then a machine-gun spluttered close to Kayburn's hand. Cross had succeeded in getting it into position again. When it ceased, Pengelly's body was hidden under the corpses of his assailants.

" Fair barmy he was, I'll allow," exclaimed Cross, as he proceeded to fit another belt of ammunition to the gun. "How's the cap'n, mate ? "

" Done in, worse luck," replied Davidge laconically.

CHAPTER XXV

VINDICATION

"BEST let me bandage your shoulder, sir," suggested Barnard.

"It's nothing much," protested Kayburn. "Clean puncture. . . . See if you can do anything for him."

He pointed to the motionless form of Captain Cain.

"Time enough to tend to the dead when we've fixed up with the living, I guess, sir," rejoined Barnard, as he dexterously cut away Kayburn's tunic. "Two down and out—gone West—and two wounded. We've paid a pretty stiff price."

"It's worth it," declared Kayburn. "Even Captain Cain would have said so. We've drawn off the attack upon the town. . . . Thanks, that feels better already," he added, as Barnard deftly bandaged the wound. "It felt like being kicked by a mule. I wonder my shoulder hadn't been blown clean away."

"Bullet went in an' out," reported the Good Samaritan. "Lucky the swine weren't using soft-nosed stuff. And Pengelly's gone!"

"Ay, the swab!" exclaimed Cross.

Kayburn turned and looked reprovingly at the speaker.

"He did his bit at the last, at any rate," he said.

"That he did, sir," agreed Cross. "An' that's his dirty work."

He pointed to Cain's body. Blood from a wound *in the back* was staining the captain's white drill jacket.

"What's that?" demanded Kayburn and Barnard simultaneously.

"Fact," persisted Cross. "It was while I was a-foolin' round with that jammed gun, Pengelly, my opposite number, markin' time as it were. When the cap'n grabbed t'other gun and got atop of that there boiler, I saw Pengelly, out of the corner of my eye, raise his pistol and shoot the cap'n down. I'd have put a bullet through the swab's head, only I couldn't very well knock off what I was doin'. Then he jumps over the barricade and makes a bolt for it. You know what happened then. Fair off his rocker, if ever a bloke was, I'll allow."

"Let's hope for his sake that he was," said Kayburn soberly. "Now, let's see——"

His suggestion was interrupted by the loud crash of a quick-firer, followed by a regular salvo of medium-sized ordnance. Shells were bursting amongst the sugar-canes to the south-east of Port Ballator, where the insurgents were congregating.

"A warship's arrived," declared Barnard. "It's all over bar the shouting."

" Let's hope they won't start strafing us in error," said Kayburn. " It'll be light in a few minutes. As soon as we can establish our identity we'll get out of this."

With the first streaks of dawn shell-fire ceased. Out of the relieved town poured bluejackets with machine-guns, Mills bombs, rifles and bayonets, all eager to punish the barbarous and blood-thirsty rebels who, but for Cain's intervention, would have burnt the town and butchered the inhabitants.

" What are you fellows doing here ? " demanded an officer, as he encountered the survivors of the airship's crew.

" Our bit, sir," replied Barnard.

" So I should think," rejoined the naval officer, glancing at the pile of corpses surrounding the improvised fortress. " Want any assistance ? You'll find our doctor in the town. Good luck ! "

The landing party swept onwards. The way to Port Ballator was open.

Carried on the shoulders of four of his devoted crew, Cain's body was taken into the town. Already a gap had been made in the defences, and through this the survivors of the airship made their way.

" By Jove ! " exclaimed a weary and hideously dirty officer of the Noyada police—the sole un-wounded commissioned officer of the eight who had been shut up in the beleaguered town, " so you are the fellows who kicked up that diversion last night ? We wondered what it could be.

You've saved the situation. We were reduced to less than a hundred rounds. If those blighters hadn't switched off to attend to you we'd have been properly in the soup. Come along! We've plenty of food and drink. You look as if you need both. What, a doctor? There's the *Jutland's* M.O. over there."

The Surgeon-Commander of the *Jutland* was having a busy time, for the casualties amongst the military and civil population had been heavy. Under his direction the light cruiser's sick-berth staff were working like Trojans. In the circumstances, Kayburn felt it advisable to wait for his wound to be dressed. There were others in greater need of medical assistance.

A lieutenant, gaitered and belted and with a service revolver strapped to his side, came limping back from the firing-line. As he passed, he glanced at the motionless form of the former pirate captain and brought up all standing.

" Excuse me," he said, addressing Kayburn, " but how did he come here ? "

" You know him, then ? " asked the airman.

" Yes," replied Broadmayne. " I had hoped to meet him again, but not in these circumstances. Is he dead ? "

Kayburn inclined his head.

" Bullet through the heart," he announced. " He was a white man, if ever there was."

In spite of his injuries, Broadmayne knelt by the side of his former captor.

" He's breathing ! " he declared. " He's not dead. Fetch the doctor, one of you."

During the brief wait, Broadmayne caught the eye of Barnard, the ex-pirate bo'sun ; but there was no sign of recognition. Both men realised that the naval officer knew the other's secret, and was content to let it stop at that.

Twelve hours later, Cain recovered consciousness to find Broadmayne standing by the side of his cot.

" So you've found me," remarked Cain feebly.

" Yes, Commander Alhampton," replied the lieutenant. " I'm awfully sorry——"

The wounded man gave a wry smile.

" I've cheated you after all," he declared. " But you might have respected my *nom de guerre*."

" No need for that," said Broadmayne. " You can honourably make use of your own name. You have received the Royal pardon, the sentence of the court-martial is quashed and you are restored to your former rank."

" A bit too late in the day," protested Cain grimly. " There are other counts to be taken into consideration. However, I'm slipping my cable. It's good to hear that I've been cleared of one accusation ; but I want to ask a favour, Mr. Broadmayne. My men : you know . . . they were with me in the *Alerte*."

" Yes, I know," rejoined the lieutenant. " They won't be penalised, I can assure you. Neither will you, sir. My skipper reported your case to the Admiralty, and on our way up from Bomanares we had a wireless to say that the Government proposed to take no further action in the *Alerte* affair, and that you would be at liberty to return to England whenever you wish."

A smile flitted over the pale features of the wounded ex-pirate and ex-Presidente.

"Life's worth living after that," he remarked.

.   .   .   .

Six weeks later, Commander Ambrose Alhampton, R.N., set foot upon his native shores.

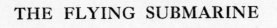

THE FLYING SUBMARINE

CONTENTS

CONTENTS

THE FLYING SUBMARINE

CHAPTER I

SUB-LIEUTENANT HOLMSBY HAS TO INVESTIGATE

"NO, no, Wapping. I don't think we need take action. Hang it all, man, what with all these tin-pot scares about foreign spies, we shall be run off our feet."

"But don't you think this is something out of the ordinary?" asked Captain Douglas Wapping, M.V.O., R.N., of his chief.

"Out of the ordinary? Yes, quite—a letter written by a gimcrack hare-brained pensioner, with the evident idea of gaining notoriety prior to calling attention to some grievance real or imaginary. I know their game. Who is this Lieutenant Haslar?"

"I've looked him up in the *Navy List*, sir. Retired on pension. He was a ranker, promoted for meritorious service in the Bangwan River affair."

"Oh yes, I remember the man. Garrulous as an old washerwoman."

" But he states sufficient in the letter to justify investigation——"

" Well, well, Wapping, have your way then : you always do, somehow or other. Hang it, man, if I had your powers of persuasion I would have received Flag rank long before I did."

That morning Rear-Admiral Pennington had received a letter from an obscure Cornish fishing-hamlet, stating that the writer, Lieutenant Haslar, R.N. (retired), had reason to believe that a mysterious submarine, owned apparently by a foreign power, had been seen cruising in the waters of St. Ives Bay, and that, moreover, a huge airship, that must have its headquarters in the vicinity, was in the habit of making nocturnal passages overland in the direction of Plymouth.

" Send one of the youngsters," continued the Chief Director. " Have you anyone in view ? "

" There's Herne, sir, or Bircham, or——"

" How about Holmsby ? "

" Well, sir——"

" What ? "

" I'm afraid I cannot recommend him."

" Why not ? "

" Personally I know little of him, but James has reported unfavourably upon him more than once."

" A fig for James, Wapping. You let that fellow lead you by the nose, as I've told you before."

" You have, sir," admitted Rear-Admiral Pennington's subordinate humbly.

" As a matter of fact, I know something of young

Holmsby. A bit high-spirited, perhaps, but after all, is that a failing ? Moreover, he came here with an excellent report from the captain of the *Tremendous.* Send him in to me, and we'll give him his sailing orders."

Accordingly a messenger was dispatched to summon Sub-Lieutenant Reginald Holmsby to report himself in the chief's sanctum, and in a few minutes the young officer was standing as straight as a dart in front of his superiors.

Recently it had been the practice of the Admiralty to appoint junior officers to the Naval Intelligence Department to assist the commanders and marine captains who had hitherto comprised the combatant *personnel* of this branch at Whitehall. It was purely an experiment, but since these juniors could be entrusted with missions of minor importance, and would gain experience to enable them to tackle more intricate matters, the scheme bid fair to prove a success.

Sub-Lieutenant Reginald Holmsby was a fine active specimen of the British naval officer. Standing five feet eleven inches in his socks, broad yet wiry in body, and with a powerful-looking face that betokened courage and sagacity, he still retained an almost boyish expression in his dark eyes. At sea he had been popular with his messmates, ever ready for a " lark " when ashore,—a propensity that more than once had led him into trouble,— but at the same time he was devoted to his profession and a hard worker. Having passed his Greenwich exams with " firsts " in seamanship, gunnery, and naval law, and " seconds " in torpedo and other subjects, and having qualified for an interpreter in Spanish and Italian, he had been appointed to the Naval Intelligence Department at the comparatively early age of twenty.

" Ah, good-morning, Mr. Holmsby," exclaimed the admiral genially. " I believe you've been on leave for the last twenty-one days. Let me see, you were in Cornwall ? "

" Yes, sir."

" What part ? "

" The north coast."

" Oh." The Chief Director raised his eyebrows slightly, then : " How did you get there ? "

" By motor-cycle, sir," replied the sub., wondering what on earth possessed his superior to evince such an interest in his doings while on leave. Then, with a burst of confidence, he added, " And I had a ripping time, sir."

" I'm glad to hear it," remarked Admiral Pennington brusquely. " Did you happen to come across a place called Pen—Pen (where's that letter, Wapping ? Ah, thanks)—Penkerris ? "

" Rather, sir. Had a mishap to a sparking-plug and had to wait there until the carrier brought me another from Redruth."

" What sort of place is it ? "

" Usual type of Cornish fishing-village, sir. A sort of a kind of a big crack in the cliffs, with a few stone cottages and a little jetty, sheltering perhaps half a dozen drifters or small fishing-craft.   When it comes on to blow, you can't go in or you can't get out, because they place huge pieces of timber across the mouth of the basin to check the force of the breakers."

" Hardly the sort of port suitable for a destroyer, for example ?   Is the harbour tidal ? "

" Yes, sir ;   dries, I should think, at three-quarters ebb."

" Well, Mr. Holmsby, you seem to have gathered a fair amount of information concerning the place, as all officers should do.   So what do you say to another visit to this out-of-the-way village ?   Now read this letter."

Holmsby took the missive and read it through carefully from beginning to end, his face betraying the interest its contents afforded.

" Now this will give you the clue to what you will have to do," continued the Chief Director. " To-day is Wednesday.   On Friday you will proceed to Penkerris in the rôle of a tourist.   Con- trive to make the acquaintance of this Lieutenant Haslar, and, without letting him know who you are, pump him concerning the cock-and-bull yarn about the foreign submarine and airship.   You might also put a few casual questions to the fishermen.   By the bye, where is the nearest coastguard station ? "

" At Polgwenyth, three miles from Penkerris, sir," replied Reginald promptly.

" Good," exclaimed Pennington approvingly. " Now I leave the matter entirely in your hands.

Use your own discretion, and if there should be any truth in this report, communicate with us by wire. If, however, you find that urgent action is necessary, get the aid of the coastguards at Pol—what's its name. Before you start, I'll give you an order to that effect, signed by the officer commanding the division."

" Am I to proceed to Cornwall alone, sir ? I venture to suggest that with a companion this business could be carried out more efficiently——"

" How ? " interrupted Admiral Pennington, in surprise. " Pray explain."

" Tourists mostly go in pairs, at least," replied Reginald. "Besides, should it be necessary to explore the cliffs, I could dispense with the aid of any of the inhabitants, who would become suspicious as to my intentions."

" I'm afraid, sir, that cannot be managed," interposed Captain Wapping. " We cannot spare anyone else at present."

" I did not mean that," continued the sub-lieutenant quietly. " I've an intimate friend—he holds a civil appointment at the Admiralty—who knows this part of the coast thoroughly. He would be only too glad to come and bear a hand."

" But he cannot be sent officially," replied the Chief Director. " Besides, is he to be trusted to share the seceret ? It's risky, you know."

" I can rely upon him absolutely," assented Holmsby, with conviction. " However, sir, if you have any objection, I will proceed alone."

" No, no, Mr. Holmsby.   You can have a free
hand.   Now you may go.   See me to-morrow afternoon and the necessary papers will be ready for
you.   In the meanwhile, should anything fresh
transpire I'll send for you."

With that Reginald took his leave, but instead of
returning to his room he made his way to another
part of the huge block of buildings that gives shelter
to the numerous and complex departments comprising the Admiralty.

" Is Mr. Tresillian in ? " he asked of a uniformed
messenger.

" I'll see, sir," replied the man, who recognised
his questioner.   " I think he's in his room."

In a few moments the messenger returned and
requested the sub-lieutenant to follow him.

" Hello, Dick; busy, eh ? " asked Reginald
breezily, as he was ushered into the presence of his
old friend, who was engaged in languidly turning
over the dry-as-dust pages of the *Home Dockyard
Regulations*.

Dick Tresillian, a tall, thick-set Cornishman, with
so swarthy a complexion that he might easily have
passed for a Spaniard, threw the book upon the
table and jumped to his feet to greet his visitor.
The son of a mine-owner, he had " passed " for
Osborne at the same examination as Holmsby, but
in the ensuing medical examination a lynx-eyed
doctor had discovered that the young Cornish lad
possessed a stiff thumb-joint.   Placing a small silver
coin on the floor, the medico bade the youngster

pick it up. Dick's efforts were unavailing, and in consequence he was " ploughed." Thereafter he was wont to bewail the fact that his career was blighted by a threepenny piece. However, he was sent to an engineering college, and in his twentieth year presented himself at the Admiralty for examination—this time for the " civil " post of Assistant Surveyor—and passed with comparative ease.

" Busy ? " replied Tresillian. " My dear Reginald, do I look it ? Look here, old man, I'm not of a grousing disposition, but honestly I'm sick of this place. Instead of surveying—I haven't set eyes on a theodolite since I joined—I've been sent to supervise a pack of clerks who know more about their work than I ever hope to."

" You've a soft time, at all events," remarked Holmsby.

" That's just what I have to complain about. Instead of using my intellect—and I suppose I have a fair share—I've got to kill time, and help to keep up the utter farce of working overtime for no reason whatever but to swell a rotten ' return.' Honestly, Rex, I don't like it, so I can only hope for a turn at foreign service. But what's up ? You look excited."

" I'm off to Cornwall again, old chap."

" Lucky dog ; but I thought you had only just returned from leave."

" So I have. This time it's official business. But to get to the point : could you possibly manage to come with me ? "

" I wish I could.   But what is the reason ? "

" Never mind that at present," replied Holmsby laughing.   " But look here :   I asked you a question. Can you manage to get off ? "

" I haven't had much leave this year.   Perhaps the chief might see his way clear to let me off from my arduous duties," said Tresillian, bestowing upon the hateful *Regulations* a lusty kick.

" Then see him as soon as you can.   I'm off to Penkerris the day after to-morrow."

" It's like the call of the blood, Rex.   Penkerris is, as you know, within ten miles of my home, and I know every inch of it."

" Couldn't suit me better.   Now cut off and see about obtaining leave, and I'll wait here."

" Cannot be done, old fellow," replied the Assistant Surveyor dolefully.   " Thanks to red tape, 'twill take a day at least to get the application through."

" Then we must leave it at that," said the sub-lieutenant, who knew full well that his friend's objections were only too well founded.   " You'll come if you can manage it.   Ten-thirty train from Paddington.   Bring your motor-bike, and don't forget this important item :   an electric torch. Let me know the moment your leave's approved."

" By Jove, this sounds mysterious."

" I hope for my own sake it is," replied the sub-lieutenant sententiously.   " But I'll tell you about it when we are fairly on our way.   Now I must be off, for there's much to be done. But remember, not a word as to where we are bound for," and with this parting injunction Reginald Holmsby left his friend to essay the prodigious task of applying for leave.

CHAPTER II

THE OUTRAGE ON THE HIGHWAY

PUNCTUALLY at a quarter to five on the following Friday afternoon the train bearing Sub-Lieutenant Reginald Holmsby and Dick Tresillian steamed into the terminus at Newquay.

The young Naval Intelligence officer had chosen Newquay as the place from which the motor-cycle journey should commence, since it was within an easy distance of Penkerris, and the arrival of two dust-covered tourists would cause less comment than if they had alighted at the nearest station and jogged leisurely to the scene of their approaching enterprise.

During the run down from Paddington Holmsby had confided to his comrade the object of his mission, and the strict necessity of using the greatest caution.

" We may as well be prepared for eventualities, Dick," he added, and unstrapping a small leather portmanteau, produced a serviceable little revolver,

" Here you are, Dick : carry it in your pocket. so that you can easily get it if required," he continued. " It's a little beauty. Takes ·202 cartridges, and will drill a hole through a two-inch deal at fifty yards."

" A neat little weapon," exclaimed Tresillian enthusiastically as he opened the chambers and examined the ends of the six copper cylinders with a critical eye. " But do you think we'll have to fall back upon this ? "

" You never know.   But you are not jibbing already, are you ? "

" Not I," replied Dick stoutly. " Although this is hardly what I expected in an out-of-the-way Cornish fishing-village.   But how about you ? Haven't you a shooter too ? "

" Trust me for that," said Reginald, tapping the breast pocket of his coat. " I've a weapon identical with yours in every respect ; so if we are disappointed, we can find some solace in a shooting match along the cliffs.   By the bye, is there a decent place where we can put up at Penkerris?   You know the place fairly well, I believe."

" When I was there last—that's two years ago— I found comfortable quarters at a Mrs. Pedler's. A homely sort of Cornishwoman, middle-aged, inclined to talk, but strictly honest."

" So much the better," remarked Reginald. " We'll sample Mrs. Pedler's Cornish pasties and cream within a few hours, I hope."

Half an hour after their arrival at Newquay the two comrades were proceeding at a modest twenty knots, as the sub-lieutenant expressed it.

Reginald Holmsby's spirits rose high as he felt

himself speeding through the bracing air in the
breezy uplands, while his companion was not one
whit the less enthusiastic at being once more in
his beloved native country. Knowing the route
intimately, he led the way with the utmost confidence, pointing out the numerous objects of interest
as they sped along.

Presently the road descended abruptly, and the
riders found themselves on a wide rolling plain,
composed mainly of drifting sand interspersed with
patches of coarse grass.

" This is a strange sort of place," remarked
Reginald. " I must have missed this district when
I came through last month."

" They say the sand is steadily encroaching. It
does in several parts of Cornwall. Over there,
although you can't see it from the road, lies St.
Piran's lost church. It was buried in the sand for
centuries, and only discovered a few years ago.
However—— Hello! Hang it, Rex, my back
tyre's down."

" Hard lines ! " ejaculated Holmsby, as he dismounted. " Here, let me bear a hand."

" No need for that," replied Tresillian, who had
already turned out his repair outfit. " I'll have it
all right within half an hour or so. Look here, if
you care to have a look at the church while I'm
doing this—it's very interesting—you can walk
there and back easily in the time."

" Thanks, but I don't think I fancy a trudge
through that desert, on the off-chance of finding the

place," replied Holmsby, glancing at the vast expanse of waving grass and soft sand. " I'll stand by and smoke a pipe."

" Please yourself, then," said Dick airily. " But I thought you were a bit of an antiquary."

" So I am, but I don't want to desert you when I might be able to help."

" Well, look here. At the fork-roads, less than a hundred yards away, is an old Roman amphi-theatre, called St. Piran's Round. That may interest you, and you can't miss it."

" You seem mighty keen on getting rid of me," remarked Reginald, with a smile. " However, I'll leave you to it, and have a look at the place."

Leisurely following the soft tract at the side of the road, the sub-lieutenant came in sight of a circular earthwork, nearly fifty yards in diameter, a worn gap in the sloping banks enabling him to gain the interior with comparative ease.

Although walking naturally, his feet made no sound upon the soft earth, and on gaining the top of the encircling bank Holmsby found that he was not the only visitor to this relic of bygone days.

Two men were seated on the grass with their backs towards the side on which Reginald was standing. Both were apparently tall and strongly built. Unless he were absolutely certain to the contrary, Holmsby could have been sure that one was his companion, Dick Tresillian, while it did not require much imagination to liken the other man to himself. Both were talking volubly, making rapid and excited gestures, while one of them was coiling away a length of insulated wire.

Struck by the resemblance, Holmsby, out of sheer curiosity, stood looking at the pair, until he became aware, from drifts of conversation that were borne to his ears, that the conversation was being carried on in Spanish.

Instantly the quick-witted young officer reviewed the situation. Here were two men, obviously foreigners, taking counsel with themselves in a secluded spot, while there was no apparent reason why they should be handling electric gear.

" To-night . . . will ascend . . . strong measures . . . Carlos with explosives . . ."

" This sounds interesting," mused Reginald. " Is it possible that these rascals are the owners or agents of the mysterious airship ? It seems to me that this Lieutenant Haslar is not so far out after all."

On first thoughts, the sub. was for slipping quietly away and bringing Dick to the scene of action ; but reflecting that the men might observe him as he crossed the gap, and also that much of the conversation might be lost, Holmsby slid softly down the remote side of the bank and listened intently. But though he strained his ears, the rustling of the wind in the grass made the conversation totally inaudible.

" May as well risk it," muttered Reginald, and, regaining his feet, he stood boldly upon the mound.

" After all, if I don't betray any interest in

them, they can't do much," he soliloquised. "I've as much right as anyone to be here."

At that moment one of the men took a small cylinder from his pocket and placed it at his side. Holmsby instantly recognised it as a detonator similar to that used in the Service and of high explosive power. As the foreigner did so he caught a glimpse of the intruder standing on the bank above him, and with a muttered exclamation of annoyance he snatched at the cylinder with more haste than discretion and replaced it in his coat pocket. Then both men started to their feet and confronted Reginald with no pleasant expressions on their faces.

The sub-lieutenant now saw that all resemblance to Dick and himself ended, for the man whose back view reminded him of Tresillian, though round-featured and swarthy, wore a short, straggling black beard. The other, equally swarthy, was clean-shaven and inclined to flabbiness.

"What are you here for?" demanded the latter menacingly, in excellent English.

"That's rather a strange question to ask me," replied Holmsby coolly. "I understand that this place is open to anyone's inspection. Have you any objection?"

Taken aback at the pointed question, the man seemed flabbergasted.

"My friend here is annoyed," said his companion, in a conciliatory tone. "We are touring, and have had trouble with the police for not carrying our driving licenses. Moreover, we have had a slight breakdown with our car." And he pointed to the opposite side of the earthwork, although no sign of the car was visible.

" I am sorry to have caused him needless alarm," replied Reginald, though he was perfectly aware of the object of the man's change of front. " As it happens, my friend, who is a skilled mechanic—purely an amateur, by the bye—is a little way down the road ; he will be most happy to give you any assistance."

" We shall be much obliged," replied the man, though Holmsby noticed that he gave a deprecatory shrug.

Leaving the two foreigners, the young officer walked across to the road, whence he could see Tresillian struggling with the refractory tyre.

" Dick, ahoy ! " he shouted, in stentorian tones. " Here, I want you."

Seeing that Tresillian had heard and was about to join him, Reginald walked back to where the twain were still standing.

" Perhaps, sir, you would like to have a look at our car," said one. " It may be that something is amiss that can easily be rectified without troubling your friend."

" He's on his way now," replied Holmsby " But I'll see what I can do, if you like."

Without replying, the two men sauntered carelessly round the embankment to where a powerful-looking car stood, bearing a registration plate marked F.O. 445.

" It is this switch that has given us the trouble," said the man who had spoken so abruptly. " See, it is useless," and jumping into the car, he thrust the lever to and fro without any apparent result.

Visions of forcible abduction made Reginald exercise a certain amount of caution, and instead of accepting the implied invitation to board the car, he stood slightly in advance of the off-side front wheel. At all events, Dick would be here soon, and they dared not——

Holmsby's thoughts were rudely interrupted by the car giving a sudden bound. Only by a quick side movement was he able to escape being crushed to death. Then, as the motor gathered speed, Reginald became aware of a rapid succession of reports like the crack of a whip. Instinctively he ducked, his cap falling from his head as he did so ; there was a momentary vision of one of the foreigners brandishing an automatic pistol, and with a skid and a bound the car dashed round the corner of the cross-roads.

" What's up, old man ? " asked Dick anxiously, as Holmsby rose to his feet, recovered his displaced headgear, and unconcernedly began to brush the dust from his clothing.

" Up ? My number very nearly," answered the sub. " They tried to run me down, and finished up by letting rip at me. How I escaped is a marvel.

Hello ! Why, there is a bullet-hole through my cap."

" Who ? " demanded Tresillian.

" How should I know ? I can only guess. Dick, old chap, we are something at last." And Holmsby proceeded to give a detailed account of what had transpired.

" What are you going to do ? " asked Tresillian. " Put the county police on their track ? There's a station at Perranporth, and in less than half an hour a description of the car will be telephoned to all the police in the duchy."

" Not I," replied Reginald emphatically. " This is our affair, and once we bring in outsiders, the whole business, and the reason for my being here, will become public property. No, Dick ; this little incident proves that something mysterious is happening, and I mean to find out what it is. But, by Jove, I believe the brute touched me after all."

Turning up the coat-sleeve of his left arm, Holmsby found that his surmise was correct. A bullet had grazed his forearm sufficiently slight to leave an angry-looking scar.

" Well, that's luck," he ejaculated. " One shot through my cap and another through my sleeve. The beggar with a beard let fly, I should think, ten shots, and it was only the jolt of the car that saved me. There's truth in the old saying that a miss is as good as a mile. But hadn't we better be getting under way ? You've finished the repair, I hope ? "

" Nearly. I've only to replace the cover and

pump up. But ought we not to make a thorough examination of this place ? It seems quite possible that, being secluded and sheltered, it might form a landing-place for this mysterious airship on its nocturnal voyages."

" By Jove, I never thought of that, Dick. We'll have a look round."

But a careful search revealed nothing. Beyond a small patch of grass beaten down by the two foreigners as they sat there was no trace of any recent damage done to the " ring." Had an airship alighted, there would bound to be traces of spilt oil and petrol and the marks of the securing grapnels.

" We've drawn blank this time," observed Dick, " So, as you say, we'll proceed."

Hardly had the two comrades left the shelter of the earthwork when a vicious shot of flame burst from above a rough stone wall at less than twenty yards distant, and a shot whistled between their heads.

CHAPTER III

THE MYSTERY DEEPENS

INSTINCTIVELY both men doubled behind the embankment, their retrograde movement being accelerated by a fusillade of pistol shots ; but unscathed they reached a place of safety.

Reginald Holmsby was perfectly cool and collected, while his companion, thanks to his previous training in the Imperial Yeomanry, was no greenhorn, although actually under fire for the first time in his life. Dick could not help experiencing a strange sensation of mingled fear and anger as the bullets whizzed past him, but on taking cover his natural sang-froid reasserted itself.

" You've your revolver, I hope ? " asked the sub., noticing that Tresillian was in his shirt-sleeves.

" Rather : I shifted it to my hip-pocket when I began to repair the tyre."

" Good. Now, we can't stop here to be potted at. These fellows will also try to cripple our bikes, I'm afraid. Will you edge away to your left and keep them in play, while I work my way round to the right and take 'em on the flank ? "

Dick assented, and, revolver in hand, took up

the position indicated. So far Holmsby had waited merely to place his cap upon a thorn bush so that it was just visible to the two desperadoes, and immediately set off to carry out his projected flanking tactics.

The appearance of the headgear was the signal for another fusillade from an automatic pistol, and in reply Dick sent three shots in rapid succession towards the spot where a thin bluish haze denoted the presence of their assailants.

Then ensued a long pause, till the sharp report of Holmsby's revolver came from the same side of the stone wall behind which the mysterious oreigners were in hiding.

" After them, Dick, they're off ! " shouted the sub-lieutenant, carried away with the fierce joys of victory.

Instantly Tresillian left his cover and ran for the stone wall. Clearing it at a bound, he saw with mixed feelings of delight and regret the forms of the two assailants disappear behind another wall at the far end of the field.

Prudence urged Dick to return to shelter, while Holmsby, having fired two more shots, " just to show there's no ill feeling," as he expressed it, rejoined his comrade. But the precaution, though judicious, was unnecessary, for in a few moments the noise of a car's exhaust was borne faintly to their ears.

" That's settled their hash for the time being, Dick," exclaimed Reginald. " You never gave me a chance, for directly you fired they bolted like hares. I could only get a flying shot at them as they ran. But why should they be so intent on sniping us, I wonder ? "

" Goodness only knows," replied Tresillian. " But let's get on the move in case they take it into their heads to have another go at us. Now it comes to the point, Rex, were we justified in firing upon the King's highway ? "

" Justified ? Gracious, man, do you think I was going to be potted like a pheasant without giving them tit for tat ? Mark my words, we haven't seen the last of these gentry."

By this time the two comrades had returned to the abandoned motor-cycles. Dick replaced the cover while Holmsby stood on the alert ; but unmolested the repair was completed, and the twain remounted.

" Not a word about this affair to anyone, mind," cautioned Reginald, as they descended into the little watering-place of Perranporth. " We may as well make a few inquiries about the car though. We can say that we are looking for our friends in a car with the registration number F.O. 445."

" What does F.O. stand for ? " asked Tresillian.

" Can't say off-hand, but here's a garage. Perhaps they have a list of registration letters. I'll ask."

Presently the sub-lieutenant returned with the information that the car was registered in Radnor.

" It's a blind for certain," he added. " However,

I'll write off at once to the office and get the chief to make inquiries as to who the owner of F.O. 445 might be. But, honestly, I believe it will be a false clue."

From Perranporth the road led sharply up the side of a steep hill. Even on low gear the cycles made hard work of it, but wild scenery amply compensated the drivers.

Away on the right, betwixt rugged cliffs that formed vast defiles, could be seen the blue waters of the Atlantic, now tinged with a deep crimson by the setting sun. To the left a chain of rugged hills, fringed by an irregular line of tall chimneys, met the skyline ; while ahead, the gorse and bracken covered downs, capped here and there by the " stack " of a gaunt deserted mine, rose in seemingly endless persistence.

" Think we'll take that without trouble ? " asked Reginald, pointing to a conical-shaped hill that reared itself to a height of nearly seven hundred feet, the white road showing clearly as it ascended a spur of the formidable beacon.

" We don't want to," replied Dick. " The road to Penkerris branches off just here. You must have missed the hill as well when you came in from St. Ives."

" Yes, you're right," agreed Holmsby. " I struck inland to avoid it. But I remember this lane well."

They had now reached the by-road, which, assuming a loose rough surface, plunged steeply down a narrow rocky valley. Ahead, the powerhouse and gaunt chimney of a still working copper mine stood out clearly against the evening sky.

To the left of the road ran a swift stream, not of sparkling water like the brooks of Devon, but of a bright crimson hue, being fouled by the mundic from a score of copper mines.

The line terminated abruptly almost at the edge of the sea, where a stretch of slate-coloured pebbles did duty for the beach. On either hand the cliffs rose sheer to a height of over a hundred feet. To the right as far as the eye could reach the cliffs continued in a succession of bold bays, while in the other direction a frowning granite headland restricted the landscape to a distance of less than a quarter of a mile.

At the base of this cliff two massive stone jetties enclosed a small artificial harbour, the only visible means of access from the shore being a series of steps cut into the solid rock and protected by a rough hand-rail, while a wooden crane afforded the means of removing the scanty catches of fish or the cargoes of the colliers and other coasters that at rare intervals put into the basin.

A few stone houses, perched on every available portion of level or slightly sloping ground, comprised the hamlet of Penkerris. Picturesque from all points of view, it would have been a popular artists' haunt and watering-place but for the presence of the mineral-charged stream. Discolouring the sea for a space of a hundred yards from the diminutive beach, it rendered Penkerris impossible for bathing. Doomed to stagnation, the hamlet was left severely alone by holiday-makers, and was fifty years behind the times even as far as the rest of the duchy was concerned.

"Here's Mrs. Pedler's cottage," said Dick, pointing to a rambling two-storeyed cottage, the granite walls of which were nearly hidden by a profusion of creepers. "No doubt she can accommodate us; if not, I'm afraid we're done, for there's not even an inn nearer than St. Agnes."

Leaving their motor-cycles outside the garden gate, the two comrades, in the now fast-gathering twilight, made their way up the irregular path and knocked at the door.

It was opened by a portly dame, who peered at the two mackintoshed-clad figures over the rims of her glasses.

"Good-evening, Mrs. Pedler," exclaimed Dick genially.

"Good-evening, sir, whoever you might be, for I can't a-bring you to mind. Ah, to be sure, 'tis Mr. Tresillian. Come in, sir, and be kindly welcome."

Within ten minutes the two comrades were doing justice to a plentiful Cornish supper, while their hostess was bustling to and fro with an almost too attentive solicitude as to their wants.

"By the bye, Mrs. Pedler, how is Sampson's Cove looking? Last time I was here it was about to be sold."

"Don't mention it, sir," exclaimed the old dame raising her hands in dismay. "A gentleman from

Lunnon 'as bought it and a rare slice of the down as well. He be a real stranger gentleman, sure, though I can't call to mind that I ever set eyes on him. But people in the village who knows says he's in league with the Evil One."

" A kind of limited liability company, eh ? "

" I can't say as I knows what that is, sir, but 'tis a real bad company whatever he keeps. What goes in there goodness only knows, for they've put a girt iron fence all around, and no one in the village 'as ever set foot inside since for nigh a twelve-month."

" Then we shan't be able to visit the cove as I used to do ? "

" No, sir, that you can't. It's fair cruel to stop up the path to the cove like that. Mr. Haslar up at Anchor Cottage is right vexed about it. But that ain't the worst. The Lunnon gentleman isn't satisfied with tearing all over the place in a motor, but he's often flying through the air in a girt thing that makes an awful noise."

" What's that, Mrs. Pedler ? " asked Holmsby, who had hitherto been patiently enduring the old lady's conversation. " Travelling through the air ? Is that a fact ? "

" As sure as I'm alive, sir ; for, though I'd told you I d never set eyes on him, his flying-machine well-nigh scared the wits out of I."

" Oh, what sort of machine is it—an aeroplane ? "

" Oh no, sir," continued Mrs. Pedler, " 'Twern't that ; 'twas more like the size of my poor dear husband's ship, and she was a brig of 200 tons register," and the old lady pointed to a gaudy oil-painting of a trader that occupied a prominent position on the wall.

" 'Twas like this," Mrs. Pedler was now in full swing, and needed no prompting. " Last June, it being my sister's wedding-day so I am sure of the date, I had been over to Redruth to spend the day. Sure as fate I mussed my train, and it was dark when I caught the next. As you know, sir, it's a pretty goodish step from St. Ann's Road station to here. Just as I were a-coming to the cross-roads I heard a most uncommon sort of floppin' in the air, and this girt flying thing comes right over my head. I were turble skeard, an' took to my heels an' ran—an' me with rheumatics in my knees an' all."

" What happened then ? " asked Reginald.

" I came straight home. Next mornin' I told the police sergeant, but he actually told me—a respectable widow—that I had been having a drop too much. 'Twas the same with everybody I told, except Mr. Haslar; but now I knows they knows I was not telling fancy tales."

At length, from sheer want of breath, Mrs. Pedler stopped and left the two comrades alone. Supper over, Holmsby suggested a stroll before turning in.

" The moon will be up by now," he remarked. " And a saunter as far as the headland will do us no harm. I'm afraid, though, we will not see anything of the nocturnal airship, unless we make a night of it; and, candidly, I've had enough excitement to last me for the present."

Accordingly, the twain took the left-hand or north-western cliff path, and in about a quarter of an hour reached the extreme point that separates Penkerris Bay from its neighbour.

Everything was calm and peaceful. Beyond the glimmer of a few lamps in the hamlet and the regular flashes of Godrevy Light almost on the horizon, extreme darkness brooded over sea and land, for the moon was obscured behind a bank of clouds.

" Quiet, isn't it ? " remarked Holmsby, puffing contentedly at his pipe.

" Simply grand," replied Tresillian. " But we've come in the wrong direction to see anything of Sampson's Cove."

" I meant to," said the young officer. " Tomorrow we'll have a quiet day and find some excuse to keep watch all night. So——"

" What's that ? " exclaimed Dick hurriedly, pointing to a faint luminosity on the water several hundred feet below the spot on which they were standing.

Following the direction indicated Holmsby saw a phosphorescent swirl disturbing the tranquil water close to the edge of the next headland. After watching it for some moments the sub. rose to his feet.

" Let's get back," he remarked. " You're getting jumpy, Dick. It's only a shoal of mackerel."

" I've never seen a shoal like that," maintained Tresillian stoutly. " Hold hard a minute."

The luminous patch, whatever it was, was slowly moving seaward, yet it retained its apparently compact form.

Just then the moon shone forth through a rift in the clouds, flooding the sea with its silvery light, and the illusion vanished.

" Come along, Dick," repeated Holmsby. " You have caught a bad nervous disorder."

But Tresillian obstinately refused to budge, keeping his eyes fixed upon the spot where he had last caught a glimpse of the mysterious swirl. For full five minutes he remained thus, while Holmsby, with ill-concealed impatience, sat down upon a piece of rock and refilled his pipe.

Just as Reginald was in the act of lighting up, a sudden exclamation from his companion caused him to throw down the match and spring to his feet. Half-blinded by the glare of the match, he could see nothing, but he distinctly heard the faint whirr of a powerful motor.

As for Tresillian he gazed in astonishment at what he saw, for apparently from the depths of the sea a dark grey cylinder had emerged, and with incredible swiftness rose in the air to an immense height, speeding rapidly in a south-easterly direction.

By the time Holmsby had accustomed himself to the darkness once more, the mysterious airship was out of sight and hearing.

CHAPTER IV

CHECKMATE

" WHAT do you think of it ? " asked Dick. Being a born diplomat, he had prudently refrained from the irritating exclamation, " Wasn't I right after all ? " but he could not help feeling inwardly elated at his discovery.

" Didn't see it at all," replied Holmsby, scorning to beat about the bush. " I was lighting my pipe and the glare of the match put me out of the running. What was the thing like ? "

" As far as I could see, it was similar in shape to our airships, only smaller. Whatever it was it shot up from beneath the sea, floated for a brief interval, and then ascended."

" Are you sure it came from below the surface ? I can understand an airship starting from a floating position on the water, but the very idea of an object possessing the extreme buoyancy to lift in the air and sufficient weight to sink in the water seems utterly opposed to every law of nature and science."

" I'm practically certain the thing did shoot up from beneath the surface."

" Then, Dick, we are on the track of an invention that will revolutionise warfare—a submarine possessing some powerful and hitherto unknown agency to make it able to resist an enormous pressure of water and also to enable it to raise itself in the air. A truly formidable tool in the hands of an unscrupulous inventor. But it's not of much use waiting for further developments to-night. To-morrow we'll pump old Haslar, and in the evening we must take steps to fathom the mystery."

That night Dick Tresillian could not sleep. The events of the day had excited his feelings to such an extent that for hours he lay uneasily in his bed listening with feelings of envy and irritation to his companion's deep, regular breathing.

At length, finding slumber impossible, Dick arose and went to the open window, where he remained lost in thought, yet hoping to detect the sound of the returning airship, till the dawn began to disperse the shades of night.

Then dead-beat he threw himself upon the bed and slept, seemingly but a few minutes, until he was roused by Holmsby's voice demanding whether he meant to spend the day in bed.

"What's the matter with you, by Jove ? " asked the sub., noting his companion's tired expression. " You look as if you hadn't had a wink of sleep all night."

"Neither have I—I simply couldn't. But I don't think we'll witness the departure of the airship to-night."

" Why ? "

" I was looking out of the window until dawn, and I can swear I never heard a sound. So perhaps she's off for good."

" I trust not. But get your things on and we'll go for a swim. There's nothing like salt water to freshen you up."

On the way down to the little harbour they met a fisherman returning from his night's work. The man greeted them civilly enough, but both remarked that he eyed them with a certain amount of suspicion.

" Perhaps he takes us for some of the new owners of Sampson's Cove," said Dick. " If so, that's awkward. We must disarm suspicion in some way."

" Mrs. Pedler will enlighten them on that subject, never fear," replied Reginald. " But here we are, and there's another boat coming in. If we can hire it for an hour we can have a decent swim without running the risk of being dyed a bright red."

Descending the steep flight of steps, the two men reached the jetty. Without hesitation the fisherman agreed to take them off, for his luck had been out, and less than half a dozen small whiting had been the reward of a night's hard toil.

" Can you run us round to that cove I see yonder ? " asked Holmsby, pointing to the mysterious Sampson's Cove. " The water seems clear enough there."

" No, I won't," replied the fisherman bluntly, resting on his oars. " You be strangers here ? "

" Staying at Mrs. Pedler's. But I remember you," said Dick. " You took me out fishing when I was here two years ago."

" Now you comes to mention it, I do, sir," replied the man. " But you ain't anything to do with they up there—are you, sir ? " and he jerked his head in the direction of Sampson's Down.

" No, we're not," assented Tresillian. " But what's the matter that you should refuse to take us to the cove ? "

" Can't do it, sir. The place has been sold, and a pretty fine sort o' chap 'as bought it. I believe he's a luney, for he's fenced the place right in and don't allow a single soul in Penkerris to set foot inside. If a boat sets her keel in the cove a lump of rock'll be sent flying from the cliff—an' who's to prove it ain't pure accident ? "

" Sounds lively," commented Dick.

" What sort of man is the owner of Sampson's ? " asked Reginald. " Tall ? Does he use a motor-car ? "

" No, he's a little 'un. Leastways, I think so, but I only just caught sight of'n once. Ne'er a blessed moty-car 'ave I seed, either."

" Surely he must get provisions from some-where ? "

" Not in Penkerris nor in St. Agnes. An' 'tis said that he only lives in a little house over t'hill.

Sure he's a real wrong 'un. There's been nought but bad luck in the fishin' since he comed here."

" How's that ? " demanded Holmsby sharply.

" Don't know," replied the fisherman with equal brevity, mistaking the tone of his questioner. " But 'ere you are, sir ; no tide fit to speak of and puffectly safe for swimmin'."

" You frightened the old chap," observed Dick on their return to the village. " He shut up like an oyster."

" Yes, I noticed that. 'Twas an unfortunate blunder on my part. However, we'll have some breakfast, then cross-examine old Haslar."

Anchor Cottage was the highest-situated building in Penkerris, standing within fifty feet of the edge of the low cliff of the north-eastern side of the beach. It was a two-storeyed stone building with a roof of thick slate slabs. On two sides there was a well-stocked flower-garden, while seaward a small lawn, with a flagstaff in the centre and half a boat that had been converted into a look-out perched perilously near the brink of the sheer cliff.

Half hidden in the profusion of flowers was a short, stocky, red-faced man with a neatly-trimmed iron-grey moustache and torpedo beard. In his navy-blue reefer coat there was no possibility of taking the individual for anything but a retired Service man.

" Can we reach the cliff by this path ? " asked Holmsby by way of opening a conversation.

" You may, sir, though this is private property. This way. I'm afraid you can't go very far because of the fence."

" Thanks awfully," replied Reginald, purposely ignoring the latter part of Lieutenant Haslar's reply. " You've a fine display in your garden, if I may be allowed to say so."

" Not bad," replied the retired officer modestly.

" I suppose you've had a lifelong experience of gardening. These rows are worth exhibiting."

" Never touched a hoe as far as I remember until twelve years ago. I'm a Service man."

" A Service man ? " Holmsby was the perfection of innocent ignorance.

" Yes, sir, a Service man. Pensioned carpenter-lieutenant from the Royal Navy. Haslar, John Haslar is my name, and I'm not ashamed to answer to it."

" Well, Mr. Haslar, we must thank you again for your courtesy—but what was that you said about a fence ? "

The old man's face clouded.

" Yes, that blamed fence you can see over there. Turns Sampson's Down, with one of the finest, if not the finest, outlook on the coast into a private arsenal or something worse."

" A private arsenal ? "

" Ay, 'tis about time the Government took steps in the matter. They aren't so particular as when I was in the Service, or they would have sent a detachment of coastguards to investigate. Instead of that the ' gobbies ' have nothing better to do than to plant cabbages. It's an outrage, sir."

" I'm afraid I can't follow you."

" Well, I know for certain that the fellow who has bought Sampson's Down and the cove is nothing less than a foreign spy, if not worse. Night after night I've seen one of those airships start off from the cove. What for ? Why, Plymouth isn't more'n two hours' run, so you can draw your own conclusions. I've written to the Admiralty about it, but beyond the usual acknowledgment they have taken no action."

" I've heard tales in the village about an airship What sort of craft is she ? Where is she kept when not in use ? "

" That's where I'm beat, sir ; never been able to make out. But might I ask why you take such an interest in the thing ? "

" It is your account that interests us, Mr. Haslar. You see we are visitors here, and never expected to hear strange tales about an airship in this out-of-the-way Cornish hamlet. By the bye, would you care to have a drink ? There's a ' pub.' in the village, I believe ? "

" The sun's not over the foreyard yet, sir."

" Very good," replied the sub-lieutenant, but the next instant he was biting his lip in his mortification : by his tacit acceptance of the pensioner's refusal he had given himself away.

" You are a Service man yourself ! " exclaimed Haslar, looking Holmsby straight in the face.

" I am," admitted Reginald. " And what is more, I've been sent down expressly by the Admiralty to investigate the facts contained in your report."

" Then why the deuce didn't you say so, instead of beating about the bush ? Confound it, you cock-sure youngsters want to pick the brains of a man old enough to be your grandfather and take all the credit. I'll be hanged if I tell you another thing."

And turning on his heel the irate lieutenant walked off, leaving Reginald and his companion standing dumbfounded in the garden.

" I've made a mess of it again, by Jove," ejaculated the former, when he had recovered his tongue. " That's twice this morning already."

" Never mind ; the old chap will open out next time we fall across him," said Dick. " But at any rate our investigations are checkmated in this direction, so we may as well start on another tack."

Armed with a pair of powerful prism-glasses, the two investigators hired a boat, and dropping anchor about a quarter of a mile from Sampson's Cove, began ostensibly to fish.

Under the shelter of the loosely furled sail they took turns to scan the frowning cliff. But although they persevered till late in the afternoon, not a single human being nor any sign of animation could be discerned.

" Evidently the place is deserted," remarked Holmsby. " The airship has either left for good or she has gone for a prolonged cruise. However, we'll renew our researches after sunset."

CHAPTER V

THE SECOND NIGHT

" ANY luck, sir ? " asked the boatman, as the two pseudo-fishermen returned to Penkerris Harbour.

" Not a single bite," replied Dick. " But we're going to try again to-night—I believe night is the best time for this sort of game."

The man looked at them with a marked shade of suspicion, but after all he was well paid for the hire of his boat, so what did it matter ? "

" It used to be a good place for night fishing, sir," he said. " Perhaps with a bit o' luck you might pick up a few bass or whiting."

" We can but try, so will you please see that the boat is ready and the bait on board by half-past eight."

" You won't be runnin' no risks wi' my boat, will 'e, sir ? You see she's all I got to keep me going."

" I'll try not to," replied Holmsby. " By the bye, what is she worth ? "

" A matter o' ten pun', seein' as she ain't no chicken," replied the man honestly.

" Well, I'll tell you what I'll do. Come with us to our diggings and I'll hand Mrs. Pedler a ten-pound note to give to you if the boat's lost—which I don't expect for a moment will be the case."

" Very good, sir," assented the man, with an air of relief. " I knew'd as you were a gentleman."

" We're making everyone in the place suspicious," remarked Dick, after the boatman had left the cottage. " There's old Haslar fairly up the pole : I wonder if he's been giving the show away ? "

" I don't mind particularly if the villagers are suspicious," asserted Reginald, " so long as we can achieve our aim ; and I mean to do it—outside influences won't affect the case. Now the best thing we can do is to have a nap after dinner till eight o'clock so that we can be fit for our night's work."

The evening was warm and balmy ; not a ripple disturbed the surface of the sea, even the usual ground-swell failing to assert itself. Quite three miles to seaward a Rochester barge, a Padstow brig, and a large barquentine were drifting idly with the flood-tide. Almost hull down, two tramps were ploughing Bristolwards, each sending up a thick column of smoke, while far away in the direction of Trevose Head the sea was dotted with the brown sails of the Padstow fishing-smacks.

" We shall only have ourselves for company," remarked Holmsby, as they surveyed the deserted sea in the vicinity of the rock-bound coast. " Even

the fishing-boats seem to give this part a wide
berth. You've your revolver handy, I hope ? "

" Trust me for that, after our meeting with
those rascals at St. Piran's Round," replied Dick.
" But here we are, and the boat's ready."

It was now barely quarter flood, and the truck
of the boat's mizzenmast projected only two feet
above the edge of the jetty. On the fore side of
her mizzen, as is usual with the fishing-craft of these
parts, a square iron frame with glass sides contained
an oil lamp. This the considerate boatman had
already lighted.

" Good-evenin', gentlemen. Everything's ready.
I'll bring her round to the steps."

" No, don't trouble," said Reginald. " We'll
slide down the shrouds. Now, Dick, inboard with
you."

This Tresillian accomplished, but to his surprise
Holmsby, in following him, awkwardly collided
with the lamp, his shoulder demolishing two panes
of the glass.

" Steady, cap'n," exclaimed the boatman re-
proachfully, as he witnessed the destruction of his
property.

" I'm sorry," said Reginald. " However, I'll
make good the damage."

" And you'll be wanting another lamp ? I'll
run and get one."

" No, we won't take another. Besides, the moon
will be up in a couple of hours."

" Not before eleven-thirty, sir."

" We'll do without a light," said Holmsby decisively.

Owing to the flat calm it was useless to hoist sail, so using their oars with a will the two comrades urged the boat through the entrance to the little harbour and gained the open sea. That they were the object of much local curiosity was evident from the fact that on a seat perched on the edge of the lofty cliff that bounded the landward side of the harbour half a dozen fishermen were watching them through telescopes and binoculars.

" Don't raise your voice above a whisper," continued Reginald. " On a fine night like this sound travels so clearly that these fellows could hear us talk when we are a quarter of a mile away. I managed that lamp very nicely, didn't I ? "

" I didn't think a sailor would be so confoundedly clumsy," was Dick's remark.

" Nor is he. I smashed it on purpose ; otherwise, we would have had to keep it burning."

" Why ? Surely we could have extinguished it if we wanted to ? "

" If we had there is a great possibility that the fishermen ashore seeing the light go out would think something was amiss and would put off to us. Now we can lie fairly safe from observation, for from a great height a small craft like this would be almost invisible even in the moonlight."

It was a weary vigil. Though both men kept their eyes glued to their night-glasses in turns and scanned the horizon and the rugged outlines of

Sampson's Down, their efforts seemed fated to be unrewarded.

Hour after hour went by. The moon rose and ascended high into the sky, throwing the bold headland into strong relief; but still no signs of the object of the night's watch.

Suddenly at about two in the morning the anchor-warp trembled violently. The boat's nose dipped to within a few inches of the water and gathering way the little craft began to shoot rapidly ahead.

"Stand by!" shouted Reginald warningly to his comrade, and grasping his knife he made his way for'ard, lying full length upon the diminutive half-deck.

Dick, hardly able to realise the situation, "stood by" very effectively by sitting on the bottom boards and gripped the thwart with both hands. He was aware that the little craft was being drawn towards the cliff at no mean speed, while a sullen agitation of the sea showed that there was some large moving body travelling beneath the surface.

Then, without warning the boat's bow dipped once more till the water swirled over the half-deck. Holmsby, his arms and shoulders immersed, slashed at the anchor-rope, and the next instant, the boat, released from the downward pressure, bolted up like a cork, well-nigh throwing the sub. from his precarious perch.

"I thought we should have to swim for it," he exclaimed. "And we've lost our anchor."

" What has happened ? " asked Dick, still remaining in his undignified position.

" Oh, nothing : only the submarine airship come home."

" What to be done now ? "

" Done ? Why wait. The fun is only just beginning. The tide's slack and with no wind the boat won't drift very far. Get the oars out, though ; we're a bit too close in."

" By Jove, we are ! " exclaimed Tresillian, as he noticed for the first time that they had been dragged or towed almost between the two horns of Sampson's Cove.

" There's one thing I've discovered. There's a submarine passage underneath the cove, and that's where the craft has gone. If I hadn't cut the rope we would have been carried down with her, and the suction would certainly have drawn us through the tunnel. Now, that's far enough : lay on your oars and watch."

For more than another hour they waited, giving an occasional stroke with the oars to counteract the tide.

Presently Reginald touched his companion lightly on the shoulder.

" Look ! " he whispered.

Standing on the summit of the cliff, his outline silhouetted against the pale dawn, was a man. For a few moments he looked in the direction of the boat, then, seemingly without the faintest hesitation, as the head and shoulders of another person appeared above a slight rise in the sloping ground of the down, the foremost man sprang into space.

Dick gave an involuntary gasp, that trailed off into an exclamation of astonishment, for the falling man's descent was gradually retarded, till it looked as if he were descending a flight of stairs. Once or twice he appeared to be drawn towards the face of the cliff, but by a movement of his arms he thrust himself clear, till he disappeared from view behind a mass of boulders fronting the base of the headland.

Then the second followed, descending in almost the same manner.

Holmsby glanced at his companion.

" What do you make of it ? " he asked. " They must have descended by a rope or steel wire, but I can't make one out : can you ? "

" I'm pretty certain there's no rope : but how did they manage it ? "

Dick was positively shivering, while in spite of his iron nerve Reginald felt a cold chill in his spine. There was something decidedly uncanny in the manner in which the two men literally threw themselves over the towering precipice and were prevented by some invisible agency from being dashed to pieces.

" They spotted us," continued Holmsby.

" Do you think so ? We're still in the gloom," said Tresillian. " But, honestly, old man, I feel creepy."

" So do I," admitted Holmsby frankly. " Still we're here, and I mean to remain till sunrise."

But though they resumed their vigil till the sun tinged the eastern sky no further developments were forthcoming.

" Let's get back," said Reginald. " I've seen as much or more than I expected, but still I'm not satisfied. To-night I mean to scale the fence and explore the top of the cliff. Are you game ?'

" Yes," replied Dick

CHAPTER VI

THE THIRD NIGHT

THE following afternoon Reginald and his
companion walked into St. Agnes, where a
telegram was awaiting them :

" F.O. 445 motor-cycle owned by Scatterthwaite,
Methodist preacher Presteign."

" That's a false scent laid bare," commented
Holmsby. " The number of the motor-car is
obviously a blind, so it would have been no use to
have attempted to track it by its identification
plate. I shouldn't wonder if the rogues kept a
stock of them. However, there is some consolation
that we need not worry about what is obviously
an attempt to lead us astray. Had we done so we
might have complications with an irreproachable
Radnor parson."

" By the bye, we may as well have a newspaper,"
remarked Tresillian ere they left the shop. " I
haven't seen one since we left town, and it's strange
how you miss being in touch with the rest of the
world."

" Here you are—read this," he continued, after
scanning the pages of a county paper.

Holmsby took the limp pages and read :

" Plymouth—Monday.—An airship passed over the town in the early hours of Sunday night. After hovering above the Citadel it headed towards Devonport Dockyard, where it descended to within two hundred feet of the ground. When last seen it was proceeding rapidly in the direction of Tavistock. Much uneasiness has been caused in official circles by its visit, since it is well known that none of the airships attached to the Port have left their sheds during the week, while the movements of Service Aircraft in other parts of the kingdom have been fully accounted for."

" That's let the cat out of the bag," growled Holmsby. " Once the papers get hold of the news our people will be spurred on to immediate action. We must look sharp or the chief will be sending a senior to investigate."

During the remainder of the walk back to Penkerris conversation was dropped. Both men were thinking deeply.

" Look here, Dick," said the sub-lieutenant at length. " I didn't want to report to headquarters until I had unravelled the mystery—since the chief treated the matter lightly. But now, for our own credit, I will draft out a full report of our investigations to date and give particulars of our impending expedition. This will satisfy the old man, and perhaps stop him from sending Boldrewood or any of the senior fellows down."

Holmsby acted accordingly, and having posted

the missive and partaken of supper, the two investigators prepared for their nocturnal expedition.

" I've commandeered one of Mrs. Pedler's footstools," remarked Reginald. " It will easily stow into this bag, and my electric lamp too. By the bye, you might run down to the harbour and get Trevaskis to lend you a coil of rope—twenty-five fathoms of inch-and-a-half stuff if he's got it."

In less than a quarter of an hour Dick returned with more than the required length slung in coils over his shoulder.

It was now dark. Dividing their burdens the two adventurers left the village and began the steep ascent that lay betwixt them and Sampson's Down. Here they rested ere descending the intervening valley.

" Stand by ; there's some one coming this way," whispered Holmsby.

For want of better shelter the twain flung themselves on the grass, while the short quick gasps of a person obviously out of breath came nearer and nearer.

Presently a short, thick-set figure passed within five yards of their place of concealment, and ignorant of the presence of Reginald and his companion, breasted the crest of the hill and descended towards the hamlet.

" It's old Haslar. I wonder what he's doing out here at this time of night ? " whispered Holmsby, as the lieutenant's outlines were lost to sight in the darkness.

" Doing ?   Why, trying to cut us out," replied
Dick, as they shouldered their loads.   " I hope he
hasn't raised the alarm."

Another quarter of an hour's brisk walk ending
with a stiff climb brought them to the fence.   It
was a formidable affair, being of the so-called
" unclimbable " variety, and consisted of double-
barbed rails seven feet in height with intervening
spikes of about two-thirds the length of the taller
ones.

Without a word Reginald wedged the footstool
upon two of the sharp prongs ; then bending down
he signed to Dick to jump on his shoulders.   The
next instant Tresillian was seated upon the precarious perch, whence he slid softly to the ground.

" Hand over the gear," he whispered.

Holmsby passed the sack containing the lamp,
but instead of throwing the coil of rope to his
companion he placed the bight of the coils between
two of the spikes.   Then gripping the upright and
inserting his foot into the lowermost portion of the
coil of rope, Reginald swung himself easily upon the
stool, thence rejoining his comrade.

They were safely within the fence, but how were
they going to get out again should they meet with
opposition ?

From this point the cliff path continued, though
grass-grown through disuse.   In places it passed
perilously close to the edge of the cliff which in
many places had recently crumbled away.

" Steady a moment while I hitch the end of the

rope round my waist," whispered Holmsby. "You hang on to the rest of the coil and walk a few yards behind me."

Presently they came to the spot immediately over the head of the cove and where the mysterious descent of the two men had occurred. As Reginald had expected, there was no sign of a windlass or any mechanical means by which a descent could be made, but instead they found a well-defined path leading up the gently-rising ground above the cliff.

"This way," said the sub. in a low voice. "We're on the track."

Before he had gone fifty yards Holmsby stopped short at the brink of a yawning shaft barely twenty feet in diameter. It had been at one time enclosed by a low stone wall, but nearly half of the stonework had been levelled.

"Stay where you are and keep the rope taut," he cautioned. "I'm going to lean well over this pit."

For nearly five minutes Holmsby listened. To his great satisfaction, he distinguished the rhythmical purr of machinery deep in the bowels of the earth, while at regular intervals came the dull swish of the ground-swell.

"This funnel communicates with the sea," he whispered, as he rejoined his comrade. "I fully expected it did. Now I'm going to attempt the descent. If this is the shaft of a disused mine there will be climbing-irons to get down by. This stump seems fairly secure. I want you to take a half-

hitch round it, and pay out the rope till I find a
foothold. When you feel the rope slacken keep on
paying out gently. If I jerk it twice in quick
succession haul up."

Dick knew that it was useless to expostulate.
He could only follow his friend's instructions, and,
as Reginald disappeared over the edge of the
chasm, he kept the rope well in check. But before
he had paid out twenty feet he felt the strain relax.

Slowly he continued to ease off the rope till
quite a hundred feet had been let go. Although the
exertion was slight the moisture stood in great
beads upon Dick's forehead.

Suddenly the rope was jerked out of Tresillian's
hands. He heard a stifled cry. Then as he strove
frantically to check the swiftly running coil he
felt that the strain had ceased. Then the dreadful
knowledge dawned upon him that the rope had
parted and Reginald had fallen to meet a terrible
fate on the floor of the stupendous abyss.

Scarce knowing what to do, Dick stood helpless.
His bewildered mind was trying to form some
plan whereby he could aid his comrade—if he were
still alive.

His agonised thoughts were rudely interrupted,
for a pair of strong hands grasped his ankles;
another gripped his throat, and a man's knee was
thrust violently into the small of his back.

Before he could utter a sound, Dick was lying
on his back with his limbs bound so tightly that he
could scarce writhe in his bonds.

In the starlight he could see that his captors were three stalwart men, but their features were concealed by thick beards and the turned-down brims of their hats. They were talking rapidly and in low tones in a language that was quite unintelligible to him, though it was evident that they were arguing as to what was to be done to their prisoner.

In a vain hope for the aid that was not to be forthcoming, Tresillian shouted as loudly as his parched throat allowed, but ere the echoes died away one of the men lifted him as easily as if he were a child and bore him towards the mouth of the shaft.

For a moment Dick felt himself being held over the brink of the horrible pit, then fear held him spellbound.

Slowly his captor leant over the abyss. Dick realised with a thrill of indescribable dread that 'twas impossible for the man to regain his balance. . . . Then, clasping his prisoner in his powerful embrace, the fellow dropped into space.

CHAPTER VII

DON MIGUEL O'ROURKE

"FOUR bells already, Stubbs ? " asked Holmsby, sitting up in what he imagined to be his bunk. Then he began to realise that he was not in his cabin on board the *Tremendous*, and that it was not his marine servant warning him for duty. Instead he found himself in a cot in a small cubicle, with Tresillian lying on a folding bed groaning most dismally ; while standing by the door was a short, swarthy-looking man of obviously foreign descent.

" Where am I ? " asked the young officer wearily ; then, his attention drawn to his comrade's moans, he demanded fiercely, " What have you done to my friend ? "

" There is no need to rise, Mr. Holmsby," exclaimed the stranger peremptorily. " Mr. Tresillian is in no danger. He is merely labouring under the effects of an anæsthetic—even as you were till within a few moments ago."

Obediently Reginald fell back upon his bunk. Somehow he had no inclination to do otherwise. So he lay and pondered, trying to recall the events of the night and endeavouring to find some reason for his presence in bed.   Then came the awful recollection of a struggle with an unseen antagonist in the depths of the vertical tunnel ; his vain efforts to prevent himself being torn from his precarious foothold ; the indescribable sensation of finding himself falling headlong . . . and then merciful insensibility.

Almost dreading to make the experiment, Holmsby drew up first one leg and then the other. Thank heavens, they appeared to be sound.   His arms, he knew, still possessed their muscular action. Perhaps, after all, in his fall he had not sustained any serious injury.

" I wonder who that little Johnny with the turned-up moustache is ? " he thought.   " Evidently he knows who I am, but how ? "

Raising himself on one elbow, Holmsby looked at the third occupant of the cubicle.   He was barely five feet four in height, yet properly proportioned. He had the olive features of a Spaniard, with dark brown eyes, straight nose, and rounded chin.   His hair was dark and crisp, growing low down on a lofty brow ; his mouth was of generous dimensions, his lips thin, while his carefully trained moustache failed to conceal a liberal expanse betwixt his upper lip and nose.

He was carefully groomed.   His clothes, well-cut and immaculately fitted, consisted of a dark blue yachting coat and trousers, a soft flannel shirt, and a crimson cummerbund ; while spotlessly clean white doeskin shoes encased a pair of violet-socked feet.

" Evidently fond of a bit of colour," commented Reginald. " Yet the fellow doesn't look like a fool. Well here goes ; I'll tackle him. Beastly awkward to find yourself in night-gear when you've to question an utter stranger, though."

" Excuse me, but where on earth am I ? "

The unknown regarded his interrogator calmly for a few seconds before replying.

" To the best of my belief, sir, you are not on the earth at all, but two hundred and fifty-nine feet beneath the surface."

The stranger spoke in sibilant tones, with the faintest trace of a foreign accent.

" Then how did we get here ? " asked Holmsby.

" Mainly through your overstrained inquisitiveness : also, I regret to say, through an equally unfortunate blunder on the part of some of my servants. But we will defer further explanations for the time being, Mr. Holmsby, for I see that your companion is about to recover his normal condition."

Holmsby turned to his friend. Dick Tresillian had rolled partly off his bunk and was moving his right hand over the floor as if in the act of writing.

" Ten thousand fiends take the Cash Account ! "

In spite of himself, Reginald smiled at his chum's antics and exclamation.

" Mr. Tresillian, like yourself, suffers from an excess of zeal at times," exclaimed the stranger languidly. " I have heard it said that your Government business methods are of the most antiquated description, and unnecessarily complicated into the bargain. Your friend evidently wished to corroborate my assertion. . . . Kindly shake him by the shoulders and he will be himself once more. We must excuse the deficiencies of your wardrobes."

Holmsby obeyed, and in a few moments Dick was awake and striving to collect his thoughts, even as Reginald had done.

" I will now leave you two gentlemen to the pleasure of your own company," remarked the unknown. " After your six hours' sleep perhaps a little refreshment will be acceptable. Meanwhile will you do me the honour ? " and producing a gold cigar-case from his pocket the speaker with a courtly bow offered it to Holmsby and his comrade.

As he opened the door the stillness of the room was broken by a loud roar—the united outburst of machinery working at high pressure and the surging of the waves in a confined space. But on closing the door after him the stranger completely shut out all noise once more. The walls of the building, though thin, were absolutely sound-proof.

" Well, we've certainly stumbled upon something remarkable," observed Dick, as he proceeded to light his cigar.

" Stumbled into it, you mean," corrected Holmsby, who could not help noticing that the desire to smoke—usually the last taste in a person recovering from the effects of an anæsthetic—was perfectly normal. " But what have they done with our clothes ? "

" Goodness only knows : and to think that we've been in a state of insensibility for six hours. But I say, Rex, old chap : what happened to you after you began to descend the shaft ? "

The two comrades exchanged the account of their experiences, without being able to satisfactorily explain how they escaped being dashed to pieces in the tremendous drop down the yawning pit.

" No, I can't understand it," concluded Holmsby. " But, by Jove, before I leave this place I'll know why. It also puzzles me to know how that polite little foreigner got hold of our names."

" From our clothing, perhaps."

" From yours, possibly ; but I make it a point never to have mine marked with my name. Perhaps we ' babbled o' green fields ' in our sleep, or, in other words, talked shop. I know for a fact that you did."

At that moment the door opened and a man entered bearing the two comrades' clothes. Without saying a word he placed them on separate chairs and withdrew.

" As silent as the tomb," commented Tresillian. " I wonder if that's one of the fellows who tackled us. However, let's dress and we'll feel more at home."

Their clothes had been carefully brushed and

pressed, but, in place of the stout boots in which they had set out, two pairs of doeskin shoes with rubber soles and heels had been brought in to them. Their revolvers had, however, been removed from the pockets of their clothes.

Hardly had they finished dressing than the same man who had brought their clothes reappeared with a tray on which were rolls, butter, eggs, Cornish cream, hot milk, and coffee.

" Gracious ! Do they run a model dairy in the bowels of the earth ! " ejaculated Tresillian. " Come, let's set-to, for I'm as hungry as a hunter."

After breakfast the comrades began a systematic examination of their room. It was about fifteen feet in length and twelve in breadth, the height being about nine feet. With the exception of the door there were no other openings, windows and ventilators being apparently unnecessary. The walls were of a hard resounding substance resembling porcelain, which Tresillian, from his professional knowledge, recognised as " Uralite "—a composition used largely in the construction of light, yet strong, fire-proof buildings. The floor consisted of solid rock covered with canvas. Tresillian tried the door. It was locked.

" Queer sort of lamps," remarked Dick. " Apparently electric, though I cannot see any wires."

" Be careful," cautioned Reginald, as his companion grasped one of the glass globes that were placed on brackets on the walls.

The warning came too late. Dick seized one of

the globes and lifted it from its shelf. There were no wires.

Even as he did so Tresillian clapped one hand to his eyes exclaiming, " I'm blinded ! "

Instantly Holmsby dashed across the room, took the glass from the hand of the unlucky investigator, and replaced it on the shelf.

" How goes it ? " he asked anxiously, for Tresillian still kept his eyes covered.

" I hardly know. I was trying to discover whether it was a carbon lamp and the beastly thing seemed to snap the optic nerve. . . . But it's getting better, I think."

' Still making unfortunate discoveries, Mr Tresillian ? " asked a suave voice, and, wheeling, Holmsby found that the mysterious master of the subterranean home of modern magic had noiselessly entered the room. " I ought to have warned you of the risk of tampering with the lighting arrangements of this apartment. Pray, allow me."

Taking a small instrument resembling an egg-cup from his pocket the unknown held Dick's head with one hand and vigorously massaged his forehead. Tresillian afterwards confessed that it was like the application of a freezing mixture ; but in a very short space of time his eyesight was restored to its normal state.

" Now, gentlemen, we will discuss the situation," remarked the stranger, motioning to Reginald and Dick to seat themselves. " I fear that I owe you an explanation."

" To come more to the point," said Holmsby, with more impatience than discretion, although his anxiety might be regarded as being sufficient to justify his unintentional rudeness. " Are we to be detained here against our will ? Why were we subjected to an unwarrantable attack by your men ? Were you justified in so doing ? "

The unknown raised his hand in a sort of dignified protest.

" Really, Mr. Holmsby, you overwhelm me with a torrent of questions," he remarked in even tones. " Please remember that *I* am master here, and need not reply to a single question unless I choose. You complain that you have been assaulted and forcibly detained here : is not that so ? Good : that is your view of the matter. Now listen to mine.

" I am not going to mince matters, for no useful purpose will be served thereby ; so I tell you that I mean to detain the pair of you until the preparations for the work I have in hand are complete."

" This is an outrage—an abominable outrage," exclaimed Holmsby.

" Undoubtedly, but you see the punishment fits the crime ; but to proceed with my explanation. First let me introduce myself as Don Miguel O'Rourke. Perchance the name is familiar to you ? "

" Oh yes," replied Reginald. " Then you are the ex-President of the Republic of Calderia ? "

" At present I am the ex-President," assented O'Rourke, with a courtly bow. " But what I hope to be in the future remains to be seen."

It was not so many years ago that the internal dissensions of the South American Republic of Calderia were the talk of the civilised world. President O'Rourke—a descendant of the famous Irishman who, with Cochrane, O'Higgins, and other British half-pay officers, had aided the South American colonies of Spain to throw off the tyrannical yoke—was no doubt a most capable ruler ; only, he lived before his time. Educated in London, Paris, and Seville, he showed promise at an early age of exceptional ability, and at twenty-five found himself installed in the Presidency of Nalcuanho, the capital of Calderia. His régime was strictly impartial, but his reforms were either regarded as too advanced by one section of the Calderians or else not sufficiently sweeping to meet with the approbation of the ultra-progressive party. Then, with the characteristic swiftness of the South American temperament, came a revolution. O'Rourke had to flee, taking refuge on board a Dutch man-of-war that happened to be lying off the coast on her voyage to Surinam. Ere long the want of the ex-President's acumen began to be felt by both parties, although a section of the Extremists retained its hostile policy. Calderia called for its former ruler—but called in vain. Don Miguel O'Rourke seemed to have vanished off the face of the earth—now he stood face to face with Sub-Lieutenant Reginald Holmsby in the depths of a Cornish mine.

"Now to resume my explanation," continued O'Rourke. "I came here and bought a piece of ground in this county, including any minerals that might be lying underneath the soil. It is well known that under Sampson's Down is a mine that years ago was flooded out by the sea. I found that my anticipations were realised ; the place was admirably situated for the purpose of conducting various experiments and scientific research. Naturally I wished to live in obscurity, but as far as I know, I broke no law of the country that had given me shelter. The place is even open to examination by your Board of Trade Officials and Inspectors of Mines, although, mind you, I did not go out of the way to show them the means whereby I could descend the shaft. Three or four times they troubled me with their attentions, till finding nothing but an apparently ladderless pit without machinery for ascending or 'descending, they regarded me as a kind of recluse or even a harmless madman—and left me severely alone.

"So far, so good. My work progressed, and I succeeded in perfecting machines capable of travelling either in air or under water—practical amphibians, in fact. But, concerning this portion of my narrative, I have said enough for the present. Then it came to my knowledge that two of my most implacable opponents had almost succeeded in tracing my hiding-place. Their avowed object was either to take my life or to destroy the work I had in hand, which they rightly guessed was to further my plans for recovering my position in Calderia.

" Naturally I took due precautions ; but, owing to a blunder on the part of my men, you were mistaken for the rascals——"

" I think we can enlighten you on the movements of your enemies," said Holmsby, and he proceeded to give a description of the encounter with the two foreigners at St. Piran's Round.

" You certainly did me a good turn, though perhaps unconsciously," remarked O'Rourke. " But, on the other hand, what do I find ? While you were lying unconscious, under the effect of a certain drug that by inoculation instantly produces utter insensibility, an agent of mine brought me word that an officer of the Naval Intelligence Department, accompanied by an assistant, had been sent down to report on my movements. Why ? I know not. In all my nocturnal excursions I have carefully avoided passing over military stations, in spite of reports to the contrary that from time to time have appeared in the papers. There is no law in England prohibiting a man from constructing an airship, aeroplane, or submarine, provided he conforms with the Foreign Enlistment Act and measures of similar import. At least, if there be, I've never heard of it. Now, suppose my secret reaches the ears of the British Admiralty :

my work would be totally undone ; unscrupulous so-called inventors would steal my plans, my inventions, my brains, and claim the credit.   Therefore, since you have fallen into my hands, I hope you will realise the importance of my resolve to keep you until I deem it safe to do otherwise."

"I quite see your point, señor," said Reginald calmly.   "But I trust you realise that by detaining us against our will you make yourself liable to severe penalties—illegal imprisonment is a serious offence, you know."

"I am perfectly prepared to accept that risk," replied O'Rourke, as he lit a cigarette.   "'Tis but a matter of a few days."

"In a day or so our disappearance will be noticed and a search party will be sent out."

"They may be fortunate : *quien sabe ?* " rejoined the ex-President with a deprecatory shrug.   "But now, gentlemen, pray be sensible.   Make yourselves at home, as it were.   If you like I can materially aid your mission by showing you the wonders of Sampson's Mine.   The knowledge will be invaluable to you, and you have my full permission to make whatever use of it that you may think fit—when the time comes.   Come now, your hand on it."

There was something about Don Miguel O'Rourke's magnetic personality that Reginald and his comrade found impossible to resist.   Both men rose and held out their hands.

"Capital!" exclaimed the Calderian approvingly, as he grasped their outstretched hands in turn. "Now, gentlemen, this way. The secret wonders of Sampson's Mine are at your service."

CHAPTER VIII

A MODERN MAGICIAN

"DO not hesitate to ask any questions, gentlemen," remarked Don Miguel. "But, on the other hand, do not take it in a wrong light should I be compelled, for my own sake, to withhold any information that I may deem prudent to do so. Here you see some strange - looking objects."

Their guide pointed to a small glass case on the wall of the room, in which were several indiarubber discs, each with a fine metal point projecting slightly from its centre.

"They look like vacuum arrow-heads—the kind of toy I used to play with as a small boy," said Dick.

"They are certainly meant to adhere to the palm of one's hand by suction—they are injectors. The fluid — composed of an extract from the deadly poisonous upas tree—passes through a minute tube in the needle. The operator merely makes one of the discs adhere to the palm of his hand and the faintest puncture in the skin of the person operated on is sufficient."

"Good heavens ! Do you mean to say you kill

people in that diabolical fashion ? " exclaimed Tresillian.

" If that were the effect of those implements, neither of you would be here now," replied O'Rourke. " The most deadly poison can, under the fostering influence of science, be made to act beneficially to mankind. Thus, one injection of that liquid produces total insensibility. Its application is not accompanied by that horrible strangling sensation produced by the use of chloroform, neither are the after-effects so distressing—in fact, there are no after-effects, as you must have realised when you smoked those strong Havana cigars."

Opening the door, Don Miguel motioned to his involuntary guests to precede. They found themselves in a large brilliantly-lighted cave, measuring nearly one hundred yards in length by about thirty in width, the roof arching irregularly to a height of nearly fifty feet. The floor for nearly half the length of the cave was smooth and gradually sloping, but a rough wall, six feet in height, hid the remaining portion from the sight of the two comrades. The nearest part of the floor was occupied by several machines all running at high speed and emitting a deep hum, but neither Tresillian nor Holmsby could discover their motive power. There was a remarkable absence of belts and shafting ; each machine seemed to be actuated independently of the others, while one man at each seemed sufficient to control the whirling complicated mass.

" What are those lamps ? " asked Tresillian, pointing to one of the globes that had previously been the means of nearly blinding him.

" My own invention," replied O'Rourke, raising his voice above the roar of the machinery. " That I will explain later. Now be careful where you tread."

Throwing open a thin sound-proof door in the wall of the cave the Calderian entered, waited till his guests had followed, and closed the door. The place was pitch dark and as silent as the tomb.

" Be careful," he cautioned. " There is a pool of water just beyond where you are standing. Now, look upwards."

The twain did so. Far above their heads they could discern a small circular disc of pale light, through which a star was faintly visible.

" The mouth of the shaft : two hundred and fifty odd feet deep. You certainly were not devoid of pluck to attempt its descent, Mr. Holmsby, but at the same time I cannot congratulate you upon your discretion. Had it not been for the action of my men you would assuredly have been dashed to pieces, for the shaft is only partially laddered, and the rungs are quite rotten in places. As it was, both of you finished your descent in this pool of water, and that was the reason why you found yourselves in bed."

" But how—— ? "

" Never mind that question at present. I know exactly what you were going to ask. The means of ascent and descent I will tell about in due course."

" It's perfectly quiet here," remarked Reginald.
" Yet I could hear the roar of the sea from above."

" Quite possible. At that moment the sound-
proof door must have been open for some purpose,
although we never prolong that operation. It is to
my advantage to stifle any sound that might
lead to the discovery of my subterranean workshop."

Re-entering the main cave Don Miguel led the
way towards the farthermost recesses. Beyond the
stone wall the floor was several feet lower, and here
were rows of retorts glowing in an electric furnace,
while on a long bench were hundreds of small
cylinders, apparently made of earthenware, surrounded by an aura of pale blue light.

" What do you imagine this to be ? " asked
O'Rourke, picking up a spherical piece of iron from
the floor and handing it to Holmsby.

" Looks like an obsolete twelve-pounder shell,"
replied the sub-lieutenant, handling the metal with
evident distrust.

" That is exactly what it is," agreed the ex-
President. " See, I remove this plug and you will
find water inside. Now, watch."

Drawing on a pair of insulated gloves, Don Miguel
took one of the small earthenware cylinders from the
bench, deftly inserted it in the iron sphere, and
replaced the plug. Then, even as the two Englishmen watched, the mass of iron began to rise, slowly
and surely. Up and up it went till it bumped
lightly against the crown of the arched cave.

Spellbound, the comrades gazed at this inexplicable phenomenon until Holmsby gasped, " You've discovered something wonderful, by Jove ! The force of gravity is absolutely overcome." The inventor beamed with self-complacent pride.

" 'Tis the most important discovery of the age," he replied. " Now what do you think is the force that enables a heavy body to be lifted by a self-contained agent ? Well, you will never guess : it's a secret compound which I have called ' Helia,' and to be brief it is an extract from the by-products of radium.

" Probably you are aware that immense quantities of pitch-blende—approximately eight tons—are required in order to produce one gramme of radium chloride. A decade ago the total quantity of radium known to be in existence was less than a quarter of an ounce. Now I have found that helia, which is compounded in fairly generous quantities from pitch-blende, when brought into contact with sea-water produces a gas that has approximately a thousand times as much lifting-power as an equal quantity of hydrogen. Unfortunately the constant waste of substance and energy in helia is quite noticeable—a contrast to the non-apparent diminution of radium—so constant charges have to be used in order to keep a heavy body afloat in the air. You will observe that the metal globe is already showing signs of returning to earth."

" Wonderful ! " was all that Reginald could exclaim, while Tresillian was quite beyond words.

" I also use helia in conjunction with other gases for the purpose of producing light. Each of those globes contains sufficient light for six weeks without recharging, the substance being contained in a vacuum in order to still further reduce the natural leakage. Now, here is another object to which I wish to call your attention."

Don Miguel held up for inspection a metal case about four inches in length, with one concave face. To it were attached four broad straps provided with buckles.

" Looks like a kind of military water-bottle," remarked Reginald. " But ten to one I'm wrong."

" You are," agreed O'Rourke. " This receptacle is a man-lifting apparatus, and contains sufficient helia to enable a person to leap fifty feet in the air. It is quite possible to increase the size of the charge, but then the danger arises that the lifting-power would be too great, the user might lose his head and, when at a great height, release too much helia with disastrous results. As a matter of fact just enough is used to counteract the force of gravity."

" Then that is how your men descended the cliff ? "

" You saw them ? " asked Don Miguel.

" Yes, the other day when we were lying off the cove in a fishing-boat."

" The incident was never reported to me," said the ex-President meditatively. " I must inquire further into this, for a public exhibition of the

important force at my command is the last thing I
wish for at present. Do you know, Mr. Holmsby,
that you owe your life to this invention ? One of
my men seized you just as you were about to
descend to a rotten step in the shaft ladder. Even
the rope would not have saved you, since your
strength would have been exhausted long before
you climbed to the surface. You were rendered
insensible by inoculation, and brought down—with
more force than desirable, I fear—while your
companion was, owing to the misunderstanding
which I have already explained, subjected to the
same treatment."

" That is what I wanted to know," said Holmsby.
" I was just conscious of being dragged from the
ladder and falling into space—then unconsciousness.
But, by Jove, of what incalculable service would
that invention prove to an aviator."

" Undoubtedly. As a matter of fact I cannot
claim to be the sole originator of the discovery.
Waechterlinck in 1910 and Hauptmann in the
following year nearly stumbled upon the use of
helia, but each in a desire to circumvent his rival,
issued a treatise on the subject ere their researches
were materialised. In the interests of humanity
I even went so far, at the great risk to the success
of my great mission in life, to hint of my discovery
to the principal Aero clubs of Great Britain, France,
and the United States—but in each case my offers
were curtly declined. No doubt I was thought to
be a madman—a common verdict on most of the

world's greatest inventors until time has vindicated the truth of their discoveries."

By this time O'Rourke and his two companions had reached the apparent end of the cave. Here a well of roughly-hewed granite stopped all further progress.

" Beyond this partition is the flooded portion of the mine," explained Don Miguel. " The water stored within is sufficient to run the electric dynamos for sixteen hours per day. For the remaining eight we have to make use of the rising tide, which here attains a height of seventeen feet. You see we are still obliged to press electricity into our service, although before long I hope to have stored sufficient energy in the form of helia to make us independent of dynamic power. Now, gentlemen, behold my masterpiece."

As he spoke O'Rourke thrust aside a sliding hatch on the floor, disclosing a deep vault that was one blaze of light. Kneeling down both Englishmen leant over the edge of the opening. Below them they saw the afterpart of a huge, grey-coloured object that might be either airship or submarine.

" The *Amphibian*," announced the inventor.

CHAPTER IX

THE *AMPHIBIAN*

WITH professional eagerness and curiosity Reginald Holmsby gazed at the monster with ill-disguised astonishment. Oblivious of the fact that he was in danger of losing his balance and falling a sheer distance of fifty feet, he remained in rapt admiration at the very brink of the yawning pit.

" Perhaps you would like to make the close acquaintance of my *chef d'œuvre* ? " asked Don Miguel.

" I should," replied Reginald eagerly.

" Then you must trust yourself to the merits of my gravity-neutraliser," continued the inventor, providing three of the small metal cases from a receptacle fixed to the wall.

In a few seconds the three men were equipped, the device being securely fastened to their backs by means of the straps.

" Be careful not to walk with a springing step— glide rather," continued Don Miguel, as he proceeded to charge the apparatus on Tresillian's back. Reginald watched him curiously.

Opening a small panel by means of a powerful cam-action slide, O'Rourke deftly thrust in a small cylinder of porous clay and instantly sealed it. This done he performed a similar operation with the case strapped to Holmsby's back, and instantly the sub-lieutenant became aware of the upward force of the imprisoned chemical.

" You saw what I did ? Good ! " exclaimed Don Miguel. " Now do you think you could do the same for me ? Otherwise I must send for one of my men."

" I'll try," replied Holmsby, and, following the examples that he had already seen performed, he succeeded in charging the Calderian's gravity-neutraliser.

" Let yourself drop," said O'Rourke, and, without hesitation, though he involuntarily closed his eyes, Reginald stepped over the edge of the pit.

Unfortunately in his grim determination the young officer stepped too eagerly, and instead of falling slowly he rose a good twenty feet in the air, descending some distance on the other side of the opening to the lower cave. Nor were his antics ended on his descent, for mechanically he bent his legs to break his supposed fall, with the result that he again performed a prodigious leap. Eager to aid his comrade, Tresillian made a rush forward, only to find himself soaring upwards. So vigorous had been his " kick-off " that he brushed the roof of the cavern.

" I think I gave you fair warning," remarked

Don Miguel without the suspicion of a smile, when the twain had somewhat gingerly gained the floor. " Now, watch me."

With a springless gliding motion the inventor slipped off the edge of the opening. Then, slowly, as if being lowered by an invisible wire, he descended to the lower level. Profiting by his example, the two Englishmen followed.

" There is no necessity to empty the charges," observed O'Rourke. " They are sufficient to last four hours at the least—but be careful to secure the belts round the iron bar. Otherwise we would have to recourse to the somewhat unpleasant operation of being hauled up by a rope."

Having taken off and secured the gravity-neutralisers, the two Englishmen walked up to the mysterious vessel, which they had beforetimes seen and heard about. Now it rested in front of them : its wondrous secret was to be theirs.

Its fabric consisted of a smooth, rigid metallic substance, lined with thin asbestos sheeting to withstand the effect of expansion by heat without the necessity of having to provide safety valves for the compressed gas. The bows were somewhat snub, the afterbody thinning off gracefully to a sharp point. Right through the centre of the bow projected a shaft, on the end of which was a two-bladed metal air-propeller.

Aft were the horizontal and vertical rudders and a four-bladed propeller for use when submerged. There was no " nacelle " or car, but in the place of a conning-tower on the highest part of the convex surface a long narrow metal hatch, projecting barely three feet beyond the outer skin, extended fully ten feet in a fore and aft direction. This raised part was provided with glass inspection-holes or scuttles.

The craft lay on a cradle that had been hauled up an inclined plane, the slipway disappearing beneath the surface of the water that covered the farthermost recesses of the lower cave, but a constant agitation of the water showed that there was direct communication between it and the open sea.

This much Holmsby took in with the eye of an expert, but there were several points on which he could not find a satisfactory solution.

" How can that huge envelope—for such I must term it, successfully withstand the pressure of the water when submerged, and also possess sufficient lightness—even taking into consideration the lifting-power of your helia—to rise in the air ? " he asked.

" The outer skin is not intended to be subjected to any great strain under water," replied the inventor. " It merely contains the helia, being divided into ten gas-tight compartments, six of which, when charged, being sufficient to raise the ship. The others are to be used in case of emergency should a leakage occur. Inside the outer fabric is the submarine proper—built of enormously strong plates of duralium. Supposing the *Amphibian* is in the air and wishes to dive beneath the sea. The helia is allowed to escape and the airship sinks till it rests on the surface of the water. Unfortunately it is not yet possible for a vessel to make a direct dive from the air into the sea or *vice versa*—unless, of course, she is an utter wreck : but that is outside my subject. So the *Amphibian* has to rest on the surface for a few minutes while water is rushing into the compartments of the outer envelope to take the place of the expelled helia. The pressure of the water is resisted by the walls of the submarine, while at the same time the presence of a homogeneous fluid inside and outside the outer skin of the airship preserves it from injury. Diving is performed by the action of the horizontal rudders, the submerged craft having a slight reserve of buoyancy."

" But when the vessel has to ascend from beneath the surface ? "

" The process is practically reversed. The introduction of a cylinder of helia into each of the six compartments causes the gas to expand in contact with the salt water, and the tremendous lifting force is brought into action. Simultaneously the water is expelled through the automatic valves, and the vessel immediately soars skywards."

" I notice that you have two propellers : the one for submarine work is not, of course, used in air, but how about the aerial propeller when the vessel is submerged ? A twin-blade of comparatively large area would be a hopeless drag in the water, besides being easily damaged should it come into contact with any substance that would not otherwise cause harm in the ordinary course of events."

" I agree with you. But I have already made due provision for this contingency. Before the *Amphibian* dives the aero-propeller folds back upon the shafting, and the whole is withdrawn into the outer envelope."

" If it is not troubling you too much," said Tresillian, who hitherto had been listening and observing in silence, " I should like to ask you one or two questions."

" As many as you like : your interest is a source of satisfaction to me and a testimony to my work," replied Don Miguel grandiloquently.

" But are you not afraid to explain all this, knowing the nature of my visit ? " asked Holmsby.

" Afraid ? No ! " exclaimed the inventor, with the utmost conviction. " You have yet a lot to learn ere you master the supreme secret of the *Amphibian*. But, to speak bluntly, I should not be at all surprised if your Admiralty did not make a hard shot at it. You English were ever good at copying. History proves it. You ' adapted ' your vaunted British bayonet from the French ; from the same nation you copied the lines of their fastest frigates in the days of Wooden Walls ; in the submarine you improved upon an American invention ; you waited till the first aeroplanes came to something like perfection ere you picked the brains of the American Wright Brothers. It's a nice policy

to wait and see, but hardly honest.   However, that's
neither here nor there at present—what did you
wish to ask me, Mr. Tresillian ? "

" If the outer skin completely encloses the submarine, how do you manage to steer the *Amphibian*
under water ; and how do you contrive to navigate
her in the air ?   Surely it is essential to be able to
observe what is taking place beneath the craft ? "

" You will be better able to understand my reply
if we board the *Amphibian*, Mr. Tresillian ; so we
may as well do so at once."

CHAPTER X

THE WONDERFUL NUTSHELL

"WE'LL find a ladder on the starboard side," continued O'Rourke. "My men are still at work with the finishing touches, besides repairing some slight damage sustained during our last experimental trip."

As the three men made their way under the tapering stern Holmsby caught sight of a familiar object lying on the slipway. It was the anchor and cable of the fishing-boat they had hired.

"That is the cause of our last mishap," remarked the inventor, pointing to the anchor. "Our stern propeller bracket fouled this kedge as we were returning to the cave."

"So I believe," replied Reginald. "It is the anchor of the boat we were in. You nearly towed us beneath the surface."

"Oh! Might I ask what you were doing in Sampson's Cove?"

"Keeping a look out for your return," replied Holmsby frankly. "You see we were not disappointed."

"Your curiosity cost us several hours of labour,"

said Don Miguel. " However that is now a thing
of the past. By the bye here is the tunnel communicating with the open sea. When I bought the
place there was only a small opening, but with the
aid of dynamite and four skilled Italian divers—who
were brought here without knowing where they
were—we soon contrived to enlarge the tunnel to
suit my purpose. The materials for building the
Amphibian, together with the necessary plant,
were conveyed to the cave in a submarine of an
antiquated pattern that I bought at a sale at
Richmond Navy Yard, U.S.A. We still use the
submarine for similar purposes. At present she is
lying in a cave to the left of this tunnel."

Ascending a ladder that had been temporarily
placed against the bulging sides of the *Amphibian*,
the three men gained the long, narrow raised platform. Here Holmsby noticed that there were
sockets fitted to receive rails and stanchions,
although the latter had been unshipped in order to
facilitate the vessel's passage through the submarine tunnel.

" You are now standing upon part of the
Amphibian that cannot be described as belonging
to either the aerial or the submarine portion. It is,
in fact, a sort of combined conning-tower, mechanical
appliance chamber, aerial observation station, and
emergency compartment. It extends right through
the central portion of both airship and submarine,
and, in case of stern necessity, when the vessel is
submerged, the whole can be released and brought

to the surface. When in the air this deck forms a promenade, and, as you can see by the mountings, we are able to fit a light pair of quick-firing guns fore and aft."

Throwing back a metal hatch, lined with india-rubber, Don Miguel motioned to his guests to descend.

" You are now in the uppermost storey or the conning-tower," he continued. " There are observation scuttles on all sides, each commanding a clear view above the turtle-deck. This lever controls the elevating planes ; this the vertical rudders. Here is the switch that actuates the submarine propelling machinery, while close to it are the appliances for feathering the aerial propeller or starting its shafting as the case may be."

" What is the motive power ? " asked Holmsby.

" Radio-electricity : we carry a supply sufficient to take the *Amphibian* for a distance of 12,000 miles, or, roughly, half the circumference of the globe. Under water the radius of action would be about one-fifth, or enough to take the vessel across the Atlantic."

" These discs," he continued, pointing to ten red-capped pushes of about half an inch in diameter that were ranged in two rows on a switch-board, " are the termination of the tubes through which the helia charges are sent to the respective ballonettes of the airship. Until ready for use the charges are stored in an air-tight magazine underneath the floor you are now standing on. To keep them perfectly dry is absolutely essential : indeed, I shudder to think what the effect would be if water came in contact with that vast store of potential energy."

The second storey was, in the absence of scuppers, lighted artificially. Here were the water-tight doors communicating with the fore and aft parts of the submarine, and also the officers' quarters.

Opening one of the slides Don Miguel showed the two Englishmen the cavern-like interior of the fore-part of the metal-sheathed vessel.

" Here the crew, nine in number, have their quarters. When submerged the air is purified by oxygen ; when the *Amphibian* is above the surface fresh air is supplied by means of automatic ventilating pipes leading through the gas chambers of the airship," observed the inventor. " Here, too, are the torpedoes for submarine attack, eight of them, charged with a high explosive and having an effective range of 8000 yards, being stored under that raised bench. You can now see the shafting of the aerial propeller. On either side of it are the two torpedo tubes."

" Have you no means of using aerial torpedoes ? " asked Reginald.

" Yes, those will be shown you shortly ; meanwhile you might as well have a look at the afterpart of the submarine, for there the propelling machinery is placed."

Retracing his way to the central section, O'Rourke carefully secured the water-tight panel.

Then, crossing to the opposite side of the compartment, he opened a similar door.

" Is that all the propelling machinery ? " asked
Holmsby in surprise, as a small six-cylindered
motor met his eye.

" More than sufficient to drive the *Amphibian*,"
replied the ex-President, with a smile.   " If you could
but see those running at 2000 revolutions per minute."

" But surely that is impossible as regards the
aero-propeller.   And, besides, the shaft ends here,
whereas the aero-propeller is for'ard."

" Quite so," assented Don Miguel.   " Part of the
aero-shaft passes outside the central compartment
and is geared up to the main shafting for the submarine propeller, thus giving the former a speed of
not more than 250 revolutions.   Also, had the shafting of both propellers been direct it would have to
pass through the central compartments, and in that
case it would be impossible to use that portion of
the vessel as an emergency compartment.   Now we
will make an inspection of the lowermost storey,
and then I think you will have had a very general
idea of my masterpiece."

Descending the third ladder the two Englishmen
found themselves standing upon a slightly concave
floor, this compartment also being artificially
lighted.

" These are four thick plate-glass observation
holes at your feet," explained O'Rourke, "only as
the *Amphibian* is on the slip we have to keep them
covered by metal plating.   Through them we can,

when in the air, command a distinct view of all that is going on beneath us. Here is the bomb-dropping gear. Observe these indicators. This one gives you the speed of the ship through the air, to which must be added or subtracted, as the case may be, the velocity of the wind. Thus, suppose we are travelling at 30 miles per hour in a northerly direction against a northerly wind of 15 miles per hour. That means that we are actually moving over the ground at a rate of 15 miles per hour. That is simple enough. Now, in addition, when dropping a bomb, we have to take into consideration the motion imparted to the projectile by the speed of the airship. Thus, suppose we were to drop a bomb when travelling at 60 miles an hour. The instant the missile left the mouth of the dropping apparatus it would have a tendency to travel in a horizontal direction at the same speed, as well as being taken earthwards by gravity. In a few seconds the latter force completely overcomes the former, but in its flight the missile's course is that of a parabola. This indicator, therefore, enables us to automatically make due allowance for the horizontal motion of the airship and ensures the bomb hitting the mark. Now I think I have shown you all that I can possibly do within the bounds of discretion, so we will now return to the quarters temporarily assigned to you."

Without another word Don Miguel led the way to the place where they had left the gravity-neutralisers. Donning these, the Englishmen succeeded in following their guide to the upper cave.

Here a man approached the ex-President and, with a salute, handed him a sealed envelope.

Don Miguel tore it open and read the contents. As he did so a deep flush overspread his olive features.

"Gentlemen, your term of detention will be shorter than I anticipated," he exclaimed. "I have just received information that Calderia is threatened by its powerful neighbour the Republic of Talpico. Now is my chance : to-night the *Amphibian* leaves for the seat of hostilities. Ere she leaves you will be escorted to the summit of the cliffs and allowed to return to Penkerris. Meanwhile, as I have urgent work on hand, I must ask you to return to your quarters until I am at liberty to entertain you."

"Look here, Dick," exclaimed Holmsby, when they found themselves alone, "I'm going to see this thing through."

"What do you mean ? "

"Why, haven't I a sort of roaming commission ? We'll have a cruise in the *Amphibian*. You can square the matter all right with your chief, and we'll have an exciting voyage, I can assure you."

"I'm game," replied Tresillian resolutely. "But will Don Miguel O'Rourke consent ? "

"Where there's a will there's a way," said Reginald, his eyes fixed upon the glass case that hung upon the wall. "I'll ask him. If he consents, so well and so good—if he does not, I'll compel him by fair means or foul to have two Englishmen aboard the *Amphibian* on her voyage to Calderia."

CHAPTER XI

HOLMSBY GAINS HIS POINT

"FAIR means or foul," repeated Dick slowly. "What do you mean ? "

" What I said. Is there anything to prevent us threatening him ? If needs be we can use one of these injectors, make him insensible, barricade the door, and hold him prisoner till he submits to our terms."

" Won't do, Rex, my boy," replied Tresillian. "Think it over. It savours of treachery, flinging yourself upon an unsuspecting man and rendering him insensible——"

" But he did not hesitate to serve us the same," expostulated Holmsby.

" Acting under a misapprehension. Remember he freely admitted his error."

" Well, go on."

" Besides, Rex, you've forgotten one incident that makes this intended *coup de main* impossible."

" What was that ? "

" We shook hands with him."

" Oh ! " There was a sincere tone of contrition in Holmsby's exclamation. He now realised, through his companion's arguments, that any course that necessitated force or coercion would be unworthy of the conduct of an English gentleman. Hitherto in his impulsiveness he had overlooked this fact.

" Hang it all, man," he continued. " You're right. But we must manage it somehow. Think, man, think as you never did before and find a feasible plan for getting on the right side of Don Miguel O'Rourke."

Thus abjured Dick Tresillian tried to form some idea of the best means of diplomatically tackling the ex-President. But though he was on his mettle the young Civil servant was bound to confess that his train of thoughts led to no satisfactory solution of the problem.

" Come on, come on ! " exclaimed Holmsby impatiently, after he had sat in a chair for a full half-hour. " Something must be done. Let's review the situation : violence barred ; strategy doubtful. Here ! Can't we manage to stow ourselves on board ? "

" We might, but to what purpose. O'Rourke would then be perfectly justified in setting us ashore on the first convenient land : convenient no doubt to him, but mighty awkward for us. We might be hopelessly stranded, thousands of miles from home, with scarce ten pounds between us, and nothing gained as far as knowledge of the *Amphibian's* capabilities as a fighting machine are concerned. My own opinion is that O'Rourke is a perfect gentleman, but if angered he would prove a nasty customer to tackle."

"Well, we must see what we can do by asking him point-blank. That's the only way I'm——"

Holmsby's words were left unfinished, for at that moment the door was thrown violently open and O'Rourke rushed in, thrust the door to, and attempted to wedge it with his foot. But all to no purpose—with an irresistible heave the door was wrenched from its hinges, and a great hulking man, his face inflamed with passion, burst into the room, brandishing a heavy, keen-edged machete in his hand.

Without taking the slightest notice of the two Englishmen the would-be murderer bounded upon the ex-President, snarling the while like a beast of prey.

Raising a chair with both hands the agile Calderian attempted to parry the savage thrusts of his opponent. It was touch and go, for in his fanatical rush the hulking body of the attacker well-nigh swept the lightly-built form of the ex-President from off his feet.

Up went the blade once more. In another instant . . .

But by this time the two Englishmen had regained their scattered wits, for the sudden and unexpected entry of Don Miguel and his assailant had taken them totally aback. Flinging himself upon the giant, Holmsby grasped the man round the neck and pinioned his right arm to his side, while Tresillian seized the man's wrist in his iron grip, receiving a clean cut in his own arm as he did so.

" Hold him tight ! " exclaimed O'Rourke breathlessly, as he slipped from the front to the rear of his assailant.

It was a difficult business, for the man was as powerful as a gorilla, his rage adding to his strength.

Holmsby was on the point of shouting to O'Rourke to help secure the struggling maniac —for that he practically was—when out of the corner of his eye he saw the ex-President dart to the wall-case and extract one of the injecting needles.

Awaiting his opportunity O'Rourke buried the point into the heaving neck of his assailant, and the two Englishmen felt the ponderous carcase, a brief instant before full of strength and uncontrollable energy, grow limp and helpless in their grasp.

" Place him on the floor," exclaimed Don Miguel as calmly as the exhausted state of his frame permitted. Then, " Thank you, gentlemen," said he.

" Good heavens, you've killed the man," exclaimed Tresillian.

" He would certainly have knifed me but for your assistance," replied Don Miguel. " No, he is not dead, though he richly deserves to pay the death penalty. In another hour he will recover his senses.

" Remove him," he added in Spanish, addressing five or six men, who, with their olive features grey with apprehension, had rushed to their master's aid. " When he comes to, place him in irons."

" You're not hurt, sir ? " asked Holmsby.

" Hurt ? No : but your friend has made the acquaintance of that rogue's machete."

" So I have," exclaimed Dick, for the first time aware that his arm was bleeding freely. " But it isn't much—merely a scratch."

" Let me attend to it," said O'Rourke. " Yes, a clean cut and nothing serious. In a day or so it will heal."

" What, might I ask, caused that man to make such a ferocious attack upon you ? " asked Reginald, as the ex-President began to wash and dress Tresillian's wound.

" *Caramba*, I cannot tell," was the reply. " I had occasion to speak to the man—his name is José Alini, and hitherto he has been perfectly satisfactory —concerning the stowage of certain gear : not at all complainingly, be it understood. Without warning he whipped out his machete and rushed at me, and this cabin being the nearest place where I could hope to check his pursuit, I ran for it. Undoubtedly you saved my life, gentlemen, and you will not find Don Miguel O'Rourke ungrateful. Anything in my power that I can do for you I will right willingly."

" Thank you ! " exclaimed Holmsby, so emphatically that the inventor started in surprise. " Thank you, Don Miguel. We'll hold you to your word. We have a request to make."

" And that is——— ? "

" That we may accompany you to Calderia on board the *Amphibian*, señor."

" *Caspita!* This is the last thing I expected," exclaimed the South American with undisguised surprise. "Have you weighed the question thoroughly ? *Bueno!* My word is my bond."

" A thousand thanks, señor. We shall be ready to start as soon as you think fit. Meanwhile is it possible to communicate with our friends and our respective Heads of Department ? "

" Our wireless telephone will be placed at your service. With it you can speak to my agent in London and he will forward any messages to their proper destination. Or, if you wish, you can write, and I will see to it that the letters are safely posted."

" The first course will be preferable, I think," replied Reginald. " We might get a reply through before we start."

" Then there is no time to be lost, Mr. Holmsby, for we start in less than five hours. It is now four o'clock."

" And the Department closes at five," exclaimed Tresillian. " There is no time to be lost."

" There never is," replied O'Rourke oracularly. " So if you will kindly write out your messages I will be responsible that they are forwarded without delay. Now, gentlemen, I must be off once more, for there still remains much to be done. Meanwhile, remember that once you have put your hands to the plough——"

At half-past eight the two Englishmen were informed by the inventor that all preparations for the voyage were complete and that they could now board the *Amphibian*.

" There has been no reply to any of your messages," he continued. " I can vouch for it that every one was sent off within twenty minutes."

" In that case we must take French leave," replied Holmsby resolutely. " For my part I can claim that I am acting within my instructions. You, Dick, being here unofficially, must make the best of things."

" I suppose I must. But, candidly, I wouldn't very much mind if I never set eyes on that rotten old office again. Now, I'm ready."

" Here are your revolvers and ammunition, gentlemen," said Don Miguel. " You will pardon my action in temporarily depriving you of these, but taking into consideration the fact that I did not know you as intimately as I do now, the precaution must be regarded accordingly."

In the outer cave the contrast was most marked. The machines had ceased their shrill whirr ; most of the lamps had been removed. In the semi-gloom the place looked ghostly.

" We're shutting down the house, you see," explained Don Miguel, with a smile. " Perhaps we may never require to use Sampson's Cave again, *quien sabe* ? "

Descending to the lower cave the two Englishmen found the *Amphibian* all a-shiver under the action of her propellers, which, at a comparatively slow speed, were being revolved to satisfy the engineers that all was in order. From a scuttle looking for'ard a powerful search-light threw its brilliant white beam upon the surface of the still agitated water. Men were running hither and thither, on deck and ashore, all intent upon the work of clearing away the dog-shores that held the cradle.

" I thought you had nine men for the crew," remarked Holmsby. " There are at least thirty here."

" Three officers—the lieutenant, engineer, and myself—and nine men," replied O'Rourke. " Including yourselves there will be fourteen persons on board. The others remain until the *Amphibian* is clear of the cave. They will then complete the dismantling of the workshop, seal up the stores, and take their departure in the submarine of which I have already told you about."

" Good heavens, what are you going to do with that ? " asked Tresillian, as the heavily-manacled form of the ex-President's assailant was led across the cave.

" I have dealt with him already," replied Don Miguel. " He will be taken on board the submarine and placed ashore at a port where he will find it difficult to return to Calderia in a hurry. He will be subjected to no further punishment, I assure you. As a matter of fact, I ascertained the cause of his act of violence: it was mental aberration, due to prolonged work at too close a distance from a powerful helia lamp. The man neglected to wear his rubber head-gear, and this was the result."

" Poor brute ! " exclaimed Holmsby, then, under his breath, he muttered, " A jolly good job for us anyhow."

" Up with you," said O'Rourke, pointing to the ladder, and in a very short space of time the two Englishmen were standing upon the narrow promenade-deck of the *Amphibian*. The inventor rejoined them, the ladder was removed, and the vessel was ready for her long voyage.

" All clear ? " shouted O'Rourke in Spanish to the men who remained. Receiving an affirmative reply he motioned to his companions to go below.

Here the brilliantly-illuminated conning-tower presented a somewhat different appearance to what it had done a few hours ago. The engineer was at his post, testing the various switches and levers, while his eyes frequently sought the array of indicators above the switch-board ; a subdued hum accompanied the slowly-running motors ; the oscillation of the whole vessel added to the general aspect of novelty.

" Now we are ready ! " shouted the inventor, as he gained the conning-tower and secured the massive, rubber-lined hatch-cover. He had to raise his voice to make himself audible above the din. " Take up your position at those scuttles and you will see the walls of the tunnel quite distinctly. . . . Now, we're off."

CHAPTER XII

THE *AMPHIBIAN* TO THE RESCUE

A SLIGHT jerk, a barely perceptible jar as the
cradle slipped down the ways, announced
to the interested Englishmen the fact that the
Amphibian's voyage had commenced.

Then, as the huge bulk slid slowly into the water,
came the sharp hiss of the air that was being
expelled from the outer envelope.

The engineer, with his right hand upon the start-
ing-lever, was watching the mercury rise in the
submersion-indicator. Slowly, yet surely, rose the
silvery column till it stood at 14 metres—at which
depth the *Amphibian* was awash. The engineer
thrust down the lever till the needle in the dial
that recorded the number of revolutions per minute
oscillated between 200 and 210, and the craft
quivered under the vibration of the powerful
propeller.

Yet the *Amphibian* forged ahead but slowly,
guided by the impassive O'Rourke, as he grasped
the spokes of the wheel and kept the craft fairly in
the centre of the vast tunnel.

From where he stood at one of the scuttles on

the starboard side, Holmsby could see the weed-covered wall of the tunnel glide past under the reflection of the powerful for'ard search-light, the displacement of the water causing the long, dark-brown tendrils to agitate like a nest of young serpents.

Suddenly a beam of subdued light flashed athwart the path of the *Amphibian*. Reginald saw that it came from the conning-tower of the submarine which was lying in the side-cave, waiting to take off the remainder of O'Rourke's men after the *Amphibian* had left. Then, an instant later, the wall of the tunnel resumed its unbroken aspect.

Holmsby glanced at the ex-President. Don Miguel seemed unconscious of his surroundings, his whole attention was directed upon the gleaming white disc ahead where the searchlight's rays impinged upon the top and sides of the cavern. Standing slightly below and in front of his chief was the lieutenant, his long, thin hands grasping the lever actuating the elevating planes and rudders. As for Dick he seemed glued to his scuttle, for, in the mirror-like reflection of the glass, Holmsby could see his chum staring at the waving masses of seaweed as if completely fascinated by his unwonted surroundings.

Ere the *Amphibian* had started on her voyage, Holmsby had, with professional force of habit, looked at the compass. The needle then pointed to " norte cuarto norte-este " (N. by E.); it now showed nearly " Norte-oeste cuarto norte " (N.W.

by N.), showing that the tunnel had made a fairly sharp curve of nearly 45 degrees in less than two hundred yards.

Looking aft, Holmsby could see nothing but an opaque body of water; even the churning of the propeller failed to produce any phosphorescent swirl on the agitated water; so, having investigated on all sides, he again directed his attention ahead.

Now, even though it was night, came a faint luminosity, showing that the open sea was not far off, and at the same time the *Amphibian* began to develop a motion hitherto unnoticed—a kind of combined pitch and roll, though not sufficient to cause the heeling-indicator to register more than 1 degree.

" We are now clear of the tunnel," said Don Miguel, speaking for the first time since the *Amphibian* had started on her voyage. " This motion is due to the undertow; when we descend deeper we will be beyond its influence."

" It must be fairly rough outside," replied Holmsby, glancing at the submersion-gauge that stood at 19 metres. " We are in fairly deep water. I didn't know such a depth existed so close inshore."

" It's merely a narrow, natural gulley not marked on the charts," replied O'Rourke. " And, as you say, it is blowing not half a gale but a whole gale from the north-east. I was going to ascend, but under the present circumstances I don't think it is advisable — at least till we get a good offing."

Then, bending towards the engineer, he motioned to him to let the motors run at full speed.

Instantly the craft, quivering like a leaf, shot forward ; but as soon as she " got into her stride," as Tresillian expressed it, the vibration practically ceased, while the motors purred so easily that conversation could now be carried on with comparative facility.

" I should like to let her rise," continued Don Miguel. " You see we are still in 13 fathoms— hardly sufficient to escape running the risk of being smashed up by a deep-drafted steamer, though I admit the probability is somewhat remote. As it is, we have only 2 metres of water under us."

" The envelope is certainly a disadvantage in that respect," replied Reginald.

" Yes, I quite admit I ought to have reduced the height and given a corresponding increase in length and beam. However, when we are in deeper water, it will not signify. But see, there is a vessel passing over us."

Giving the search-light a slight upward inclination, Don Miguel pointed through the for'ard scuttle. In the powerful beam the two Englishmen could see the wildly-pitching heel of a tramp-steamer as her single screw alternately raced and gripped in the heavy sea.

" No doubt her officers will enter a note in the·

log to the effect that they passed through a luminous patch in Lat. 50° 15′ N.; Long. 5° 25′ something W.," said the inventor. "But I wonder if they have any idea of what was but a few feet beneath their keel ? "

"She was throwing herself about," remarked Reginald. "But here down below there is no indication of the weather."

"We'll soon have a sample of it, Mr. Holmsby," rejoined O'Rourke. "We have placed a fair space between the *Amphibian* and the shore, so we'll let her ascend. But be prepared for a bit of a rough tumble : we are bound to have it fairly thick while we are resting on the surface."

For the next few minutes all was in a state of apparent confusion—the officers shouting. men running hither and thither as far as the limited space permitted. The submarine propeller ceased its rapid revolutions ; the six helia cylinders were thrust into their respective ballonettes, while under the action of the powerful pumps the surplus water was ejected from the outer envelope.

Like a huge bladder the *Amphibian* was tossed upon the crests of the mountainous waves, drifting rapidly to lee'ard the while as her crew hastened to manipulate the air-propeller gear. Rolling well-nigh on her beam ends, the giant craft was almost at the mercy of the elements. It was a risky course, for had there been a craft in her path it would have been certain destruction.

"It is thick, by Jove ! " exclaimed Reginald,

bawling into his friend's ear. " If the aerial part of the programme is not better than the transitory stage I would rather that the *Amphibian* remained beneath the surface."

" I'll be hanged if I care for it at all," admitted Dick. " This is more than I bargained for. Oh! That was a brute!" he added, as the crest of a vicious wave caught the cork-like *Amphibian* on her quarter and threw her quite ten feet clear of the water.

" She's rising," replied Reginald cheerfully. " Hold on tight."

" That's what I've been doing for the last ten minutes," gasped Tresillian, as his legs shot from under him for the tenth consecutive time.

Again a wave dashed against the huge bulk, only to flick harmlessly under her. The *Amphibian* had begun to feel the upward force of the helia, and was now well clear of the surface of the cauldron of seething water.

Still she rocked as the eddying currents of air seemed to smite her on all sides. Then came a sharp detonation as the first cylinder fired, a whirr, and the air-propeller shafting began to revolve.

Bringing the now tractable airship head to wind, Don Miguel allowed his crew to take a well-earned spell ere the south-westerly course was resumed.

" It's the first time we have attempted to rise in a gale," he explained, turning to the two Englishmen. " I don't think I'll try it again, unless under stern necessity. What it must be like ashore, goodness only knows. I pity any aviator or aeronaut who attempts to try conclusions with a sixty miles an hour gale ashore."

With that Don Miguel left them to make a tour of inspection, but having satisfied himself that all was in order he returned.

" Perhaps, gentlemen, you would like a turn on the promenade deck ? " he inquired.

Holmsby and Tresillian looked at him in amazement : surely the Calderian was joking.

" There is no danger," continued the ex-President.

" Danger ! " exclaimed Holmsby, bridling at the suggestion. " We are ready, sir, to brave the elements."

" Shall we require oilskins ? " asked Dick. " You see we brought none with us."

" I think not," replied O'Rourke. " There are thick coats at your disposal. The night air at this altitude may be somewhat raw. For myself I will go as I am."

So saying the inventor unbolted and threw back the hinged hatch and gained the deck. Unwilling to seek additional protection from the raging elements when their host had scorned to do so, the Englishmen followed holding their caps tightly to their heads in anticipation of a hurricane.

But to their surprise, instead of having to hold on like grim death against a howling gale, they found themselves standing in an almost perfectly calm atmosphere. The stars were shining brightly, and a barely perceptible breeze, warm in spite of the altitude, fanned their faces. Instinctively Holmsby looked for the Ursa Major making the astounding discovery that the *Amphibian* was heading dead in the eye of the supposed north-easterly gale.

Except for the starlight and the light filtering through the scuttles, the deck of the *Amphibian* was in darkness.

Holmsby walked to the rail and leant over. Far beneath him, as far as the eye could reach, was a vast bank of rugged clouds, torn here and there with wide ever-changing rifts.

" Have a cigar, gentlemen ; it's quite safe," exclaimed Don Miguel genially, as he produced his inseparable gold case. " You will appreciate a weed in this pure and mild atmosphere. Somewhat of a surprise, eh ? "

" I suppose we have struck a stratum of calm air ? " asked Dick, as he held a lighted match in his upturned hand.

" I think not," replied the inventor, with a smile. " Otherwise these wind-torn clouds would be ramping past us. As a matter of fact, we are at this moment travelling stern-foremost over the earth at an estimated rate of fifty-five miles an hour."

" Great Scot ! " ejaculated Tresillian. " Is that so ? "

" At present we are travelling through the air at five miles per hour; the propeller is revolving at a comparatively low rate of speed, you will observe, barely sufficient to give the vessel steerage-way. Her direction is against the real direction of the wind, which we estimate at sixty miles an hour. By simple subtraction, we arrive at the fact that our speed over the land—or sea, rather—is practically fifty-five miles per hour in the same direction as the wind."

" I see," replied Dick. " Had the propeller not been working we would be in the position of a non-dirigible balloon floating in calm air notwithstanding the force of the wind."

" Precisely. Once clear of the earth, the wind being free from eddies, there is no danger of being overcome by the wind. It is only when leaving or returning to earth that is dangerous."

" It never struck me in that light before."

" Probably not. But, look, there is a light below us ! "

The three men leant over the rail. Nearly half a mile beneath them, betwixt a rugged rent in the apparently stationary clouds, a blinking light seemed to move in the same direction that the *Amphibian* was heading for, although infinitely quicker.

" A lighthouse ! " exclaimed Dick. " A fixed red light and a flashing white one. What is it, I wonder ? "

" You've seen it times before, Dick," said Holmsby in mock reproof. " That's Godrevy Light—a white flash every ten seconds."

" I don't remember the red light," replied Dick.

" Perhaps not, it is only visible across the reefs lying N.N.W. off the lighthouse: consequently we are somewhere above that danger."

" You can judge by the speed that light appears to drift ahead of us that we are travelling fairly quick," said Don Miguel. " Already we are half-way across St. Ives Bay."

" Why are we going so slowly and against the wind ? " asked Tresillian.

" To give the crew a chance for rest. They've been working splendidly for nearly twenty hours. But we are descending, I fear. If we are not careful we will find ourselves scraping the dirt off your Cornish hills. See, there is another light below us."

" A flare ! " exclaimed Holmsby. " Some vessel in distress."

" If that be so we will descend still farther," said O'Rourke decisively. " To aid a ship in peril is a universal duty."

So saying he led the way below, till they reached the lowermost of the central compartments, pausing to give the engineer directions as he did so.

Almost immediately the *Amphibian* shot ahead, and soon attained a velocity equal to that of the estimated rate of the gale, while, swooping through the thick bank of clouds, she hovered a good two hundred feet above the sea.

Meanwhile the inventor had thrust back a long

sliding panel, disclosing a large square of plate glass.

"Don't be afraid to tread on it," he remarked. "It's tested to 400 lb. to the square inch. By the way, would you mind touching that switch?"

Holmsby did so, and instantly a brilliant searchlight beam was directed vertically from the underbody of the *Amphibian*.

For a few seconds only it swept the surface of the storm-tossed sea, illuminating the foaming breakers and the flying spindrift with silvery light. Suddenly Holmsby gave a warning cry:

"There she is."

With her decks almost hidden by a smother of foam lay a small ketch. Her mainmast had gone by the board, and she was riding to the wreckage with comparative safety for the time being, although drifting rapidly towards the iron-bound coast. Her mizzen was still standing, a closely-reefed sail having been set to keep her head more to the wind, while aft were three men clad in oilskins and lifebelts, clinging with the strength of despair to the iron horse that crossed the deck abaft the battened fish-well. Lashed to the stump of the mainmast was a still-smoking tar-barrel, but the waves had already extinguished its warning glare.

This much Holmsby saw by the aid of a pair of night-glasses. Instinctively he wondered how the *Amphibian* could render aid to the unfortunate toilers of the deep. He looked round for O'Rourke, but the Calderian had gone.

Presently he returned, having roused the sleeping crew.

" We are all ready, Mr. Holmsby," he exclaimed. " You are used to this kind of thing "—and he held up a megaphone. " Give them a hail to tell them to stand by for a rope."

As he spoke Don Miguel unfastened a dead-light in the floor of the compartment and slightly to the side of the glass panel. A perfect whirlwind, the first audible intimation of the strength of the wind, screamed through the aperture.

" Ahoy, there. Stand by for a rope ! " shouted Reginald in stentorian tones.

" They can't hear us ; we'll forge ahead to windward," bawled O'Rourke. " Now, try again."

This time the hail was successful. One of the men raised his arm, and proceeded to make his way for'ard, followed by one of his companions.

Then from the afterpart of the *Amphibian* a barrico, to which was attached a stout grass hawser, was paid out, till it trailed to lee'ard of the disabled craft.

Skilfully manœuvred the airship forged ahead once more till the rope dragged across the stranger's foredeck. Once more the oil-skinned figure raised his hand, while, with a succession of blows with an axe, his mate cut away the raffle of cordage that held the floating gear.

With a jerk that well-nigh capsized Holmsby as he knelt at the open dead-eye, the *Amphibian* took the strain of the tow.

" Don't be alarmed," exclaimed Don Miguel, who had regained the lowermost compartment. " She'll stand it all right : this is not your *Mayfly*."

Reginald shut his jaws tightly at these words, but the Calderian was not slow to notice his guest's umbrage.

" Forgive me," he exclaimed; " I meant no offence. It was merely to give you confidence. A thousand pardons for my ill-placed remark."

" Don't mention it," replied Reginald unhesitatingly. " But where do you propose taking them to ? I thought you meant to sling them aboard on a bowline."

" It would have meant a tedious delay ere the weather moderates sufficiently to land them," said O'Rourke. " I would only do that as a last resource. No, my plan is to tow the craft into St. Ives Harbour."

" It's dead to lee'ard, and there's a heavy breaking sea between the harbour piers," exclaimed Holmsby. " I know the place. Besides, with this wind the *Amphibian* would travel at such a speed that even if the ketch escaped being swamped she would carry too much way and smash herself to pieces ashore."

" You're right," assented Don Miguel. But what alternative can you propose ? "

" If you could spare a barrel of lubricating oil," replied Holmsby, " we could veer the craft in——"

" Excellent," exclaimed the Calderian warmly. " Your resourcefulness is remarkable."

Still forging ahead the *Amphibian* reduced her speed till the force of the wind drove both her and the towed vessel rapidly to lee'ard, the strain on the hawser being just sufficient to keep the ketch's head to the breaking seas.

Now through the mirk the red sector of St. Ives light appeared to view, while on either side the breakers thrashed themselves upon the rocks in a smother of milk-white foam.

" Port your helm slightly, sir," cautioned Holmsby. " That's better. Now the light shows white. It's straight in now."

Apprehensively the men on board the ketch cast their eyes towards the smother of foam that lay betwixt them and safety. *They* knew the danger.

The upper search-light, which hitherto had been unused during the act of rescue, was now switched on, and its beam directed upon the massive stone pier that now lay dead to lee'ard. In spite of the clouds of spray that from time to time completely hid it, the structure was black with people, sheltering under the lee of its protecting wall, for the lifeboat had already gone on an errand of mercy, a large brigantine having grounded on Hayle Sands.

Meanwhile O'Rourke had ordered a barrel of oil to be brought from the storeroom and placed on the lowermost floor close to the still-open dead-light. With a swinging blow of his axe one of the seamen stove in its head and, tilting the cask, allowed the oil to fall in a steady stream through the aperture.

In a very short space of time the oil spread over the water, beating down the spiteful crests in a marvellous fashion, so that the rescued craft, instead of being swept from end to end, now pitched sluggishly in the unbroken waves.

Still slowly backing, the *Amphibian* allowed the disabled ketch to be veered right between the harbour lights. Ropes were flung from the lee of the outer pier, and, amid the hearty cheers of the crowd, the almost exhausted crew were helped ashore.

Meanwhile the *Amphibian*, held by the hawser, was battling manfully against the gale. Yet, in spite of Don Miguel's most careful helmsmanship, the huge bulk was slowly yet surely beginning to slew broadside on. Once the wind caught her thus, her immense lateral structure would be swept landwards encumbered as she was by the heavy grass rope.

" Cast off the hawser, you idiots ! " yelled Holmsby through the megaphone ; but either his words failed to carry or else the people on shore would not slip the rope from the bitts.

" We'll be broadside on in a moment," exclaimed O'Rourke excitedly. " If we do, there'll be some damage done ; but not to the *Amphibian*. Give them another hail, Holmsby."

Again Reginald shouted, all to no purpose. The *Amphibian's* bows were ten points off the wind.

Don Miguel gave a hurried order to his lieutenant. The officer rushed off and inserted another helia cylinder into one of the spare ballonettes. Then, as the huge vessel rose still higher in the air, a vicious squall took her on the port bow.

In a moment she literally scudded over the pier-head. There was a wild stampede on the part of the spectators to escape being capsized by the bight of the hawser—men falling over each other in all directions.

Then as the rope began once more to tauten the bight got foul of the lighthouse at the pier-head. The stone structure stood the strain, but as the rope ran up the column, the lantern was swept away. For a brief instant there was a heavy jerk as the whole bulk of the *Amphibian* told upon the hawser. Something had to go—and something went.

Like pieces of matchwood the oaken bitts of the rescued ketch were torn away from the deck, and freed from any restraining influence the *Amphibian* bounded upwards for a distance of nearly a thousand feet and, ere she could be brought head to wind, had drifted far beyond the little town.

" Great Scot ! that was a holy smash," ejaculated Dick. " The lighthouse knocked clean out of action."

" It was not our fault," remarked Don Miguel. " We gave them fair warning. I could, of course, have slipped the hawser ; but since it is the only one of that length and size we have on board I was not going to lose it."

Just then one of the crew approached, saluted, and in a low, excited tone spoke a few words to his

superior. Holmsby caught the words " aqua "
and " merma."

" Something's sprung a leak, Dick," he explained,
after Don Miguel had hurried away. " It seems
serious, I should think, judging by the expression
on his face. If we're obliged to attempt a descent
here, I won't give much for our chances, by Jove ! "

CHAPTER XIII

AN EXCHANGE OF SHOTS

"WE'VE had a somewhat unfortunate mishap, gentlemen," announced Don Miguel on rejoining his guests. "Somehow or the other our main freshwater tank has started, and its contents have escaped into the limbers of the submarine. Consequently, since it is not clear enough to pump back, we must repair the tank and wait till the weather moderates before we refill and resume our voyage. I thought of bringing up over the Scilly Isles."

"I believe fresh water is scarce there," said Holmsby.

"Where, then, could we replenish the tank ? "

"There's a good supply in the hills above the village of Zennor," said Tresillian. "I know the place well. We would also be fairly protected from the wind, if it remained in this quarter, and there is little chance of being seen."

"I do not mind publicity now," replied Don Miguel. "Nevertheless your proposal seems good We'll wait till daybreak and see where we are."

Accordingly the aerial propeller was run at

sufficient speed to counteract the drift caused by the force of the wind, and having given Don Carlos, his lieutenant, instructions as to course and altitude to be kept, Don Miguel and his guests retired to the officers' quarters.

Just before sunrise Holmsby awoke. His companions were still sleeping soundly, so, without disturbing them, he dressed and made his way to the lower storey.

The sliding panel still remained open, allowing a wide view of the country beneath to be made through the plate-glass window.

The *Amphibian* was going ahead very slowly. Possibly the gale had moderated, but it certainly had changed slightly in direction, for, instead of floating over the northern coast of the " toe " of the duchy, the airship was immediately over the town of Penzance.

Holmsby could discern the outlines of the coast with the utmost ease, the range of vision at an altitude of 1500 feet, embracing the whole of Mount's Bay, including St. Michael's Mount and the villages of Newlyn and Mousehole, while the rocks and submerged shoals of the bay were visible with startling clearness against the pale green sea.

So rapt was his attention at the unfamiliar sight of a familiar coast that Reginald was unaware that O'Rourke was standing behind him.

" Admiring the English Bay of Naples, Mr. Holmsby ? " he asked, with his customary affability.

" It's stunning, sir; but haven't we got a bit out of our course ? "

" Nothing to speak of. Don Carlos carried out his orders faithfully, but the wind veered slightly in the night."

" The *Amphibian* will cause a little excitement to the inhabitants of Penzance, I fancy."

" It's early yet ; but no doubt some of the crews of the fishing smacks yonder have observed us. Seamen, as you know, use their eyes : it's part of their education. But I'm willing to wager that I would bring the *Amphibian* over an inland town and descend to within five hundred feet, without attracting attention, though, mark you, once one individual saw us the news would spread like wildfire, and the whole town would soon be gazing upwards with eyes and mouth agape."

" But the gale is moderating fast. We will drop to lee'ard a little and come up head to wind under the shelter of Land's End."

By the time the early breakfast had been done justice to, the *Amphibian* was over the village of St. Buryan. As Don Miguel had said, the wind was piping down, but its velocity was still too great to warrant a descent.

" If I were the commander of a fleet of hostile airships operating against your country that building would be one of the first I would destroy," observed O'Rourke, pointing to a house snugly sheltered betwixt two rocky headlands.

" The submarine and wireless telegraphy station

of Porthcurnow—however did you know that ? "
asked Tresillian.

" You English are apt to despise the poor
foreigner—it's a common failing with you, I fear,"
replied Don Miguel. " But the average foreigner
—especially if he be a seaman—knows far more
about your country and its defences than ninety-
nine per cent. of its inhabitants. I once met the
skipper of a German trader, who boasted, not
without cause, that he knew the position of every
fort between Aberdeen and Falmouth, and that
even if the buoys were removed, he could navigate
a vessel into every harbour on the south or east
coast of Great Britain. Yes, gentlemen, the destruction of that place would mean that submarine communication with South Western Europe
and Madeira would be almost impossible : the only
working line remaining being that between Falmouth and Bilboa—and Porthcurnow is absolutely
without means of defence. Well, you must excuse
me, for I have to do the rounds : I think that is
what you naval men term it."

O'Rourke had not been absent many minutes
ere he returned.

" I've just been speaking with my London
agent," he exclaimed. " He tells me there's a fine
dust up about you. The authorities received
your message, but seem to have regarded it as a
hoax. More, there has been a serious shooting
affair at Sampson's Down, and a troop of cavalry
has been sent there from Exeter. No further

details are obtainable at present. *Madre!* I wish I could get hold of a newspaper," he added tentatively.

"The London papers do not reach Penzance till late in the forenoon," said Dick. "Perhaps we might be able to get one, but at the present moment I don't know how."

"If you don't mind, I think you would be the best man to get one," said the ex-President. "There's not much wind under this hill. I'll bring the *Amphibian* as close to the ground as I dare and lower you by a rope. Take one of the gravity-neutralisers with you for your return, in case we have to ascend, but it's not advisable to use it for the descent. We will await you here."

"I'll do it," replied Dick resolutely. "But I think I know of a better plan. I'll walk into Penzance, get the papers, and take train to St. Ives. In the meantime you can take the *Amphibian* to Zennor Hill and carry on with the watering. It's a fairly short distance from St. Ives to Zennor, and I'll be back before four o'clock."

"You might take letters for us," added Reginald. It would be a good plan to confirm our previous messages."

"You'll return to us, I hope ? " said Don Miguel. "Nay, pardon me, regard my remark as unsaid."

"I'll return sure enough," replied Dick. "Am I the man to break his word or desert his comrade ? "

Accordingly the *Amphibian* was brought within twenty feet of the ground above a gently-sloping field. Tresillian, with the uncharged neutraliser slung on his back glided down the rope and reached the earth in safety ; then, with a reassuring wave of his hand, he started to walk rapidly in the direction of Penzance.

An hour later the wind had subsided sufficiently for the *Amphibian* to risk a descent. At an elevation of less than a thousand feet, she headed rapidly northwards towards the rugged hill that Tresillian had pointed out.

As the huge airship passed over the main road to Land's End, Don Miguel called Holmsby's attention to a couple of motor coaches lumbering along towards the Mecca of Cornish tourists—the most westerly point of England. Through his glasses the sub-lieutenant watched the holidaymaking freight, but, sure enough, though out for sight-seeing, not one of the occupants of the coaches chanced to look aloft at the greatest marvel of the twentieth century that was gliding serenely over their heads.

On arriving at the chosen anchorage the *Amphibian* manœuvred until the copious stream was found, then, dropping her bow grapnel, shut off the motors and swung head to wind. For nearly a hundred yards the grapnel found no grip in the sun-baked turf, till, engaging in the top stone of a weather-worn cromlech, it allowed the huge vessel to ride motionless in the now almost still air. Then, with a barely perceptible jar, the *Amphibian* sank gently to earth.

Meanwhile the crew had been actively engaged in repairing the leak in the water-tank, and ere the landing operations were effected the work was completed. Four or five short lengths of hose were coupled up, a powerful centrifugal pump was set to work, and the fresh sparkling liquid flowed rapidly into the tank.

In less than half an hour the *Amphibian* was ready for her ocean passage. All that was to be done was to wait patiently for Dick Tresillian's return.

Holmsby and his host had taken the opportunity of " stretching their legs ashore," but on the completion of the tank-filling operations they boarded the *Amphibian* and took up their position on the promenade deck, where, by reason of the height of the aircraft, they were able to command a long stretch of the granite road that wended its way down Zennor Hill in the direction of St. Ives.

It was now nearly four o'clock, but still no signs of Dick Tresillian. Presently a motor-car was to be seen breasting the spur of the hill. When as close to the *Amphibian* as it could possibly be without leaving the road the car stopped and its three occupants regarded the huge craft with apparent curiosity.

After waiting for five minutes the car was set in motion, and was soon lost to sight in a dip in the road.

" Still no sign of your friend, Mr. Holmsby," remarked O'Rourke, after carefully scanning the

distant highway through his field-glasses. " I
trust that he has not met with a mishap."

" Perhaps there was not a convenient train
or——" Reginald's words were interrupted by the
zipp of a bullet whistling past his ear, while, with
the sound of a sharp report, a volley of shots
struck the bulky target presented by the *Amphibian*. Some of the missiles passed from one side
to the other of the outer envelope, others cutting
their way almost without resistance through the
duralium skin flattened themselves against the
proof metal sheathing of the submarine.

" Lie down ! " shouted Holmsby to his companion, and instantly Don Miguel complied, calling
at the same time for the rifles to be served out.

Through the hatchway swarmed the lithe
Calderian crew, each man with a Jansen automatic
rifle. Though they lacked the calm deliberation
of the British seaman the men were not deficient
in courage. Taking advantage of the scanty cover
afforded by the turned-up edges of the deck, they
began a rapid fire upon their practically invisible
enemies, their bullets cutting up the turf all
around a natural embankment behind which
Holmsby had detected the movement of a man's
cap.

Realising that the more they fired the better
able were they to keep down the fusillade from
their unseen foes, the crew shot rapidly and well.
As for their assailants they had hoped to take the
airship by surprise, send in several destructive

shots, and get clear away in their car ere the *Amphibian* could reply ; but so prompt were the crew that their treacherous attackers were literally trapped since they could not retire without offering a tempting mark as they drew clear of the sheltering bank of earth.

" Who are these fellows, I wonder ? " asked Don Miguel of Holmsby, who had taken up a rifle and was joining in the firing. " Some of your Government friends ? "

" No," replied Reginald. " Otherwise I would not be using this rifle. Unless I'm very much mistaken they are our old acquaintances of St. Piran's Round with motor-car F.O. 445."

" Hello ! " he exclaimed, after a pause. " There's Dick coming along the road. Now what's to be done ? He'll be trapped to a dead cert."

CHAPTER XIV

DICK TRESILLIAN'S ESCAPE

THERE was no time to be lost. Ordering four of the seamen to follow him, Don Miguel went below. In a few moments the bow rope was paid out sufficiently to enable the stern grapnel to be broken out and hauled on board; then, as the *Amphibian* rose twenty feet in the air, the air-propeller began to revolve, and the gigantic vessel forged slowly ahead, the fusillade being maintained almost as lustily as of yore.

The care which Don Miguel had taken by securing the bow anchor in the cromlech now proved a source of difficulty, but, after a considerable amount of manœuvring, the refractory instrument was shaken clear and secured to the bow of the vessel.

Thanks to the ingenious composition of the fabric of the outer envelope, the small-bore pistol-shots from the attacking party did but little harm, the punctures closing automatically with but little escape of helia. Nevertheless O'Rourke took the opportunity of inserting a charge into the seventh ballonette.

" Now we'll punish the rascals," he exclaimed,

as the *Amphibian* soared aloft and the men on deck now, being in no position to use their rifles, descended to the lowermost compartment whence they could continue their fire with good effect. "I'll fly right over their heads, and I'll simply wipe them out."

Seeing their danger the three assailants broke cover and ran towards the motor-car. One of them fell and lay writhing on the grass, but the others, heedless and regardless of their companion's fate, gained their desired refuge.

Now the shots from the *Amphibian* rained thick and fast upon the car, but the occupants had already provided for their personal safety. An armoured hood had been drawn over the vehicle, successfully stopping the bullets in spite of their high velocity and powers of penetration.

Then as the *Amphibian* headed towards the spot where Dick, scenting danger, had stopped, the F.O. 445 started in pursuit, jolting over the rough grass-grown down, one of the occupants using his automatic pistol while the other steered.

Seeing the airship coming in his direction, and the car bumping along in its wake, Dick realised that something was amiss, especially as, for the first time, he heard the noise of the firing.

Knowing that it would be impossible to charge the gravity-neutraliser while it was fastened to his back, Tresillian did the only thing possible. He strapped it across his chest, inserted the charge, and waited, wondering what would happen if he miscalculated the speed of the *Amphibian* and jumped wide.

" Stand by ! " shouted Holmsby, who had once more taken up his station on the promenade-deck. "Now ! "

The bow of the *Amphibian* was nearly fifty feet in a diagonal distance from the waiting man : the car but a hundred yards off. Unhesitatingly Dick bent his knees and leapt.

Fortunately for him the occupants of the spurious F.O. 445 were somewhat astounded at the apparently supernatural appearance of a man leaping ten times his own length in air ; but, quickly recovering from his surprise, the man with the pistol, having just recharged the magazine, let fly as fast as the automatic mechanism would permit.

" Good heavens ! " muttered Holmsby. " If a single shot should pierce the neutraliser."

Strange as it may appear, he never gave one thought to the fact that one of the stream of bullets might hit his comrade in some vital part : he only contemplated the possibility of a fearful fall to earth should the supporting medium be damaged.

Up shot Dick, sprawling on his back as it were, with arms outstretched, for the lifting apparatus, being designed for the wearer's back, now showed a tendency to capsize him.

Just as he reached the highest point of his flight, Don Miguel had the whirling air-propeller stopped, and, adroitly manœuvring the *Amphibian*, brought her smartly underneath Tresillian's descending body. Ere Dick rebounded, Holmsby held him in his powerful grasp, safe and sound upon the deck.

With a swift rush the *Amphibian* shot a thousand feet skywards, presenting a target that it was almost impossible to hit.

"Now to have my revenge," exclaimed Don Miguel, and, bending over the hatchway, he gave orders for the bomb-dropping gear to be brought into action.

"Watch the effect of one missile—utter annihilation," he exclaimed.

"Excuse me, señor; you must not," said Reginald quietly.

"Must not?" replied the ex-President hotly. "Pray, why?"

"Look down," continued the sub-lieutenant. "The car has stopped close to that little village. Would you, in your desire to revenge yourself upon two worthless scoundrels, wipe out perhaps forty or fifty harmless people?"

For an instant the two men looked each other in the face—the cool Saxon and the impulsive Creole.

"You are right," replied Don Miguel, after a pause. "Nevertheless I'll have them in my power ere long."

"Ay," assented Holmsby. "You'll have them right enough—in due course. Even I am as anxious as you to settle old scores, but there is a time and place for all things.'

Without another word O'Rourke went below, and in a few minutes the *Amphibian* turned till her bow pointed south-west. Then, with a whirr as her propeller ran at top speed, she cleft the air in the direction of the broad Atlantic.

The Englishmen endured the hurricane caused by the speed of the craft through the air as long as they could, then, going below, took up their position at the observation panel in the floor of the lower compartment.

" How did you feel when you were being shot at in mid-air, Dick ? " asked Reginald, as the last outlying rocks of the Scilly Islands were left astern and nothing but an unbroken expanse of water was to be seen.

" A sort of a kind of a first of September partridge feeling," replied Tresillian all in one breath. " No more of that for me. The shots almost grazed my upturned nose."

" All's well that ends well," said Holmsby complacently. " But you brought the papers ? "

" Yes, and read them. A pretty kettle of fish, I can assure you."

" Where are they ? "

" O'Rourke has them, I believe."

" I don't think I'll trouble him just yet : he seems somewhat crusty. Tell me——"

" Mr. Holmsby ! " came Don Miguel's voice from above.

" Ay, ay, sir," replied Reginald promptly, as he sprang up the ladder.

The commander of the *Amphibian* was standing in the conning-tower, grasping the steering-wheel. Seated on a bench by his side was Don Carlos, looking ghastly pale, and with his right hand swathed in bandages.

" I regret to have to inform you that my lieutenant has been badly wounded, Mr. Holmsby," began Don Miguel. "During the last exchange of shots a bullet severed two of his fingers. Without saying a word to anyone he continued to superintend the seamen under his orders, and it was not until we were fairly out to sea that he collapsed through loss of blood. I've rendered such surgical assistance as lies in my power, and can only trust that the natural healing will be a matter of time. But, meanwhile, Don Carlos will be totally unfit for doing any work, so I ask you as a favour to take his place until his recovery."

The sub-lieutenant hesitated. Visions of the dire penalties threatened by the Foreign Enlistment Act, the Naval Discipline Act, and a score of other formidable Acts flashed across his mind.

" I know what you are thinking of," continued Don Miguel. " But you need not trouble on that score. Whether you take up arms against a friendly state or not depends entirely upon yourself. There is this knowledge, however," and the Calderian pointed to the two newspapers lying on the table. " Both you and your comrade are officially dead."

" What ? " gasped Holmsby.

" Dead as my illustrious ancester, Don Patrick

O'Rourke, as far as the British Admiralty is concerned, I fancy. Read this."

Holmsby took the paper. Printed in bold headlines he read :

" STARTLING DEVELOPMENT IN THE CORNISH
    MYSTERY. — SUPPOSED MURDER OF TWO
    ADMIRALTY OFFICIALS. — A NAVAL PEN-
    SIONER FOUND DANGEROUSLY WOUNDED.

" ST. IVES. *Tuesday noon.*—Our special correspondent telegraphs that the mysterious events centring around Sampson's Cove have developed with startling rapidity. On Monday night two visitors to Penkerris, who, it appears, had been sent from the Intelligence Department of the Admiralty to make inquiries concerning the presence of a mysterious airship that had been seen in various parts of Cornwall, left the village with the supposed purpose of conducting their investigations. With them, apparently, was Lieutenant Haslar, R.N. (retired), whose intimate knowledge would prove of great assistance to the Admiralty officials.

" Failing to return on the following morning the services of a party of coastguards were requisitioned and a search made of the fenced-in portion of the ground. Lieutenant Haslar was discovered, dangerously wounded and insensible, outside the fence and close to the edge of the cliff. He was promptly removed to his house, and on the arrival of a doctor was found to have been shot with a small-bore bullet through the left lung. Up to the time of

wiring he has not recovered consciousness, so that
the events of the previous night must at present
be left to conjecture.

" Presumably the three men were suddenly
attacked, Mr. Haslar falling as he attempted to
escape, while the other unfortunate investigators
were hauled over the cliff.

" It is well known in the district that Lieutenant
Haslar gave frequent warnings to the authorities
of the danger to the community at large by the
presence of a band of desperadoes with the most
potent instruments of science at their command.
Now the gallant officer has set the seal to his
assertions, possibly at the cost of his life.

" We understand that cavalry are to be brought
into the terrorised district, and in the meanwhile
armed parties of coastguards are actively engaged
in patrolling the cliffs in search of the missing
officers and their assailants. The next few hours
may produce startling developments."

" What do you think of that ? " asked Don
Miguel, when Reginald had finished reading.

" Absolute rot ! " replied the sub. " Someone's
on the wrong tack. But I'm sorry about old
Haslar, even though he was a surly bear."

" Who's Haslar ? I see his name mentioned
once or twice. Did he accompany you ? "

Holmsby hastened to explain that he and the
pensioner were practically rivals.

" It's strange," he added. " We passed him

going homewards as we made for Sampson's Down. He must have returned. I wonder who shot him : none of your men ? "

" Most emphatically no," replied Don Miguel. " But here is another paper — the *St. Ives Romancer.*"

" THE MYSTERIOUS AIRSHIP ATTACKS ST. IVES. WANTON DESTRUCTION OF THE LIGHTHOUSE.

" Late last evening, or rather in the early hours of the morning, the mysterious airship, which has recently been prominently brought before the notice of the public, showed herself in her true colours. During the height of the north-easterly gale that, as related elsewhere in our columns, wrought havoc on our coasts, the airship, manned by a crew of desperadoes, wantonly destroyed the lighthouse on the pier-head. By what means she succeeded in performing this wilful act of destruction—an undoubted outrage against all nations—remains a mystery. Many of the spectators avow that it was by the agency of an electric discharge. Fortunately the damage was confined to the lighthouse, the gale sweeping the sky-pirate over the town ere she had time to continue her deeds of inexplicable destruction."

" More bungling. That editor ought to be made to swallow his confounded paper," said Holmsby savagely. " Here, Dick, come and see the account of your premature decease."

" I've already done so," replied Tresillian, as
he rejoined his companion.   " Dulce et decorum
est pro patriâ mori.   But, seriously, Rex, who
could have winged old Hasler ? "

" Give it up ; unless it were our old friends
F.O. 445.   There's one consolation : our letters
will reach the Admiralty to-night, and will help
to clear up several false impressions."

Dick's face suddenly paled as he clapped his
hand to his breast-pocket.

" I'm a regular ass ! " he exclaimed.   " I've
forgotten to post them.   What's going to happen
now ? "

" That remains to be seen, as the ship's cat said
when it upset the ink over the commander's log-
book," replied Holmsby.   " At any rate we are
both officially dead, and there is a vacancy in the
Active branch of the King's Navy to say nothing
of one in the hard-working Civil Service."

" Then I would suggest that present complications are considerably simplified, Mr. Holmsby,"
remarked Don Miguel.   " Until you are resurrected you have no official status : your very
existence is denied.   Therefore, it seems to me,
there is no reason why you should not accept my
offer and become lieutenant of the *Amphibian* for
the time being."

" May as well go the whole hog," replied
Holmsby, with forced cheerfulness.   " I'll accept,
subject to one condition."

" And that—— ? "

" That should the *Amphibian* become embroiled in a conflict with any nation, except with the rebels of Calderia, we can claim the right to be set ashore or on board any craft we may happen to fall in with."

" Agreed ! " exclaimed Don Miguel O'Rourke, extending his right hand

CHAPTER XV

THE TALPICAN AEROPLANES

SWIFTLY the *Amphibian* sped on her course towards the distant Calderian shores, and once clear of the recognised trade routes hour after hour passed without sign of a vessel upon the vast expanse of ocean.

On the evening of the second day after leaving the Cornish coast the airship passed beyond the range of her wireless telephone, and from that time until her arrival off the port of Nalcuanho all communication with the outside world was practically impossible.

Early on the morning of the third day the Bermudas hove in sight, and flying at an altitude of nearly 2000 metres, the *Amphibian* passed directly over the town of Hamilton, unnoticed by any of the inhabitants.

The same evening she flew high over Moro Castle and the town of Havanna. Don Miguel gave orders for the lower search-light to be switched on, and instantly the town was swept by a dazzling ray of light.

By the aid of their glasses the Englishmen could

see the Plaza crowded with creoles and negroes taking their evening promenade. At the first flash, falling apparently from the sky, shouts of terror rose from the superstitious Cubans. Some fell prostrate on the ground, others ran shrieking to the shelter of the narrow streets, and in a few seconds the Plaza was deserted.

" If that had been the Talpican army we would have gained a splendid moral victory," exclaimed Tresillian.

" Unless I'm much mistaken the Talpicans are made of sterner stuff," replied Don Miguel. " We will not be able to clear them off Calderian territory without bloodshed, I fancy. Now, gentlemen, it is about time the watch is set, and those off duty take their rest. This will be the last opportunity of undisturbed repose for some days to come."

At sunrise Holmsby was out upon the promenade-deck, marine-glasses in hand. Away to the south-west there appeared to be an irregular crimson cloud. It was the snowclad peaks of the Calderian Sierras tinged with the glow of the rising sun.

" Quite seventy miles off, I reckon," commented Reginald. " Another half-hour and we'll be on the scene of hostilities."

The crew of the *Amphibian* were already busily engaged in clearing for action. Speed was reduced while the two 0·755 centimetre quick-firers were brought from below and mounted on the promenade-deck. Racks of sinister-looking polished shells were ranged alongside the guns and secured by strong lashings ; while amidships a Maxim was mounted on a light tripod and placed in such a position that it could command a wide arc of fire on either broadside.

Just before eight o'clock Don Miguel O'Rourke, now attired in a gorgeous gilt-braided uniform, came on deck, and as eight bells struck the Calderian ensign was run up to a small staff abaft the promenade-deck.

Then, with the flag blowing out as stiff as a board, the *Amphibian* resumed her greatest pace direct for the city of Nalcuanho, now barely twelve miles distant.

"By Jove, señor, I believe we are too late," exclaimed Holmsby, as the two stood at the for'ard scuttles of the conning-tower. "The place is already in flames."

Such evidently was the case, for in the almost calm air a thick column of flame-tinged smoke soared skyward.

"We are not too late for revenge, Mr. Holmsby," replied the ex-President.

"Revenge," thought Reginald. "This fellow seems to think of nothing else. All his power, riches, intellect seem to exist for that one purpose."

"They are still firing," exclaimed Don Miguel. "See, there are shells bursting away to seaward."

" Yes, and do you see what they are firing at ? " asked Holmsby quietly. " See those little black dots, like a swarm of flies, flopping up and down ? "

" *Caramba !* " muttered the Calderian. " They are aeroplanes."

" Talpico has evidently made strides in the science of warfare since you left Nalcuanho, señor," remarked Reginald. " However, we must be careful. What do you propose to do ? "

" Stand on and see what happens. I hope they'll turn tail when they see the Calderian ensign floating in the air. See that the men at the quick-firers have the correct range, Mr. Holmsby."

But ere Reginald could leave the conning-tower, Don Miguel shouted to him to return.

The Englishman was surprised at the change in the Calderian's features. The deep olive tint had given place to the sickly yellow of terror. In the hour of peril the vaunted rescuer of his country completely lost his head.

" What must we do, señor ? " he gasped, pointing to the Talpican aeroplanes, which, having formed into two long lines *en échelon*, were advancing straight for the *Amphibian.*

" Do ? " replied Holmsby, almost roughly, for the sight of the craven ex-President provoked his deepest resentment. " Do ? Why, act, man, act ! "

" I cannot."

" Shall I, then ? "

Don Miguel gave a feeble gesture of assent. Reginald immediately sprang to the wheel, put the tiller hard over, elevated the planes to their highest capacity, and shouted to the engineer to charge the four remaining ballonettes.

" Look sharp, Dick," he shouted. " Serve out the neutralisers. We'll rise till we drop those fellows —or bust in the attempt."

Like an arrow from a bow the *Amphibian* darted upwards, just missing a rocket from the nearest aeroplane of the starboard division, the hissing missile of destruction passing a few feet below the envelope. Had the rocket engaged it would have burst a hole through the duralium with the greatest ease in spite of the asbestos sheeting for, by an ingenious mechanical device, the heads of these newly-invented anti-airship weapons were provided with a sharp rotary drill. The impact would be sufficient to enable the point to obtain a grip, and its spiral action would speedily enlarge the aperture, through which the unquenchable flame of mingled petrol and sulphur would pass, causing the total destruction of the best-protected aircraft in existence.

" Ugh, you brute ! " ejaculated Holmsby, who alone had noted the *Amphibian's* narrow escape.

It seemed as if the whole fleet of aeroplanes were falling seawards, so swift had been the airship's vertical leap. In less than half a minute the hostile fleet looked no bigger than a covey of partridges, as, superbly managed, they circled in ever-ascending spiral curves in fruitless pursuit of the Calderian airship.

Suddenly, and without orders, one of the crew released a bomb from the lowermost deck. The gunner evidently knew his work, for, in setting the fuse to explode at 5000 metres, he gauged the distance to a nicety.

With a roar that was greatly intensified by the rarefied atmosphere the highly-charged missile exploded in the midst of the pursuing aeroplanes.

Holmsby, in the conning-tower, was in ignorance of what had occurred; but Tresillian had run to the floor-panel and saw the tragedy enacted.

The blinding flash was instantly concealed by a thick yellow cloud mingled with fragments of the annihilated machines. Some, beyond the actual zone of explosion, were capsized by the blast of displaced air, their occupants falling to a quick yet horrible death; others had their planes burnt and rent by the spurting flames, and like flies shorn of their wings plunged swiftly downwards; while four only, rocking violently in their endeavour to counteract the air-eddies, succeeded in recovering their balance. Terror-stricken, their occupants executed a terrific *vol-plané* till they almost reached the surface of the sea, whence they fled for safety to the lines of the Talpican army.

" What's wrong with Don Miguel ? " asked
Dick, as he joined his comrade in the conning-
tower with the news of the appalling disaster to
the pursuers.

" Blue funk ! " whispered Reginald.

" I don't wonder at it : I feel as sick as a dog
after seeing that," and Dick made a downward
motion with his hand. " If that's war I want
to see no more of it."

" Our friend yonder had his attack before the
scrap began," said Holmsby, contemptuously
glancing in the direction of Don Miguel who still
remained huddled up on the floor. " Just fancy,
Dick, I'm in command of this caboodle now.
Here we are at 4000 metres above the sea-level,
and in danger of the envelope bursting at any
moment. I wonder what old Pennington would
say if he could see me now ? "

" Don't stop to think, old chap ; but for
goodness' sake let's descend a few miles. See,
already there is ice forming on the turtle-back
deck."

Realising the urgent necessity of following
Tresillian's advice, Holmsby ordered the engineer
to release the helia from the four now-superfluous
ballonettes.

The man instantly grasped one of the levers
actuating the valves ; but though he used
considerable force the steel rod remained immovable. The others he tried with the same
result.

" Pardiez, señor, I cannot open the valves," he gasped. " They are frozen."

Holmsby glanced at the aneroid. The *Amphibian* was still rising. Would the envelope withstand the terrific internal pressure ?

CHAPTER XVI

A SWOOP FROM THE SKY

" Señor O'Rourke ! "

Bending over the almost motionless body of the terrified inventor, Holmsby called him by name. There was no response.

" He ought to be made to rouse himself, Rex," said Tresillian. " Hang it all, man ; it's his invention, isn't it ? Why can't he be made to control it ? Shake him."

Thus abjured, Holmsby turned Don Miguel over on his back. The man's eyes were wide open, his teeth chattering like castanets, his face absolutely devoid of colour.

" Come on, get up and play the man ! " shouted the sub. " We're in a bit of a hole. Don't be afraid—the aeroplanes are smashed to a jelly."

The Calderian gave no sign of intelligence. He lay, breathing heavily, yet apparently devoid of all his senses.

Drawing his revolver from his hip pocket, Reginald held it to O'Rourke's temple.

" Get up, you white-livered scoundrel," he said sternly, " or, by Jove, I'll——"

149

The sub. paused to note the effect of the threat ; but his action and words were wasted. Don Miguel was temporarily dead to the world.

" Confound the fellow," he grunted. " We must leave him alone : he's properly off his head. Here, Dick, give me a hand with this lever. Ah ! That's good."

By their united efforts the Englishmen succeeded in reversing the elevating planes, but the helia release-valves obstinately refused to move.

" Now we'll try the motor and see if we can descend in spite of the lifting power of the ballonettes," exclaimed Reginald. " Perhaps we may succeed in striking a warmer zone of air and thus melt the ice."

Cautiously running the motor at half speed, since he feared that the vibration might complete the anticipated rending of the envelope, Holmsby noticed with intense satisfaction that the *Amphibian* was beginning to gather way and descend obliquely ; but in a few moments the huge fabric began to tilt so steeply that the sub-lieutenant had to re-trim the planes to prevent the craft from assuming a vertical position.

" Now what's to be done, Dick ? " he asked. " It's evident that she won't descend in a proper manner. If she tilts too much I'm afraid the motor will be wrenched from its bearers or some of the heavy gear will be started. Look, it's 4900 metres now."

" Couldn't we hack one of the ballonettes through from the outside ? "

" Impossible, I'm afraid, Dick. The men had to take shelter below by reason of the intense cold when we were at only 3000 metres. They could scarcely breathe."

" We'll both have another shot at the valves. Something is bound to go if we heave for all we're worth."

" All right—but one moment : are all the neutralisers served out and charged ? "

" Served out, but not charged."

" Then I'll give the order for that to be done. If the ship gets out of control and makes a down-ward plunge it may be possible to save our lives before she plunges into the sea. She may fall gently or she may go with a terrific smash— it all depends on how the ballonettes stand it."

In a few minutes the crew were ready for the unhoped-for emergency, Holmsby and his com-rade having likewise provided for the expected catastrophe.

" By Jove, Rex ! " exclaimed Tresillian, as they made their way towards the valve-levers, " I don't think this apparatus has the same buoyancy as it had before."

" I'm certain of it," replied Holmsby. " It is doubtless due to the rarefied condition of the atmo-sphere. If we leapt overboard it's a moral certainty we should fall like a stone for a few miles till we entered a stratum of normal density. By that time we would not be worth much, I fear."

" Then how is it that the helia in the *Amphibian's* ballonettes has a comparatively greater lifting power ? "

" It hasn't—bulk for bulk. That's what I'm afraid of. If we cannot open those valves the helia which is sufficient to support the *Amphibian* in a rarefied atmosphere will assuredly burst the envelope in denser air. Already the interior pressure is about as much as the fabric will stand. So the sooner we start the valves the better. Now, all together."

Desperately the Englishmen tugged at one of the refractory levers, but all to no purpose. The steel rod bent to almost a semicircle, but the actuating rod remained fixed as if an immovable part of the airship's frame. The effort well-nigh left the two men breathless ; the thinness of the air rendered breathing a matter of difficulty, and for some minutes they could only sit down, gasping for breath while beads of perspiration froze on their foreheads.

" Try the motor once more," at length suggested Dick. " Tell the engineer to run half speed astern and see if the *Amphibian* will keep her balance better that way."

But after several attempts to start the engine the engineer made the startling discovery that the petrol had become frozen. Holmsby looked at the thermometer. Even within the confined space of the conning-tower it registered −15° centigrade.

" How long will it be before the natural leakage of the helia will be sufficient to cause the *Amphibian* to descend ? " asked Tresillian.

" Goodness only knows. Don Miguel might, but —well, look at the man."

" Then we are like Mahomet's tomb—floating betwixt heaven and earth—until something happens to——"

A vicious hiss—the sound of escaping helia interrupted Dick's words. The next instant officers and crew were flung violently against the forward bulkheads of the compartments.

One of the after ballonettes had burst, fracturing four others. Instantly the *Amphibian*, her buoyancy being contained in the five 'midship and for'ard helia-chambers, tilted nose upwards, and began to fall swiftly towards the dark blue expanse five miles beneath her—to wit, Mother Earth.

Helplessly the despairing men held on to whatever came nearest to their hands. Even had they retained their presence of mind and attempted to leap from the falling aircraft, the rush of air past the conning-tower hatch prevented it from being opened. From intense cold the temperature, suddenly raised by reason of the friction of the air, changed to extreme heat. The blades of the huge for'ard propeller were compressed against the curve of the *Amphibian's* bow as she plunged to an apparently unavoidable fate upon the soil of Calderi.

Even in this moment of peril, Holmsby kept his eyes upon the clock and the barometer. In one minute and a half the mercury had risen over twenty-three inches, representing a fall of four miles, at a mean rate of 160 miles an hour.

Then it was that Holmsby became aware that the awful velocity was being retarded. The buoyancy of the still undamaged ballonettes was sufficient to break the final plunge.

With newborn hope he reached up to the elevating levers. Thank heaven they were still in order. Scarcely daring to hope, he gently deflected the two nominally horizontal rudders. The *Amphibian* made a decided movement towards regaining her normal position of equilibrium ; but the unequal balance of the buoyancy chambers still gave her an oblique inclination of her major axis. Still that was enough to break her fall.

" Dick ! " shouted the sub.

There was no reply. Tresillian was lying by the side of the craven Don Miguel. The strain had been too much for him : he had swooned.

" Look alive, men ! " shouted Holmsby in Spanish, but of the crew only two showed signs of intelligent movement and came crawling through the narrow hatchway betwixt the conning-tower flat and the 'midship compartment. Instinctively they pinned their hopes on the coolness of the young English officer.

One glance through the for'ard scuttle showed Holmsby that the *Amphibian* was not now in danger of falling upon hard ground. Could her present oblique course be maintained she would strike the water some distance outside Nalcuanho Harbour.

"Secure that hatch!" continued Reginald, pointing to the only means of egress which, though closed, was not held firmly in position by its locking-levers. Then, having satisfied himself on this point, Holmsby kept his attention upon the disabled airship's course.

Now, but eight hundred yards beneath the falling *Amphibian*, he could see the six battleships and cruisers of the Talpican navy steaming in single line ahead, with a dozen destroyers spread out on their seaward side. The fleet had been engaging the Calderian batteries, but on discovering the crippled *Amphibian* they had ceased firing to see the result of a headlong plunge from the sky.

To Holmsby it seemed as if nothing could prevent the *Amphibian* from falling athwart one of the hostile craft, but in a few minutes the ever-decreasing distance showed that there was room and to spare betwixt the ships should the direction of the diagonal flight be kept under control.

Fortunately the Talpican fleet did not possess quick-firers mounted so as to enable them to repel the aircraft, their extreme elevation being not more than 45°; but, recovering from their surprise, the crew of the *Puebla*, the leading ship of the line, prepared to hazard a broadside from their secondary armament ere the hapless airship struck the surface of the sea.

Suddenly a gust of wind caught the falling

craft, and instead of descending when Holmsby had hoped, the *Amphibian* swerved For one brief instant it seemed as if she would descend upon the *Libertad*, the second ship in line.

Her crew had a momentary vision of the gigantic airship swooping down athwart her tapering masts; there was a series of crashes as the raffle of wireless gear came tumbling from aloft, a resounding splash like the blow of a whale's tail, and the *Amphibian* disappeared beneath the waves in a cauldron of boiling foam.

CHAPTER XVII

"WE HAVE STILL THE SUBMARINE"

THE wreck of the *Amphibian* rested on the ocean bed eleven fathoms beneath the surface. The shock of the impact was not sufficient to deprive the gallant sub-lieutenant of his senses, and, keenly alert to the urgency of immediate action, he instantly rallied those of the crew who were capable of understanding and acting upon his orders.

"Close No. 4 starboard valve," shouted Holmsby, for under the terrific pressure water was hissing like escaping steam through the practically-closed apertures in the 'midship section of the submarine.

Fortunately, though Reginald was unaware of it, this leak had proved to be of inestimable service to the hapless *Amphibian*. It destroyed her slight reserve of buoyancy, otherwise the craft would have risen to the surface ere the crew could take steps to prevent her so doing, and thus prove an easy target for the guns of the Talpican squadron. As it was, the flow of water was checked just at the right time.

Having ascertained that the hull of the submarine was perfectly sound and watertight, Reginald turned his attention to his companions. Tresillian was his first care. The Cornishman lay perfectly motionless, the sudden change of temperature, combined with the confined air within the submarine craft tending to prolong his state of insensibility. His face was pale and pinched ; his eyes dull ; pulse almost imperceptible, and breathing very feeble, while Holmsby could scarcely detect any signs of respiration or circulation of the blood.

Placing his comrade's body in a horizontal position with his head slightly raised, Reginald bared his patient's neck and chest and proceeded to chafe his limbs. For nearly a quarter of an hour he persevered, leaving off only to administer an occasional teaspoonful of brandy—all apparently to no purpose.

"Try the oxygen, señor," suggested one of the seamen, who was engaged in trying to revive one of his comrades.

Holmsby made the experiment almost in fear and trembling. To him the use of the gas was like treading . upon dangerous ground, but in the absence of the necessary fresh air the course seemed the only possible one.

To his unbounded delight the experiment proved successful, and Dick opened his eyes.

"Where am I ?   Am I still alive ? " he muttered fearfully.

"Alive, ay," replied Holmsby encouragingly, " and as safe as the Bank. Now lie still and don't ask any more questions for some time to come."

But Tresillian would not be quiet. Possibly the use of the oxygen hastened his recovery, for in less than a quarter of an hour from the time he opened his eyes, Dick was, to use his own words, " quite chirpy."

Meanwhile most of the Calderian crew had recovered from the effect of the terrible strain upon their nerves, for beyond a few slight contusions few had sustained injury. Don Carlos, the incapacitated lieutenant had, however, received a nasty gash across the forehead ; for, having his hand bound up in splints, he had been unable to take a secure hold when the *Amphibian* began her earthward flight.

As for Don Miguel O'Rourke, he, too, had partially recovered from his attack of abject terror, and lay on the floor crying silently, ignorant and heedless of the circumstances of his surroundings.

" I say, Rex, old fellow," began Dick, as Holmsby returned from holding a consultation with the engineer, " where are we ; and what has happened ? Don't be afraid to tell me, for I feel as fit as a fiddle."

" We fell, Dick—nearly crashed on top of one of the Talpican battleships. At present we are lying at the bottom of the sea in eleven fathoms of water."

" Lying *en perdu* till the enemy give us a chance

to ascend, I suppose. Then we can try the effect of a few more bombs."

" Lying here because there's no help for it, Dick. The *Amphibian* belies her name. As an airship, her days, I fear, are over."

" But we have still the submarine."

" True ; and what is more, I mean to let those Talpican rascals know it, if they give any more cause. They were not content with seeing the *Amphibian* fall helpless from the clouds, but they must needs prepare to hull her with their quick-firers at close range."

" Did they ? "

" No, but it wasn't their fault that they didn't."

" How is Don Miguel faring ? "

" Don't mention him," replied Holmsby con-temptuously. " He may be a most clever inventor, but he has no physical courage. His nerve failed him at the moment when it was most required."

" So did mine, Rex."

" But you are differently situated. You did not boast of revenge ; you did not aspire to taking this marvellous fighting machine into action : he did both, but when it came to the point—well, you saw what happened."

" What do you propose to do now ? "

" Do ? Why, carry out my promise to Don Miguel. Give him a fair chance to regain the presidency, support him as well as I can bring myself to do without losing my self-respect, and then, Dick, we'll make tracks for home."

" Is the *Amphibian* much damaged ? "

" The envelope is, I fear ; but the submarine part seems as sound as a bell. The motors, too, are in working order ; at least, so the engineer informs me, but the aerial propeller is done for. If you feel equal to it, look through the conning-tower scuttles and see the extent of the damage."

" Of course I feel equal to it," replied Tresillian, but as he rose to his feet Holmsby noticed that he staggered more than once.

The glare of the bright tropical sunshine was sufficient to penetrate the water even to the depth at which the stricken craft had sunk. Peering through the thick plate glass, Tresillian could form some idea of the extent of the damage.

The *Amphibian* was lying on an almost even keel, with her bows somewhat depressed and with a slight list to starboard. For quite twenty feet the fore turtle-back deck had been rent, the duralium plating resembling the jagged edge of a saw. Beyond this cavity, through which the helia from the five injured ballonettes had forced its way, no other fracture of the envelope was visible. Only one blade of the aerial propeller remained, but that was so badly twisted that it would be useless even had the *Amphibian* been capable of supporting herself in the air. The remaining ballonettes were sound, but useless for lifting purposes until the balance of the craft had been restored by the repair of at least two of the for'ard ones.

It was indeed fortunate that the two members of

the Calderian crew who had retained their senses had the presence of mind to open the valves of these compartments ere the *Amphibian* struck the water, otherwise the buoyant afterpart would have floated like a cork—an easy target to the guns of the Talpican fleet.

While the two Englishmen were looking through the scuttle, a polished cylinder, followed by a wake of eddying water and air-bubbles, flashed through the transparent sea barely twenty feet above the *Amphibian.*

" Heavens ! " exclaimed Tresillian. " A torpedo. The beggars are trying to settle our hash. Luckily we are too deep down for a torpedo to strike us, even when run at its maximum depth of submersion. I hope they won't attempt to use electro-contact mines, though."

"How have they spotted us ? "

" Probably they heaved a mark-buoy over the spot where we disappeared ; or we may be visible from their mastheads. It's remarkable how deep one can see from aloft in tropical seas. All right, my beauties," he exclaimed, as he made his way to the hatchway communicating with the forepart of the submarine. " I'll teach you a lesson."

The Calderian crew, now recovered from the effects of their fright, were at their posts. In a few moments the bow torpedo tube was launched back and a deadly cigar-shaped missile placed in the tray. Holmsby's only fear was that the weapon in leaving the tube would strike the débris of the aerial propeller, for owing to the injuries it had received it was found impossible to withdraw the shafting and feather the remaining blade.

Meanwhile the principal centrifugal pumps were engaged in throwing out the water that had made its way into the submarine through the improperly-closed valve ; and as soon as the huge metal cylinder began to grow " lively," Holmsby ordered the engineer to restart the motors.

He was now back in his place in the conning-tower, his right hand grasping the steering-wheel, his left on the lever controlling the horizontal planes, while his eyes were fixed upon the ap-parently unbroken expanse of semi-opaque water ahead. It mattered not to him whether the *Amphibian* was encumbered with a framework of useless plating, or whether she would never again soar in the air. His comrade's words rang in his ears : " We have still a submarine." A submarine ? Yes, and, by Jove, he meant to make good use of her.

Slowly the *Amphibian* rose from her ocean bed, then, gathering way, crept over the bottom of the sea—so close to it that the wash of her following wave stirred up a long wake of sand-discoloured water.

By sheer good luck the submarine was heading straight for the battleship *Libertad*. From the fore-bridge her navigating-officer saw the tell-tale swirl, and, in a panic, signalled to the engine-room for full-speed ahead. A warning blast from the syren of the

Paulo told him that his vessel was heading straight for her consort. There was not sufficient space to up or down helm. Full-speed astern ! With the foam bubbling in cascades on either side of her quarter the *Libertad* slowed down, stopped, then began to gather stern-way.

Suddenly Holmsby, from his post in the conning-tower, caught sight of a dark, indistinct mass looming through the water. It was the *Libertad.* Now he could discern the swirl of her port-propeller as it strove to check the momentum of the forward motion of the ship.

Slightly elevating the bows of the *Amphibian*, Holmsby gave the order to fire, and with a sharp detonation, followed by a characteristic hiss, the torpedo left the tube. The range was short—almost too close for the rule-of-thumb " margin of safety," but, being without a periscope and not daring to rise till the top of the conning-tower was awash in order to take his bearings, the sub-lieutenant was compelled to take the risk.

At that distance a miss was almost an impossibility. Ere the Calderian engineer could obey Holmsby's order to reverse the submarine, the deadly missile struck the Talpican warship fairly amidships and about twelve feet below the armoured belt.

Instantly there was a tremendous explosion, followed by another equally terrific as the primary shock affected the warship's magazine with disastrous effect.

The concussion caused the sea to be violently agitated. Even the submerged *Amphibian* rolled like a striken porpoise as she backed from the scene of her exploit.

The *Libertad* had been literally torn to pieces both above and below her armoured belt. Ere the fragments of metal had fallen from the immense height to which they had been hurled the shattered hull sank like a stone.

The result of the sharp stern lesson justified its application. Panic seized the surviving vessels of the Talpican squadron, and, steaming at full-speed ahead, their funnels belching out thick clouds of black smoke tinged with deep red flames, they headed for the doubtful security of Sta. Cruz Roads.

Reginald was perfectly satisfied with his victory. The Calderian coast had been freed from the presence of the powerful hostile fleet. Pursuit would have been useless, the *Amphibian* being, in her damaged condition, capable of doing a bare seven knots ; but the terror of the mysterious vessel that had dropped apparently crippled from the clouds and yet retained the means of sending one of their finest battleships to the bottom was sufficient to totally demoralise the Talpican fleet.

Slowly rising to the surface, the *Amphibian* shaped a course towards the harbour of Nalcuanho. In less than an hour, Calderia would have its former President within her territory. What would be the nature of his reception ?

CHAPTER XVIII

DON MIGUEL TAKES THE FIELD

"I FEEL quite sorry for that poor O'Rourke," exclaimed Dick. "He's sitting in his cabin looking the very picture of misery. I can quite sympathise with him."

"Yes, it's hard luck when you lose your nerve," agreed Holmsby, for now the excitement of the flight and subsequent attack was over the British officer looked at Don Miguel's failings in a different light to what he had hitherto done.

Holmsby had relinquished the wheel to the Calderian quartermaster on approaching the harbour of Nalcuanho. He had never before negotiated the intricate entrance, and, unwilling to take further risks, had left the navigation in the hands of those who were more capable of taking the crippled *Amphibian* betwixt the rocks and shoals that, for a distance of three miles, render the channel to the harbour of the capital of Calderia one of the most dangerous of all South American ports.

"Look here," continued Holmsby. "I'm

horribly sorry for the poor fellow, too. Suppose we try and buck him up."

It was a very dejected Don Miguel who rose to meet the two Englishmen as they knocked and entered his cabin. He was certainly calmer, but was still labouring under the agitation of his mind.

" Gentlemen," he began, " I must most deeply apologise——"

" No need, Don Miguel," exclaimed Holmsby briskly. " We have come to tell you that we are about to enter Nalcuanho Harbour. In another half an hour Calderia will greet its deliverer."

" Yourself."

" No, señor : you are the person whom I refer——"

" But after my regrettable——"

" That, señor, is a closed book. You can and must play your part."

" My part," repeated the Calderian bitterly. "My chance is gone. I am disgraced, not only in your eyes, but in the sight of my crew. In another hour the news will be shouted from all the house-tops of Nalcuanho. You, Mr. Holmsby, will be the hero of the Calderian people."

There was nothing hypocritical in Don Miguel's words. It was a straightforward declaration of incompetency. The man realised his position.

" Take another view of the situation," said Reginald. " Your chance is only just about to take place. It was your brains that evolved the

Amphibian—that you must admit ? Good. Now,
to continue : an unfortunate attack of nerves incapacitated you. More by sheer luck than anything else I managed to see this business through.
That was all. Both Mr. Tresillian and I saw your
state and knew the reason ; but of the crew,
though they saw you lying on the floor of the
conning-tower, none knew what had happened.
Supposing we treat your case as an injury to the
head received in action ? "

"You mean it, señor ? " asked Don Miguel, hope
reviving in his breast.

"Certainly. But, remember, another time you
must act the man. I'll say no more, Don Miguel.
We are nearly in harbour now, so pull yourself
together. For our part we'll do our utmost to
see you through."

With the Calderian ensign flying proudly in the
breeze, the shattered *Amphibian* passed between
the crowded pier-heads and moored alongside the
Inner Mole.

Calm and collected, yet deathly pale, Don Miguel
O'Rourke, dressed in his gorgeous uniform, accompanied by his two English companions, appeared
on deck.

In an instant Calderia recognised the commander of the vessel that had driven off the hostile
fleet as its former President, and, with loud and
repeated " Vivas," the crowd pressed and swayed
on the quay-side, their shouts absolutely drowning
the Calderian National Anthem that was being

played by a military band with all the power at
its command.

" You are all right now, señor," whispered Dick
encouragingly. " The people are solid for you."

As O'Rourke stepped ashore, the Alcalde greeted
him warmly in the name of the people, and,
almost mobbed by his enthusiastic compatriots,
the ex-President was carried shoulder high to a
carriage.

" Where are my English friends ? " he shouted,
and the cry was taken up by the crowd, " El
Englese, el Englese."

Reginald and Dick had modestly retired to the
seclusion of the *Amphibian's* conning-tower ; but
in spite of their protestations they were made to
come out of their retreat and escorted to the
carriage in which Don Miguel and the Alcalde were
already seated. Preceded by the band, and
escorted by the excited populace, who insisted
upon unharnessing the horses, the carriage was
drawn in triumph to the City Hall.

During this semi-regal progress, Don Miguel had
much food for reflection. He pictured the self-
same street a few short years ago, when he was
stealthily creeping along the deserted thoroughfare
by night to escape the fury of the mob, perchance
composed of the same men who were even now
cheering him to the echo.

As for Tresillian, who knew not the Calderian
temperament, he " rather enjoyed the fun," as he
afterwards expressed it ; but Holmsby, with his

characteristic manner, was making good use of his
eyes by noting the effect of the bombardment.

Altogether the Republic of Calderia was in a
strange predicament. There had been a revolution within a revolution. The Extremists, who
had been so active in the downfall of Don Miguel
O'Rourke, found that their ideas did not at all
coincide with those of the former co-revolution-
aries—the Retardists. There was a split. The
Extremists sought the aid of the neighbouring
Republic of Talpico, while the Retardists, com-
promising with the Moderates—the party who
wished for the recall of Don Miguel O'Rourke—
found themselves beset by the Talpican navy and
army and threatened by civil war to boot.

The subsequent bombardment of Nalcuanho,
though interrupted by the timely arrival of the
Amphibian, had caused considerable damage, not
only to the fortifications, but to municipal and
private buildings as well; but, curiously enough,
the popular outcry was not against the sister
republic but against the Extremists whose action
had been the means of causing the Talpican
invasion.

But though the city of Nalcuanho was for the
present relieved of the horrors of bombardment
and investment, a real danger still existed within
the boundaries of Calderia.

The Extremists, under the leadership of the
President of their choice, General Guzman Lopez,
held the southern portion of the Republic in con-

junction with the Talpican army. Even if the allies
did not carry out their boast of marching upon
Nalcuanho, no peace could be assured until the
work of driving the insurgents and their Talpican friends through the passes of Sierra was
accomplished.

Don Miguel could not have arrived at the capital
at a more opportune time. Amid the acclamations
of the populace, he was once more made President
without the necessity for an election—for the simple
reason that there was no one in Nalcuanho to
oppose him.

Steps were immediately taken for the suppression
of the insurrection and the expulsion of the Talpican
army. The Third Reserve was called out, the forces
of the Republic reorganised, and in less than a week
the Calderian troops were ready to take the field,
led by the President in person.

But during that week Don Miguel had been busy
in another direction. The *Amphibian*—the Republic's greatest asset—was being repaired, under
his personal supervision so as once more to bear her
part in the air; but, with considerable forethought,
it was given out that her sphere of operations would
be confined to the sea, with a view to making a
salutary attack upon the Talpican fleet.

This had the effect of keeping the fairly powerful
Talpican fleet within its harbours, for the *Amphibian*
was regarded with feelings of terror by the seamen
who had witnessed the appalling destruction of the
Libertad. Talpico had still a strong squadron,

whereas Calderia, with the exception of a few river gunboats, had no warships.

True to their word to see the President safely through, Reginald and Dick offered to accompany Don Miguel to the front.

"I have better work for you, señors," replied Don Miguel. "Within three days the *Amphibian* will, I trust, be again fit for service. Since you, Mr. Holmsby, know almost if not quite as much about the handling of her as I do myself, I wish that you will take command of her and bring her to the fighting-line. I am indeed grateful for your aid. Your advice to play the man I mean to follow. If, therefore, in action I am fated to fall, I trust it will be with my face to the foe. Should total defeat overtake my army, all will be lost as far as Calderia is concerned. My ambitions will be crushed, my life's work ended, for I vow never to leave the field alive and dishonoured. Should that unfortunate event take place, please understand that the *Amphibian* is yours to do with as you wish. Moreover, I have written to my agents in Paris—here is their address —telling them, in the event of my death, to hand over to both or either of you the documents relating to the secret of the composition of helia. Now I think I have made myself clear. To-morrow we set out for the frontier. Within a week we ought to be in touch with the enemy, and by that time I can hope for your co-operation with the *Amphibian*."

"Good luck to you, señor," exclaimed both

the Englishmen. "For our part we'll do our best."

At daybreak on the following morning the van of the Calderian army entrained, a single line of rails communicating with Estores—a town fifty miles from Nalcuanho on the edge of the vast plain that stretches from the Rio del Este to the foot of the sierras. Throughout the day train after train left the capital, each packed with troops. The men, though somewhat lacking in discipline, were full of ardour and well armed with modern rifles. The majority were mulattoes; a few of the picked regiments only being composed of creoles. Nevertheless, they compared favourably with the land-forces of the Republic of Talpico, and, under the usual conditions, could be relied upon to give a good account of themselves.

Loyally Holmsby and Tresillian stuck to their task of superintending the repairs to the *Amphibian*. Day and night they took turns to keep the Calderian workmen at high pressure till the reconstruction of the envelope and aerial propeller neared completion.

Every day for five days messengers reached the town of Estores with news of the advance of the army, whence the information was telegraphed to the capital; but on the sixth day came an ominous break in tidings from the front. Excitement was at fever-heat, but throughout the tension of public alarm the Englishmen kept cool and collected, directing their attentions solely to the matter entrusted to their care ; and at daybreak on the morning of the seventh day following Don Miguel's departure, the *Amphibian* rose majestically in the air and headed towards the distant sierras.

CHAPTER XIX

THE VINDICATION OF THE PRESIDENT

IN less than seven hours the *Amphibian* covered the distance that had taken the Calderian army seven tedious days to accomplish, and shortly before noon the blue outlines of the rugged sierras appeared in sight.

Holmsby had already given the order to clear for action. The quick-firers were placed in position, and every man was at his post, equipped with a neutraliser in the event of a catastrophe to the airship, the speed having been reduced to twenty miles an hour so as to enable those on the promenade-deck to conduct their observations in comparative comfort.

It was a broiling day. The sun's rays poured vertically upon the huge bulk of the *Amphibian*, and in spite of the draught caused by her passage through the air, the metal deck plates and stanchions were almost too hot to touch with the hand, while the rubber-soled shoes of the officers and crew were rendered almost viscous by contact with the deck.

Suddenly above the sharp buzz of the aerial

propeller, Tresillian detected the long-drawn sound of artillery and musketry fire.

"They've started, Rex," exclaimed Dick, pointing to the still distant range of mountains.

"Eh? What direction? Where's my glass?"

"Away more to the right, I fancy," replied Tresillian, handing his comrade his binoculars. "Can you see anything?"

"By Jove, I can," replied Holmsby. "One of the armies, at any rate."

"Then where's the other?"

"Entrenched or hiding in the long grass, I fancy. But what a one-sided place to choose for a battle: where the mountains meet the plain. One side is nothing but good cover and the other is as flat as a table."

Side by side the two Englishmen stood looking through their glasses at the still-indistinct line of grey-coated troops while the *Amphibian's* course had been altered so as to take her to the scene of battle.

Presently Holmsby brought his open hand down heavily upon the stanchion rail.

"Now I see what it is," he exclaimed. "We're a trifle too late to be of much use. That line we see is in reality both armies. They are having a fine set-to, but, by George, what a disregard for all modern tactics."

In a very short space the *Amphibian* was hovering over the battlefield at an elevation of nearly five hundred feet. It was as Holmsby had remarked, a hand-to-hand fight : the science of present-day warfare was totally lacking.

Don Miguel had opened the attack earlier in the day by a furious cannonade upon the Talpican defences. The invaders, possessing only light mountain artillery, were completely outranged, but in spite of their terrible ordeal stuck gamely to their trenches and the splendid cover afforded by the natural ruggedness of the ground at the base of the sierras.

At length, after four hours' incessant artillery fire, Don Miguel, unable to restrain the ardour of his troops, gave the order for a general attack, and no sooner did the bugles blare out the advance than the whole army, save the artillery, dashed forward with the utmost *élan*.

The sight of their advancing foes was enough for the Talpican soldiers. They, too, did not hesitate, but, firing an irregular volley at 800 metres, rushed pell-mell to engage their attackers.

The total length of the line of attack was barely two miles, the men being bunched together in close formation instead of the recognised open order, and in less than ten minutes from the beginning of the Calderian advance the opposing forces met.

It was more like a conflict between two savage tribes than a battle between two armies equipped with modern weapons. Beyond the first two or three straggling volleys few shots were fired on either side, but with bayonet, clubbed rifle, or the equally formidable machete, the foes met in deadly earnest.

Up and up swarmed the light grey clad soldiers of Calderia, only to be hurled back by the dark grey troops of Talpico, till the long line of struggling men appeared like a vast writhing serpent when viewed from the *Amphibian*, whose crew could see everything with the greatest ease, yet could not lift a finger to help in the conflict lest they should injure friend as well as foe.

Slowly yet surely the Talpicans gave back under the relentless fury of their attackers, but even as they did so the ground was dotted with grey figures, silent in death or writhing in agony.

Unseen in the heat of the battle the *Amphibian* hovered above the hardly-contested field, the Calderian crew hardly able to control their feelings at the undoubted success of their compatriots, while the Englishmen, calm and collected, were trying to distinguish the figure of Don Miguel O'Rourke. There was nothing to give them any sign of the President's presence, for neither side bore the colours of their respective republics, while officers and men were, in active service, dressed almost alike, the former being invariably dismounted.

Suddenly the left wing of the Calderian army began to give back. The Talpican right flank, reinforced by the rebel Extremists, instantly took advantage of the retrograde movement and pushed home a counter-attack with irresistible force till the light greys turned and fled in utmost disorder·

The cries of dismay and rage from the crew of the *Amphibian* increased when they saw the Calderian centre begin to waver. Should the panic spread, the day would be hopelessly lost. Some of the men went so far as to beseech Holmsby to drop one of the high explosive bombs upon the Talpican wing ; but this he sternly refused to do, knowing that in the terrific explosion friend as well as foe would be involved in certain destruction.

" We'll drop to within 30 metres," he assured his crew. " No doubt the mere sight of the *Amphibian* will turn the fortunes of the day."

" Look ! " exclaimed Dick. " There is Don Miguel."

" Where ? "

" Stand here and look just above this stanchion More to the left—do you see that knot of men wedging their way into the dark grey troops ? See that man with his handkerchief bound round his head ? That's O'Rourke : I saw it was he when he turned his face just now."

" So it is, by Jove ! " said Holmsby. " He's fairly in the thick of it."

The sub-lieutenant spoke truly. Almost surrounded by the hostile troops, the butt of every bayonet and clubbed rifle within arm's length, the President of Calderia seemed to bear a charmed life. Already a bullet had grazed his forehead, but maddened rather than hurt by the wound he threw himself into the thickest of his foes. Nothing seemed able to withstand the sweep of his sword, while his example served to encourage his discomfited followers. Taking heart they rallied, and by a supreme effort thrust back their opponents till the Calderian centre pierced the Talpican line.

Meanwhile the enemy's right flank had strayed far from its original position in pursuit of the demoralised wing. Unless the fugitives could be brought to rally, the centre would be threatened with a flank attack.

" It's about time we stopped this useless slaughter, Dick," exclaimed Holmsby. " We'll give them a shot or two."

With the Calderian ensign floating proudly aft, the *Amphibian* swooped down to within two hundred feet of the ground, and at Holmsby's order the crew let fly two rounds with the fore quick-firer, the shells bursting harmlessly at a distance of three hundred yards to the rear of the Talpican centre.

Although the rifle firing was very desultory, cold steel doing most of the work, the din raised by the combatants almost drowned the sharp reports of the airship's gun. But the detonations were sufficient to attract attention. Both sides temporarily ceased their desperate attack and counter-attack and gazed skywards.

A yell that was meant for a cheer burst from the throats of the Calderian troops, while the Talpican forces, having a wholesome dread of the vessel that had paralysed their naval strength, gave back and soon broke into headlong flight.

Most of the Talpican officers made for their horses, mounted and galloped off for dear life, leaving their men to shift for themselves. Throwing away their arms as they ran, the fugitive soldiers made for the mountain pass, the mouth of which was barely two miles from the field of battle. Had Holmsby wished he could have dropped a high explosive charge into the gorge and sealed the demoralised invaders in a trap ; but this he humanely refused to allow his crew to do. Even as it was, many of the fugitives were shot down by their victorious pursuers, who gave no quarter, ferociously slaughtering every wounded Talpican they came across.

" What bloodthirsty brutes ! " ejaculated Tresillian, as he gazed at the scene of slaughter below them.

" They are," assented Reginald. " It's their nature. During their war of independence a hundred years ago their forefathers fought thus, giving and expecting no quarter, and a century of republicanism has apparently changed them but little."

" This will end the war, I think," said Dick. " Those unlucky beggars have had quite enough. The question is, Rex, what are we going to do now ? "

" Do ? Go home again, of course. I've carried out the instructions of my superiors to investigate— although I don't mind telling you I fancy I've somewhat exceeded my orders—so there's nothing left but to return and make out my report."

" You're following the example of Nelson at Copenhagen, Rex—interpreting your orders in a somewhat peculiar manner."

" Then I hope the sequel will be as successful, old man. Even Nelson would have found himself in a hole had he bungled over the business. But what's amiss now ? "

Several of the crew grouped upon the forepart of the promenade-deck were gesticulating violently and pointing in the direction of the tallest peak of the sierras. Following the direction indicated, Reginald and Dick simultaneously gave vent to a surprised whistle.

Soaring over the mountains, and looking like a small dot in the brilliant sky, was an airship.

CHAPTER XX

TREACHERY IN THE AIR

" WHAT'S her little game, I wonder," exclaimed Holmsby. "An airship in these
parts is a bit of a novelty. We must push forward
and see what her intentions are."

" Hadn't we better signal to Don Miguel first ? "
asked Tresillian. "It would be well to warn him,
since I don't suppose she is yet visible from the
ground."

" It will mean descending again till we get within
hailing distance," objected Holmsby. "Since the
wireless telephone was knocked out of gear during
our fall from the sky we have to rely upon the
megaphone or the semaphore. During that time
this mysterious craft will have sailed right above us,
and that is like the advantage of the weather-gage
in the good old days of sailing line-of-battleships.
So up we go."

Ordering another helia charge to be inserted in
one of the reserve ballonettes, Holmsby took his
place in the conning-tower. In a few minutes the
Amphibian rose vertically to a height of 3000 metres

and at a speed of ten knots forged ahead to meet her supposed rival.

"Stand by with the for'ard quick-firer," was Holmsby's next order in Spanish. "But don't fire till I give the word."

The oncoming craft was now clearly visible. She was at least four hundred feet in length, and of the non-rigid type. She differed greatly in appearance from the *Amphibian*, having a slung platform in place of the latter's promenade-deck, while the motive power was imparted to four propellers, two on either side of the long "nacelle." On this platform were three fairly large deck-houses, the foremost being triangular in shape so as to offer less resistance to the wind. As far as Holmsby could see, she carried no guns, but on each side of the for'ard deck-house was a search-light, capable of throwing a beam well ahead with a good elevation, abeam, or vertically downwards.

When within half a mile the strange airship suddenly ported her helm, and, describing a half-circle, brought up broadside on to the *Amphibian*. As she did so the stars and stripes of the U.S.A. fluttered in the breeze.

Holmsby immediately put his helm hard-a-starboard, with the result that the two vessels were now slowly gliding in parallel lines at a distance of about eight hundred yards apart.

"Airship ahoy!" hailed Reginald, who had gained the promenade-deck. "What craft is that?"

" The *Black Eagle* of Boston, U.S.A.," was the reply, every word being clearly audible in the rarefied air in spite of the intervening distance. " Is Don Miguel O'Rourke on board ? "

" No," replied Holmsby, surprised at the question.

" Then I reckon I'm tongue-wagging with Sub-Lootenant Reginald Holmsby ? "

" You are," assented Reginald, still more surprised at the American's latest question. " How did you know my name ? "

" Well, considering that you and Mr. Tresillian have had your names given in every paper as being kidnapped by an airship belonging to Don Miguel, it's not to be wondered at."

" We heard we were dead."

" P'raps," replied the American. " But we're here to see something of the scrap : all picture rights reserved for the Boston and Salem Electric Star Picture Company."

" Take care you don't get a shot through your gas-bag," cautioned Reginald. " It's a risky business getting within rifle range."

During the conversation the two craft had converged, so that they were now less than two hundred yards apart. There were four men only visible upon the platform of the *Black Eagle*, the individual who had hailed leaning against the bulkhead of the 'midship cabin.

" Say, are you certain the President isn't aboard your hooker ? " he continued.

" I said he was not," replied Holmsby, somewhat nettled at being doubted.

" That's a great pity."

" Why ? " asked Holmsby.

" This ! " shouted the man, dodging behind a
screen.

Before Holmsby could act or even utter a warning shout a flash followed by a deafening report
leapt from the 'midship cabin of the airship, and
a two-pounder shell struck the *Amphibian* just
abaft the conning-tower.   Penetrating two of the
ballonettes and one side of the inner shell that
formed the body of the submarine it burst with a
terrific detonation, shaking the *Amphibian* like a
leaf from bow to stern.

Giving a sharp list to port the victim of the
treacherous attack began to drop rapidly earthwards, while, simultaneously with the discharge
of another gun, the projectile of which skimmed
harmlessly over the *Amphibian's* deck-rail, the
mysterious airship dropped several bags of ballast
and shot upwards for nearly another thousand feet.

Even as she did so three men emerged from the
deck-house and waved their hands at the stricken
Amphibian.

In the midst of peril both Holmsby and Tresillian
recognised the miscreants—they were the oceu-
pants of motor-car F.O. 445.

Fortunately the engineer, in response to Holmsby's orders, thrust another helia cylinder into
another of the reserve ballonettes, which had been

unaffected by the concussion, and at less than three hundred feet from the ground the *Amphibian* recovered herself, though still retaining a decided list.

" Let her down gently," ordered the sub., and with hardly a tremor as the helia hissed through the valves the *Amphibian* sank gently to earth on a broad ledge betwixt two towering peaks of the sierras. By this time the treacherous airship, heading rapidly southwards, had vanished beyond the saw-like crests of the mountains.

Directly the vessel was made fast bow and stern, the Englishmen, accompanied by the engineer and the bo'sun, entered the wrecked portion of the submarine. No doubt the rogues thought that the gas in the *Amphibian's* ballonettes was highly inflammable, and that the explosion of the shell would ignite the contents of the envelope ; but, although they saw that the anticipated disaster did not take place, they were convinced that their diabolical plan had succeeded inasmuch as the *Amphibian* appeared to fall, completely wrecked, upon the jagged rocks of the sierras.

The damage was serious enough. The projectile had bored a small circular hole through the metal plating of the submarine, but had failed to penetrate the other side ; the explosion had practically wrecked the whole of the interior abaft the central compartments.

The motors had been rendered unserviceable, the main shafting was fractured in places, while the stores, flung from their duralium cases, littered the floor, the provisions being badly spoiled by the thick brown dust from the explosion.

The Calderian engineer burst into tears and began wringing his hands at the sight of his crippled motors. They were done for, he declared —they would never be of use again. The *Amphibian*, perched half-way up the precipitous sides of the mountain, would be helpless.

" It might have been worse, Rex," said Tresillian. " Imagine the result if the shell had burst in the for'ard part where all our explosives are stored."

" It's a mystery to me how the concussion failed to explode them," replied Holmsby gravely. " We've still a lot to be thankful for."

" What's to be done now ? "

" Done ! why to get back to Nalcuanho as soon as we can," said Reginald resolutely.

" How ? We can't use the motors."

" True ; but where there's a will there's a way We must wait for a favourable breeze, and then we'll sail back. The *Amphibian* is still capable of being supported in the air; it is merely a question of time."

" Time, yes : but in the meantime we may starve."

" Dick, you are a confounded pessimist. Have faith."

" Faith won't feed an empty stomach, my dear fellow."

" Think yourself fortunate that you still have

the faculty of feeling the pangs of hunger. Now to work. I'll send in some of the crew and you can see that they clear this awful muddle away. Examine the stores; if they are spoiled, heave them overboard. We can't afford to carry useless lumber. If not, put them by. Meanwhile I'll see if the outer envelope and the two damaged ballonettes can be temporarily repaired."

" All right, Rex. I'll do my part. But when we reach the capital what do you propose to do ? "

" Do ? Why, what do you think I ought to do ? I'll tell you. In less than a week after our return the *Amphibian*, with myself in command, will be off in pursuit of the treacherous airship. I fancy I've a few old scores to pay off against Messrs. F.O. 445 & Co."

" Rex, I thought you were not revengeful," said Tresillian in mock reproach.

" Neither am I. But you can't always twist a dog's tail and not expect him to bite. Now, I'm off. Keep those fellows at it, for every moment is precious."

So saying Holmsby re-entered the central compartment and, ascending the iron ladder, gained the promenade-deck. It was a strange sight that met his gaze. The *Amphibian* was lying upon a broad ledge of grass-grown earth that was shut in on three sides by the almost sheer cliffs towering to a height of three thousand feet. On the remaining side was a corresponding drop of over a thousand feet. Far below, Holmsby could see a fertile valley through which a mountain torrent leapt like a silvery thread till lost to sight behind a rugged spur. Beyond the valley the mountains towered almost as high as the one on the side of which the *Amphibian* had found a place of refuge.

"This place is well sheltered from all but northerly winds," thought the young officer. "And a north wind is not what we want. The bother is that with a favourable breeze there will be no wind at all on this side of the cliff, or, what is worse, a baffling eddy. Ah, that reminds me. If the so-called *Black Eagle* should return and drop half a hundredweight of explosives on the *Amphibian* while she's lying here it would be a case with us, I fancy. I think I'll send a man up the cliff to keep a look out—No, I won't, by Jove. I'll go myself."

"Dick!" he shouted down the hatchway. "I'm going aloft."

"Aloft, where?" replied Tresillian, who was busily engaged with some of the crew in shovelling a sticky mixture of calcined bread and oil and dust into buckets.

"Up the cliff. I'm going to have a look round."

"Shall I come with you?"

"Better not."

"Is it safe?"

"Safe as anything. I'll be back in less than a couple of hours."

Taking with him his revolver and twenty-four rounds of ammunition, a pocket compass and his binoculars, Holmsby gained the ground by means of a rope ladder, while one of the crew followed with two neutralisers.

Both of these the sub-lieutenant fastened to his back. One was charged; the other, for use in case of emergency, was not; while, as an additional precaution, Holmsby thrust four spare cylinders into his coat pocket. In his hand he carried a short staff shod with a steel point and bent prong somewhat resembling a boat-hook.

Giving one upward glance to see that no projecting crags impeded his way, Holmsby leapt. Fully fifty feet he shot up, then, as he was on the point of returning earthwards, a gentle thrust with the pole gave him a fresh impetus. It was exhilarating yet almost tireless, Holmsby thought, as, leaping from crag to crag, taking advantage of every crevice and assisting his ascent by clutching at the tufts of coarse grass that festooned the face of the cliff, he rapidly left the *Amphibian* far beneath him.

In exactly fifty-five minutes from the commencement of his climb, Holmsby reached the summit of the cliff, and, holding on to the scanty herbage, lay at full length in order to remove and secure the still buoyant neutraliser.

There was no sign of the treacherous airship. As far as he could see there was nothing but a saw-like ridge of gaunt peaks, some considerably higher than the rest being snow-capped.

" There's not a thing that I can lash this contrivance to," remarked Reginald to himself, as he looked about him. " I don't want the thing to break away and soar skywards, even though I've a spare neutraliser. Well, I suppose I must drive this spiked staff into a cleft in the rock and make the thing fast to it."

Acting on his impulse, Holmsby rose to his feet and began to walk cautiously along the mountain-top, but, though rugged, there was no fissure deep enough to receive the pole and keep it securely.

Suddenly a gust of wind swept over the summit of the cliff. Holmsby heard it whistling ere the blast reached him, and, realising his danger, threw himself forward. But owing to the retarding influence of the neutraliser the movement was necessarily slow. Before he could secure a grip the gust caught him, and, lifted like a feather, he was in a moment whirled far out over the cliff. Beneath him was a sheer drop of nearly four thousand feet.

CHAPTER XXI

THE PRESIDENT'S CHOICE

DESPERATELY gripping his boat-hook like the proverbial drowning man grasps at a straw, Holmsby found himself being twisted and turned in all directions by the powerful wind-eddies. At first he feared that he would be swept far across the valley to the corresponding range of mountains; but by degrees he felt himself dropping lower and lower till the cliff from which he had been hurled began to break the force of the wind. His descent was more direct and rapid now that he had struck a belt of comparatively still air. Yet this rate of his downward fall was not great enough to cause him any discomfort beyond the anxiety as to what would happen when he reached the ground.

The descent was even more exhilarating than the ascent, and Reginald found himself wondering whether the general use of the neutraliser would in days to come evolve a new pastime. Ski-ing and tobogganing were not to be compared with it, he decided.

As he neared the ground the air in the lower

part of the vast gorge was considerably denser than at the greater altitude, and in consequence his fall was retarded to such an extent that the impact with the ground occasioned him little more discomfort than a leap of six feet under ordinary conditions.

Holmsby had fallen at least two hundred yards from the base of the cliff, the intervening distance being thick with thorn-bushes. Realising that it would be a matter of considerable difficulty to crawl through this almost impassable barrier, hampered as he was, Reginald decided to release the remainder of the helia charge from the neutraliser.

Over and over again he had to retrace his steps and attempt another route, while at times the bushes were so tall and thickly leaved that the towering cliff and the blue sky over his head were both invisible, but, guided by his compass, Holmsby stuck gamely to his task.

It took him quite half an hour to traverse two hundred yards, and it was with feelings of relief that he found himself on an open space close to the base of the cliff. Evidently this was a path through the mountain-pass, for there were signs of horse-traffic, although not sufficient to check the growth of weeds and thistles. A little to his right was a scar or projecting ledge of rock beyond which the rough path was lost to sight.

" Although these neutralisers are marvellous devices they are a regular nuisance," he remarked, as he began to recharge the one that had served him so well. "Why can't they be charged from the front ? I am afraid I shall have to use it in the same manner as Dick when he escaped from our old acquaintances in F.O. 445."

Just then the withered stump of a tree caught his glance.

"Good idea. I'll lash the neutraliser to this tree, charge it, and slip the belts over my shoulder. Then I can cut away the lashings and make a fresh start."

Acting on this inspiration, Holmsby walked over to the stump and tested its condition. It was sound enough for his purpose. But when he searched for some cord, which he had felt certain he had placed in one of his pockets before starting, the desired article was not to be found.

"I must sacrifice my handkerchief, I suppose ; and here are some withies—as strong as an inch rope," he thought.

Just as Holmsby had securely fastened the neutraliser in position and was about to insert the helia cylinder, the distant clatter of horses' hoofs caught his ear. There was no time to unlash the metal case, so, hastily covering it with a handful of rushes, the sub. made a dash for cover behind the intervening crag.

Nearer and nearer came the sound, now sharp as the iron-shod hoofs struck the bare rock, now deadened as they sank upon the soft earth ; but just as Holmsby expected the horsemen to appear in view, he heard a voice exclaim in Spanish, " Halt ! "

"This is a regular nuisance," said Reginald to himself. " I don't want to be penned up here for the next hour or so while those fellows are having a meal. I may as well have a look at them and see who they are."

Holmsby looked at the crag above him. Close to where he stood was a fissure extending in a diagonal direction almost to the top of the rock, a distance of twenty feet from the ground. Stealthily he ascended, making good use of his steel-shod pole, till, unnoticed and unheard, he gained the summit of the projecting ledge. Here, without much fear of discovery, he could command an almost uninterrupted view of what was going on beneath him.

There were nearly a dozen Talpican irregular cavalry ; some were engaged in collecting wood for a fire, others were hobbling their horses and unloading their packs ; but two of them, evidently officers, were talking in a threatening manner to a prisoner.

The prisoner was Don Miguel O'Rourke.

The President of Calderia was in a most un-dignified position. He was on horseback, his legs fastened under the animal, his arms secured behind his back, while a guerrilla with his rifle grounded stood ten feet behind him.

Don Miguel showed no signs of fear ; there was a

look of haughty indifference on his face, although he answered his captors readily enough.

" You see, señor," said one of the officers. " You are entirely in our power. Consider your position. Your wonderful airship is hopelessly destroyed, your English friends are dead, but that is a pity since I should like to see them taken prisoners and shot as filibusters. We make no secret of the fact that Don Robiera Sanchez, who, after attempting to prevent the *Amphibian* from leaving England, came here in the airship *Sol d'Este*, was responsible for that achievement. His mechanical skill and ingenuity almost rival your own. But to proceed. Our fleet, now free from attack, will proceed to Nalcuanho and complete the work that it had begun. Talpico will have ceded to her the territory she demands, and in return Don Robiera Sanchez will occupy the presidential chair of Calderia. Now, this is our alternative. Give us the secret of the mysterious agency that enabled you to raise the *Amphibian* from the depths of the sea——"

" Never, señor——"

" Not so fast, Señor O'Rourke. Either the secret or the garotte. Picture yourself in the centre of the Plaza, the public indignity, the first squeeze of the instrument—and, señor, having your throat compressed by an ever-tightening metal collar is not at all pleasant—then a hasty burial in an unmarked grave."

" Three times you have placed your base pro-

posal before me, señor," replied Don Miguel
calmly. " In every case my reply has been, and
will be, the same. I, perchance, have failed, but
there are others to carry on my work. Rest
assured that the desired secret will never be known
to any Talpican, nor will Talpico occupy a foot
of Calderian territory unhindered while a single
Calderian remains in arms. So, I beg of you, save
your breath for other purposes."

" *Caramba!* To-morrow you'll tell another tale,
Señor O'Rourke. We rest here this night; at
sunrise we start again, and ere noon will be at El
Cayo. See, the sun is sinking behind the sierras.
Take heed lest you see it set for the last time."

During this conversation Holmsby's brain was
actively thinking. Don Miguel must be rescued—
but how ? One way would be to recover the
neutraliser, scale the cliff, and bring the crew of the
Amphibian to the aid of their President ; but the
risk of Holmsby being discovered, and also the fact
that night was approaching, negatived the proposal.
There was another way.

Placing his spare cartridges beside him on the
rock, and making a cursory examination of his
revolver, Holmsby braced himself for the coming
ordeal. He had no qualms at suddenly opening
fire on the unsuspecting guerrillas, since they had
threatened their helpless captive with death. Also,
he was perfectly aware that had either he or Tresillian fallen into their hands they would have been
summarily shot.

Resting the barrel of his weapon upon the edge of the rock, Holmsby depressed the muzzle till the sights were in line with the intersection of the guerrilla captain's cross-belts. A gaudy clasp on one of the leather straps made a splendid mark, yet the Englishman hesitated to press the trigger.

The Talpican was indisposed to leave his captive in peace.

" You dog—obstinate mule ! " he exclaimed. " I am of a mind to have you whipped to help you change your mind. Curse you ! Why do you treat me as dirt ? Why won't you answer ? "

Urging his horse nearer to the captive the guerrilla captain raised his clenched fist. Holmsby could not see Don Miguel's face, but by his attitude it seemed that the President never quailed.

Before the threatened blow fell, the Englishman pressed the trigger, the heavy weapon kicked, and ere the bluish haze had cleared away, the coward lay writhing on the ground. Five times more the revolver spat viciously, and all but one shot took effect.

Jerking open the chambers and allowing the ejector to throw out the still smoking cylinders, Holmsby began to reload ; but before he had completed this operation the survivors of the party were in flight. Some leapt into their saddles, others crouching ran by the side of their horses abandoning their fallen comrades, baggage, and prisoner in their panic to escape from what they imagined to be a numerous party in ambush.

But to Holmsby's consternation the steed upon which Don Miguel was bound began to follow the fugitives—hesitatingly at first, then increasing its speed. It was a risk, but the Englishman took it. Raising his revolver he aimed rapidly and deliberately at the retreating animal and fired. The horse staggered a few yards, sank on its forelegs, and rolled over on the ground with Don Miguel still bound in the saddle.

Sliding from his elevated position with more haste than caution, Holmsby gained the ground and ran to aid the Calderian President.

With another shot he put the struggling animal out of his misery, then with a swift slash of his knife severed the thongs that bound O'Rourke's ankles.

" Señor Holmsby ! " gasped the rescued man in astonishment.

" Hurt, señor ? " asked Reginald, who saw that Don Miguel's face was deathly white.

" My leg is broken, I am afraid," replied the President. " The horse falling on it—but I heard you were killed ? "

" Never in better health. The fresh air of the sierras suits me," assented Holmsby. " But we must be off in case these rogues pluck up courage and return. In another quarter of an hour you will be safely on board the *Amphibian*, I hope."

" The *Amphibian* ? Do I hear aright ? "

" Certainly, in spite of what you have just heard from that rascal," replied Holmsby, pointing to the motionless form of the guerrilla captain. " She's damaged—badly, I fear—but I have hopes of getting her back to Nalcuanho. Now, Don Miguel, let me assist you."

The President, however, could not put his foot to the ground. His fears were realised : his ankle was broken.

Holmsby looked upwards at the dizzy heights, then at the sky. The sun had disappeared behind the sierras, and darkness might set in at any moment.

" There's no harm in trying it," he muttered, and, darting off, he made his way to the spot where he had concealed his neutralisers.

Strapping one to Don Miguel's back, he charged it, then, replacing the one he had previously worn, Holmsby requested his companion to insert the helia cylinder. This done he picked up two rifles that the guerrillas had left in their flight and withdrew their ramrods. These he bound tightly to O'Rourke's injured limb, at the same time passing a leather belt under the patient's foot, so as to take the strain in mid-air.

" Now, señor," exclaimed Reginald.   " Hold on tightly to me, and grin and bear it. Either we gain the *Amphibian* in another ten minutes or we will have to spend a most uncomfortable night with those dead Talpicans for company."

" I am ready," replied the President.   " But can you manage to climb up with me on your back ? "

" I'll have a good shot at it," said Holmsby resolutely.   " Look here—I suppose we can't place two cylinders in one neutraliser ? I have some spares."

" It's not worth the risk," replied Don Miguel. " There are two dangers : too much buoyancy and also the great possibility of the appliance bursting."

" Then that settles it," rejoined Reginald. " I don't fancy a thousand-foot drop. So, stand by— now."

And, kicking off with a vigorous thrust, Holmsby with his companion gripping him round the shoulders, began the hazardous ascent.

CHAPTER XXII

THE PERILS OF THE ABYSS

UP and up the almost sheer cliff Holmsby
made his way, taking advantage of every
convenient crevice or projection. Often he was
compelled to stop, clutch at the rock with one hand
while he wiped from his eyes the particles of dust
that fell from above.

For the first five hundred feet the ascent was
comparatively easy, although more than once
Reginald had to ask his companion not to clasp
him so tightly. Beyond that neither man spoke,
nor durst they look down at the yawning gulf
beneath them.

Holmsby was practically supporting a dead
weight of a pound—the difference between the
combined weight of the two men and the upward
force of the neutralisers. It seemed but slight, but
to lift even a pound up a vertical height of one
thousand feet was in itself a severe strain.

Gradually it began to dawn upon the sub-
lieutenant that something was amiss, but trying
to console himself that it was the telling effect of the
continuous strain, he stuck to his stupendous task

with determination. But ere he gained another hundred feet the truth became apparent : one of the neutralisers was leaking.

Resolving not to say a word to alarm his companion, Reginald held on to a rock and rested a few moments ere he resumed his strenuous efforts, but his anxiety not to inform Don Miguel of the impending danger was relieved when the latter exclaimed :

"*Dios*, Señor Holmsby ! My neutraliser is almost exhausted."

"I feared that it had been getting weaker for some time past. But courage; it is only a short distance to the summit."

Reginald spoke boldly, but he knew full well that it was a full three hundred feet to the broad ledge on which the *Amphibian* rested.

"Perchance the charge has been in use for some time," suggested O'Rourke.

"Impossible. I put a fresh cylinder into the neutraliser you are wearing. But I have some more in reserve. Can we recharge the thing now ? "

"We must be careful to allow the helia to totally escape," said Don Miguel. "But what is to happen to us in the meantime ? One neutraliser will not suffice for both."

"I see a fairly wide cleft just above us," exclaimed Holmsby. "So hold on while I make another effort."

It was now as if Holmsby were climbing alone without the aid of the neutraliser, and burdened in addition with a load on his back. Scrambling, clutching, heaving, and raising himself by sheer physical strength, he climbed foot by foot, his breath coming in laboured gasps.

" Good-bye, old comrade," exclaimed Don Miguel suddenly. " It's too much for us both. I'm going to let go."

" You'll do nothing of the sort," gasped Reginald. " Hang on like grim death. I'm still going strong."

" No, Señor Holmsby, I know you cannot do it, burdened by my weight ; so good-bye once more."

" Stop that," almost shouted the Englishman in desperation. " Stop that and hold on, or—or, I'll punch your head ! " Ludicrous as the threat was under the circumstances, O'Rourke gave in to his companion's superior will, and Holmsby at length succeeded in gaining the scanty shelter afforded by the fissure in the face of the cliff. With a groan of utter bodily exhaustion he placed his living burden on the slightly-shelving rock and threw himself down beside his almost helpless companion.

It was indeed a place of refuge and that was all. The cleft was about four feet in height and three in breadth and extended inwards till the sloping floor met the also converging roof at a distance of not more than ten feet from the edge. Besides sloping outwards, the floor was fairly smooth, affording no foothold save the slight projection which Holmsby had made good use of when gaining the place of shelter. A slip would result in a headlong plunge upon the rocks several hundred feet below.

Cautiously loosening the valve of Don Miguel's

neutraliser, Reginald allowed the remaining helia to escape and then withdrew the porcelain cylinder. It was perfectly dry. The fault lay not in the exhaustion of the chemical but in the fact that the water in the apparatus had either leaked or evaporated.

" All the spare charges we have will not help us now," exclaimed O'Rourke.

" Then it cannot be helped," replied Holmsby. " Supposing I give those fellows above a hail. They will either lower a rope or else another neutraliser.

Both men shouted again and again, but no welcome response came in answer to their appeal for aid. Strange as it may seem, the *Amphibian*, tucked away on the ledge, was completely inaccessible by waves of sound travelling upwards along the face of the cliff.

" Look here ! " exclaimed Holmsby, after a few minutes' anxious wait. " I'll scale the remaining part of the cliff and bring assistance. My neutraliser is still active."

" For Heaven's sake don't leave me here helpless and alone," implored Don Miguel, his courage failing him after a struggle to keep up his spirits.

" Nonsense, man," exclaimed Reginald, almost roughly. " It's the only thing to be done unless we have to stay in this hole for the night."

" I cannot," almost screamed the now nerveless man. " The horrible gulf seems to want to drag me into its depths. Don't leave me, señor, I implore you."

" Very well, then," replied Reginald savagely, for, iron-nerved himself, the sight of a man in a pure funk always exasperated him. " We must make the best of it ; but I warrant you'll be sorry for it before morning."

Since there was no place to secure his neutraliser, Holmsby released the remaining helia and un-strapped the apparatus. Then, better able to gain a footing on the shelving ledge, he gently dragged his helpless comrade as far from the brink as possible. He knew what to expect when a man with a broken limb has to pass many long and weary hours with-out medical attention ; so to safeguard himself as well as his companion, Holmsby deftly passed the strap of O'Rourke's neutraliser round the ankles of the late wearer, placing the second belt in readiness should it be required.

Barely had he completed these preparations when the brief twilight deepened into night and intense darkness brooded over the valley. Though the horror of the gloomy depth beneath was hidden from sight, the thought of the awful gulf but a foot from where they were lying remained. Sleep was, of course, impossible, since the slightest involuntary movement might result in the two unfortunate men rolling over the brink of the tremendous cliff.

" Are you hungry ? " asked Holmsby, after a while, anxious to break the dismal silence.

" Not very," replied Don Miguel. " Though it was early this morning since I had anything to eat. You see we started the attack upon the Talpican position at six. But I am thirsty—my throat seems as if it's full of burning sand."

This was a bad sign, Holmsby thought. He would have given much to have one of Don Miguel's injectors at the present moment. Had he one he would not have hesitated to render its inventor insensible and risked the remainder of the ascent in the darkness in order to obtain aid. He was also curious to learn the circumstances under which the President had fallen into the hands of the Talpicans, but, forbearing under present circumstances to question O'Rourke on this point, he wisely determined to let that information stand over.

Slowly the hours of darkness passed, till shortly after midnight a vivid flash of lightning blazed across the sky, throwing the valley and the outlines of the distant mountains into strong relief, then leaving the two men blinking in the corresponding intense darkness.

The heavy peal of thunder that followed seemed to shake the solid rock. Holmsby gave an involuntary gasp and dug his heels more firmly into the precarious foothold. The vibration, intensified by the helplessness of their position, made it appear as if the ledge was on the point of bodily giving way.

Then the storm burst. Flash succeeded flash with great rapidity, the thunder rolled, and the rain descended in sheets. Fortunately there was no wind, although Holmsby momentarily expected the sudden vicious squall that almost invariably occurs during some period of the thunderstorm. He wondered what would happen to the *Amphibian*, only insecurely anchored in a dangerous position, where one blast from the northward would hurl her bodily against the rugged cliff.

Presently a steady stream trickled from the roof of the fissure and gradually increased in volume. This was to a certain extent beneficial, since Don Miguel could slake his thirst. Even Holmsby was beginning to feel the pangs of hunger and the want of something to drink, but when availing himself of the now copious gush of water, he could not help wondering what would happen if the stream became a torrent and swept the refugees from their confined haven of rest.

At length the storm passed, and although the water continued to run steadily it did not increase in volume. Nevertheless the rocky ledge was rendered so slippery by the moisture that the precarious holding-ground was made even more unsafe. Then, as Holmsby had expected, his companion began to grow restless. Symptoms of fever were beginning to appear, and ere long Don Miguel would be delirious.

Holding the hand of the tormented man, Reginald strove to calm his fears, both real and imaginary, and as he waited thus the peaks of the distant mountains began to grow visible through the darkness.

" Surely it is not daybreak," thought Holmsby, but as the light increased he saw that it was caused by the rising moon. In less than a quarter of an hour the valley was bathed in mellow light. This was comforting, and even the injured man seemed to find ease of body and mind with the welcome change.

But the rally was only temporary.

" Mr. Holmsby," he whispered, " the pain is returning. I fear it is more than I can bear. Place your hand in this pocket and you'll find a case. Inside is an instrument that you know how to use, so make good use of it."

The tortured man pointed to a small pocket behind the knee of his riding-breeches, so cunningly placed as to be easily overlooked except by a most careful search. In it was a thin case about two inches square, and to Holmsby's satisfaction an injector was within.

" I carry it as a last resource," explained the President. " That needle is charged with a most virulent poison."

Holmsby's face fell.

" Here, this won't do," he exclaimed. " I'm not going to kill you, if that's what you want me to do."

" I do not. Be careful. In the lining of the case is another needle which will inject the anæsthetic only. It will keep me quiet for a few hours at any rate."

" You are quite sure about the needles ? "

" Perfectly ; now please hasten, for the agony is becoming intense."

Carefully extricating the needle and pneumatic

pad from the case, Reginald stuck the point into the nape of Don Miguel's neck. The effect was instantaneous : the Calderian President was dead to all pain.

" A few hours, he said," thought the operator. " By Jove, I'll risk it."

It was a comparatively easy matter to charge and buckle on the neutraliser. Kept by its own upward pressure against the sloping roof of the hole in the rock it presented no difficulty to Holmsby, who, setting his back against it, drew the straps across his chest. In a few moments he was making his way up the face of the cliff, keeping as straight a direction as possible, in order to find the crevice again.

Good luck favoured him, for he gained the ledge upon which the *Amphibian* rested without much trouble. In the moonlight the huge bulk seemed to tower higher than usual, while from the conning-tower the beams of the two search-lights shot diagonally upwards. On the promenade-deck, silhouetted against the illumined face of the cliff, were the crew, all intently gazing upards. Holmsby understood : the faithful fellows were watching and waiting for his return, only he came from a direction whence they least expected him.

" Hi, there, you Tresillian. What d'ye mean by switching on those search-lights ? " he bawled. " Do you want the airship to find you out and blow you to smithereens ? "

And with a magnificent leap Reginald gained the

deck of the *Amphibian* and grasped his comrade by the hand.

Dick could not bring himself to utter a sound. He merely used Holmsby's arm as a pump-handle, while it was with the greatest difficulty that he could prevent himself from blubbering like a whipped schoolboy.

"It's all right, Dick. I'm not a ghost. If I am, I'm a pretty solid one, I assure you," his comrade expostulated; then, turning to the crew, he told them in a few words of the precarious position of the President of Calderia.

For the next few minutes all was confusion and bustle. Men ran hither and thither, some donning their neutralisers, others bringing coils of ropes from the ship's store. While these preparations were in progress, Holmsby went below and helped himself to some food and a stiff dose of Calderian wine.

"Going down again, Rex?" asked Tresillian. "Can't I go and you stay here and superintend operations?"

"Impossible, old chap; you wouldn't find the place. I'm as fit as anything now. You stand by with six of the men. I'll take a length of fine cord with me. When I give three tugs, haul away on the life-line."

The rescue of Don Miguel was soon accomplished. Secured by a rope and buoyed up by a neutraliser, his apparently lifeless body was hauled up the remaining portion of the cliff, Holmsby and the men who accompanied him ascending with hardly an effort by merely holding on the same rope that was attached to the President's body.

On regaining the *Amphibian* the wounded man's limb was set in splints, and the bullet graze on his head carefully dressed, but Holmsby and Tresillian agreed that the sooner O'Rourke received proper medical attention the better it would be.

The return to Nalcuanho must be made at all costs, but how ? Provisions were running short, the supply of water, though augmented by the torrential rain, was steadily diminishing, and unless a favourable breeze sprang up the crew of the *Amphibian* would be compelled to abandon their craft and make their way back to the plains on foot.

Three days passed, but still the north wind held with aggravating persistence. On the morning of the fourth day one of the crew raised the alarm that an airship was in sight.

Rushing on deck, Reginald brought his glasses to bear upon a small speck in the sky. The Calderian was right. Making her way rapidly in a southerly direction was the airship commanded by the treacherous Don Robiera Sanchez, the erstwhile owner of the fictitious F.O. 445. Either the airship was on the look out for the supposed wreck of the *Amphibian* or else it was on its way to assist in the second attack upon the capital of Calderia. The *Amphibian*, helpless to repel an onslaught, was in a perilous situation. Should the Talpican airship discover her she was doomed to destruction ; on the other hand, ere the crippled vessel could return to Nalcuanho, she would have to run the gauntlet since her rival had placed himself between the sierras and the capital.

" What's to be done now ? " asked Tresillian.

" Done ? Give me a favourable breeze, Dick," replied Holmsby, " and, by Jove, I'll make a fight for it."

CHAPTER XXIII

THE AIRSHIP THAT PASSED IN THE NIGHT

EARLY on the following morning Holmsby went on deck and, after receiving the reassuring report from the look-out that nothing untoward had occurred during the night, anxiously scanned the sky. There was not a breath of wind under the lee of the cliff, but at a great altitude light fleecy clouds were moving slowly in a northerly direction. What wind there was above was certainly favourable, but the vital question arose : whether the Talpican airship would intercept the *Amphibian* ?

The latter was now little better than a balloon. The damaged compartments had been temporarily repaired, although patching the metal shell of the submarine was under the circumstances impossible. Motive power there was none, the airship being at the mercy of the winds. No doubt she could more than hold her own if attacked by her rival in mid-air, since by her superior raising-power she could easily outsoar any hydrogen-filled craft, while her armament was still intact. But Holmsby did not wish to run unnecessary risks. For the time being, and until the *Amphibian* was thoroughly repaired, he would rather that Don Robiera Sanchez and his treacherous gang laboured under the delusion that the dreaded *Amphibian* was no more.   There was also another reason.   Should the Talpican airship discover the *Amphibian* scudding helplessly before the wind, she could easily keep to windward of her and wait till either the Calderian craft was blown out to sea or until she attempted a descent in the vicinity of Nalcuanho.   In that case the *Amphibian* could be easily destroyed before the Talpican airship came within range of the high-angle firing guns of the forts.   To men who were being attacked by the gnawing pains of hunger the prospect of being unable to take advantage of a wind that would soon blow them to the fertile plains of Calderia was exasperating in the extreme ;   but on Holmsby explaining the dangers and difficulties of a flight by day the Calderian crew readily gave way to the judgment of their English adviser.

Meanwhile Don Miguel was progressing favourably in spite of the lack of medical attention.   The pure mountain air worked marvels, and, unless complications followed, his cure bid fair to be rapid and lasting.

Yet the mercurial temperament of the man fell very low, and Holmsby could see that he was in a fit of depression.

" I'm not fated to be a leader of men, Mr. Holmsby," he said plaintively.   " At times I feel I have the energy and the power of mind ; but when it comes to the point, alas. I know I am a miserable failure."

" Don't talk like that, señor," said Reginald. " It is only owing to the result of your condition. No man could have led his troops more gallantly than you did the other day."

" You saw me then ? " asked O'Rourke brightening up.

" Saw you—of course we did. You fought magnificently——"

" And allowed myself to be taken prisoner a few minutes after the battle had been won. Again, my courage failed me utterly during the ascent of the cliff. I am no hero. As an inventor, with a knowledge of science, I hope I am above the ordinary, but as President of Calderia I feel that the realisations of my lifelong ambitions have fallen short of my expectations. Without the aid of you and your friend where should I be now ? "

" You never know your luck," replied Holmsby sententiously; then, anxious in his modesty to divert the channel of Don Miguel's expressions of gratitude, he asked :

" How did you find yourself in such an awkward position after the victory ? "

" I can hardly remember. The wound in my head was troubling me, although during the attack I scarce noticed it. Our men were in pursuit of the enemy. Somehow I found myself well in the rear, attended only by an orderly. I was on the point of going to rejoin General Saldanha and the rest of my staff, who were trying in vain to keep our men well in hand, when a volley from a thicket bowled the orderly over. Ere I realised it I was surrounded, made prisoner, and thrown upon a horse. My captors were all mounted and, riding with the greatest audacity round our straggling right flank, soon placed a safe distance between them and the battlefield."

" Couldn't you shout when they made you ride past the flank ? "

" Shout, señor ? My word ! With a revolver pointed at one's head one does not care to waste breath in more ways than one. Those guerrillas are most daring men, and it was with the intention of either killing me or taking me prisoner that they lay in ambush while the rest of the Talpican army fled. Was it not your Shakespeare who made one of his characters say, ' I would give all my fame for a pot of ale and safety ' ? I would willingly give all I possess—even the secret of my great invention—to live my student days over again. But what do you propose to do now, Mr. Holmsby ? "

Reginald told him of his plan of action.

" Excellent. You are what I ought to be, my friend. I have the initiative but lack the strength of will to carry out my intentions : you have both."

" Well, señor, I must be off, for there still remains much to be done. By the bye—have you a drawing of the motors on board ?   If so, we ought to be able to make a speedy job of assembling the new parts."

" My drawings are here," replied O'Rourke, tapping his forehead.   " It is the only safe place as far as I am concerned.   But since I am at present incapable of attending to my work I must needs leave it to others.   Within three hours I will make rough drawings sufficient to enable the parts to be turned out or cast ; but please remember that until I give you leave to do otherwise the secret of the motive power of the *Amphibian* rests solely between you and me."

It was half an hour before sunset that the crippled *Amphibian* rose slowly in the still air. Fearing that ere she cleared the top of the cliff she might sustain damage by colliding with the precipice, Holmsby had caused large sacks filled with grass to be slung around her bulging sides, while men armed with long poles were stationed on the deck to fend her off.

All went well till the airship was within fifty feet of the summit.   Here the wind blowing strongly over the peaks of the sierras eddied treacherously. At one moment a fierce gale would strike the craft on the bow, at another the afterpart would be caught by a vicious blast.   Swaying, pitching, and rolling, the huge bulk was helpless in the wind ; but just as it seemed to be on the point of crashing into the rocky face of the mountains the true wind caught the *Amphibian* on the beam.   The next moment the peril was past and the airship was being whirled rapidly northwards.

Holmsby gave a sigh of relief as he realised that all cause of anxiety was at present at an end, and rejoining Tresillian on the promenade-deck he had for the first time for some days a minute to call his own.

" Isn't that magnificent ? " exclaimed Dick, pointing to the jagged peaks of the sierras, that alone of all the landscape were bathed in golden sunshine.

" Fine," replied Holmsby shortly. He had no inclination to study picturesque effects : his sole thoughts were on the question of whether the *Amphibian* would reach Nalcuanho before the moon rose.

" We don't seem to be moving very fast," continued Tresillian. " It seems more like being on a merry-go-round at a country fair, only no blaring organ to liven things up."

The *Amphibian* was slowly see-sawing, her bow describing a double loop while at intervals she would make a complete revolution on a horizontal axis ; but, looking over the side, Holmsby noticed that the country beneath was apparently slipping past at a great speed.

" We're doing all right," he exclaimed cheerfully. " Forty miles an hour at the least. The nearer we get to the sea the steadier the breeze will be."

" But forty miles an hour is too great a rate for us to descend ? "

" True ; but with luck we ought to be on the coast at sunrise. In this country, like many other tropical parts, every evening the wind blows towards the sea, since the land gives off its heat quicker than does the water. Soon after sunrise the conditions are reversed, but ere the change takes place there is a lull for some hours. This calm I mean to take advantage of, if possible. Now, I'm going to turn in. Keep the watch on deck up to the scratch, and don't forget the barometer. So long as we are ten thousand feet in the air we won't come to much harm. But should anything unusual occur call me at once."

Bidding his comrade good-night, Reginald went below and turned in " all standing," so as to be ready for an emergency.

Left to himself, Dick paced the afterpart of the promenade-deck. His knowledge of Spanish was limited to a few words picked up during his stay on the *Amphibian,* sufficient to give a few orders, but not enough to engage in conversation. For'ard the watch on deck were talking volubly, but keenly alive to their duties, they maintained a sharp look out.

Darkness had now set in, and, though the airship's erratic behaviour was still noticeable, it was not so uncomfortable as it had been during the day when the sight of the earth beneath increased the sense of motion.

Hour after hour passed. Not a light was visible from the land, nor was the cheery glimmer of a lamp permissible on board. The crew, too, were deprived of the solace of their otherwise ubiquitous cigarettes. At what rate or in what direction the *Amphibian* was being blown it was impossible to tell. To Tresillian it seemed as if the vessel was floating idly in a void of impenetrable darkness ; the stars, even, were invisible, for the stratum which the airship was drifting was dense with a moist, freezingly cold vapour.

As Dick was emerging from the conning-tower, whence he had gone for the twentieth time that night in order to read the barometer, he hailed the look out. There was no necessity to go for'ard. Away on the beam, miles away it seemed, a pale gleam of light was visible beyond the horizon.

Getting his night-glasses to bear upon the spot, Tresillian saw that it was a search-light flashing intermittently at an immense distance off. Every time it shot skywards it threw into relief the outlines of a long, low-lying line of buildings.

" Surely that cannot be Nalcuanho already ? " he muttered, as he dived below to rouse his comrade.

Hastily springing from his bunk, Holmsby rushed up the ladder and gained the deck. For some moments he looked in the direction Dick had pointed out, till one of the crew shouted out that the light now bore dead astern. During the interval between Tresillian last sighting the beam and his reappearance on deck, the *Amphibian* had described an arc of 90 degrees.

Reginald's first act on spotting the light was to take its bearings with the standard compass. It bore N.E. by N., so that, making due allowance for magnetic variation, Holmsby knew that its true direction was due north.

" What do you make of it ? " asked Tresillian, but Holmsby, with his night-glass glued to his eyes, silenced him by a gesture.

" K.L.V.P. — stop — V.M.C.G.B. — stop — T.Z.J.," he read. " No intelligible meaning. They're signalling in cipher. That search-light is coming from one of the warships lying off Nalcuanho Harbour."

" One of the Talpican fleet ? "

" Shouldn't be surprised ; but keep a bright look out. There'll be a reply from another ship shortly."

The coded message now ended, and the darkness seemed blacker than before.

Suddenly, at a distance of about a thousand feet beneath the *Amphibian*, a vivid flash of light streamed diagonally upwards. For a few seconds the beam remained stationary, then broke into a succession of " dots and dashes."

" Silence, there ! " exclaimed Holmsby sharply as some of the men began to talk in quick, excited sentences.

The *Amphibian* was floating almost directly over her rival, the Talpican airship.

Swiftly, yet as noiselessly as possible, the crew cleared away the quick-firers, the search-lights

were screened and connected up ready to direct
their penetrating beams upon the floating monster
beneath.

Yet Holmsby forbore to give the order to open
fire. Not from any motive of humanity : the
despicable treachery that accompanied their former
meeting had put Don Robiera Sanchez outside the
pale. But, knowing from his previous experiences
afloat, the great difficulty of hitting a source of
light at a practically unknown range, the sub-
lieutenant decided not to take the risk.

The next instant he regretted his decision, but
it was too late to drop an explosive upon the
hydrogen-charged airship. Holmsby recognised a
new danger. The Talpican aircraft was running
slowly dead against the wind, while the *Amphibian*
was drifting, absolutely beyond control, straight
for the path of the beam of the former's search-
light. It would be useless to ascend : no matter
the altitude the penetrating rays would make the
grey hull of the *Amphibian* appear as if sheened
with silver. In another half a minute—

" After gun, there—stand by. Elevate your
sights to 800 metres."

Since it had to be done, Holmsby wisely decided not to wait till his gun's crew were " spotted "
and dazzled by the glare of the search-light.

Now or never. With a fervent prayer for a
successful shot he was on the point of giving the
order to fire when the Talpican airship's search-
light was suddenly screened. With a grunt of

disappointment the Calderian gun-layer stood back
from the night-sights and rubbed his eyes, while
the captain of the guns promptly dropped the
firing-key lest a spasmodic action on his part
would release the charge and send it hurtling aimlessly through space.

The next five minutes was a period of anxious
suspense. Holmsby could see the blinking of the
distant search-light. At any moment it might
cease and the Talpican airship would reply. Even
in the bitterly cold air Reginald could feel the
perspiration standing out in beads upon his
forehead.

Then the expected flash leapt skywards, but,
hurrah ! far astern of the rapidly drifting *Amphibian*. In that five minutes the Calderian airship
had passed through the normal path of her rival's
search-light, and nothing short of a deliberate
alteration of the powerful beam would reveal her
to her antagonist.

" I'd give twelve months' seniority to know
what those fellows are saying," he exclaimed.
" Ten to one, Dick, they are planning a combined
attack upon the forts of Nalcuanho."

But Holmsby was wrong in his surmise. The
Talpican airship had notified her maritime consorts
that her supply of hydrogen was getting low, and
that she intended to return to the depot at San
José to replenish her gas-chambers.

When the Talpican flagship again replied,
Holmsby once more took a bearing.

The compass gave exactly the same bearing as previously, so that to his great satisfaction Reginald knew that the *Amphibian* was still keeping to the desired course, unless—an extremely improbable event—the wind had changed and was blowing in exactly the opposite direction.

Soon the flashes ceased, and Holmsby fancied that he heard the deep buzz of the airship of which they had so nearly fallen athwart; but after a further short interval the noise ceased and the *Amphibian* was left floating and drifting in soundless, impenetrable space.

"We may as well drop down a few thousand feet," remarked Reginald, before returning to his bunk. "There's nothing to fall foul of at two thousand : that will afford a safe margin. If nothing occurs in the meanwhile turn me out at daybreak."

At length the pale dawn glimmered in the east, and as the twilight quickly changed to day the crew of the *Amphibian* could determine their position. Nothing could have been better.

The crippled craft was floating in the now light breeze immediately over the city of Nalcuanho. The Talpican airship had disappeared, while seaward a haze of black smoke showed that the blockading squadron had temporarily retired in order, presumably, to replenish their coal and fuel.

"Let her come down !" exclaimed Holmsby, who had, in accordance with his instructions, been

roused from his slumbers.   " Bring her down on
that piece of ground alongside the inner basin."

As he spoke, a puff of smoke burst from one of the
batteries on the landward side of the city, and a
huge rocket came soaring skywards.   It struck the
Amphibian on the port quarter, spluttered venom-
ously for a few seconds, then shot earthwards.   Had
the *Amphibian's* outer skin been made of anything
but asbestos-lined duralium and had the ballonettes
consisted of hydrogen or other highly-inflammable
gas her destruction would have been swift and
complete.

" What are those fools firing for ? " asked Holmsby.   " Surely the place is not in the hands of the
enemy ?   Here, run up the ensign.   They are
mistaking us for the enemy."

Ere this could be done another rocket whizzed
past the airship at less than ten yards' distance ;
but on the Calderian ensign being displayed a bugle
could be distinctly heard calling the " Cease fire ! "

The mistake was, under the circumstances,
justifiable.   The rumour that the *Amphibian* had
been totally destroyed had already reached the
capital, and the sudden appearance of an airship
was interpreted as the first phase in the threatened
assault by air and sea upon the forts and batteries of
Nalcuanho.

Holmsby's doubts were now at rest.   On all the
forts the Calderian ensign was hoisted, while by
means of his glasses he saw that the troops wore
the light grey uniforms of the Republic.

Consummately handled, the *Amphibian* descended, her speed through the air now allowing the steering-rudders and elevating-planes to be brought into action, and with hardly a jolt the huge vessel was brought to earth and securely made fast in the desired mooring-ground.

It was with difficulty that the troops were able to keep back the throng of excited citizens, whose delight at the *Amphibian's* return was doubly increased by the good news that their President, though wounded, was once more in their midst. As soon as the lofty gangway could be rigged up and placed in position, Don Miguel was carefully lifted out on a stretcher and taken to his official residence. But before he went the promised rough drawings of the *Amphibian's* propelling machinery were placed in Reginald's hands.

" If these are your rough drawings I wonder what your finished plans are like, by Jove ! " exclaimed Holmsby, for the draughtsmanship was beyond reproach. How a crippled and pain-racked man could produce such careful and elaborate workmanship passed his comprehension.

There was no time to be lost. If the long-threatened attack upon the capital was to be averted the *Amphibian* must be refitted with the least possible delay. Swarms of artisans took her in hand. The shattered plates of the submarine hull were removed, the damaged shafting and propellers were removed to serve as patterns for a new forging, while under Holmsby's personal supervision the motors were taken to a jealously-guarded workshop where the separate parts were carefully copied by the skilled mechanics. The actual assembly of the parts was to be undertaken by Holmsby and the engineer of the *Amphibian*.

Thanks to his training in the workshops of Osborne and Dartmouth the sub-lieutenant was well conversant with the nature of the work, and in less than a week, working at high pressure, the motors were again in position. All that remained was to wait until the extensive damage to the inner plating had been made good, a task that would take not less than another eight days, and then only if no unforeseen hitch occurred.

On the day following the completion of the reconstruction of the propelling machinery a motor-launch arrived at Nalcuanho harbour, after having made a hazardous passage from the Talpican port of San José. Her crew consisted of three Calderian mining-engineers who had been taken prisoners and sent to San José during the initial stages of the war. They had succeeded in breaking out of prison, and with the greatest audacity took possession of the motor-boat and ran out of the harbour in broad daylight. Their flight was not discovered until well beyond the range of the forts and, though chased by a Talpican torpedo boat, they contrived to shake off their pursuers. They reported the *Don Robiera Sanchez* airship had returned to San José, having developed a leak in one of the gas-chambers, and that some days must elapse ere the craft would be ready for service.

That afternoon Holmsby strolled down to the quay in order to look at the little craft in which the prisoners had effected their escape.

It was barely twenty-four feet in length, with a sharp entry and exceptionally clean run aft. Save for a short turtle-back deck for'ard and a small space decked in aft, the boat was entirely open. Her motor, made by a well-known British firm, consisted of six cylinders developing 200 horse-power, and capable of driving her at anything between twenty and twenty-five knots.

As Holmsby looked at the little craft a thought flashed suddenly across his mind. He had an idea : the idea developed, and in less than five minutes he was making his way to the quarters of the Commandante.

CHAPTER XXIV

HOLMSBY'S RAID

GENERAL ALONZO SALDANHA, the Commandante of the city of Nalcuanho and
Acting-Commander-in-Chief of the Calderian army,
was a short, pompous-looking man of about sixty
years of age. His bronzed features, iron-grey hair
and fiercely up-turned moustache gave him a very
martial appearance, and in truth he was possessed
of no mean military skill. But his creed was
" Calderia for the Calderians," and although he was
implicitly trusted by the President he harboured an
intense dislike for the two Englishmen on whom
Don Miguel set such store.

Nevertheless he greeted Holmsby with punctilious
courtesy.

" I have just been to see the motor-boat in which
the prisoners escaped," said Holmsby, "and it struck
me that with a crew of determined men much could
be done with her. I understand that the airship of
Don Robiera Sanchez is at San José, and is very
carelessly guarded. With ordinary luck it would be
possible to land a few miles from the town, destroy
the ship, and re-embark on the motor-launch before
the enemy could realise what had happened."

" I, too, have been planning a raid into Talpican territory, Señor Holmsby," replied the Commandante, unwilling to be thought lacking in initiative. " I thought of sending half a dozen picked men by motor-car to the base of the sierras. Thence they could make their way through one of the more neglected passes, seize horses and make a dash for San José. What do you think of that ? "

" They would have to go a long way from their base of operations, Commandante," observed Reginald. " And you must also take into account the difficulties occasioned by the use of wireless telegraphy and telephony in modern warfare."

" True, but for every man who can be of use in a boat we have a hundred skilled in guerrilla warfare and accustomed to making long journeys on horse-back. As you are aware, our navy was not to be compared with the Talpican fleet, and now ceases to exist. In fact I know of no one capable of leading an expedition by sea. Don Carlos is, as you know, still incapacitated by wounds."

" It is my intention to ask your permission to make the attempt," said Reginald calmly.

" You ! " exclaimed the Commandante, sitting bolt upright and tugging at his moustache. General Saldanha's first thought was that this young Englishman would add to his already coveted reputation should he succeed ; then, on the other hand, the business would be an extremely hazardous one. The chances were that Holmsby would fall into the hands of the Talpicans, and then—but the

Commandante was, after all, a soldier and he thought it his duty to warn even the man whom he had long regarded as a dangerous rival.

" You will be shot as a filibuster if you are caught, señor," he added.

" That is a risk which I have taken into consideration, Commandante," replied Reginald. " The fact remains that with this means of offence in our possession we ought not to let a chance slip. As for the *Amphibian*, she will not be ready for quite another week, and in the interval my companion, Mr. Tresillian, will superintend matters. So there is no reason why I should not make the attempt."

" Very well then," said General Saldanha. " I will write out an order handing over the boat to you. You may also take four men with you."

Overjoyed at his good fortune, Holmsby bade the Commandante farewell and took his leave. On returning to the *Amphibian* he informed Dick of what he proposed to do, steadfastly refused to let his comrade accompany him, and then set about to pick his crew. The four men he required were soon forthcoming, for Holmsby did not want to have any but those who were serving on board the airship. Fortunately two of them were conversant with the handling of a marine motor, while all, making allowances for the mercurial Calderian temperament, were to be trusted.

Before noon the motor-boat was taken out for a trial spin, and Holmsby was very well satisfied with her speed and seaworthiness. Stores, a large supply of petrol, arms, and ammunition were placed on board, and everything was in readiness to make a start for San José early in the afternoon.

Holmsby had hoped to keep the object of his expedition a secret, but greatly to his annoyance the news leaked out, and before the start was made the intelligence was all over the city. This was more than annoying, for it was well known that there were spies especially amongst those of the Extremist section of the revolutionists who still remained at Nalcuanho. There was no time to be lost if the raid was to be carried out before the Talpicans heard of the departure of the daring adventurers.

At exactly two o'clock the motor-launch started on its long voyage. If all went well Holmsby hoped to arrive off the Talpican coast about an hour after sunset and reach the harbour of San José at about two in the morning. Fortunately the sea was as smooth as glass, and the boat, dashing along at twenty knots, soon began to lessen the distance betwixt her and her destination.

Presently one of the crew, who had occasion to look for something in the space under the turtle-back deck, told Reginald that there was a man lying under the folds of a tarpaulin. Unceremoniously the stowaway was hauled from his place of concealment, and Holmsby recognised him as being one of the three men who had escaped from his prison in San José.

The man was frank in his explanation. He had

heard of the object of the raid, and, having a score
to pay against his former captors, he meant to
become a member of the expedition.

" You see, señor," he exclaimed extending his
hands, palms uppermost, and shrugging his
shoulders deprecatingly, " I know much of San
José : therefore I am of much use to you. Moreover
did not I, with my two comrades, take possession
of the boat ? Have I not a right to be in it ? "

Holmsby was annoyed at first, but since he could
not get rid of the man, who, after all, might prove
of great service by his intimate knowledge of the
town of San José and its vicinity, he resolved to
make the best of the business.

Night succeeded day, and still the launch
maintained her rapid pace through the water until
an alternating red and white light appeared above
the horizon.

This, Holmsby knew to be the lighthouse on the
Sobra Shoal, a dangerous ledge of rocks extending
seaward and for nearly a cable's length from the
western side of the entrance to San José Harbour.
Presently the shore lights began to loom up : the
motor-boat was approaching hostile waters.

Slackening his speed to seven knots Holmsby
steered the craft closer in-shore till the roar of the
ground swell could be distinctly heard. This was
another item in the raiders' favour since the noise
of the surf drowned the pulsations of the motor.

" There is the creek we are looking for, señor,"
exclaimed one of the men pointing to an ill-defined

gap in the white line of broken water. "It is less than twenty minutes' walk from the town."

Round swung the launch and with barely sufficient speed beyond what was required to give her steerage-way she headed for the opening. Within the entrance the place appeared absolutely deserted, and Holmsby was about to congratulate himself upon this fact, when there was a dull, grinding sound. The little craft trembled from keel to gunwale, then lifted by a wave was thrown into deep water. She had bumped heavily upon a submerged rock, and ere the shore was reached it was apparent that the boat was badly damaged.

"Stuff your cap into the hole," exclaimed Reginald in a low voice, but before the seamen could raise the floor boards the water was level with the engine-bed. Nothing could stop the incoming flood ; the motor gasped spasmodically, then stopped.

"We'll have to swim for it," exclaimed Holmsby "Make sure that you have your revolvers."

As he spoke the gunwale of the waterlogged craft dipped and she sank in three feet of water. Her crew, holding their pistols well above their heads, waded ashore.

They were, indeed, in a precarious position : fifty miles from the frontier, their retreat cut off, and within a short distance of a hostile town. The Calderians looked at one another in blank despair. The sudden reverse of fortune had completely unmanned them.

"Come on, men," shouted Holmsby encourag-

ingly. " We'll do what we can. If we are taken
they can't hurt *you* " ; but he knew full well that
the Talpicans were perfectly justified in shooting
him on sight—a subject of a neutral country
taking up arms against a friendly state.

" Now, señor," he continued, addressing the
former prisoner, who seemed fated to return to his
place of incarceration, " lead the way to the spot
where the airship is lying. Stand to your arms,
men; but, remember, not a shot till I give the word."

Led by the mining-engineer the raiders followed
in Indian file. The path from the creek ascended
a steep hill that was thickly clothed with young
olive trees. Here a hundred men could find
shelter; but on gaining the summit of the rising
ground the adventurers found themselves deprived
of cover. The town of San José, now shrouded
in darkness, lay beneath them.

Cautiously the six men descended the gently
sloping ground. Twice they threw themselves
flat upon the grass, fearing that some belated
Talpican was passing that way ; but their alarm
was unnecessary. All was quiet.

Now they were threading their way through the
narrow squalid alleys on the outskirts of the town.
Well it was that the ex-captive had accompanied
them, for in that maze of buildings they would
otherwise have been hopelessly lost.

" Here we are, señor," whispered the guide, as
the raiders halted on the edge of an open square.
" The airship should be lying on our right."

" Carry on, then," replied Holmsby briefly, and treading close on one another's heels the Calderians followed their intrepid leader.

Suddenly the guide halted—so abruptly that Holmsby nearly ran into him. Peering through the darkness the Englishman could discern the figure of a sentry. The Talpican was leaning against a porch, his rifle with its long sword-bayonet held carelessly in the hollow of his arm, while, utterly unsuspecting danger, he was humming softly to himself.

Holmsby gauged the distance. Could he cover the intervening space before the man could recover from his surprise and give the alarm ?

Presently the man shouldered his rifle and moved on—not, as Holmsby expected, to walk his rounds, but to shelter from the now keen wind on the other side of the porch.

Softly treading on the sand that bordered the tiled path the sub-lieutenant gained the spot where the sentry had been standing. His men followed, till the angle of the wall was inconveniently crowded.

But instead of returning, the sentry stood still. Holmsby saw a faint glimmer, followed by an impatient *Caramba*, while the rank smell of a South American match was drifted to his nose.

Keenly on the alert, Reginald waited till the sentry struck another match : this time with better results, for he proceeded to light a cigarette.

Blinded by the glare, the soldier was scared out

of his wits to find a powerful grasp upon his neck
and a heavy hand crushing the cigarette and
clasping his mouth. Thinking that he had been
caught by one of his officers, the man did not
attempt to struggle till it was too late ; in less
time than one could count he was lying gagged
and bound upon the ground.

Still advancing cautiously the raiders gained
the side of the airship. It was not partially deflated as Holmsby expected, but was straining on its
securing ropes. "Men," he whispered, "here lies our
way of escape. We'll board her and cut her out."

The long bridge-like "nacelle" was within ten
feet of the ground. A light was burning in the
'midships cabin, but no one was visible either on
the airship or on the ground.

Swiftly the lithe Calderians clambered up the
ropes. Two made their way for'ard, their keen
machetes in their hands, two ran softly aft, while
Holmsby and the mining-engineer, with their
revolvers ready for instant use, took their stand at
twenty feet from the door of the occupied cabin.

Suddenly the after part of the airship gave a
sickening heave and reared itself so high in the
air that Holmsby and his companion had to hold
on like grim death. The stern, liberated before
the bows, was tilting upwards ; but the men
for'ard were not much behind their comrades with
their keen blades, and like a clay pigeon released
from the trap the airship leapt a thousand feet
in the air.

As it did so the door of the cabin opened and a man looked out. The light streaming over his shoulders fell upon the Calderian uniforms of the two seamen who had completed their work aft and had rejoined their leader. With a yell the man, ignoring Holmsby's demand to yield, sprang forward, then placing one hand on the rail surrounding the " nacelle," vaulted—not as he thought for a distance of ten feet to the ground—but into space.

" Mind, señor, there is still someone within," cautioned one of the men as Holmsby was about to explore the still lighted cabin."

" Surrender, señor : the airship is ours," shouted Reginald.

In reply a tall broad-shouldered man appeared from behind the door, and, brandishing an automatic pistol, fired rapidly and indiscriminately at the group confronting him. Holmsby felt a bullet plough through his hair, while a sharp cry behind him told him that one of the shots at least had taken effect.

Holmsby raised his revolver and pressed the trigger. The bullet struck his antagonist's automatic pistol, knocking it from his hand, and being deflected passed through the partition of the cabin ; and ere the Talpican could draw his knife, Holmsby threw himself upon him.

Fiercely they struggled upon the swaying floor, until the Calderian crew, coming to the rescue, bound the still resisting man hand and foot and unceremoniously bundled him into the cabin.

Telling one of the men to guard the prisoner, Reginald made a hasty inspection of the captured craft, but no more Talpicans were found. Having found the valves regulating the supply of hydrogen, the prize crew took steps to check the still upward tendency of the airship, which had now reached an altitude of seven thousand feet. This done the propelling gear was inspected and found to be in working order, and in less than an hour the captured vessel, with her four propellers running at 500 revolutions per minute, was shaping a course towards the frontier.

Having detailed three men, one of whom had received a slight flesh wound in the shoulder, to keep the vessel on her course, and one to attend to the motors which required frequent lubrication owing to neglect on the part of the late owners to take proper care of the intricate machinery during the time the vessel was under repairs, Holmsby entered the 'midships cabin where the mining-engineer was mounting guard over the prisoner.

Now in the lamplight, Reginald recognised his captive. It was Don Robiera Sanchez, the owner of the bogus F.O. 445, the prime mover in the treacherous attacks at St. Piran's Round, at Zennor Hill, and again in the air above the sierras, The recognition was mutual, but Don Robiera. beyond giving Reginald a look of venomous hatred, said not a word; while Holmsby on his part refrained from crowing over a fallen rival. The other occupant of the car on the occasion of their

first meeting was the man who had leapt to his
death when the airship was boarded by the raiders.

Holmsby knew that he had no option but to hand
his prisoner over to the Calderian authorities. Of
his fate there could not be much doubt. Don
Robiera Sanchez was a Calderian Extremist, who,
not content with taking an active part in the civil
war, had used his influence, only too well, to induce
the Republic of Talpico to invade his country. But
for him the invasion, that was all but successful,
would never have taken place. As a traitor to the
Republic of Calderia his doom was practically
sealed.

The captured airship, the *Sol d'Este*, was not to be
compared with the *Amphibian* either in speed,
capability of handling, or in aggressive or defensive
power. As it was, pounding against a strong hard
wind, she made so little progress that daylight
found her still twenty miles from the frontier.

Keeping fairly close to the ground, for Holmsby
wisely decided to retain as much ballast as possible
until the surmounting of the sierras had to be
accomplished, the *Sol d'Este* presently passed above
the camp of the Talpican army, for after their defeat
the invaders had fallen back across the frontier
until the result of the threatened sea and air attack
upon Nalcuanho was known.

Thinking the airship was on her way to act in
consort with the fleet, the soldiers turned out of
their tents and cheered lustily. But their enthusiastic demonstrations were quickly changed

into yells and shouts of execration when Holmsby,
with pardonable pride, caused the Calderian ensign
to be hoisted over the green and white flag of
Talpico.

The troops were restrained by their officers from
opening fire upon the airship ; no doubt they feared
the possibility of having dynamite bombs dropped
amidst them, but Holmsby, finding that there was
no actual hostile action, refrained from taking
advantage of the powerful means of offence at his
command.

It was late in the afternoon that the sentries on
the batteries and forts of Nalcuanho saw the airship
appearing from the south. The greatest excitement
prevailed, for should the apparently hostile craft
succeed in escaping the defensive fire of the rockets,
the city would be at its mercy. But when the on-
coming craft, flying low as if scorning the threatened
fire of the batteries, was seen to display the
Calderian ensign over the Talpican national flag,
Nalcuanho gave itself over to unrestrained enthusiasm.

The *Sol d'Este* was brought to earth just beyond
the outer line of defences, and Holmsby and his five
comrades were received with open arms. But in
the midst of these demonstrations of joy there was a
certain section who bit their lips at the Englishman's
unforeseen good fortune.

General Alonzo Saldanha and a few of his staff
were already resolved to check the influence and
popularity of Reginald Holmsby.

CHAPTER XXV

A TRAITOR'S DOOM

" HOW is the work progressing, Dick ? " asked Holmsby, after the first greetings between the reunited pair were said.

" Better than I expected," replied Tresillian, who, clad in blue overalls and smothered with grease and dirt, looked little different from the Calderian mechanics. " We ought to have everything shipshape again by the day after to-morrow. But what's to be done with your prize—is she going to be employed against her late owners ? "

" I scarcely know. You see it's hardly my affair; but since the *Sol d'Este* is not a patch on the *Amphibian*, and is moreover a hydrogen-inflated craft, I think it would be preferable to dismantle her. Should it blow hard when she's under way she can't make headway ; where she is now lying she is at the mercy of the next strong wind, while the presence of a huge bag of highly explosive gas is prejudicial to the safety of the city. I mean to point this out to the Commandante and suggest that he has the envelope deflated. At some future time, with helia ballonettes and better propelling

244

machinery, she ought to make something of a show."

"How about that rascal Don Robiera Sanchez? What are they going to do with him?"

"I hear he's to be brought to court-martial this afternoon. Somehow or other I feel sorry for the poor brute. I almost wish it hadn't fallen to my lot to capture him. Hello, what's this?"

An orderly, bearing two official envelopes, walked up to where the two Englishmen were talking at the foot of the *Amphibian's* gangway, and with a salute handed one to each of the comrades.

The documents were summonses for Reginald and Dick to appear as witnesses at the forthcoming trial of Robiera Sanchez, a subject of the Republic of Calderia, on a charge of conducting traitorous correspondence with a hostile state and with taking up arms against the Republic.

"Hang it all!" exclaimed Holmsby. "Can't we manage to wriggle out of this? Surely they've enough evidence to shoot the man without dragging us into it. I'll run over and see the Commandante."

But the sub-lieutenant's mission was fruitless. General Saldanha, on the grounds of absolute necessity, refused to dispense with the evidence of the two Englishmen.

At two o'clock that afternoon the Court assembled. Even Don Miguel, carried thither on an ambulance, had to be present. Compared with a British court-martial, the trial was almost a farce

There were five judges, all of them officers of the Republican army. Altogether twelve witnesses were called for the prosecution, but no one was allowed to give evidence on behalf of the prisoner.

Don Robiera, in spite of the knowledge that the verdict was a foregone conclusion, defended himself with admirable coolness and skill, basing his plea upon the fact that when he took action against the so-called Government there was no President ; consequently the constitution of the Republic of Calderia was not legal.

But when asked to explain why he attempted to harm the life and property of Don Miguel O'Rourke on British territory the prisoner merely shrugged his shoulders and stated that he had a private feud against the inventor of the *Amphibian*, and since the vendetta, in a modified form, was still recognised in Calderia, his action was therefore justified.

" Nothing more nor less than this—Don Miguel O'Rourke robbed me of my secret, and the *Amphibian* is the result of my discovery which was stolen from me."

A hush of deep amazement swept over the crowded court. Don Miguel, pale and shaking with emotion, attempted to rise, but in vain.

" If your assertion be true," continued the senior judge, " How comes it that your airship, the *Sol d'Este*, is admittedly inferior to the *Amphibian* ?"

" There was neither time nor opportunity to apply my invention to that particular craft."

" Your Excellency : you hear what the man states ? " asked the prosecution. " It merely requires your word on oath to give him the lie direct."

" I can safely assert that I never had any communication whatsoever with the prisoner on the subject of either his or my invention," replied Don Miguel slowly and emphatically. " I was unaware, up to this moment, that he had any pretensions with reference to scientific invention. And, above all, I cannot express myself too strongly in words that the suggestion that I robbed him of the fruits of his enterprise is utterly false."

" But I can prove it to be otherwise," stoutly asserted the prisoner. " If I may be provided with paper and ink I will write down the formulæ on which the principles of Don Miguel's so-called invention are based. If Don Miguel will also write down his formulæ, the two can be compared, and the truth of my assertion vindicated."

" In the interests of the Republic I cannot accede to the prisoner's request," said Don Miguel. " But if Don Robiera will, on his part, write what he has suggested, I swear by the Virgin that I will truthfully give my opinion upon the merits of the formulæ."

Writing materials were thereupon handed to the prisoner, and, after scribbling vigorously for some time, he handed the paper to the President of the Court, who in turn passed it on to Don Miguel.

Holmsby, who was watching O'Rourke, particularly noticed that his face paled even more than hitherto, and his hands trembled slightly as he held the paper.

" Señors ! " exclaimed Don Miguel, " only one formula out of five has any worth. Collectively the results derived from them would be useless," and deliberately tearing the document into small pieces he thrust them into his breast-pocket.

" Rather a high-handed proceeding, Rex," whispered Tresillian, and Holmsby acquiesced with a nod.

Don Robiera, who had hitherto preserved a dignified demeanour, now burst into a torrent of expletives directed towards his rival the President of Calderia. He even tried to throw himself upon Don Miguel, but was prevented by the soldiers who were guarding him.

The rest of the trial was of the briefest description, and the anticipated verdict of guilty was followed by the sentence that the prisoner was to be shot within the walls of the prison at daybreak on the following day.

As Holmsby and his companion were leaving the court, General Saldanha beckoned to them.

" You must be present at the execution, señors," he began when the Englishmen had crossed over to where he was standing.

" Is it necessary, Commandante ? "

" It is the President's wish that you should do so."

" But why ' must ' ? " asked Holmsby pointedly. " Supposing we refuse ? "

" You are temporarily in the service of the
Republic of Calderia ; under what circumstances
or conditions I know not, nor do I feel inclined to
discuss the matter. But as servants of the State,
since your presence is required, you must be
present." And with the air of a man who had
said what he meant to say and no more, General
Saldanha turned on his heel and walked towards
his quarters.

" What an old fire-eater, Rex," exclaimed
Tresillian. " I suppose we must go."

" I mean to see Don Miguel first," replied
Holmsby. " There are one or two questions I
should very much like to ask him. They've just
carried him back to his quarters, so wait here a few
moments and I'll look him up."

Holmsby had no difficulty in gaining admittance
to the President's presence. Don Miguel greeted
him cordially and expressed his highest admiration
for the way in which Holmsby had effected his great
coup.

" And it's in consequence of that business that
I'm here now," said Reginald. " Now, look here,
Don Miguel, I've always found you straight, and I
hope you have the same opinion about me. I want
to ask you two questions : first, why did you tear
that paper up ? "

" To safeguard my interests and those of the
Republic," replied Don Miguel, with a suspicion of
hauteur.

" I fancy I've heard those words before," replied

Reginald grimly. " To me the affair looks somewhat suspicious. Were Don Robiera's formulæ similar to yours ? "

" I have already sworn that they were not, Mr. Holmsby. But in confidence I may tell you that they were so near the right thing that for the moment I was on thorns. He nearly made the discovery, but one small yet important detail was omitted. You doubt me, señor ? "

" Your action seemed suspicious."

" I told you that at some future date I would hand over to you my supreme secret : the formula for the preparation of helia. My promise I mean to perform, but in the meantime I will also give you these fragments of paper. They can be easily pieced together and deciphered. When the time comes, Mr. Holmsby, for you to have my formula you will then see that I have vindicated myself. Is that sufficient ? "

Holmsby bowed.

" I hope it may be so," he replied. " No doubt Don Robiera imagined that he had a grievance and made the accusation. Now, my second question, señor : why did you order us to be present at the execution ? "

" I did not order : I merely requested that you should be there."

" And why ? "

" That requires an explanation. Ever since my return after the victory over the Talpicans I have had doubts as to the loyalty of the army—and the

Commandante, General Alonzo Saldanha in particular. Something seems to tell me that my influence and popularity are on the wane. Tell me what is your private opinion of the Commandante?"

"Not a bad old sort as far as Calderian officials go," replied Reginald, with typical British candour. "A bit pompous, perhaps, but keen in the execution of his duties. You must be labouring under a delusion, Don Miguel. Is it likely that, with the war progressing favourably and with every prospect of success, the people wish to change their President?"

"You are not acquainted with the true Calderian temperament as I am," said O'Rourke. "In success or misfortune there is a constant desire for social upheaval. It is part of their nature. Therefore I should not be surprised if I were not shortly asked to take my departure. Fortunately I have made all preparations for that probability; but, at the same time, I still wish to retain my position. Saldanha may be a good general, but he would never make even a passable President, so I have no fears that he will supplant me. But there is one man whom I have occasion to fear as long as he remains alive: and that man is Don Robiera Sanchez. I have reason to believe that Saldanha has a secret understanding with that rogue; therefore I ask—not command—Mr. Tresillian and you, as the only persons I can implicitly trust, to see that the sentence of the court-martial is properly carried out."

" Under the circumstances I suppose we cannot refuse, although this business is not in my line, señor. But, at the same time, I hope your fears are ungrounded ? "

" With Don Robiera dead my mind will be easier," replied Don Miguel.

" But mine won't," muttered Holmsby under his breath. " I feel almost responsible for the whole concern." Then aloud he added, "I will make my report at eight o'clock to-morrow, señor. At eleven, with your permission, the *Amphibian* starts for San José. Within a week I hope that the war will be over and all differences settled to your satisfaction. Then, having carried out our part of the compact, Mr. Tresillian and I will return home."

" Much to my regret, Mr. Holmsby."

Taking leave of the wounded President, who was still making rapid progress towards recovery, Reginald hastened back to his comrade and informed him of the reason that Don Miguel gave for wishing them to be present at the execution.

Tresillian had little sleep that night. The shadow of the tragedy weighed heavily on his mind. Holmsby, on the contrary, betrayed no emotion. He had witnessed similar spectacles in West Africa, when, during the Bangwan River Expedition, four deserters from a West African regiment were shot for taking up arms against their former comrades.

Just before sunrise the two Englishmen were aroused and, proceeding to the prison, found that the preparations for the carrying out of the sentence

were already well advanced. Five feet from a blank
wall in the prison-yard a grave had been dug, while
at ten paces from it a dozen rifles were placed upon
the ground. The Commandante with several of the
staff were already present. Outside the walls a
vast concourse of people had collected, filled with a
morbid curiosity to hear the death-dealing volley,
while many were the complaints that the good
citizens of Nalcuanho had to be deprived of a
spectacle which they regarded as a right to be
allowed to witness.

Presently a file of soldiers, accompanied by an
officer, entered and were drawn up two paces in the
rear of the rifles ; a drummer began beating a loud
roll upon his side-drum, and escorted by two
gaolers and accompanied by a priest the condemned man appeared.

He looked wonderfully self-possessed, and unhesitatingly took his place in front of the wall. A
handkerchief was bound round his eyes, and his
attendants retired to a safe distance.

The officer in command of the soldiers drew his
sword, the men stooped, picked up their rifles and
held them at the ready.

A quick word of command, the sword flashed in
the air, and like a single shot the rifles delivered
their volley.

Don Robiera remained standing for nearly three
seconds, then, falling forwards, pitched headlong
into the trench.

Without a moment's delay the Commandante

shook hands with the two Englishmen, thanked them for their presence at the unavoidable incident, and escorted them to the gate.

Tresillian was shaking like a leaf. Holmsby was softly humming a tune, while his face bore a curious smile. Dick turned on him almost savagely.

" You are a callous brute, Rex."

Holmsby stopped and faced his comrade squarely.

" Dick, we can make allowances for you, but when the Commandante takes me for a greenhorn he's jolly well mistaken."

" What do you mean ? "

" Mean—why Don Robiera is no more dead than you and I are. I used my eyes. The rifles did not kick : they were loaded with blank cartridges. A bullet from a modern rifle would pass clean through a man and knock chips out of the wall behind him : the plaster was not scratched. Don Miguel is right after all. That fellow Saldanha is up to some nice little game."

CHAPTER XXVI

A BLOODLESS VICTORY

A T exactly eight o'clock Holmsby and his companion were ushered into the President's presence. Don Miguel's face wore an anxious look, and as Holmsby entered he could scarce control his impatience to have the expected news confirmed.

" We both saw the sentence carried out, señor," began Reginald, and a gleam of positively diabolical delight swept over O'Rourke's features. The Calderian President, in spite of his European education, still retained the fierce characteristics of his fellow-countrymen, and he listened eagerly to Holmsby's narrative.

" Now, señor," continued Reginald. " Having described to you how I carried out your request we will now discuss our plan of campaign. I take it that these gentlemen "—bowing towards a group of officials who stood by the President's couch— " will withdraw, according to custom, when matters relating to the *Amphibian* are broached."

The Calderian officials had no option but to retire as decorously as they could, although they were incensed at the manner in which they were compelled to give place to two aliens.

Then in a few words Holmsby told Don Miguel what his impressions were of the mock execution.

" That is what I expected, Mr. Holmsby," exclaimed the President. " The Commandante is in league with that arch-rogue Sanchez. Ere I am fit to move there will be another revolution."

" Wouldn't it be advisable for you to be taken on board the *Amphibian* and clear out before the storm breaks ? Revolutionaries have been known to shoot their late Presidents before now."

" I would willingly, but for one reason," exclaimed Don Miguel. " As long as the Talpican army threatens our land frontiers and her fleet hovers off the capital my duty to what is undoubtedly an ungrateful country demands that I should see her through her ordeal. It is improbable—unless a serious reverse overtakes our arms —that the conspirators will take definite steps until the war is concluded."

" If I were you, señor, I would let Calderia burn her fingers."

" That I am prepared to do, should occasion arise, Mr. Holmsby ; but till then my work lies in compelling Talpico to cease from her aggressions."

" Then I am at your service. Everything is prepared, and the wireless telephone is again in working order. You can rely upon it that you will be kept closely in touch with everything that takes place during the *Amphibian's* next cruise, and within a week you may be prepared for glorious news."

" I trust so, Mr. Holmsby," replied the President warmly, as he bade the two Englishmen adieu.

Directly the *Amphibian* was clear of the Calderian coast, Holmsby called the crew aft and explained to them that their President was in danger of being deposed. The men who had followed Don Miguel into exile and had loyally supported him during the construction and subsequent commission of the *Amphibian* were highly incensed. Some of them proposed that they should return, take Don Miguel on board, and wreak vengeance upon the Commandante ; but when Holmsby explained the nature of the President's wishes they readily consented to perform their duty to their country and trust to fate to keep Don Miguel in the presidential chair.

At midnight the *Amphibian* was brought head to wind a thousand feet above the town of San José, and through the intense blackness of the night two powerful search-lights directed their beams upon the houses, forts, and harbour. Instantly all was confusion in the Talpican town. Fearing an irresistible onslaught from the skies, the inhabitants poured from their houses and ran for the open country ; the troops manning the batteries cowered in the bomb-proof vaults or joined the civil population in their flight ; while the warships, unable to cross the bar for want of sufficient tide, were huddled hopelessly together in so small a space that one of the powerful missiles from the *Amphibian* would have put them out of action or at any rate crippled them so severely that escape would be impossible.

By means of the international code, Holmsby flashed a message to the Governor of San José, stating in emphatic terms that if a single ship opened fire or attempted to leave the harbour the *Amphibian* would at once commence her work of destruction ; but that if no hostile act were committed by the Talpican forces generous terms would be offered to the otherwise doomed town.

Promptly the answer was returned that San José was prepared to surrender unconditionally. For the rest of the night Holmsby was in constant telephonic communication with Nalcuanho, and an hour after daybreak the Calderian terms were presented to the Governor, who had meanwhile received authority from the President and Government of Talpico to treat on behalf of that Republic.

Don Miguel's terms were certainly moderate. They were : the surrender of one half of the effective ships of the Talpican navy ; indemnity of 100,000 dollars for damage done by the Talpican army during the occupation of Calderian territory, and that a portion of the Talpican frontier, that formed a wedge into Calderia, was to be ceded to that Republic, so that the land frontier was clearly defined and strongly protected by the sierras.

Before nine o'clock Holmsby telephoned that the rough draft of the terms of peace had been signed, and asked that prize crews should be sent from Nalcuanho to man the surrendered ships. The young Englishman had good cause to feel proud of his achievements. He had won a decisive yet bloodless victory, and had secured a balance of power between the two neighbouring republics that neither would feel bold enough to disturb.

But although Holmsby patted himself on the back the news of the terms of peace was received by the populace of Nalcuanho in a manner that would have unfavourably surprised him. Once more he had under-estimated the Calderian temperament. He had imagined that since that Republic had been freed from fear of invasion, placed in possession of the nucleus of a fleet, given a slice of territory and a large sum as indemnity, national pride would be fully satisfied. But an important item in Calderian characteristics had been overlooked—revenge. Nothing short of the complete and final subjection of Talpico would satisfy the people who a few weeks ago trembled at the thunder of the Talpican gun without their gates. A bloodless victory did not appeal to their hot-tempered instincts : they wanted revenge.

For three days after the signing of the treaty of peace, Holmsby held frequent converse with President O'Rourke, but on the morning of the fourth day there was no response to Reginald's call. Whether the wireless instruments at Nalcuanho had broken down or the threatened trouble had fallen upon the ill-starred President, Holmsby knew not. He could only wait until the prize crews arrived to take possession of the ceded portion of the Talpican fleet, when he would be at liberty to take the *Amphibian* back to Nalcuanho.

At length the expected ships' companies arrived; but since they had left the capital before telephonic communication was interrupted they could give no further information, although Holmsby, who now shared the President's suspicions, detected a distinct aggressive manner in their replies.

It was like groping in the dark. Cut off from all communications with Calderia, Reginald was in utter ignorance of how events were trending. Nevertheless he waited until the surrendered ships, now displaying the Calderian colours, had cleared San José Harbour and were well on their way towards Nalcuanho.

He waited still longer: until the 100,000 dollars indemnity had been paid in bullion, and with this sum safely stowed on board the airship he bore away to the capital of Calderia.

It was late in the afternoon ere the *Amphibian* came in sight of Nalcuanho. Both Englishmen were on the promenade deck, eagerly scanning the city through their powerful glasses.

There was something strange about the appearance of the place. The plaza and the olive-lined boulevard fronting the quay—usually the favourite places of assembly in the cool of the day of the easy-going pleasure-loving Calderians—were deserted. Most of the windows of the houses were protected by planks, while at the end of each of the broad streets converging on the quay barricades had been erected and field-guns mounted behind them. Soldiers there were in large numbers, but hardly a civilian was to be seen.

" Something has gone wrong : that's a moral cert," exclaimed Tresillian.

" Undoubtedly," replied Holmsby. " We must take necessary precautions," and raising his voice he called those of the crew who could be spared from all but the most important duties to muster aft.

In a few words he explained what he thought to be the actual state of affairs and which subsequently proved to be correct. The army, at the instigation of the Commandante, had mutinied, Don Miguel was deposed, and Don Robiera Sanchez, resurrected with dramatic effect, was literally thrust into the presidential chair. Of Don Miguel's fate there was no inkling, but the crew of the *Amphibian*, vowing vengeance should a hair of his head be harmed, called upon their English commander to take the *Amphibian* right up into the city.

In a few minutes the all-powerful airship, fully cleared for action, was floating two hundred feet above the government buildings of Nalcuanho.

CHAPTER XXVII

" I GIVE YOU ONE MINUTE TO DECIDE "

THE *Amphibian* was indeed in a curious position. On all sides light guns for discharging either six-pounder shells or rockets were trained upon her; but two reasons prevented the rebels from proceeding to extremities : they wished to gain possession of the powerful airship in an intact condition if possible; they also feared the result of the terrific explosion of her stores of highly-charged projectiles. Yet the situation was desperate. An excitable gunner might unconsciously press the trigger of the electric pistol attached to the quick-firer; an impulsive officer, without regard for the consequences, might order his men to open fire, in spite of the fact that the Calderian ensign was still displayed from the *Amphibian.*

Realising these possibilities Holmsby resolved to execute a daring manœuvre, and skilfully handling the huge airship brought her to earth in the centre of the quadrangle enclosed by government offices. Here, safe from artillery fire, she lay, with barely twenty yards betwixt her bow

and the windows of the Assembly Chamber. Her
for'ard quick-firer was trained point blank at that
part of the buildings, while the gun's crew of the
aft quick-firer brought the sights of that weapon
to bear upon the offices of the Minister of War.

" Now," exclaimed Holmsby with fierce delight,
for his blood was up, " we can sit tight. One single
act of aggression and we'll blow the revolutionary
headquarters to Hades."

He had not long to wait. Attended by several
of the numerous generals of the Calderian Army
the Commandante entered the quadrangle.

" Welcome to Nalcuanho once more, señor," he
began. " The Republic pays tribute to your deeds
of valour and discretion."

" I am sorry I cannot return the compliment,
General," replied Reginald bluntly.

" My friend, you are over hasty. Since you take
this tone I must call upon you in the name of the
Republic to relinquish your command of the airship
Amphibian."

" And if I refuse ? "

" Then I must take steps to compel you."

Holmsby laughed. The little Commandante,
bristling with fury, spluttered vain threats against
the young Englishman ; then he appealed to the
crew of the *Amphibian* to give up their alien commander, threatening, if they failed to do so, that
they would all be taken prisoners and shot.

The men treated the proposal with contempt, and
raised loud shouts of " Long live President Miguel."

" There is now no President Miguel," announced the Commandante. " President Robiera is now the head of the Republic. Surrender your foreign officers, men, and take the oath of allegiance to the new President, and you will have no cause to regret your actions."

" Here I stand unarmed : why do not the crew of the *Amphibian* accept your conditions ? " demanded Holmsby calmly. " I will tell you. They will not be gulled by that rascally son of a peon the Commandante."

Stung by the insult, for General Saldanha prided himself on his direct descent from a hidalgo of Spain, the Commandante fairly danced with rage. Then turning to one of his officers he spoke a few words. A bugle blared and instantly three field-pieces were run out into the quadrangle, unlimbered and trained upon the huge bulk that overshadowed the greater portion of the confined space ; while at every window commanding the *Amphibian* soldiers with loaded rifles simultaneously appeared.

" Have a care, men," shouted the Commandante addressing the crew of the *Amphibian*. Escape is impossible. Either surrender your officers or die. I give you five minutes to decide."

Holmsby calmly took a cigarette from its case, deliberately lit it, extinguished the match, and flicked the still smouldering fragment of wood to the ground.

" Five minutes is a long time in an affair of this sort, Commandante," he said, raising his voice that

all could hear him. " I, too, have something to say.
Now listen : I need hardly remind you that stored
within the *Amphibian* are explosives sufficiently
powerful to destroy the whole of these buildings and
shake Nalcuanho to its foundations. One shot and
the trick will be done. It's a quick death, Commandante, but the thought of it is terrifying to a
coward. No, don't attempt to move," for General
Saldanha and several of his officers showed unmistakable signs of executing a strategic movement
to the rear. " You are fairly cornered, Commandante, five rifles at least are covering you. One
more step and it will be your last. Ah ! That's
more reasonable. Stay where you are, and it rests
entirely with you how you get out of this business.
" Now I will resume my interrupted remarks.
Kindly order those guns to be limbered up and
those soldiers to remove their greasy-looking faces
from the windows. I know you would not wish for
so large an audience to witness your discomfiture.
Hurry up, please, three minutes out of the five you
graciously offered us are already up."

There was no help for it. The muzzles of the
rifles of the *Amphibian's* crew formed a powerful
incentive. The Commandante falteringly gave the
order, the field-pieces and troops seemed to melt
away, and empty windows overlooked the quadrangle.

" Now we have quite a happy family gathering,"
continued Reginald cheerfully, while the Calderian
crew, their faith in their English commander

rapidly gaining strength, began to see that Holmsby held the whip hand. "Before we proceed any further I may as well tell you how we stand. No doubt, with your born cupidity, my dear Commandante, you hoped to reap the profits of my work on Don Miguel's behalf. You may, if you behave yourself, get out of this mess unharmed. You hoped to derive some benefit from the Talpican indemnity. You won't : the whole of the 100,000 dollars is at this very moment on board the *Amphibian* and will be used solely for the benefit of Don Miguel and the crew who so loyally stand by him.

"That reminds me. How is Don Miguel ? I hope for your sake that he has not had an—shall I call it—an accident ? "

"He is no worse, Señor Holmsby," faltered the now frightened Commandante.

"Very good thing for you he isn't," replied Reginald, stepping towards a locker and extracting his revolver. "Now, General, our conversation is becoming more personal when we discuss the position of a mutual friend. If you and two of your fellow rascals will do me the doubtful honour of coming on board, we will go more into this matter."

The Commandante hesitated. Even the sight of the menacing rifles would not tempt him to put his head into the lion's jaws without a guarantee of safe conduct.

Some of his staff began to edge towards the door through which they had entered the quadrangle.

"Come back, you ! " shouted Holmsby.

Most of the terrified officers stopped, but one, bending as he ran, darted towards the opening. Even as he gained the lowermost step Holmsby raised his revolver and fired. The fugitive, shot through the knee, pitched on his face.

" It's no use trying to play the fool," said Reginald sternly. " Two of you go and pick that fellow up—two of you, I said, not half a dozen—that's better. Now, General, step this way, please."

This time there could be no hesitation. The Commandante, attended by two of his gold-laced minions, ascended the rope ladder and gained the deck of the *Amphibian*.

" To resume our little conversation," continued Holmsby. " There is no necessity to be alarmed. If you get into an awkward predicament it is your own fault. Now, tell me, where is Don Miguel ? "

" He is a prisoner in his quarters."

" And what did you intend to do with him ? " asked Reginald sternly. " Shoot him ? Come, speak up, and don't hesitate."

" Perhaps," mumbled the Commandante.

" It's a wonder you haven't done so already," rejoined Holmsby. "But you see we are here to shake things up a bit. Now here are pens, ink, and paper. Write an order for Don Miguel's release and give orders that the warrant is carried out."

" Don Robiera Sanchez is now the President : he alone can order Don Miguel's release," expostulated the Commandante.

" Don Robiera is the puppet and you pull the strings. I know that perfectly well. It's jolly lucky for you that Don Miguel is still alive. Do you know what would have happened had it been otherwise ? From a height of six thousand feet the *Amphibian* would have dropped a hundred kilos of explosives in the government buildings, and the Republic of Calderia would have to look both for the fragments of her former officials and for others to take their places. But I am wandering slightly from the point, Commandante. You gave us five minutes to decide whether the crew should hand over the *Amphibian* to the revolutionaries. Incidentally I may mention that the five minutes have now expired and the *Amphibian* is still in the possession of Don Miguel's adherents. I give you one minute to decide : sign the order I require or I'll dangle you by the neck from underneath the *Amphibian*, and at a sufficient height for every person in Nalcuanho to see. After that I'll gain my end by other means."

Without a single word in reply, General Saldanha feverishly gripped a pen, scribbled a few hasty lines, signed the paper and presented it to his conqueror.

" Thank you, Commandante ; until the order is executed you must be detained here. By the bye, a polite note to President Sanchez, informing him that you are in a slight difficulty and requesting his presence, would also be in accordance with the present run of things."

" It would be of no use, señor."

" What ! The performer cannot now control his puppet. Anyway, have a shot at it."

Thereupon the Commandante wrote as Holmsby had suggested, and the two letters were handed to the General's staff with instructions to carry out the orders they contained ; while, under guard, the three hostages were sent for'ard.

" By Jove, Dick ! " exclaimed Reginald, when the two comrades found themselves alone. " I never talked so much in all my life. I think I must chuck the Service after this—if I am not chucked out—and go in for public speaking."

" You fairly frightened the old rascal, although I wonder you didn't mention that you knew all along that he tried to fool you over that mock execution. You see my knowledge of Spanish has increased enough for me to follow much of the conversation."

" I might have done, but I didn't want to rub it in too thick."

" If that's what you call rubbing it in lightly I should like to know how you let yourself go, Rex," replied Tresillian. " But the main thing is that it looks as if we shall rescue Don Miguel. What's going to happen next ? "

" Wait and see," replied Holmsby oracularly.

CHAPTER XXVIII

DON MIGUEL'S REVENGE

WITHIN a quarter of an hour, one of the revolutionary officers re-entered the quadrangle.

Halting at the foot of the *Amphibian's* ladder, he held up a sealed letter, which was taken from him by one of the crew and handed to Holmsby.

"Bring the prisoners aft," he ordered, and when the Commandante and his two companions had taken their places between the double line of the airship's crew, Holmsby opened the missive.

"I am sorry your authority has so little weight, Commandante," said Reginald. "According to this letter President Sanchez has already deemed it advisable to leave you in the lurch. The last seen of him was that he was riding as fast as his horse could carry him in the direction of Estores. Presumably he is on his way to Talpico, but I am afraid that to his surprise his reception will be totally different to his former one. I expected it would be so. However, since I've had you brought here again, you may as well wait till the second messenger returns."

But the second messenger did not return. Having played a somewhat prominent part in the latest revolution he thought it best to follow the example of President Sanchez ; so having delivered the Commandante's order he rushed off to the railway station and shook the dust of Nalcuanho from his feet.

The order had the desired effect, for presently Don Miguel, carried on a stretcher, was brought into the quadrangle. The loyal crew of the *Amphibian* gave vent to lusty shouts of delight as they hastily prepared for the return of their idolised master, and assisted by willing hands the ex-President was hoisted on to the deck of his airship.

In a few words, Holmsby informed Don Miguel of what had transpired, and learnt in return of the events that had taken place subsequent to the *Amphibian's* departure for San José.

It was as Holmsby had pictured. The moment the prize crews had left Nalcuanho and the revolutionary generals concluded that the indemnity had been paid, the revolution broke out. Troops seized the government buildings and threw up barricades across the principal streets. The bulk of the civil population, still favourably inclined towards President O'Rourke, came into collision with the military but were dispersed with great loss of life, and in less than an hour from the first shot the revolution became an accomplished fact.

Taken prisoner Don Miguel was confined in the

city gaol. His brutal captors made no secret of the intention of the revolutionaries to shoot him as soon as the *Amphibian* was made to surrender. This the Commandante believed would be a comparatively easy matter, but he had learnt to his cost that he had a brave and resolute Englishman to deal with.

" Well, Don Miguel," said Holmsby, when O'Rourke had finished his narrative, " the matter rate, entirely in your hands. Here is the prime mover in the revolution."

" I did not think that my confidence in you," said Don Miguel, addressing the trembling Commandante, " would have been so vilely abused. As a traitor and murderer—for at your command hundreds of the citizens of Nalcuanho have been shot down—you richly deserve to suffer the same fate as you intended to inflict upon me : there would be no mock execution, I can assure you. But although I mean to have my revenge, I give you your life. My revenge is this : I am resolved to leave Calderia for ever. She can struggle out of the throes of internal dissensions as best she may. By freeing her from foreign aggressors I have done my duty. Your punishment will be at the hands of those who will be incensed at your diabolical action in causing the benefactor of the Republic to abandon a part of his task. I wish you joy of it. Now go, and may I never see your face again."

Absolutely bewildered by this totally unexpected clemency the Commandante backed from the presence of the man whom he had so despicably served. But the crew of the *Amphibian* were for the first time out of hand. Throwing themselves upon the Commandante they tore the medals and decorations from his breast and trampled them on the deck ; they wrenched the buttons and gold lace from his uniform ; they drew his sword and broke the blade in two. Not content with this, two of the men, regardless of the risk they ran, seized the shorn general, dragged him through the War Office buildings, and presented him at a window to the dense crowd of curious and excited citizens who thronged without.

To Saldanha, the martinet, the pompous Commandante, the humiliation was almost unbearable ; but he had tasted only of the first-fruits of Don Miguel's vengeance. The rest he had to suffer at the hands of the people whose confidence he had abused.

" We must do something, señor," said Holmsby, after the excitement within the quadrangle had subsided, although the tumult of the crowd without still sounded like the subdued roar of breakers on a rocky shore. " We cannot possibly stay here. What do you propose to do ? "

" I have already mentioned that I have done with Calderia," replied Don Miguel. " I must find an asylum—a quiet retreat—in another country ; and the one that most appeals to me is Great Britain."

" You are no stranger to it," observed Tresillian.

18

" No ; I presume my title to Sampson's Down still holds good. I can there live in retirement and devote my days to my favourite pastime of scientific research. Fortunately I am not in want. On the contrary, I have taken care to provide against emergencies. My crew will doubtless go with me and find a home in Cornwall, but they will not suffer for their loyalty. As for the *Amphibian*, I mean to hand her over to the British Government as a sort of peace-offering, and, Mr. Holmsby, that act will be performed through your mediation. The secret of the preparation of helia will be entrusted into the hands of yourself and Mr. Tresillian : that alone, which ought to be worth thousands will, however, scarcely pay the debt of gratitude I owe you both. At the first opportunity on our arrival in England I will send for the necessary documents from my Paris bankers. Now Mr. Holmsby, I think I have made myself clear. If you will kindly muster the crew aft I will put my proposition before them."

Both Reginald and Dick thanked O'Rourke as well as they could find words to express their thoughts for his generosity ; then Holmsby told him of the bullion he had on board.

" It affords me much satisfaction that the indemnity has not fallen into Robiera's hands," remarked Don Miguel. " Personally the money is of no particular consequence to me. If you require any of it, you have but to ask."

Both Englishmen refused, saying that Don Miguel had already been over-generous.

" Then I will divide part of it amongst the crew
and devote the rest to charitable purposes," announced O'Rourke. " Now, Mr. Holmsby, if you
will please do as I request you."

In less than half a minute the crew were formed
up on the afterpart of the promenade-deck, and
their master briefly told them of his intentions,
leaving out, for the present, all mention of the
proposed division of the indemnity. Without exception the men expressed their utmost willingness
to follow the fortunes of their chief, and their
delight was unbounded when Don Miguel completed
his address by announcing that fifty thousand
dollars would be divided between them. Even the
noise of the crowd without was hushed into silence
as the men gave three ringing shouts—the nearest
approach to a hearty British cheer that Holmsby
had ever heard.

" All clear fore and aft ? " asked Holmsby, when
the preparations for the departure were completed.

" All clear, sir," reported the quartermaster.

The engineer deftly inserted the two helia
cylinders that alone were required to give the vessel
the necessary buoyancy, and gracefully the *Amphibian* rose from the ground, and remained poised in
the air at an altitude of five thousand feet. Don
Miguel was carried to the rail to take a farewell
glimpse of the country he wished to serve so well,
then carefully handled by four of his men was
taken below to his cabin.

The huge propeller began to revolve, and the

Amphibian, rapidly gathering way, headed in a north-easterly direction. Upon the crowd of citizens who lined the quays of Nalcuanho a strange silence descended. Instinctively they realised that they had lost their former President for ever.

CHAPTER XXIX

HOLMSBY'S RETURN

FIVE days later the *Amphibian* sighted the Lizard. Off Rame Head she overtook the British dirigible, *Gadfly*, pounding against a strong east wind. It was like a motor-car overtaking a lumbering stage-coach, and even though the sight of the ensign fluttering from the *Gadfly's* stern filled Sub-Lieutenant Holmsby with an indescribable yearning, he could not repress his satisfaction that the *Amphibian*, the vessel that he was to hand over to the British Navy—was immeasurably superior to the latest production of gas-inflated dirigibles.

Without attempting to communicate, the *Amphibian*, with the Calderian ensign still flying, passed the British dirigible and soon left her far astern.

Off Portland the First Division of the Home Fleet, steaming in double columns, in line ahead, hove in sight. Wishing to demonstrate the manœuvring power of the *Amphibian*, Holmsby brought the airship to rest upon the surface of the sea. Then diving, he steered the craft underneath the Fleet and ascended two miles in their wake.

In the gathering twilight of a dull November afternoon, Portsmouth had a momentary view of the *Amphibian* as she headed towards London. Then the gathering darkness hid her from further observation.

" Here we are, Dick," exclaimed Reginald, as the *Amphibian* descended into the vast natural hollow of the Devil's Punch Bowl, where she lay sheltered by the towering masses of Hindhead from the blustering wind. " I must ask you to stay another night on board, although the temptation to spend an evening in Town must be very great. I mean to surprise the Chief a bit. You can manage the *Amphibian* as well as I can, so I want you to bring her up to-morrow."

" Where to ? " asked Dick.

" Let her rest on the Thames opposite the Houses of Parliament. That's about the best place I can think of. Try and get there as near as possible at eleven o'clock."

" All right, old fellow," replied Tresillian cheerfully. " But what do you propose to do ? "

" Walk to Haslemere, take train to Town, and advise Admiral Pennington of the result of my investigations. I'll tell you all about it later on."

Accordingly Holmsby, clad in a thick coat in addition to his ordinary clothing—for he felt the sudden change from the warm air of Calderia to the raw atmosphere of his native land—descended the rope ladder and was soon making his way through the thick, rain-sodden gorze.

At Haslemere he had to wait for a train, but in the interval he was soon deep in the news of the day. Even during his short absence everything seemed strange : he had lost the thread of current events. But there was one paragraph that especially interested him : a report from Plymouth stating that the *Gadfly* had been overtaken by a mysterious airship that answered to the description of the one that caused such commotion in Cornwall in September last.

It was late in the evening when Holmsby found himself in London. His first inclination was to go to his club, but on second thoughts he decided to make for his " shore quarters " at Dulwich. But reflecting that his landlady could not be relied upon to keep the news of his return he finally decided to call upon a brother-officer, Sub-Lieutenant Diver of the Hydrographers' Department.

" Good heavens, Holmsby, is it really you ? " asked that astonished officer.

" I don't think it's anyone else, George," replied Reginald. " Look here, I know you can keep a secret. I don't want a word about my being in Town mentioned until I've seen old Pennington. How did my Chief take it ? "

" I hardly know, not being in the same branch. But I heard he was awfully cut up about your supposed death. Of course he had a message purporting to come from you; but not being authenticated he naturally thought it was a bogus report to throw him off the scent."

For quite two hours Holmsby related his adventures to his wonder-stricken friend. Now that the responsibility of the *Amphibian* was removed from his shoulders, Reginald's almost boyish character was beginning to reassert itself.

" Can you lend me your full-dress uniform, old fellow ? " he asked. " I can't get mine as it is at my digs : that is if my people haven't sent for my things."

" Certainly, but what for ? "

" I'm going to have a little game with old Pennington—that's all."

Shortly after nine on the following morning, Holmsby, attired in his friend's uniform, entered the offices of the Intelligence Department. Save for the messenger the place was deserted, for it was the practice of the staff to arrive just before ten.

When the head messenger had recovered from his astonishment, Holmsby impressed upon him the absolute necessity for strict official reticence and reserve concerning his presence, as he particularly wished to announce his return to the Chief in person.

But instead of going to his own room Holmsby went straight to the Chief's sanctum. It was a large apartment. A mahogany table and half a dozen arm-chairs filled the greater part of it, but

CHAPTER III

THE *ALERTE* SAILS

THAT same afternoon, there being a full moon on the previous day, the spring tide was at its highest at about six o'clock. The conditions being favourable, R 81 was moved into the covered-in slip, while the shell of R 67 was placed in the berth vacated by her practically intact sister.

When employed as active units under the white ensign, these boats had a surface displacement of 420 tons; submerged, this displacement was increased to the extent of 80 tons. Their speed when on the surface was 15 knots; while submerged, this was reduced to nine. The propelling machinery consisted of semi-Diesel engines for surface work, 13 tons of oil being carried for that purpose. In diving-trim this class relied upon electric motors, the " juice " being kept in numbers of storage batteries that had frequently to be recharged.

In her present state, R 81 retained her engines. To get these tuned up was not a difficult matter. The batteries had deteriorated to such an extent as to be useless.

Trevorrick decided to scrap them. He had no

within the next few days and sound your pal,
Port—What's his name ? "

" Porthoustoc—Silas Porthoustoc."

" That's the fellow. We'll want him and his
lugger. He's sound, isn't he ? "

" Do anything," replied Pengelly. " If he were
put to it, he'd be a second King o' Prussia.[1]
Nod's as good as a wink to him—at his price."

" I wouldn't let him know too much," suggested
Trevorrick. " At least, not at first. Once I get
him in my power sufficiently, I can put a half-
nelson over him in double-quick time. Then he
daren't open his mouth—price or no price."

Pengelly eyed his companion dubiously.

" You're not going to try that game on me, I
hope ? " he asked.

Trevorrick brought his huge hand heavily down
on his partner's shoulder.

" Come now," he exclaimed. " You know the
saying, ' Honour amongst thieves ? ' Aren't we
sworn comrades under the Jolly Roger ? "

Pengelly nodded.

" I'd like to remind him of another saw," he
soliloquised. " ' When thieves fall out.' But
perhaps I'd better not."

[1] King of Prussia : soubriquet of John Carter, a noted Cornish
smuggler, who in the latter part of the eighteenth century held
and fortified Porth Leah, a few miles east of Marazion, as a
smuggling base. On one occasion he fired the guns at a revenue
cutter. On another he broke into the Custom-House at Penzance
and recovered various contraband goods which the Excise
people had seized, taking only " his own " and no more. Carter
was a sort of Cornish maritime Robin Hood. Porth Leah is
now called Prussia Cove in memory of this daring smuggler.

immediately opposite the door was a small library, partitioned off by a heavy curtain.

Behind this curtain Holmsby took up his position. Two months previously he would not have dared to take such liberties with the much-to-be-feared Chief Director of Naval Intelligence ; but emboldened by the success of his undertaking Reginald had now no fears on the point.

Precisely at ten the great man entered, but instead of following his usual custom and devoting half an hour to the daily paper, he rang his bell and asked for Captain Wapping.

" Ah ! Good-morning, Wapping. I see that confounded airship has turned up again."

" Yes, sir, I saw that in last night's paper. By the description it seems to be identical with the one that poor young Holmsby lost the number of his mess over."

" Yes, unfortunately——"

At that moment the First Sea Lord burst into the room. A visit from this high and mighty one was most unusual. Captain Wapping began to back from the room. Even Holmsby's courage oozed from his finger-tips when he recognised the newcomer's bull-voice.

" Good morning, Pennington. Don't go, Wapping, this might interest you," exclaimed the First Sea Lord handing an official message to the Chief Director. " Read it, Pennington, read it aloud, so that Captain Wapping can express his opinion on it."

Thus commanded, Rear-Admiral Pennington

began to read the dispatch, while the First Sea Lord, sitting cross-legged in the easiest arm-chair, drummed his finger-tips on the table in his obvious excitement.

" From Admiral commanding First Division of Home Fleet, Portland (by wireless).

" Report on 19th inst., St. Albans Head bearing NNW½W distant 12 miles, sighted airship flying Calderian colours. Airship apparently disabled, fell into sea, and sank. Detached *Onyx* to render assistance, but could find no trace of wreck. Eleven minutes later airship reappeared, gained an altitude of two thousand feet, and proceeded East. Request strict look out be maintained by detached units, and coastguard informed accordingly."

" Now what do you make of that ? Where, by the bye is Calderia ? " asked the First Sea Lord, whose geography was limited to the North Atlantic and Indian Oceans.

" Calderia, sir, is a rotten little Republic in South America. Always having revolutions, I'm told."

" I wonder if there's any truth in the newspaper report that the airship resembled the one that was reported in Cornwall in September ? "

" Shouldn't be surprised, sir. The description also tallies with my late subordinate's last report— that was just before he met his death."

" Of course, I remember now. A smart young officer, I believe. Wasn't his name Holmsley ? "

" Holmsby, sir; a most promising officer. His last report—I have it before me—shows wonderful powers of discernment. I took the greatest interest in his career——"

" Thank you, sir ! " exclaimed Reginald.

CHAPTER XXX

THE *AMPHIBIAN* HAULS DOWN HER ENSIGN

" BLESS my soul, it's Holmsby ! " exclaimed the Rear-Admiral, while the First Sea Lord sat bolt upright in his chair, jammed a monocle to his eye, and coughed severely, until he realised that it was the much-lauded sub-lieutenant who stood before him.

" Explain yourself, Mr. Holmsby," began the Chief Director.

" I'm sorry, sir, but I did not expect to find——"

" Never mind about being sorry—that can wait Explain how you escaped from your supposed death."

" It's a long story, sir," replied Holmsby, looking at the clock. " But I've completed my investigations."

" Carry on then, and let us hear what you've done."

Thus enjoined Holmsby began, and although his distinguished listeners followed him with rapt attention, Reginald had the greatest difficulty to keep his eyes off the clock, as the hands slowly approached the hour of eleven. Almost exactly to the minute a messenger knocked at the door and made the startling announcement that a foreign airship was on the Thames.

" On the Thames ? " demanded the First Sea Lord, absolutely bewildered with the rapid chain of events.

" I think, sir, I can explain," said Holmsby.

Meanwhile the news had spread like wildfire through the various Admiralty departments. In the Accountant-General's branch half a dozen highly-paid officials were gravely deliberating whether a workman should receive threepence farthing or threepence and three-eighths for working in a hazardous place. The conference came to an abrupt ending, and the debaters, clapping on their hats, hurried off to see the strange sight. In the Works Department an animated discussion was going on as to whether a poorly-paid clerk should receive threepence or fourpence a day increase of pay after four years' service. Here again there was a hurried exodus. It was the same with the other branches, the chiefs hurried off, and the subordinates followed at a discreet distance.

The War Office dignitaries, aroused from their slumbers, deserted their snug offices, and joined the Thames-ward throng, which had already assumed tremendous proportions.

Westminster and Lambeth bridges were packed, all vehicular traffic being suspended. Every vantage-ground on the Surrey side was crowded, while some of the more daring spectators actually invaded the sacred precincts of the terrace of the House. Even the river teemed with life, bargees reaping a rich harvest from the sightseers who were fortunate in getting standing-room in the unwieldy lighters.

Making their way across the surging tide of hurrying people the First Sea Lord, Rear-Admiral Pennington, Captain Wapping, and Reginald reached the Embankment by a circuitous route, and had to walk as far as the Temple Pier before they could find a River Police launch—the only craft available.

Pushing its way betwixt the dense pack of small craft that surrounded the *Amphibian*, the launch ran alongside. The aircraft was floating on the swift-flowing tide, moored head and stern abreast of the Victoria Tower.

Received with naval honours by the Calderian crew, the Admiralty officials clambered up the rope ladder and gained the deck of the mysterious craft, and were introduced to the still crippled Don Miguel.

In a few well-chosen words the ex-President expressed his wish that the *Amphibian* should be taken over by the British nation, and on behalf of the State the First Sea Lord accepted the gift.

Thereupon the Calderian National Flag was lowered slowly from the ensign staff, and Holmsby with his own hands hoisted the White Ensign in its place.

Only one in a hundred of the spectators fully realised the meaning of this action ; but a wild storm of cheering burst from the assembled throngs. The *Amphibian* had taken her place as the most powerful unit of the British air fleet.

Taking the discarded ensign over his arm, Holmsby returned to where Don Miguel was lying and gave it into his hands. Keenly observant, Reginald noticed that the eyes of the dapper little man were filled with tears : the sacrifice he had made was no light one. He had handed over the choicest gem of his life to the care of the foreign country that was to be his by adoption.

.   .   .   .   .   .

Don Miguel, or Michael O'Rourke, as he is now called, carried out his intention and settled down in a modest country-house on Sampson's Down. There is now no mystery about his presence in the Duchy of Cornwall. He has earned the esteem of the villagers of Penkerris by his general de-meanour and liberal generosity. Even Lieutenant Haslar, now in receipt of a Greenwich Hospital pension, in addition to his well-earned Service pension, is on intimate terms with the smartly-dressed little man who walks with a decided limp —for Lieutenant Haslar has learnt that this assailants were Michael O'Rourke's foes. And the Penkerris fishermen now shoot their nets in Sampson's Cove, for the fish are not now disturbed by the movements of a mysterious object beneath the waves. Penkerris has had a " boom."

Tourists flock to it in order to gaze with more than discreet curiosity upon the little man who created the *Amphibian*, the prototype of Britain's omnipotent air fleet—and, in consequence, Mrs. Pedler has started a select boarding-house.

A few miles from Penkerris are the spacious works of the Helia Company. Dick Tresillian had his wish, and promptly " chucked " the department for work of a more congenial nature. He is now managing-director of the Helia Company, and is reported to be rolling in money. He is a frequent and regular visitor to Sampson's Down.

As for Reginald Holmsby, he is making rapid progress in the air fleet. Already his name is high on the list for Flag rank. He, too, whenever his arduous duties permit, makes frequent visits to Sampson's Down, where, in the company of Michael O'Rourke and Dick Tresillian, he delights in recalling their adventures in the *Amphibian*.